LOVE AND LIBERATION

to Mike —

A proud tale
of your heritage
from a liberated daughter
and granddaughter —

Ralph Plenty

8/14/01

LOVE AND LIBERATION

WHEN THE JEWS TORE DOWN THE GHETTO WALLS

A Historical Novel
by Ralph David Fertig

Writers Club Press
San Jose New York Lincoln Shanghai

Love and Liberation
When the Jews Tore Down the Ghetto Walls

Writers Club Press
an imprint of iUniverse.com, Inc.

For information address:
iUniverse.com, Inc.
5220 S 16th, Ste. 200
Lincoln, NE 68512
www.iuniverse.com

Cover picture: Honore Daumiere, *The Uprising*

The Phillips Collection, Washington, D. C.

ISBN: 0-595-16383-1

Printed in the United States of America

To Marjorie

my collaborator,
my editor,
my love.

I love thee now and always

"Minds are conquered not by arms,
but by greatness of soul"

Baruch Spinoza,
The Ethics, IV, App., 11

CONTENTS

LIST OF ILLUSTRATIONS

PREFACE

This is a love story, the romance and adventures of a group of central European Jews who helped bring about vast changes from the oppression of feudal bondage to the realization of personal freedoms.

It is an historically faithful account of the times. The rulers, their rules, the battles and shifting borders, the major events, public figures, literature, all of the quotations attributed to historic figures, attitudes and architecture of the period are authentic as reported. A bibliography provides the sources of attributions and background facts.

Those of the characters who are fictitious tell their stories as representative of ordinary people of the era. They are composites or adaptations of real people who lived in central Europe from 1769 through 1807. Family trees of the key figures appear at the conclusions to Chapters II and IV.

A glossary translates Yiddish and German expressions.

$$* \qquad * \qquad *$$

For almost two millennia, Jews were barred from citizenship, land ownership, the professions, most occupations, trades, institutions, and the marrow of the European economy by the laws of nations, local governments, and Ecclesiastical authorities.

Throughout central and eastern Europe, Jews were confined by law to *ghettoes*, walled enclaves in the cities, from which they could not emerge at night, on Sundays, or during periods of Christian celebration, or to *shtetls*, defined settlements in rural areas, small towns, and villages. Outside their restricted quarters, they had to wear yellow stars, circles, or hats, items of ethnic identification designed to invite deprecation.

Organized violence against the Jews, sanctioned by state and church, was perpetrated by military forces and mobs under the protection of local rulers.

The easing of restrictions began in central Europe with the Enlightenment and emergence of capitalism in the late eighteenth century. But emancipation arose as a product of the French Revolution and spread across the continent with the advance of the armies of Napoleon who tore down the ghetto walls and ordered the removal of symbols and strictures of servitude.

Poverty, isolation, religious fundamentalism within the Jewish community, and subjugation from without gave way to economic opportunities, participation in the mainstream, the beginnings of Reform Judaism, and the extension of civil rights.

For Jews of the German states, this period of emancipation was a brief one. The Congress of Vienna in 1815, rescinded the obligation of any nation to grant citizenship or rights to Jews. Although the ghetto walls remained down, and Jews retained some rights as citizens in western Europe, it was not until the 1870's that personal freedoms were fully restored to Jews in Germany.

The genocide of the Nazi era grew easily from the soil in which persecution of Jews had been cultivated for centuries. In the 1930's, the German government withdrew the short lived rights of Jews to citizenship, education, and occupations, reinstituted insignias of deprecation that Jews had long been forced to wear, rebuilt walls of containment, and organized the obliteration of Jews with an efficiency honed in the new industrial age. The Third Reich merely had to build upon a heritage of hatred against which the Jewish families of this story struggled in the heartland of Germany at the dawning of the Era of Enlightenment.

ACKNOWLEDGMENTS

The passage from concept to publication can be made only with many helping hands, and I have been lucky to have had the generous and skillful support of numerous good and accomplished people. My wife Marjorie provided inspiration, humor, and ongoing challenge in the editing of phrases, slashing of rhetoric, and shaping of tone. Gloria Goldsmith, playwright and friend, honed the work further. Adriana Shaw, producer/distributor and friend believed in the manuscript and brought it to my agent, Christina Arneson, who made everything else happen. Special thanks go to Michael Altman of iUniverse.com who gave personal attention to production details.

Others read early drafts and their comments and encouragement shaped the telling of the tale: Actor/ writer Susan Anspach; Cantor and biblical scholar, Jay Frailich; Rabbi Allen Freehling, my spiritual guide; Rabbi Chaim Beliak, a role model for Jewish social activism; author and friend Irene Dische, whose personal accounts of overcoming obstacles to publication gave me the determination to keep at it; Carolyn Anagnos, Lynn Braun, Lydia Brazon, Lila Garrett, Marvin and Esther Schachter, and Kani Xulam.

I am enduringly grateful to each.

*   *   *

At the dawn of the last century, my father left his grandparents' backwater farm near Ratibor to find the mother who had abandoned him as a child. In the bustling city of Breslau, liberated from the provincial Jewish orthodoxy of his youth, he embraced the rich, romantic German culture. When his search brought him to America, he found instead a sense of family in German-American communities that nourished a nostalgia for a homeland that he came to believe included him.

My mother was the child of an assimilated Jewish middle class family in Berlin whose men fought for the Kaiser and whose women held salons. While visiting America after World War I, she met my father and they settled in the Midwest where he had become the publisher of German language newspapers.

In the 1930's, when Hitler assumed power, even the German American Bund rallied behind the Third Reich and my father was rent from his dreams and his work, an outcast in a strange land. He and my mother became part of a colony of refugees, convinced that Nazism was an aberration, inconsistent with the rich cultural and scientific legacy of which they had thought they were a part.

I grew up in Chicago, in a household cluttered with shattered people struggling to reconcile the roots they had romanticized with the mordant reality they fled.

This book began with my search to understand my heritage and their turmoil.

RDF

Chronology of Characters

(the order of their personal appearance)

Jonah, a lad of nine in the Breslau ghetto,1778; the chief protagonist of the story.
Zelda, his mother
Joseph ben Jacob, Senior Rabbi of the Free School
Leah, his wife
Natalie, Sarah, and Hadassah, Joseph and Leah's daughters
Yankel, the butcher
Nehemiah, the tailor
The woman raped in a pogram in 1769
The old Rabbi and Rebittsin (who accompany the woman on the road to Breslau)
Aaron, the woman's son, born 1770 (we come to know him in 1778)

Reuben and Miriam, Jonah's grandparents from Prague
Ephraim, their son (Jonah's father)
Heinrich Nachrader, a Prussian farmer

Mordecai Friedlander (we meet him in Berlin in 1778)
Izaak, Mordecai's father

Ezra and **Raizel**, Izaak's mother and father (Mordecai's Grandparents)
Samuel Stern, a one-time "Court Jew" from Vienna
Naomi, Samuel's daughter (who married Izaak and became Mordecai's mother)
Rivkah, Mordecai's wife
Moses Mendelssohn, the philosopher
Nathan, son of Mordecai and Rivkah (8 years old in 1778)

Dorothea Mendelssohn, daughter of Moses Mendelssohn
Hoshea, the cobbler
Joachim Gauner, Attorney at Law and his Clerk

Pinkus, the pawnbroker
Vlad, a Ukranian emigre
Stas, a Polish blacksmith
Hans, a Prussian schoolteacher
An **ex-convict**

Feigel, the Breslau matchmaker
Leib Meyer of Amsterdam
Rebekkah and **Zacutus Meyer**, Leib's parents
Hanni, the Amsterdam matchmaker
Levi da Costa, an Amsterdam publisher

Erna Sacks, a Berlin dilettante
Karl Wilhelm Friedrich von Schlegel, a lecturer at the University of Jena
Johannes Sacks, Erna's father, a Berlin banker

Eleazar Pistron, a feed salesman from Ratibor
Reinhardt Vertreter, Chief Detective of Breslau

Madam Rosa of Jena
Dolly, Myrna, Kitty, Polly, Gina, and **Lisa:** ladies of the bordello
Wilhelm Sacks, son of the banker, Johannes Sacks

Jean Claude Boudin from Alsace   } denizens and
Carlo Regnini from Genoa   } members of
Pier Vandergryft from Amsterdam   } the Frankfort cell

Dr. Langkau of Breslau
Dr. Leibowitz of Ratibor
Judith, daughter of Hadassah, born 1792
Adam, Aaron's son, born 1792
The **Rabbi of Ratibor**

Georges Jacques Danton, Jacobin Deputy to the Assembly of France
Wilma Krankenschwester, a wet nurse
Rosalie, her charge
Smul, Samuel's valet
Jabal Rosenkohl, a fugitive
Fruma Klatschbase, the informer

Napoleon Bonaparte
Anna, wife of Carlo Regnini of Genoa
Giuliano, Anna and Carlo's nine year old son (we meet him in 1796)
Chassidic adherents and their rebbe
Crazy Salvatore, Ox of the Quay

Mother Superior of the Genoese Orphanage
Fr. Ludwig of Breslau
Chajjim Wolfssohn, Adam's classmate
Abraham Furtado, President of the Assembly of Notables, Paris, 1806
Friedrich Wilhelm, King of Prussia

The Monsignor at St. Berhardin's
Prince Jerome Bonaparte of Westphalia, brother of Napoleon

A Graduate Research Fellow in the University of Jena
David Frenkel of *Sulamith*
Rabbi David Zinzheim of Alsace   } the Presidium of
Rabbi Abraham de Cologna of Mantua   } the Grand Sanhedrin
Joshua Benzion Segre   } Paris, Feb. 9, 1807

Marshal Lefebvre, conqueror of Danzig, 1807
Censor No. Eleven
Henrietta Hertz of Berlin

Panoramic view of Breslau in the 18ᵗʰ century

The ghetto is in the foreground, just to the left of the
Schweidnitzer Gate [#4] guarding the bridge at center.

I

The Schoolmaster's Daughters

The assault of pushcarts on cobblestones jolted him into the new day. As peddlers' chants urged the dawn, Jonah tugged clothes over his nightshirt and stretched his feet to fill the oversize boots encrusted with mud from the damp dirt floor. A scrawny lad of nine, he stood to empty his bladder into the night bucket, hauled the pail up the steps to the *Judengasse* and, amid retreating shadows, emptied it into the stinking trench.

With sunrise, the ghetto gates spread open to the city of Breslau. Light filtered through the grime of the basement window upon Zelda, now awake, heating kasha and water on the cast iron stove his father had built. Pale yet handsome, his mother moved quickly about the dim quarters, straightened their bedcovers, poured water into a washbowl, brushed his bristly, tangled hair, and arrested by his eager eyes, returned a broad, pleased grin as she served the warm cereal and hot tea-in-a-glass.

Her son filled the chasm of her loneliness and protected her from the dread of desperation. His youthful energy was her spark of hope. In turn, her unequivocal love gave the boy confidence to face the world.

They set out on the Judengasse, now teeming with people who hawked wares, hauled jars, sacks, and crates, begged for coins, and poured up and down teetering staircases that hugged the outside walls of towering apartment buildings enclosing each side of the street. As the limited space for Jews had filled up, Christian landlords had added floor upon profitable floor. Where the street widened stood the grand Breslau Synagogue, *mikvahs* for ritual bathing, the Jewish hospital, a *yeshiva*, and an inn where members of the *Judengemeinschaft* met to manage and tax residents of the ghetto.

The lad dashed ahead, up the stairs to the top floor of the Free School, home of its Senior Rabbi and his family. Joseph ben Jacob was a huge man whose voice boomed from behind an abundant beard that hung in a great semicircle of glistening black curls from one ear across his barrel-shaped chest to the other. His wife, Leah, a heavyset woman of high energy, always out of breath, coached Zelda and her son through itemized lists of chores.

Jonah scooped ashes from the stove, carried loads of wash to the well, and bore basins of water for Zelda to scrub floors and clean utensils. He had mastered the skills of balance and torque to climb out on window sills and rub panes clear of coal fumes and grit. From his perch high above the ghetto walls, he gazed across the rooftops and fortifications of the city to boats and barges on the Oder. Below him, just beyond the hated gate, a boisterous gang of Gentiles hiked up Graupenstrasse to the coach terminal. Jonah sneered good riddance to the sons of Silesian peasants, bound for Frankfort where they would join the Hessians as mercenaries for the British to fight revolutionists in far-off America.

Within the apartment, three children stared at the young athlete reaching to the sky from their window frames until their mother swept them off, giggling and fussing, to their room. So large a family was rare in the ghetto. Married Jewish couples, on payment of 160 thalers, were allowed to raise one offspring. The burghers charged 70,000 thalers for each additional child who remained in Breslau upon becoming an adult. Few Jews could afford the sum, so when most extra children passed puberty, they were exported to other locales as brides or as workers.

Couples prayed for a son who would bring a daughter-in-law into their homes and care for them in old age. The community honored males. Only a boy could recite the mourner's *Kaddish* for a deceased father, become a *bar mitzvah,* and help form a *minyan,* the minimum of ten men essential to conduct religious services.

Throughout his years in the yeshiva, in worship, and in the Free School, Joseph was surrounded by men; they read, debated, chanted, danced and drank together. He wanted a son.

Strictly following the guidance of the Talmud to produce a boy, he had waited to the very middle of Leah's cycle to consummate their marriage. Upon discovering the joy of copulation, he returned to his wife's bedside to repeat the glorious act *every* night, even as the miracle grew within her, until the bursting of Leah's water brought forth: a girl! Convinced it was God's punishment for his unrestrained lust, he named her Natalie (after Nathan, through whom the Lord reproached David for his lechery).

Leah consoled Joseph: their daughter would marry well, and perhaps *she* would produce a son. But Joseph could not wait eighteen years for "perhaps." "Let us save what funds we can to build a proper dowry so that, before she comes of age, she can be married to a good man in a shtetl not more than three or four days from here. Now, we shall try again for a son!"

He limited his effusion to *only* the very middle of her cycle, abstained from all other contact, and fervently, intently, prayed. At the first sign that his seed had sprouted, Joseph suppressed his hunger for Leah's flesh; he dared not touch her until after the birth of his heir. When the time came, he pressed his ear to the door of the birth chamber, waiting for the precious moment of delivery, hoping to glean the child's gender from its startled cries. The midwife, with a smirk of perverse satisfaction, hinting at the superiority of her sex, announced the arrival of Sarah.

"It was intended," Leah reassured her distraught husband, "that you who must be a father to all the boys of the school not be distracted by a son on whom you would heap special favor as your own." She urged him to educate Natalie in the Holy Scriptures as he would a son, and she would train their second daughter to be a good wife to a proper man in a distant Jewish community.

Not to be thwarted by his wife's interpretation of the will of the Divine, Joseph convinced her to join him in one more try for a son. He secured an ancient elixir from the apothecary. Again, they counted the days, matching them to the congruent phases of the moon and carefully clocking the hours. On the fifteenth of Av, at 11:00 a.m., he swallowed the elixir, and vomited. Terrified that this was a bad omen, they waited another month.

Each day, Joseph joined arms with the men of a minyan and shouted to God for a male descendant. For two days before their union, he took only barley water. On the fourteenth of Elul, at 10:48, he consumed the elixir; it stayed down, and by 11:00 o'clock they mated. Joseph continued the daily prayers with his minyan as Leah's body slowly expanded for the mystery within her through three seasons of the year.

On the twelfth of Ivar, Leah gave birth to Hadassah, an enchanting May Day child. Laughing with tears, now certain that it was God's will that he have no son, Joseph vowed to enjoy her until she, too, could be found an appropriate match abroad.

Making the best of his lot, Joseph taught all of his daughters to read. Natalie, a shy, slim wisp, spent so much time in books she was fitted with glasses by the age of eight. The spectacles reinforced her isolation just as they brought her closer to the printed words. Certain that she was the chosen one who alone would not be exported, she stood in her father's shadow, helping him teach her younger sisters, grading papers of the boys whose school she could not attend, following his recitations as though they were the voice of God.

Though raised to help in routine chores, Sarah was consumed with the realization that she would have to know everything about keeping house in a distant place. She became relentlessly inquisitive about each herb, fruit, and vegetable; where it was grown, in what kind of soil, with what kind of care. When sent to bring home a chicken for dinner,

Yankel the *shochet* had to tell her how it had been raised before he could cut its neck and drain the blood. At Nehemiah the tailor's, Sarah inspected the stitching and learned about the origins of every piece of apparel.

Hadassah, the effervescent child, lit up the house with her laughter and teased everyone into pleasing her. She loved humanity and it loved her back, nourishing her sublime sense of self-assurance. She would not bother her head with the prospect of exile. She was young, and she would be young forever.

On this Friday afternoon, at work in the schoolmaster's study, Jonah furtively unraveled the holy scroll of the Torah. He gazed in awe upon the words of God whose letters he could not decipher. The *Judengemeinschaft* would have paid his tuition to the Free School, but Jonah had to work while others were in class.

"I could teach you to read," a gawky, erudite Natalie intruded.

Embarrassed at being discovered, Jonah summoned a pose of nonchalance, rolling up the scroll as though it were a routine task, and dismissed out-of-hand the prospect of being taught by a girl. "My father will teach me to read."

"Ephraim is a criminal," the graceless girl leaned into his face. "He will never come back."

His nonchalance dissolved. "My father never did anything wrong and he will prove it!" bellowed the defiant son of a servant, his face taut with fury. "You and all the fancy Jews who leave him there to rot can't hold a candle to him. You're all a bunch of cowards! You grovel before the Prussians and lick their boots."

In tears, more from Jonah's rejection than his rhetoric, Natalie ran to the kitchen, alarming the women who were preparing the Sabbath evening meal, refusing to tell anyone why she was whimpering. Leah took her daughter in her arms. Women of Leah's generation were not expected to be literate, but she had felt a tinge of sorrow as her children slipped away from her into the pages of books she could not comprehend. She relished this rare moment, mothering her precocious child.

In the dusk that decreed the onset of *Shabbat*, carrying her usual portion of *schalet* for tomorrow's dinner, Zelda returned with her subdued son to their basement flat. "What did you do to Natalie to throw her into such a frenzy?" she asked Jonah.

"That snotty, conceited girl spoke lies about my father."

No more was said, nor should be said or spelled out such that Zelda would have to respond further. She needed the work given her by the schoolmaster's wife. But she needed far more the honoring of her husband's name and was proud of how deeply her son respected Ephraim.

That night, Jonah tossed in his bed, dogged by anger and humiliation. How could a girl read the Holy Writ, while he was blind to the simplest words? *How dare she accuse his father!*

For a long while, he ached with bitterness, fighting off fatigue until the cries of babies in tenements above him merged into soothing maternal sounds. He drifted off in a reverie of lullabies his mother used to sing.

In the depths where weariness had plunged him, Jonah walked with Ephraim among the cedars of Lebanon and then his father disappeared into the trees and became their trunks, his beard their leaves, his shoulders the Mount of Olives, and his strong back the eastern wall. Ephraim *was* the promised land.

The interior of the Breslau temple: Engraving by Johann Christian Sander, 1746. From the HUC Skirball Cultural Center, Museum Collection, Los Angeles, CA.

II

Jonah and Aaron

Nine years earlier, Zelda and Ephraim had brought Jonah to the Breslau Temple to enter into his covenant with God on the altar of circumcision. It was on that same dry August day of 1769, in a church cut into the crags of the Corsican coast, that Letizia and Carlo Maria Buonaparte brought their first son to the altar to be baptized Napolione.

While far to the East, in the Pale of Settlement, a woman staggered from a burning *shtetl*, unable to weep or speak or close her lifeless eyes. While a dozen men, those too ancient or infirm to flee, held the mourner's Kaddish for her husband and all those who had perished, she wandered into the woods.

No one knew how long it was before the *rebbitsin* came upon her, took the fragile frame into her ample arms, forced droplets of water and bits of bread into the doleful woman, sprinkled and purified her body, bruised by the lust of marauders, and washed her clothes clear of their stains of abuse.

Each day from dawn to dusk, the compassionate rebbitsin walked hand in hand with the woman and old rabbi, a stooped man whose long white beard disappeared into his vest. While he chanted and mumbled, his wife invoked the wrath of a vengeful God upon the Cossacks, appealed to His lovingkindness for comfort, and praised His almighty power for the miracle of their survival. The woman removed a ring with a pale rose red stone from her finger and pressed it on the rebbitsin.

Faintly inscribed inside the metal band were the words, "*To a woman of valour: Proverbs 31.10.*"

Moving westward, they arrived at shtetls not yet raided, were given lodging for the night, and journeyed on. Winter storms came and their stopovers grew longer. There were always families ready to trade room and board for lessons, divine guidance and resolution of nagging questions on fine points of scripture. Their journey took months. By springtime, it was clear that the woman was with child.

The baby was born on the outskirts of Breslau. Squalling, he emerged with bright red hair as his mother gasped her final breath.

Under cover of night and a gentle rain, they buried her in a potato field where the rabbi said the Kaddish.

The rebbitsin took the new born infant in her arms, named him Aaron, and together with her husband, walked to the city gates. Although the toll for Jews was set above that for cattle, more than they could afford, the guards accepted the tarnished ring with its rose red stone as payment for their entry.

Tonight would be *erev Rosh Hashanah,* the beginning of the new year. In solemnity and awe, guided by the sight of soaring tenements, they entered the ghetto, shielded by walls that abutted the city's fortifications along the Ohlau, a tributary of the Oder.

On either side of a street paved in cobblestones were buildings of brick and mortar inscribed as institutions of learning and holiness. Though people strode at various paces, none walked in fear. Everyone spoke loudly and freely. Jewish shops carried Jewish goods crafted by Jewish artisans. At the center of everything, stood a grand baroque Temple. Overwhelmed, the old rabbi knew he had found the promised land. He would trudge no further.

On the eve of the Day of Judgment, he filled out the forms in flawless Hebrew calligraphy, stood erect, spoke clearly with the authority of a master, and petitioned the Judengemeinschaft for permanent residence.

He was engaged to teach at the Free School in exchange for food and lodging for himself, his wife, and the child.

His classroom became their home; after the last student left, they curled up on the benches and pulled woolen covers about them. Aaron grew up under the tutelage of the old rabbi and the rebbitsin, who were looked upon as his grandparents. Everyone knew the story of the slaughter of Aaron's father and the rape of his mother in the Polish massacres. No more was ever said about his parents, but there were whispers about his parentage.

The rebbitsin became ill with consumption. From the age of six, when other boys hauled coal, helped their parents set up their push-carts, and worked at odd jobs, Aaron was a nursemaid to her, spending little time outside the quarters occupied by the school. Within a year, she was dead. She had given him the only love he ever knew. Numb with emptiness, Aaron moved his bench closer to the rabbi who, choked by his own grief, could offer only commentaries in place of affection. All day and into the night, he sat at the old rabbi's feet, listening to discourses on the Torah, the Talmud, and the Midrash, folktales that amplified the stories of the Hebrew Scriptures whose characters became his family.

He was on his way to shul, through snow turned grey by the fumes of ten thousand coal stoves, when Aaron stumbled into another boy. Before he could stammer out an apology, the boy pushed him into a manure-crusted mound of ice. A third lad, bellowing curses, lifted the assailant off Aaron and booted him on his way. Jonah ben Ephraim held out his hand, pulled Aaron to his feet, brushed him off with frozen willow branches till he was presentable for shul, and walked with his new friend to Shabbat services.

Before them stood statues of Moses and Aaron, the first high priest, flanking Frederick the Great as though he were king of the Jews. Jonah detested the Prussian invasion of his temple, so he looked up and found comfort in the overhead figures of *real* Kings: Solomon and David.

Although he could not read, he had memorized some of the chants and traditional prayers and followed Aaron's cues on when to seesaw on his feet or bow his head.

The reader began the week's section of the Torah, Exodus, 16: "*He that stealeth a man, and selleth him, or if he be found in his hand, he shall surely be put to death.*" Jonah set his jaw, certain that God ordained him to avenge Ephraim.

"*And he that curseth his father or his mother, shall surely be put to death.*" The boy swore an oath that he would not admit any foul thoughts nor let anyone ever speak ill of his father.

Trumpets blared, drums rolled, and the cantor concluded, "*thou shalt give life for life, eye for eye, tooth for tooth, hand for hand, foot for foot, burning for burning, wound for wound, stripe for stripe.*"

With clenched fist, Jonah bobbed in obeisance to each degree of retribution, confident that he would be the agent of God, visiting eternal damnation upon those who had falsely imprisoned Ephraim.

That afternoon, Aaron and the old rabbi began teaching Jonah the name for each Hebrew character. All through the week, as he helped his mother scrub floors and windows, he practiced the sounds that went with the symbols, writing a chet, a vet, a raysh and a dahlet with strokes of soap, then rubbing them off as he pronounced the letters with different vowels. Each Saturday, after services, Jonah learned how to unite the sounds to make words.

His regard for the quirky, cloistered Aaron deepened with his comprehension of aleph, bet and gimel. The boys read to one another, first words, then prayers, and finally tales from the Bible. Jonah entered a new and seemingly boundless world. But it was one in which Aaron had felt trapped. With no other friend, no family or roots, only the verses of scripture to relate to, he craved stories of the earth from which Jonah had been shaped.

Together, they set out on a search.

*   *   *

As the evening gate closed upon the pushcart vendors returning from the city, the two boys ran among them. "What are the Germans like?" Jonah shouted to Hoshea the cobbler who had spent the day fitting peasants into secondhand boots.

"They are the same as us, except they are free," said the shoemaker.

"Then how can they be like us?" snorted Pinkas the pawnbroker who stood nearby to collect his debts and hand back the trinkets he held as collateral.

"The *burghers* may be free," said Nehemiah the tailor as he counted his share of pfennigs from the sale of the tired garments he had mended to look new. "But most of the poor bumpkins who buy from us are serfs from the farms; they are almost as poor as we are, and they are trapped by the same forces."

Jonah threw himself into Nehemiah's long, bony outstretched arms. He loved the lanky old widower with his crisp, certain, and unorthodox views of everything. The tailor had been like an uncle to him and to his father before him.

"Tell us about those forces and why they lock us up in this stinking pit."

With permission from Zelda and the old rabbi, Nehemiah took the boys, one on each hand to Naaman's *Knishery* where he filled a sack with potato dumplings, and then led the boys up the creaky stairs to his capacious apartment. Through looms, stacks of old clothing and new bolts of cloth, the trio made their way to the front room where a great window looked out upon a vast, brilliant firmament. Sitting with their legs tucked under them, noshing on knishes, Jonah and Aaron faced the old man, his figure framed by the mesmerizing glimmer of the sky.

"Life hasn't always been like this. I was born in the flourishing Jewish community of Prague. Although we had to live behind ghetto walls, Jews were admitted to the trades and we became doctors, teachers, and merchants. With the approval of the Hapsburg Empire, we built a great center of learning. We worshiped in our synagogue and lived well, though our dead were confined to a small plot of land, buried five deep, one on top of the other.

"I was the son of a woodcutter, but I wasn't much good for my father's kind of work. My thin, delicate fingers were more suited to the refining of lumber than to the hewing of it. So my papa hired me out as an apprentice to Jonah's grandfather. Reuben was a ruddy, pipe-smoking, muscular gnome who stood no higher than the head of a goat. He was so skilled a carpenter and cabinet maker that weavers from every corner of Bohemia sought his spinning wheels. His wife, Miriam, towered half-a-meter above Reuben, a height he found useful for reaching his tools and stringing his wheels.

"The year was 1744. Jonah's father, Ephraim, was a babe in the crib created by *his* father, Reuben, when Frederick the Great, king of Prussia, marched into Prague. Throughout history, invaders had pillaged ghettoes, slaughtered our men and raped our women. Fearing the worst, we bolted doors and shutters and hid in our cellars. But after several days of bewildering quiet, the strongest men cautiously emerged, looked about and saw that our houses were untouched. Slowly, we resumed our occupations. Frederick was much more interested in the crown jewels of the Schatzkammer and the riches of the Hofberg Palace than with the miserable possessions of petty Jewish merchants and artisans!"

Relieved, the boys attacked their knishes.

"Still," Nehemiah went on, "I remember how Reuben clutched his hammer when Prussian Guards looked down at him from his doorway. He relaxed his grip when they decreed they'd come to engage his serv-ices. Over the next nine months, we labored day and night, Reuben, Miriam and I. We built wonderful, elegant sturdy chests for the king. Each morning, officers arrived, ordering us to work faster. No sooner had we finished one cabinet than it was hauled off and we constructed another. As they carried away the last container, we heard distant thunder that we knew meant the return of the Austrians.

"The snows came early that year and soon the roads would be impassable. The whole town watched Frederick's royal cavalry depart for Berlin, his royal wagons sagging under the weight of Reuben's handsome chests filled with Hapsburg gold. We were left exhausted, unpaid, and answerable to a new master."

"What happened to you then?" Aaron choked on his knish. Nehemiah lowered his voice and pulled a cloak across his shoulders.

"Maria Theresa, the Empress of Austria," he stood up to emulate an evil queen, "hated the Prussians. She charged all the Jews of Prague with having helped Frederick, her worst enemy.

"It was the harshest, most bitter winter in years." Nehemiah wrapped the cloak about him for warmth. "But Maria Theresa didn't care. She ordered our immediate expulsion. In a single stroke, she ended eight centuries of Jewish settlement.

"My father, the woodcutter, hid with my mother, deep in the woods he knew so well." Nehemiah turned his head to look wistfully away. His voice broke slightly and dropped to a whisper. "He knew I was too frail to survive in the forest."

Recovering, the tailor playfully tapped Jonah on the chest. "So I joined your grandparents and we tramped with twenty thousand other Jews across treacherous, ice-covered roads that twisted, rose, and fell away from Prague. Everywhere we walked, we stumbled over bodies turned stiff." The tailor stumbled across the floor, recalling the journey. "All along the way, we urged those who lingered or rested, the weary and the ill, to go on. Only the need to protect little Ephraim drove us and kept us going."

Jonah squirmed with delight in the knowledge that their love for the child who was his father had given them the will to live.

"We knew that no town would accept thousands of Jews. At every fork, we prayed for deliverance, then split into groups, each taking a different path. It was Miriam's idea to follow the deep ruts in the ice, left by the great weight of the king's wagons loaded with Reuben's chests. Day after day, across mountains and fields, we trailed Frederick's troops to the banks of the Oder, where we camped, determined to petition the king for the right to enter the city to which he had returned."

"Weren't there Jews already living in Breslau?" asked Aaron.

"Only sometimes, and always under the heels of others. We were here long before there was a ghetto. Five hundred years ago, the Lateran Council ordered these walls be built to lock us in. Still, one conqueror after another drove us out. When we were a part of Poland, a Franciscan friar, John of Capistrano, charged forty-one Jews of Breslau with desecrating the host. The city fathers burned them all at the stake, seized their young children, brought them up as Christians, and banished the rest of us from the city.

"For a long while, our ghetto stood empty. Hungary invaded the city, then Bohemia and Austria. Jews filtered back, always at their sufferance, never allowed to own homes or shops. Whenever it looked like Jews could become a viable community, they thinned us out. In 1741, Frederick the Great marched in and relaxed the restrictions.

"But when he left to conquer Prague, the burghers reinstated the old rules, limited Jews to twelve families, and evicted all the rest. We followed Frederick back from Prague and sent a delegation to meet with his councilor. Reuben was one of our spokesmen, and he argued that the king should give us sanctuary, since we had been made expatriates only because we had helped him. Gentile landlords wanted renters for their vacant buildings in a ghetto nobody else would occupy. Given all these considerations, Frederick granted us asylum. He let us build our new synagogue and to assure him of our gratitude and loyalty, the Judengemeinschaft placed that statue of him in the center of it."

"I hate it!" volunteered Jonah. "They lock us in this putrid sinkhole, let us have one beautiful building of our own to worship in, and we have to muck it up with a false idol to thank a distant, Christian king for letting us be here!"

Aaron could not be outdone in the purity of his devotion. "That statue," he pontificated, "violates the sanctity of our temple!"

"Before all other commandments comes the injunction to survive." Nehemiah put one arm on each of the boys, "so that we can carry out all the others. As bad as Frederick was, he offered us the protection of life and the right to publicly assemble in prayer. We need his protection. It has been the local burghers of Breslau, who have made our life even more difficult. They resented but had to accept their king's order, but then imposed conditions upon us to keep us from competing with their control of the land and the marketplace. That is why we cannot enter any profession or trade except for tailoring or shoemaking.

"But we survive. I was able to put my fingers to work as a tailor's apprentice, married my employer's daughter, and moved into this flat with my late wife's prosperous family. Listen! Their ghosts linger here, still." The boys looked about nervously.

"They would not let us sell new commodities, so Reuben collected and refurbished secondhand chairs, tables, cabinets, and clocks. We could not open shops outside the ghetto, so Miriam became a peddler. She wheeled Reuben's wares into town each day and pushed the cart back behind those creaking gates before each evening's curfew.

"Ephraim grew up in the workshop at the back end of his parent's flat, breathing his father's tobacco smoke, learning about furniture, appliances, and all devices made by man and dissected by Reuben. He became a mender of things and soon earned enough to take a wife. Your mother was exported from Leipzig, and surrounded by your parents and aging grandparents, you were born, Jonah, in a flat like this."

Jonah could barely remember his grandparents, and could not recall ever living in such luxury, but he loved listening to Nehemiah's narrations of the past. The night was still young and there were more stories for the old tailor to tell.

Joseph & Leah's family:

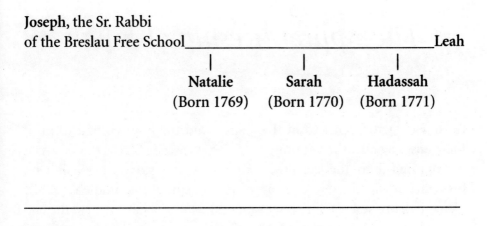

Joseph, the Sr. Rabbi
of the Breslau Free School_____Leah

| Natalie | Sarah | Hadassah |
| (Born 1769) | (Born 1770) | (Born 1771) |

Jonah's forebears:

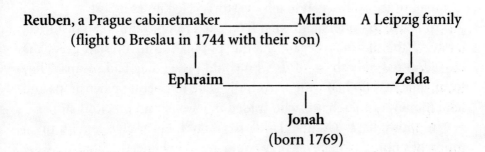

Reuben, a Prague cabinetmaker_____Miriam   A Leipzig family
    (flight to Breslau in 1744 with their son)

Ephraim_____Zelda

Jonah
(born 1769)

III

The Apprenticeship of Jonah

A falling star dropped from the galaxy, and the boys rushed to press their noses against the window, watching it cascade across the sky. As it disappeared into the cosmos, Aaron told the story of Elijah who brought down fire from heaven to consume the godless. While Nehemiah brewed tea, Jonah sat rapt in the biblical tale. "And at the end of his life," Aaron concluded, "Elijah was swept up into heaven by a whirlwind, in a chariot and horses of fire."

"I will ride against the godless, and bring fire down upon those who unjustly imprisoned my father," Jonah announced, "and maybe I, too, will be borne up to heaven."

"Tell me about your father," Aaron pleaded.

Jonah urged Nehemiah to tell the story. "He knows it best."

"You have to understand what happened to Ephraim in an historical context," the old man began. "As our population in Breslau grew, the city admitted only those of us who could prove they had means. They let anyone in who had orders from the state to operate pawnshops and lend money, or merchants who traded in jewelry and precious stones.

"In those days, Gentile landlords could evict any tenant on a moment's notice, whenever they could get a higher rent. Since we were confined to the ghetto, in houses we could not own, we ended up bidding against one another for living space.

"Reuben's fingers had grown stiff and his legs no longer carried him. Now, Ephraim had to provide for his parents, as well as a wife and child, with little money left over for rent. He could not compete with others who could pay more for his apartment, so the landlord set all the contents of his workshop and the family's personal effects out on the Judengasse in a Silesian snowstorm. Miriam was haunted by recollections of their trek from Prague, and was convinced that they were again being sent into exile. She gave up. With a broken heart, Reuben followed his wife to her grave."

Aaron put his arm about his friend. "But at least you had your mother and father," he comforted Jonah. "Is that when you moved into the basement?"

"It took everything Ephraim had to pay for that miserable hovel." The tailor gritted his teeth. "Infuriated, Ephraim told the story of his parents' martyrdom to everyone who would listen. He spent day and night organizing tenants least able to pay the rent. They filled the synagogue and demanded that the rabbis invoke the ancient Jewish law of proprietary rights. With that kind of pressure, the Judengemeinschaft agreed to protect existing occupants against overbidding and exploitation.

"Nobody was permitted, under any circumstance, to offer a higher rent than that being paid, or to do anything that resulted in expropriating the lease from the current resident. An occupant could give away or sell his lease, he could include it in a dowry for his daughter or pass it on by heredity to his son, but so long as the rent was paid, his tenure was secure.

"The idea spread to other ghettoes and became the rule throughout Prussia. But Ephraim was marked as a troublemaker. It became ever more difficult for him to find work in Breslau." The old man rose from his chair and paced angrily about the room.

"Just beyond the city," Nehemiah pointed to land across the Oder, "Heinrich Nachrader, a small farmer, hired Ephraim to set new beams in his roof, reconstruct his dilapidated fence, rebuild a pen, and repair a broken carriage. With each new job, Nachrader agreed to pay him a fixed sum… But the payments never came.

"Jonah, your father worked on Nachrader's farm for months with nothing to show for it. One afternoon, as he headed back to the ghetto before curfew, Ephraim dug up an apron-full of potatoes from Nachrader's farm…He was caught and thrown in jail.

"Before the magistrate, he argued he was entitled to these potatoes and more, for his months of uncompensated toil. Nachrader denied that Ephraim had ever been hired for any work, and accused your father, Jonah, of coming on his land to poison his well. Ephraim was detained pending charges of theft and, outrageous as it sounds, *intent to murder*!

"The leaders of the Breslau ghetto dared not come to his defense. The law of collective responsibility holds all Jews accountable for the transgressions of any one of us. We were blamed for the Black Death. In Chillon, the entire Jewish community was massacred on the wild tale that a Jew had concocted a poison out of spiders, frogs, lizards, human flesh, the hearts of Christians and consecrated Hosts. They said he dropped the toxin into wells from which Christians drew their water. The tale traveled throughout Europe. All the Jews of sixty large communities and of one hundred and fifty smaller locales were massacred. Many cities swore they would never harbor Jews in their midst again.

"When Ephraim was accused of that same mythic crime, Zelda turned to the Judengemeinschaft for help. The major contributors appoint its Administrative Council, and they, in turn control all contact any of us have with the outside world. They trembled in their boots at the thought of a trial of Ephraim. It could set off all those macabre, medieval misgivings against us. It could give Christian extremists a pretext to wipe us out.

"So the Judengemeinschaft issued a declaration, washing their hands of any responsibility for Ephraim's acts, and placing their trust in the so-called fairness of the judicial system.

"It has been three years," Nehemiah cursed the air, "and Ephraim still sits in the Breslau prison, awaiting a trial that will never come, while Zelda scrubs floors to make ends meet."

"Someday," Jonah pointed his finger to the certain future, "my father will be proved innocent. Someday," he pressed his hands in prayer, "my father will be free and my mother will be relieved of her toil. Someday," he whispered hoarsely as he made a fist, "I will avenge them!"

Aaron stared in awe at Jonah, admiring his passion and choking with envy of one who could love and be so loved by his parents. They sat in silence for a long while, watching the stars fade as the glow of the eastern horizon pushed back the night. With thanks to Nehemiah, the boys stood up and hurried to their flats before the rays of the sun would command their diurnal duties.

*   *   *

From the moment that she first stood up and walked, Zelda had been trained to suppress her emotions. Like most second or third daughters born in a ghetto, she was sculpted in ice for export. As a servant to her elders, she had to be a young adult. In matters of religion, she had to remain a child forever: pious and illiterate. There were no matters of the heart. Still, she grew up with the dread of leaving everyone she knew, upon becoming eighteen. But when she came to experience desire of the flesh, she secretly invested her inevitable betrothal to a stranger with feelings she dared not reveal. By the time Feigel the *shadchen* arrived to take her to Breslau, Zelda was torn between her grief over leaving all that was familiar, and a wild hope that she might find expression for longings that welled up inside her.

Reuben and Miriam embraced their daughter-in-law with uninhibited zeal. The easy, open ways of their household liberated her spirits, and Ephraim fulfilled her most sensuous dreams. She discovered her capacity to love. Jonah was conceived in a burst of passion. Those first few years were the happiest of Zelda's life.

Even when troubles came, she could withstand the anguish of eviction and the despair of Miriam and Reuben's death, so long as she had her husband and son at her side. She encouraged Ephraim to organize the tenants and was proud of his accomplishments. She consoled him when he came home empty handed from Nachrader's farm.

But when her husband was arrested, Zelda's world collapsed. She was despondent, isolated and ostracized. Only Nehemiah came to her assistance. Successful in his work, he had become an iconoclast. He was bitter about the ease with which an empress could order the collapse of a great Jewish culture and was fed up with the delusions that Jews had invented to justify their exclusivity. Personal loyalty to his friends was the only value he treasured. He sat and sewed and had no use for social niceties, gossip, or convention. Nobody could recall when he had last been at services; there were rumors that he was not a true believer and that he even stitched garments on the Sabbath. The wealthy Jews did not care about his personal habits, or if he violated Shabbat. They were grateful that the tailor produced their finished apparel promptly.

Nehemiah prevailed upon some of his customers to engage Zelda as a servant. Those who hired her did so knowing that because her husband was in jail, they could pay her less. And, she came with a vigorous son to help her.

*   *   *

"If you learn to read," Aaron ventured, "you may someday become a lawyer for your father."

"They will never let us be lawyers. And with what I earn from a pail, I can never raise the funds to hire a Christian attorney, especially with the extra fees they charge a Jew. Somehow, the Judengemeinshaft must be convinced to help my father."

"Then *write* to them," the single-minded Aaron tried to focus his pupil on the possibilities of the pen.

"Eh! They won't listen to *me*!" At that instant, he knew what to do. Each evening, while his mother slept, he went over it again, making sure that it was clear and correct. On Shabbat, just before daybreak, he slipped out of his cellar chamber and carried it, rolled under his arm, along with his father's hammer and four pegs.

Before the cock crowed, Jonah nailed it to the front door of the synagogue. In bold block Hebrew letters, he had printed:

JEWS of BRESLAU:
EPHRAIM BEN REUBEN IS IN JAIL BUT HE IS INNOCENT
PLEASE TELL THE JUDENGEMEINSHAFT
TO DEFEND HIM!

It was the consuming topic of conversation from the moment the congregants arrived for services until after the last cup of tea was drained from the urn at the *oneg Shabbat*:

"What impudence for a child to question the eminent leaders of our community!" "What heresy to profane the shul with political propaganda!" "What can you expect from the son of a thief?" "Where is the mother in all this?"

As soon as the sun set on Shabbat, the Administrative Council met on the question of what should be done with Jonah ben Ephraim for his outrageous, seditious conduct.

"We can no longer allow so rebellious a boy," said Yankel the schochet, "to go into the homes of the better families."

"We cannot let him spend his time on the streets where he would rile up the beggars and the discontented," argued Pinkas the pawnbroker. "He should be in school where he can be supervised."

Joseph agreed that he no longer wanted Jonah working in his house, near his daughters, but hastened to add, "It would be dangerous to put him in the Free School where he could spread his ideas among vulnerable students."

"Then he should be expelled from Breslau," snapped Yankel.

"We cannot cast out a child of ten from our community without his father," said the Chief Rabbi. This was an unusual case.

After hours of Talmudic exploration and tormenting debate, the Council called in Zelda and warned her she would have to control her son or face the possibility of expulsion along with him. Terrified, Zelda ran to Nehemiah. How could she control her unruly son? How could she leave Breslau while Ephraim was still in prison?

For years, Nehemiah had quietly nurtured Jonah's fervor for justice. As the boy grew, he had filled him with accounts of inequities and implanted seeds of dissent. Now, the old tailor faced up to a sense of profound responsibility: this was a predicament he had helped to create.

"With all the new settlers pushing into the ghetto," he told Zelda, "I have been getting more orders than I have time to fill. I need an apprentice, and Jonah is just the right age to begin to learn the trade. I cannot pay him, but I can watch him like a hawk, feed him, keep him out of trouble, here in the workshop of my apartment seven days a week. At the end of his training, he will be a real *mensch*, ready to earn his own way!"

Zelda threw her arms about her old friend, weeping with gratitude and relief. She would find the energy to do the housework without Jonah. Her employers would not have to pay her as much.

The protective rules for which Ephraim had fought allowed Nehemiah to keep his entire flat, even after his wife and her family had passed on. He emptied out a storeroom with a window on the airshaft. The stench of turd at the bottom of the shaft mingled with the aroma of cabbage, rutabagas, onions, and garlic that poured out of the other apartments. But the room became Jonah's citadel. It was an elegance he had never known.

Nehemiah immediately put him to work and Jonah was not seen again at the shul. It would be years before he saw Aaron.

IV

The Enlightenment of Berlin

Mordecai Friedlander considered himself the most fortunate of men. God had provided him with a wise father, a mother of wealth, and had brought him forth in the stately city of Berlin just as it was opening up for Jews with entrepreneurial skills. He rubbed his circumcised penis, bringing it to erection, so he could secretly admire his full manliness in the bedroom mirror.

This was 1776 and a whole new world was dawning. The old *Generalreglements* that had controlled and assessed the Jews with special tolls was now eased. Synagogues were at last permitted.

His family had come so far since Grandfather Ezra had to beg for old rags at the back-doors of affluent Christian homes. At night, locked in the ghetto, he sorted and scrubbed the better scraps to fetch a decent price from Jewish tailors who were confined to the use of secondhand clothes. Each morning, he set out on a predetermined route, but one day of the week was special. On Wednesdays, he carefully scoured all his sweat-points, buffed his boots, shook out his coat, brushed his beard, and pushed his locks under the obligatory yellow hat.

At the stroke of nine, he rapped on the kitchen door of a half-timbered house just off Potsdammer Platz. Raizel, a Jewish servant, always had garments to put into his sack, along with a kind word. In the winter, she offered Ezra hot coffee; in the summer she greeted him with an inviting glass of cool water. After two and a half years of resolute Wednesdays at nine, he spoke to her of marriage.

Under state law, Jewish servants could not marry or have children. But Raizel could leave her job if Ezra could afford her.

As resourceful as she was ripe for matrimony, Raizel harvested a better quality of hand-me-downs from her employers and their neighbors so that Ezra could peddle them directly on the streets of Berlin. Within six months, they garnered the funds to pay both the special tax for a Jewish marriage certificate and the tariff for the marriage itself. Ezra and Raizel worked steadily to transmute rags into raiment. Months after they paid the levy for the birth of the one child allowed for Jews of their class, they produced Izaak, the son into whom they poured all their love and dreams.

While he was still an infant, Izaak rode on his parents' pushcart while they hawked their used apparel through the bustling city streets from dawn to curfew. When old enough to be left behind to attend the Berlin Free School, he peered through the ghetto gates at the emerging wealth of the city.

The Thirty Years' War was over, the Great Elector, Frederick William Hohenzollern, had conquered the Polish Duchy of Prussia, and Izaak witnessed the rebuilding of the German capital. The Oder-Spree canal linked Berlin with Breslau at one end and Hamburg at the other, making it the center of trade and the vital hub of the new empire, one extending to the Russian border. Izaak envisaged himself a part of that elegance and might. Jolting him from his fantasy, an intrusive neighbor grabbed him by the ear and marched him through the boisterous, backward, fetid alleys to Hebrew class.

When finished with daily lessons and chores, Izaak ran to the Oder-Spree canal and listened to the tantalizing tales of sailors, their descriptions of exotic people and strange products from far away places. Little by little, he perfected his German, befriended the longshoremen, and accumulated odd leftover lots of silk cloth that sailors brought from the east. As he grew into his teens, Izaak came to know the different qualities and strands of silk, their sources and characteristics. He acquired his own pushcart for the specialized peddling of silks.

*   *   *

Mordecai's mother, Naomi, was born in Vienna, the daughter of Samuel Stern, a bald, rotund supplier of uniforms to the Austrian Royal Army, *a Hofjude,* or "Court Jew," in the reign of Maria Theresa. Court Jews were unique figures who had emerged in the Middle Ages to serve kings and princes as financial agents, civilian quartermasters, or doctors.

Maria Theresa, committed to the preeminence of the Catholic Church, was uneasy with her Court Jews. They shunned the wearing of yellow armbands and their women no longer wore yellow ribbons in their hair, as required of all other Jews throughout the provinces of Austria. She wrote to her son, Crown Prince Joseph, that without "a dominant religion, tolerance and indifference would spread, and these were just the very means to undermine everything." She barred synagogues from Vienna, reduced the city's Jewish population to five hundred and fifty, and made conversion to Christianity a condition for continued protection of the *Hofjuden.* Faced with the choice of abandoning their heritage or giving up their advantages, the Sterns were among fifty Hofjuden families who refused baptism. Furious, the empress expelled them all from Austria.

Frederick William, the Great Elector of Protestant Prussia, welcomed the exiled Jews to Berlin. Their capital and knowledge would help him develop his nation's economy. Drawing on his experience in supplying the Austrian army, Samuel negotiated with the shepherds of Brandenburg for their wool, hired and organized spinners and tailors, and brought finished fabrics to market.

The Great Elector had assumed that given such prerogatives, Samuel would become a good Christian. When he did not, his business and properties were expropriated by the crown and local officials forced him into the ghetto along with other Austrian Jews who refused to convert.

But before the former Hofjuden could form bonds with their oppressed coreligionists, a new regent, Frederick the Great, acceded to the throne. Although he had contempt for the "religious superstition" of Judaism, Frederick cleverly distinguished between the mass of Jews whom he would enslave and the wealthy few to whom he could sell entitlements to advance the interests of the state.

His *Generaljudenprivileg* of 1750 was described by Voltaire as an instrument of torture. It burdened and controlled the vast majority of Jews, banned them from most crafts, agriculture, and every occupation in which there were guilds or professional associations of Christians. Jews were assessed countless taxes not required of others. Poor alien Jews could never enter the country.

On the other hand, Frederick invited select Jews to help bring the industrial revolution to Prussia. For 25,000 thalers a year, one could buy a *schutzbrief,* entitling him to secure credit and do business with anyone under the protection of the crown for the specific purpose of establishing a factory. However, no Jew could have anything to do with the commerce or manufacture of wool.

Samuel's pleas to officials for permission to resume his wool trade went unheeded. So long as he would not accept Jesus, he could not touch the fibre of the lamb. Though not a pious man, Samuel had been expelled from Austria rather than deny his heritage. He could not now forsake his religion, merely for personal profit.

In the streets of Berlin, he came upon Izaak, peddling his odd lots of silk. Samuel fondled the material and asked about its origins. Izaak explained that the textiles were spun in Italy and Switzerland from raw silk of the Orient, the cloth came from husks of reeled cocoons, damaged and unreelable cocoons, and from floss and other wastes. One could produce better silk fabric than this by reeling it from very long, continuous fibers. Such products would have more beauty, strength, and brilliance than those which were spun. But who could afford the equipment for the reeling process?

Samuel Stern had capital and considerable know-how for the weaving of textiles. Izaak Friedlander knew which sailors and captains to trust. Samuel would develop a trade with Constantinople where he could buy the best continuous fibers of raw silk from China, Japan, Bengal, and the Levant. He hired Izaak to be his assistant, and a working relationship was formed.

Samuel was quick to secure the letter of protection for the manufacture of silk textiles, and with that, the "Berlin Silkworks" was born. He oversaw the building of the factory, the looms and throwing mills, and supervised the manufacture of the textiles. The raw materials were treated by methods analogous to those of weaving, were dyed and made into fabrics. The spun silk was sent to market, while reeled silk went to the finest tailors in Berlin.

Izaak managed the importation of raw silk from the east and assisted in the promotion and sale of the finished product. As the company grew from planning and organizing to reality and success, Izaak became a steady guest in the home of his employer.

Samuel's comely daughter, Naomi, had always been a child of privilege, shielded from any sense of oppression, even in the Berlin ghetto where the Viennese exiles preserved their own enclave. Izaak worshiped her casual indifference. A man of the streets where passions openly erupted and anger was one's defense against fear, he mistook her aloofness for aristocracy. Samuel grew fond of Izaak and was well rewarded by the young man's energies and effectiveness in the business. Izaak's marriage to Naomi assured the future of the firm.

Her pregnancy was made easy by hovering servants, and the finest physician in Berlin was charged with having her deliver Mordecai without any sense of labor. Mordecai was raised never to impose himself, his emotions, or immature demands upon his mother. At the appropriate time, she arranged his marriage to Rivkah, the daughter of a proper goldsmith.

Following the wedding ceremony, Naomi ran off with the footman.

It would be years before Izaak no longer blamed himself for her desertion. Throughout his married life he had withheld his passion, believing his wife to be fragile. Samuel, humiliated and abashed, ordered that his daughter's name never again be mentioned in his house.

Mordecai filled a void in his grandfather's life; he became the child on whom Samuel could lavish luxuries and from whom he could expect admiration. The grandson thrived in Samuel's salon, comfortable more among the flirtatious women than the literati who flocked to Berlin, the new cultural center of Europe.

Although Jews were still restricted and segregated, those in Samuel's class became a part of the city's intellectual discourse. Jewish scientists and sages drawn to Berlin, entered through the gate designated for Jews, paid the special tolls, and found work as scribes, chemists, and tutors. Samuel sought out the finest minds among them for use in his enterprise.

So it was that he gazed into the deep, penetrating eyes of Moses Mendelssohn, a biblical scholar from the ghetto of Dessau. A short man with a humped back and an open mind, eager to learn the ways of industry, he had come to Berlin to integrate his Talmudic heritage with the fresh spirit of rational inquiry. He began as a bookkeeper at the Berlin Silkworks and slowly moved up the ranks to management, spending his evenings in the study of German and French. Soon, he discussed his translation of Rousseau's *Discourse on Inequality Among Men* in Samuel's drawing room, stirring visions of equal rights. Among the guests was Gotthold Lessing, the Christian poet who would bring Mendelssohn, and through him, Jewry, into the Enlightenment.

In industrialized, sophisticated Berlin, the church was less intrusive, less of a presence in one's daily life. Jews no longer wore the badges or yellow hats. Mendelssohn, like the modern Jews of Samuel's circle, was clean shaven and wore tailored clothes. They considered themselves German while remaining Hebraic in religion.

To reconcile Judaism with contemporary thought, Mendelssohn translated the Pentateuch into German with a modern commentary in Hebrew. His writings guided Jews to the language of their oppressors and fueled the quest for equality. Jews could be the peers of Christians without abandoning their religious tenets; differences lay only in forms of worship.

In 1763, Mendelssohn's study on *Evidence in Metaphysics* had captured the prize of the Prussian Academy of Sciences against the competition of Immanuel Kant who described Mendelssohn as a genius "destined to create a new epoch." Mendelssohn's *Philosophic Discourses* won him the respect of academic circles and an invitation to the court of Frederick the Great. The parochial persuasion of any individual mattered less to the king than the obedience and fidelity of his subjects. Coached by the cynical Voltaire, Frederick saw all religious conviction as childlike, with ambitious priests and anachronistic rabbis invoking revelations and miracles to gullible masses. His disparagement of the Jews, based on his view of Jewish devotion to dogma, did not extend to men of culture and wit like Mendelssohn.

How Samuel yearned to be like him. Fabrics produced by the Berlin Silkworks were now featured at court; someday soon, Samuel would also appear among the stars. Mendelssohn's Judaism was not the blind adherence to scripture, rejected by the Enlightenment, but more an attachment to an ethic and a heritage.

Izaak, on the other hand, had come to doubt the value of the Enlightenment.   Naomi's abandonment of him, his son, and their lifestyle jolted Izaak to rethink his values and his lifelong ambition to be part of Berlin society. He retreated to nostalgic thoughts of his simpler days in the ghetto.

Unlike his father, Mordecai, now the firm's assistant sales manager, had no problem with moving out into the sunshine of the glittering city.

Slowly encasing his pubic prominence with soft silk undergarments, a product of the union between his father and his mother's families, he withdrew from his reflections in the mirror, and looked out the window onto the market opportunities of a thriving Berlin.

Mordecai lived in a house in Kreuzberg, at the edge of the city, shaved his beard daily, wore the latest styles to flaunt his prosperous, ample figure, and strode, cane in hand, to the Berlin Silkworks' display shop off the Mariannenplatz. Each day, he presented samples and took orders for silk fabrics from Christians and Jews. Each night, he sat down to a kosher meal with his tiny wife Rivkah, and his young son, Nathan. On Saturdays, Mordecai attended shul. And on special occasions, he took his best customers to the opera. He knew he was the most fortunate of men in this most cultivated time and place.

The forebears of Mordecai and Nathan:

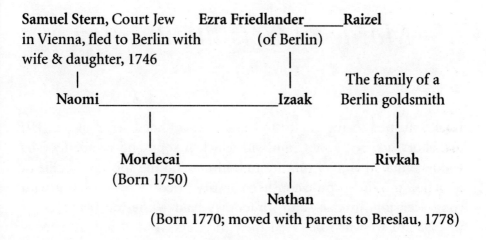

Samuel Stern, Court Jew
in Vienna, fled to Berlin with
wife & daughter, 1746

Ezra Friedlander_____Raizel
(of Berlin)

Naomi_____Izaak

The family of a
Berlin goldsmith

Mordecai_____Rivkah
(Born 1750)

Nathan
(Born 1770; moved with parents to Breslau, 1778)

V

Mordecai Gets the Business

Izaak returned to the ghetto to nurse his wounded sense of self. His neighbors hovered about him with chicken soup and sympathy. The widow Shua, in crepe from top to bottom, and the spinster Shullie in bleached muslin to proclaim her chastity, tried to console him with condescension. In black and white, they babbled he was blameless; it was Naomi who had betrayed their marriage vows. No, he was convinced, he had betrayed her. Fascinated by her elegance, he had paraded her as a bauble. It had been of no concern to him that she might have appetites and dreams, and he ached now that he had never been a part of them.

Izaak stared fixedly at his parents who still plied their pushcart, passing judgment on no one. His fateful infidelity had been his rejection of their values: they looked up only to God and spoke straight to all people. In his vaingloriousness, he had tried to be a part of a world that would never accept him as he was.

No one in the ghetto was better off because, for a time, he had stepped beyond its walls. Gentile crews on the canal still charged the extra toll for bringing materials to a Jew. The factory still had to give preference to Christians who barely disguised their contempt for Jewish bosses. Imperial authorities still called for annual payment for the letter of protection which granted rights but not respect. The Silkworks could only operate with continuing bribes and payoffs to those who would expropriate it all on a moment's shift of Prussian politics.

Izaak became embittered with the delusions of the Enlightenment. He found it painful to attend his father-in-law's salons. The occasional inspiration of a visiting intellectual was diluted by the overarching importance of appearances and the shallowness of relationships. He had helped to make his only son into a dandy; Mordecai relished the glamour and status of his life, so far removed from his father's origins.

As his rancor gave way to resolution, Izaak realized that he had to wrest Mordecai and his grandson, Nathan, from the chimera of Berlin gentility. They would have to learn the value of hard work and the integrity of their heritage.

He set about to convince Samuel that they needed to expand the business. The market to exploit lay in the east where there was a growing demand and little competition. Breslau was well situated at the end of the Oder-Spree canal, the key to Silesia. Surely, for the right price, the king would grant a *schutzbrief* to Mordecai for industrial development in the far reaches of the kingdom.

Samuel derived pleasure from impressing Mordecai and savored his deference. However, embarrassed to admit to such vanity, the old entrepreneur responded to Izaak in terms of the work ethic to which they were both committed. "I need Mordecai here in Berlin to learn the business so that some day he can take it over."

"What better way to groom him," Izaak countered, "than to have him develop a subsidiary plant and business network on his own?"

The two men finally agreed to assign Mordecai to the project for a limited period of time. Samuel purchased the *schutzbrief* for the development in Silesia which Mordecai could retain as a lifetime estate, even after he returned to Berlin.

With reassurances from his father that he was taking the Berlin Silkworks to imperial heights, and with promises from his grandfather that he could visit Berlin as frequently as his obligations permitted, Mordecai Friedlander set forth to build a silk factory for the firm in Silesia.

Although Jews were ordinarily forbidden to ride in carriages, Mordecai enjoyed his special station. He appeared at *Das Niclas* gate of Breslau elegantly attired, with his exquisitely costumed wife and properly suited son, in a leather-upholstered landau drawn by four straight-backed horses. Such appearance, enriched by his impeccable German and his excellent position with the Berlin Silkworks would guarantee the appropriate deference.

Once he had paid the required toll and showed his passport, the guard unceremoniously directed the family to vacate the coach and walk to the ghetto,"where you belong." Mordecai was stunned, certain that there was a mistake, humiliated in front of his wife and son. He tried to argue with the Prussian guard who repeated the order, shoving his rifle butt hard against the open carriage door.

The three terrified occupants stumbled out into a world they had not known, one that belonged to an earlier time. Men smelling of bratwurst and beer surrounded the trio, laughed at their inappropriate elegance and offered to carry their oversized luggage for overpriced fees. Mordecai dared not trust these ruffians, and instructed the coachman to hold onto the trunks until he could send porters from the ghetto.

The skies opened, and Mordecai held Nathan high up on his chest, shielding him with his hat, while Rivkah pushed her skirts through the swelling mud. After an agonizing trek through the downpour, they reached the offices of the *Judengemeinschaft*, presented their credentials, and sent for their bags.

Impressed by Mordecai's *schutzbrief,* the members of the Administrative Council welcomed him heartily. Yankel the *shochet* invited him to join the *Judengemeinschaft*, with an apology that the ghetto was overcrowded and no housing was immediately available. Among the elderly tenants, one was certain to die soon, and until then, the Friedlander family could be accommodated at the Inn. It provided simple quarters, but they were dry and relatively clean.

When the porters arrived at the city gate, the coach was gone. Guffawing maliciously, the guard advised them they were too late. Others had already picked up *Herr* Friedlander's possessions. In the blinding torrent, it was impossible to know who they were.

Over the next few days, Mordecai presented himself to a tailor, met with the burghers, and sent for a replacement of his stolen goods from Berlin. The Breslau government granted him the right to rent an old warehouse outside the ghetto that he could convert into a factory to provide jobs to the townspeople. But he, Rivkah, and Nathan would have to live among the Jews.

Recalling the large apartment occupied by the tailor who was fashioning his new suit, Mordecai offered to hire him in exchange for subleasing most of his flat. Nehemiah would supervise the stitching of silk fabrics at the incipient factory.

The tailor's apprentice would have to be moved out of the apartment to make way for the Friedlander family. Concerned that Jonah remain under his watchful eye, Nehemiah suggested that the lad be housed at the factory where he could double as the night-watchman. After the theft at the city gates, Mordecai agreed he needed someone he could trust to guard his precious silks and looms.

He pleaded with the City Council to allow one Jew to spend nights outside the ghetto. With the promise of additional revenues to the city coffers, the Council's interest in expediting jobs for Breslau workingmen, and with assurances that the night watchman's quarters would be bare bones (a space in which no Christian would want to live), permission was reluctantly granted.

Jonah scoured, insulated and improved an old shed on the factory roof, formerly used for pigeons. Nehemiah brought Jonah a chest, bunk, blankets, a table, and an oil lamp salvaged from the storage and work rooms of his apartment.

The tailor quibbled with Mordecai over every detail of sub-dividing the space, working out the barriers and points of access. Mordecai paid dearly for the room with a window on the Judengasse. Nehemiah held onto the only remaining room with a window, the one vacated by Jonah on the turd-stenched air shaft. Rivkah hired Zelda to scrub the walls and floors and threw herself into creating a tasteful if cramped space for her family.

As the looms arrived, Mordecai set about to organize the new silk factory, hiring local townspeople to spin the lengths of continuous lustrous fibers shipped from Jews in Constantinople.

Mordecai Friedlander struggled to keep his anger and outrage within him. Each day, he strode forth with his cane in hand, playing at being charming to his employees, tradesmen, and prospects beyond the ghetto walls, feeling within himself that he was groveling, coming across as obsequious to heathens. He read ridicule in their faces. He knew they suspected his every word and held out for every advantage. Each night, seething with indignation, he returned to the ghetto, hunched over the cane with which he pushed away the debris of the Judengasse, the cesspool to which he was confined.

As deeply as he resented the contempt of the Gentiles, he loathed even more profoundly their equating him with those of the ghetto who spoke the guttural tones of Yiddish and hid behind unruly beards and forelocks that cascaded over smelly, stained, black, baggy, woolen clothes, worn day after day.

His wife, Rivkah, confined to their new environment, found ways to negotiate it. She incorporated the inflections of Yiddish into her Berlin German, found warmth and comfort with the old ladies in babushkas, met Feigel the shadchen who told her everything she needed to know about every family and shopkeeper in the ghetto and where to get the freshest produce. On a side street off the Judengasse, she discovered the old well. While no longer safe for gathering water, it provided a roof under which the more informed women (some of whom knew how to read) gathered and gossiped.

To enroll their son in the Free School, Mordecai and Rivkah met with Joseph, the Senior Rabbi. His clean white shirt, polished boots, and precise German diction distinguished Joseph as a cut above, a reasonable, if somewhat culturally limited man. Although there were no other choices, Mordecai sought assurances that his son would benefit from a school that privately he viewed as semi-primitive. Joseph described a broad curriculum, but of course, Nathan would have to catch up with the other boys in his grade, "to learn about his heritage." He would need a tutor. An old widowed rabbi lived on the ground floor of the school with his grandson, a redheaded boy about the same age as Nathan. So it was arranged.

Every day, after school, Nathan brought his lessons and his questions to the old rabbi. "How is it, Rabbi, that we are asked to be humble, to not take credit for what we have done, and to think of ourselves as never having done enough, and yet when we take the Torah out from the Ark, we pray to God, *May it be Your will to prolong our lives in happiness, and that I may be counted among the righteous?*"

"We ask not for ourselves as individuals, but as members of a group," the old rabbi explained. "It does not detract from personal humility to appreciate others as righteous and deserving, and if we are unified with them, then we can ask for our share in the communal blessing."

For a while, Aaron sat by and listened. Little by little, he entered into the discussions. At times, Aaron helped to express the pupil's concerns to the old rabbi, and explained the tutor's more enigmatic replies to the boy from Berlin.

"How does prayer work, Rabbi?" Nathan asked.

When the old rabbi raised his arms in exasperation, Aaron spelled out what was gnawing at his young companion.

"He wants to know, is God subject to change? When we ask God for something, do we change His mind?"

"The rays of the sun," the old rabbi proclaimed, "can darken one object yet bleach another, and heat can melt one substance while solidifying another."

Dumbfounded, Nathan's jaw dropped. Aaron unobtrusively came to the rescue. "One gets different results according to the object that receives the radiation. What he means is, that prayer isn't just asking for something; it can be our way of expressing hope or trust, or awe of God. Prayer can bring about changes in us, and as we change, the Divine emanations may be more favorable to us."

After the sessions with the old rabbi, the two boys chatted over tea about other things. Nathan acquainted Aaron with the middle class trappings of his parent's apartment: padded furniture and real beds, carpets and decorative ceramics, fabrics of silk, and an engraving of the Berlin Opera House.

The two argued about ultimate meanings and enjoyed each other's wit, each sharpening his own thoughts through parrying with the other. Nathan taught his companion chess and Aaron was soon his match. He told Aaron about the exciting new developments in Berlin and changes in the ways Christians were coming to regard Jews. Aaron did not believe that Christians would change: "I do not trust them or want to live among them!" He found explanations for everything in Scripture, the very documents Christians wanted to destroy.

When Mordecai brought his son to the Silkworks to show him the business he would someday inherit, Nathan was intrigued by a Jewish boy who worked with his hands and his back. To earn extra income, Jonah repaired the looms and stoked the coal fires along with his duties as an apprentice tailor to Nehemiah. Nathan, who did not work at all, would someday sit in a chair and exert only his head. Coming from the cultivated center of Prussia, he boasted of the freedom and cultural riches of the Jews in Berlin.

Jonah was not impressed. "You're a Jew, same as me," he snapped, "and they hate you as much as they hate me. This is Breslau," the apprentice scoffed, "under the iron control of the burghers, not the fancy capital of Frederick the Great. Your father may have a *schutzbrief*, but he pays the king dearly for it, and the local townspeople resent it, you, and your father. They laugh about the *schutzbrief*; it only protects your father from some obligations to the crown. The burghers can do as they like. Nothing here will change for the Jews, and that includes you!"

Nathan ran to his father in fright, alarmed by Jonah's deprecating diatribe and the defiance with which he delivered it. Mordecai summoned the young apprentice and warned him sternly *never* to speak to his son like that again. He consulted Nehemiah about whether the young man should be replaced.

"Ha! You'd have to hire one of *them*," Nehemiah bit a thread to tie it. "Remember, they made an exception, letting you bring just one Jew out of the ghetto to oversee the delivery of your equipment and watch your supplies; are you now ready to trust a Gentile?"

Mordecai dropped his head in resignation. But still, he thought, such rudeness towards his son could not be tolerated; some punishment was called for.

"Why did you recommend this young savage in the first place?"

The old tailor told the story of Jonah's father, of Nachrader's accusations, and of Ephraim's wasting away in jail. "Four times a year, on a Sunday, when the Gentiles allow visitors," Nehemiah spat contemptuously, "Jonah takes his mother to see his father. Each time they go, Ephraim appears more beaten, more emaciated and sallow, festering with more disease and bitterness. But the sight of his son growing bigger, stronger and more capable infuses him with hope and the will to keep going.

"Jonah saves most of his wages so that someday he can hire a lawyer. He is convinced that once Ephraim is brought to trial, he will prove his innocence. It is crucial that Jonah keep this job. As a father, yourself, you cannot, must not shatter his dream."

Mordecai thought for a while. "There is no excuse for his being uncivil to my child," he blurted out. But he knew in his heart he could not punish the lad. "You," he demanded of Nehemiah, "will have to teach him civility!"

Each day, after work, the old tailor met with his apprentice with lessons to bring him into a civilization beyond the struggle for survival. He began with Mendelssohn's translation of the Torah into German. Jonah would learn the language of the oppressor through the voice of one dedicated to his liberation.

*   *   *

A great division arose among the Jews of eastern and central Europe. Israel ben Eliezer, a charismatic figure, the "Baal Shem Tov" emerged from Poland. He taught that piety was superior to scholarship and that any man, however ignorant or poor, could commune with God. Thousands of Jews joined his movement; they were named *Hassidim,* the Pious. They believed that spiritual exaltation and complete surrender of self could bridge the gulf between heaven and earth through the guidance of a Righteous One. The *zadik* acted as an intermediary between mortals and the Almighty. His power could only be passed on by heredity.

On the other side were the *Misnagdim,* the opponents who denounced the new sect as irrational and heretical. The Senior Rabbi of the Breslau Free School was among the Misnagdim, but many of the students and some of the faculty sided with the Hassidim.

Aaron threw himself into the debate. He was repulsed by anything that came from Poland and angry at those who proposed shortcuts to unrelenting study. Yet, deep inside, he struggled against the temptation to lose himself in the ecstasy and abandonment offered by the Hassidim in their feasts and rapturous songs and dance. Embarrassed by his feelings, Aaron caught himself. He was determined to prove that only through coming to know the *words* of God could one come to know God. His ardor for Truth would validate the rationalist approach.

He so excelled in the debates that he came to the attention of the Senior Rabbi. Joseph listened to Aaron's arguments, was pleased by the way the young man marshaled authorities to support his contentions, and arranged for him, upon graduation from the Free School, to enter the yeshiva, the college for Talmudic study.

*   *   *

From the old well of the women to the offices of the Judengemeinschaft, whispers of liberation sweetened the air. Stories flowed in from all across Europe. The Jews of Alsace had prepared a petition for Moses Mendelssohn to present to the King of France. Mendelssohn turned to the Prussian councilor Christian Wilhelm Dohm to champion their rights. In 1781, Dohm had published *On the Civic Improvement of the Jews*, documenting the oppression of Jews throughout the German states, and calling for new laws aimed at complete emancipation. In nearby Austria, with the death of Maria Theresa, her son, Joseph II succeeded to the throne. In a letter to Count Blumegen on October 19, the new emperor wrote of liberating Jews from "humiliating and oppressive laws." Two days later, the law requiring Austrian Jews to wear a yellow badge was abolished. Soon thereafter, the body tax on Jews was removed.

Each day, Mordecai brought news of the latest developments to Nehemiah and his apprentice to convince them that Jews would soon become full fledged citizens of Prussia: "Germans, as good as any of them!" But Jonah saw tracts that the German workingmen brought into the factory, heaping scorn upon the Jews. He did not wish to be a part of their society. His dreams of liberation were of his father set free, of his mother lifted from her wretched state, and of his becoming the equal of the indulged Nathan. Nehemiah grumbled to himself that it would be too late for him.

Mordecai found a more receptive audience in his son, firing Nathan with the enthusiasm of impending opportunities. On the October day that the yellow badges in neighboring Austria came off, Nathan rushed to the schoolhouse to tell Aaron, "Perhaps, someday in Prussia..." He found his friend weeping.

The old rabbi was dead. He lay there now, in eternal sleep on the bench from which he taught. After a bleak service and burial organized by the school, Aaron, though not yet an adult in the eyes of the faith, sat *shivah*, frightened, and mourned for seven days in the icy, barren classroom, an orphan on the eve of his *bar mitzvah*.

But Aaron was not to enter adulthood alone.

As Joseph joined in the mourning, he bowed in awe to the providence that had brought him a *son*. Here was a child to be rescued, one who could not be counted by the authorities, subject to tolls or export. He praised God with every fiber of his being and took Aaron into his home.

A corner room of the Senior Rabbi's apartment, just off the top of the stairs, had been used to store books, piled, one on top of the other, from floor to ceiling. Joseph helped Aaron build bookcases along the walls, put the books onto the shelves, and moved him into the liberated space. A new life began for Aaron.

Leah's glorious dinners, Joseph's wise musings on scripture, the excited chatter of three young women, and Natalie's predictable knocks on his door (to borrow this or that manuscript or commentary), gave Aaron a sense of family for which he had yearned, a completeness he had never known.

But all too soon, a new and terrifying experience visited him. Aaron awakened with a great, throbbing enlargement between his legs and a sticky wetness across his belly. For a while he lay there, feeling a consuming shame as he recalled, and then tried to block out his recollection of lascivious dreams. He bounded out of bed, furtively rubbing his bedclothes dry, praying for forgiveness, scanning scripture for understanding. He could find nothing to comfort him, and so he returned to his studies, burying his anguish in verses from Job:

Lift off thy heavy hand, scare me not with thy terrors,
Then will I answer thy summons —
Tell me all I have done wrong, let me know what sin I am guilty of…

A few nights later, it occurred again. His dreams were even more vivid, carrying him down to sinfulness, and a viscous explosion thrust the slime of iniquity upon his thighs. He trembled that some evil force had taken possession of his reverie and his loins. Again, he sought refuge in the Prophets, searching among the many ways that God guided heroes and redeemed those who had failed Him, but it was all in vain.

As the pattern repeated itself, he discerned a palpable pleasure, a realization that plunged him into an abyss of even greater despair. Was he devolving into some base creature, made alien from his God?

He found it torturous to face his new family or his teachers. Surely they would notice changes in him that were forcing his descent. He slumped his face toward his plate at dinner, scarcely looking up. He stammered in reciting a Psalm of David in class.

When he fumbled at chess with Nathan, he stalked moodily away. Suspecting what it was that disturbed his naive friend, Nathan pursued him into the stairwell, determined to pierce Aaron's petulance. Grabbing Aaron by the arm, Nathan proclaimed with unseemly hubris, "I have become a man!"

"What do you mean?" asked his dumbstruck companion.

With unbridled joy, Nathan boasted about the sensation of his ejaculations. When he was a youth in Berlin, Zev, the sophisticated *mohel*, had told him that some day his testicles would ripen and he would be able to emit the divine seed that God had planted within them. "The Lord," Zev whispered, "would make such emissions pleasing so that we would perform the very first of the six-hundred and thirteen commandments of our Torah, at Genesis I, 28: *Be fruitful and multiply.*"

A great relief settled over Aaron; he was *not* cursed but had foolishly failed to recognize a blessing. God was forcing him to distribute his seed. But as he pondered this revelation, he again became confused and distressed. He could not waste his seed, like Onan. Yet he was not ready to take a wife.

The urbane Nathan had an answer for that, as well. There were women who were widowed or who had been passed by, well into their twenties or beyond, still not married. Such women were available for young men. The women were, of course, not Jewish; God would not want Jewish women to be used for practice or to waste their bodies for men who could not marry them. This was how some of the Gentile women earned their living. It was only fair that they be paid. While Aaron did not trust the Christians, he let Nathan convince him that this was a service they could perform to help him become a better husband to the bride who would someday be selected for him. It was a necessary step.

Alone, late at night, under a candle, Aaron read the Song of Solomon with rapt anticipation and a conscious hardening of the organ with which he would celebrate the mission of the Lord. Sometimes assisted, the nocturnal emissions continued. He now reassured himself that they were but preparations for carrying forth the First Commandment, and he thanked the Lord for making him worthy, even as he carefully cleaned up so that his family would never know.

Nathan got his father to find chores for Aaron to perform at the Silkworks, and the young scholar saved the pennies he earned until he could pay what some unknown woman would deserve. It took months, but each boy prepared himself with increasing dedication.

On the morning after their night-long Passover Seder, a feast of gratitude for being freed from the bondage of slavery, the two boys slipped out of the ghetto. Concealing the yellow patches still required in Prussia, they strode confidently to the place they had heard about in bawdy quips of workingmen, a neighborhood of wooden shacks alongside the docks of the Oder.

In front of one shed after another, sat a woman on an upturned barrel or crate, staring emptily ahead. Nathan and Aaron stood back, peering through the slats of a cart, sizing up first one prospect, then another. The first was too tough. The next, too innocent. The third, too old. And so they worked their eyes down the row to a shed with its door closed.

"Now *that's* a good sign," Nathan observed, irreverently, "she must be a chosen person."

"Or a very tired one, from too much of that stuff," volunteered Aaron, sending them both into seizures of nervous sniggering.

The boys found other excuses to eliminate each remaining candidate, stalling to see if the mysterious door would open before they rejected all their options and would have to go scurrying back behind the ghetto gate, reassured that at least they had tried.

Just as they came to agree that the last woman on the row was not to be trusted ("she probably has a man inside ready to strike you dead and take your money"), the door of the occupied shack flew open. And there, backing out, enveloped in raucous laughter, was Nathan's father, Mordecai Friedlander.

The boys ran through the streets of Breslau, not knowing or caring where they were going, until first one, and then the other collapsed, out of breath. They sat drained of feeling for a long time.

The revulsion that slowly welled up within Nathan gave way to tears of betrayal. The anxiety that had dominated Aaron from the dawn of their venture now melted into compassion for his friend. Silently, they stood up and found their way back to the Judengasse.

VI

The Maturation of Nathan

Nathan kept running. He went on the road for the Silkworks, introducing its products to tailors throughout Silesia and Saxony, serving ever more customers, courting new clients, overseeing deliveries. In Leipzig, he learned the lure of silk lingerie led him to the boudoirs of sophisticated ladies whose husbands were oblivious. In Dresden, he discovered the delights of coitus in the sensuous creases of silk sheets. In Weimar, widows wove his silk sacks into concupiscent condoms.

By the time he entered Brandenberg, silk and lasciviousness had merged into an orgy of prodigious promotion. Cocksure, he reported to Berlin and prepared to meet the elegant society surrounding his great-grandfather.

In his best patrician manner, Samuel strode up the grand staircase of the *statoper,* his shoulders arched back, introducing his handsome great-grandson to friends every step of the way. They shared their box with Moses Mendelssohn and his daughter, Dorothea, whose thick, wavy hair flowed to the edges of her tantalizing bosom. Nathan was speechless in the presence of a beguiling woman whose lips pronounced words like "Montesquieu."

"We cannot forget that Montesquieu denounced the Inquisition," she declared. "One must not condemn him just because he wrote that the national character of the Jews is particularly obnoxious. He explains, in *Esprit des Lois,* how centuries of subjugation shaped despicable traits.

What other great writer tried to understand how those poor wretches in the ghetto got that way?"

Nathan agreed; he knew and understood many such wretches.

The musicians took their places, the curtains lifted, and the tale of *Don Giovanni* unfolded. With each aria, Nathan sank deeper into his seat in the realization that Mozart's libretto was about *him*. At first in farce and then as an object of contempt, Giovanni was the kind of rogue Nathan had become. He felt the eyes of Dorothea Mendelssohn peering into his soul, knowing him for the knave and fool he was. As the opera moved from comedy to tragedy, he struggled against the sentence of eternal damnation. For a long, haunting moment, Nathan knew he was no better than the father from whom he had fled.

As others stood in applause, shouting for curtain calls, he sat in a daze, consumed with specters of betrayal: Don Giovanni's callousness, Mordecai's disloyalty, his *own* villainy in the beds of his clients' wives, and now his counterfeit obsequiousness to Berlin intellectuals. He wondered about Grandmother Naomi who ran off with the footman. Had she deceived her husband or had she pursued some deeper truth?

In the morning, Izaak greeted him in his flat made comfortable in the ghetto. Of his wife, Naomi, he would say only that she would be thrilled to know she had such a fine grandson. At the grave site of his own parents, he fired Nathan with stories of their struggle and sacrifice so that he could have a better life.

"Ezra and Raizel," he reminisced, "were simple, loving people, not appreciated by the current crop of rich Jews so quick to condemn their forebears as provincial and naive."

Nathan dropped his head in shame. Only last night, he had been ready to write off his great-grandparents as poor wretches of distasteful character.

Nathan felt torn between the worlds of Samuel and Izaak. Great-grandfather Samuel luxuriated in the salons of the literati, sat with Moses Mendelssohn, a Jew who had an audience with the king and a brilliant daughter who explained away anti-Jewish expressions of the Enlightenment as part of its hostility to *all* religion.

Grandfather Izaak, on the other hand, saw in the Enlightenment a new kind of contempt for Jews, not as a religion but as a race of Semites. "Their *Encyclopedie,*" he pointed out, "describes the Jewish "national character" as 'disgusting, dishonest, and greedy.' Even when they excuse us with some historic justification, they think of us as a *breed* of people. It's not just our beliefs that they hate."

That night, at his salon, Samuel toasted the new Emperor of Austria whose *Edict of Toleration* admitted Jews to a few crafts, encouraged them to help develop his economy and enrich his state.

Izaak dissented. "The Edict still bars Jews from becoming master craftsmen, asks us to replace Hebrew and Yiddish with German, to attend only German schools, and to assimilate in everything but religion, which the emperor dismisses as 'an evil which has to be made innocuous.' Yes, we can enter agriculture, but only in Jewish communities. In Vienna, we are forbidden from having public religious services and from increasing our population.

"And here, in Prussia, we are still not admitted into schools or crafts unless we forswear our religion and accept baptism into theirs. We should be able to be Jews and still be accepted as human beings," Izaak argued. "I do not want to be baptized. I do not want to assimilate in the hopes that I can be cleansed of an undesirable national character. I want to be able to worship on *my* Sabbath day, to pray in *my* synagogue, to dance and sing Yiddish songs and still enter *any* school, craft, or profession for which I have the brains. This they will not allow!"

"Soon, soon, it will all come," Samuel urged patience. "They are in charge, and have been for eighteen centuries! It is finally in their interest to offer economic opportunities to us. The Enlightenment is not just some intellectual exercise. Frederick will get the burghers in line because he wants Prussia to become a world power. They need us to develop the nation. Then, once we have economic power, they will *have to* give us *real* freedom."

When he returned to Breslau, Nathan tried to sort out the Samuel from the Izaak within him. He talked with Jonah, now a journeyman tailor, responsible for the growing inventory of towering spools of silk. With Nehemiah's prodding, the two young men had slowly developed a respectful relationship, sharing an occasional lunch hour on the factory roof.

Nathan was sure that soon they would be free to live outside the ghetto, own land, and go to universities. More skeptical, Jonah swore that such changes would come about only through organized resistance to the burghers and the king.

Nathan looked over the edge of the roof at the city below them and lowered his voice. "If you demand too much now, you'll get their backs up, and we'll get nothing."

"If we remain silent," Jonah pounded his fist, "we will be ground up in the order that *they* build, fodder to their might and power, tools of their exploitation!"

Shaken, the young merchant pointed to the factory below and warned, "Don't ever let our Christian workers hear you talk that way! They'd take your rhetoric as proof that Jews are all radicals. We *will* make progress, not by undermining them, but by becoming part of their economy. And be careful that my father never hears you speak like that or he'd turn you in. He's *all* business."

Having learned to be *civil*, Jonah remained silent.

*   *   *

His bright red uncut *payess* spilled out between Aaron's wide brimmed black hat and his long black caftan. A *yeshiva bucher*, he learned to walk with downcast eyes, impressing others that he was absorbed in some Talmudic problem, never looking at a woman. Each morning began with early prayer, each day was absorbed in rigorous study with the rabbis, and each evening he arrived home after the others had finished dinner. Natalie was always there to bring food to him. She was plain, sallow and studious with a self-effacing tone that masked her generosity. In the menacing privacy of his room, they dared not exchange glances.

After Sabbath services, Aaron relaxed over games of chess with Nathan while they each stole secret glimpses of Hadassah, nurturing parallel desires. She had developed from a playful child to a voluptuous young woman, moved about gracefully and unabashedly, so unlike the other women of the ghetto who had been trained to avert their eyes from men and to avoid expressing emotions in front of them. She was the free spirit Nathan admired and Aaron feared.

Aaron dared not speak with Hadassah, doggedly suppressing his excitement at the sight of her. But in the fantasies with which he still prepared himself for marital blessings she was his private muse, a dream whose shame he relished.

Nathan, on the other hand, invented ways to dazzle her with his erudition. At Leah and Joseph's dinner table, he read aloud his letters from Berlin. Although centered on commerce, the missives were peppered with references to the changing styles and gossip. He could not get Hadassah to care. Natalie the Profound was abruptly dismissive of such profane matters. Sarah was fascinated. She pushed away her apfel strudel and reeled off unsolicited ideas on how Nathan's manufactory could benefit from the latest styles.

Intending to impress Hadassah with the wealth that would someday be his, Nathan invited the three sisters and Aaron to visit the factory. They arrived, as planned, while Mordecai was in Berlin. Nathan took charge, confidently leading his four guests on a tour of the production facilities, proudly strutting his command of advanced technology.

In the office, where steaming bowls of mushroom barley soup were served for lunch, Sarah asked a hundred questions about how the plant was run, how it guaranteed its supply, how it developed and served its market, who were the employees, what were their needs, and how he and his father selected and managed them.

Flattered by Sarah's attention and intrigued by her quick wit, Nathan found himself drawn to this extraordinary woman.

Uninvolved in the discourse, Aaron meditated aloud, reciting a Psalm of David. Natalie repeated the Psalm; the two uttered the lines in unison a third time, then fell silent.

Hadassah wandered aimlessly across the plant floor, watching weavers and dyers when, turning a corner, she came upon a fresh faced, bare chested man pushing heavy slats of a giant loom into place. She had never seen a man in such nakedness before.

His muscular body, covered with beads of perspiration, reflected the glow of a swaying oil lamp overhead. Intoxicated, she steadied herself against a crate.

When he realized he was being watched, Jonah slowly lowered the slat, returned a penetrating gaze at the elegant, immobilized lady, and disappeared behind an oversized vat.

Hadassah returned to the office, flushed with excitement, struggling to conceal her exhilaration. It was the heat, she explained to Sarah and Nathan still engrossed in shop talk, and to Natalie and Aaron who remained oblivious, seated in silent meditation.

For a long time thereafter, Hadassah revisited the plant floor in her mind, lingering where the big looms sit next to the oversized vat.

VII

Ephraim and the Rule of Law

In the cavernous recesses of the Breslau prison, Ephraim prepared himself for the quarterly visit of his wife and son. He was cramped into a small cell with three others, all foreigners, neither one speaking the language of any other.

In the winter they froze, sleeping on the floor without mattresses. In the hot, unventilated summer they fought off vermin and mosquitos who bred in the lingering pools of urine. The bucket for their excrement always overflowed. Ephraim was forever hungry and had long since given up rejecting any part of the maggot-laden crusts tossed to him by his better fed cellmates.

When he asked for something to drink, the jailors stood just outside his cage and mockingly drank tea; sometimes they threw steaming hot water in his face. Often, in the middle of the night, he or one of the men in his corridor would be taken away, beaten or raped, then returned whimpering and pathetic.

Each morning, they were awakened at 5:00 by drunken guards coming off their shift, shouting military songs. They were ordered to salute the captain's dog, a German shepherd who was trained to nip at their genitals. After being left without food for several days, the jailers brought a head of dirty lettuce, full of soil, to each prisoner and made him eat it as it was, unwashed. They knew that the convicts would spend the night in their excrement.

Most of the food his wife brought four times a year was divided among the guards before it came to him. It was divided again with his wretched cellmates. No matter how big the basket, Ephraim always received the same small fragment.

On this visit, Zelda brought a tribute from Hoshea the cobbler, Ephraim's comrade from his tenant organizing days. The cobbler had set aside the best leather he could find and, noting that Jonah's feet were the same shape as his father's, he waited for them to grow to be the same size. When the day came, Hoshea tested the pattern against Jonah's toes, heels, and arch. For a month he worked far into the night and meticulously crafted the finest pair of boots in Breslau.

Straining to look presentable for his wife and son, Ephraim picked off the feces encrusted in his skin. Again and again, he jumped in his shackles and beat his head and beard to shake off clusters of lice. He folded his arms over the most worn-out parts of his shirt, turned inside-out, and was ready when the guard came to shove him through endless corridors up winding stairs to the visiting room.

Slowly, as his eyes adjusted to the shock, the people he loved more than life emerged from the dizzying haze of sunlight. He clasped the change of clothing from his son, grown taller, and gaped at the magnificent new pair of boots presented by his wife, grown lovelier. For a few moments, the years of torment melted away.

In their inflexibly rationed minutes, Jonah spoke quickly. At last, they had money enough to hire a lawyer! Into his notebook, he scribbled his father's responses to every question the attorney could ask before he would accept the case: each detail of the jobs that Ephraim had performed for Nachrader; the terms of employment; precise hours and days of work; and who would be the most reliable witnesses. Ephraim had barely finished, had not yet exchanged words of love with his wife or hosannas for the gleam of hope, when the guard poked him back to the archway at the end of the room.

Though the shackles restricted his feet, Ephraim shuffled with his head held high, hoarsely shouting farewells.

Nehemiah arranged for Jonah to take time off from work. Now with his cash firmly tucked in his Sabbath trousers and his notes in hand, the lad sat on a polished oak bench in the high-ceilinged waiting room outside the office of Joachim Gauner, Attorney at Law.

Through a long day of well-dressed Gentiles coming and going and staring at the lad from the ghetto, he silently rehearsed his answers to the questions Herr Gauner would surely ask. A thousand times, he ran his fingers through the coins that bulged in his pockets, counting and sorting them invisibly by size.

It was dusk when a pale, skinny, aged man, in a frock coat whose tightly starched collar held his neck from collapsing beneath his bent shoulders, stepped out to peer through a monocle that wobbled perilously in its socket. The wraith bade him wait a while longer.

After darkness fell, long after the antechamber had emptied out, after the lamplighter lit alternate lanterns along the wall to provide just enough visibility for the washerwoman to scrub the day's traffic from the floor, the bony, hunched being behind the teetering monocle ushered him into an office with paintings on the ceilings, gilded panels on the walls, and velvet drapes sagging from the tops of tall window frames.

Behind an enormous oak desk on which piles of neatly arranged papers announced his importance, sat a broad-beamed, squinty-eyed gentleman whose upturned nose seemed out of harmony with his drooping jowls. Through the fluffy lace cuffs that embellished his precisely tailored suit, Herr Gauner pressed the pink fingertips of one hand against those of the other.

Shifting uneasily from his left foot to his right, Jonah blurted out his father's predicament. He started to recount details of Ephraim's unpaid service and offered the names of witnesses, all the while assuring Herr Gauner of his father's innocence.

The lawyer cut him short. "I cannot take your father's case," he snapped with a terrifying tone of finality. "Nor will any other lawyer in Silesia." He set his pink fingers flat on the desk.

"But why, why not?" stammered the boy, "Do you think I do not have enough money? Look here." He emptied out his pockets, strewing thalers between the well-organized piles of paper, promising to provide more if only the lawyer would tell him how much was needed.

The sight of money always softened Herr Gauner, and he set about explaining, in a calmer, almost consoling tone. "You simply cannot match the money or power that seeks to prevent your father's case from ever coming to trial." He asked Jonah to be seated while he went over the law and the facts in the case of *The Council of the City of Breslau v. Ephraim, a Jew.*

"In his *Generaljudenprivileg* of 1750, Frederick the Great had ordered that all members of a Jewish community shall be held collectively responsible for offenses committed by *any one* of them," Herr Gauner began. "Certain prominent Jews dare not risk a finding that a member of the Breslau ghetto tried to poison Heinrich Nachrader's well. They have paid us to keep the case from ever going to trial. So long as the charge is not officially litigated, there can be no finding and everyone is safe."

Jonah exploded, demanding to know who paid him to block justice for his father. Raising his pink forefinger to his pursed, tinted lips, Herr Gauner hushed the lad. He could not disclose any names. It would violate his ethical code (not to mention threaten a source or two of income).

"But there is more. Your father made some powerful enemies when he organized Jewish tenants against Christian landlords. He has quite a reputation. No attorney can afford to be branded as the defender of a radical. He would be rendered useless for any other client. It would never do for business.

"The truth," Herr Gauner explained, "does not matter. The law requires only what can be proven. Your father cannot prove what he did not do. The prosecutor would whip up the passions of the people of Breslau. They would fill up the courtroom and shout down any testimony by a Jew. Who do you think the court would believe?"

The lawyer concluded his sermon: It was best this way for all concerned, even for Ephraim, who was better cared for with a charge pending than he would be if he were convicted.

"No!" Jonah shouted, "You cannot imagine how miserably they treat my father *now*. No human being can go on suffering like that!"

The alternative, Herr Gauner coldly reminded the hot-blooded boy before him, was the noose. He scooped up the coins, thanked Jonah for payment of his legal services, and showed him to the door. Jonah's savings dissolved along with his hopes.

It was dark and he had to make his way to his night post at the factory without being caught on the streets of the city. Barely able to see through the torrent of his tears of despair, Jonah edged nervously along one wall after another. He stumbled against a harlot, excused himself, and piteously added that he had no money, anyway. "That's nothing to cry about," she shouted, and for a moment Jonah found something ghoulishly comic in the nightmare through which he walked.

Securely inside the plant, his furor uprooted one loom after another, cursing the elite little nest of cowards of the Judengemeinschaft. They had condemned his father rather than stand up for his rights and theirs. His tongue discovered oaths his voice had not before known. He raged until his breath gave way to his fiercely pounding heart.

Slowly, he came to the realization that though he was the captive of the merchant Jews, they in turn were captives of the Christian burghers. Would both someday be captives of a regent beyond their reach? He was a slave of slaves. He would care for his mother and try to keep his father alive. There was nothing more he could do.

As dawn broke through, he started to set the looms straight. When the workers arrived, he explained he had knocked them over while chasing rats. They sneered about his clumsiness, vociferously agreeing with one another that the Jew-boss would let only a Jew-boy get away with such incompetence.

When Jonah told his mother what he had learned from Herr Gauner, she accepted it with the understanding of a loyal servant who justifies the sins of her master. "They are responsible for protecting all of us," she explained the acts of those who guide the community. She and Jonah should seek a higher authority.

They would consult a man of God.

The prickly-whiskered Assistant Rabbi of the shul urged them not to endanger their neighbors. "Remember the massacres! It only took a charge; nobody ever proved it and they never have to."

The massive, tented Cantor embraced them, commiserated on what good people they were, and led them in prayer to accept God's will.

The deep furrows in the Chief Rabbi's face cascaded into his unending beard as he rocked back and forth, reciting a midrash to inspire them with the constant presence of divine purpose in even the most acrimonious adversity.

Perhaps they could get a fresher view from one not yet corrupted by the established conventions. In an instant, Jonah recalled his childhood friend, now studying for the rabbinate. They found Aaron at the yeshiva.

Upon hearing the full story, Aaron suggested a course of action. They should appeal directly to Heinrich Nachrader. As a Christian, he would not want to be responsible for another man's unjust suffering. They would promise to drop the claim for wages if Nachrader agreed to withdraw his charge of attempted murder. Surely Ephraim had served enough time for the theft of the potatoes and would be released if no other charge was pending.

They followed the path through the woods until, on their right, beyond a crude dam of rocks pitched at all angles to hold up the hill, they could see the city. On their left, stood the sturdy wooden fence built by Ephraim in the dawn of his distress.

At the edge of his farm, leaning on a hoe, the crusty Prussian smirked at the sallow, redheaded alien in the caftan leading two loathsome Jews to his gate. "No Yid may step foot on my property," Heinrich snarled, "the last one tried to kill me!"

"Please, sir," Aaron implored him. "It is about Ephraim that we have come to seek your help. This is his wife and son, and they join me in begging your forgiveness. Ephraim has been suffering these many years in prison for the crime of taking potatoes from your land. It might have been a dreadful deed, but in our teachings, the hungry may take from the surplus of a land. Surely, he has paid enough for his offense."

"It was not just the potatoes," the farmer railed, "He tried to poison my well!"

"How do you *know* that Ephraim's tried to commit so horrific an act? Did he carry a potion? Did he threaten any evil intent?"

"I don't need to prove anything to you, Jew," Heinrich sneered. "Who are you to question my word? Now, get away from my property, or I'll have you all charged with disturbing my peace."

Every night for ten bitter years, Jonah had soothed himself to sleep with the promise to set his father free. Each day he had labored to contain his malignant hatred of Nachrader.

Now, only the barrier built by his father separated Jonah from the incarnation of evil. With his dreams in shreds, all restraint evaporated; the loathing vented on looms a fortnight ago surged back through his veins. He wrenched a board from the farmer's fence, brandished it above his head, and lunged toward Nachrader shouting, "I'll give you something *real* to charge me with!"

Zelda screamed and pushed hard into Aaron, throwing him against her son. All three fell onto the jagged rocks that bruised and stabbed them till they bled into each other's wounds.

Ripping his shirt into strips, Jonah tended to his mother's cuts and scrapes, reassuring her he would never threaten the bastard again.

Zelda pleaded with Heinrich. Her son was all she had.

Aaron prayed.

Shaking but resigned, Jonah knelt before the Prussian.

A loud crack split the air. With strong, steady strokes, Nachrader brought a gnarled, deformed branch down upon the naked back of the defiant Jew. Only Zelda's cries, muffled against Aaron's shoulder, broke the sound of the bludgeon tearing into Jonah's flesh. Finally exhausted from the expenditure of his venom, the farmer rested against a fencepost.

"If you *ever* come anywhere near my farm," he warned the lad, "I'll make sure you spend the rest of your life with your father!"

They trudged home, bowed more from their realization of futility than from the humiliation of defeat.

*   *   *

Word came to Ephraim that his family had approached Nachrader, appealed to him to drop the charge, that his son had lost his temper, was beaten, and very nearly arrested.

"It could only have happened," the father reasoned, "if Jonah had found that there is no longer any hope in going to the court."

"He is a good son," Ephraim mused, "he will not give up. Jonah will try to help me somehow, again. And again, he will come up against those who keep me locked up, so long as I am here. Inevitably, Jonah will get into trouble and will end up in here with me." Ephraim repeated the thought, "*so long as I am here.*"

His cellmates were fast asleep when he removed the clothes brought by his wife and son. Shivering in the darkness, he knotted the pieces tightly into a cord.

In the morning, they found Ephraim hanging from the bar at the top of his cell door, wearing only his new pair of boots.

VIII

Nehemiah's Secret

Zelda had been a good and loyal wife. She had attended shul regularly and scraped out contributions from her meager day wages to put in the *pushke* for charity. She had worked reliably for influential Jewish families, and they trusted her with their silverware and jewelry. Now all she wanted was a proper burial for her husband. Her request presented a conflict between religious custom and temporal concerns.

Halakah, traditional law, was interpreted by the Chief Rabbi. On worldly matters, however, he sought the advice of the Judengemeinschaft. Its Administrative Council debated the budget, building repairs, allocations of the welfare fund to the needy, and relationships with the Gentiles and their many governments. They discussed the likely costs and benefits of each possible course of action. *He* then decided which option was right for the synagogue. (The Council provided him with cover for an unpopular decision, while everyone celebrated his wise determinations).

On July 17, 1789, the Council and the Chief Rabbi deliberated: could Ephraim's widow bury her husband in consecrated ground? The Council agreed the theft of potatoes would not exclude him from a religious interment; he had taken the food for a hungry family. But when he put himself in the position of being charged with an attempt to poison Nachrader's well, Ephraim created a dangerous threat to the very survival of the entire Jewish community.

"On one hand," said Pinkus the pawnbroker, "he never came to trial, so he was not found guilty of that horrible crime."

"On the other hand," responded Mordecai, "We are still subject to the law of collective responsibility. We had to pay the Gentile lawyer with money we could have used for the new roof! A trial could have ignited all of Breslau against us!"

"His hanging himself," asserted Yankel, "was an act of contempt against those who imprisoned him. To the Catholic Church, suicide is the one unforgivable sin. This is their town, and we live here, under their system of law. If we honor him with services at our shul and a burial in our graveyard, what will they think of us?"

Joseph looked about the room at his fellow councilmen. He believed their fear came from a captivity more compelling than that which had held Ephraim. These were good people, generous in their support of the Free School, now begrudging a widow her right to *tzedaka*, compassion which is best expressed by helping one's fellow being. "Tzedaka," he gently reminded them, "is the obligation above all commandments, for Jews to establish justice by being righteous.

"Ephraim took his life," the schoolmaster raised his voice, "to protect his son and, ultimately, to shield us from the consequences of finding him guilty for a crime we know he did not commit. Ephraim suffered for *us*. We dared never speak in his behalf while he was alive. Let us respect him now. Let the holy *Kaddish* be uttered for him in our House of Prayer."

The Chief Rabbi braced his arms against the seat of his chair and slowly, carefully, rose to his feet. Holding onto the shoulders of those who quietly formed about him, he worked his way to Joseph and placed his lips upon the schoolmaster's forehead. The matter was settled.

*   *   *

Proud and erect with his mother in her mourning clothes on his right side, and Aaron in his caftan and broad-brimmed hat on his left, Jonah wheeled Ephraim's draped, barefoot body from the prison through the streets of Breslau. As they arrived at the ghetto gate, the Judengasse emptied out before them. Many, like frightened mice, scurried into shops, houses, and up the stairs to tenement apartments where they huddled, slyly peering through broken shutter cracks to the scene below.

A few, a noble few, bowed their heads, ripped a shred from their shirts, and chanted *Kaddish* as they joined the procession: Joseph and his entire family, Nathan, Nehemiah with three strangers, Hoshea the cobbler, Pinkus the pawnbroker, and a scattering of scrub women, day laborers, and apprentices.

Most of the ghetto elders such as Mordecai, Yankel, and other members of the Judengemeinschaft, craftsmen, and people of the better families kept a respectable distance. At the entrance to the shul, Nehemiah and the strangers stepped aside. Disheveled but dignified, the entourage filed into the synagogue.

The men stood with Jonah, rocking back and forth on the balls of their feet as they intoned ancient prayers. Above and behind them, in the ladies' balcony, the women swayed and hummed the cantilations in unison with those from below.

From behind her widow's veil and through tears of grief, Zelda gazed down upon the wooden casket. Ephraim was gone from her forever. She fretted over his missing boots and felt a secret sorrow that he would meet his maker without her final gift to him.

Leah peered over the edge of the balcony, proud that her Joseph had made this service possible. Natalie looked down upon Aaron, feeling virtuous that her special friend was at the side of the bereaved. As Sarah beheld Nathan praying for the martyred Ephraim, she realized how important it was to her that he stand among the righteous. Transfixed, Hadassah's heart leaped: the son of Ephraim was the beautiful bare-chested man from the factory!

At the burial site, the gravedigger muttered that the Breslau prison should be torn down, brick by brick, the way the Parisians leveled their

Bastille. Startled, Jonah asked, "What happened in France?" "They've had a *revolution*!" Hoshea piped in. "Yeah," grumbled a workingman, "*their* revolution."

*   *   *

Aaron was about to become a rabbi, but he had failed himself in his first real test. It was his advice that had brought them to Nachrader. He had intended to plead with the Christian on the basis of his religious beliefs. Instead, Aaron had become argumentative, challenging him on points of evidence. It was he who had made the farmer defensive. He had caused the encounter to escalate into a confrontation that led to Jonah's beating and to Ephraim's death. He had bungled unforgivably.

Something died inside Aaron with the burial of his friend's father. He withdrew to his room, shaved his payess, and shed his caftan. Early the next morning, wearing ordinary street clothes, he stole out of the house before Joseph's family awakened.

Wandering through the streets of Breslau, he came upon *Gustav's Gaststatte*, a seamy tavern at the waterfront. Abjuring his convictions, he gorged on non-kosher food, then rushed to the wharf to throw it up. Rugged hands grabbed the miserable fellow and steadied him against falling in. Offering thanks, Aaron recognized his rescuer as one of the mourners who had walked with Nehemiah in the funeral procession.

The tall dockworker whose Adams apple popped out between a stained turtleneck blouse and a jutting lantern jaw was Vlad, a Ukrainian emigre. He led Aaron back to Gustav's where Nehemiah sat with his morning coffee.

"You are returning to us?" the old tailor wryly acknowledged the absence of Aaron's parochial robes and forelocks.

"Yes. No. I don't know," stammered the fugitive yeshiva bucher.

Nehemiah had been told every detail of the disastrous venture. He surmised that Aaron held himself personally responsible.

"There is hatred out there which you cannot change except by personal example," the tailor began. "Nothing you could have said would have reached Nachrader. Nothing."

"But I should have faced him alone. I knew that Jonah, as a child, had a hot temper. I should not have allowed him to come with me. I wanted so much to please him, to be his friend again. I wanted to be his hero. Instead, I became his father's hangman."

Swearing it was kosher, Nehemiah acquainted Aaron with rot gut whiskey. As the yeshiva bucher dulled his misery, the old man expounded, "What you did was an act of love. Never regret loving.

"I once heard a great Talmudic scholar say that each man must love himself and desire whatever leads him to a greater state of perfection.

"But it takes more than impulse or feeling to achieve that perfection. Only the action of reason will set you free. Go back to the yeshiva, Aaron."

Stroking his own sideburns to mimic Aaron's missing payess, Nehemiah chortled,"and you *don't* need to engage in more self-castigation."

That night, tossing in his bed, surrounded by books, Aaron knew this was his place. He would perfect himself through study, and would do so with the woman he had come to love.

The next morning, he asked Joseph for the hand of his daughter Natalie.

*   *   *

"Why did you not come into the synagogue?" Jonah later asked his mentor. "And who were those men with you?" Everyone knew that Nehemiah eschewed formal religious practice, but Jonah felt deeply hurt that his father's dearest friend had stopped at the entrance of the shul and refused to join the service.

The tailor put down his stitching and looked off into a space beyond the factory walls.

"What would you do, Jonah," he asked after a long moment of silence, "if you learned something about me which could keep you from ever having contact with me again?"

"Nothing," his stunned protege swore, "could ever do that. Is it not enough that I have lost my father? You have been to me all *he* would have been. No person, fact, or force can drive me from you."

Moved, Nehemiah looked the scamp up and down. "Perhaps it is time that you know," he whispered, "but you must never tell anyone. For once you have found out and have *not* rejected me, you too will be subject to ostracism from the entire Jewish community."

With that, Nehemiah revealed his secret: he and the companions with whom he walked at Ephraim's funeral were adherents of Baruch Spinoza. Jonah knew the name only as an abomination. Anyone connected with Spinoza was barred from entering the synagogue. How could the gentle tailor he loved be linked to such a man?

Nehemiah placed his hand on Jonah's shoulder. "Spinoza," he explained, "was a Talmudic scholar of the seventeenth century. His writings convey a vision of God, man, and the universe which is so progressive that it threatens many rabbis and those who run the institutions of the ghetto."

The ordeal surrounding his father had kindled a revolutionary zeal within Jonah. He was eager to know more about this mysterious philosopher who had the power to intimidate the elite.

The tailor began with a strong admonition: "Once you start, know what dangerous ground you may tread."

"I am not afraid," said Jonah, "I want to walk with you."

Nehemiah read aloud the *1656 Resolution of the Amsterdam Ecclesiastical Council* which still resonates in Breslau today:

> With the judgment of the angels and the sentence of the saints, we anathematize, execrate, curse and cast out Baruch de Espinoza...May he be accursed by day, and accursed by night;

let him be accursed in his lying down, and accursed in his rising up; accursed in going out and accursed in coming in. May the Lord never more pardon or acknowledge him; may the wrath and displeasure of the Lord burn henceforth against this man...

Hereby then are all admonished that none hold converse with him by word of mouth, none hold communication with him by writing...and no one read any document dictated by him, or written by his hand.

Here was a Jew who was the enemy of Jonah's enemies. He *must* read the forbidden texts! The tailor resumed his role as teacher, bringing the young journeyman writings of Spinoza to study through his long nights as watchman to the establishment.

In *A Treatise on Religion and the State*, Jonah read that the language of the Bible is deliberately metaphorical; its stories are allegories to appeal to the imagination of man. To Spinoza, it is not the interpretation of events as *miracles* that proves the existence of the Divine, but rather the realization of universal and invariable laws of nature that establishes the oneness of God. The Almighty is revealed through *the processes of nature.*

Jonah's spirit soared: he could understand the words of the Torah as parables created by *human beings*, not the literal revelations of a man-like apparition in the sky. God is everywhere, a force, not a creature who must be obeyed. And so, rules passed down by the rabbis are *their* interpretations of writings left by fallible mortals and shaped by cultural traditions.

In Spinoza's *Political Treatise*, Jonah found a credo he could fight for: the ultimate end of the state should not be to dominate men, nor to restrain them by fear. Rather, it should be an instrument to free one from fear, to live and act with security and without injury to one's self or his neighbor. The state should enable its citizens to live by, and exercise, free will that they may not waste their strength in hatred, anger and guile, nor act unfairly toward one another. Thus, the end of the state ought really to be liberty.

He did not yet know how he would do it, but he would dedicate himself to help build *that* kind of regime.

*   *   *

Half a continent away, the Count Honoré Gabriel Mirabeau echoed the vision of the excommunicated Jewish philosopher: the state should guarantee liberty, equality, and fraternity for all. At the Court of Frederick the Great, Mirabeau had met Moses Mendelssohn who inspired him to write a tract advocating full citizenship for the Jews of France. Now, as President of the French National Assembly, Mirabeau urged support for the petition presented by Jews from Alsace-Lorraine to be granted equal rights.

*   *   *

Each Thursday, at *Gustav's Gaststatte,* Jonah lunched with Nehemiah, Vlad, Stas, a broad-faced, balding, muscular Polish blacksmith, and Hans, a short, cigar-puffing Prussian schoolteacher in a white shirt and a three piece suit. Over sausage and beer they argued the works of Goethe, Lessing, Hamann and Herder and exchanged the latest reports from France.

Every night, Jonah savored the thoughts he discovered in literature. Every Thursday, he was energized by the spirit of revolution. As the two currents fused within him, he found hope for the redemption of his father in a political movement emanating from the other end of Europe.

*   *   *

In early autumn, the Jews of Breslau were given permits to build *sukkahs*, booths of branches and twigs, in the nearby woods to celebrate *Sukkot*, the Festival of Tabernacles.

Joseph and Leah stretched out on the mossy floor of their hut, staring dreamily through its flimsy roof to the clouds that floated just below heaven.

Aaron and Natalie, promised to each other, prayed that the Jew whose death would grant them their turn for a marriage license be one who was old, ready to join the Lord. They could wait, they told God and each other.

Sarah wrapped twigs of palm, myrtle, and willow in one hand, held the traditional citrus in the other, and paraded with her neighbors among the sukkahs.

Hadassah wandered down a path to the creek. Alone, in the sunlight that filtered through red and golden leaves, stood Jonah. Hadassah had dreamt of this moment for so long, had wondered how she would reach out to him, how he would respond.

"I am so sorry about your father," she ventured.

"Thank you for coming to the service," Jonah dug one foot into the soft clay of the bank, "you and your family. It was courageous of you to be there with us."

"My papa believes your father was innocent," she explained. "He told us that Ephraim suffered for the rest of the community and we owed him our gratitude and respect."

"My father could *not* have tried to poison that Prussian's well. Nobody who ever knew him would believe that! I remember, as a child, how straight he was. With everyone. Once, when he redeemed his watch from the pawnbroker, Pinkus wanted to waive the interest, but Dad insisted on paying the full amount.

"What's right is right," he told me, "Pinkus is entitled to a return on the risk he took for holding my watch."

"And there was the time when Yankel put his thumb on the scale and overcharged Simka the scrubwoman for ground meat.

"My father caught him at it and Yankel was infuriated. But he re-weighed the meat! Yankel never again spoke to my dad and whenever my mother went into his shop, he grumbled about how her husband was everyone else's avenging angel, so why didn't he provide better for her?"

Jonah's voice choked and his eyes moistened. "He tried to provide for both of us, not just in material ways…"

He talked a long while about his father as he and Hadassah worked their way between the thick undergrowth and the river bank. Where the path narrowed, he took her hand, and where the embankment became steep, he held her waist.

They left the riverside for the protection of the dense foliage. He enveloped her in his arms. She stroked his hair, touched his cheek, and tasted his lips on hers. He gently caressed her wonderful breasts and eased her onto a bed of leaves.

She trembled, opened to him, and felt him deep within her. Time stood still for God is love. Nothing else existed.

Their eternity was arrested by a wind from the west stirring the forest to life.

*   *   *

Into *Gustav's Gaststatte,* late one afternoon, wandered a hideous scabby-faced hulk wrapped in a shroud of rags that concealed all but the shiny tips of his black boots. Through an infested beard, a toothless mouth uttered words Stas understood to be Ukranian. The Polish schoolteacher signaled the wretch to wait while he ran to the docks to fetch his friend.

When he returned with Vlad, the two men from the Ukraine chatted easily in their native dialect. Between gargantuan gulps of beer, the stranger explained he was looking for the coach to Kiev. He had just been released from the Breslau prison where he served two years for trying to steal a piglet.

"It was just a *little* squeeler," he complained. "It got away, but I didn't. It must be a big swine by now, and I have lost as much weight as the hog has gained." He pulled back a section of his shabby sheathe to bare discolored flesh sagging from a once fuller frame.

Dusk was settling into darkness and the pathetic churl would never find his way through the maze of convoluted and dead-end streets to the eastern coach. Feeling compassion for anyone who had spent time in a Teutonic dungeon, Stas and Vlad volunteered to escort him to the boarding point.

Along the way, he moaned about conditions in the prison, how he was cramped in a single cell with a Yid and two murderous thugs, everyone speaking a different language.

"We slept in our own crap. Imagine, being locked up with a dirty Jew and no way to wash! Even the food was filthy, and never enough. The portions were so stingy, you could starve to death."

Vlad patronized the offensive scoundrel. "How did you survive such hardship?"

The ex-convict explained that luckily, one of the guards was Ukranian, and favored him. With diabolic glee, he recounted how the guard gave him most of the food allotted to the Jew.

"And what he didn't give me, I took." He raised his mangy mantle to his knees and pointed to a remarkable pair of brand new boots into which he had squeezed his grotesque feet.

"The old fool hanged himself, and wasn't going to need *these* any longer!"

They walked a long while in silence. A dog wailed, pigs snorted, thunder heralded a rainstorm. Under a dense, black sky they twisted through back alleys and groped their way across deserted fields, taking shortcuts to the coach stop known only to Vlad.

*   *   *

The next morning, under a bright sun rising from the east into a clear new day, Vlad and Stas appeared at the Silkworks.

Grinning broadly, the two conspirators handed Jonah his father's boots. They could never go back to Gustav's.

IX

Sarah's Misfortune

Never did Feigel the *shadchen* work so hard to find a match. Soon, Sarah would be an adult, and everyone in and around Breslau knew she was far too self-willed to be controlled by an ordinary husband. Joseph wanted a man of erudition for his daughter but any Talmudic scholar expected a grand dowry and financial support from a wealthy family. The schoolmaster was respectable but poor.

How imprudent of Joseph and Leah to have let their daughter become a well educated woman. She could not be molded to serve a Jewish husband and his mother.

Beginning with the surrounding region, and expanding into ever wider concentric circles across the Germanic states, Feigel wrote to other shadchens for viable prospects.

*　　*　　*

Ever since Leib had begun to talk, he spoke with snorts and whistles. His parents, Rebekkah and Zacutus Meyer, found the sounds endearing in a child, something he would outgrow. The school teachers with whom they left him from dawn till dusk could do nothing to help Leib overcome the peculiar sounds. He became an object of taunts and derision by his classmates. From the moment he learned to read, Leib found comfort in quiet communion with books. It was his good fortune that his home town of Amsterdam had become the literary center of the Jewish world.

Portuguese speaking *Sephardic* Jews who had fled the Inquisition were welcomed in Amsterdam where they built the Talmud Torah Community in the Jueden-Bort.

To consolidate their power, the regents of the Jewish community invoked *herem*. Jews who discussed theology with the Gentiles, sold, gave, or lent books to them, or gave haircuts to their women could be excommunicated for days, months, or years.

Leib's family had come to Holland in the wave of Yiddish speaking *Ashkenazic* Jews from Germany early in the century. Together with Jews escaping massacres in Poland, Galicia, Lithuania, and the Ukraine, they formed their own neighborhood within the larger, more prestigious Sephardic Amsterdam community. Into this mix, rabbinical scholars and writers converged from all over Europe. Learned and religious works rolled off its busy multilingual presses, and Leib consumed all he could acquire from each of the diverse Jewish traditions.

To bring the energy and skills of the Jews into the economic mainstream, Dutch city authorities called upon them to interact with Gentiles and limited the right of the regents to excommunicate their own people. Freed to reach out beyond the Jueden-Bort, Rebekkah and Zacutus visited the surrounding countryside, gathered fresh produce, and intermingled with the Christians.

In the nearby province of Overijssel, they made friends with farmers, peasant weavers, and merchants. Through the spring and summer, they watched the production of linen, from the planting and gathering of raw materials to the spinning of the final product and its sale in the village stores.

When the English wrested control of shipping and international commerce from the Dutch Indies Corporations, prosperous Sephardim turned to the Ashkenazim to help forge new economic opportunities. With their knowledge of the production of linen and their contacts in Overijssel, Rebekkah and Zacutus induced Sephardic investors to put up money for yarns which they delivered to the peasant weavers and to pay them for their work, becoming the link between the isolated countryside and the city.

Leib's career as a scholar was cut short. He was needed to run the Amsterdam office full time, keep the accounts, organize the inventory, note which cloths and dyes were most popular, and advise suppliers to meet the demand of the Dutch market, while Rebekkah and Zacutus moved between the peasant weavers of Overijssel and the growing group of investors in Rotterdam, Groningen and Zwolle.

In the course of building the business, Leib had to neglect not only his studies, but also his personal life. It was now time to take a wife. Even more than providing him with an heir, he wanted a woman who would share his interest in literature.

Hanni, the sophisticated shadchen for Amsterdam's Ashkenazic community, was commissioned.

The task proved daunting. Well-educated and middle class Jewish families of Holland did not consider a snorting, whistling bourgeois businessman worthy of their daughters. For months, Hanni shopped about for women in the lower classes where they might overlook Leib's curious impediment for obvious economic advantage. But she could not find one among them who could meet her client's unalterable prerequisite for intellectual zeal.

When the inquiry from Feigel of Breslau reached Hanni, the elated Amsterdam shadchen raced through icy streets, skidding and stumbling on frozen canals, arriving breathless at Outerdek Road where the Meyer's shop stood on the edge of the city. In Leib's astonished face, she flaunted Sarah's incredible resume. Here was the cultivated daughter of the Senior Rabbi of the Breslau Free School, experienced in business, and she kept books! For such a prize, the customary dowry was happily waived. Hanni submitted her client's resume, along with character references from the investors.

Sarah would be cared for in a cultured if distant environment. Her marriage to an educated, well-to-do Dutchman would take place concurrently with the union of her sister Natalie and Aaron, the only son of deceased parents. Joseph arranged for the double event at the grand new Sklowar Synagogue.

*   *   *

In 1790, the king ordered Jews throughout Prussia to follow the lead of those from Berlin and other sophisticated centers, and take proper German surnames. Joseph became a Lehrhaupt, the head of persons who teach. Jonah took the name Schneider, meaning tailor, Yankel became Fleischmann, the butcher. And so it went, throughout the ghetto. Special commissions were appointed to supervise the procedure. Should anyone resist, a name was created for him and registered, often with ludicrous results.

Aaron had grown up without a patronym. He never knew his mother's family. Although raised by Joseph, he dared not register as a Lehrhaupt lest he be considered a sibling to his betrothed. He was not yet in a profession, had no trade, possessed no skill, owned no property. He had, "nothing," he told the commission, "on which to base a surname. I am simply not prepared." The chief commissioner laughed, "You're prepared!" And with that, he became Aaron *Fertig,* German for "ready."

*   *   *

It would be a long and expensive trip to Breslau. Tolls were charged at the border of every duchy, province or township that had to be crossed. Leib would take a route that made its stopovers only in those select locales across Germany which had allowed a few Jews to settle. While the coachmen, horses, and other passengers rested at the inn of the town, he would seek lodging in its ghetto.

Before boarding his coach in Amsterdam, Leib was handed a gift by an investor, Levi da Costa, a Sephardic Jew who ran a publishing house.

With a skill in many languages, honed over his sixty years, da Costa had translated some of the works of Baruch Spinoza from the Latin (in which they were originally penned) into Yiddish. He trusted that they would be good reading for the journey.

*   *   *

Predictably, Mordecai and Rivkah expected their son to marry a woman of high breeding from Berlin. They wrote to cousins and received a glowing description of a fine woman, a bit older than Nathan. Erna Sacks had been tutored in French as well as German, knew all the plays and novels of the day, and dressed impeccably. Although Erna had been married before, the union was annulled upon discovery that her hapless husband was homosexual (one could assume she was still a virgin).

Thus, along with the benefits of maturity, she could promise him freshness as a woman. More to the point, she was the daughter of a banker, and would bring about a fine alliance between the Silkworks and an important financial institution.

Since that memorable Passover of his father's betrayal, Nathan had come to see his parents for what they were. While his mother basked in pleasing his father, she had not one whit of understanding or interest in what he did. She was a bauble, displayed by a powerful man who, in turn, found physical satisfaction along the Oder, in the arms of whores. The few tedious hours Mordecai spent with Rivkah were devoted to trivia.

Influenced by Goethe and the romantic novels of the day, Nathan wanted a different kind of relationship. He envisaged a woman with whom he could share ideas as well as passion.

Whenever his parents broached the subject of marriage, Nathan adroitly found avenues to avoid it. Confronted by his mother, he suggested they wait for his father. When Mordecai brought up the subject at work, the young man insisted, in deference to his mother, that they wait to discuss it at home. On such evenings, he was certain to challenge Aaron to a game of chess.

In the warmth and intellectual stimulation of the Lehrhaupt household, Nathan chatted with Aaron and Joseph on the role of the Jew in the changing world. Often, Sarah turned the conversation to ways in which the Jew could help change the world. If Nathan, for example, would convince his father to improve the working conditions of the men in his silk plant, this would enhance both their regard for the Jews *and* the productivity of the business. She had more ideas about improving the skills of the workers, their health and living conditions, many ways in which the industry could be a force for *tikkun olan*, the ancient injunction for Jews to heal, repair and transform the world.

"It's all right for her to sound the reformer," Nathan thought to himself. "She is an educated woman. Lucky she's engaged to an intellectual in liberal Amsterdam. Things are different here in Breslau." Still, he enjoyed her zest and teased her to be more practical. Aching with the thought that soon she would be gone with a Dutchman he decided to hate, he realized he was jealous.

He lost badly to Aaron at chess, defeated by impossible images of Sarah, and made his way home as the candles in the windows along the Judengasse belched their last gusts of flame.

When it became clear that Nathan would resist any effort by his parents to match him with a woman of their choice, Mordecai contrived a ruse. He would send his son to Berlin, ostensibly to entice a banker, Johannes Sacks, to invest in the Breslau Silkworks. Nathan, his father advised him, would have to be subtle; an obvious overture could offend a cosmopolitan man of means.

Nathan would join his great grandfather Samuel at a salon given by Herr Sacks honoring Moses Mendelssohn. The great man of letters who had achieved international eminence still managed the Berlin Silkworks. While Sacks might be interested in investing in the enterprise, it would be gauche to discuss business in front of the esteemed philosopher. That was where Nathan came in.

Mordecai engaged the best tailor in Berlin to fashion a suit and cloak for his son in the latest style, using only the finest silks from the Breslau factory. His ensemble would be so exquisite, Mordecai assured him, that his host would be bound to ask about its origin. This would give Nathan the opportunity to provide Herr Sacks with all the details on the silk and fine workmanship which he personally oversaw at the Breslau plant. "This was the way," his father expounded,"that gentlemen did business."

Though he protested that he loathed the intrigue, Nathan could not resist the prospect of parading himself before Dorothea Mendelssohn (surely her father would bring her) and the literati of Berlin in an outfit tailored to define the fashion of the day, at the very moment Sarah was to be locked in matrimony to a damned Dutchman she didn't even know. He read every review on Montesquieu's works printed in German.

Mordecai and Rivkah drank a quiet toast. Their son would be won over by Johannes' daughter Erna and the refinement for which they themselves had yearned throughout their years of exile.

*   *   *

Ralph David Fertig

Henrietta Hertz   Rahel Levin
Leaders of the Berlin Salon

Moses Mendelssohn and Gotthold Lessing playing chess

Lost in the profundity of Spinoza, Leib rode through one duchy after another. The philosopher made no separation between Old and New Testament, looking upon the Jewish and Christian religions as one, "each proclaiming love, joy, peace, temperance, and charity to all." Paradoxically, he wrote, Jews endured chiefly because Christian hatred of them compelled a solidarity for survival. Spinoza believed that Jews and Christians should be able to live together in harmony, and Jews could begin this, he said, "by recognizing the nobility of Jesus, the greatest of all prophets, a mortal whose wisdom was evidence of the power of God."

In the liberal environs of Amsterdam, Leib had known many Gentiles, but only formally and in the context of his family's business. He arrived in Berlin determined to offer his complete fellowship with the communicants of Christ.

Burning with evangelical zeal he strode through the streets of the cosmopolitan city until he came upon a Lutheran Church. With outstretched arms, Leib ran to the alter, loudly chanting praises to Jesus. Outraged at an obnoxious Jew mocking Christian beliefs with grotesque sounds from his nose and mouth, the Pastor ordered his removal at once.

The Yiddish Dutchman was seized by angry congregants who unceremoniously threw him down an imposing staircase into a mound of ignoble mud.

That night, shaken but undeterred, he read da Costa's translation of Spinoza's *Ethics*. His life took a new turn when he discovered that mind and body are aspects of one another; that the decision of the mind and the determination of the body are one and the same thing. Will and intellect are identical, "since a volition is merely an idea which, by the richness of associations or the absence of competitive ideas, has remained in consciousness long enough to pass over into action.

"What is called *will*, the impulsive force that determines the duration of an idea in consciousness," Leib read as though an experience of revelation, should be called *"desire...*the very essence of man."

He read and reread that section throughout the next day on the coach. When he opened his mouth to talk with the ashen-faced man in furs stuffed into the seat beside him, no snorts or whistles came out. "I am cured!" Leib shouted to the Polish passengers, who understood not a word, no matter how loudly he repeated the news of his habilitation.

Only the dread of Poland as they neared the frontier propelled him into silence. He had taken the chief route to Breslau, going by way of Poznan. At the border, Polish sentries who searched his bags, forced Leib to strip before the snickering, fully clothed, Slavic passengers. He was in the land of the enemy.

He rode in quiet humiliation to the gates of Poznan.

At the inn in the lively ghetto of Poznan, he sat across from a guest clutching a recent critique of Montesquieu's *Espirit des Lois*. Here was a fellow intellectual with whom he could celebrate his personal triumph of will. The stranger was a family friend of Moses Mendelssohn whom Leib knew as the wise old hunchback who had convinced Mirabeau to take up the cause of the Jews of France.

When the Dutchman raised a second tankard to celebrate his forthcoming marriage, Nathan realized this was Sarah's betrothed. He studied the businessman from Amsterdam, loathing his seeming likability. "Tell me, sir," Nathan asked testily, "What exactly do you do *for your workers?*"

*   *   *

Nehemiah and Stas stood at the door to The Cafe of the Collegium Maximum, screening students, artisans, and workers anxious to hear the Jesuit priests' translation of the latest journal from Camille Desmoulins. After the presentation, Hans led a discussion calculated to expose the political values of each participant. If one's support of the struggle appeared unshakable, he would be probed privately on his knowledge of Marat's *L'Ami du Peuple* and Robespierre's *Defenseur de la Constitution*. His background would be checked and only on the solemn guarantee of a sworn member of the covert Jacobin society, would he be considered for membership in the outlawed group.

At dusk, on appointed days, Jewish members of the cell knelt with their Christian comrades in the Jesuit Church near the riverbank. Under cover of night, at a signal from Vlad, one by one they crept to the Silkworks. Jonah listened through the aperture in the door for the whispered password, opened the portal and studied each face before admitting anyone, directing new recruits to Nehemiah.

Stas began the meeting with news from Paris. Mirabeau, Clermont-Tonnerre, Robespierre, and the Abbé Gregoire were locked in battle with the Bishop of Nancy and the conservative deputies in their effort to emancipate the Alsatian Jews. In his *Courrier de Provence,* Mirabeau summarized the call for religious freedom. The Berlin cell had translated the summary and sent copies by the usual route to Hans. After the meeting, Gentile members of the cell cautiously filed out, distributing the pamphlets throughout the city of Breslau. Their Jewish compatriots, not daring to be caught beyond the ghetto walls at night, secreted themselves in the Silkworks until the edge of dawn. Before the workmen arrived at the plant, they departed, the circulars tucked into their clothing. Soon, the ghetto was awash with propaganda for emancipation.

*   *   *

Joseph welcomed Leib Meyer at the coach terminal, warmly embracing his prospective son-in-law while the porters unloaded the luggage.

"No, sir, those are *my* books," Leib intervened as his bag was about to be given to a stranger. Hans apologized and pointed to a package of similar appearance waiting for him.

Leib handed Joseph the bundle of books and hauled the large, heavier valise himself as they walked together to the inn, pausing to *daven* at the grave site of Yankel Fleischmann's wife whose passing had cleared the way for Natalie and Aaron, setting this glorious date for the double wedding.

The Senior Rabbi of the Free School was pleased that Sarah's fiance was a literate man. Later, they would discuss all these books. In the meantime, he let the weary traveler relax.

Feigel had no such compunctions. "Nu, so where is the ring?" the shadchen began her catalogue of inquiries. Befuddled, Leib asked her to point the way to a jeweler.

"Before the sun sinks into the Sabbath, you only have time to go to Pinkus," she remonstrated."God willing, he will have a ring."

The pawnbroker had just the thing. He dug deep into the trove of jewels on which lenders had borrowed funds until at last, he found it. Years ago, a Gentile had defaulted on a ring bearing a pale rose red stone. Pinkas polished the metal and found it to be silver. Its inscription,"*To a woman of valour*" would please Sarah.

Leib returned to the inn with barely enough time to unpack, change, and arrange his *tallis*. Following special Friday night services, Leah laid out a feast on embroidered linen tablecloths sent by Rebekkah and Zacutus Meyer, stretched across tables, extending end-to-end through two rooms of the Lehrhaupt apartment.

Sarah, her parents, sisters, brother, and the academic staff of the Free School took their places. His betrothed was comely, charming, eager to assist him in his business, and spoke as a thoughtful person. But Leib's inexperience with women, his natural shyness and deference to customs he associated with central European Jews dictated he keep her at a cautious distance.

Invigorated by the intellectual milieu, Leib urged the schoolteachers to tell him all about their curriculum.

Zelda, hired to help serve, brought in the brisket, steeped in Leah's special gravy, and Joseph stood to offer a toast.

"Don't you teach anything about Spinoza?" Leib's words remained suspended in space, hovering in a vacuum of incredulity.

The glass in the hand of Joseph's upraised arm plummeted, shattering crystal and sweet wine onto the fine Dutch linen.

"What kind of man are you?" thundered the schoolmaster.

Leib was enveloped in a terror of silence. He felt the lacerating stares of the teachers; the pity in the eyes of his fiancee and her sister, Hadassah; the wonder of it all in the eyes of Aaron and Natalie; the anguish in Leah's bearing; and the paralyzing outrage in Joseph, whose arm collapsed, sending his hand onto the shards of crystal, spewing fresh drops of blood. Zelda unobtrusively backed out of the room while Leib struggled to reply.

"A Dutchman, sir." There was nervous sniggling.

"A Dutchman! A Dutch *man*, you say; not even a Dutch *Jew*? Do you Jews who are Dutch dare to touch one leaf of the writings of that heretic anathematized by your own Ecclesiastical Council?"

"Well," Leib faltered, "He was a Talmudic scholar who…"

"Who desecrated the Talmud!" Joseph boomingly interrupted the bewildered simpleton before him. "Leib Meyer, in the name of the Divine One, blessed be His name, I ask you, have you read any of the documents ever issued by that cursed apostate?"

The teachers bowed their heads in unison. Aaron gaped in amazement at Joseph. Leah and Natalie withdrew from the room, gesturing in vain for Hadassah and Sarah to follow, but the two younger sisters fixed their gaze on Leib, wondering how he would reply.

Between whistles and snorts, the man who would be his son-in-law blurted out, "I have read many of his works."

Joseph sank into his chair, pressed his wrists to his forehead, tore a strip from his shirt, and chanted the prayer for the dead.

Trying to rescue the situation, Aaron turned to the dazed and floundering Dutch Jew. "Then do you denounce and repudiate that disciple of darkness? Do you seek the mercy of the Almighty, blessed be His name, for forgiveness, acknowledging your error; will you seek to cleanse yourself from such transgression in whatever way the rabbis may guide you?"

The teachers joined Joseph in the *Kaddish.* Sarah and Hadassah clutched each other.

Leib saw his dreams of a normal married life crushed in the granite of wine, crystal and blood. This was a good family. But it was far removed from the world he had discovered through da Costa's translations.

His lifelong affliction had returned full force. He would be repulsive to everyone until he could regain that inner peace he had found in the writings of one whom he was asked to disavow.

He had never thought of himself as courageous, or even stubborn. But in this, he had to be truthful.

"I shall always," he wheezed and snorted between whistles, "honor Baruch Spinoza as a great Jewish theologian."

"You must leave this house," an exasperated Joseph demanded between teeth clenched to contain himself from further soiling of the Sabbath.

"You must never look upon my daughter or any member of my family. You must leave this town. And may the Divine one, blessed be His name, have mercy on your soul!"

Leib staggered back to the inn and tore open his book bag as if to project blame on the words which had given him inspiration. Neatly bundled leaflets dropped out, calling for freedom from religious oppression.

X

A Case of Mistaken Identity

Nathan realized he had been set up.

The salon began with a recital by a lavishly ornamented, abundantly overweight Erna Sacks, mutilating the harpsichord while singing mercilessly off-key. During the coffee and brandy break, the colossus pursued him through a jungle of overstuffed furniture, unyielding in her chatter: who wore what at which recent event; who made the latest gaffe; who was seen with someone else's husband; and what was wrong with the latest play. He guessed that her painted cherubic cheeks belied her age and her incessant prattle, strewn with feigned French phrases, intimated an ingrained ignorance.

He was saved by Dorothea Mendelssohn's introduction of her lover, Karl Wilhelm Friedrich von Schlegel, whose poetry had just been published in the *Athenaeum.* The son of a highly respected Lutheran Pastor (who had recently been assaulted by a deranged Jew in his own, very refined church), he lectured at the University of Jena in the same department with the great Friedrich Schiller. Seated among the guests in the salon, Nathan listened to Karl Wilhelm read excerpts from his works, calling for the celebration of free love. He would take Dorothea back to Jena with him, where she would compose paeans of passion without promise.

When he discovered that Herr Sacks was already an investor in the Silkworks, Nathan felt angry, used, and foolish in his overly elegant silk. He took the Sunday morning coach to Poznan.

* * *

Sarah buried her rage and shame beneath blankets on the bed she shared with her sisters. Sick of compliant Natalie's assurances that Papa had saved her, and unable to grasp Hadassah's foolish, romantic visions, urging her to run off with her "one chance for a new life in Amsterdam," she writhed in humiliation. Their father had held her up to ridicule! Everyone in Breslau would know that the best match she could get was a snorting, whistling dolt who put a heretic ahead of her.

She could do nothing. All Jewish women had been weaned on their duty to keep the culture alive, to maintain a tradition that put them on pedestals and confined them. She had been raised with the additional responsibility of being a child born beyond the quota. A surplus daughter of a schoolmaster, she had prepared herself to be placed with an appropriate man in another community.

Yet the closer she had come to the date of her wedding with Leib, the clearer it became to Sarah that she was deeply drawn to another man, one who lived in her own ghetto yet breathed the air of affluence. She dreaded having to leave Nathan, dear, dashing, Nathan. She had teased him with exhortations and prodded him with suggestions for the business she had dreamed of someday sharing with him. But the chasm between them loomed larger than the distance between Amsterdam and Breslau.

Now that the misguided arrangements with the bizarre Dutchman had collapsed, she was destined for deportation to Aunt Sophia in Krakow. She would never see Nathan again.

*   *   *

The moment Shabbat services ended, the worshipers poured onto the platz in front of the synagogue to whisper and embellish details: the man Sarah was to have married is a heretic; his tongue is cursed by the Almighty; he brays like a jackass; he has the evil eye; his stare caused Leah's crystal to shatter. Joseph, God bless him, saved his daughter from disgrace; a single woman, she will have to be exported to live with pigs in Poland.

The wedding will be for Natalie and Aaron alone. But it should be a grand feast. They should not be made to suffer. It is important to show Joseph and Leah our support.

The innkeeper, unnerved by the tales of his guest's depravity, ordered Leib to leave, forthwith. In spite of the denunciations (or perhaps, reinforced by them), Leib still considered himself a Jew. He would not travel on the Sabbath, though he had no idea where or how he would find food or lodging until the Sunday morning coach.

He had just completed packing when Zelda appeared at his door, bringing the linens which the Lehrhaupts had asked her to return. Neatly folding them one way, and then another, she helped Leib try to force the tablecloths into his valise. It was no use; they were too bulky. As they broke down in laughter at the absurdity of their efforts, Zelda felt a pang of pity.

Emptying out the contents of his book bag to free it up for the linen, Zelda sprang back in horror. "Those pamphlets! Where did you get them? You *cannot* leave them here. No one must see them!"

He explained that there must have been a mix-up at the carriage yard, these were not his. Someone else has *his* books.

Zelda knew. She had kept her silence, but had found leaflets like these crumpled in the pockets of clothing her son had left with her to wash. She stuffed the circulars back in the bag, tied the linens in a separate bundle, and bade Leib follow her. They left his valise and linens in Zelda's flat, and, with the book bag under Leib's arm, made their way through the streets of Breslau.

Observing the kosher laws, they ate fresh fruits at a café in the bustling marketplace, surrounded by Renaissance and Baroque burgher-houses that flanked the Gothic City Hall. Zelda wanted to know all about Leib, and he painstakingly told his story. She was not put off by his snorts and whistles, attending only to his words. And sensing that Zelda was more than a scrubwoman, Leib wished to hear about her. She talked about her life with Ephraim, his imprisonment and death, and her pride in Jonah. The Lehrhaupt daughters (she was so sorry he did not get to know Sarah) had taught her to read. Ever since Jonah moved into the Silkworks, she spent evenings alone in her flat, studying the Torah.

At the close of her narrative, Zelda stood up, took the book bag from Leib, asked him to wait, and disappeared into the crowd. He drank his beer slowly, barely aware of the multitude streaming by or the chimes of the Church of St. Mary Magdalene. He reflected on the fullness of the simple cleaning woman. She had been so kind and accepting when all the Breslau ghetto had risen up against him.

It was dusk when Zelda returned with his bag of da Costa's translations. He was in awe of her resourcefulness.

He spent the night in her flat. She spread his linens lengthwise on one side of the bed. As he studied her in the flickering candlelight, he felt a yearning for this tender, courageous woman.

Zelda was young when she had married Ephraim; Leib was old for a bachelor. The decade between them melted away as he seized her in his arms. It had been many years since she had been touched by a man. He had never known the thighs of a woman and she guided him. Their lovemaking was soft and gentle. His ecstasy was boundless.

*   *   *

As the third star brought an end to the Sabbath, the guests began to arrive at the synagogue. Natalie looked magnificent in the silk bridal dress that was a gift from Nathan, away in Berlin on business. It hurt Aaron that his friend was not at his side. They had never spoken of it, but he suspected that Nathan could not bear to see Sarah beneath the *chuppa*, exchanging vows with another man. Aaron thought, "If only Nathan knew that this moment was for Natalie and me alone, he would be here with us."

The wedding was dignified and somber. Clouded by the disaster that befell Sarah, propriety took the place of joy.

Still, the marriage feast proved Joseph undaunted. The sins of a man from Holland would not stain his good reputation, or afflict his family, and he toasted vintage wine to the happy couple.

They had been like brother and sister, and their vows gave perpetuity to their companionship. Natalie and Aaron would be good for one another. Everyone agreed.

* * *

Sundays belonged to Hadassah and Jonah. He loved her for the straightforward and spontaneous spirit with which she greeted the world, and the special way she embraced him. She loved him for his exuberant commitment to life, his vulnerability to the pain of others, and his tenderness with her.

They talked easily about everything and nothing, delighting in the sounds of one another's voice. The shed upon the roof was their secret island, protected by a sea of passion from the strictures of the hostile, parochial mainland.

They adored one another's bodies and lay shamelessly naked upon the fine Dutch linen his mother had brought him earlier that morning. His eyes danced as she taunted him with caresses making ever smaller circles to his tantalizing erection. She laughed aloud as he ran his tongue around her nipples and across her flesh, down, down to her magical place. Possessing him, feeling his throbs within her, she found rapture. Surrounded by her, he exploded with fulfillment.

* * *

In the twilight of Sunday afternoon, Nathan made his way to the Poznan ghetto inn. Halfway between Breslau and Berlin, he was in a world different from either. Although Poznan had been the home of great rabbinic academies, Jews had not yet recovered from the late seventeenth century looting and massacres by Cossacks, Swedes, and Russians. They were so impoverished and economically exhausted that only loans from the Catholic clergy made it possible for Jews to try to rebuild their community.

How different, he thought, was the plight of the Jews in Germanic states. A Berliner by birth and allegiance, Nathan believed in the Enlightenment and the opportunity it offered his people to enter the economic and intellectual mainstream of Western Europe. Even Breslau boasted a Collegium Universitat where the words of Lessing, Dohm, and Mendelssohn were studied. Friedrich Gottlieb Klopstock himself, the patriarch of German poetry, wrote of the suffering of Jews in his great epic, *Messiah*:

> Who is not seized by the shudder of compassion when he sees
> How our mob dehumanized the people of Canaan?
> And doesn't it engage in it because our princes
> Lay upon them too heavy chains?
> You, Savior, loosen the rusty,
> Tightly fettered chain from their sore arm.
> They hardly feel it, don't believe it. So long
> Has it rattled on the miserable ones.

Such people would inevitably relax restrictions against the Jews. He was proud that Breslau was German. It was the Poles (whose city it had once been) who were the real enemies of progress. Feeling innately superior, he pitied the Jews who were under Polish rule. He heard the sounds of one of them in the dining room, so oppressed that his speech was obfuscated with snorts and whistles.

*   *   *

Aaron brought Natalie into their wedding chamber, the old book room, strewn with treatises and commentaries. Good friends, they were shy and awkward in the realm of intimacy. She lovingly fingered the manuscripts he treasured, tentatively read aloud to him and they fell into each other's documents. They tried to find in one another the passion they felt for the word of God.

*   *   *

All the way to Breslau, Nathan was consumed with images of Sarah. What consummate luck to have run into the Dutchman! How incredible that Leib let his absurd loyalty to an obscure, castigated pedagogue of the last century come between him and so wondrous a woman.

He thought of her deep set eyes graced by enchanting, long lashes and dark brows. He loved the gentle, deliberate way in which she moved. She was not meant to be confined to the ghetto. Sarah was sensitive, yet the epitome of the new rationalist approach. She was real, so unlike the fatuous Erna or the self-indulgent Dorothea. He knew it was not the pretentious salon, but the production of goods and profits and wages that gave meaning and support to the Enlightenment.

Through their industry, he dreamt that he and Sarah would help build a new era. She might push him with extravagant ideas about the workers, but she would be reasonable. How lovely and wise was this schoolmaster's daughter. Would she have him? His desire for Sarah intensified as his carriage brought him closer.

That evening, Nathan pounded on the door of Aaron's book room/boudoir. Rushing at the astonished, nearly naked newlyweds with neither an apology nor a word of congratulations, he pulled his friend down the stairs into the fetid air of the Judengasse. Pacing frantically back and forth, he poured out his heart.

"Aaron, tell me Sarah has not yet left for that vile place in Poland! I must see her. I must tell her how much she means to me."

Clutching his blanket about him, his dazed friend pressed one cold bare foot against the warm calf of the other. "It will take the Breslau bureaucracy weeks to invalidate her marriage license, reinstate her status, and schedule Sarah for export."

"Do you know how she feels about me? Would she have me?"

"Anytime you come into the room, Sarah lights up, becomes animated, self-conscious, and aware of herself as a woman. She always targets you for conversation. I've known for a long time that you two were destined for each other. It is ordained by God, blessed be His name."

Aaron embraced his childhood friend. "We will be brothers!"

"After the disaster with Leib due to *his* beliefs," Nathan winced, "what would Joseph think of a rationalist as a son-in-law?"

"Sarah's marriage to you would keep her in Breslau. Leah would not let Joseph block it, and he would have to consent so long as you keep kosher and promise to raise the children in the tradition."

Nathan found that convincing Mordecai was another matter altogether. "What! My son married to a schoolmaster's daughter!"

Knowing that love meant little to his father, Nathan addressed Sarah's potential value to the business. "You don't need to marry a clerk," the merchant blustered, "we *hire* people for that!"

"Father, Sarah would bring a new level of sophistication to *management*," the son countered."She is a highly intelligent woman."

To Nathan's amazement, it was Rivkah who brought her husband around. While Mordecai had immersed himself in the world of commerce she had found human warmth in the ghetto and learned that the quality of people transcended class. She reminded her husband that *his* father, a fine man, was once a peddler. Izaak had married into Jewish aristocracy; could not Mordecai's future daughter-in-law do the same?

Charging it to the business, Mordecai paid 70,000 thalers to the city of Breslau to permit Sarah to remain. Between them, Joseph and Leah emptied a bottle of schnapps. Last to be asked, though she knew what was happening at every step, Sarah was euphoric. Nathan registered for the license and waited for a Jew to die.

*   *   *

As she wrote the letter to Leib about Sarah and Nathan, Zelda reflected on their scandalous night and their frantic dash to the Sunday morning coach. She cherished those moments; there could be nothing sinful in making love, even (or especially) at her age. How dear of Leib to insist that she have the silver ring with a rose red stone. Still, she had declined his entreaties to flee with him. It was all too sudden. She had many obligations and people dependent upon her in Breslau. Those who demonized Leib would never understand his innocence. (Jonah tactfully described him as one caught in the interstices of ideals and reality). Her son had been good to her. She could not leave him. Not yet.

*   *   *

On April 4, 1791, hundreds of thousands of Parisians joined with the Jacobin Societies, the King's Ministers and Municipals, and all members of the National Assembly in a funeral procession for Mirabeau, its fallen president. This would be the last time aristocrats, bourgeoisie, and proletarians would march together. The hope for building a constitutional monarchy was fading.

On June 20, near midnight, disguised with their two children, the King and Queen stole out of the Tuileries to join Bouille's army of the east, hoping to overthrow the revolution. The landlord of the post house at Sainte-Menehould recognized the king, passed the word, and the royal family was intercepted at the bridge to Varennes and returned to Paris. Vast crowds received the royal coach in silence.

Now that the King could no longer be trusted, the division between the people and the nobility deepened. The masses rallied behind the

Jacobin Party and its commitment to build a republic. Royalists and officers loyal to the crown fled to Treves, sought arms from the crowned heads of Europe, and prepared to restore the autocracy.

On August 27, the King of Prussia and the Emperor of Austria declared that "the restoration of the monarchy is a matter of interest to all sovereigns." They invited other royal powers to join them in gathering armies to attack France. The new Legislative Assembly prepared for war, and Frenchmen mobilized.

In the spirit of liberty, equality, and fraternity, the National Guard of Paris, foot-soldiers of the Revolution, conducted a referendum on Abbé Gregoire's petition to extend the rights of man to the Jews. Of the sixty *Arrondissements* in the Paris Commune, fifty-three voted overwhelmingly in favor of complete Jewish emancipation!

Representing the guardsmen, the Abbe Malot moved the Assembly to grant all privileges of full citizenship to the Jews. When the clericists tried to block action on the resolution, the Jacobin Deputy Duport demanded that their motion for postponement be withdrawn. Regnault de Saint-Jean, President of the Assembly, ruled that to oppose the motion was equivalent to opposing the Constitution of the Republic.

On September 28, 1791, Jews were declared to be equal with all men and free citizens of France.

*   *   *

Throughout an October night, the cell posted leaflets on walls in every corner of Breslau and slid them under every door in the ghetto demanding the same rights and status for the Jews of Prussia. Nathan burst into the Lehrhaupt apartment, hailing the news. "For the first time since the fall of Judea, we have been granted full citizenship! Prussia will have to follow!"

Aaron and Natalie did not share his enthusiasm. They would welcome the removal of special taxes and restrictions, but were skeptical about many of the changes Nathan craved. Aaron wanted no equality with those whose baseness denied his God and devastated everything his Supreme Being stood for. Most loathsome, was the notion of fraternity with those who had butchered and oppressed his family and co-religionists, raped his mother, and left him with the private, secret shame of a life generated by polluted seed.

He and Natalie turned to one another, reinforcing their isolation. They studied and loved and slept among books that promised a connection with the Divine. The idea of liberty threatened their shelter.

*   *   *

Emancipation for Jonah and Hadassah meant that one day they could be together in the sunlight. For now, the tyranny of oppression held them hostage to the rules of the state and the conventions of her family. As an excess daughter, she would soon be of an age requiring emigration from the city. Her parents had consulted Feigel the shadchen to provide Hadassah with a respectable husband in a nearby shtetl. Even if he were to somehow come up with 70,000 thalers, her family would never accept Jonah.

The lovers dreamed of running off together, but she could not bring shame upon her family. Their Sundays became more precious. They clung to each other. Their love on the island was doomed. Only liberation of the mainland could set them free.

Jonah became increasingly involved in the insurgent activities of the cell.

*   *   *

As her wedding day approached, Sarah glowed with more confidence and delight. Mordecai became resigned and then appreciative of the skills she would bring to the business. Rivkah scrutinized, came to respect and cherish the woman who was to become her daughter-in-law. Nathan felt the exhilaration of having taken control of his own life.

It was at the wedding feast that Hadassah first saw Eleazar Pistron, a rough-hewn widower in his forties who collected and distributed feed for livestock in nearby Ratibor. He examined her like a mule skinner surveys an animal at a distance, to avoid being kicked before mounting her. She shuddered at his glance and turned to watch the men dance, relieved that Jonah was among them.

Chastened by his encounter with Leib, Joseph would not make the same mistake again. He knew his daughter, Hadassah, had a wild streak and wanted her married before she did something foolish on a romantic impulse with some stranger. She needed a strong husband who could take her in hand. Eleazar was a pious man of moderate but adequate means, with an enterprising spirit, who would maintain a disciplined household. Best of all, Hadassah would be in Ratibor, a part of Silesia, just two days from Breslau. She would have to be persuaded.

*   *   *

For their wedding night, Sarah and Nathan were given the run of the Friedlander apartment while Mordecai and Rivkah stayed at the inn with their out-of-town guests. Giddy from the wine, aroused by the promise of fulfillment, the groom slowly, mischievously unraveled one layer of finery after another from his wife, stripping himself with the same gentle teasing, tossing each article of clothing into a different corner with erotic abandon.

Modestly, Sarah doused the candle. Boldly, Nathan relit it. For a long, palpitating moment, he gazed upon the alluring curves of his woman. He led her to the sofa where Rivkah had placed a sheet to receive the evidence of her virginity. Sarah lay invitingly before him, and as he brushed his hand across the hairs of her mound, the front door crashed open.

The Breslau police fell upon a dumbfounded Nathan. Sarah, terrified, wrapped herself in the wedding-night sheet and leapt from the sofa. She cowered against the wall, watching as they upturned furniture, emptied out drawers and closets, and cursed the traitorous Jews. The invaders gathered up papers while Nathan clutched a shirt to his crotch and grabbed his boots. As they hauled him out the door, the thugs snarled something about acts against the state. They were gone with the sound of hooves clopping on the Judengasse.

From the other side of the partition, Nehemiah heard the loud commotion. Only carriages for the police were admitted into the ghetto at night. It was clear to him what had happened, and the tailor slipped out into the dark and through his secret passage from the ghetto into the streets of the city. He tapped the secret code on the door of the Silkworks.

"You must leave this place," he warned Jonah. "Somehow the police have found out about our meetings here. They've stupidly arrested Nathan and are bound to figure out it is *you* they want. There's no time. Gather what you need and let's go!"

Jonah ran to the shed, pulled back the floorboard to recover the remaining leaflets, the cash he had saved, and his love notes from Hadassah. Swiftly donning a long black coat and his father's boots, he seized his mother's linens and left the factory behind him forever. Nehemiah led the young radical through back alleys to a shack in the shadow of St. Berhardin's Church where Vlad answered the faint rapping at his window.

∗   ∗   ∗

The boisterous celebration suddenly fell quiet when a disheveled Sarah staggered into the dining hall of the inn. Mordecai and Rivkah choked at the thought of their son's excess. "Where is Nathan? What did he do to you?"

Heaving and gasping for breath, she struggled to find the words. "The city police…They took Nathan away."

"Impossible!" stormed Mordecai, as he heard the word *sedition*. "Oh, no, not us!" moaned Rivkah at the description of the havoc. "Typical!" muttered Grandfather Samuel of Berlin at the officer's anti-Semitic remarks. They tried to comfort Sarah, assuring her it had to be a mistake. At dawn, when they could leave the ghetto, they would engage Joachim Gauner to make inquiries and secure Nathan's release.

* * *

While Vlad shaved Jonah's beard and cropped his hair, Stas crafted a new passport. Hans drilled him with names and directions to a series of safe houses they dared not put on paper. He would flee westward, toward the Rhineland. Vlad provided a sketch of routes to avoid Prussian checkpoints. The loyal Nehemiah had delivered the linens and Jonah's sealed note to Zelda, removed all hints of her son's partisan activities from her apartment, and returned with a ring bearing a rose red stone.

"She wanted you to have this. Perhaps you can buy some safety with it, along the way."

The men embraced, swore fidelity to their cause and to one another and, tormented by thoughts of losing Hadassah, Jonah solemnly pledged to return in the vanguard of the revolution.

As he scrambled through the underbrush, Jonah found himself alongside Nachrader's farm. He climbed over his father's fence, looked cautiously about, lowered his trousers, and took a long, steady, satisfying piss into the Prussian's well.

* * *

Upon pocketing his fee, Herr Gauner asked Sarah, Mordecai, Rivkah, and the grandparents to be seated while he untangled it all. "For some time," the lawyer explained, "officials of the city of Breslau have been trying to track down the Jacobins who post seditious circulars on walls and slip them under doors, calling for violent overthrow of the government. The police determined that it took more than Jews to carry this out since the leaflets were always disseminated under cover of night, when Jews are safely locked up."

Herr Gauner paced back and forth."Reinhardt Vertreter, chief detective assigned to this case, reasoned that the distribution of flyers throughout the town was so thorough and quick, the effort required the work of a number of people. He further deduced that since the conspirators had to coordinate their efforts, there must be a central meeting place. He set out to find it.

"A few nights ago, Vertreter was found unconscious near the Schweidnitzer Gate. He had been struck on the head. The police carried him to his home and sent for a doctor. Just last night, he regained sufficient coherence to give his report. From his bedside, he told the police that on the night he was wounded, he had been conducting a surveillance far from the Gate.

"The chief detective watched while several figures came out of the shadows to enter the building which he suspected was the lair of the subversives. They had their backs to him, and in the light of the doorway, he could see only the face of a young man who admitted them, one by one.

"On his way to the police station to get constabulary support, Vertreter heard a woman scream, 'Stop! Thief!' and saw a hideous-looking man, bandaged about his head, barefoot, and in a patchwork of rags running down the street with a hefty full-grown pig in his arms.

"The chief detective shouted for the man to stop, but when that proved to no avail, pursued him toward the Schweidnitzer Gate. At its approach, the thief turned and, in a Ukranian dialect said something that translated as 'I have already served time enough for the swine,' and he struck Herr Vertreter full force with the squealing sow. As he fell, the chief detective's head hit a rock.

"Now of course, you, like the police, want to know *where* did this surveillance take place?" The barrister paused, savoring the suspense, relishing the authority with which he would resolve the mystery. He continued the tale, step by step.

"Vertreter first explained to the police how he came to the suspected site. He had always been convinced that a Jew had to be at the bottom of this, and you, Herr Friedlander, are one of the few Jews who has a base outside the ghetto."

At this, Mordecai sprang from his seat to protest. "I would *never* have anything to do with such treachery." Turning to his family, he pleaded, "All of you know I would not jeopardize our business by allowing people of such ilk into our plant!"

Herr Gauner motioned him down, "As it happens, Herr Friedlander, the police do not have any evidence against you. They initially thought it was your son, with his liberal ideas, who was receiving a group of revolutionaries into your factory after hours.

"Last night, as soon as the chief detective told his story to the police, they went straight to your flat, looked for signs of Nathan's involvement and took him in for questioning. Your son denied all knowledge, none of the papers they seized revealed anything, and this morning, when Herr Vertreter *saw* him, he told the police that Nathan was not the young man in the doorway.

"Apparently it was your nightwatchman who let people into the Silkworks, and he has disappeared. They are looking for him now, and when they catch him, they will get to the bottom of this. For your sake, Herr Friedlander," the lawyer chuckled," I hope he was hosting a party for pinochle, opium, or sex! It would go easier for you than harboring saboteurs.

"They have released your son, and I have sent my aide to bring him here to my office from the lockup. There will be a slight charge for the trousers I've provided him." Herr Gauner prepared the family. "Before they could be sure he was not guilty, the police had to be thorough in their interrogation."

When Nathan appeared, his shirt was in shreds, his face bruised, and his back purple from scalding water and the stings of a whip. In pain and exhausted, he buried his head in Sarah's lap.

*   *   *

In the note to his mother, Jonah begged her understanding for his abrupt flight and bade her farewell, adding: "Mother, I have never asked how you received these linens, but now you are free to follow them to their source. The enclosed poem is for my beloved Hadassah. I know you will keep our secret."

That evening, Hadassah drew Jonah's mother to her bosom as she read his words aloud:

I love thee now and always
Wherever I shall be
From deep within,
From all that's been,
And all will ever be.

I love thee now and always
For everything thou art:
Thy hopes and fears,
Thy smiles and tears,
Thy kind and loving heart.

I love thee now and always
With everything that's me:
My soul, my dreams,
My being; it seems
The best of me is thee.

I love thee now and always
From lands to which I flee:
Thou art my life,
My rightful wife,
As ever thou will be.

She sensed his stirrings inside her, counted the days since she last dripped menstrual blood, and felt her breasts hardening.

If only she knew where he was, she would go to him. But if she searched for him, she could be followed. If he heard that she was seeking him, if he learned that their child was growing within her, he would jeopardize his safety to come to her.

She cared not what would happen to her. Before God, Jonah was her true husband.

Hadassah told her father that she would accept Eleazar Pistron's offer.

XI

Jonah's Flight

Joseph was drafted to write the resolution. It was vital, the Administrative Council agreed, that the Judengemeinschaft disavow any connection with those persons seeking violent overthrow of the state. "Only through legal and socially appropriate means," the statement read, "do we wish to address the continuing improvements between the Jewish community and the citizens of Breslau."

A thorough search of the Silkworks had revealed no evidence of Jacobin activity. But mindful that the law of collective responsibility was still on the books, everyone in the ghetto prayed that Jonah would never be caught. "Like father, like son," they whispered. And, "Can you trust the mother?"

One by one, Zelda's customers found other women to clean their homes. She helped Hadassah prepare for her wedding, tearfully saw her off to Ratibor, and sat alone in her apartment.

For a moment, it seemed that she would be rescued from impending poverty when Yankel Fleischmann asked her to be his housekeeper. On her second day at the widower's flat, however, Yankel emerged from his bedroom fully nude and chased her about the apartment. As she ran into the Judengasse he shouted out the window, "What did you expect? Nobody will bring you into their homes for anything else!"

Zelda wrote Leib and sold the linens for a one-way ticket to Amsterdam.

*   *   *

The heavy snows covered his tracks and discouraged search parties. Wearing his father's wonderful boots, Jonah trudged ever west, past the safe houses of Silesia, into Saxony, avoiding roads and population centers. Many nights he slept in a stable; one night, outside Bautzen, he stayed in a choir loft; near Dresden, he had a bed in an orphanage; near Rosswein, he spent the night in a crypt. He learned that Jesuits were more likely to give him sanctuary than diocesan priests. As he moved into Lutheran territory, he found the Catholics more sympathetic to a stranger than Protestants.

His passport identified him as Johannes Schultz, a denizen of Frankfort-am-Main (It would be assumed he was a Christian, since permanent residence was not given to Jews). His cover story was that he had gone to Gorlitz to bury his father, was robbed by highwaymen, and was now heading back to his wife and children in the Rhineland.

He nearly froze one night under a lean-to in the woods near Meerane, then crossed the heights into Thuringia. His chill became a fever and in the stable of a bordello just outside Jena, he fell into a delirium.

It took little professional discernment for the ladies of the house to discover he was a Jew, but the tough Madam Rosa ordered them to nurse him back to health and to closely guard the secret of his presence and his faith. When he regained consciousness, she demanded he tell her the truth. Upon hearing his story, the cynical Madam revealed a comforting side, applying compresses and soothing him back to sleep.

As he recovered, he came to know each of the ladies and to realize that they, too, were victims of an unjust system. Dolly had been raped nightly by her father, Gina by her mother's boyfriends, one after the other. Myrna's father marketed her body to coal miners in Silesia. Kitty never knew a father and her mother was in a lunatic asylum. Polly was sent out to beg for a hungry family; many of those who gave, took her first. Lisa was abandoned as an infant. Each had been on the streets, forever doomed to lives of prostitution, exploited and abused by pimps.

Once violated, there was no way out of servitude. Madam Rosa offered them protection, cared for them when they fell ill, screened the clients, and watched over them zealously.

Jonah saw how the Madam audaciously ushered out one College Lecturer who tried to get violent with Myrna. "He writes about free love," she groused, "so he thinks when he pays for it, he can go crazy. But not in this house, not with my girls!"

"If he is such a proponent of free love," Jonah naively inquired, "then why does he pay for it here?"

"Because the lover he gets for free is an overbearing, self-indulging snob from the salons of Berlin who is better at talking about passion than providing it."

For a fortnight, Jonah grew stronger and wiser in the ways of a different world. His skills as a journeyman tailor helped him earn his keep; he repaired torn garments and stitched new gowns for each of the ladies. With remnants from each, he created a scarf of many colors for Madam Rosa. It was time to continue his journey.

Pressing the ring inscribed "*To a woman of valour*" into the Madam's hand, his body refreshed and his boots resoled, Jonah waved the ladies farewell. His note of thanks promised to return on the wings of liberation for all, and it ended with "Verses to Vice:"

With fondest admiration,
And great appreciation,
I leave thy habitation
To fight for liberation

Forever will I treasure
Ye women, fine and fresh;
O, thee who bringest pleasure,
Ye helped restore my flesh.

Under a bright sun, he entered the Thuringian Forest, climbed the foothills of the Bavarian Alps, and followed the river Main as it cascaded down until, at Bamberg, it became navigable. He joined the crew of a barge, hauling hides and furs to Frankfort.

*   *   *

Forsaken in the Breslau Inn, she braced herself against the smell and mass which had become her husband. From the sewing set Nehemiah had given her as a wedding gift, Hadassah removed a fine needle and placed it under the connubial sheet. In the darkness that modesty required, Eleazar lifted his nightshirt and entered his wife just as she pressed the steel into her buttocks, shouting the requisite cries of pain and producing the blood to prove her worthiness. The next morning, arching his back in triumph, Eleazar packed his conquest into his wagon and set out for Ratibor.

The trip to the shtetl was a long road back in Time from the Breslau ghetto whose rich diversity of workers, bourgeoisie, tradesmen, and scholars crackled with dialogues of politics and change.

In Ratibor, everyone was poor, fundamentalist, and superstitious, resisting anything new. Although the Jews lived in separate, wooden frame houses, spread out across the snow, they were always in one another's homes. In Breslau, where the Jews were densely packed into a small ghetto, living one on top of the other, Hadassah had more privacy than she would know from the invasive, peering, opinionated women of Ratibor.

Eleazar had selected his first wife, Zilpah, because her name suggested that she would bear him two sons. The wretched woman bore him none, so he had let her wither away with consumption. "She is in the hands of the Lord," he said to himself, having saved the cost of the doctor he did not trust. "God will give me another chance to produce a son."

When, a month later, Hadassah told her husband she was with child, he guffawed at the stupidity of Dr. Leibowitz. That ass had told Eleazar *he* was the infertile one. For the next seven months, Eleazar Pistron was gentle with his wife.

*   *   *

Mordecai insisted that Nehemiah be fired. "I gave Jonah the chance of a lifetime," he roared, "on the strength of Nehemiah's assurances that he could control the ungrateful scoundrel."

Sarah, who had not left her husband's side since his release from the lockup, and Nathan, who had become utterly dependent upon her, urged moderation. "Nehemiah took Jonah under his wing when he was a mere lad. As an adult, Jonah is responsible for his own deeds," the daughter-in-law pleaded. "You can't put an old man out on the street!"

Nathan reminded his father that their occupancy of the flat was conditional upon Nehemiah's employment at the Silkworks. "Have you forgotten that he is our landlord? If you cancel your contract with him, *we will all* be out on the street."

Relenting, Mordecai growled, "All right, all right. But he's got to go to the police, he's got to tell them everything he knows about Jonah or they will suspect *us* forever."

Nehemiah knew he was on the list, but he dared not speak with Reinhardt Vertreter. What could he tell the chief detective that would not provide a clue? Would he be able to conceal his true beliefs from a professional interrogator? When they worked him over as they did Nathan, would he be able to keep from naming others? They would follow him night and day, recording his every move, his every contact. He dared not risk communication with any of his co-conspirators. He was too old to run away.

He stared with endless fascination at snowflakes melting in his hand. The thought of flight across the snow gave him the idea.

The next day, Nehemiah sent word to Vertreter to meet him at high noon at the Church of the Holy Spirit, on the banks of the Oder. He would have an important message for him.

The chief detective arrived just in time to see Nehemiah step out onto the ice that hugged the shore.

"Look, all ye people of Breslau," the old tailor shouted, "here is another Jew walking on water!"

He continued out to where the ice ran thin until the river swirled about him.

*   *   *

Across the continent, on the pretext of restoring the King of France to his full regal authority, German forces mobilized. On December 14, Louis XVI issued an ultimatum to the Elector of Treves to disperse those who had gathered there to march against France, or be treated as an enemy. The Elector promptly banished the royalists into the Rhenish snowfields.

*   *   *

Aaron did not know the sturdy, unassuming man, who he was or where he came from. His Polish accent, filtered through a hoarse whisper, confided that Jonah was now safely out of the country, but had often spoken warmly of the Talmudic scholar. He knew Aaron could be trusted. The stranger described how he had dredged the icy waters with a dockworker to recover the body.

"Nehemiah died to shield men who struggle for the right of Jews to *be* Jews without restrictions. It is fitting that you conduct the burial service." The lifeless eyes of the old tailor stared up at Aaron as the stranger disappeared into the dusk.

The young man wrestled with his heart. Could he, a devout believer, lead the Kaddish for a Jew who had abandoned his faith?

Natalie was pregnant, more pious than ever, and anxious that he not jeopardize his career. "Surely the rabbinic authorities," she cautioned, "would object to a religious service for someone who is not religious!"

"But Natalie, what is *more* of a religious act than to sacrifice one's life for those who take risks, whoever they are, so that we can practice our beliefs?

"Listen to our religion." Aaron read from *MICAH, 6.8:*

It hath been told thee, O man, what is good
And what the Lord doth require of thee:
Only to do justice, and to love mercy,
and to walk humbly with thy God.

Aaron still felt pangs of guilt for having set in motion the series of events that drove Jonah into the arms of radicals. And Nehemiah had been like a father to his friend. He would stake his career on assuring that the tailor who did justice, loved mercy, and walked humbly received a decent burial. "God," Aaron concluded, "walked with him."

It was Nehemiah's first time in the synagogue in decades.

*   *   *

In Berlin, a charming young fop with an uncontrollable stutter boarded Leib's coach. Wilhelm Sacks and his new travel companion quickly relieved each other of any discomposure due to impediments of speech. The two became fast friends. Wilhelm was bound for Amsterdam to set up a branch of his father's bank.

At night, they shared a bed in the inns of ghettoes along the way and engaged in boyish erotic pleasures. Leib discovered that it was sex he loved, not any particular person or gender.

When he arrived home, filled with Spinoza and sexuality but without a bride, his family promptly disowned him and sat *shiva*. Leib went to live and work with Johannes Sacks's son; the two found genuine affection in one another.

Upon receiving Zelda's letter, Leib consulted Levi da Costa who agreed to hire her as his housekeeper. When Leib steered Zelda to the book publisher, she struggled to conceal her initial disappointment. Over time, da Costa made up for her sense of loss, delighting her with endless storytelling and providing her with a comfortable home. She came to know and love Amsterdam.

*   *   *

Frankfort stood alongside the Main river, the chief waterway draining the streams of central and southern Germany into the Rhine and the vital point where major east-west and north-south roads of central Europe converged. Protestant refugees from Spanish- controlled Holland built its commercial core, plundered the ghetto and drove out all the Jews.

When the Emperor of Austria made Frankfort his imperial city, he allowed a few Jewish families to return. After the Thirty Years War, trade fairs brought thousands of visitors and foreign firms to Frankfort each year, making the city a vital financial center. Jews expelled from Nurnberg, Ulm, Augsberg, Mainz, and Cologne filled the city's ghetto; their trading and money lending extended throughout Europe. Still, they could not own land, were banned from agriculture, most crafts and retail trade, had to wear large yellow circles and were confined to the ghetto every night, and on Sundays and feast days. Johann Wolfgang von Goethe described the scene:

> It hardly consists of anything more than a single street which, in early times probably had been hemmed in between

the city wall and moat as in a prison. The narrowness, the filth, the crowded conditions, the accent of a disagreeable language, all together made the most unpleasant impression…It was a long time before I dared to enter alone and I did not return after I had escaped the importunities of so many men, untiringly asking or offering to shop and trade…

*   *   *

As church bells heralded Christmas Eve, royalist refugees, evicted from Treves, sought room at the inns of Frankfort. Officers of the Austrian Imperial Brigade, sympathizers and carolers welcomed them at the western gate and paraded them through snow covered streets. Priests, on their marble steps, blessed the crowd as it stomped by. Ravenous merchants rubbed their hands, inviting the wealthy emigres into brightly decorated shops, while anxious peddlers hurried their carts to the ghetto before revelers, constables, and night could descend upon them.

Amid the clamor, Jonah slipped through the eastern gate with minimal scrutiny.

The denizens' quarter was home to select aliens, mostly men in low-wage jobs, granted residence from Holland, Italy, France and from other Germanic states. At the back cellar door of a red brick rooming house, Jonah tapped the secret pattern taught by Hans.

The portal creaked open just enough to reveal a gritty, heavyset woman with a mop in one hand and a bucket in the other. No sooner had Jonah uttered the obligatory password than she hooked him in with the head of the mop and shoved him into a subterranean room. He waited in silent darkness.

In time, a lantern floating above a stately nose betrayed a tall, austere figure. As light spread through the chamber, the wraith passed the lamp into the heavy woolen gloves of a curly haired companion. Behind them stood a sentinel coated in sawdust whose intense blue eyes pierced Jonah's skin.

The towering presence led the questioning. He wanted to know all about the young lad in elegant boots who sought access to a Jacobin hideout at the very moment Frankfort was swelling with Bourbon benefactors.

Calloused hands with wood splinters frisked Jonah while the curly-haired confederate left to find the captain of the barge and question him about "Johannes Schultz." Awaiting his report, the tall patrician interrogated Jonah on Jewish customs and ritual.

The report from the docks corroborated Jonah's account of his voyage from Bamberg. Now, the committee of three let the adventurer with the counterfeit papers tell his story from the beginning.

The day-to-day details of his journey, with names of those who had given him safe haven, validated Jonah's credentials. His compassion for the women of the brothel attested to his humanity. And, as he told the story of his father whose boots had brought him to them, they saw Jonah's passion and dedication to the revolution.

The chief inquisitor introduced himself. Jean Claude Boudin was born and raised in Metz where the Alsatian Ashkenazim had acquainted him with Jewish culture. His ease with many languages gave him work as an interpreter. As a stevedore, Carlo Regnini, a genial native of Genoa, knew everyone on the docks. The piercing blue eyes belonged to Pier Vandergryft of Amsterdam, a carpenter who built booths and displays for the fairs.

One by one, they embraced their new comrade.

Beyond the ominous basement, legions of worshipers filled the churches of Frankfort in a midnight mass to the Holy Trinity. In their underground chamber, the revolutionaries drank to Marat, Danton, and Robespierre.

The Frankfort Ghetto: 19th century engraving by Dielmann; photography by Lelo Carter. From the HUC Skirball Cultural Center, Museum Collection, Los Angeles, CA

XII

Aaron's Epiphany

"They crushed your eggs," said Dr. Langkau, clasping Nathan's scrotum in his hand. "It is unlikely you will ever be able to procreate." Nathan shivered as he recalled the repeated blows of the truncheon to his genitals by the police.

The holiest part of him, the source of life for generations to come, was shattered on his wedding night. He had been taught to feel pious when he grasped his testicles in testifying to God, but now he felt only bitterness and anger while he groped, between his forefinger and thumb, to find fragments of his seed.

As he buttoned his trousers, Nathan simmered with curses of Jonah and his pack of hotheaded zealots. It was *their* impatience, *their* taking risks on *his* property, that doomed him to emptiness.

The brutality of the police was widely known; they were doing their job. He was offended by their anti-Jewish innuendos, but that was the way of uneducated Gentiles. No Jew could ever advance if he took such rebukes too much to heart.

"Of course they grabbed me," he thought, "they mistook me for that ill-bred traitor! It was *Jonah* who should have been horse-whipped and robbed of *his* dreams. Jonah and his gang are not content to wait for the Enlightenment to take root in Breslau. They tear everything down. Not only do they jeopardize *me*; they subvert our only opportunity to achieve real progress!"

He sought out Aaron, his friend and confidante, before confronting Sarah.

*　　　*　　　*

Each egg was roasted and fertilized with a splash of saltwater, garnished with a sprig of parsley, and set on the tray with matzo, lamb, bitter herbs, and *charoses*. Jonah served cups of wine to denizens from many lands, toasted the legacy of a people committed to emancipation, and began *his* interpretation of the *seder*.

"They say that Moses was found among the reeds of the Nile and adopted by the daughter of the King of Egypt who had him raised in the palace by a Hebrew slave. He came to think of her as his real mother. But I believe he was a man much like the late Honoré Mirabeau, who, while reared with the comforts of royalty, found his true origins lay with the workers and the poor. Both understood that their power and wealth was created by the toil of others. Moses was ashamed. When he saw an agent of the Court strike a slave, he slew the guard and joined the underclass.

"Hebrew slaves, like many of the people of France, were at first too frightened to shield an insurrectionist from the mighty Pharaoh who, long before the Bourbons, had the idea of the 'divine rights of kings.' Moses fled into exile, much like Jean Paul Marat wandering, not through underground sewers, but across the high dunes of a desert. He came upon a wonderful bush, like the torch of liberty, that burned and was not consumed. Through its light came an inspiration, directing him to return to the populace and lead them out of oppression."

After they drained a cup of heady wine to Moses, a second to Mirabeau, and another to Marat, Jonah continued.

"Moses invoked an invisible force of righteousness, like that described by Jean Jacques Rousseau as the 'Divine Being.' With an ardor like that of Georges Jacques Danton, he tried to sway the Court and arouse the slaves. None of his appeals succeeded. So he organized ever escalating acts of terror, like the Committee of Safety, to undermine the control of the aristocracy. Only when an Angel of Death took up arms for the Israelites, did the Pharaoh release them from bondage. Seizing their liberation, the Hebrew people abandoned the kingdom."

Full cups were raised high with gusto to Danton, with respect to Rousseau, and with reverence to the Divine Being.

"Even then, after the people had tasted freedom, the Pharaoh, like Louis, tried to regain his power over them. Before the blood of the people's uprising had dried, he sent his Imperial Army to recapture the Hebrews and return them to serfdom.

"With the regent's chariots at their backs, the children of Abraham came to the shore of an impassable sea. It was like the despair that blocks some of our comrades today from taking action.

"But the faith of the Israelites parted the waters, and they passed through. When the regal guard followed them into the breach, the sea closed in, drowning them in their armor of aristocracy."

Jonah and his comrades celebrated the miracle with another anti-royalist round.

"Leading his people through the desert into an uncertain future," their narrator concluded, "only the demands of Moses for absolute loyalty to the principles of the revolution, like those called for by Maximilien de Robespierre, brought them to the promised land."

Sated and euphoric, the group collapsed into a triumphant, bacchanalian bliss.

*   *   *

On May 15, 1792, Judith was born in Ratibor. As she suckled her babe, Hadassah felt the thrill of Jonah.

Doctor Leibowitz kept her secret. He assured Eleazar that the child was premature. Though he had never trusted the physician, Eleazar *knew* his wife had been chaste on their wedding night.

The old wives of the shtetl were not so sure: "The baby is too robust for seven months," they said."The mother came with all those airs from the big city where (may the Lord forgive me) they do such things!""The poor *tsedrayter* doesn't know the tricks of a *gozlin*." whispered the yentas. "It's Zilpah's revenge!"

Eleazar heard the cackling. It fed his foreboding.

Disappointed with a daughter, he would try again. Eleazar would prove his virility and have a son. For a while, Hadassah resisted her husband. When he threatened her and raised his belt, she shuddered and acquiesced. Month after month, as his efforts bore no fruit, his skepticism mounted. Not satisfied with her denials, he began to beat her. When Hadassah begged him to stop his assaults in front of the baby, Eleazar dragged her outside and whipped her before the approving eyes of the neighbors.

Even the rabbi counseled: "It is the duty of a wife to obey and accept her husband as he is. If Eleazar beats you, then you must ask what you have done to offend him. Look to the Almighty, blessed be His name, for mercy upon you both."

Only the love of her baby and letters from Zelda and her family kept Hadassah going.

*　　*　　*

The Duke of Brunswick, Commander of the allied forces of Austria and Prussia, demanded the French restore Louis XVI to power and accept the invading army in peace. Otherwise, resisters would be shot and Paris utterly destroyed. His manifesto hinted of covert support from French royalists who looked to the Allies to rescue them from the radicals.

The Jacobins charged Louis with abusing his constitutional privileges and secretly aiding the enemy. They intercepted letters from Marie Antoinette in which she begged the Allies to hasten their march upon Paris. Enraged, the people of France rose up against the King and Queen.

While members of the Assembly debated the fate of the royal family, the demand came from Marseilles to depose the king. A battalion of five hundred men, well furnished with patriotism and munitions, set out for Paris, rousing all France with their infectious anthem, the *Marseillaise*.

*   *   *

July 14 was celebrated in the imperial city of Frankfort with the arrival of Francis, the newly elected Emperor of Austria, nephew of Marie Antoinette, for his coronation. It took all the forces of the royal troops and local *Polizei* to restrain the cheering throng from enveloping the royal carriage, drawn by twelve white stallions through the Romerberg to the Kaiseraal.

Most of the soldiers garrisoned at the fort in nearby Sachsenhausen had joined the parade. On the south bank of the river Main, just below the armory of the fort, Jonah and Carlo released tricolored balloons emblazoned with the militant maxim that was sweeping Europe: *Freiheit, Gleichheit und Bruderschaft!*

Guards abandoned their sentry post to pursue the offenders while Jean Claude and Pier emerged from the underbrush, laid explosives alongside the ammunition storage tower, ran the fuse down the hill, lit it, and plunged into the Main.

Hugging close to the far side of a passing barge, Jonah felt a surge of triumph as the entire region lit up with fireworks spewing from the emperor's arsenal. He had read, run, and recited rhetoric for the revolution, but now he experienced the thrill of combat. It was a sensation he would savor and seek to relive in the years of battle which lay ahead.

In the name of his father, he had become an *avenger of blood*, entitled by the Torah itself to slay those who had condemned Ephraim to his death.

*　　　*　　　*

Bastille Day was celebrated in Paris with the arrival of the first flanks of the Federated National Guard. Thousands of the citizen soldiers joined the Revolutionary Commune led by Danton. On August 10, they stormed the palace, overthrew the monarchy, and took the royal family to the ancient tower of the Temple. The Assembly abolished feudalism and confiscated lands held by the nobility.

Nine days later, Brunswick's army crossed the frontier into France. Ordinary citizens, freed from the bonds of servitude and fired by their zeal for the emerging republic, stood against the professional armies of Prussia and Austria.

Confident of their superior training and artillery, the Prussians advanced toward Paris. At Valmy they discharged one cannonade after another, expecting to frighten the French into retreat. Instead, the French repulsed the invincible allied army. As the barrage died at Valmy ridge, the poet Johann Wolfgang von Goethe told his comrades, "From this place and date begins a new era in the world's history." Elated with victory, the French pressed on and by October, they were in Frankfort.

*　　　*　　　*

Just before midnight on July 26, 1792, after hours of agonizing labor, Natalie delivered a healthy, squalling infant with bright red hair. Aaron cooed to his son, held him close against his chest, and rocked with reverence for the Divine source of all life.

When he placed the child at Natalie's breast, he saw that she was bleeding and writhing in pain. The midwife sent for the doctor.

"Her contractions did not expel the afterbirth," Dr.Langkau explained. "There is nothing we can do. It is in God's hands." Aaron tried frantically to reach the hands of God with his own. Before her husband and her family, Natalie slowly bled to death.

Melancholy pervaded the service. The piercing cries of the baby gave voice to the torment in his father's soul. As Natalie became part of the earth, Aaron named their child Adam.

For seven days, the family sat *shivah*. In torn garments and cloth slippers, Joseph and Leah huddled together on a low wooden bench, Sarah and Nathan on another, while Aaron curled into himself on a footstool. Mirrors were covered. No mourner could work or read, except for certain sections of the Torah in which Aaron could find nothing.

Bearing candles with loaves of bread, cakes, hard-cooked eggs, and plates of potato latkes, friends, teachers, students, yeshiva buchers and neighbors poured into the flat. In hushed tones, they offered words of praise for Natalie. No other conversation was permitted. The mourners could not offer or acknowledge greetings. Tradition dictated that they be preoccupied with their grief and the memory of the departed.

Each morning and evening, a *minyan* of ten men came from the shul to the apartment to recite the Kaddish and hold services.

Sheloshim, a thirty day period of lesser mourning, followed. For Aaron, the sheloshim was even harder to bear; he was expected to socialize and could not.

With a sense of futility, he could only stare at the innocent infant whose emergence had brought death to his wife. He was dimly aware of Leah and Sarah reaching out to his baby and to him.

Although reading was permitted during the sheloshim, he turned away from it. Aaron and Natalie had shared Judaic literature. Without her, it would have no meaning.

To avoid facing others, Aaron wandered into the city. People laughed in the sunlight."How can they? How can there be gaiety?" He was pushed along aimlessly beyond the marketplace. Staring up at faces of death carved into the cornices of the Rathaus, he turned and looked into the eyes of Nehemiah.

It was the man who had brought him the old tailor's body. Stas turned on his heel, and Aaron, shouting for him to stop, chased after him down streets and through the massive doors of St. Elizabeth's Basilica. The Talmudic scholar entered a Church for the first time in his life.

Stas slipped into a confessional booth and Aaron deftly stole into the other side. "You! You knew Nehemiah!" gasped Aaron. As the blacksmith reached for the curtain, Aaron implored him, "Please, please my friend, don't go!"

"Hush. You've no right to be here." Stas tried to calm him, to convince the overwrought Jew he had mistaken him for someone else. But Aaron knew. He was the one who had drawn Nehemiah from the water. Somehow, he was connected to Jonah and the tailor. Aaron *had* to engage him. Stas dared not make a scene. He listened quietly.

"My wife and I believed deeply in our God. Our love was an expression of our passion for Him. But at the moment that should have been our greatest joy, He abandoned us."

The Polish workingman remained silent.

"I grew up hating the fact of my conception, an act of violence against my mother. I was haunted with the knowledge that my birth caused her death, and searched in our scripture for an explanation. Natalie helped me to see that my mother's suffering will be avenged. I was comforted in the belief that our Lord is a just God. But now, my own son has become the instrument of death for *his* mother. Where is the justice? Why has God deserted me?"

Through the aperture of the confessional came a voice: "Look within yourself."

A strange, majestic sound filled the huge stone chamber. Chords emanating from heaven reverberated through every bone in Aaron's body. He stumbled out of the confessional booth to trace the source of the music to a priest hunched over the keyboard of an elaborately carved piece of furniture attached to columns of pipes that vaulted ever upward toward the dome of angels and cherubs far above.

Parishioners filed in for late afternoon vespers. A priest bearing incense led acolytes through the nave. Moses on the Mount stared down from a stained glass window. Stas had disappeared.

Trudging back to the ghetto, Aaron pondered the words, *Look within yourself*. He struggled for a reference point. Where was he to look? He had never known or reached into himself. He had been carefully taught by the old rabbi to place his soul in the lap of God, to trust Him, for God loves the victims of oppression. How he had languished in his victimhood, grateful to the Divine force that protected him from his anger. Only once, when he overstepped his knowledge and misguided Jonah, had his moral, rational compass failed him, and even after that, God took him back.

Look within yourself. What kind of *man* was he? The word frightened him, he a creature of God. But he came back to it, haunted by the denial of the hot blood he had envied in the Chasidim, suppressed in his visions of Hadassah, almost let loose in the lair of whores along the Oder, finally brought under Divine control in his union with Natalie. And as he dwelled on the meaning of their bond, he could not escape the overwhelming realization that he had been betrayed not by God, but by his own clinging to artifices and self-pity. He had never experienced his own humanity.

Aaron would languish in the culture of suffering no longer.

*   *   *

Eleazar's intransigence, his refusal to let her go to Breslau to sit shivah for her sister, galvanized Hadassah. She vowed that she and

Judith would leave Ratibor. She would not live out her days with a man she had come to loathe. She would not raise her daughter in a hamlet of narrow-minded harpies.

Once she had reached her resolve, she could withstand his abuses; it was only a question of *how* to get out. Each day, after Eleazar left to ply his trade, Hadassah wrote a letter to her sister, Sarah. Every evening, before he returned, she tossed it into the fire. Eleazar screened everything she wrote and she dared not use the coach that picked up mail from the shtetl.

Dr. Leibowitz found a note in his physician's satchel and duly dispatched the accompanying letter from the next town.

*   *   *

At last, there was one place among the German states where Jews were offered freedom. In the defeated imperial city of Frankfort, Brigadier General Custine granted all Jewish inhabitants the right to leave the ghetto. But they were afraid to leave the prison which had become their sanctuary. Some feared that accepting favor from the French invaders would anger the burghers. The Jewish community declined the opportunity and instead, swore allegiance to the allied powers of Prussia and Austria.

"Caged birds," remarked the French Brigadier General, "whistle the tunes that are played to them."

Before the dead of winter, the Prussian army stormed the gates of Frankfort. As the French were driven back across the Rhine, Jonah and his comrades retreated with them.

*   *   *

Joseph's shame gave way to outrage. He had been too anxious to protect Hadassah from her impetuous self, too worried that she would have to be exported to a distant place, and too easily taken in by Eleazar. Nathan hired the carriage to take Sarah and her father to rescue Hadassah. All the way to Ratibor, Joseph rehearsed his speech to Eleazar, citing *Halakah*, Jewish law, for the violation of his promise to honor and protect his wife.

Barred from post houses along the way, they spent the night under blankets in the landau, arriving in Ratibor just as Eleazar was starting out with his wagon load of feed.

Joseph intercepted his son-in-law. Sarah rushed ahead into her sister's home. While her neighbors stared at the handsome coach waiting in front of the Pistron's, Sarah embraced Hadassah, took Judith in her arms, and carefully examined the stripes across her sister's back. Joseph demanded that he and Eleazar go directly to the rabbi of Ratibor to dissolve the bonds of matrimony.

He was astonished by Eleazar's ready acquiescence. All the neighbors knew that he had married the wrong kind of woman, one who had produced a daughter of dubious parentage. While the slurs offended Joseph, he found himself curiously comforted by the thought that Judith might well be the daughter of another man. He dared not pursue it further.

Everyone in the shtetl gathered before the rabbi of Ratibor.

"We are a simple people," he explained, "but we have sustained ourselves in a hostile world for countless generations. We live by a code that protects our way of life. Hadassah is a proud and independent woman who cannot bend to assuage the rancor and bitterness in her union with Eleazar. She does not adopt the traditions of the community into which she wed. Eleazar, too, is proud, but he yearns to be a part of the world of his fathers, a step he cannot make with a wife who tugs at him from a culture as foreign to us as that of the Gentile. We cast out this strife and pray that the Lord, our God, blessed be His name, will help each of you to find yourselves in the lives in which the Divine One intended you to dwell."

On their way home, Joseph explained that the war against France was yielding benefits for the Jews. "In order to coordinate his forces, the king has centralized the power of Prussia in Berlin. He took local control away from the burghers and, following the lead of the Austrian emperor, began to ease some disabilities against us. Perhaps he wants to assure our loyalty. Otherwise, we might be drawn to the French by their promise of emancipation. Everything has changed, Hadassah, you may not have to be exported!"

*　　　*　　　*

The Breslau Free School began its new term after the High Holy Days of Rosh Hashanah and Yom Kippur. Aaron was selected to greet the students for the Hebrew year of 5453.

"We were slaves in Egypt," he began with a traditional theme. "And we are slaves here, today," he struck a new chord. "We are slaves to those who confine us behind ghetto gates, limit us to servile occupations, and restrict us from realizing our promise to God and fulfilling ourselves as men.

"But we are also slaves to our own timidity and fear, to our acceptance of injustice. God made us in His image, with the powers of reason and free will so that each of us is accountable for our selves. We blaspheme when we blame Him for our tribulations.

"Our ancestors accommodated to bondage of the flesh but never yielded their commitment to our holy ethic. The world they built was a shelter for survival, and we survived inquisitions, exiles, pograms, and disabilities, but it was never intended to be a shield against action.

"We may be forced to accept the temporal rule of passing potentates, but we forsake our God when we accede to their degradation of our character.

"For we are all equal in the eyes of God, all of us and all of the Gentiles and all the kings and their lords and ladies because we shall have no other Lord before Him, not lords of our manors, the lords of Breslau, nor the lords of Prussia.

"We were chosen, not to be special in God's grace, but to carry forth His message of social justice. We who have just completed the fast of Yom Kippur, are reminded by ISAIAH, 58.6-7,that the true fast chosen by the Lord was meant:

To loose the fetters of wickedness,
To undo the bands of the yoke,
And to let the oppressed go free,
And that ye break every yoke
…deal thy bread to the hungry,
And…thou bring the poor that are cast out to thy house
When thou seest the naked, that thou cover him,
And that thou hide not thyself from thine own kin.
Then shall thy light break forth as the morning,
And thy healing shall spring forth speedily;
And thy righteousness shall go before thee.

"Let your study here prepare you for the day, and it is coming soon, when we shall vindicate the sacrifice of our forbears. We shall blast like the trumpet of Joshua to bring down the walls that isolate and impound us."

XIII

A Bullet for Danton

There once was a rabbi named Aaron
Filled with compassion and carin'
   He taught with such candor,
   Refusing to pander,
The school thought it ought to forswear him.

(*Written on the back wall of the Breslau Free School*)

Joseph agonized. On the one hand, he felt boundless affection for Aaron, whom he took in as a son, who married his Natalie, the child with whom he had most richly shared devotion to Holy Writ, and who fathered his grandson. He empathized with Aaron's pain and outrage at her unjust death and understood why his son-in-law spoke out as he did to the entering class.

But, on the other hand, it was a reckless speech. God willing, it would not be reported to the burghers. The Administrative Council of the Judengemeinschaft, suggested that Aaron's tenure at the school be reviewed.

The family met around the dinner table. "Let us intervene with the Council," offered Nathan, Sarah at his side. "Aaron, you have got to come to your senses! Explain to the Judengemeinschaft you were overwhelmed by grief and didn't realize what you were saying. Tell them you never intended to put the school in jeopardy. Beseech them for the opportunity to redeem yourself. Both my father and I carry some weight there, but we need your help to convince them to give you another chance."

"You don't understand, Nathan. I do not regret and I could not take back a word. No, I should resign," Aaron responded, "I will leave Breslau and take my son with me."

Her heart aching, Leah pleaded with her son-in-law not to go.

Hadassah had always thought of Aaron as a youthful version of her father, devoted to learning, but rigid, moralistic, and bound to tradition. She found his new openness refreshing.

"How dare you patronize Aaron," she scolded her brother-in-law, "he doesn't need to be rescued! Aaron! Don't you even *think* of groveling *or* of walking away from this fight."

Her family stared at Hadassah in shock. She swore that if they tried to dump Aaron she would go directly to the students and ask them to publicly demonstrate their support for him. He was far and away their favorite teacher. Joseph could not dissuade his daughter. Her threat to mobilize the students put everything in a new light.

Instead of trying to appease the Judengemeinschaft, Nathan and Sarah appealed to them to leave well enough alone. Malcontents like Aaron had long been part of the Jewish rabbinical tradition. In any event, the Gentile authorities were preoccupied with their expansion into Poland and their war against France.

*   *   *

All of Europe was in flames. The execution of Louis XVI and the excesses of the Reign of Terror brought England, Spain, and Sardinia into an uneasy alliance with Prussia and Austria in their war against France. In the north, the French freed the Dutch from Austria while England grabbed the Dutch Indies. In the south, French forces overran

Savoy and Nice and advanced into northern Italy to face the Austro-Sardinians. In the east, Russia and Austria marched on Poland.

Instead of coming to the aid of her allies on the western front, Prussia deployed her regiments eastward, to help Russia and Austria carve Poland into thirds.

*   *   *

Frankfort had welded them into a covenant. Elbow to elbow, they enlisted in the new French National Guard. Based on his multi-lingual skills Jean Claude Boudin was appointed lieutenant, in charge of training recruits from many lands, formed into the 224th Battalion. Privates Jonah Schneider, Carlo Regnini, and Pier Vandergryft served proudly under his command.

It was a new and different kind of army. An alloy of peasants, workers, and professional soldiers, volunteers and conscripts were backed up by a full mobilization of national resources. Royalist officers had deserted, proprietary rights were abolished, and in their place deserving soldiers were promoted from the ranks.

The army outgrew its old linear organization. Improvised troops of temporary divisions gave birth to the modern system of war. In place of costly, burdensome hauling of wagon loads of tents, food, and supplies, they lived off the land. Their rapid movement and bivouacs and their requisitions on local communities for the support of troops enabled immediate decision-making in the field.

In contrast, the Allies maintained small, cautious, centrally controlled troops, trained to march at a steady 120 paces per minute, laden with cumbersome tents and full rations. They relied on evasive strategies, risking little to gain little.

Starting with drill book form, Jean Claude deployed half the battalion to fire in line and ordered the other half to form neat columns to support them. Raw and awkward, the trainees of the polyglot 224th stumbled over one another and broke up into confused, shapeless swarms. Jean Claude threw away the drill book.

Noting a vast range of differences in skills, he organized a new kind of formation, putting sharpshooters like Pier in a leading line to serve as skirmishers, backed up with the larger number of closely-massed foot soldiers. The increased flexibility let them charge and fire close order volleys. The best marksmen took their shots while the rear forces were kept under control in the field, ready to deliver the decisive blow with rifles and bayonets. Jean Claude was made a full captain and his concept for combat spread throughout the French National Guard.

The 224th Battalion was sent to join the ragtag army of Frenchmen facing the disciplined Hanoverian forces of the Duke of York in the Netherlands. When, at Hondschoote, Hessians moved forward in the ceremonial slow march, the defending French General Houchard froze. The distinguished Deputy, Georges Jacques Danton, sent from Paris by the Committee of Safety to oversee the expedition, rode up and down the lines, blocking Houchard from a retreat, imploring recruits who fled from the field to hold their ground.

Exasperated, Danton shouted to the Captain of the 224th, "My authority overrides the General's; I order you to attack at once!"

Under cover of Pier and the sharpshooters, Jean Claude led his battalion in a wild irregular bayonet charge. Mounted on his white horse with a tricolored sash and plume, Danton followed into the fray.

Swelling with the exhilaration he had first felt at the diversion in Sachsenhausen, surrounded by his comrades who drew inspiration from Danton's bold intervention, Jonah lunged forward.

A musket shot intended for Danton struck Jonah, throwing him to the ground in a pool of blood and torn flesh. The Deputy yelled out for the name of the hero who saved his life.

"Jonah Schneider, a Jew from Breslau," shouted Jean Claude.

Danton's horse reared and off he galloped, leading the charge of French troops as they returned to the front in hundreds, routing the Hanoverians.

Carlo ripped his shirt into strips, wadded it into bandages, and applied pressure to the wound to staunch the flow of blood. Easing Jonah onto his shoulder, he carried him, unconscious, through the bushes to safety.

The battle of Hondschoote had defined the determination of the New French; it was a turning point for the war. Back in Paris, Danton spoke of the courage of Frenchmen and of those from foreign lands who together fought for the revolution's promise of freedom. His story of the Jew from Breslau, who gave his life for France, appeared in journals of the day.

*   *   *

Hadassah and Aaron raised Judith and Adam together, living in the same apartment, sharing Leah's meals and Joseph's grace. As the children began to explore their world, the parents grew in their appreciation of one another. Aaron's earlier secret attraction to Hadassah had been tempered by his shyness and her self-assuredness, a quality not thought to be appropriate in a woman. He had been drawn, instead, to the piety and feminine diffidence of her older sister. Now, as a more confident man, he relished Hadassah's directness and was flattered by her advocacy on his behalf. And he was alone.

Hadassah enjoyed Aaron's companionship, but she privately kept herself for Jonah. There would never be anyone else.

On the streets of the ghetto, she heard the news. The Yiddish language press reported that Jonah Schneider had become a martyr in the French cause.

Hadassah walked through a vast emptiness. All around her debates raged on Jonah's heroism (or sedition). Not daring to reveal her grief,

she erupted in anger when the Judengemeinschaft officially disassoci-
ated the Jews of Breslau from Jonah, acquitting her outrage as one
against injustice and war. Only in the solitude of her room, as she clung
to their sleeping daughter, or in affectionate letters to his mother, could
Hadassah mourn.

*　　*　　*

Mordecai was spending more of his time in Berlin. His aging father,
Izaak, was no longer able to work, and his father-in-law, Samuel, was no
longer interested in working. The two senior partners of the Silkworks
wanted Mordecai to take over the business. Nathan and Sarah could
manage the Breslau operation. He and Rivkah could come home.

As she helped her mother-in-law get ready for the move, Sarah was
haunted by visions of encroaching loneliness. She foresaw years of
following her husband to the factory. He would meet with workers on
the floor and customers in the community, while she balanced
accounts, alone in her cubicle. She would come home to an empty
apartment and wait long hours to serve Nathan a late dinner.

The liveliness in her parents' home had shifted to the next generation. Judith and Adam were going their own way, well cared for by the
strange partnership of Hadassah and Aaron. Sarah desperately wanted a
family of her own.

Rivkah commiserated with her daughter-in-law, but it was Mordecai
who proposed adoption. He knew of places in Berlin and would use his
connections. Sarah should consider a daughter (boys, he assured her,
were hardly ever given up for placement). Swept up by Mordecai's
enthusiasm, Sarah and Nathan authorized him to make inquiries on
their behalf.

Upon his return from Berlin, Mordecai told them of a two-month
old girl, cared for in a secluded area on the outskirts of the city by a
private nurse, a widow whose husband and infant recently perished in

a carriage accident. The parents' identity was unknown, but since the nurse received a decent stipend, it was clear that the infant came from a good family.

A nervous Sarah accompanied her father-in-law on his next trip to Berlin. Poznan had become a part of Prussia and the stopover was combined with new business opportunities. But all Sarah could think of was the child. Would she be healthy? Would the child like her? Would she like the baby? Was this the right thing to do?

They took a private carriage to a farmhouse well beyond the city walls. A corpulent matron, still in mourning, whose heaving breasts burst the buttons of her soiled, sour smelling outfit of black crepe, held the baby in swaddling clothes with one hand and threw open the door with the other. Perspiring profusely, Wilma Krankenschwester handed the sleeping infant to a bewildered Sarah and pushed her erupting bosom down into her bodice.

Sarah held the baby close and watched her waken. She kissed the little fingers and found herself in love with her new daughter. With an uncanny resemblance to the Friedlander family, the child would fit in well. Mordecai handled the legal details and Sarah brought Rosalie home to Breslau with the capable Wilma.

*   *   *

Yankel Fleischmann felt a lift whenever Hadassah came into his meat market. She had always seemed superior and unreachable, but lately she appeared more solemn and subdued. He had been a widower long enough. A magnanimous man, he was prepared to overlook the disgrace of her status as a divorcee.

When he asked Joseph for Hadassah's hand, the Chief Rabbi of the school approached his daughter. Hadassah would never agree to marry Yankel.

Since the butcher was a major contributor to the school, Joseph needed a good reason to reject his offer. Hadassah told her father she would marry Aaron.

She set the terms: they would be partners but not lovers. (In their marriage without intimacy, she would fulfill her private promise to Jonah never to have another man).

Aaron cursed Eleazar, believing it was her former husband who had deadened Hadassah's interest in carnal affection. Aaron wanted her, but he comforted himself with the knowledge that in restraining his flesh, he would remain true to Natalie.

*   *   *

On April 5, 1795, Prussia agreed to peace with France. The 224th Battalion joined the army of occupation in the Netherlands and Pier, now a lieutenant, was assigned to his home town. He reflected on the wild stories Jonah had told him about another resident of Amsterdam, Leib Meyer, who wandered into a pious Silesian ghetto, innocently mouthing the phrases of a heretic and unknowingly carrying literature of the revolution. Pier set about looking for him among Jewish linen merchants.

Although Zacutus Meyer denied any connection to his son, his wife, Rebekkah followed Pier out to the street and directed him to Levi da Costa. A housekeeper, in mourning, showed the lieutenant into the sitting room where the winsome host welcomed him.

As she brought in the tea service, Zelda overheard first the name of Leib Meyer and then, that of Jonah Schneider. The tray fell to the floor as she grabbed Pier's lapels, "You knew my son?"

With a flourish, Levi da Costa announced, "Let me introduce you to the late Jonah Schneider's mother."

Pier sank into his chair. "Late?" he asked in shock. "He was doing so much better when I saw him in the hospital less than a month ago."

Mouth agape, Zelda stood stunned and speechless. Levi da Costa intervened, telling Pier about the article in the Yiddish language press. Jonah was a hero!

The lieutenant agreed his comrade was heroic, but that he was very much alive in Lille. None of the men in the ranks read newspapers or had heard the erroneous accounts of Jonah's death, a matter chiefly of interest to the Jewish community.

He described how Carlo had carried his gravely wounded friend to safety. For weeks, Jonah was in and out of consciousness. Pier reassured Zelda that her son grew stronger every day.

Sobbing with joy, Zelda threw her arms around Pier, then Levi, and the three planned her trip to Lille. Pier secured the passes while da Costa arranged the coach. Zelda shed her black and emptied out her closet, selecting clothes of bright colors. She would bring her son back to Amsterdam where the boy could recover.

Her coach had just left when a letter arrived for Zelda from Breslau. Levi held it for her return.

*　　*　　*

The word of the Lord came unto Jonah: Arise, go to Nineveh, that great city, and proclaim against it…

He had failed the Lord and fled from Breslau and now he was cast into the dark and retching belly of the whale. Many times, he was regurgitated onto a battlefield only to be consumed by renewed dread and pain. When, at last, the leviathan gave him up, he lay strapped upon a narrow beach, praying for the soothing calm of night to protect him from the searing ache in his right flank.

For a long time it seemed that he was just hanging on to a dream. He tried to return again and again to the vision of Hadassah but cold-handed creatures kept pulling him away, forcing vile liquids through defiant lips, tormenting him with sharp prods. And then she was there, reaching out for him, but he could not come. His feet could not carry him, the relentless pounding would not subside. "Stay," he implored her, "stay."

He became accustomed to the sounds of boots and heels on wood and knew which ones preceded the damp cloths on his face, the taps on his chest, the changing of his sheets. And as soon as the delicate heels with tough, rigid fingers pulled the container sloshing with his waste from between his legs, he could resume his communion with Hadassah of the faraway ghetto.

He lived for the day his arms could enfold her, for that magic moment on the other side of battlefields and revolution when her image would become flesh. It was his determination to breathe life into his longing that brought him past the critical weeks of low blood pressure and excruciating agony, through successive weeks of raging fever from infection of his open gut.

When at last he put faces to the footsteps, sat up for ever extended periods of time, and lifted a spoon to his mouth, he knew that his mission was to return to Nineveh and preach the words of deliverance to the heathens, for only then would there be a reality to share with Hadassah.

He read every book on the hospital cart, improved his French, greeted visiting comrades, and in time, graduated to crutches.

Shafts of sunlight streamed through the unwashed windows of the hospital ward as Jonah's mother, dressed more fashionably than he had ever seen her, appeared before him. The apparition spoke, wept, and stroked his cheek before he knew it was real.

Her timidity, lest she touch a wounded spot, melted away as he grabbed and lifted her into his lap. They laughed and hugged one another with unrestrained delight.

Their stories tumbled out…about his flight and hers, about his adventures and her new position, about the false news of his death, and Pier's visit. And finally, what he was bursting most to know.

"Hadassah is well and back in Breslau with her parents after a brief marriage and divorce to a feed salesman in Ratibor."

"But why?" Jonah's heart sank. "We *belong* to each other. Every battle I fought was for the day we could be together. She *swore* she'd wait. What kind of man…"

"It had nothing to do with him, Jonah. She loves only you."

"Were they about to export her? Sarah could have found a job for her in Berlin. She could have waited for me there."

"Jonah, she *had* to marry. She was carrying your child. Your daughter was born on May 15, 1792. Judith is a healthy, bright little girl. I've saved Hadassah's letters, detailing her every step, every word. Hadassah *is* waiting for you. Now, with Prussia and France at peace, you can write and tell her you're alive!"

He broadcast his paternity to every patient on the floor while his mother arranged for his discharge from the hospital. After a round of thanks to all the good staff, he threw his belongings into a sack and hobbled off with Zelda to the waiting coach.

It was the most glorious spring day of his life.

XIV

The Truth Comes Out

Hadassah had known love, love that filled her soul and drove her to want to be with Jonah forever, touching, watching, listening to him, laughing, fussing and playing, arguing and dreaming. He and he alone upon her breasts and round her naked body, his wonderful face above hers, the beat of him deep inside, the consuming serenity alongside him.

The rules of their culture and those of the state which confined them would not let their love abound and he was now gone.

So she had acquiesced to the ways of her society and learned the bitterness of a brokered marriage: forced labor, broodmare to her husband's desires, and chattel to his cruelty. It was an enslavement known to the great majority of the women of her day.

She would never again be hobbled to any man. Her alliance with Aaron would protect her against lechery and exploitation.

The pristine nature of their union helped Aaron focus on his mission to find new ways for expressing Talmudic social justice. And there it was that Hadassah found a role.

He had won the right to teach, but they both knew the school could not long withstand his way. To Aaron, the legacy of Moses and the Prophets mandated action against the forces of oppression to which the institutions of the ghetto had accommodated. Out of his love for Hadassah and Aaron, Joseph would stand by them. Out of theirs for Joseph they could not let him.

Together, they looked for new opportunities for a rabbi to serve a fresh population of Jews.

Burgeoning industries mandated by war needed workers just as Prussian youth were marched off to the front. To fill the void, thousands of Jewish men, barred from armed service, left shtetls to converge on factory towns like Breslau.

The rigid demands of organized Jewry on diet and dress, its schedule of rituals and Saturday Sabbaths, interfered with jobs and promises for career advancement. Men without families formed their own associations, unrelated to synagogues. Working long hours in factories alongside Gentiles, many found it easy to assimilate. Conversion was an easy way out of the fetid ghetto. Often, they married Christians, damning Jewish maidens to eternal spinsterhood.

In Berlin, David Friedlander (Mordecai's pedantic cousin) had become Moses Mendelssohn's successor and advocated *Bildung*, a new form of Jewish identity, focused on the formation of the individual. Appealing to the growing number of secular Jews, it shed antediluvian practices while sustaining the basic beliefs of the faith. Men could shave and trim their hair, dress in the styles of the larger culture, and hold worship services on Friday evenings, free to compete in the factory or marketplace on Saturdays and be part of the economic mainstream.

Hadassah had learned to detest the established synagogue. It had ostracized her beloved Jonah and his father; its petty yet powerful code of morality had forced her into a brutish marriage; and, but for the intervention of her family, the myopic omnipotence of the Ratibor Rabbi would have kept her in eternal vassalage. With Aaron, she found a partner to challenge the unyielding dogmatism of the orthodoxy. They would build a new kind of shul, one that upheld the basic beliefs, celebrated the core values and traditions, yet accommodated to social and economic changes.

Pinkas the pawnbroker guided Hadassah to workers, apprentices, scrubwomen and widows who savored the awe and the rhythm of worship, but felt shame for their lack of understanding of its liturgy. They were excited by the prospect of a different kind of service but had no funds to contribute to it.

Hoshea the cobbler had an enticing proposition. He was losing his sight, and needed an assistant. If Rabbi Aaron would be willing to learn the shoemaking trade, he could earn a modest income. Hoshea would assemble interested people after work to sit on benches and packing crates in the back room and receive instruction in the Bible and contemporary Jewish thought.

It was quite a comedown for a graduate of the yeshiva to work with his hands, but just the way to throw in his lot with the workers and great majority of the residents of the ghetto, who were poor and uneducated.

While her mother, Leah, minded Judith and Adam, Hadassah set off each day, mingling with customers and passersby at the cobbler's shop. She visited the old well to talk with women who welcomed the interest of a rebbitsin, and she recruited those who thirsted for knowledge. She called on the elderly and infirm, confined to rabbit-warren flats in creaking, urine-stained buildings. She found infants tied to door-latches while their parents were away at work, and discovered children in dirt-floor cellars, hidden from the civic authorities.

Hadassah arranged for some of the elderly to watch over the infants and appealed to the Judengemeinschaft to pay the body taxes for the hidden children. Wherever she went, she spread the word of her husband's nightly workshops.

On three evenings each week, women who had been isolated from the world of study became part of an academy. On three other nights, men who were laborers or beggars and had never held a quill in their hands learned to write Hebrew. On the seventh night, women and men, seated across from one another, crowded into Hoshea's back room for Shabbat services.

Aaron believed fiercely that the Torah was the word of God and that it commanded action. Each week he read aloud a passage from the Pentateuch and led a discussion on what it meant.

One night, they debated whether the sins of Prussia were greater than those of Sodom and Gomorrah. Gatam the beggar yearned for brimstone and fire to descend upon Breslau. "What they've done to us is more sinful than anything those shikkers and shtupers did to each other."

"But Gatam," Pinkas leaped to his feet, "the conflagration would take us with them."

"So be it. What kind of life do we have that we should worry about our skins when our souls are enslaved?"

At another session, some of the women identified more with Esau, the victim robbed of his birthright, than with the cunning Jacob. But in Jacob's wrestling with the angel of God, the workingmen saw the promise of their own struggle.

The story of Joseph advising Pharaoh to store wheat harvested in years of plenty and to distribute it to the poor in the lean years led to talk about the rich sharing with the poor. In the many weeks devoted to Moses, they rediscovered their right to liberation and grappled with concepts of justice through universal laws.

In time, Aaron became known as the "Red Rabbi of Breslau." Chief Detective Vertrater would make inquiries.

*   *   *

Rivkah had so yearned to return to the glamour of her youth in Berlin she failed to notice both had passed on. She was now well past middle age, and the salons no longer greeted her with adoration and hints of romance. Her old friend, Rahel Levin, had encountered Goethe in Karlsbad, and introduced him to Berlin. Now, every Jew in her circle was expected to read his every word.

The confidantes with whom Rivkah had shared girlhood secrets had become authorities on Friedrich Schiller and his literary discovery of the Jews. They quoted his lines on the "eternal rights of humanity," portraying them as a still suppressed people; he would crusade for their freedom from enslavement. She was expected to understand Kant and to participate at Henrietta Hertz's receptions where the philosopher's thoughts were discussed by his Jewish disciples: Solomon Maimom, and Lazarus Bendavid. As one who had been subjected to the harshness of the Breslau ghetto, it was assumed that she would have profound opinions on religious reforms.

Rivkah felt herself a bumpkin hausfrau from the provinces, more isolated among the glittering set of her childhood companions than she had been in the protected community of the Judengasse.

Now she understood the plight of her mother-in-law, Naomi, who had run off with the footman; Rivkah harbored dreams of rescue by some simple seraph who would demand nothing of her but tenderness.

*   *   *

Zelda crumpled the letter from Hadassah. She could not bring herself to tell Jonah that his beloved had married his friend. Not now, while he needed all his strength. She convinced her son to defer writing his sweetheart until he was able to walk unaided and could report he was whole. If she knew of his injuries, Hadassah would rush to him across perilous Austrian lines.

Jonah read and reread earlier letters that recounted Nathan's barbarous arrest, Nehemiah's martyrdom, Hadassah's suffering in Ratibor, Natalie's death, and the transformation of Aaron.

He basked in the story of Hadassah's rescue and in each miracle of their daughter's unfolding.

As soon as Lieb Meyer heard that Zelda's son was alive and at da Costa's, he came to visit. "You haven't been to see me," Zelda gently scolded. In a great flurry of shutting doors and whispering between whistles, Leib pulled his chair close to Zelda. "I've been so absorbed with Wilhelm's sister. She was in hiding with us until she delivered her bastard child.

"You must not tell anyone," he shook his finger. "When Erna went back to Berlin, she left us with the baby and an enormous, whimpering, recently widowed wetnurse. Wilhelm took them to a place outside Berlin where the mother could secretly see her. It's all very hush-hush. Her family would *die* if word got out."

*   *   *

Da Costa guided Jonah to Germanic writers, hostile to the atheism of the Enlightenment, who found in Judaism the roots of Christian morality.

Johann Georg Hamann helped to make the long scorned Old Testament fashionable in literary circles. Redemption, he held, did not come from the Greeks, but from the Jews.

Johann Gottfried Herder introduced poetry of the Hebrews to the Germans, praised their heritage, and advocated the slow, gradual admission of Jews to carefully selected occupations so that, in time, they would deserve equality.

Jonah especially enjoyed Goethe whose writings drew heavily on Old Testament stories. Overcoming his initial prejudices, Goethe befriended Jews and filled his life with attractive Jewish women.

Friedrich Schiller invoked the spirit, images, and language of the Bible and paid homage to the Hebrew people for bringing the doctrine of one God to the world. He condemned the barbaric treatment of Jews by ancient Egyptians, a metaphor for their persecution by the Europeans in crowded, segregated quarters. Reason and natural law, he said, commanded that Jews be dispersed throughout the nation and granted full equality.

Immanuel Kant sought harmony with Jews through amalgamation. While disparaging the Jewish character, he held out hope that "purified religious conceptions" would awaken them and "upon accepting the religion of Jesus, they could become an educated, well mannered people, capable of all rights of citizenship."

At a dinner party, called to hail Jonah's first steps without a crutch, da Costa toasted the post-Rationalist writers for their hints of compassion. His was the long view. Jonah responded that the German authors were patronizing and self-justifying. He wanted simple emancipation everywhere. No compromises, no probationary period to prove oneself, no forced assimilation or amalgamation. He would settle for nothing less.

Leib and Wilhelm were just glad to be in Holland where the benefits of the French Revolution were extended to Jews.

Pier was not interested in academic arguments. His rifle was a great leveler, and it alone had brought liberation.

*   *   *

On his frequent trips to the capital, Mordecai had developed his reputation as a successful businessman, ready to enter the international stream of commerce. Now, as head of the firm and a permanent resident of Berlin, he enjoyed the salons as a place in which to make more contacts. He was not concerned with political dimensions or literary pretensions.

Rivkah felt increasingly alone. She could neither participate in her husband's business promotions in the smoking rooms nor in flirtations in the drawing rooms. Unprepared for intellectual discussions, feeling herself a china doll, she wondered if this was the kind of life which her mother-in-law had renounced. She determined to find out all she could about Naomi and the footman.

Smul, Samuel's valet, had been in service to three generations of the Stern family. At every opportunity, Rivkah pleaded with him to divulge what he knew. Only after he saw the desperation in her eyes and was convinced that she would replicate Naomi's flight unless he told her, did he relent.

Meeting at an undistinguished cafe in the market, he looked nervously about, removed his hat, bowed his head, and told the story.

Jabal Rosenkohl was an impetuous young rascal who grew up with Naomi in Samuel's household. The son of a servant, he was her playmate, at her call, tugging at her sash and her heartstrings. They were adolescents when Samuel was expelled from Vienna, and Jabal remained behind, at the center of Naomi's romantic reveries.

She became an object to be shown and served, first by her father and then by her husband. No one tugged at any part of her.

Years later, a fully bearded Jabal arrived in Berlin and by a trick of fate, found employment at the Silkworks. From the moment he saw Naomi, visiting her husband at the plant, his childhood fantasies were re-ignited and he contrived ways to be near her.

One evening, certain Izaak was away, Jabal hired a coach and told the servants he had been sent by Herr Friedlander to deliver his wife to the opera. Bewildered but convinced that she must have forgotten the date, Naomi allowed him to escort her to the carriage, curiously drawn by the messenger's mischievous charm. He followed her into the cab and drew the curtains.

Naomi arranged for Jabal to become her footman. He was often, scandalously, seen entering the coach with her.

Smul told Rivkah that Fruma Klatschbase knew everything that took place in the old Berlin ghetto. Rivkah found her, an elderly, withered crone, leaning on two canes in front of a window overlooking the Judengasse, her crow's nest to all that went on below. Frau Klatschbase pointed with her head to the flat where, over the years, Naomi and Jabal spent many a night.

"After your wedding to Mordecai," Fruma recalled, "the police came looking for the missing Naomi and her jewelry, but she and her lover had fled.

"We learned, some time later, that Jabal was run down by a carriage on a limestone hill at the edge of Jena. He had to scurry out of town before sunset. Even the great Schiller," Frau Klatschbase grumbled, "condoned the law that barred Jews from staying the night in his old university town!

"Jabal's family traveled to Jena to pick up the body. There was no sign of Naomi or her jewels."

Disheartened, Rivkah looked about her. The Jewish section of Berlin, while no longer walled in, appeared more depressing than she remembered it from decades ago. Unlike the Breslau ghetto which had a mix of classes bonded by a common religion, the Berlin Jewish quarter was packed with the latest arrivals from the east, the poorest, sickest, and oldest of the Jews. Those with money were quick to move out, leaving a despondent horde of beggars, peddlers, and those completely dependent upon the support of rabbis, daily wage earners, and a few stubborn souls like her father-in-law, Izaak.

Rivkah realized that in her search for her mother-in-law, she had been seeking a part of herself. Izaak had managed to fill the void in his life by giving himself to a community in need. She would follow his example As the resident trustee of the Jewish Aid Society, Izaak was delighted to involve his daughter-in-law. Her contacts among the Jewish middle class would enable Rivkah to raise funds for the Society's work. With a renewed sense of purpose, she set about to organize a charity ball.

In the course of her rounds to the homes of prospective sponsors, Rivkah came upon her husband's coach, parked in front of Johannes Sacks's residence. She was at first confused when the maid advised her that neither the banker nor his daughter Erna was in. Provoked, she demanded to see Mordecai. A flustered, disheveled Fraulein Erna appeared, assuring Rivkah that Mordecai was not there. He had, however, sent her home in his coach from the factory where, earlier, she had accompanied her father on a review of his investment. Herr Sacks would bring Mordecai to his carriage when the two men concluded their work at the plant.

On leaving the Sacks household, Rivkah's suspicions mounted. At the plant, she asked for Mordecai and found he had not been present since lunch. When she learned that Herr Sacks had not been on the premises all day, Rivkah went home to pack.

She had no romantic footman, only anger and pain. But Naomi had shown her the way: Rivkah emptied all her jewelry and Mordecai's, along with the best of their silverware into her bag. She would return to Breslau to help Sarah and Nathan with the raising of her granddaughter, Rosalie.

*   *   *

The months with Levi had so immersed Jonah in literature and publishing, that he tried his own hand at it, editing the drafts of other authors and writing about his experiences at the front. Da Costa offered him a job with his publishing house, and Jonah welcomed it as a platform from which he could campaign for emancipation.

He would compose articles for both Jews and Gentiles, and encourage their interaction with one another. Their isolation was legion. None of the Jews of Metz, for example, liberated in 1791, had yet left the ghetto, so accustomed had they become to imprisonment, and so afraid to expand their boundaries. He would urge all Jews to enter the mainstream, to fear neither the Gentile nor the loss of heritage in casting off their shackles.

He was well enough at last. His letter to Hadassah, dispatched by da Costa's private courier service, was writ large with joy and passion.

Soon, they could be together. While awaiting her reply, he penned poetry of love.

*   *   *

As Hoshea's back room filled up with increasing numbers of students, Aaron suggested stacking the crates and bringing in more benches to create additional space. "Wait," said the cobbler, sternly, "wait until after class tonight. Say nothing about moving a thing."

When the last student left, Hoshea locked the door, dropped the blinds, and pushed back a crate, half-filled with odd pieces of leather, to expose a trapdoor. Aaron lifted the portal and, with an oil lamp in one hand, eased himself down a ladder into an empty cellar. Hoshea followed, pointing out a large wooden disc in the dirt floor, which covered access to the sewer system of Breslau, an escape route worthy of protection.

Back on the ground floor, the two consolidated the contents of assorted crates to create more space. With the wood of the emptied crates, they built a *bimah,* mounted the ark containing the Torah upon it, and set the modest altar over the trapdoor.

As they left, late that night, Aaron noticed a Gentile loitering across the street. Were they being watched? Casting about for a familiar face, Aaron seized upon Gatam the beggar and announced in a loud voice, "We have been building a bimah so we can conduct a proper worship."

"Nu?" Gatam replied, "Will it feed my mother?"

*   *   *

"Your brother-in-law," Chief Detective Vertrater lit his cigar, "has been stirring up the scum of the ghetto. Does he think that his rabbinical robes protect him from laws against sedition?"

Nathan explained that Aaron's teachings were grounded in the Bible, certainly not part of the Enlightenment's attack upon established institutions. Nor were they in any way directed by interests seeking the overthrow of Prussian rule. "He is trying to make the poorest and least educated of our people useful as workers and contributors to your society and ours."

"But he is not content to stay in the Judengasse," the chief detective retorted. "He has been conferring with Jesuits in Breslau, involving them in the filth you people have created. What do you suggest I do with this information, Herr Friedlander?"

Nathan implored him not to charge his brother-in-law. "You owe me," said Nathan in despair, recalling his arrest.

"Au contraire." Herr Vertrater stretched out his hand, "It is you who owe *me*." Gritting his teeth behind a forced smile, Nathan emptied out his purse.

*   *   *

Hadassah whirled about her room in unqualified euphoria. Her beloved was alive and safe. She had remained true to him, yielding her body only to Eleazar to protect the honor of Jonah's child. Her partnership with Aaron, an arrangement to shield her from other men, had merely provided a vehicle to carry out the kind of work to which her lover was dedicated. He would be so proud of her!

The pounding in her heart slowly gave way as she fought to control the quill in her hand to frame words of passion and explanation. How could she make him understand her love for him and the impossibility of her situation? How could she reconcile the two? One draft after another shriveled in the fireplace.

Despondent, she turned to her aging father and told him everything. Joseph soothed his youngest daughter. He had long suspected that Judith was not the child of Eleazar, and found some comfort in the fact that his granddaughter's father was a Jewish renegade. Joseph was tired of acquiescing to forces of hostility. He had found inspiration in pamphlets circulated by underground forces, in the news from France, and even in Aaron's rebellion.

Joseph reminded his daughter that the news of Jonah's death had relaxed the threat of holding *all* Jews collectively responsible for his acts against the state. He could not now appear in Breslau without jeopardizing the entire community.

"Moreover, if the authorities found out that you had a personal connection to Jonah, they would identify you as a crucial link between him and Aaron, whose work they have already put under surveillance."

Joseph cautioned her to tell no one, *especially Aaron*, that Jonah was alive. Aaron's sense of honor, his inclination to step aside for her and her lover would imperil them all. It was safer for him to know nothing.

Joseph arranged for Hadassah's letter to travel through confidential rabbinical networks, beyond the reach of Prussian censors.

*   *   *

Nathan and Sarah welcomed Rivkah into their home. They asked no questions until Mordecai appeared, outraged, and demanding his studs, tie clips, and silverware. Familiar from childhood with the whispered legend of his grandmother and the footman, Nathan pulled his mother aside:"Was this a family tradition?" Reassuring him she had no lover of her own, Rivkah told her son the story of Naomi.

"And so she tired of being a showpiece," Rivkah concluded, "in a world that meant nothing to her, populated by those who could not see beyond the precious stones men used to adorn and possess women. Ironically, her jewels gave Naomi freedom.

"Although I, too, took my gems to enable me to stand on my own two feet, the situations are quite different," she explained.

"I could not live up to the expectations for a woman in the Berlin of today. And I have never been a pretty ornament for your father. Now I can live a full life with you, Sarah, and Rosalie. The silverware is your inheritance. It belongs here, not in Berlin. I will return your father's jewelry which I took in a fit of anger. But that is between the two of us."

In a private meeting with Mordecai, Rivkah demanded that he set up a trust fund, guaranteeing her a monthly allowance, or she would seek a divorce in the Berlin Synagogue, naming "that woman."

Rivkah found her place in Breslau. Her friends still gathered at the old well. Hadassah enlisted her in visits to those in need, and once a week, she attended religious classes in the cobbler's shop. She oversaw the household and her thriving granddaughter. Wilma Krankenschwester, still serving as Rosalie's wet nurse, her year of mourning over, became engaged to Yankel Fleischmann.

*   *   *

He read the letter over and over again. Her expressions of joy in finding him alive were buried beneath Hadassah's regrets and self-recriminations. Jonah raged like a trapped, wounded animal.

He gave not a damn about the rationale for her marriage. With or without intimacy, Hadassah was married and raising their daughter with his childhood friend who had the impudence to be a decent man. He could not so much as *see* her without placing her in mortal danger. He could never claim her or their child!

The temporary truce between France and Prussia had done little to advance personal freedom. The Jews of Berlin, to their credit, had rejected offers by the king to remove many of the disabilities in exchange for "dry baptisms," an acknowledgment of the sanctity of Jesus. Jonah would still be viewed as an agent of sedition in Breslau, and he would have to cross the principal battleground of Europe, the crumbling Holy Roman Empire, to get there.

Little more than a geographical expression, the Empire consisted of some 350 states. They ranged in size from the electorate of Brandenburg ruled by the Prussian king, and the Austrian duchies controlled by the Hapsburgs, to independent lordships or counties a few miles square.

Hopelessly divided, prey to the competing forces of Prussia and Austria, each State throughout Germany eschewed the Jew as an alien, denied him entry, restricted and contained him in walled ghettoes. Only a liberating force from outside could rescue him.

That force was now marshaling troops in France, ready to march against Germans of many jurisdictions: Austrians, Silesians, Prussians, Saxons, Rhinelanders, Hanoverians, through any or all 350 boundaries. The 224th Battalion had been assigned to the French Army of Italy, poised to penetrate Hapsburg-dominated Tuscany under the command of a new Major General, Napoleon Bonaparte.

Jonah tore up the drafts in which he had appealed for international moderation and understanding.

His comrade, Pier Vandergryft was a first class marksman.

"Teach me how to handle a rifle well," Jonah implored him. "I'm going to re-enlist. I want to try to level things your way."

XV

Allons, Enfants

Any prospect of victory appeared dim. The French Army of Italy had fought over the same ground for two years. The soldiers were unpaid, destitute, and hungry. Thousands were barefooted, hundreds without muskets and bayonets. Even the horses were too thin and weak to haul the meager and poorly maintained artillery. No one had regular uniforms; Jonah and Carlo wore old blue army coats over their civilian clothes. If only the army could break through the wall of the Apennines into the rich plains of Piedmont or Lombardy, they would have food and feed. Setting out from Nice on April 2, 1796, Napoleon addressed his troops:

"Soldiers! You are hungry and naked. The government owes us much but can give us nothing…I will lead you to the most fertile plains on earth. Rich provinces, wealthy towns, all will be yours for the taking. There you will find honor and glory and riches."

To finance his campaign, Bonaparte sent Regimental Commander Jean Claude Boudin and an elite corps of the 224th Battalion to the neutral Republic of Genoa. The wealthiest merchants agreed to lend the needed funds, and the Genoan Senate granted permission for the French to cross its territory to attack the enemy in Lombardy.

At the front of the crowd assembled before Genoa's Palazzo Municipale, cheering the emissaries of the 224th as they marched triumphantly from the council chambers down the grand marble staircase, were Anna, Carlo Regnini's wife, and their nine-year old son,

Giuliano. Carlo had returned to his home town, a hero in the vanguard of the forces that would liberate all of Europe.

With a few hours of leave in Genoa, Jonah was drawn into the vitality of the Regnini family. Knowing that his parents needed private time, the street-smart Giuliano pulled Jonah to the Palazzo Rosso and great Romanesque and Gothic churches and campaniles. They paused before Giulo Romano's painting of the martyrdom of St. Stephen in Santo Stefano's, and the great Rubens in the Church of St. Ambrose and St. Andrew. From the Cathedral of San Lorenzo to the Palazzo Doria in the Piazza del Principe, the lad strutted in proud imitation of his father's bearing. They wound through a confusion of narrow streets, lanes, and alleys and climbed stairways up steep slopes to out-of-the-way churches. Giuliano pointed out discrete local sights like the brothel where Columbus spent nights. Crossing bridges that spanned the deeper valleys, they came upon a panoramic view of the harbor.

A great orange sun fast sinking before them, they hurried through a network of *carugi* above the wharf to the warmth of the one room flat, where they were enveloped by Anna's open arms and the seductive redolence of fresh sweet basil and garlic. On a table wedged between two beds were platters heaped with Genoan trenette al pesto and steaming bowls of glorious zuppa di pesce made from a rich assortment of fish scraps that Anna, who worked as a scaler at dockside, had garnered for the occasion. They toasted friendship and victory in the coming battle.

A few days later, Jonah and Carlo joined their battalion at Savonna, striking with the force of a battering ram against the stiff columns of an Austrian army. Advancing into the Apennines, they seized Cherasco, a major stronghold with its rich store of munitions, cannon, fresh horses, and food. Demoralized and terrified by reports of pillage, King Victor Amadeus of Sardinia, broke with his Austrian allies and sought an armistice at Turin. Bonaparte won the right to cross the Piedmont to the Po.

To his troops, Napoleon praised the battles they had won without cannon, recalled the rivers they had crossed without bridges, the forced marches they had trekked without shoes, drink, or bread. He urged them on, pursuing the Austrians across Lombardy and marching on the Papal states. To the people of Italy, he offered liberation from chains of feudal bondage. By May, they took Milan; by August, they were in Verona.

In city after city, wildly enthusiastic crowds of Republicans welcomed the French troops. Everywhere, "Liberty Trees" were raised up for the people, arm in arm, to dance around, flourish tricolored French cockades and shout themselves hoarse with the *Carmagnole*, the song of the revolution.

Wherever Napoleon's army went, it singled out the Jewish community to prove its commitment to liberty, equality and fraternity. In Ferrara, Jean Claude ordered Jews to tear off their yellow badges of shame, worn since the order of the Lateran Council in 1215. Jonah and Carlo helped lift the ghetto gates off their hinges, never again to be shut. In Modena, the city proclaimed: "Every man is born and remains free, and should fully enjoy all rights. Jews are citizens and must be recognized as such in society, received in all occupations, and welcomed into the Civic Guard."

Outnumbered and outflanked, Napoleon attacked the enemy bridgehead on the Adige river at the village of Arcola, and drove the Austrians northeast. Throughout the next eight weeks, each side cared for its wounded, received reinforcements, and girded for the next battle. It came on January 8, 1797. Marching north, hauling artillery and supplies across snow-pelted mountain trails, Napoleon confronted three columns of the Austrian army at Rivoli, just east of Lake Garda. The fighting began lightly and soon escalated to hand-to-hand combat, with Napoleon in the thick of battle, losing two horses under him as he rallied his troops.

Jonah would die for this man whose determination and idealism mobilized every fibre in his body. He advanced with bayonet drawn against the hated German oppressors when Carlo, alongside him, was struck by flak in his right shoulder, shattering the socket. Jonah fell on top of his comrade, shielding him from further fire, as the battle raged on around them.

A lethal stream of case shot decimated two Austrian columns at point-blank range and blew up their ammunition wagons, as French cavalry charged through the Austrian lines. With the enemy dispersed, Jonah lifted Carlo, groaning in pain, and carried him to the medical tent at the edge of the battlefield. His arm could not be saved, but Carlo would survive the injury. He was taken to a military hospital in Verona.

After three days of battle, one flank of Austrians surrendered at La Favorita. Ravaged by famine and illness, the remaining garrison of thirty thousand men surrendered at Mantua.

Jonah brought the news to Carlo in Verona. Napoleon had forced the doge and senate of Genoa to abdicate, transformed it into the Ligurian Republic with a new, liberal constitution, and posted a French garrison to protect the city. Carlo had lost an arm but gained a nation.

The two friends talked about Carlo's return to Genoa after the war, where funds saved from his army pay would buy a fishing boat. He could still toss nets with his left arm. Anna would be there as his better right arm. He would raise Giuliano in a free republic with the hope that his son would grow up to be like Jonah.

Napoleon pressed on. When he entered Venice, a Liberty Tree went up in Piazza San Marco. Christians marched to the Northwest corner of the city where, together with Jews, they removed and burned the gate, and tore down the walls of the ghetto, brick by hated brick. In the ashes of the gate, a Liberty Tree lit up the old Campo di Ghetto, and for the first time in the city's history, Jews and Gentiles embraced one another.

Promenading about the Liberty Tree, they held hands, chanted hymns of one another's faith, and sang one round after another of the

Carmagnole. Everything Jonah had fought for and believed in came to life, vindicated his struggle, appeased his anger, lifted his spirit. No force on earth could stop him now.

The crusade went on. As he advanced on Vienna, Napoleon dispatched a courier to Archduke Karl, calling for a truce. On April 7, French troops seized Leoben, only seventy five miles from Schonbrunn Palace. The Austrians agreed to peace talks, scheduled to begin on the 18th.

On April 17, while the strongest units of the French troops were withdrawn, a rebellion known as the "Veronese Passover" broke out. Propertied people of Verona, outraged that their riches had been appropriated, slaughtered Frenchmen on the streets and soldiers recuperating in the beds of the military hospital.

Carlo Regnini, a simple dockworker who fought for freedom and yearned to become a fisherman, lay lifeless in a pool of blood, his one arm dangling over the side of his bunk.

The war was over. Countless villages and the old order lay in ruin. New republics and hard fought rights emerged. And Jonah would carry the remains of his dearest friend and comrade-in-arms back to his family in a one-room flat, somewhere in a network of carugi above the wharf in Genoa.

*   *   *

With the expansion of Prussia into Poland, entire communities of destitute Polish Jews, fleeing pogroms and seeking jobs in German industry, had swarmed to the congested Breslau ghetto. One-family flats were crammed with families of three generations. Beds that had been shared by two were put on shifts to accommodate six or more. Lines formed outside the bathhouses at all hours of day and night. The stench of human waste, garbage, and unwashed sweat-stained clothes permeated every corner, cubicle, and cobblestone of the tightly contained community.

Unlike the earlier wave of German Jews, Polish Jews brought new accents and old customs. Many were Chasids, all were steeped in folkways of the shtetl. Shunned by the older settlers, the newcomers set up their own places of worship in overcrowded apartments. The German Jews resented, more than ever, their confinement in a ghetto inundated by Jews from the East.

*   *   *

"Yes, Herr Friedlander, I know that you are different, you are not at all like them," Joachim Gauner, the lawyer, reassured Nathan. "But the law is the law, and if you want to remain Jewish in Breslau, you must be content to live among the Jews."

It was only their common roots in religion that locked him and his family behind ghetto gates with the most wretched, impoverished, parochial rabble of eastern Europe. The Enlightenment had made it easy and profitable for affluent Jews to convert to Christianity, without having to take the vows seriously. But Nathan could not abandon Judaism. He felt solace in the chants and rhythms of the familiar ritual and was comfortable among the men he met for prayer. A trustee of the synagogue, he was pleased by the respect it brought him from his friends and family.

Nathan had lost some of his workers to the Prussian army and had to hire more personnel to meet an escalating demand for silk, to be made into German officers' shirts. In a slight easing of the disabilities, he was allowed to hire those who had not already been preempted by the burghers. That left him with the dregs: those whose black raiment, fur hats, draping forelocks, unkempt beards and foreign ways had put off the Prussian entrepreneurs.

Sarah suggested he seek Aaron's aid to recruit and screen job aspirants from the Chasidic horde. Her brother-in-law would know how to talk with them and assess the capabilities of individual applicants to work in a modern setting.

Aaron climbed five flights to the Chasidic quarters. On every step, disciples hovered, ceaselessly celebrating the Divine One. His ancient biases melted in the warmth and openness of their love of God. Though the words they uttered were pregnant with a mysticism he could not indulge, he envied their passion. His own zeal to fulfill God's commandments was channeled into intellectual exercises for social justice.

At the sight of the Chassidic rebbe, he was overcome with poignant memories of the old rabbi and rebbitsin.

Aaron recited parables, chanted psalms, and danced with the men until he fell into feather-stuffed cushions. After hot-tea-in-a-glass, sipped through a sugar cube in his teeth, he spoke of job possibilities at the Silkworks. The rebbe summoned a mechanic, three weavers, a cutter and two stitchers. As soon as the mechanic assembled a loom, the weavers began working yarn through its slats. The cutter produced a bolt of cloth, sheared it, shaped it, and presented the pieces to the stitchers who deftly assembled a blouse and woven belt for the rebbe.

The next day, Aaron marched the bearded band of applicants of strange appearance and attire to the Silkworks where they repeated their presentation before a flabbergasted Nathan who hired all seven on the spot.

Heretofore, at the edge of dawn, Nathan had routinely nudged his way past burdened pushcarts poised to descend upon the city. As the ghetto gates opened, he had quickly put a proper distance between the peddlers and himself, striding to his factory, cane in hand, like his father, a proud entrepreneur. Now, seven figures, cloaked in heavy black, followed him to the plant, emitting guttural sounds all the way.

Nathan oversaw their work, and as their craftsmanship proved their worth, he gradually overcame his embarrassment at having placed them alongside Gentile personnel.

Each evening, before all of Breslau, he trudged back to the detested ghetto in the wake of a stench that testified to the day's toil and adhered to the workers' indeterminate layers of clothing. He had hired them solely because of their skills. *He was not one of them.* Once inside the ghetto gate, they went to their separate flats and separate lives in separate communities.

*   *   *

On February 15, 1798, French forces declared Rome a republic and ordered the Jews to rip off their yellow badges forever. In tricolored French hats, waving Republican flags, Jews raised and festooned a Liberty Tree. As Pope Pius VII was led in captivity from the Eternal City, General Berthier read Napoleon's Proclamation granting Jews full and equal rights.

*   *   *

At the Peace Congress of Rastatt in 1798, Christian Grund urged the great powers to extend human rights to the German Jews. His pleas fell on deaf ears.

Within Prussia, there was little impetus for reform. Germany had won her intellectual and ethical independence, and ceased to look to France for leadership in literature or philosophy. Goethe, Schiller, Lessing and Herder gave Germany a place beside the literature of France and England; Kant's teaching dominated the thinking of the most educated minds. The German language had reached its full maturity as an instrument for the expression of lofty ideals and the interpretation of individual experience. The romantic movement nourished a new German patriotism with poems and folk tales, giving Germans a stronger feeling for their land.

Intellectual Jews yearned to be a part of German culture but almost all were still confined to ghettoes. It would take a great force from outside to bring about social change in Prussia.

*   *   *

Giuliano ran down the hillside from his school to greet his Mama and Jonah, tacking their vessel toward the fishermen's docks of Genoa. He had grown tall and scrawny since that day when Jonah brought his father's remains, and Anna held him close at the grave site, while soldiers shot bullets into the air.

She had christened her vessel *The 224th Battalion* after her husband's comrades who had dipped into their spoils of war to buy the fishing boat for which Carlo had fought and dreamed. Always in her widow's black, Anna trimmed the sails close to the wind while Jonah tossed the nets and pulled them in with a skill matching that of any fisherman in Genoa. The old dockhands exchanged salty quips about Jonah going to sea with a woman, but no one dared to confront the husky soldier from the army of liberation.

With merchants and restauranteurs, Anna haggled for the best prices, offering to clean the fish for a little extra. While Jonah tended to his nets, Giuliano raced up and down the pier to survey the competition and hawk his mother's catch.

During two glorious years of peace, they became a family, sharing each day's labor, plans, and dreams.

Although she never ceased mourning for her Carlo, and he never faltered in his love for Hadassah, the two eventually yielded to intimacy. In a curtained-off section of the one-room flat, they found a tenderness in one another.

On March 1, 1799, the War of the Second Coalition intruded. Russian armies, enlisted by the emperor of Austria and subsidized by

England, marched south through Galicia against France, and Jonah was called back to battle.

Anna went to the docks to seek a partner in hauling the nets.

No self-respecting Genoese fisherman could have a woman run the sails for *him*. Anna would not remove Giuliano from school. He was, she thought, too young to handle the nets and too vulnerable to the inevitable catcalls from the fishermen.

She hitched her boat to its moorings and returned to her post, ready to clean fish. But the men saw her in a different light. She was a plump morsel who had forsaken her widowhood to sleep with the Jew, and now it was *their* turn. They began with lewd banter and, as each fisherman competed to sound more outrageous than the other, quickly escalated to demands for obscene acts. While she scaled their fish, they encircled and tried to scale her, grabbing her bosom from behind, rubbing their crotches against her buttocks, reaching under her garments.

From his perch on the sea wall, Crazy Salvatore sprang into action, threw each offending fisherman against the dock and planted his enormous frame in front of Anna, daring any taker to approach her. Nobody would mess with the "Ox of the Quay" who had hauled, set, and replaced each boulder in their wharf. Groaning, muttering, excusing it all as, "just in fun," the fishermen dispersed.

That day, and every day for a week Salvatore watched over Anna and every night he followed her home, making sure she was safe. He stood outside her door, arms folded, lips pursed, until the moon set over the harbor. When it was clear she would not invite him in, he began banging on the door, shouting for all to hear, that she was his. Little Fr. Angelino had to calm him down.

The next day brought the summer storms. Anna rushed to check on her boat just as it slipped away on the tide, the cable to its moorings slashed and floating at its anchorage. She grabbed a dinghy, furiously rowing into the swell. Great gusts of wind shoved the *224th Battalion* beyond the breakwater and she followed her boat out into the open sea.

All she had of Carlo was adrift, its spars rising and falling on a horizon ever beyond her reach. Her breath grew shorter, but still she rowed. The downpour became a torrent. Her arms ached and became heavier with each stroke, but still she rowed. For a moment, she seemed to be gaining, and then her beautiful boat broached to. Her back throbbed with pain, and still she rowed.

The deluge from the sky merged with the sea, swamping her dinghy, filling her lungs. The last thing Anna saw was the main mast of the *224th Battalion* lit up gloriously in a shaft of lightning that stretched from merciless heavens to the deep.

The nuns took Giuliano to the orphanage. He did not speak a word to anyone until the following June.

*   *   *

The War of the Second Coalition left feudalism in ruins. The system of neatly tiered authority, based on ownership of land, from the sovereign through noblemen who oversaw their serfs, could not withstand the onslaught of citizen armies or the power of an ascending industrial revolution.

Frederick William III was timid, but he wanted to improve the Prussian economy and saw capitalism as the wave of the future. The Enlightenment and the war convinced him to encourage economic development by a new source of affluence, the bourgeoisie, whose capital built factories to produce arms and commodities for trade.

Stas and Vlad were part of an incipient class of workers bred by the manufacturing process, the proletarians, whose labor was unrelated to the land. Together with Hans, an enlightened pedagogue, they believed that liberty could be won only through full equality and brotherhood, and called for the overthrow of royalty, its privileges and rank.

Hauling a sack of beloved booklets, Hans crawled through the underground network linking the sewers of the city to the chamber below the cobbler's shop, now the Breslau Landessynagoge. He brought the words of Thomas Paine, calling for armed struggle to redeem the rights of man. "The Enlightenment," he cursed, as he emerged from the cellar, "has done *nothing* to help the general population, the peasants, workers, *or* the Jews."

"But the way of revolution has lost all credibility," Aaron countered. "The violence of the Jacobins and the looting and pillage by the French army has so terrified the German people, they have closed ranks behind the king. Why should we continue to distribute pamphlets and risk our lives for the ephemeral idea of a republican government?"

"With the kind of people the Prussians are likely to elect to their parliament," Hoshea speculated at the end of a pipe, "the Jews might be even worse off."

"We do it," Hadassah spoke with resolution, "because we have no other choice. Only in a republic, will we be able to demand the right to participate!"

*   *   *

Cut off by the war, Amsterdam had come through an economic depression. Vessels entering Dutch ports had declined by two thirds. Trade with Russia alone, which normally took 430 ships, had dropped to sixteen. The Dutch East India Company fell into ruin. The Bank of Amsterdam nearly folded. Poverty overtook the city, though agriculture flourished in the countryside.

Leib's parents, the Meyers, had maintained their contacts with the farmers of Overijssel who provided them with ample food. The elimination of ghetto barriers allowed the Meyers to move freely back and forth, fill their outworn pushcarts and bring provisions back to Amsterdam for themselves, their closest friends, and clients.

Accepting their contributions of food gratefully, da Costa pleaded with Zacutus Meyer to become reconciled with his son who lay starving, nearby. Faced with the thought of losing him forever, the rigid old Dutch Jew clasped Leib to his breast, kissed him, and asked his forgiveness. From that moment on, Leib never snorted or whistled again.

*   *   *

On November 9, 1799, the 18th Brumaire of the French Revolutionary calendar, Napoleon took command of France.

By May, 1800, he descended from the heights of the grand St. Bernard Pass into the valley of the Po, and forced the Austrians to abandon all of northwest Italy. On June 2, Bonaparte entered Milan and nine days later, after the battle of Marengo, the armistice was signed.

In the treaty of peace at Luneville, Austria recognized the Dutch Republic and guaranteed peace for Amsterdam.

The war had lasted fifteen months.

XVI

Jonah's Return

Giuliano's first words, muffled against Jonah's shoulder, reunited the two with inseparable bonds. They hugged, openly wept, talked for hours, mourned and planned together. Early the next morning, they rowed out beyond the breakwater, laid boughs of flowers upon the sea, prayed in Hebrew and in Latin, stripped down, and dove in to mingle their flesh with Anna's. Back in the boat, they shared their picnic lunch with the fish. In the afternoon, Jonah took Giuliano to be fitted for a fine set of clothes. They dined in splendor at the best restaurant in Genoa.

Past all decent hours, they arrived at the orphanage to run headlong into Mother Superior, impatiently tapping her foot on the front steps. She had been simmering ever since she was told Giuliano was missing. Wrenching her ward by the ear, she reminded him of procedures that had never meant anything to him before. He had not sought permission or filled out forms. But in any event, they could not release a child to someone not his relative, not even for a day trip.

"I am deeply sorry to have caused you distress," Jonah apologized. "We were carried away at seeing one another. We had so much lost time to catch up with. Now that the war is over, I plan to adopt Giuliano and raise him as my son."

"That," snapped Mother Superior, "is completely beyond the realm of possibility! Neither the ecclesiastic nor the civic authorities would ever allow a Catholic lad of Genoa to be adopted by a Jew from Breslau."

The following evening, a hooded Fr. Icarus from the Seaman's Mission, where they had held rites for Anna (as they do for all poor souls lost at sea), asked in the name of his mother, to speak with the troubled orphan.

The two were last seen walking together in the garden.

By dawn, Jonah and Giuliano had crossed the French frontier. No one would stop a fully uniformed sergeant bringing his son home to Amsterdam.

*　　　*　　　*

In separate treaties with Prussia, Russia, and Austria in March, 1803, France redrew the map of Germany and the result was the dissolution of the Holy Roman Empire. One hundred and twelve states disappeared and the alliance with the Church, on which the empire had rested, was destroyed. The Catholic control of both the College of Princes and Ecclesiastical Electors gave way to Protestant majorities.

In absorbing Westphalia and other states, Prussia welcomed 500,000 new German inhabitants to offset and assimilate their Slavic population, spoils acquired in the partition of Poland. Increasingly, German nationalism took the place of sectarianism. One's religion was no longer a matter of state.

*　　　*　　　*

For the Church to survive in this era of Enlightenment, revolution, and nationalism, Fr. Ludwig believed it had to be more flexible, more humanist, more willing to reach out. The prematurely bald, bespectacled cleric had set out on an errand of discovery and gaped in wonder at the bustle before him. He had never seen so many Jews, all of them busy, all of them talking at once.

Women in babushkas, bossing their boisterous children, hauled sacks, baskets, urns, and clothes still dripping from their wash at the well. Beggars came off their stoops with mawkish pleas and outstretched hands to men in black outfits and fur hats, who argued loudly with one another at the head of processions of chattering wives and children. Husky men in overalls shouted achievements, complaints, and warnings as they ran up and down the stairs of buildings that stacked one floor atop another.

Grandmothers leaned out of windows, calling stragglers to dinner. Peddlers, hoarse from hawking their wares, bellowed in vain, "Step aside!" to kaftaned students absorbed in chants. The stentorian tones of a towering patriarch were punctuated by animated assents of gesticulating, head-bobbing minions.

A Jewish dignitary, a rococo cane protruding from his velvet cloak, pompously demanded ruffians to clear the way. Young people flirted as they emptied buckets into the reeking open trench. Fr. Ludwig worked his way past doddering men and women carping and moaning, as they leaned on warped rods and one another. Upon reaching the Free School, he climbed its stairs to the Lehrhaupt apartment and to a Friday night dinner.

Well-worn upholstered chairs were pushed into corners to make way for benches set about a carved oak gate-leg table, stretched open for dinner. An indoor stove in the next room bulged with crockery, pots and pans, sacks of flour, cereals and salt. Urns filled with water stood alongside a washtub. Leah, Hadassah, and Sarah formed a caravan bearing bowls of hot soup, roasted chicken, cabbage, beets, and kasha.

The priest had befriended Aaron, sensing in him a denial of self, parallel to his own Thomistic ideals. How much more was he intrigued by his host's asceticism when he observed the enchanting beauty of his wife as she offered the prayer and lit the Sabbath candles. From the head of the table, Joseph poured wine for the priest and pontificated.

"Judaism is more than a form of worship. It is a comprehensive way of life embracing age-old traditions..."

At the far end of the table, the children giggled at Adam's schoolmate, Chajjim, as he transformed his dinner napkin into a mask, then a babushka, a telescope, and a flag. Judith and Rosalie made faces imitating the adults engrossed in unfathomable argument.

Though the quarter moon could barely pierce the heavy clouds, the lights of the city beyond their walls helped them find their way to the Breslau Landessynagoge in the back of a cobbler's shop.

Aaron introduced his envoy of interfaith understanding citing LEVITICUS 19.33-34:

> And if a stranger sojourn with thee in your land, ye shall not do him wrong. The stranger that sojurneth with you shall be unto you as the home-born among you, and thou shalt love him as thyself; for ye were strangers in the land of Egypt...

"We are part of a nationwide movement to transform religious services and education," Aaron began his sermon, "to uphold our religious commitments and the values of Judaism while freeing us to participate in the secular German culture.

"The centuries of isolation are past. Yes, for fifteen hundred years, we justifiably retreated from the assaults of Gentiles beyond our prison walls. But we grew to accept those barriers of stone as our protection.

"A far more devastating, everyday assault," he looked into the eyes of his congregants, "lies in the fact of our pervasive poverty *because* we are trapped in this ghetto. Good jobs and decent housing elude us. Among our able bodied men, almost one in five is a beggar, three in ten are peddlers.

"*Because* we are a people set apart, they will not let us grow food, raise cattle, work in agriculture, own land, enter most occupations, trades, or professions. Fewer than one in a hundred of us can afford to pay, year after year, for a schutzbrief to manufacture only what they let us.

"We cannot care for all our sick and aged, or educate many of our young. Half our families cannot put food on their tables. Prussia flourishes only for those outside these walls.

"So long as we are treated as a nation-within-a-nation, a *separate* people, we will be denied opportunities available to others with whom we dwell in this land.

"Today there is a movement, with good people like Fr. Ludwig, to open the gates forever, if only we have the courage to step out into the sunlight. We *can* be Jewish in our faith *and* Prussian in our nationality. That is why I ask you to join in our effort to become citizens of our great kingdom."

Aaron passed a parchment to his brother-in-law, seated in the first row. "This petition is being circulated throughout ghettoes and shtetls from Frankfort and Berlin to Ratibor and Koenigsberg. It asks that Jews be granted the right to vote as Prussians. We will present all the petitions to the *Reichsdeputation* in Regensburg. I urge each of you to sign."

Nathan realized however far he tried to distance himself from those who trailed him from the ghetto each morning, he was, nonetheless, forced to follow them back behind its gates each evening. He could never leave the ghetto until they could. He could never be free until they were. The right to vote was a reasonable first step. Signing the petition, he joined in solidarity with Jews of East and West.

Someday soon, the walls would have to come down.

*   *   *

Chajjim's father, Feitel Wolfssohn, had brought his son from Laslo in the district of Rybnik, where Jews were denied access to schools and jobs, to enroll him in the Free School. Knowing of the vacant room once occupied by a tailor, Joseph had arranged for Nathan and Sarah to rent it to Chajjim. The new boarder and Adam became inseparable.

With Chajjim's spending money, they plied Feigel the shadchen with jelly doughnuts in exchange for secret stories about Judith's father, Rosalie's mother, Mordecai, and Rivkah. At each telling, according to her state of mind (and the quality of the jelly doughnuts), the stories became more tantalizing, more scandalous, more lavish, more apocryphal. They sneered at the mention of Eleazar, applauded enthusiastically to accounts of Jonah, rolled on the floor in laughter over tales of Leib, and bit their lips in reverence when Feigel whispered the mysterious legends of Nehemiah.

On Thursday afternoons, Yankel Fleischmann went to purchase Sabbath hens and left his wife in charge of the butcher shop. When Wilma lowered the blinds, the pubescent boys presented their pfennigs for a quick nuzzle into the chasm of her bosom.

After Joseph drilled them for their forthcoming bar mitzvahs, the boys matched wits each evening in an innocent game of chess.

On Saturday afternoons, the entire family celebrated Sabbath dinner at the Friedlanders. The young rascals locked arms with the men, and, goaded by the women, danced feverishly through the apartment.

On Sundays, it was now possible to venture out into the streets beyond the ghetto gate, so long as they wore the yellow insignia of subservience. Adam and his new friend ran through the streets of the sprawling city, grabbing for abandon. But they were besieged by the same demons Chajjim thought he had left behind in Laslo. From somewhere in a crowd of Churchgoers, came the gibe, "Look at the dirty Jewboys!"

In the parks, strictly *verboten* to Jews, where grass beckoned to be rolled upon and trees begged to be climbed, indignant adults and children drove them off. At the marketplace, where fresh, succulent fruits glistened in the sunlight, merchants shooed them away. The boys dared not touch produce at the town markets. Any Jew who did so, had to pay for "soiled" fruits or vegetables.

"Some day," Adam reassured Chajjim, "we won't have to display these despicable badges. They won't even know who we are."

*   *   *

"The Enlightenment," Jonah explained to Giuliano in far-off Amsterdam, "promised me the right to become as good a Christian as anyone else. The Revolution granted me the right to remain a Jew and still be a citizen and a free man."

"But what do you mean," asked the child, "by saying you are Jewish? You don't go to synagogue and you don't even keep kosher!"

"It's my *identity*, Giuliano, it's who I am."

*   *   *

Napoleon, himself, would raise the issue of Jewish identity. On May 30, 1806, the emperor called for a convocation of the leading Jews of France, Holland, and the German Rhineland. As a distinct nationality, could they assure him of their loyalty to France?

Levi hired Jonah to serve as his clerk at the Assembly of Notables. Having a veteran of the French army of liberation would enhance their cause. Jonah met with Jean Claude Boudin, now a general, to learn of the intrigues and key individuals in Bonaparte's cabinet who threatened the rights of Jews.

In Paris, on July 12, 1806, one hundred and twelve dignitaries elected Abraham Furtado, a wealthy Portuguese Jew of Bordeaux as their president and Levi da Costa of Amsterdam, their secretary. They were addressed by Imperial Commissioner Mole who, with thinly veiled contempt, advised the Jews that the emperor wished them to become Frenchmen, but warned they would be deprived of the honor, should their actions prove unworthy and their responses to his questions unsatisfactory.

"Did French Jews feel any obligation of loyalty to France?" They would have to provide written details of their commitment.

There were questions on the willingness of Jews to participate fully in French society: "Was a Jewess allowed to marry a Christian?"

Regarding their adherence to French law: "Were Jews allowed to be polygamists?"

With respect to whether Jews entertained special entitlements for themselves: "Did Jewish law bar usury from Jews but allow it from Christians?"

Most important of all, "Would they develop a plan to stimulate the Jews of the empire to enter the crafts and professions, so they could learn to substitute dignified callings for the disgraceful occupations to which they had devoted themselves for centuries?"

In formulating a response to each of these questions, the Notables debated how they could best prove their devotion to France, the nation that had given them freedom at home and fought for their rights abroad. Jonah took notes, helped da Costa draft a plan for moving Jews into useful vocations, and on September 17, the Assembly presented its answers and recommendations.

Napoleon was pleased. He especially welcomed their proposals to make patriotic and productive Frenchmen of Jews. To give their commitments the force of religious sanction, the emperor called upon the Notables to convoke a *Grand Sanhedrin.*

They agreed to bring together representatives selected by Jewish communities throughout Europe. It would be the first gathering of the ancient High Council of rabbis and Jewish lay leaders in seventeen centuries.

Their efforts were temporarily interrupted by the resumption of war.

Friedrich William of Prussia sent an ultimatum to Napoleon, demanding as a condition of peace, that he withdraw French troops across the Rhine and acknowledge the formation of a North German Confederation. Instead, Napoleon mobilized.

At last Jonah could return, as part of an army of liberation, to the land he had been forced to flee. He would fight his way across Prussia to his beloved and their child.

* * *

Tutored by da Costa and indulged by Zelda, Giuliano had become a smart, sturdy, handsome eighteen year old who could not be deterred from joining his father in Company B of the 224th Battalion. He stood tall in Ephraim's indestructible boots, passed on to him by Jonah for the special protection they would provide his son, as they had him. They would take on the Germans together.

The Prussia which Frederick the Great had made into a great power lay before them. Friedrich William III had changed it hardly at all. He saw no reason to modify the condition of the peasants or to abridge the privileges of the nobles. His chief concern was to have peasants enough to meet the requirements of his recruiting system and nobles enough to command them. He would not expect men of the citizen class to serve in the army, and they, in turn, viewed the fate of military ventures with indifference.

The Prussian army, 250,000 strong, was numerically equal to Napoleon's, but peasant soldiers, often ill-treated by their masters, had little enthusiasm to follow *any* nobleman into battle. It was no match for a modern French army brimming with men of revolutionary zeal drawn from many nations, men like Jean Claude, Jonah, Giuliano, and Pier.

Most of Friedrich William's generals were exceedingly old and had neither the energy nor the initiative to manage or lead even half the troops in the field. His commander in chief, the Duke of Brunswick, defeated at Valmy, was overawed by Napoleon, and moved cautiously, lest he lose his precious duchy in a war he would rather not fight.

As Napoleon's troops advanced from the Rhineland, the King of Prussia felt that honor dictated his presence in the field. His assumption of command displaced Brunswick. Prince Friedrich Ludwig zu Hohenlohe refused to serve under a Duke who was no longer Commander in Chief, so a separate army corps had to be constituted for him. All Prussian campaign plans were delayed, repeatedly changed, and orders countermanded. 200,000 troops were made weary from trudging week after week: south from Berlin to Dresden; west from Dresden to Bamberg; back east to Dresden, and west again to Bamberg. Councils of war debated endlessly.

Napoleon's army streamed onto the plains of Saxony, behind the Prussian lines. Rather than engaging the French, the Germans debated once more. Anxious to avoid battle, Friedrich William withdrew from Bamberg and led his army north, through Jena, back toward Berlin. To block Napoleon's pursuit, Prince Ludwig's Corps took a defensive position on a plateau west of Jena.

French troops, under Marshal Davout's command, had already advanced northward, east of the Prussian columns of retreat. At Auerstadt, twelve miles north of Jena, Davout's Corps met Friedrich William's retreating army. Although half their size, the French routed the Prussians. Brunswick fell, fatally wounded in battle. Neither the King, nor anyone, could bring unity to his campaign.

On October 14, Napoleon attacked and demolished Prince Ludwig's corps at Jena. Soldiers of Friedrich William's army fleeing Auerstadt ran into Prussian fugitives from the field of Jena. Panic-stricken and hopelessly disorganized, they all fell back, threw away their weapons, and went home.

* * *

With his arm slung over Giuliano's shoulder, Jonah led the young man across the rapidly clearing field of battle to a house he remembered fondly. A long line of soldiers stood in single file, each shifting from one foot to the other, exchanging embarrassed chuckles and boasts of grandeur. At the head of the line, waving her scarf of many colors, Madam Rosa cried out for patience.

"There is plenty for everyone. You will each get a turn," she reassured them, as she moved down the line collecting cash deposits. The moment she spotted Jonah, she flew into his arms. Over the groans and catcalls of the other men, she pulled him and his young ward straight away into the house.

"Tell me all about yourself! Is this your son? Are you here to liberate us? Really, Jonah, we need to be liberated. Just as times are good, with all the soldiers paying fine prices and leaving generous tips, life is horribly rough for the girls. There's not a moment of intimacy, it's all so quick. You saw that mob out there? How can a woman go on, hour after hour, soldier after soldier, and not become a living corpse?

"You remember Polly? Poor Polly is in your old sick room, dying from syphilis. Kitty is a walking ghost, like her mother. Who can blame her? Gina and Lisa each ran off with customers. Lisa came back with all her teeth knocked out. The police found Gina's body in a ditch.

"Most of the girls are new, women deflowered by soldiers, then left behind. What future do any of them have? Oh, but Myrna and Dolly will be so happy to see you!

"Myrna takes time with the customers, she charges more but she's good. She would be perfect for your son. Will this be his first? It's on the house, my treat!"

In a glorious tour of orifices and protuberances, Giuliano discovered the rapture of flesh on flesh. In Myrna's comforting arms he had found God and gone to heaven.

Jonah would later tease him that this was his *bar mitzvah* since *bar* in German means "bare," and *mitzvah* in Hebrew, a "good deed." No boy ever entered manhood happier.

"It hasn't always been this easy," Madam Rosa sat Jonah down for a late dinner. "It was hard to provide for the girls when the army took all the men away. The professors from the university never pay much, and they always take too long.

"The ring you gave me, Jonah, helped to carry us through the dry times. I don't know if you realized how valuable it was. That was a *real ruby*! I sold it to an old geezer who comes here once a year from a far off shtetl. He wanted it for his young daughter, and paid full price!"

"Where did you learn about jewels?" asked her amused admirer.

"I grew up with them in Berlin. They were lavished on me," she reminisced, wistfully. "It was a very elegant home."

"And you gave up such luxury for this?"

"No. I gave up being a bauble for real love, for the love of my life. I fled the vacuousness of drawing rooms.

"We wandered about like vagabonds while my lover recited the poetry of Goethe, Klopstock, and Herder as though the lines were written for me. Those were the happiest days of my life.

"We came here because he wanted to hear Friedrich Schiller lecture on his *Mission of Moses*. But at the University, they humiliated my love. They would not let him enter the lecture hall.

"'Jew, get out of the town of Jena.' they told him, 'before nightfall.' He started to run. He must have been blinded by tears of anger. He didn't see the carriage hurtling toward him!"

A look of pain-that-knows-no-end passed over Madam Rosa's face.

"I waited a long time, just outside the city gate. When they told me, I could not even claim his body because we were not formally married. I could never go back to Berlin. *But I had my jewels.* They paid for this house. There was nothing else for a woman of my class to do."

Deep into the night, after the last raucous customers had stumbled into the soft October flurries, Dolly entered his bed, stroked his loins and reawakened his flesh. It had been years of steadfast sublimation since Jonah had tasted the joys of passion, and she brought him unencumbered warmth and acceptance.

Between torrents of rediscovered pleasure, he poured his heart out, telling Dolly about his enduring love for Hadassah. He had fought the revolution and joined the armies of liberation for the right to love Hadassah, free from the constraints of an order he would help to destroy.

They lay in each others arms, the worldly wise prostitute and the earnest idealist, until a bright dawn called him back to his battalion, ready to march with Giuliano and his comrades toward Silesia and the emancipation of his beloved.

XVII

The Siege of Breslau

All of Breslau bristled with trepidation: the French were coming. Consumers drained every bushel of food from the marketplace. Churches surged with confessors. Peasants in uniform strutted behind aging Prussian generals through city streets. And Jews grappled to get out of the way.

In the nadir of a night filled with biting insects, scratching branches, and twigs that crunched beneath them, Jonah's squadron crept to a wooded knoll above the west bank of the Oder and waited. At daybreak on October 28, 1806, the fortifications of Breslau loomed above the sun-sparkled river before them.

Giuliano, crouched in Ephraim's illustrious boots, pointed to a farmer digging potatoes from his ground beyond the knoll. "Yes," Jonah acknowledged, "that is him. We are on his land." Upon sighting the invaders, Heinrich Nachrader ran, cursing all the way, into a dilapidated farmhouse and slammed its warped door shut.

It had been thirty years, Jonah counted back, since his father had put the last coat of paint on that house. Few flecks survived the snows of winter, torrents of spring, and hot summer sun. Nothing of his father remained but the beams of the farmhouse roof.

The hatred that burned within him still had been kindled here. For all his conscious life, Jonah had loathed Prussians because of Nachrader's exploitation and lies, acts supported by a culture of tyranny and a system of serfdom. At last he could avenge his father's unspeakable torment and death, his mother's subjugation, his own humiliation. So hopeless did it seem only fifteen years ago.

But now, armed with muskets and grenades, part of the vast, unconquerable army of liberation, he could avenge his father with impunity. Nachrader stood for everything the revolution was against. Jonah had fought him in cities and on battlefields across the continent. With a gesture, the sergeant could command his squadron to obliterate the farmhouse and all its occupants.

Giuliano grew up with stories about Heinrich Nachrader, the quintessential Kraut they loved to hate. Never was there a nemesis more deserving of annihilation. The lad joined his comrades circling the house, asking each other. "Are there others inside with Nachrader?" "Are they armed and ready to fire?"

"Never question who else is in your target," the manual instructed. "Your goal is to destroy the enemy. Demolish the structure and have muskets trained on whoever comes out."

Overriding the textbook strategy, Jonah walked through the encirclement of soldiers to the cabin door, his bayonet raised. This was his personal mission, his moment of deliverance.

With the heel of his musket, he rammed the door open. A grey spotted cat screeched, arched its back and leapt upon a urine stained mattress alive with vermin. Atop a fusty, crumb-infested table, a putrid wedge of cheese drew a cloud of rapacious gnats. Cowering in a corner, behind a broken chair, the villainous Nachrader shat into his overalls.

The tyrant who had so long obsessed Jonah was pitiable. He was not worthy of the accumulation of the many years of contempt.

"Who are you?" gasped the reeking figure.

Jonah stared at him and saw only a fool, one who had been used by those who consumed them both.

"What will you do with me?" pleaded the decrepit despot.

It had already been done. Nachrader's world was crumbling, taking him with it, down the sinkhole of oblivion. In Frankfort, French artillery had demolished ghetto walls. In Cologne, the French commissioner declared all men equal before the law. Jews, banned from that ancient city since 1426, began their return. Westphalia liberated Jews completely; Mecklenberg, Baden, Wurttemberg, and Bavaria followed. At this moment, French artillery was taking up positions against the city of Breslau.

"You stare at me, soldier, as though I were some spectacle. I have seen those eyes before."

Jonah's gaze reached past Nachrader to the innocent faces of young French, Italian, Dutch, even Austrian infantrymen, who had fallen on fields of battle as though sacrificed to bring him here.

"I know you! You are that Jew-boy I thrashed. The son of the repairman. You have come for your vengeance!"

In the Book of Jonah, when God saw that the people of Nineveh listened to His prophet and turned from their sinful ways, He "repented of the evil which He said He would do unto them, and He did it not. But it displeased Jonah exceedingly and he was angry."

Jonah Schneider remained silent. *Was he, like the biblical Jonah, clinging to righteousness as he defined it, finding in this vestige of a dying order a pretext for personal revenge?*

As Giuliano entered the house, he heard Nachrader offer not repentance, but abject self-justification.

"I had no money to pay your father. Half of what I earned went to the bloodsucking Jew money lenders."

He denies my father any obligation, thought Jonah, *because they have taught him that he doesn't have to owe a Jew anything. They can beat, cheat, and murder us, regarding us as less than human because we have not their Christian souls.*

Banned from most other forms of livelihood, we are compelled to be their money lenders. Forbidden by their church to lend money, they are obliged to borrow from us. They despise us because they need us. The nobility uses us to gain economic advantage abroad. The burghers tax and control us. Their soldiers and peasants kill us to wipe out their debts.

"He stole my potatoes," cried Nachrader. "He had no right to take food from my ground."

Ephraim had put in honest weeks of work to enrich the farmer, thought Jonah. *Wis wife and son went hungry because this man had violated the commandment set forth in* DEUTERONOMY 24.14:

> *Thou shalt not oppress a hired servant that is poor and needy, whether he be of thy brethren, or of thy strangers that are in thy land within thy gates. In the same day thou shalt give him his hire, neither shall the sun go down upon it, for he is poor, and set-teth his heart upon it: lest he cry against thee unto the* LORD *and it be sin in thee.*

Eprhaim had earned the right to compensation, and he took it.

"He was a Jew," Nachrader ranted, "He poisoned more than my well. You people contaminate us and our whole way of life."

Squinting to see where his father had mended the beams of the ceiling, Jonah thought: *They confine us, slaughter us, yet fear us. They will absolve us of all pernicious implications if we join in their communion, consuming the flesh of their god and drinking his blood. Is that not a toxin more dreadful than any they accuse us of?*

"You killed the only begotten son of our Lord and now you are going to kill me," Heinrich wailed, stifling his sobs with straw pulled from the mattress.

They cannot forgive us for maintaining the seed out of which their God emerged. That is the poison they fear: He may arise from us once again and judge them!

"I did what I had to," Nachrader fell to his knees, clawing at the floor-boards, "to hold onto this land. It's all I have. I work day and night to produce enough, or it will revert to my landlord."

Alone, clinging to dust, Nachrader never really had anything. He would have to be judged by another court.

"Wash him off!" Jonah commanded Giuliano, and he turned on his heel.

He had better things to think of. Exiled and embattled, Jonah had found fulfillment in a cause, joined with men and women of different lands, committed to building a better civilization. His true, enduring love and their daughter were just beyond that bridge, and soon he would hold them.

"Private Giuliano, son of the sergeant," the lad introduced himself, seized Nachrader by the scruff of his neck, and marched him to the well.

"Let us see if it is poisoned," he taunted, slowly lowering an old oak bucket down a dark, moss-eaten shaft.

* * *

Just before the dawn, the scream of roosters signaled the onslaught to come. Anticipating another day of terror, horses whinnied, asses brayed, pigs squealed, and dogs howled, transforming the city of Breslau into a primeval wilderness.

The sun rose with the roar of cannonades, shattering wood and stone and iron. Startled structures collapsed onto shrieking people, crushing cobblestones and churning up debris. Overturned stoves lit tinderbox houses driving tenants into streets strewn with rubble. The collective forces of France, Bavaria, and Wurttemberg battered the feudal fortifications and the city beyond.

"These," Nathan assured his family as they huddled each morning beneath a barricade of furniture, "are the sounds of liberation." Clasping each other's hands, they braced themselves against the cataclysm.

Hunched under the table, Rivkah calmed herself in a reverie of happier times: She was in her kitchen, preparing *schalet*. To the potatoes and lamb, she added beans, barley, carrots, and spices, then set it in a slow oven for the next day. How everyone praised her at Sabbath dinners, week after week. Then came the panic. She grabbed the last of Yankel Fleischmann's lamb and rushed to the marketplace. The burghers had emptied all the stalls of potatoes. She could not make a true Jewish casserole! Was this a fore-shadowing of the world to come? Schalet without potatoes, Jews without their traditions? She smiled to herself, pleased that she had smeared drops of the lamb's blood onto the side post of their door and prayed for the Angel of Death to pass over.

*   *   *

As the earth shook, stacks of books fell upon the Lehrhaupts, cramped together in the basement storeroom of the Free School. Joseph had dismissed classes and sent his students home for the duration of the siege. "They will not return," he lamented. "Nothing will be the same."

A new order was marching across Germany. Smiling sadly at Adam and Chajjim, Joseph realized they were among the last of his pupils. The Free School, which had been his life and the mainstay of continuity in the Jewish community, would be meaningless to the younger generation who saw Judaism as merely a religion.

Embarking on a program of forced assimilation, the Prussian government had required the Jewish community to provide the funds for its recently established *Wilhelmschule* of Breslau, a secular school for Jews. In place of the comprehensive Jewish curriculum which Joseph had provided to three generations, Jewish children of Breslau would now receive a German education. Graduation from such a school could secure their admission to German universities. Jews could prepare for careers in professions no longer closed to them.

Would this, Joseph worried, be the doom of Judaism, or the salvation and rebirth of a people?

*   *   *

As the sound of explosions moved closer, Aaron called on the wrath of Jehovah to destroy the ghetto walls. "Liberate us from the shackles of confinement and the control of the Orthodoxy! Free us to return to the basic teachings that You handed down to Moses and the Prophets."

Lazarus ben-David and liberal theologians in Berlin were building a new kind of Judaism. But in the Breslau ghetto, the Orthodox saw their movement as apostasy. Aaron's congregants were refused relief; their sick were not cared for by the Judengemeinschaft and they were denied burial in the cemetery.

At night, while the great guns rested, Aaron and Hadassah moved furtively from one tenement to the next, spreading their ever thinner store of staples to those most in need. To conserve the dwindling supply of fuel, they gathered the ill and elderly in a single flat kept barely warm. Only the grievously injured and pious were admitted to the Israelitische Krankenverpflegunganstalt, the old Jewish hospital.

*   *   *

Heinrich Nachrader, bound hand and foot, cringed in a corner of his farmhouse where Jonah's squadron had made their bivouac. Unversed in French, he could communicate only with Giuliano, the son of the sergeant whose life he had plagued; Jonah spoke not a word to him. Released into the howling snow to perform his bodily functions, he was even then under gunpoint. Helpless, he watched the invaders consume his storage of food and beer, and roast his poultry and livestock in his fireplace with logs from his woodpile.

Enraged and embittered, he spent his time concocting schemes to seize a rifle and exterminate his captors, to set the house on fire and escape into a snowdrift, or die in the flames with them. Unwilling to accept the reality of it all, he stopped eating. Eventually, he fell into a delirium.

*   *   *

Dark, chilling, numbing days of hunger shrouded the chaos of cannon fire until, as Christian armies approached the Christmas holidays, their guns fell silent. For those few days in which they revered His birth, the Emperor of France and the King of Prussia deferred to the Prince of Peace.

In the Jewish quarter, this was the time for the festival of lights, a celebration of religious freedom.

During the lull of battle, congregants assembled at the Landessynagoge to hear Aaron tell the Chanukah tale of recovering the ancient Temple from heathens. Hadassah listened in awe to her husband's interpretation of the two thousand-year-old legend.

"Our ancestors found that there was only enough holy oil to burn for one day. But it miraculously glowed for eight days until a runner brought a new supply to keep the flame eternally lit. From this we learn that we have within ourselves the energy to illuminate our world far beyond apparent limitations."

With his family gathered about him, Joseph told how the Jews in 165 B.C.E. purified the Temple and rededicated themselves to the traditions which had been eroded by assimilation with the Hellenic Syrians. "We light the menorah," he explained, "with an additional candle each night to affirm an increasing commitment to our origins. Let us *always* remember our mission as the people chosen by *Adonai*, blessed be His name, to bring His Radiance to the world."

On the banks of the Oder, Jonah regaled the members of his squadron with the saga of the Maccabean uprising, describing heroic battles against thousands of warriors, many mounted on fierce elephants. Mattathias, and then his son, Judah, triumphed over Antiochus to free the Judeans.

"Just as we will soon free the Jews of Breslau," he exulted.

While his comrades celebrated Christmas Eve, Jonah cradled Heinrich Nachrader in his arms, gently dripping brandy through the farmer's parted lips. With the coming of dawn, the old Prussian was reborn in the lap of an iconoclastic Jew.

For seven glorious days following the birth date of his Savior, Nachrader gained strength. Chicken and potatoes from his domain became broth with which his adversaries nursed him back to life. Observing the filial bond between Jonah and his young Italian aide, he reminisced about the daughter who had left him long ago.

He grew accustomed to the banter of young recruits who crowded into his house for warmth after setting their cannons upon his property, aimed at fortifications across the Oder. Now, avenging shells from Prussian batteries would rain down upon him. The farmer found himself curiously allied with these *auslanders* in preparations for their mutual defense and in prayer.

*　　*　　*

During the interval in the fighting, tradesmen, managers, and professionals returned to their workplaces to take inventories, repair doors and windows, and collect whatever of value had been left behind. The Breslau police were everywhere. Property and people had to be protected, vandals rounded up, and most important of all, sedition had to be suppressed.

On New Year's day, Nathan and Chajjim, now his assistant, led Chasidic workmen back to the Silkworks to board up broken windows. Through a blinding blizzard, they shoved pushcarts loaded with timber, scavenged from the debris of combat.

The cutter assembled remnants of various textiles which the weavers stitched together and bound to wooden frames crafted by the mechanic. They hammered the wooden sash with its pane of many fabrics into cavities where windows once stood. Nathan pored over the books with Chajjim, unable to distinguish the pounding of a truncheon at the door from the racket of the hammers. When at last they responded to the demand for entry, Chief Detective Reinhardt Vertreter, and great gusts of snow, burst in upon them.

Angrily brushing himself off in Nathan's office, the policeman warned, "This time, your brother-in-law will not get away so easily. The garrison has ordered us to shoot all suspected subversives at dawn. It's no longer just up to me. I need to pay off ten others, and that will take ten times what you've paid me before."

Herr Vertreter responded to Nathan's anguished moan by poking his night stick into the merchant's groin. "How many eggs do we have to break to scramble one Jew?"

The sadism of this tinhorn tyrant suddenly energized Nathan; he had a plan. "That is a great deal of money, Herr Vertreter. You will have to excuse me while I go to my vault in the cellar."

"You want to disappear on me so you can run to warn Rabbi Aaron without paying me! Oh, no. We'll go to your vault *together*."

Nathan stood up to lead the official into the plant, pausing at his assistant's desk. "We are, *cholilleh*, going down to the vault. Give me your candle, please. Herr Chief Detective thanks you for the *chmallyeh*."

To Vertreter, he boasted loudly, "Chajjim is a good boy, he always knows what to do."

"Will you Yids never learn proper German?" the detective grumbled as they stepped out onto the factory floor.

"This city cannot hold out much longer. Our defense forces have deserted to Poland. I count on you to tell the French of the risks I have taken on your behalf, how I have *helped* you. Soon, we will be on the same side. But now, I have to compensate others, or they will suspect my loyalties."

They proceeded past the Chasidic workmen to the stairs at the far end of the factory.

"I trust *you*, Herr Chief Detective, but once you have my money, how can I be sure that Aaron will not be shot by *another* officer?"

The candle flickered as they descended into subterranean corridors, zigzagging through endless chambers.

"Tomorrow morning the shelling will resume. No one will ask *how* anyone was shot. It is a much more efficient way of dealing with dissidents than taking them into custody. We know when and where the cell meets. 'Stray fire' will take care of them. As curfew approaches, I will follow you back to the ghetto and watch. When the gates are locked, you may tell Rabbi Aaron to get under cover and to stay there. Tell him *nothing* of our plans. If you do, he might try to be noble or send a messenger to alert others. If *anyone* steps out of the ghetto tonight, his blood will be on your hands."

They seemed to be doubling back. Increasingly impatient, the extortionist demanded to know where he was being led.

"The vault is just ahead," Nathan assured him. "Will you hold the light while I try the key?"

As he reached for the candle, Vertreter fell forward, struck by a blow, a *chmallyeh,* from behind. The Chasids deftly tied and gagged the chief detective as Chajjim, holding the candle high, laughed in triumph.

"I told you. *Cholilleh*, he has no vault!"

Wrapped tightly in rolls of silk and crowned with a yellow hat, the struggling body was loaded onto a pushcart and delivered through the blinding snow to a quiet chapel in the rear of the Church of St. Berhardin.

Returning to the ghetto, the Jews of the Silkworks, for the first time, walked together with Nathan. With wry references to the bundling of the Chief Detective, Chajjim explained that on this day, Christians celebrated the Feast of the Circumcision.

At the Landessynogoge, Nathan warned Aaron, and told him the full story of his encounter with Vertreter. With a nod to Aaron, Hadassah slipped through the secret passage to alert the members of the cell. Their meeting place, in the rarely used chapel of St. John the Baptist, at the rear of St. Berhardin's, was no longer safe.

"So, what can he do to me?" Nathan asked. "Admit that he's been on my payroll for months?"

"The big question," Aaron responded,"is what will the *French* do?" He locked the door behind his brother-in-law, lowered himself into the chamber below the bimah, and waited anxiously until, as though they were ringing in a new year, Hadassah, Hans, Stas, and Vlad emerged from the network of sewers to join him.

That night, feeling a miraculous tingle in his testicles, Nathan seized Sarah, carried her to the sofa that had been waiting since their wedding night, and rediscovered the joy of carnal lust.

XVIII

The Liberation of Breslau

The woolen muffler drawn across his face concealed Mordecai's glee while dour Berlin gentlemen recoiled at the impertinence. Napoleon's stallion had dropped turd at the Brandenburg Gate. The silk merchant stood with men of Prussia against the cold winds of October 25th to protect German women, lest they be bothered or beguiled by Frenchmen.

Bonaparte led two hundred thousand virile soldiers through the capital, pressing their victory into the pavement of Unter den Linden, as though it were plaster of Paris. Friedrich William had ignominiously fled to East Prussia, freeing additional French troops in the southeast to reinforce their siege of Breslau.

Through a bitter fall and early winter, alone in his house in Kreuzberg, Mordecai prayed for the safety of his family. In rambling missives to Rivkah, he poured out regrets, begged for forgiveness, recalled happy occasions, reminisced on moments with their son, asked about their granddaughter, and pleaded to be reunited.

Mired in her despair of impending disaster and relentless hunger, Rivkah read her husband's letters repeatedly, clinging to the remembrance of better days. Honoring Chanukah behind the barricades, she was reminded of its commitment to rebuild on the basis of one's past. She began to write and offered some hope, but warned she would never again be embarrassed or ignored by him.

She would not end up like his mother Naomi who had to find love outside her marriage. When Rivkah wrote her husband all she had learned of Jabal Rosenkohl and the tragedy in Jena, Mordecai vowed to find his mother.

* * *

On January 2, 1807, with frightening fury and painstaking accuracy, the bombardment resumed.

By the light of a single candle, Hadassah gazed aimlessly at her husband, surrounded by the group of revolutionaries, as he propounded the commandments of a God in which neither she nor they had faith. Trapped in the bunker, she ached to get to her children and to those in the ghetto who depended upon her. After each new fusillade, she ascended the steps and thrust herself against the trap door, held in place by the bimah from above. Each time, the men pulled her back; she could not jeopardize their security. The weight of men and religion had always held her down.

Isolated from battle, waiting for the din to subside, there was nothing any of them could do but wait; their future lay with the military forces confronting one another on the banks of the Oder. If, after the guns fell silent, Hoshea did not come to let them out, they would have to retreat back through the subterranean tunnel of waste to the tyrannical Germany they had sought to escape.

While anticipating liberation from outside, Aaron decried despotism from within. "Jews who try to adapt Judaism to the world of today are forced by the rigidity of the Orthodox to escape into Christianity, or are driven away from religion altogether."

"Why not let your people decide for themselves whether they want to remain Jews?" countered Hans. "Surely, emancipation should give them the freedom to be Germans of any persuasion."

"So long as the Orthodox control our religion and Christians control our lives, Jews have no real choice.

"Those who leave our faith do so chiefly because of its outer trappings, not its inner commands. As a rabbi, I want to offer a Judaism that sees the Bible not as an absolute, but as a palpable, divinely inspired document, subject to interpretation."

"But what of those who believe in no Divine Being?"

"Jews do not have the luxury of being atheists! We are forever stamped as Jews unless we convert to Christianity. Our new form of Judaism helps those who would otherwise leave the faith to find God, to discover Him in our *own* roots."

Despondent and tired of the incessant intellectualizing, Hadassah found solace in dreams of her lover. The conflict that had kept them apart for fifteen years now raged just beyond the bimah, at the doorstep of the onetime shop in which the remarkable boots had been crafted, the boots that had carried him away.

*   *   *

It was his reawakened manhood, Nathan was sure, that gave him the omnipotence to provide sanctuary for the family in his embrace.

The angel of death would pass over their household, and the fire outside, he vowed, would be the last of the plagues before freedom. Nathan was a new man for the new era.

His ardor comforted Sarah. She smiled deeply within, recalling his return to the ghetto last night, arm in arm with the eastern Jews. Was it the spark of impending emancipation that ignited his passion for her? Pleased with the prospect of life beyond the bombshells, she playfully tousled the hair of their thirteen-year- old daughter.

*   *   *

Between tremors that capsized piles of books in the wake of each new salvo, Joseph Lehrhaupt conducted lessons for Adam, Judith, and

Chajjim. His commitment to Judaism transcended differences in forms of worship. He taught the lore of Jewish people as a folk with a heritage of four thousand years across many lands. Whatever was to happen in the next generation, his pupils would be prepared to pass on their ancient legacy.

*   *   *

Giuliano tucked Heinrich Nachrader into a clean blanket on fresh straw in the corner furthest from the field of battle. Every night, the farmer moaned in the most piteous, heartwrenching tones for Myrna, begging forgiveness. On this morning, he looked into the eyes of his young captor. In Latin, they recited Roman Catholic litanies. In the German he had learned from Jonah, Giuliano talked with his slowly recovering patient. He wanted to know what made such a man tick, and he was consumed with curiosity about Myrna.

Over the following days, Nachrader told the lad his life had been endless drudgery to keep his land, pay feudal duties to his oppressive landlord, and harvest a crop. His wife died in delivering the daughter he raised alone, a winsome, vivacious child with golden hair, Myrna of his paeans. He would say no more about her.

He had been taught by priests to see Jews as the Antichrist, proper game for abuse and worthy of his basest fears. But he was now bewildered that the mighty armies of Christendom had placed the son of Ephraim upon his land. What did this league of Christ and Antichrist have in store for him?

Looking across the river to the ramparts that separated him from his beloved, Jonah ordered the discharge of cannonades against the high walls of the city. In response, a great volley from the Prussian batteries knocked Jonah unconscious as a cannonball found the farmhouse behind him.

Within the house, Giuliano and Nachrader were pinned between the wall and upended beams that fell from the ceiling. Other timbers fell into the hearth, spreading flames to the entire structure. This was it! Nachrader knew he would surely burn in the fires of Hell. "Giuliano, you must receive my confession, you must grant me absolution from my sins!"

Although the lad was not a practicing Catholic, he had been baptized in the Church. Facing his own inevitable demise, he agreed to provide the sacrament.

Terrified, in agony and remorse, Nachrader told the story of Myrna. She had been his light and inspiration. He had to put food on the table, keep a roof over their heads, and though he went to certain houses to engage in carnal practices essential to a man, his daughter was the essence of purity. He borrowed heavily from Jews to assure her the best of everything in clothes and comfort, buy her a riding habit and her own white gelding. All his labors, all his compromises to virtue were made to protect and adorn her.

When he discovered that she had been violated by the landlord, he went to kill the man, but she blocked her father, boasting that she had *liked* it! Suddenly, everything he had worked for turned to dirt. The child for whom his wife had given her life and to whom he had devoted his, was just a tramp!

Since she *liked it*, he hired her out to Silesian miners to pay the debts incurred for her pleasure. He became his daughter's whoremaster until she ran off on the gelding. She is a prostitute today, in a brothel just outside Jena.

Giuliano gasped. With flames advancing ever closer, he had to tell Nachrader the truth or he, too, would burn in Hell. "Heinrich, I know your daughter! Myrna is a good and unsullied woman. It was she who brought me into my manhood. She was delicate, affectionate, and sweet as she led me into paradise. Whatever the Church says, there was nothing immoral about it. But how can I can give you absolution after I have been with your daughter? Perhaps I should ask *you* for forgiveness."

In their absorption with one another's confessions, the sinners had not noticed that the huge snowdrift on the roof had begun to melt from the heat of the fire. Suddenly, a great gush of water pulled a mountain of wet snow through the hole left by the collapse of the beams, and extinguished the flames. Jonah's comrades hoisted the fallen beams, and the two men were freed.

Soaked and chilled, they laughed with relief. Nachrader had been forced to divulge his deepest shame, but the lad who knew his Myrna did not condemn him. Once again, he was saved by those he had known only as the enemy.

"Myrna is well cared-for and protected by Madam Rosa. Go to Jena!" Giuliano urged Heinrich. "This is a new day and you and your daughter must try to make new beginnings. But first, you will have to seek redemption from Jonah for your crimes against his father. *He* is the one to whom you will have to make a complete confession."

The old farmer shivered. Everything he had believed had gone up in smoke. Could he cope in this curious world?

*   *   *

Only that obscure corner of the church was struck by the hail of gunfire, the alcove where Fr. Ludwig had let the band of fallen-away Catholics and Jews come together to discuss Divine Rights. The Monsignor had often warned the priest about them, but Fr. Ludwig believed it was better to have men of conscience *in* the Church than organizing against it. Approaching the cloistered chapel, he saw the head of St. John the Baptist lying in pieces among shards of stained glass and fine marble.

Picking through the flotsam, Fr. Ludwig came upon the unconscious, wounded body of a Jew, bound and wrapped in ceremonial silks.

Undoubtedly, anti-Semites had deposited him at the feet of St. John, as a warning to the dissidents who had met here.

The Monsignor rebuked his associate with a stream of "I-told-you-so's," but the two agreed that the authorities should *not* be summoned to St. Berhardin's. They removed the silk (which would find better use as an altar cloth), untied the poor victim, and, with the yellow hat of Judaism snug upon his head, transported him to the Israelitische Krankenverpflegunganstalt.

*   *   *

On January 5, 1807, the city of Breslau capitulated to Jerome Bonaparte, brother of the Emperor of France. Stifling their humiliation, old martinet generals led dazed green recruits, the dregs of a Prussian army (most of which had fled to Poland), in a closeorder drill of surrender. As the defeated laid down their muskets, the victors pulled up their stakes, disassembled their camps, and prepared to march forward into the conquered city.

Jonah ordered his unit to harvest all of the potatoes left in Nachrader's soil. Breaking frozen crusts of earth with their bayonets, shoveling with the butt of their rifles, they filled all the sacks and baskets they could find with rich, bulbous spuds.

On January 6th, the Day of The Epiphany, when the Magi bore gifts to Jesus, French troops entered the city, bringing potatoes to the chosen people.

A sky clear of snow and exploding shells had dawned upon the walled enclave of the Jews. Creeping out from under their table, the Friedlanders peered through broken window panes. Below them, French officers emptied bushels of potatoes onto the Judengasse. Rivkah leaped at the sign of deliverance. It was the replenishment of oil for the temple! Throughout the lean months of siege, she had longed for the day when she could serve up a true schalet. She ran out into the gathering swarm of celebrants.

Joseph Lehrhaupt neatly restacked the books one final time and led his coterie onto the street where it seemed that all the Jews of Breslau, men and women, whatever their class or origin, joined hands, shouting and weeping with joy as they passed handfuls of potatoes to one another.

Shoving his way through the multitude from the gate that stood open at the end of the Judengasse, Nathan shouted til he was hoarse, "The guard is gone! The guard is gone!"

Hoshea appeared in a shaft of blinding light. "Our liberators have come," he turned the cellar door back on its hinge, "bringing manna from the soil of Prussia!" On either side of him, with outstretched hands to deliver their parents from the darkness, stood Judith, a broad smile on her ingenuous face, and Adam, a tricolor yarmulke riding on his red curls.

A violin began the strains of an ancient hymn. A fife, then a flute, trumpets, bugles, a clarinet, drums, a cello, more fiddles, and an accordion joined in, harmonized into folk songs, then erupted with raucous improvisations. Adam grabbed the arms of Chajjim and two old men and all four kicked their feet into free air. Aaron, Hans, and Hoshea gathered boards and slats and set about building a Tree of Liberty.

In the platz before the main synagogue, the Sergeant of the French Guard stood erect, his eyes flashing with excitement, the welcome sun bouncing off his brass buttons. In a voice bold and self-assured, he ordered the leadership of the Judengemeinschaft to assemble in the sanctuary of the main shul.

Hadassah grasped Judith's shoulders to keep from fainting or shouting his name, or running to him. How could she quiet the clamor of her heart? His eyes found hers, dark and deep, permeated with their dreams.

For this glorious moment, he had fought across half the continent: to be near his beloved, after all that Time had stolen from them. Surely, that was their daughter, a young lady now. She had her mother's fine features, but those high cheekbones were his.

The mob pressed forward, following the Sergeant of the Guard and the Administrative Committee of the Jewish community into the great sanctuary. Two infantrymen presented Joachim Gauner, attorney-at-law, and his aide, a scribe. The people whispered, "Herr Gauner in the ghetto!" "What brings him here?"

From her seat among the women in the balcony, Hadassah watched a handsome young soldier, in boots that were unmistakably Jonah's, lead an aged German farmer to the bimah.

The old man faced rabbis, yeshiva buchers, Chasids, Yiddish workingmen, portly bourgeoisie, moneylenders, peddlers, beggars, and a sea of babushkas.

Herr Gauner's scribe took out his quill.

"And now, Herr Nachrader," demanded the Sergeant of the Guard, "tell the people to whom you have contributed your harvest of potatoes the true story of my father."

Terrified more by the awesome power of these aliens than by the gravity of his crimes, the farmer pled for forgiveness, first of his God, then of those he had wronged.

Before people he had denigrated all his life, under oath administered by Herr Gauner, slowly so that the scribe could record his every word, Heinrich Nachrader confessed his false accusations against Ephraim.

As he did so, a murmur quickly swelled into shouts: "That's Jonah Schneider! Ephraim's son!"

"We thought he was dead!"

"Great is the power of the Almighty, blessed be His name!"

Convinced a miracle had taken place, Aaron bowed his head in reverence. Here was his loyal friend, back from the departed, to rescue even those who had cast him out.

Believing, until now, that Jonah was dead, Nathan had suspended the anger that, for so long, had gnawed at him. Outraged, he despised the onetime cheeky apprentice whose betrayal had led the police to brutalize him on his wedding night. Seeing Jonah alive, and in command, reawakened years of resentment. How dare he assume the role of liberator! Nathan seethed as he watched Jonah shame the leadership of his community.

Joseph regarded Jonah in the same light as he viewed emancipation, knowing that each brought both immense opportunities and untold conflicts. He alone knew of the illicit bond between his daughter and the reincarnated hero. What would liberation mean to the Jews — and to his family? Would either hold together?

Nachrader signed his confession and Herr Gauner announced that the document would be filed with the Court. Ephraim would be exonerated. From Hoshea and the workingmen, from Hadassah and the ladies in the gallery, out onto the platz where those unable to cram into the shul stood by, a cheer spread and rose to ever higher pitches of exuberance. Freedom had brought justice.

The fiddlers picked up where they had left off. As other instrumentalists joined in, celebration filled the Judengasse.

*   *   *

He wandered in nighttime shadows, down streets and alleys, the cold, crisp air clearing his lungs of the lingering stench of gunpowder. The glow of candles and fireplaces in Christian households guided his way through a world so long forbidden to him, until he arrived at the Silkworks of his youth.

A gaping cavity appeared where an incipient effort to seal off windows blown out by the shock of cannonades had been abandoned. He climbed the mound of hardened snow to the opening. Entering the factory, he walked among looms draped in cobwebs, every step stirring images of her. Ghosts and dreams led him up the narrow stairs to his shed on the roof.

She was there, silhouetted by the fire in his old stove.

Their embraces awakened a deepened love. There was so much to say, yet for a long while they spoke only of the moment.

Under unending tiers of stars they lay naked, soaring to constellations beyond Time.

As an amber moon dropped behind the western forest, they talked of their daughter, of duty, and of the great transformations that had melded their island into the mainland.

Wrapped in each other's bodies against the winds of Silesia, they fell blissfully asleep.

In the morning she was gone.

XIX

Judith and Giuliano

Eleazar Pistron planted his hickory stake firmly in the rubble of Antonienstrasse and dragged first one bowed leg forward and then the other. Step by painful step he approached the open, unguarded gate. Feigel, among the first to see him, ran ahead to tell Judith that her father had come.

He had camped out at the edge of Breslau for days, worried about his only child, and now greeted her with as much solemnity as joy. She embraced the withered old man, and with her arm locked in his, the two made their way to Naaman's Knishery.

They feasted on potato dumplings and borsht. He savored her every word and wondered about what might have been, until it was time to start for the terminal for the afternoon coach to Ratibor. He was satisfied that she had survived the siege and was well.

Just before boarding his coach, he looked into her eyes. "Your mother was never happy with me," he said. "She had to marry someone, or face export. It was different, then. Nobody talked about love. But you, my child…someday, a fine young man will ask for your hand and you will be free to decide if he is the right one for you."

Eleazar put a ruby ring in Judith's palm. "Let him put this ring on your finger, and wear it always, with the knowledge that liberation brought the possibility of love."

Through tears of regret that she had never really known him, she watched his coach pull away. The pale rose red of the stone glinted as she turned the ring to read the inscription inside.

Trumpets at the Schweidnitzer Gate announced the entry of Jerome Bonaparte, Regent of Westphalia. On her way home from the terminal, overcome by her meeting with Eleazar, Judith lingered in the crowd to watch the grand processional for the self-proclaimed Protector of Breslau moving into baroque Hatzfeldsche Palais.

Life will be better, she thought, humming the *Marseillaise*, while loosening her yellow bonnet of servitude. For hours, she watched Prince Jerome's Guard strut beneath fireworks, amid nighttime revelries from which, until now, she had been barred.

It was late when she approached the bonfire blazing at the edge of the Judengasse where a multitude had gathered around an incendiary speaker. The firebrand read from a pamphlet by Johann Gottlieb Fichte, the leading German philosopher of the day:

> "There is spread throughout nearly every country of Europe a powerful inimical State which wars continually against all others, and often succeeds in bitterly oppressing their peoples."

He pointed to the tenements beyond the open gate of the ghetto.

> "This state is Jewry. The only way I can see to give the Jews civil rights is to cut off their heads in a single night and equip them with new ones devoid of every Jewish idea. To protect ourselves against them, again I see no means except to conquer their Promised Land and pack them all off to it."

"Until then, lock them up," shouted someone in the mob.
"Seal the gates," yelled another.
"Let them wallow in their stinking ghetto!"

"There's one of them on our streets, now," shrieked a hideous, scabby-faced hulk wrapped in a shroud of rags. "Let's drive her back where she belongs."

Tearing rocks from the dirt, the swarm advanced toward Judith, frozen in terror. In an instant, soldiers of the Royal Guard descended upon the horde and Judith was lifted up onto the neck of a plumed charger by a young private in remarkable boots. Her rescuer galloped across the Oder, carrying her to safety.

Prince Jerome's newly appointed Chief of Intelligence took charge. Reinhardt Vertreter (known to have been wounded in his heroic defense of the Jews), lined up all those with cinders under their fingernails.

He assailed the scabby-faced thug with a sneer. "I've been *looking* for you, pig snatcher!" Whereupon he clubbed the miscreant and took him into a very long period of custody.

*　　　*　　　*

In the house of a farmer who had gone to Jena, Giuliano eased his jacket onto Judith's shoulders, built a fire, and gently lifted the yellow bonnet of stigma from her head. They huddled together, watching it dissolve in the flames of Nachrader's hearth.

Their night was filled with each other. Though she was born in Ratibor and knew her father only through a stream of letters, she was delivered to Breslau where her mother's second marriage to a visionary rabbi made her "the daughter of a mission:" she grew up in service to a multifaceted community with unquenchable needs, and nostalgically recounted specific acts of outreach. He recalled the splendors and tragedies of Genoa, his rescue by Jonah, and the warm, stimulating home in Amsterdam.

His eyes shone with tales of his adoptive father. He had basked in grandmother Zelda's tenderness and stood in awe of the font of wisdom that was da Costa. Her grandmother Leah, of the same generous nature as Zelda, helped to raise her. It was as though the women knew one another. Her grandfather Joseph could be a brother to da Costa.

She held his hands in hers, thanked him over and over, and fell soundly asleep on his shoulder. Filled with boundless affection, straining to temper his passion, Giuliano reflected on how this lovely creature had come into his life.

Earlier that day, before reveille, Jonah had awakened him in a soft, slow, determined voice. "I must leave immediately for combat on the eastern front. I cannot remain here. You, my boy, must stay in Breslau to protect Hadassah and her family." The older man kissed his son on the cheek and forehead, and then he was gone, leaving Giuliano's new orders on his cot. He had been transferred to Prince Jerome's Royal Guard at the Hatzfeldsche Palais. Giuliano puzzled: *Why did Jonah seem so in despair? Why did he leave me?*

Now, with Judith's head resting against his cheek, all Giuliano's bewilderment evaporated.

A single loon yodeled in the rafters. Frogs hiccoughed at the pond. He lay there, with her in his arms, listening to the descending wail of an owl, and to his heart. She barely stirred as he cautiously carried her on his horse across a moonlit field of fresh snow. In a trance, she found her way up the steps to her parents' apartment, daring not to waken lest she lose the dream.

*   *   *

Fr. Ludwig led the march. From throughout Breslau, Christians gathered in front of the ghetto to join hands with Jews, determined to purge the hatred that had been unleashed there the night before.

After more than 540 years of confinement, Jews, with their new Christian comrades, ripped the gates from their moorings, lifted them aloft, and hurled them into the Ohlau.

The Ninth of January, 1807, would long be remembered as the day Prince Jerome ordered destruction of the city's fortifications. Stationed on the Judengasse, the artillery of the Royal Guard fired cannonades, leveling that corner of the ramparts which had long served as walls to seal the ghetto from the shallow tributary of the Oder.

Blind Hoshea began it, pounding his cobbler's hammer at the ancient rocks that separated the other side of the ghetto from the city. Jews and Gentiles took up clubs, axes, rakes, hoes, pieces of broken furniture, and rocks, and tore down the remaining walls, bit by loathsome bit.

The Judengasse would henceforth be known as Wallstrasse.

Adam stood alongside Joseph, silently watching the collapse of containment. "Does this mark the loss of our innocence?" asked the yeshiva student. "I fear," his grandfather responded, "it is the beginning of the loss of our moral authority over our people."

*　　　*　　　*

Neither the hospital nor any doctor in Jena had a record of Jabal Rosenkohl. By law, there had been no Jewish community in the town, and thus, no way to trace the relatives who, thirty-five years earlier, had claimed the remains.

In the course of his inquiries, Mordecai learned of a plaque at the University, bearing the name of the former footman. Obscure among the ivy, on the wall of the Fuchs-Term (Fox Tower), celebrated for its student orgies, a corroding brass plate read:"*Jabal Rosenkohl died for our sins.*"

A graduate research fellow in "The Jacobin Influence on German Literature" delighted in telling the story to Mordecai. A wealthy woman had made the caustic tribute to Rosenkohl a condition of her generous and anonymous endowment.

"Schiller bemoaned that the poor devil had been killed because we drove him from the University," said the student, "due only to the fact that he was a Jew. The professor claimed to tell the tale to raise student consciousness. But most of us thought he told it to assuage his guilt. It seems that it was *his* lecture from which the chap was expelled. Anyway, the mysterious donor was known only to Schiller, a secret he took with him to his grave. He died, you know, a year and a half ago, in nearby Weimar, shortly after he brought his epic, *William Tell,* to the stage."

After a week in Jena, Mordecai was ready to call it quits. From the spot where Jabal had been run down, he hailed a coach and set out for some relaxation in a place just beyond the city limits, well recommended by academes and his innkeeper. The brothel, he was told, had been recently remodeled, thanks to the largess and libidos of soldiers from many lands.

A well-seasoned looking woman named Dolly, acting for the Madam who would shortly return from the bank, ushered Mordecai into a richly draped anteroom where he joined university professors and officers from the garrison. Sprawled comfortably on plush divans, the men engaged in philosophic and racy conversation, sipping Ashbach ur Alt while awaiting their turn upstairs. Only one patron seemed out of place, a simple bumpkin who loudly and repeatedly insisted on waiting for one of the girls named Myrna.

An amply proportioned woman beckoned Mordecai to follow her to a room furnished with only a bed and a table, on top of which stood a basin of warm water. After rendering the routine ablutions, she offered herself for his pleasure. He took little time.

Upon descending the staircase, Mordecai came upon a tumultuous scene. Several soldiers were restraining the now belligerent oaf, wildy shouting for Myrna, while the Madam, her back to the silk merchant, was resolute. "Your daughter," she explained, "does not want to see you. She says that it was you who forced her into this trade. She fled and came here to be protected from you."

The lout fell to his knees. "Tell her, please tell her, I beg her forgiveness. I swear by the Holy Virgin I never touched her. After she gave up her maidenhood to the landlord, I was devastated! What man would want her for anything else? When she said she enjoyed doing it, I went crazy. I always thought she was so innocent. I owed money to everyone because of all the sacrifices I made for her. I wanted her to pay. I *made* her enjoy it with the miners from the coal pits. They lined up, and the marks they shoved out saved the farm."

"Myrna claims the miners abused her and you did nothing to stop them. Here, we do not allow such conduct."

"I was wrong! How I have suffered and rebuked myself all these years. I've hated myself and hated everyone. But now, everything is different; I'm a changed man. Tell her, I want to make it up to her. I love my daughter and want her to come home with me to the farm. Someday, it will be *her* farm."

Above Mordecai, on the stairway, Myrna wept. "Papa, I don't know what to do."

Madam Rosa turned to calm her, and upon seeing Mordecai, collapsed into the lap of a Professor of Antiquities. A handsome, plump woman with few wrinkles and styled white hair, her face was drained of color.

Aghast, yet not quite trusting what his eyes informed him, Mordecai let out a moan, as much a query as a lament.

Myrna ran past him down the stairs to her father, still held by the soldiers, and sobbed into his chest. Taking charge of the anteroom, Dolly guided Myrna and her father into the kitchen and restored order among the patrons. Trembling, Mordecai helped the amazingly recovered Madam Rosa to her private office.

It had been thirty-seven years since he had last seen her at his wedding to Rivkah, but it was indisputably her.

"Mother!" he raged, "how could you do this?"

"How dare you judge me, minutes after you used one of my girls! Tell me, "she taunted, "after a lifetime of indifference, what brings you here now? Love? Passion? Maybe a little innocent sexual fun? I provide clean girls to *any* man seeking the same thing, so long as he has the price and behaves decently."

"I've been in Jena for days looking for you, Mother. I tried to track you through Jabal. *Now* I see, 'Rosenkohl' became 'Rosa.'"

"Jabal. He was a man who knew what it meant to love, to really love a woman. In his way, your father may have *thought* he loved me. I was good to look at. I made sure of that. But your father never *saw* me, a woman with desires, interests, even ideas. I needed so to be respected, listened to, to be *cherished.*"

Her words fell on deaf ears. "Mother, you are not that kind of woman. Women of your class don't act in this way."

"Class! What do you know of class? Here, I am hostess to some of the most influential men in Germany. Not as an ornament, but as a true companion. In this house, Schiller read aloud his *Wurde der Frauen,* a personal tribute to me. We worked on his drafts of *Wallenstein* together, and it was *my* idea to recast them into three parts. And you talk to me about class?"

"Mother, you don't have to stay here. Father is still in Berlin, aging and alone; he will take you back! Or you can come with me to Breslau, where you have a married grandson and an adopted great-granddaughter! Let me take you home."

"My home is here. My girls need me, and here, I have found my place in life. Never would I go back to the old ways."

"But the old ways are changing, they're granting us freedom!"

"Nobody can *grant* you freedom. The only real freedom is what you find through love. I have that. Now, tell me about my grandson and great-granddaughter."

The morning coach to Breslau bore only two passengers: a morose Mordecai Friedlander, shrunk in the corner opposite Heinrich Nachrader, who shouted hilariously to Myrna, as she rode alongside on her aging white gelding.

*   *   *

Each time she heard Judith retell the romance of that night, and the stories of Giuliano's adoptive father, Hadassah choked with her deepest, hidden longings. Exhilaration collided with panic.

Would her daughter live out the desires she had suppressed? Would her excitement give her away? Was this a trick of fate, or had Jonah deliberately guided his heir to her daughter, a drama he had staged to give expression to *their* love?

She could say nothing of her inner turmoil to Judith, and urged her not to speak to Aaron of her obsession with Giuliano. He would neither understand, nor approve of her attraction to a Gentile boy from another land.

But the infatuation could not remain secret very long. The next day, Judith saw Giuliano in the marketplace, laughing uproariously, his arm playfully locked about an alluring older woman. Her eyes swelling with tears, Judith ran headlong into a stand of rutabagas. Suddenly, he was there, picking up the odious yellow turnips she had strewn onto the platz. Tenderly, he kissed the tears from her cheeks, her eyelids, her lips. Before everyone, Giuliano professed his love for Judith and begged her consent to seek her father's permission for her hand in marriage.

The older woman, daughter of the farmer who had exonerated Ephraim, led the delighted crowd in raucous accolades of approval. Giuliano had been listening to Myrna's story of how her father brought her back, and she, in turn, had heard nothing all morning but his out-pouring of love for Judith.

Giuliano and Judith spent the day roaming the streets of Breslau, planning their future. He would join her faith and bring her to Amsterdam where people of different backgrounds and beliefs worked and dwelled together in peace. She would never again have to endure anti-Semitic assaults.

Snowflakes drifted from the sky and clung to their cloaks, but to them, it was Spring enveloping them in shimmering leaves of silver. A cold, bracing wind from the city swept through open spaces where ghetto barriers once stood. A merciful cover of ice muted the stench of the sanitation ditch. Their world smelled sweet.

He would wait at the foot of the stairs until after her family had completed its supper.

Word of the scene in the marketplace had made its way back to the family. Seated at the dining table, sputtering with outrage, Aaron forbade his stepdaughter to see the Christian infantryman.

"Father, it is too late," she asserted imperiously. "Before all of Breslau, Giuliano asked me to marry him, and we have committed ourselves to each other.

"Giuliano," she acidly informed her stepfather, "is not just some Gentile who risked his life to help free us."

"He is not," she taunted him, "merely a member of the Royal Guard who personally saved me from a lynch mob two nights ago.

"Papa!" she blurted out, "he is also the ward of your oldest friend, Jonah, and has been raised in a Jewish household by Zelda and the great Levi da Costa. He will formally convert to Judaism, and he wants your help. He is waiting to see you and to ask your permission for my hand."

Aaron was dumbfounded. He had been publicly committed to the proposition that Judaism was principally a religion, that we were the same as all other people but for a difference in faith. Here was the Christian scion of his old rebellious friend, ready to embrace Judaism, putting him to the test. He was, preeminently, a rational man and would analyze the matter reasonably. After dinner, he would talk with Giuliano.

Adam expressed a different opinion. He saw the loss of his sister as a premonition that portended the dissolution of his family. Choking back an inexplicable pain of rejection, Adam argued that the acceptance of non-Jews into the community was an insidious form of assimilation; it would dilute the solidarity that came from their common experience of suffering. "How can Giuliano," he asked his sister, "understand how it *feels* to be a Jew? Nothing father could teach him will make him a true member of the tribe."

"But Adam," Hadassah interrupted, "this is the very reverse of assimilation! It is bringing one who respects and loves us to participate with us in our faith. It is proof of the compelling power of Judaism."

"Is it really *Judaism*," asked Adam, "that he is pursuing, or is it *Judith*? Does he want our God, or one of our women?"

"The BOOK OF RUTH reminds us," Joseph spoke with authority, "of a convert who joined our faith because of her devotion to a good Jewish woman:

> *whither thou goest, I will go; and where thou lodgest, I will lodge; thy people shall be my people, and thy God my God.*

"Ruth became one of us because of her commitment to Naomi. She was drawn first to *thy people*, followed by *thy God*. And she was chosen by Adonai, blessed be His name, to be the great-grandmother of our beloved King David.

"Do not judge Giuliano too harshly, Adam," Joseph admonished. "With his conversion, he will suffer enough the opprobrium of his comrades and the enormous Christian world, but he will assure the raising of another generation in our heritage."

"And I will teach him," Aaron affirmed, "and hold him to the strictest standards before allowing him to take a Jewish name."

It was rare for Leah to enter any debate, but buoyed by Joseph's comments, she turned to her grandson. "Giuliano," she said, "has told Judith he wants to follow her in the traditions that molded her and others he has come to love: Jonah, Zelda, and da Costa. Someday, Adam, you and he will come to respect one another. Give your sister your blessing and your support."

Adam walked over to Judith. With tears in his eyes, he hugged his sister and wished her well. Torn but resigned, he descended the stairs to invite his future brother-in-law to join the family at the table.

With a barely discernable smile Adam asked, "Are you ready, Giuliano, for your *bris*?"

XX

Napoleon's Conquests

Jonah stumbled among frozen faces clinging to skeletal remains of bodies stripped naked by pillagers and ravaged by beasts of the Pomeranian forest. Petrified French, Italian, and Polish eyes stared at Russian boys who would never be men. Wolves, undisturbed by his plodding through the fields of Eylau, tugged at the flesh of unknown Giulianos. He vomited into snow veined by blood and gunpowder. He had grown sick of this war.

On the other side of Orion, she would be laughing with their daughter in a land he had helped to free. He cursed the ache in his gut. He would live to be with Hadassah and to tell Judith that she was his.

It was February 7, 1807. Napoleon had fought General Tolstoy's Russian army to a standstill in the bloodiest battlefield Europe had ever known.

*　　*　　*

Two days later, in the Paris synagogue, Rabbi David Zinzheim of Alsace, holding a Scroll of the Law, offered a special prayer for "our immortal Emperor, "for the victory of his army, and for blessed peace. Rabbi Abraham de Cologna of Mantua praised Bonaparte, "the creative genius, who, of all mortals in the world, is the best created in the image of God. He lifted us, the repudiated people from the depth of our humiliation, and granted us the life of citizens. We will have to prove deserving of such grace by sending our youth to military service under the glorious banners of Napoleon the Great."

Levi da Costa had spent the last weeks of his life, working with the outreach committee of Portugese, German, and Italian Jews, issuing the call to every synagogue from Bayonne to Warsaw, to send delegates to the Grand Sanhedrin.

Just days before it convened, he looked upon the promised land and heaved a final sigh of contentment.

Da Costa had lived a good and full life.

He left his house and a modest pension to Zelda. As she brought da Costa's remains home to Amsterdam, Aaron and Adam set out from Breslau to the historic event.

In Leipzig, David Frenkel boarded their coach. The editor of "*Sulamith,* a periodical to develop culture and humanism among the Jewish People," Frenkel would cover the first gathering of the High Council of rabbis and lay leaders since the dispersal of the Jews from Judea in the year 70 of the common era. They rode together, locked in conversation, forging a friendship all the way.

The convocation would be the true interpreter of Jewish law. It would provide the emperor with a sanction as valid as the Talmud itself.

In velvet cassocks with wide sashes and fur trimmed hats, Zinzheim, Cologna, and Joshua Benzion Segre, the Presidium of the Grand Sanhedrin, led forty-three rabbis in black cloaks and black hats from France, Germany, and Italy, twenty-five laymen, and ten candidates to the Hotel de Ville. For a month, they met in open session before Jews and Christians from across the continent.

Aaron and Adam arrived early each day to secure their seats alongside David Frenkel.

The answers given by the Assembly of Notables to Napoleon's twelve questions were unanimously confirmed and expanded to serve as "instructive resolutions."

Jewish religious laws were upheld as everlasting, independent of time and place. But those which were political were declared archaic; the Sanhedrin ruled that they were products of an earlier epoch of independent government and "have been inapplicable since the time that the Jewish people ceased to be a national body."

Even religious laws, such as those barring intermarriage, were abandoned where they did not adapt themselves to the law of the nation. "We'll lose our community," Adam complained. "Now Judith could marry Giuliano in a civil ceremony, and even if we did not sanctify their union, we could not proscribe it."

"Isn't it better," Frenkel responded, "for your sister to marry Giuliano without fear of ostracism?"

Jewish soldiers were exempted from religious rituals incompatible with military service.

"If the war is still on," Adam scowled, "in two years, I will be drafted. So long as I kill for the emperor, cut my beard, eat pork, and fight on the Sabbath, I can still be a good Jew!"

"If our demands for equal rights are to be considered legitimate by the nation in which we live," explained Frenkel, "we must claim it as our homeland. Having made that claim, we must recognize our duty to defend it."

Still, Aaron believed that the Sanhedrin too readily compromised religious canon to the state. Military forces could make *some* accommodations to forelocks, beards, and yarmulkes.

In its longest, most heated debate, the Sanhedrin adopted sanctions against those Jewish usurers and old-clothes dealers who, by their behavior, brought about complaints and cast aspersions upon their co-religionists.

"Where is the shame to be focused?" asked Adam. "It is the Christians who forced us into these roles and they who issued a decree just last May 30, suspending payment of all debts to Jews!"

"It is in our *own* tradition that money lenders are condemned," Frenkel argued. "Only *He that putteth not out his money on interest,*" he invoked the Fifteenth Psalm, "*is entitled to sojourn in the Tabernacle of the Lord.*"

"That," countered Aaron, "is not the point of the resolution. I believe our new, middle class Jews are too consumed with securing acceptance by Gentiles to have compassion for those who have done their dirty work through generations of oppression.

"Pinkas, a pawnbroker in our ghetto, kept Jewish beggars from starving. The Christian decree wiped him out. Now he, too, must beg. Our community depended on old-clothes dealers because the merchants of Breslau wouldn't allow us, the best tailors in Europe, to sell new clothes. *Of course* these were odious occupations. *We hated them.* But they were the only way we could survive. Let us not now heap scorn on those who had to resort to them."

In the course of the month-long conference, father and son grew closer. But they differed. Aaron was heartened by recognition given to the concept of *Bildung*, development of the individual, and the tempering of political control by the Orthodox establishment. However, he was disturbed by the tone of the proceedings.

Adam was disgusted. "We groveled," he complained, "for rights that should be ours as men. We were led to the slaughter as tools of Napoleon's ambition! Think of it. We're giving up *our* nationhood for *his.*"

"It is not so simple," Aaron cautioned, "the Sanhedrin declared we have the right to be citizens of the country in which we live. Other nations will now compete for our allegiance and will have to grant us freedoms. They will let us worship as we choose."

"Papa, you're dreaming."

* * *

The havoc to French troops had been so severe that for six merciful weeks they regrouped and rested. Giuliano's letter caught up with

Jonah; he read and reread it, beaming like a newly delivered father. The boy he had raised would marry the woman he had conceived.

Reinvigorated, Jonah marched his new squadron of eager sixteen-year-old volunteers through unscarred forests to Danzig where, on March 18, they set siege. Each day, he commanded the firing of cannons against the walls of the citadel, tearing down barriers between him and his desire. Each night, he wrote greetings to Giuliano, Judith, his mother, Zelda, and finally, a carefully worded congratulations to Hadassah and Aaron.

*   *   *

From the heights of his royal palace at Kassel, Jerome Bonaparte emancipated the Jews of Westphalia and Silesia:

> *All our subjects, who profess the Mosaic Law, will enjoy in our land the same rights and freedom on a par with the rest of the subjects.*

"*The Jewish cult,*" Prince Jerome proclaimed:

> *must be subject to our supervision just as are all the other cults, so that there be no contradictions between the cult and the legislation, as well as the social ethics which have to serve as a guide for all peoples and to create a single political society.*

The Prince authorized The Royal Westphalian Consistory of the Mosaic Faith, based in his capital city of Kassel, to administer the spiritual affairs of all Westphalia and to assure that rabbis:

> *preach obedience to the laws, particularly those pertaining to the defense of the fatherland; they should teach that military service*

is a holy duty, the observance of which frees one of all religious rituals which are incompatible with this service.

David Frenkel was appointed the lay leader of the Royal Consistory. For as long as the French occupied Germany, his decrees would compel Orthodox Jews to abandon outmoded forms of liturgy, dress, and diet. In each city, he designated a single school to teach religion and Hebrew. For general education, everyone, Jewish and Gentile, was to be taught in German. He permitted worship in approved synagogues only, those organized to reform traditional Jews and bring back secular Jews into a modern mosaic.

*　　*　　*

Bolstered by a defense pact with Prussia, negotiated secretly with Friedrich William at Bartenstein on April 26, Czar Alexander marched 115,000 soldiers against Napoleon.

Jonah dug his squadron in against the assault.

The Grand Sanhedrin: Etching by Damame dé Martrait, Paris, 1807. From the HUC Skirball Cultural Center, Museum Collection, Los Angeles, CA; Photography by Lelo Carter.

XXI

A Woman of Valour

The gaunt old clerk, hunched in a frock coat, fumbled with his monocle as he ushered Judith into the most magnificent room she had ever seen. Lightly clad nymphs danced on the ceiling, above walls of gold. Velvet drapes were drawn back to tease light from a reluctant sun.

Herr Gauner stepped from behind his massive oak desk to press his lips to her hand and show her to a high-back chair with a satin cushion. Was this how Gentiles greeted strangers? She could not comprehend why the attorney had summoned her to his chambers.

"As his only heir," proclaimed the lawyer, "your father, Eleazar Pistron, left you everything he had."

Stunned to learn of her father's death, Judith could barely make sense of the words that droned from Herr Gauner's peculiar face. "Your father saved all his money, and in his final years, when the laws permitted it, he acquired a farm of forty acres with a house, barn, livestock, and a team of horses."

It was just outside the shtetl from which her mother had fled.

Assuring Judith that the will had provided for payment of his fee, the lawyer handed her the deed and all the papers she would need to study and showed her politely to a richly painted door with a porcelain doorknob.

Adam accompanied his sister to Ratibor. At Eleazar's grave, he gathered a minyan, chanted the Kaddish, and sat shivah with friends of the deceased. He came to love the Jews of Ratibor whose commitment to ancient tradition was immutable. Running the soil of the farm through his fingers, he felt the embrace of Eden.

Judith could never live here. Her heart was with Giuliano, in a different century, and they would dwell in a different world. When her brother came running with the news that the Rabbi of Ratibor had invited him to be his assistant, she knew what to do. In an act of love, Judith gifted the deed to Adam.

*   *   *

"Seven weeks after the people of Israel fled Egypt, "Aaron intoned, "they stood at Sinai to receive their spiritual freedom. *Shavuot,* the Festival of Weeks, exalts the budding of new life. We laud the sweetness of the Torah with the Song of Songs":

Thy lips, O my bride, drop honey —
   Honey and milk are under thy tongue
And the smell of thy garments is like the smell of Lebanon.
   A garden shut up is my sister, my bride;
A spring shut up, a fountain sealed.
   Thy shoots are a park of pomegranates,
With precious fruits......

After the last congregant left, Aaron drained the carafe of sweet wine. Inebriated from the celebration of fertility on the eve of Judith's wedding, he staggered up the stairs to his wife's bedchamber. Gazing hungrily at Hadassah, he chanted, first softly:

How beautiful are thy steps in sandals,
   O prince's daughter!
The roundings of thy thighs are like the links of a chain,
   The work of the hands of a skilled workman.

His voice rose as he stumbled, pursuing her about the room:

Thy navel is like a round goblet,
    Wherein no mingled wine is wanting;
Thy belly is like a heap of wheat
    Set about with lilies.

"No!" she cried, "This was never in our agreement!"
Now bellowing the Song, Aaron tugged at her bodice:

Thy two breasts are like two fawns.
    That are twins of a gazelle.
Thy neck is as a tower of ivory;
    Thine eyes as the pools in Heshbon…

He thrust himself at her. "I cannot touch you," she pulled away.
"I love Jonah. I have *always* loved Jonah! It is Jonah who is Judith's father. I belong to him. Forgive me, Aaron, forgive me," she sobbed.

Aaron's legs gave way, he fell to the floor, his very being crumbled. All those wistful, wasted years. He had adored Hadassah as a virgin queen, had recoiled at the iniquity of her former husband who had violated her under cover of a marriage forced by Prussian mandates. Ever since her return from Ratibor, he had been her protector.

He had honored her restored chastity by channeling his urges into degrading onanistic rituals. Now he cursed the semen spilled in vain, and damned the pride that had blinded him to her lasciviousness.

Making his way down the stairs, he groaned in the knowledge that she was not really his wife but belonged to a coarse, tempestuous rogue who played at being a great liberator. How ironic that Jonah was once his friend and defender.

He loved Judith as his own, the child of an innocent birth. What force of God or blood had drawn her to the man most like her real father? Was she destined to repeat the sins of her mother?

Long after the last candle sputtered into its glass, he sat in his study on the first floor of the Free School that, all his life, had been his home and was now his prison. He could not go upstairs. He lurched out into a drizzling darkness, headed for the shacks on the Oder where, years before, he and Nathan watched the whores.

*   *   *

Nathan and Sarah threw open their shutters to welcome the scent of spring. Rosalie awakened to the fragrance of lilacs. The odious sanitation ditch had been sealed by rocks and bricks that once formed the ghetto wall.

Across the river, wild strawberries climbed the hill to a purple-green grove of crabapple trees where scarlet flowers danced in slender white cups. In the crowded cemetery beneath their window, edelweiss clothed the graves of Ephraim, Natalie, and Nehemiah.

Sturdy pea shrubs guarded the entrance where the gatehouse once stood. On the avenue leading into town, dark green leaves of majestic linden trees framed clusters of modest white buds.

Aaron felt the touch of Joseph's hand upon his shoulder, welcoming him back from a deep and tortured sleep. Joseph knew. He had always known. Aaron had become his son in so many ways but his marriage to Hadassah was not to be. Joseph was grateful that Aaron, by Natalie, had provided him posterity in so fine a young man as Adam.

The two embraced, wept, recalled good times and bad, and sat staring beyond each other in long periods of quiet reverie, warmed by the piety of Natalie and chilled by the fire of Hadassah.

There was nothing, they agreed, that anyone could do now. As rabbis, they knew the importance of appearances; they had to get through the wedding. There would be time enough later to tell Judith and Giuliano.

*   *   *

Family, friends, and congregants filled the pews in the new home of the Landessynagoge, a onetime workhouse, set in a courtyard between Autonienstrasse and Wallstrasse.

Feeling debased and cast aside, Aaron dared not look at Judith, exquisite in the silk gown, a gift from Sarah and Nathan. He led her down the aisle to a future that held no place for him.

Taut with the awareness of her consummate vulnerability, Hadassah watched the husband she had deeply hurt bring her daughter to the chuppa. Afraid to stir, she held back even ordinary tears required of the mother of the bride.

As proud of his anticipated connubial bliss as he was of his conversion, Giuliano burst the buttons of the wedding suit made to his measurements in Amsterdam, where the tailor, engaged by Leib and Wilhelm, had not allowed for the groom's extraordinary hubris.

Grandfather Joseph, venerable and implacable, conducted the service in the grandeur of a tradition he would never forsake. *Let everyone know that the shattering of ghetto walls opened up Judaism to all, as was made manifest by the determination of this bright young man from the vanguard of the army of emancipation.* Invoking the wisdom of the sages in living Hebrew, he united a son of the revolution to a daughter of the ancient, battered tribe of Israel.

With his handsome dress boots, crafted by Pinkus, now an apprentice to the blind Hoshea, Giuliano crushed the marital goblet into thousands of facets reflecting the many dimensions of their love.

"*L'chaim!*" shouted Fr. Ludwig. "*L'chaim!*" echoed the guests.

Zelda sent elegant Dutch linens, with personal instructions to Judith, to use them for both board *and* bed on her wedding night. "It is," she confided, "an old family tradition."

All the lamb in Yankel Fleischmann's shop and all the potatoes that Myrna and Heinrich could haul, went into every pot that Leah could squeeze onto the heavy-duty stove. Rivkah supervised the creation (and steady replenishment) of her special Sunday stew, for the guests who lined up beyond the kitchen door.

Mordecai downed his fifth cup of wine. "These silver serving pieces," he announced to those holding out their plates, "are a family heirloom to be used at happy occasions."

Reaching around Feigel's hind quarters as she ladled out the casserole, his fingers gathering her skirts, he told of his relentless search throughout Germany for his wayward mother.

"God rest her soul," he pinched the shadchen's flesh, "she may well be decaying in the dirt of an unmarked pauper's grave."

As Feigel let out a squeal, Mordecai withdrew his arm, slipped it under a scarf cascading over Wilma's shoulder, and, without missing a beat, continued his tale. "In an antique store in Weimar," his hand working its stealthy way into the ample bosom of the butcher's wife, "I saw our family silver, which my poor mother must have been constrained to sell for the mundane necessities of life."

Wilma affected a blush and Mordecai a sigh of sorrow. "It was all of her I ever found."

In the modern style of the Gentiles, Chajjim held Rosalie by the waist, and together they attempted a waltz. Young men and women from the Wilhelmschule of Breslau, joined them in the new dance, to the tune, *Ach! Du lieber Augustin,* made popular at the Paris Opera by Gardel's *La Dansomanie.* Their elders politely averted their eyes.

Presents to the couple were piled alongside the neatly folded linen in a horse-drawn wagon, Adam's wedding gift from the farm he had received from Judith. When Hans, Vlad, and Stas stepped forward to present Judith and Giuliano with a specially bound collection of pamphlets, for which they and Jonah had once risked their lives, Hadassah could no longer contain herself.

She took Aaron by the hand. "It is time," she said, and with the bride and groom, they climbed into the wagon, waving cheerful goodbyes. Aaron led the mare past pea shrubs, onto the streets of the city.

Shielded by lofty linden trees, Hadassah told her daughter and son-in-law the story of those months, so many years ago, before Judith was born, and of her love affair with Jonah.

As they turned down into side streets, Aaron, his back to the three passengers, spoke somberly. "Judith, Jonah is your *real* father. Not Eleazar. Not I. I love you not one whit less, but you must know that the rascal who had to flee Breslau because he fought for our freedom, the man who raised your Giuliano, the sergeant who helped liberate us, who is fighting for us still, *he* is your father."

They were alongside the Silkworks when Judith climbed into the seat beside Aaron, grabbed the reins, and pulled the mare to a halt. Drenched with tears, she faced the man who had nurtured her from her earliest memories. "You are my father," she stroked his grey hair. "You will always be my father."

Judith had grown up with the belief that her mother's marriage to Eleazar was a means to avoid exportation to Poland, and that she was *their* child. She tried to sort it all out, electrified by the discovery that she was the creation of her mother's secret passion.

She dabbed Aaron's damp face with the folds of her gown. "Nothing between us is different, Papa. You are both my father."

Biting his tongue to keep from shouting, Giuliano ripped the remaining buttons off his suit and threw them to the sky. The man he loved most in life was the father of the woman he adored!

"You must know something else." Hadassah stepped from the wagon and walked around to address her daughter. "I respect and admire

Aaron. He has been a sensitive, fine father to you and to a whole, wonderful congregation. He is good and wise and gentle.

"But Judith," her mother looked up longingly at the roof of the Silkworks, "I love Jonah still. I have always loved him. I can no longer live the lie that has deprived Aaron and wounds everyone I cherish most."

Judith reached out to her mother. The bride's ring slid off her finger as the horse took off in a trot. Hadassah picked up the fallen ring and, from the steps of the Silkworks, watched her daughter disappear.

Fondling the ring, she read its inscription, "*A woman of valour,*" and smiled as she recalled the rest of the verse from PROVERBS: "*...who can find? For her price is far above rubies.*"

XXII

Deliverance

Snow stained with gunpowder disintegrated in spring rains and drained into the Vistula, as General Kalkreuth hoisted the white flag of surrender above the citadel at Danzig. Jonah's squadron marched behind Marshal Lefebvre through the Hohe Tor, down the stately Langegasse, into the heart of the medieval city.

Gone were the cheering crowds and brightly lit Liberty Trees that had greeted them in a different time and place. Now they hunted out sullen, frightened people hiding in cellars and fields.

Warriors had always confiscated food, personal necessities, and articles of battle from those they defeated. The legions of Napoleon took luxuries from the rich, commercial enterprises, and churches to support and reward victorious troops, send appropriations of war back to the motherland, and redistribute wealth to the peasants and urban poor of the lands they had conquered. Women were routinely bribed and coaxed into providing carnal pleasures.

Somewhere along the line, things had changed.

Forlorn, unable to intervene, Jonah watched frantic French and Italian foot soldiers pillage and loot all they could carry from grand patrician Hanseatic houses and go on to shops, cottages, pens, chicken coops and hovels, leaving even the poor with nothing to eat. Boys with acne and peachfuzz on their faces, and rifles on their shoulders, dropped pants smeared with feces, in which they had slept for months, and inflicted their filthy nakedness onto screaming maidens.

When had the forces of liberation become armies of conquest and occupation? How had the vanguard of the revolution degenerated into vassals of the empire?

He trembled with a profound sense of betrayal and tried to unravel his own role, to confront his culpability, to assuage his guilt. It was hopeless to appeal to Marshal Lefebvre to restrain the debauchery of his troops. The ogre of Austerlitz smiled with amusement from the balcony of the Junker-hof.

Jonah was responsible only for a squadron of dumb kids who had been dragged into combat from farms and slums, with promises of glory, and no preparation for death or trauma, with no sense of mission, of history, or of justice.

He could not find a way to tell them why they should be satisfied to sit in their shit, day after day, fearing it would be their last, and then, when the yoke was lifted, for a fleeting, ambiguous moment, *not* go wild and grab onto life in its crudest, most palpable form.

There would be a time when he would have to praise them for their sacrifice of arms and legs to serve some finer purpose. There would be letters to write with words of comfort and reassurance to mothers that their sons died good men and brave soldiers. On so many evenings after so many battles, he would have to report to his commander how their valor helped take a hill, when there were thousands of hills to take.

Now, he would have to get them through this ungodly mess and pray the war be over soon.

Jonah led his squadron east from Danzig to join the mighty army of Napoleon as it amassed for a final march against the Russian Imperial Guard.

*   *   *

Hadassah retrieved the ring from the gutter and walked in freedom through the dark city from her erstwhile rendezvous of love. But she would not be free to face the light of day in her home in the liberated ghetto.

Soon, Judith would join Giuliano in Kassel, where he had been dispatched to complete his service in the Royal Guard of Jerome Napoleon. Hadassah could not accompany her daughter to the city where her estranged husband would also relocate. Too humiliated to remain in Breslau, Aaron had accepted a position as David Frenkel's assistant at the Royal Westphalian Consistory of the Mosaic Faith in Kassel.

Adam would settle in Ratibor, return to his roots and plant new growth. Giuliano would endow him with Ephraim's legendary boots "so that German soil could be turned under proper Jewish feet." A man, especially one with a farm of his own, could do well in Ratibor. But Hadassah would not live with her son in so rural a setting, especially one so near the shtetl of her ordeal.

Jews had come a long way from the beginning of the century. Peddlers became salesmen or tradesmen, former beggars took over the pushcarts, and poverty was so contained that the Judengemeinschaft distributed welfare to members of the Mosaic faith, without regard to their religious practices. All those in want of health care could be served by the Israelitsche Krankenverpflegunganstalt.

There was no longer need for Hadassah's private social work.

As they evolved from the stark poverty of the ghetto, Jews exuded a spirit of economic enterprise. In the past, their involuntary separation, in widely dispersed walled enclaves had assured their oppression. Now, those very settlements became links that stretched across Europe, forging an international network, an advantage in the competitive world of commerce and industry.

Sarah and Nathan would help Hadassah enter that world. They would find work for her in Berlin and she could occupy the Friedlander house in Kreuzberg.

*   *   *

It had been a dull and tiring day for Censor No. Eleven. Few letters contained prurient passages or delicious obscenities. His eyes grew weary, trying to decipher the illegible handwriting of peasant soldiers. His fingers ached from manipulating scissors to slice open envelopes and excise any unknown or unreadable words lest they contain forbidden references.

It was late in his shift when he came upon a two-page epistle from a Dutch soldier with an Italian name to a French sergeant with a German name whom he incredulously addressed as "father."

The first page consisted of a dull description of his wedding (the chap provided no titillating details) and some outrageously fawning expressions of delight that this unlikely father was *also* his wife's father.

On his second page, the incestuous blackguard disclosed that he had been reassigned within the Royal Guard to Prince Jerome's castle, where he was taking his wife/sister and a rabbi (whom he also called father!) who was leaving the other father's lover. This presumed rabbi was allegedly coming to Kassel to assist a Royal effort to Germanize the Jews. (Who could possibly believe so transparent a ruse?) Censor No. Eleven was nobody's fool.

The writer was clearly describing troop movements, bound for Kassel, to a secret society in which key members were called "father." Page two went into a special file on Giuliano Regnini. *Military Intelligence.*

*   *   *

Under a bright, star-filled East Prussian sky, Jonah held the page cleared by the censor, electrified each time he read Guliano's account of Judith's discovery that he was her father.

Before dawn, he would pit his squadron against Cossacks and mujiks in one corner of the mightiest battle of the war. In the moments before the discharge of cannon fire, he found a calm in his son's message, and reflected on the reply he had posted, repeating to himself the two quatrains with which he had closed:

> *If I should not return, don't mourn;*
> *I've fought and been redeemed.*
> *Through thee my quest has been reborn*
> *Far more than I had dreamed.*
>
> *Protect thyself and her, my boy*
> *To whom thou pledged thy troth*
> *Know always that ye brought full joy*
> *To the father of ye both.*

*   *   *

At Friedland, on June 14, boys who never knew a cause gave their lives and limbs to slaughter peasants who fought for land they never held.

For twenty hours, Bonaparte pressed his raw recruits and regulars beyond exhaustion to a searing, resounding French victory.

"This is no longer warfare," the weary, defeated General Benningsen lamented to Archduke Constantine, "it is a veritable bloodbath."

There would be peace at last. The armistice was signed on June 22, 1807.

*   *   *

It was a long, dreary march back from Friedland, shunned by those they had conquered, from whom they had pillaged and whose women they had ravished. Reappearing at harvest time, they stripped the farms of produce. Returning through defeated cities, they stripped the people of their pride.

With each step, Jonah hated the war to which he had given himself. It was over and he was spent.

Before the ground grew cold, he was in his mother's arms.

*   *   *

From the Hatzfeldsche Palais in Breslau, Jerome Bonaparte ended vassalage in the Germany occupied by his forces. The government appointed by Napoleon to rule the Grand Duchy of Warsaw issued a new constitution abolishing serfdom.

As bondage crumbled throughout French dominated Europe, fearing that his discontented peasants might revolt, Friedrich William of Prussia signed the *Emancipation Edict*. On October 9, 1807, ancient distinctions between peasants, citizens and nobles for holding land and choosing one's occupation were removed. Noble estates, whose owners were impoverished, passed into the hands of entrepreneurs with money to develop them.

The *Municipal Ordinance* of the king extended the possibility of freedom to all who lived in the cities of Prussia, contingent on the approval of local burghers:

> ...rank, birth, religion and personal circumstances have no bearing upon the acquisition of civil rights...Soldiers, minors and Jews *may* be granted civil rights.

It was a short-lived era of deliverance. Jews who moved quickly into the burgeoning middle class were resented by the newly liberated peasants, who had nothing without their land. Those who stoked the flames of German nationalism to rise up against Napoleon, pointed to the avaricious Jew who had found favor in the French invasion.

The days of emancipation were fraught with fortune but they would be few.

*　　*　　*

Changes wrought by the French Revolution and the new economy took root in Amsterdam.

Jonah Schneider orchestrated the enterprise. Wilhelm Sacks arranged the financing through his father's bank. Pier Vandergryft negotiated terms with Dutch shipping companies for the importation of cotton from America. Leib and his parents, Rebekkah and Zacutus Meyer, drew on the network they had developed for the linen trade: the peasants of Overijssel provided the skilled labor, while the merchants of Rotterdam, Groningen and Zwolle furnished the markets.

But it was Jonah, whose knowledge of factory production of textiles and experience in management of personnel honed in the army, who made Amsterdam a center for the manufacture of fabrics.

Once *Schneider, Meyer, Vandergryft & Sacks* was underway and met with success in the marketplace, Jonah convinced his old comrade, Jean Claude Boudin (who had become a field marshall) that the plant could supply shirts, stockings, and undergarments to the troops. The contract provided jobs for families in the Jueden-Bort, a rich return to investors, and prodigious wealth to Jonah and his partners.

*　　*　　*

Hadassah had spent years matching the sizes of poor people in the ghetto to apparel which was donated by working families or discounted by peddlers of secondhand garments. Sarah and Nathan persuaded her to apply that skill to the expanding market of widows on fixed income and upwardly mobile Berliners wanting something a cut above home-knits, yet not able to afford a tailor of their own.

The Berlin Silkworks found Hadassah's refinement and attractiveness well suited to a position as sales clerk in its new retail store. It was the first shop in Berlin with fashionable "ready-to-wear" clothes.

Hadassah quickly developed a steady clientele. One stylish lady named Dolly, appeared with regularity every three months, always asked for her, and bought dozens of petticoats and twenty pairs of elegant silk stockings to go with each dress she selected for her friends in Jena.

Henrietta Hertz also became a regular customer. Her celebrated salon had dissolved on the death of her husband, and she now lived on a modest widow's pension.

She found in Hadassah a woman of culture beyond that of an ordinary shopgirl, and they became fast friends, sharing secrets of lost lovers and dreams of rescue.

The Holiday season had provided a brisk, prosperous, and grueling market. As Hadassah locked up the store on Christmas Eve, drained and desperately alone, Henrietta Hertz appeared with two tickets to that evening's performance of Gluck's *Orfeo ed Euridice,* a gift from some undisclosed admirer.

Curious and excited for her friend, Hadassah was pleased to join her at the Staatoper. They were directed to an usher in a velvet suit with lace cuffs who personally escorted them, up a private red-carpeted staircase, to a private box among those reserved for Prussian nobility and the affluent families of Berlin. With a bow and a click of his heels, he was gone, leaving them to speculate on the identity of Henrietta's suitor.

The opera house glimmered with candelabra that lit displays of holly and mistletoe, and fell upon finely dressed cognoscenti, aristocrats with their retinue, and generals with their wives.

On one side of them sat a baron with his mistress, on the other, a banker and his irrepressible, obese daughter against whom Henrietta held her fan lest she be recognized and drawn into some banal conversation.

Thankfully, she was rescued when the conductor tapped his baton; silence drowned the murmur, attendants snuffed the flames in all but the grand chandeliers, and slowly, majestically, the overture filled the house with its magic.

In the oratorio, Orfeo, grief-stricken by the death of his wife, Euridice, is permitted by Amor to descend to the other world to regain her, on one condition: he must not look at her until he has brought her back to earth.

But as Orfeo conducts Euridice through the caverns of Hades, his wife, convinced that he loves her no more because he will not look at her, becomes so distraught that Orfeo forgets the condition and gazes upon her.

When Orfeo, upon losing his adored one a second time, electrified the house with the haunting aria, *Che Faro senza Euridice,* Hadassah was blinded by uncontrollable tears of torment.

A confident, caressing hand behind a soft linen handkerchief lifted her tears away.

As Amor, on the stage below, moved by the great love of the protagonists, yields and returns them safely to earth, Jonah gazed upon the face of his beloved.

EPILOGUE

Charred, naked stalks of wheat jeered at the "Grand Army" of Napoleon. The largest battle force assembled in modern times trampled through ashes of a burnt September harvest. No longer able to live off the land, the emperor sent for provisions and pressed his troops ever forward across desolate, abandoned plains. Finding Moscow deserted, the troops sacked and burned the city, then lingered perilously for five weeks. Their supplies never came.

On October 18, 1812, Napoleon began his disastrous retreat, leaving half a million once spirited young men, artillery, cavalry, and all hope for a continental empire buried under relentless Russian snow, frozen in barren sheets of ice.

The shattering of Bonaparte's ambitions fueled German nationalism. On January 22, 1813, while his capital was occupied by French troops, Friedrich William slipped out of Berlin and rode to Breslau for a clandestine meeting with emissaries from Austria and Russia to plan the overthrow of Napoleon. With the czar's promise to restore its pre-1806 borders (including Silesia), Prussia again declared war on France. Friedrich William's appeal to the people to rise up against the French galvanized his subjects.

Now that they were citizens, German Jews rushed to prove their gratitude and allegiance to the fatherland, lined up to join the Prussian army, sang old German war songs, and marched into battle.

England and Sweden joined the campaign against Bonaparte. Guaranteed by the allies that their independence would be respected, the Dutch drove the French out of Holland.

Desperate, Napoleon had conscripted young men before their time and sent them into battle untrained and ill-equipped. French troops, alternately commanded to attack and forced to retreat were demoralized and in disarray. Bonaparte's generals could not stem the desertions or the tide of defeat.

As the cost in human lives mounted, Napoleon lost popular support at home. Although willing to make sacrifices to preserve their independence and their own land, French legislators opposed continuing the war on foreign soil.

Czar Alexander and Friedrich William entered Paris in triumph and restored France to the crown. On April 1, 1814, Vice Grand Elector Talleyrand convened the Senate which summarily appointed a provisional government, deposed Napoleon, and relieved soldiers from their oath of obedience to him. Louis XVIII, brother of the guillotined Louis XVI, was recalled from exile to become king under a new constitution. The battles of 1813 had resurrected Austria and Prussia as great powers.

The acceptance of Jews by Germans prior to the clash of battle was short-lived. Their swift rejection was mirrored in the posturing of Baron Karl Friedrich vom Stein. During the era of reform, under French influence, his municipal ordinance offered Jews in the cities hope for equality. After the fall of Napoleon, he declared, "No Jew could be accepted on the basis of full equality," and proposed that emancipation be revoked.

In 1812, the Burghers of Frankfort am Main had extracted an exorbitant payment from the Jews (equal to twenty times their annual special protection dues) in exchange for a grant of equal rights. But when German troops entered Frankfort, Vom Stein became its administrator. On July 19, 1814, he allowed the city to once again suppress Catholics and Jews, and to reestablish the ghetto.

In 1815, at the Congress of Vienna, Great Britain, Austria, Russia, Prussia, Spain, Portugal, Sweden, and Louis XVIII's France crushed the political ideas of the revolution and every trace of the free spirit that had inspired Europe since the Enlightenment.

The *Holy Alliance* formed by Russia, Prussia, and Austria reinstated the ties between church and state. Containing nine-tenths of all the Jews in Europe, these three states wielded oppression on a new scale, one that would not tolerate those who would not bow to Jesus.

To the idea of a Christian state, Napoleon's wars had added the dimension of a *national* state. In most German jurisdictions, Jewish emancipation had been granted by regimes installed by the French. Over anguished protests of Jewish delegates to the Congress of Vienna, rights conferred by occupying forces were invalidated. Freedom for most Jews was no longer protected by law.

Throughout Germany, Jews were now worse off than they had been before France crossed the Rhine. Prussia, having regained all its former provinces as well as parts of Westphalia, Saxony, and the Rhineland excluded Jews from civil and academic appointments, most professions, trades, and the army. Jews were supervised by eighteen different constitutions, were slaves to the monarch in the free cities, and restricted to individual provinces, not allowed to move from one to another.

All benefits of emancipation were denied to the 80,000 Polish Jews in the Prussian province of Poznan.

A wave of chauvinism and anti-Semitism throughout Prussia heaped scorn on Jews who had acquired their rights as a result of Napoleon's conquest. They were seen as opportunists and money-lenders who had profited from the French conquests. With the French safely back home, the rage of a robbed and betrayed people fell upon Jewish shoulders. The medievalism of German romantics, the economic protectionism of craftsmen and petty merchants, and the new nationalism joined in a common cry against the Jews.

*   *   *

In August, 1819, mobs chanting, *"Hep, Hep, Jews, Die a Miserable Death!"* stormed through streets in cities throughout Prussia, broke into Jewish homes and shops, pillaged, beat, and mutilated inhabitants. Joseph stepped out onto Wallstrasse reciting lines from Herder and Schiller that authenticated the Mosaic commitment to social justice, and to reason with the hoodlums. The thugs taunted the old schoolmaster, seized a menorah from the cobbler's shop, and battered him with it mercilessly. Joseph never recovered.

*   *   *

One safe haven was Holland, where Jewish emancipation became entrenched. Napoleon's consistories were abolished and rabbinical authority reaffirmed traditional Judaism. Jews were free citizens of the country.

With the dissolution of Napoleon's army, Jonah and Leib's textile business lost its prime customer for shirts, stockings, and undergarments. It was Giuliano's inventiveness that saved the company from collapse. Nostalgically roaming the docks of Amsterdam, he noted the increased frequency with which mariners mended sail cloths that had ripped from the strain of the new flexible rigs. Back at the plant, he directed the tight interweaving of the best cotton threads with the strongest linen to produce a firm, tough canvas. The company's sturdy sails would supply the merchant vessels of Holland.

*   *   *

Thrusting himself between Wilma's generous thighs, Mordecai's heart gave out. Parents shielded their children from the sight of Yankel the butcher hauling the merchant's carcass from his flat. Not to be humbled by the scandal, Rivkah insisted on a respectable burial. She retired to Berlin where her son ran the firm.

After his mother's death, three years later, Nathan accepted baptism in the Lutheran Church. (It was good for business). Shaken by the beating death of her father, Sarah held on to Judaism, even after her friend, Henrietta Hertz, converted to Christianity.

In the flush of first acceptance of Jews by the Germans, Chajjim Wolfssohn had changed his name to Heymann Lassal (after his home town of Laslo). He became a wholesale silk dealer and married Rosalie Friedlander. Their son, Ferdinand Lassalle, would lead the crusade for social democracy in Bismarck's united Germany.

*   *   *

The struggle for equal rights had expanded the awareness of Jews. It transformed the sense of being Jewish from an allegiance to religious forms to membership in a group with a shared heritage. Jews became increasingly identified by the culture that had evolved through their segregation and oppression.

When they were regarded as chiefly a religious group, Jews could enter the mainstream through conversion to Christianity or through changes in their own forms of worship. To the dedicated anti-Semite, however, assimilation had worked too well. Suspicious of apostates who became Christians for personal convenience rather than true belief (and anxious to keep Jews in their place), Friedrich William widened the gap. His 1823 edict ordered Jews to worship according to "traditional ritual without the least innovations in language, ceremony, prayers, and liturgy." Even sermons in German were prohibited. Everything reverted.

It would not be until 1871 that Jews would secure equal rights, a status that survived for sixty-two years, until Adolf Hitler and his eager followers tapped into the hatred of the Jew that had permeated centuries of German consciousness.

*　　*　　*

The Royal Westphalian Consistory of the Mosaic Faith in Kassel was closed, the Free School in Breslau was no more. Aaron retreated, pained and disconsolate, to his son's farm in Ratibor.

His last words to Adam were, "To be born and die a German Jew is to have lived a life of contradictions."

*　　*　　*

Jonah and Hadassah's love deepened. Levi da Costa's old house became their new island, nourished by the canals of Baruch Spinoza.

In 1829, on his sixtieth birthday, surrounded by grandchildren, Jonah reflected on his life and wrote:

We have many birthplaces:
The Garden of Eden, the Valley of the Nile, Jerusalem.
We are constantly reborn—
My blood flows from Breslau

But the fountain of my soul is Paris, where love is exalted
And where rationalism, emancipation from bondage,
Equality, and brotherhood of humanity
Burst forth and had its turbulent beginnings.

The people of Paris
began with tearing down walls of oppression, prisons, and ghettoes,

and we have picked up the pace against new bastilles and bastions
Finding love in liberation, becoming liberated through love.

At Notre Dame in Paris there is a marker,
and at every kilometer you step away from Ile de la Cité
there is another kilometer stone to tell you how far you have come
From Our Lady.

We pause with recognition at each kilometer stone we reach,
Proud that we have advanced from a source that set us on our life,
And those who have helped us along the way, celebrate
that we have come with them, thus far.

No person ever makes the journey alone.
Those whose bodies created us shape our capacities to venture.
So many others fill us with reasons and dreams and urges to go on.

People we love point us in the directions we take,
Teach us how to climb hills and cross rivers,
Give us our road maps and backpacks,
And nurture and enrich us along the way.

And at each kilometer stone we pause and celebrate,
Sensing how far we have come,
Recalling the bumps and delights,
The narrow scrapes and transforming experiences,
And thanking those who have helped to bring us to this point.

We never know how many more kilometer stones we will reach,
But as our passage nears the sea, we linger more with each step
Savoring the moment,
Finding love in liberation, becoming liberated through love.

GLOSSARY

*(words are from the Hebrew or
Yiddish unless otherwise indicated)*

Adonai: In the Bible, there are many words designating God. The most popular is the Tetragrammaton consisting of the four consonants, *Yod, Heh, Vav, Heh,* punctuated to be pronounced *Jehovah* but read traditionally as *Adonai.*

Aleph, bet, gimel; chet, vet, raysh and dahlet:

Names given to specific Hebrew consonants.

Ashkenazim: Jews of central and eastern Europe; their vernacular is Yiddish.

Auslander: German for a foreigner.

Bar mitzvah: A boy who reached his thirteenth birthday and is thereby duty-bound to observe the commandments of the Torah and is subject to punishment for his misdeeds. Also used to designate the religious initiatory rite and celebration of the attainment of maturity by a Jewish boy.

bris: Ceremony for circumcision of the male, performed as "the seal of God" to embody the obligation for Jews to observe the Covenant between God and Israel.

charoses: A condiment made of nuts, fruits, and spices mixed with wine, eaten at the *Seder* to symbolize mortar used by Jewish slaves in building the pyramid.

cholilleh: A folk expression for "God forbid that should happen."

chmallyeh: A severe blow or clout.

chuppa: A canopy under which the bride and groom take their marital vows.

daven: To pray.

Freiheit, Gleichheit, und Bruderschaft:

German for "Liberty, Equality & Fraternity"

Gaststatte: German for Public House, restaurant.

gozlin: One who outwits others.

Halakah: Rabbinical codification of Jewish law and accumulated jurisprudence.

Hassidim: "The pious," the name of a movement that spread throughout eastern Europe in the eighteenth century, begun by Israel ben Eliezer, the "*Baal Shem Tov*," a mystic who preached a folk gospel different from the rabbinical emphasis on formal learning. Instead, the Baal Shem Tov sang the praises of simple faith, joyous worship, and celebrated everyday pleasures through ecstatic songs and dances.

Judengasse: The main street in most German Jewish ghettoes

Judengemeinschaft: Organization which ran everything, taxed all the residents of German ghettoes, and represented the Jews to outside authorities.

Kaddish: The prayer for the dead.

Kehillah: The corporate body of the Jewish community in Polish settlements.

knish: Little dumplings filled with groats, grated potatoes, onions, chopped liver, or cheese.

Knishery: A bakery that produces knishes.

Krankenverplegunganstalt: German for institution for taking care of the sick or wounded.

L'chaim: To Life! A popular toast.

mensch: An upright, decent, honorable person.

Midrash: An interpretation of the Holy Scriptures, usually by a rabbi: a parable, allegory, illustrative story, or folktale that spoke directly to the common people.

mikvah: A pool or bath-house maintained by the Jewish community for ritual purification.

minyan: Ten male Jews (who must have reached their thirteenth birthday) required to conduct any religious service.

Misnagdim: "Opponents," applied to those who opposed the Hassidim (see **above**).

mitzvah: A divine commandment, it also means a meritorious act, one that expresses God's will; a virtuous, kind, ethical deed.

oneg shabbat: A term used to designate the Sabbath joy experienced through singing and instruction over the third Sabbath meal; adapted to refer to Saturday afternoon genial get-togethers.

payess: The untrimmed sideburn-locks and unshorn ear curls worn by orthodox Jewish men.

pushke: The container in which money is deposited for charity.

rebbe: The spiritual leader of a Hassidic group, not necessarily ordained; distinguished from a *rabbi* who is one learned in Jewish law, graduate of a seminary, who teaches in academies or synagogues. While both may perform the standard functions of a clergyman, the *rebbe* is often venerated and may even inherit his role, the *rabbi* is an employee of the academy or synagogue and enjoys no priestly privileges.

rebbitsin: The wife of a rabbi.

schalet: A casserole, a one-meal dish consisting of meat, potatoes, and vegetables. Often, though not always, cooked on a slow stove all day Friday to be ready for Sabbath, a day on which cooking is forbidden.

seder: Meaning "order of procedure," the term is used broadly to refer to the combination banquet and religious service commemorating the Passover, the flight from Egypt.

Sephardim: Jews from Portugal, Spain, Southern France, North Africa, and the Middle East(many of those from Spain and Portugal fled to Holland, Northern France, England, and their colonies at the time of the Inquisition); their vernacular is Ladino.

Shabbat: The Sabbath, seventh day of the week, a day of rest. Like all days in the Jewish calendar, it runs from sundown, the appearance of three stars(in this case, on Friday)through sundown of the next day (Saturday).

Shadchen: A professional matchmaker.

Shivah: The first seven solemn days of mourning for the dead.

shochet: The authorized slaughterer of animals, according to kosher requirements.

Sheloshim: The first thirty days after a funeral which are observed by mourners.

shul: Synagogue; the center of Jewish communal life where day and night men sat, read, prayed, studied, discoursed and debated. While the word, "Temple" classically refers only to the First or Second Temple of ancient Jerusalem, popular usage invokes the term almost interchangeably with shul or synagogue.

shtetl: A small town or village in which most or all of the inhabitants were poor, fundamentalist Ashkenazic Jews.

Sukkot: A thanksgiving holiday, held at the time of the full moon, when crops have been harvested. For the week, a pious family eats its meals in a *sukkah*, or booth set up out-doors, roofed with branches so the stars may be seen from inside, decorated with flowers and fruit.

tallis: A prayer shawl, used by men at religious services.

Talmud: A compendium of rabbinical thought on law, theology, ethics, poetry, diet, and guides to everyday living. It consists of the *Mishna*, a record of learned debates, dialogues, conclusions, oral law, and commentaries codified about 200 A.D.,and the *Gemara*, commentaries upon the Mishna by Palestinian and Babylonian Scholars.

Torah: The Pentateuch, the first five books of the Bible, the written record of the revelation associated with Moses and Sinai. It derives from *yarah*, meaning to direct or teach, and thus denotes divine teaching.

Tikkun olan: To mend, repair, and transform the world.

tsedrayter: A confused man.

tzedaka: The obligation to establish justice by being just, righteous, compassionate, and, above all, by helping one's fellow being.

yenta: A gossipy woman.

Yeshiva: A rabbinical college or seminary.

Yeshiva bucher: A young man who is a student at a Yeshiva.

Yom Kippur: The Day of Atonement, the most solemn of Jewish holidays on which Jews fast, confess, and pray for forgiveness of their transgressions.

Readings from the Torah are followed by the story of the prophet Jonah, whose theme is God's mercy even to the wicked city of Nineveh, a mission he initially shunned.

Only after Jonah realized that his avoidance of the direction set for him by God brought havoc on him and those about him did he re-set his course. Tossed into the sea and into the mouth of the leviathan to save those others, he experienced turmoil and rededicated himself. He was returned to the course initially set out for him.

The keynote of the concluding Yom Kippur service is "Open the gates to our prayers, Oh God, as the day wanes."

And then, the gates, as in this story, are opened.

BIBLIOGRAPHY

H.G. Adler, *Jews in Germany*, University of Notre Dame Press, Notre Dame, IN 1960.

Archibald Alison, *History of Europe from the Commencement of the French Revolution to the Restoration of the Bourbons*, William Blackwood & Sons, London, 1849.

Nathan Ausubel, *Pictorial History of the Jewish People*, Crown Publishers, New York, 1954.

Leo Baeck Institute, *Year Books*.

Thomas Carlyle, *The French Revolution*, Charles Scribner's Sons, New York, 1837.

Simon Dubnov, *History of the Jews From Cromwell's Commonwealth to the Napoleonic Era*, Translated from the Russian, Fourth Definitive Revised edition by Moshe Spiegel, Thomas Yoseloff, Publisher, Cranbury, N.J., 1971.

Dutch Jewish History, Proceedings of the Symposium on the History of the Jews in the Netherlands, November 28 - December 3, 1982, Tel Aviv, Hebrew University of Jerusalem, 1984.

Encyclopaedia Brittanica, Eleventh Edition, Cambridge, England, at the University Press, 1910.

Encyclopaedia Judaica, Keter Publishing House Ltd, Jerusalem, 1971.

J. G. Fichte, *Beitrage zur Berichtigung des Urteils des Publikums uber die Franzosische Revolution...*, *Fichte's Samtliche Werke*, Berlin, 1846 (the citation appearing on page 226, above, may be found at vol. 3, pp.147-148).

Ruth Gay, *Jews of Germany - A Historical Portrait*, Graphics-Halliday, West Hanover, MA, 1992.

H. M. Graupe, *The Rise of Modern Judaism, An Intellectual History of German Jewry, 1650-1942*, Robert Krieger Publishing Co., Huntington, N.Y., 1979.

Gunter Elze, *Breslaum Biographie einer deutschen Stadt*, Verlag Gerhard Rautenberg, Leer, Germany, 1993.

H. Holtzhauer, ed., *Dichtung und Wahrheit, Goethes Werk*, Berlin and Weimar, 1966.

The Holy Scriptures, Delair Publishing Co. Melrose Park, IL, 1988

Jewish Encyclopedia, Funk & Wagnall, New York, 1916.

Jacob Katz, *Emancipation and Assimilation Studies in Modern Jewish History*, Farnborough, Gregg, 1972.

Friedrich Gottlieb Klopstock, "An den Kaiser," *Samtliche Werke*, Leipzig, 1855 (the quotation cited on p.103, above, is found at vol.4, pp. 262-263).

Alfred D. Low, *Jews in the Eyes of the Germans*, Institute for the Study of Human Issues, Phila. PA 1979.

Marvin Lowenthal, *The Jews of Germany*, Longmans, Green and Co., New York, 1936.

Emil Ludwig, *Napoleon*, Garden City Publishing, New York, 1926.

Jehuda Reinharz and Walter Schatzberg, eds, *The Jewish Response to German Culture From the Enlightenment to the Second World War*, University Press of New England, Hanover, 1985.

Leo Rosten, *The Joys of Yiddish*, McGraw Hill, New York, 1968.

Cecil Roth, *History of the Jews*, Shocken Books, New York, 1963.

Gerhard Scheuermann, *Das Breslau-Lexikon*, Laumann-Verlag Dulmen, Germany, 1994.

Friedrich Schiller, *Samtliche Schriften*, Goedeke, ed., Stuttgart, Germany, 1867.

Alan Schom, *Napoleon Bonaparte*, Harper Collins, 1997.

Friedrich Schleiermacher, *Aphorismen zur Kirchengesichte, gesammelte Werke*, Reimer (ed.), Berlin, Germany, 1843.

Gerald Lyman Soliday, *A Community in Conflict: Frankfurt Society in the Seventeenth and Early Eighteenth Centuries*, Brandeis University Press, 1974.

David Sorkin, *The Transformation of German Jewry, 1780-1840*, Oxford University Press, New York, 1987.

Baruch Spinoza, *Treatise on Religion and the State;*
                  The Improvement of the Intellect;
                  The Ethics;
                  Treatise on Politics;
Everyman's Library, J. M. Dent & Sons, Ltd., London 1910.
                  Philosphy & Theology
Ernest Rhys, ed., Everyman's Library, London, 1913.

Zosa Szajkowski, *Jews and the French Revolutions*, Ktav Publishing House, New York, 1970.

H. Treitschke, "Ein Wort Uber Unser Judentum" in *Preussiche Jahrbucher*, Nov., 1879.

The Universal Jewish Encyclopedia, Universal Jewish Encyclopedia, Inc., New York, 1941.

N. Waldman *Goethe and the Jews*, New York, 1934.

H.G. Wells, *The Outline of History*, Triangle Books, New York, 1940.

Robert S. Wistrich, *Socialism and the Jews: The Dilemmas of Assimilation in Germany and Austria-Hungary*, Associated University Presses, London & Toronto 1982.

Michael M. Zachin, *Jews in the Province of Posen*, a thesis submitted in partial fulfillment of the requirements for a Ph. D. in the Dropsie College for Hebrew and Cognate Learning, Philadelphia, 1939.

Mehdi Zana, *Prison No. 5*, Blue Crane Books, Watertown, MA, 1994.

ABOUT THE AUTHOR

 Ralph David Fertig is a retired federal Administrative Judge. Although he has issued countless opinions, published many articles on human rights, social welfare, politics, and the law, and the historic background for this book is faithful to the facts, it is his first acknowledged work of fiction.

In the spirit of *Jonah*, Fertig has been a life long crusader for social justice. (He is seen here in Chiapas, among the Zappatistas). Early in the civil rights movement, he sat in, marched, picketed, formed the Chicago Freedom Action Committee, became a Freedom Rider, and upon returning from Selma, was asked to leave his job as Research Director of the Chicago Commission on Youth Welfare by Richard Daley because his activism unsettled the Mayor. He moved to Washington, D.C. to run a settlement house in the Anacostia ghetto and transmuted it into a center for social action, mobilizing residents to demand jobs, housing, and welfare rights, bringing Martin Luther King and other human rights leaders to Southeast D.C., and initiating programs that became models for the "War on Poverty."

For his efforts to tear down the ghetto walls in D.C., the *Washington Post* dubbed him the "conscience of Washington[1]." Robert Kennedy hailed him for the "…efforts that he has made and the inspiration that he has given to people."[2]

As Washington area President of the National Association of Social Workers and a member of the Leadership Conference on Civil Rights, he fought for passage of the Civil Rights Acts. Fertig serves on the national board of Americans for Democratic Action, presided over its Greater Washington and Los Angeles chapters, and is slated to receive its Eleanor Roosevelt Award in 2001. He is President of the Humanitarian Law Project, a non-governmental organization in the Human Rights Subcommission of the United Nations, through which he campaigns for the rights of Kurds and oppressed peoples of the Americas. He serves as a Trustee and Chairman of the Social Justice Committee of University Synagogue in Los Angeles, and on the boards of Americans for Peace Now and the Progressive Jewish Alliance.

In the essence of *Aaron*, Fertig sought truth in academia. His Columbia Master's thesis on Black-Jewish Relations, and his post-graduate work at the University of Chicago examined race and class. But it all spilled over into student activism in organizing resistance to McCarthyism. When he returned to UCLA for his JD, he fought to sustain the University's commitment to affirmative action. Fertig taught part time at Georgetown, UCLA, USC, and the Universities of Illinois, Indiana, Maryland, and the District of Columbia. For his teaching and work as a civil rights lawyer, he received the Clarence Darrow Award from Peoples College of Law.

His entrepreneurial self has been more like that of *Sarah* than *Nathan*. He ran the combined anti-poverty programs for the city and county of Los Angeles, has consulted with the Office of Economic Opportunity, Peace Corps, Departments of Housing and Urban Development, Health, Education and Welfare, and Labor.

His *Hadassah* is Marjorie Hays Fertig, whose idealism and grace was manifest in the text and in her behind-the-scenes coaching, critiquing, and confirmation of every clause and its context. Some of *Giuliano* might be found in his son, David, a civil rights attorney in Pasadena. Those familiar with his other four children might discern similarities with other characters in the book.

His mother's family worked in the Berlin silk industry and opened the first ladies' ready-to-wear shop in that town. His father's family claims descent from the union of *Rosalie Friedlander* and *Heymann Lasall* (his father was an avid leader in the Young LaSalle League in Breslau and later in New York) and from the Fertig farm in Ratibor.

He has never known *Madam Rosa*, but perhaps his paternal grandmother who ran off to America......

---

1. *Washington Post* Editorial, July 24, 1973.
2. U.S. Senate Committee on Labor and Public Welfare, April 27, 1967.

MODERN NOISE, FLUID GENRES

Modern Noise, Fluid Genres

POPULAR MUSIC IN INDONESIA,

1997–2001

Jeremy Wallach

THE UNIVERSITY OF WISCONSIN PRESS

This book was published with support from
Bowling Green State University,
the Gustave Reese Publication Fund
of the American Musicological Society, and
the Center for Southeast Asian Studies
at the University of Wisconsin–Madison.

The University of Wisconsin Press
1930 Monroe Street, 3rd Floor
Madison, Wisconsin 53711-2059

www.wisc.edu/wisconsinpress/

3 Henrietta Street
London WC2E 8LU, England

1   3   5   4   2

Printed in the United States of America

Library of Congress Cataloging-in-Publication Data
Wallach, Jeremy.
Modern noise, fluid genres : popular music in Indonesia, 1997–2001 / Jeremy Wallach.
p.   cm. — (New perspectives in Southeast Asian studies)
Originally presented as the author's thesis (Ph. D.) — University of Pennsylvania, 2002.
Includes bibliographical references and index.
ISBN 978-0-299-22900-9 (cloth: alk. paper)
ISBN 978-0-299-22904-7 (pbk.: alk. paper)
1. Popular music — Indonesia.   I. Title.   II. Series.
ML3502.I5W35   2008
781.6309598 — dc22
2008011974

FOR

JONATHAN

Nations are mythical creatures, gaseous, and sometimes poisonous. But they start to solidify when diverse people have moments when aspirations coincide.

Binyavanga Wainaina

CONTENTS

ILLUSTRATIONS

Tables

Figures

PREFACE

Modern Noise, Fluid Genres is a study of Indonesian popular music and its audiences written by an American anthropologist and amateur musician. The book is divided into two parts. The first half examines the cultural dynamics of particular sites for the production, mediation, and reception of popular music, including record stores, recording studios, video shoots, roadside food stalls, and other public and private spaces where music is performed, consumed, discussed, and debated by Indonesians from all walks of life. The second half of the book investigates specific live performance events as occasions when musical production, mediation, and reception processes occur simultaneously. The chapters in that half focus on three major youth-oriented popular music genre categories: dangdut, pop, and "underground" rock.

Through the book's focus on concrete sites and practices, I attempt to illuminate the complex affective politics of identification and exclusion that characterizes responses to contemporary popular music genres among people from different social classes in Indonesia. I conclude that access to globally circulating musics and technologies has neither homogenized nor extinguished local music making in Indonesia. Rather, I argue that this access has provided Indonesians with a wide range of creative possibilities for exploring their existential condition in a time of political transition and heated debate over Indonesia's future as a multiethnic, democratizing nation in a globalizing world. Moreover, the book posits that the popular, inclusive nationalism implicit in nearly all national Indonesian popular musics provides a viable alternative to the various forms of extremism and exclusivism (religious, regional, ethnic) that continue to threaten national integration, social justice, and democracy in post–New Order Indonesia.

In the acknowledgments to *The Religion of Java,* a landmark study of Javanese village life during Indonesia's last great experiment with democracy, Clifford Geertz (who sadly passed away while I was completing the final revisions of this book) thanks the many ordinary Indonesians who assisted him in his research and wrote of his "hope that in some way [his] book [might] contribute to the realization of their aspiration to build a strong, stable, prosperous, and democratic 'New Indonesia'" (1960, x). I humbly wish the same for the present study, which portrays life in Indonesia once again during a time of cultural ferment, political upheaval, and cautious hope for a more just and democratic future. It is my hope that this book will advance scholarly understandings of Indonesian national culture as it evolves in the current era, and that it will serve as a model for ethnographically grounded popular music research in contemporary urban settings throughout the world. Most of all, I hope it will bring to the attention of the scholarly community the diversity, creativity, and exuberance of Indonesian popular music and reveal how an informed understanding of this music can forcefully challenge ossified, monolithic Western preconceptions of Muslim and Asian cultures.

ACKNOWLEDGMENTS

This ethnographic study, like any other, would have been impossible without the aid and support of a vast number of individuals and organizations. The length of the following list of thank-yous attests to the amount of assistance and encouragement I enjoyed during the long process of researching and writing this book.

First, I am forever indebted to a multitude of figures in the Indonesian music world for their input, gracious hospitality, and boundless patience and generosity with their time and their craft. I wish to thank in particular Edy Singh, Cahyo Wirokusomo, Edo, Donny, Patty, Raymond, Sonny, Pak Cecep, and Pak Hassanudin at 601 Studio Lab; Pak Paku of Maheswara Musik; dangdut artists Oppie Sendewi, Iyeth Bustami, Titiek Nur, Lilis Karlina, and Murni Cahnia; Dessy Fitri; Bagus Dhanar Dana; Mas Puput; Pak Jerry Bidara; Yukie Pas; Richard Mutter, Helvi Sjarifuddin, and Uki of Reverse Outfits; Robin Malau and Arian Tigabelas; Dwiki Dharmawan; Trie Utami; Pra Budidharma and family; Wendi Putranto; Nugie; Adam Joswara; Rully Rohmat; Andy Atis, Amanda, and Anggie; Benino Aspiranta and Titie; Sabdo Mulyo; Melly Goeslaw and Anto Hoed; Ari Lasso; Candra Darusman; Jan Djuhana and Lala Hamid of Sony Music Entertainment Indonesia; George Effendi; Iwan Fals; and the late Harry Roesli. Many thanks also to the following bands and their management: Bantal, Betrayer, Cherry Bombshell, Eternal Madness, Karnaval, Koil, Krakatau, Kuch Kuch Hota Hai, Netral, OMEGA Group, Pas, Pemuda Harapan Bangsa, Potret, Puppen, Ramirez, Samudera, Slowdeath, Soekarmadjoe, Step Forward, Tengkorak, Tor, and Trauma. *Ribuan terima kasih, dan saya mohon maaf sebesar-besarnya kalau ada yang saya lupa untuk menyebut di sini.*

I am grateful as well to Dean Tanete Adrianus Pong Masak, Dean A. Agus Nugroho, and the other members of the Faculty of Business Administration, Atma Jaya University (Jakarta), for their logistical support and intellectual engagement with my project. Thanks are also due to Ian White, an Australian filmmaker creating a documentary on the Balinese underground music scene, for sharing his unreleased film footage with me. I am grateful to the regulars at three *warung* in Santa,

Kebayoran Baru, South Jakarta, for sharing their time, wit, and music. Last, I would like to extend my heartfelt thanks to Ahmad Najib, Guntoro Utamadi, Paramita Prabarathayu, Donny Suryady and family, and Haryo Koconegoro and family for their friendship, hospitality, and invaluable assistance with my research.

In the United States, I first and foremost thank my dissertation adviser Greg Urban and the other members of my dissertation committee, Sandra Barnes, Webb Keane, and Carol Muller, for their support, guidance, and helpful suggestions during the lengthy process of researching and writing the doctoral thesis upon which this work is based. I am also grateful to Randal Baier, Charles Capwell, Steve Ferzacca, the late Clifford Geertz, Ellen Koskoff, René T. A. Lysloff, Peter Manuel, Thomas Porcello, Guthrie Ramsey, Marina Roseman, Peggy Reeves Sanday, Anthony Seeger, Gary Tomlinson, Deena Weinstein, Sarah Weiss, Deborah Wong, and Philip Yampolsky for their intellectual inspiration and encouragement. I owe a special debt of thanks to R. Anderson Sutton for his support over the years, and for inviting me to submit a manuscript to the University of Wisconsin Press. I wish to thank as well my three undergraduate mentors: Richard Freedman, Wyatt MacGaffey, and Bill Hohenstein. A musicologist specializing in the French Renaissance, a British social anthropologist, and a maverick sociologist, these three scholars first set me on the path that led years later to the completion of this book.

I owe a debt of gratitude to David Harnish for his review of an earlier draft of chapter 1 and to David Novack for his detailed, insightful comments on an earlier version of chapter 4. I would also like to thank profusely Benedict R. O'G. Anderson, R. Anderson Sutton, Andrew Weintraub, and Sean Williams for their extensive feedback on earlier versions of the entire manuscript, and for their invaluable advice on translations and a wide range of Indonesian cultural, musical, and linguistic topics. Sharon Wallach patiently read every single word of this manuscript multiple times and, with her insightful and incisive comments and corrections, helped make this book far better than it otherwise would have been. Special thanks also go to Maxine Barry and Ken Jurek for their assistance with the music compact disc that accompanies this volume.

Research and travel funds were provided by the United States Indonesia Society and by the University of Pennsylvania Department of Anthropology. I am grateful for their assistance. During my years of graduate study, my fellow students at the University of Pennsylvania in the Department of Anthropology and the Department of Music provided me with intellectual stimulation and camaraderie, especially José Semblante Buenconsejo, Matthew Butterfield, Jacqueline Fewkes, Paul D. Greene, Deanna Kemler, Alexander "Lex" Rozin, Nastia Snider, Matthew Tomlinson, Elyse Carter Vosen, and especially Sarah Morelli. I will always be grateful for their friendship and for their thoughtful comments on my work, often requested at the last minute. Friends and colleagues from other departments and universities who kindly provided input, advice, and suggestions for this project include Harris M. Berger, Jennifer Connolly, Nicholas Crosson, Sara L. M. Davis, Kai Fikentscher, Peter Furia, Andrew Jewett, Eric A. Jones, Keith Kahn-Harris, Elisa von Joeden-Forgey, Richard Miller, Gabriel Morris, Norman Morrison, Sarah Moser, Jennifer Munger, Karl von Schriltz, Patricia Tang, Emily Vartanian, Michael Vartanian, Cynthia Po-man Wong, Juliet Wunsch, and the late Lise Waxer. Any shortcomings that remain in the text are entirely my fault.

At the Department of Popular Culture at Bowling Green State University I found a collegial and supportive environment in which to pursue this project. I thank all my past and present colleagues in Popular Culture and those in several other departments at BGSU as well, especially fellow ethnomusicologist and Indonesia specialist David Harnish in the College of Musical Arts, for their input and valued intellectual comradeship. I would also like to thank my hardworking graduate research assistants, Wei-Ping Lee, Michael Mooradian Lupro, and Adam Murdough, for scholarly and editorial assistance ably provided. Adam's work was so impressive that I asked him if he could prepare this book's index. He agreed, and did the job with his usual care and thoroughness. Finally, I would like to extend my thanks to all my students over the years, in particular the participants in my spring 2004 and 2006 graduate seminars on genre and authenticity in world popular music studies and the students in my spring 2005 graduate proseminar on popular music scholarship.

Portions of this work have been presented in various forums, including colloquia at the University of Wisconsin–Madison School of Music, the University of Pennsylvania Department of Anthropology, the Haverford College Center for Humanities, and the Bowling Green State University Department of Popular Culture. I am grateful for the feedback I received on those occasions. I am especially indebted to my fellow participants at the Royal Netherlands Institute Seventeenth Annual International Workshop on South-East Asian Studies, particularly organizers Bart Barendregt and Kees van Dijk, for their detailed comments on my research and ideas.

The publication of this work was made possible by subvention grants from the American Musicological Society, the Bowling Green State University Scholars Assistance Program, and the Center for Southeast Asian Studies, University of Wisconsin–Madison. I am most grateful for the support of these organizations. I would also like to convey my heartfelt thanks to Gwen Walker, Sheila Moermond, Barb Wojhoski, and the rest of the staff at the University of Wisconsin Press who worked on this volume for their patience and invaluable assistance bringing the project to fruition. Portions of the following work have been published in earlier forms. The material in chapter 3 first appeared in the journal *Indonesia* (volume 74, October 2002), and portions of chapter 4 were published in the edited collection *Wired for Sound* (Greene and Porcello 2005). I thank Cornell University Press and Wesleyan University Press for kindly granting permission to reprint parts of these articles.

I would like to thank my parents, Paula and Lawrence Wallach, my brothers Matthew, Ted, and Jordan, my sisters-in-law Cristina, Leah, and Diana, my grandmother Sara Shapiro, and the rest of my family for their support and for believing in me and cheering me on through many long years of study.

Finally, this book is dedicated to my wonderful son, Jonathan, who one day I hope will enjoy reading it.

MODERN NOISE, FLUID GENRES

Introduction

A BRIEF HISTORY
OF POPULAR MUSIC AND SOCIETY
IN INDONESIA

This book is an ethnographic investigation of Indonesian popular music genres and their producers and listeners during a period of dramatic political and cultural transformation. Through a ground-level examination of the production, consumption, and discursive representations of popular musics in Indonesia, I hope to shed light on complex cultural processes that play a vital role in contemporary young urban Indonesians' imaginings of the Indonesian nation, its place in the world, and its future. Furthermore, I intend to show how young Indonesian women and men from various social classes use popular musics to reconcile their disparate allegiances to and affinities for local, global, and national cultural entities.

The notion that cultural production and reception are linked to identity formation has become a commonplace in cultural studies, anthropology, ethnomusicology, and other human sciences. Such a premise suggests that the *actual encounters* of producers and consumers with particular artifacts—in situations both mundane and spectacular—should be taken seriously by scholars wishing to explore the construction of identity in particular times and places (see Porcello 1998). This ethnography, then, aims to highlight the social and experiential context of subjects' encounters with cultural objects, thus grounding its interpretations of those objects in the details of concrete settings and everyday experience. The interpretations of Indonesian popular musics contained in these pages are also informed by another key insight of cultural studies: due to the contested nature of its meanings and ownership, popular culture (especially popular music) is an important site of cultural struggle, and it can reveal a great deal about gender, class, and other social divisions characterized by unequal power relations operating in a society (see Frith 1981; Frith, Straw, and Street 2001; Middleton 1990; Ross and Rose 1994; and Walser 1993).

Inspired by recent work on the production, circulation, and reception of mass-produced cultural artifacts in modern societies (e.g., Anderson [1983] 1991, 1998; Appadurai 1996; Mahon 2004; Mazzarella 2003; F. Miller 2005), this study takes a "sonic materialist" approach to popular musics in Indonesia, examining the processes by which musical sounds—understood as forms of audiotactile material culture—are created, mediated, and disseminated, and the ways in which these sounds become meaningful in diverse everyday contexts.[1] Particularly valuable to this project is anthropologist Greg Urban's account of the production, discursive framing, and social circulation of cultural forms in modern complex societies (2001). Urban characterizes contemporary, mass-mediated societies as operating under a "metaculture of modernity" in which cultural forms (such as popular songs) are both *disseminated* as mass-produced artifacts (such as music recordings) and *replicated* through the creation of similar yet novel forms (for example, new songs in a familiar style). Urban argues that unlike societies that operate under a "metaculture of tradition," which value the precise reproduction of expressive forms (such as the recitations of myths), contemporary complex societies emphasize innovative elements when producing cultural objects, and the successful circulation of culture in such societies depends on these innovations and on how they are interpreted by audiences.

This ethnography aims to examine the processes of production, dissemination, replication, and interpretation of popular musics in Indonesia by tracing how these processes implicate and connect producers, performers, and listeners—all of whom play an active, creative role in the ongoing circulation of musical culture. To arrive at an understanding of these complex processes, this ethnography for the most part adopts a street-level perspective, engaging with the concrete details of the everyday lives of individuals in specific social settings. Thus the following investigation differs from the many anthropological studies of cultural processes under modernity that adopt a macro-level—often transglobal—analytical perspective. Instead, this book is composed of situated ethnographic narratives that illuminate the lives and concerns of actual people involved in the various stages of those cultural processes. As such, it seeks to reinsert human agency into our understandings of processes of cultural production and reception, which are too often reducible to a reified dialectic of commodification and resistance whose totalizing logic tends to discourage the sensitive, nuanced empirical inquiry that constitutes the ethnographer's greatest contribution to the study of modern national cultures.

In every context explored here, perceptions of *genre* connect sounds with particular meanings, and preoccupations with the maintenance or transgression of genre boundaries play a vital role in everyday understandings of popular music (Frith 1996, 75-95). Music scholar Richard Middleton writes, "A genre can be thought of as analogous to a discursive formation, in the sense that in such a formation there is regulation of vocabulary, types of syntactic unit, formal organization, characteristic themes, modes of address (who speaks to whom and after what fashion), and structures of feeling" (1999, 144-45). Music genres are discursively linked in complex ways to particular social categories, including class, gender, and ethnicity, and their reception among Indonesians from different walks of life can reveal a great deal about how they view themselves and others in their society. Unlike the majority of existing ethnographic studies of popular musics in non-Western countries (e.g., Atkins 2001; Meintjes 2003; Schade-Poulsen 1999; Stokes 1992; Waterman 1990; Waxer 2002; Yano 2002), this study does not focus on a single genre but rather investigates the relationships among different national and international genres relevant to the lives of urban Indonesians, particularly young people in the capital city.[2] Viewing the entire national popular "musicscape" as an arena of contestation, hybridization, and accommodation, I demonstrate the social and ideological significance of popular music genres in contemporary Indonesia and their intimate connections to competing, historically situated conceptions of nation and modernity.[3]

In doing so, this book joins a growing number of ethnographic and historical studies that examine the relationship between popular music and the formation of modern national identities (e.g., Greene 2001; Turino 2000; Yano 2002; Zuberi 2001). These works seek to understand the complex local-global relationships that constitute music genres perceived as somehow representing a nation-state and the values and aspirations of its people (see Turino 1999). In this study, I view national music and the nation as *mutually constitutive:* each is simultaneously a reification and a palpable presence that relies on the other to provide a legitimating framework. Thus "Indonesian" popular music appears to validate a particular sense of Indonesian-ness, just as the sense of Indonesian-ness generates a need for a recognizably Indonesian popular music.

Methods and Theories

> There is nothing very precise, repeatable, predictable, verifiable, law-seeking, etc. about finding another person and talking with them [*sic*] about music.
>
> Charles Keil (in Crafts et al. 1993)

> It seems to me that our ethnographic and historical expertise in musics of the world must function as something more than raw data to be plugged into Western philosophical modes of understanding and conceptualization.
>
> Monson 1999

As these quotes suggest, both methodology and theory have become epistemologically and ethically controversial subjects in contemporary ethnographic music research. Sherry Ortner has defined ethnography as "the attempt to understand another life world using the self — as much of it as possible — as the instrument of knowing" (1995, 173). In that spirit, the most important data source for the present study is classic ethnographic participant observation — interacting with Indonesians in a variety of contexts while paying close attention to verbal and expressive behaviors that shed light on the social meanings of popular musics in those settings. These data are supplemented by formal interviews with key figures in the Indonesian popular music industry, aspiring semiprofessional and amateur musicians, and ordinary fans from diverse backgrounds. Happily, I had little difficulty finding consultants for my research project as I traversed the various social networks of friends and collaborators that made up the relatively finite universe of Indonesian popular musicians. In fact, it was not unusual to encounter a musician or industry type who was well acquainted with several of my previous contacts, even if he or she was involved with a different music genre than they. These unexpected connections were an early indication of how barriers between music genres in Indonesia often were more apparent on the level of marketing discourse than on the level of social and musical praxis.

I first visited Indonesia in September 1997 to conduct what turned out to be a most rewarding dissertation pilot study. During my visit I was amazed by the level of musical creativity I observed in a range of popular genres and by the willingness of Indonesian musicians (including some of the country's most renowned recording artists) to take the time to speak with me about their music. I was also astonished by the large number of ordinary Indonesians who openly and bitterly spoke out against the then ruling Soeharto regime in their conversations with me. I returned to Indonesia to commence my dissertation fieldwork more than two years later, in October 1999. Between my two visits, Jakarta and other major cities were engulfed by catastrophic riots, and President Soeharto's New Order government (which had seemed to me so utterly entrenched and permanent during the fall of 1997) collapsed after thirty-two years in power. Indonesia then entered a tumultuous period of sociopolitical transition from which it has yet to fully emerge. Shortly after my second arrival in Jakarta, the People's Consultative Assembly selected progressive Muslim intellectual Abdurrahman Wahid (popularly known as Gus Dur) to replace B. J. Habibie, Soeharto's hastily chosen successor. Gus Dur thus became Indonesia's fourth president, an event that marked the start of a new democratic era in Indonesian history.[4]

From October 1999 to August 2000, I lived in a rooming house (*rumah kost*) in Kebayoran Baru, a South Jakarta neighborhood, and devoted my time to attending concerts, observing recording sessions, interviewing musicians (amateurs, professionals, and stars), and interacting with young people from different social classes in neighborhoods around the city. I engaged in similar research during frequent trips to the West Javanese provincial capital of Bandung (home of a remarkably disproportionate number of Indonesian popular musicians) and during visits to Yogyakarta, Surakarta, Surabaya, Madiun, Denpasar, and the Javanese towns of Pekalongan and Ngawi.

Ethnographic studies of complex societies cannot, of course, stop at the level of face-to-face interactions. Over the last two decades, anthropologists have increasingly recognized that in addition to everyday "forms of life" (Hannerz 1992) such societies possess public cultures mediated by texts and other circulating cultural objects, and that these have a transformative effect on everyday life and everyday experiences.[5] During the course of my fieldwork, I amassed a collection of over 250 commercially released cassettes and compact discs, to which I added my own field recordings of live performances and several compilations of unreleased or out-of-print songs kindly assembled for me by the artists and producers who originally recorded them. Thus the arguments I make in this study rely on both ethnographic and artifactual evidence, though I ultimately privilege the former as a necessary prerequisite for interpreting the latter.

In addition to analyzing music recordings, I examined a number of written sources to investigate the meanings of contemporary Indonesian popular musics. Indonesia enjoys a high literacy rate, particularly among urban youth, and newspapers and magazines play a vital role in conditioning the production and reception of music genres. In this book I also interpret what could be called "vernacular texts." These include T-shirt slogans, graffiti, stickers, posters, banners, decorations on vans and buses, and other forms of informal public print culture that often represent views different from those propagated by the elite-controlled official mass media (see Jones 2005). Such texts are often overlooked in studies of urban societies, yet they are an important semiotic resource, their ubiquity masking their significant influence on consciousness.

Last, the Internet has become an increasingly important resource for research into popular music in Indonesia. After I left the field, I attempted to keep abreast of developments in the Indonesian music world through a rapidly increasing number of Indonesian-language Web sites dealing with music and popular culture, as well as through regular e-mail correspondence with many of my research consultants. As a result of this research in cyberspace, by the middle of 2001 I concluded that the Indonesian popular music universe, while in many ways confirming predictions I had made in the field, had evolved into something different from what I had experienced during my time in Indonesia. As a result, mid-2001 marks the cutoff point for the period of time covered in this study.

Although I arrived in Indonesia with a list of familiar theoretical concerns absorbed in graduate school—globalization, identity, modernity, nationalism, youth culture—during my research I made an effort to listen to what Indonesians themselves considered significant about their music and not to impose a preset framework on what I encountered. The resulting work is a rather different study than the one I had originally proposed to carry out, particularly with regard to the importance I assign to socioeconomic class differences—perhaps the least developed area of inquiry in anthropological studies of Indonesia—relative to other types of social differentiation. Similarly, although I had anticipated that I would find a link between Indonesian popular music and the inculcation of an ideology of "modern individualism" among Indonesian youth, in fact I found music to function primarily as a tool of sociability, for collective enjoyment rather than private aesthetic experience. This ethic of sociality, about which much is written in the following pages, is ubiquitous in everyday Indonesian social life, and it extends even to activities of musical production in environments characterized in the West by creative isolation and carefully guarded privacy, such as recording studios.

The Backdrop: A Summary of Events in Indonesia, 1997–2001

Zaman Edan: kalo ngga' ikut edan, ngga' ngetrend!

[A Crazy Time: if you don't join the craziness, you're not trendy!]
T-shirt caption, Jakarta[6]

It used to be the New Order, now it's the Order of Renewal [*Orde Pembaruan*]!
Teris, a Tegalese migrant in South Jakarta

Democrazy
painted on the front windshield of a Jakartan *mikrolet*
(minibus used for public transportation)

In many ethnographies of Indonesia, especially those written during the seemingly quiescent years of the New Order (1966–98), current events are distant background noise if they are present at all. But during the years when my fieldwork was conducted, their impact was real and momentous. The following brief historical sketch is intended to contextualize the musical practices that this book investigates.

Indonesian popular music, like Indonesian society, was in a state of transition during the time period covered in this book. From the beginning of the Asian currency crisis (*krisis moneter* or *krismon*) in late 1997 to the political maneuverings and continued economic misery at the beginning of the new century, this transitional period for most Indonesians was characterized by occasional bouts of euphoria more than matched by feelings of disillusionment and despair (see Dijk 2001).[7] In 1998, after thirty-two years under President Soeharto's authoritarian, corrupt, developmentalist New Order (Orde Baru or Orba) regime, economic crisis and political turmoil overtook Indonesia, and the aging dictator was forced to heed widespread demands for his resignation.

T-shirt design, Jakarta. The caption reads: "Crazy Time: If you don't join in the craziness, you're not trendy!" See page 282, note 6, for a more complete explanation of this image.

Political graffiti on a wall encircling the Atma Jaya University campus, Semanggi, Central Jakarta. The slogans include: "Reject the military regime"; "Eject the Indonesian Armed Forces from Parliament"; and [General] *Wiranto + Habibie Go to Hell* (in English).

Amid violent student protests and rioting and mayhem in cities throughout the country—especially in Jakarta—Soeharto stepped down on May 21, 1998.[8] His successor, B. J. Habibie, faced a public eager for change and suffering greatly from conditions resulting from the monetary crisis that caused the Indonesian economy to shrink an appalling 13.5 percent in 1998 after decades of impressive growth.[9] After a turbulent year and a half in office, facing further student protests and the threat of national disintegration, a visibly relaxed, even jocular, Habibie publicly announced two days before the October 20, 1999, election that he would not seek another term.

The decision was greeted with cheers from reformers and activists, for during his short time in office Habibie had been the target of much criticism. Many claimed he was little more than a puppet of the former regime, and the ways in which Habibie appeared to be protecting Soeharto, his old boss, from prosecution enraged the activists who had forced Soeharto from power. But Habibie's administration also allowed freedom of the press, and for the first time in three decades Indonesians were offered a wide range of opinions and political orientations to choose from. Habibie's much-maligned term in office also saw the release of political prisoners, Indonesia's first free and open democratic elections since the early 1950s, and the resolution of the conflict over East Timor, when the former province's long-suffering population chose independence from Indonesia in a formal provincewide referendum. Nevertheless, Habibie failed to solve the country's economic woes, failed to bring corrupt officials to justice, and was unable to halt the escalating violence in Maluku, Aceh, and other troubled regions in the archipelago. Worst of all, Habibie did not prevent the horrific slaughter and destruction in East Timor carried out immediately after the referendum by the Indonesian armed forces and local pro-Indonesia militias as retribution for the East Timorese people's decision to secede.

Habibie has been all but forgotten. President Abdurrahman Wahid had slightly more success at fighting corruption and significantly reduced the military's role in politics, yet he did not make progress in strengthening Indonesia's devastated economy nor in stemming the rising tide of separatist movements in the outer provinces. Moreover, ex-president Soeharto was never brought to justice during Gus Dur's time in office either. A year after Abdurrahman Wahid's election by the People's Consultative Assembly, much of the euphoria of Reformasi ("reform" or "reformation," the rallying cry of those who supported the political transition) had evaporated, replaced by uncertainty and trepidation, and many ordinary Indonesians became bitterly disillusioned with national politics. In an example of the word games characteristic of Jakartan street corner society, a cigarette-stall worker told me sardonically that Reformasi really only stood for *repot-repot cari nasi* (much trouble to find rice), an allusion to the economic hardship that persisted in the country, seemingly heedless of who happened to be in power. As in the days of the New Order, many Indonesians regarded the *elit politik* (political elites) as a corrupt, self-serving clique absorbed in petty squabbles with little regard for the wishes or priorities of the so-called little people (*rakyat kecil*). After Gus Dur had served only eighteen months of his allotted four-year term, the People's Consultative Assembly impeached him and gave the presidency to Megawati Soekarnoputri, his former vice president.[10] A daughter of Indonesia's first president Sukarno, Megawati, known to her supporters as Bu Mega, once enjoyed tremendous popular support despite (or perhaps because of) her tendency to maintain an enigmatic silence in the face of political controversy. Unfortunately, Bu Mega's administration was no more successful than Wahid's in confronting Indonesia's myriad problems, which had become so serious that many Indonesian news commentators began to speak of a "multidimensional crisis" threatening the nation.

None of the national leaders mentioned thus far successfully addressed the most glaring social issue threatening Indonesia's stability: the widening gulf between the haves and the have-nots, the latter comprising the vast majority of Indonesians. Thus many Indonesians remained unconvinced that their leaders possessed a social and political vision for Indonesia that included not only the elite and middle classes but also the *rakyat kecil* (also known as the *wong cilik,* a loan phrase from Low Javanese), who make up most of the country's population and who had borne the brunt of the suffering created by the economic crisis. Indeed, the extreme class prejudice of New Order ideology, which viewed the poor as "backward" (*terbelakang*) and mired in obsolete ways of life, has persisted in Indonesian society and arguably still threatens the viability of Indonesia's fledgling democratic polity.

Slowdeath, a death metal band from Surabaya, East Java, describes the threat that the *social gap* represents to the Indonesian nation in their 1998 song "Crisis Prone Society," which alludes to the sporadic looting and violent unrest that characterized urban Indonesia at the time (original lyrics in English, reproduced exactly as printed in the cassette liner notes):[11]

> *Look at the exhausted and dejected poor*
> *Soon they'll lost* [sic] *their strength to endure*
> *So hard they work no difference they make*
> *Such grim fate must they take*
>
> *Crisis strikes hard with no warning*
> *The anger ends up in burning*
> *Primordialism becomes the key*
> *To solve this falling society*
>
> *This social fabric is being ruptured*
> *Overburdened and overload* [sic] *with prejudice*
>
> *This widening social gap is a perfect*
> *Breeding place*
> *For vehemence and hatred, burying the*
> *logical sense*
> *Crisis prone society*
>
> (From the album Learn through Pain [1998])

Turn-of-the-millennium Jakarta was indeed an unruly place. Frequent political demonstrations (*demo*), many orchestrated by politicians using paid demonstrators (cf. Ziv 2002, 32–33), worsened the city's already severe traffic problems. Street crime of all types increased exponentially, and with it, brutal, widely reported acts of retaliatory vigilantism. Yet life went on, and during the period of my fieldwork the city remained remarkably free of large-scale political unrest of the sort that had engulfed it in 1998. There are still those who remain hopeful that conditions will improve in the capital, even as others, mindful of the persistent social gap, await the next major cataclysm.

The Music Industry in the Era of Reformasi

The demise of the New Order occasioned a great deal of public debate and speculation among intellectuals, bureaucrats, composers, and journalists on the role that a new democratic and decentralized government might play in promoting traditional music and performing arts. Ultimately, however, market forces continued to dominate the Indonesian mass media, just as they had under Soeharto (Kartomi 2002, 141–42). After the fall of Soeharto, and especially during the period of optimism immediately after Gus Dur's election in October 1999, many companies in Indonesia's commercial music industry began a rebuilding phase. Despite skyrocketing prices resulting from the ongoing monetary crisis, they began purchasing new studio equipment from overseas and made plans to release new albums once more. An example of this new optimism is *NewsMusik,* a glossy Indonesian-language monthly music magazine modeled after *Rolling Stone,* which published its first issue in January 2000. The magazine covered both foreign and domestic popular musicians, privileging the latter, until it ceased publication in late 2002.

Though Indonesia's economic crisis continued, the country's music industry appeared to partially recover in 1999–2001, as evidenced by the number of successful new albums released in those years. By 2001, music sales had rebounded, though they had not risen back to precrisis levels. One notable development with regard to the music itself is that compared to the late New Order period, far fewer new recordings of protest songs were released by the mainstream music industry in the immediate post-Soeharto period (Kartomi 2002, 125). This decrease notwithstanding, the word *Reformasi*—well on its way to becoming an empty slogan—was frequently (sometimes cynically) employed to sell rereleased protest songs by Iwan Fals and other popular recording artists

(Barendregt and Zanten 2002, 72; Dijk 2003, 59; Sutton 2004). By contrast, Indonesian underground rock groups recorded a large number of highly political songs during this same period, including some in Indonesian rather than in English (Wallach 2003a). One reason for this was that these groups were freer to do so than during the New Order period, when writing protest songs against the government, especially in the national language, could land one in prison.

The existing literature on national popular musics in Indonesia consists primarily of article- or chapter-length historical/stylistic surveys and textual analyses (e.g., Barendregt and Zanten 2002; Bass 2000; Becker 1975; Frederick 1982; Hatch 1989; Kartomi 2002; Lockard 1998; Manuel 1988; Pioquinto 1998; Piper and Jabo 1987; Sutton 2004; Wong and Lysloff 1998; Yampolsky 1989, 1991). Although some valuable historical and sociological studies of popular music and its audiences have been written by Indonesian scholars (e.g., Kesumah 1995; Suseno 2005), most relevant works in Indonesian are standard popular biographies of major recording artists (e.g., Kartoyo and Sedjati 1997; Sumarsono 1998). A full-length, comprehensive history of postindependence popular music in Indonesia has yet to be written in either English or Indonesian, and it is beyond the scope of this study to attempt such a history here. However, although I focus on a recent historical moment in all its complexity, some additional information on the development of popular music in Indonesia is needed to situate what follows.

Unlike his nationalist predecessor Sukarno, who during his presidency (1949–66) crusaded against Western pop music, referring to it as a "social disease" and famously describing the rock and roll music of the era with the pejorative onomatopoeic phrase *ngak-ngik-ngek* (Sen and Hill 2000, 166), President Soeharto (1966–98) did not prevent international record labels from selling their wares to Indonesian consumers, nor did his government discourage Indonesian musicians who emulated international styles.[12] Also, beginning in the 1970s, the availability of inexpensive cassette players made recorded music artifacts accessible for the first time to a large percentage of Indonesia's population, part of a worldwide cassette revolution that dramatically transformed the popular music industries in developing nations (cf. Manuel 1988, 1993; Wong 1989/1990; F. Miller 2005). As in India, Thailand, Yemen, and other countries, the affordability of cassettes permitted the emergence and commercial viability of regional and working-class-oriented styles in the Indonesian market. Conversely, this new consumer technology allowed ordinary people easy access to the sounds and performance styles of globally circulating popular music—including the potentially populist, unruly noise of rock.

Under Soeharto's New Order, popular musicians constantly faced the threat of punishment or censorship by the government. This did not keep some of them, including Rhoma Irama, Harry Roesli, Iwan Fals, rockers Slank, and the *pop alternatif* group Dewa 19, from performing songs that could be construed as criticizing the Soeharto regime. Indeed, commentators who claimed that dissent was largely absent from late New Order society were clearly not paying attention to developments in popular music. Despite occasional harassment, censorship, and even imprisonment of the most brazen critics of the regime (for example, the late avant-garde composer and pop star Harry Roesli was imprisoned twice for criticizing the government), popular musicians for the most part enjoyed a degree of creative freedom that recording artists living under other totalitarian regimes would envy (Sen and Hill 2000, 184). During the same time, Indonesia also had an active musical avant-garde that specialized in combining international experimental music trends with indigenous aesthetic traditions (Kartomi 2002, 137–40). Thus neither social criticism expressed in song nor radical sounds were wholly absent during the New Order.

One major problem that has long plagued the Indonesian recording industry is rampant piracy (*pembajakan*), which severely limits the ability of record companies to generate revenue from their products. In postcrisis Indonesia, I was told by insiders in the music industry that the actual ratio of legitimate music cassettes sold to pirated copies sold was about 1:8; in the early 1990s, before the *krismon*, the ratio was closer to 1:6. As a result, despite a potential national market of roughly 225 million people, the music industry of the world's fourth most populous country was fairly small and decentralized (though still the largest in Southeast Asia by far [Sen and Hill 2000, 169]). No single record company dominated, and the major multinational music corporations (WEA, Sony, BMG, and Universal/Polygram, all relatively recent arrivals to Indonesia) had to compete with large, well-established national independent labels like Aquarius, Musica, Bulletin, and Virgo Ramayana, as well as with hundreds of smaller-scale, often quite specialized operations. Unlike the Indonesian film industry, a more capital-intensive enterprise that was virtually annihilated by the flood of Hollywood films and other foreign movies into the country (and by the meddling of the acquisitive Soeharto family), the various players in the Indonesian music industry have survived (and sometimes prospered) despite the conspicuous, well-publicized presence of foreign music in the Indonesian music market.

In 1995, MTV began to be featured on Indonesian national television (Sutton 2003, 324). This had a dramatic effect on the new generation of Indonesian recording artists, who, like young people throughout capitalist Asia in the 1990s (cf. Stocker 2002), were coming of age in an increasingly globalized mediascape. Slickly produced music videos broadcast on national television became a crucial means for promoting albums, and the influence of up-to-the-minute international musical trends intensified in Indonesia and other countries across the continent (see Chun, Rossiter, and Shoesmith 2004). Indeed, the political transformations of 1998–99 seem to have had less impact on Indonesian popular music than the introduction of MTV, though one reason for this is that Indonesian popular music was already highly cosmopolitan and often politicized long before the fall of Soeharto.

Music, Gender, and the State

Like most other aspects of public life, the realm of Indonesian popular music performance and production is dominated by men. Yet this patriarchal structure is nonetheless dependent on the talents and contributions of women not only in their roles as singers and dancers, but also as audience members and consumers. Popular music in Indonesia, as elsewhere, provides a site for both reinforcing and challenging gender ideologies through performance. Contested Indonesian notions of femininity and masculinity are constituted in musical performance, and such performances index the conflicts between indigenous and Western gender codes. Furthermore, genre ideologies and gender ideologies intersect in complex ways, and the limits of acceptable (and transgressive) behavior in performance vary greatly among the different genres of popular music.

A further clarification is in order here regarding the role of the Indonesian state in what follows. Much of the existing scholarship on Indonesian popular culture has focused on the intrusive role of the state and its attempts to construct its citizens (e.g., Mulder 2000; Murray 1991; Pemberton 1994b; Weintraub 2004; Widodo 1995; Yampolsky 1989, 1995). In these studies, the project of forging an Indonesian national culture tends to be regarded as sinister and hegemonic, and the rhetoric of culture is viewed as a tool of state domination (cf. Steedly 1999, 441–44). The present work differs in that I focus on a part of Indonesian popular culture characterized by a relative lack of state interference during a time when the ideological hegemony of the state was breaking down (at least in major cities), and I therefore take a more benign view of national cultural production. Indeed, far from encountering a timid generation brainwashed by years of New Order propaganda, I found Indonesian youth boldly experimenting with the myriad possibilities of identity in a postauthoritarian historical moment while at the same time maintaining a strong affective investment in the utopian nationalist project of Indonesia. Therefore, while the construction of national identity and belonging is of central concern to this study, neither the New Order government nor the more democratic administrations that succeeded it take center stage. Instead, I focus squarely on the voices of regular Indonesians involved with making and listening to music.

I readily acknowledge that the approach I have taken in this study has several limitations. First and foremost, the fact that my ethnographic research was largely confined to urban areas on the islands of Java and Bali, and mostly Jakarta and West Java province at that, obviously limits the applicability of my interpretations to the lives of Indonesians elsewhere in the country, although the products of the Jakarta-centered Indonesian national music industry do reach audiences all over the archipelago. A further shortcoming is the relatively short time frame of this inquiry—Indonesian popular music has a rich and inadequately documented history that is only alluded to in the following ethnography. My aim has been to provide a snapshot of a specific cultural moment in all its lived richness, and thus at times I have chosen to attenuate discussions of longer historical trajectories. Despite these shortcomings, I hope that the following study can raise productive new questions about popular music, national identity, and the cultural dynamics of contemporary complex societies in Southeast Asia and the world.

Outline of Chapters

This book is composed of two parts: "Sites" and "Genres in Performance." Part 1 explores a series of locations and describes the activities and interactions that take place there, the participants, and the particular musical forms that circulate within them. I discuss the meanings and social functions of these cultural forms and the behaviors associated with them within each particular context, connecting them to discourses on class, modernity, gender, and nation in contemporary Indonesia. Part 2 shifts the analytical focus from places to particular events unfolding in time, examining the specific and contested ways in which popular music genres are performed by musicians and received by audiences at live concerts.

The first chapter attempts to place the major Indonesian popular music genres in a broad historical and sociocultural context. Chapter 2, "In the City: Class, History, and Modernity's Failures," departs from strictly ethnomusicological concerns in order to provide a more detailed cultural account of this study's main field site: Jakarta, Indonesia's capital city and undisputed political and economic center. Through a cultural analysis of the diverse languages, spaces, and soundscapes of the Indonesian metropolis, I explore the role of socioeconomic class in fundamental urban processes of social differentiation (often based on a deceptive village/urban dichotomy) and the oft concealed but powerful role of class in the hegemonic discourses of modernity (*kemoderenan*) and development (*pembangunan*) so influential during the New Order. This chapter sets the stage for the ethnographic portraits that follow, which depict the many types of musical encounter that transpire in urban spaces.

Throughout the book I argue that musical phenomena must be comprehended through the social spaces they occupy and the varied material forms they take. Also, assessing music's meanings requires an understanding of the social activities and interactions involving musical forms that take place in particular social settings. Chapter 3, "Cassette Retail Outlets: Organization, Iconography, Consumer Behavior," focuses on the first of these settings. In this chapter I explore an obvious yet frequently overlooked site of musical encounter: stores that sell music recordings. The chapter describes the spatial organization, classification schemes, iconography, and behavior patterns that characterize these spaces and relates them to local understandings of musical genres. A wide range of retail outlets is included, from shops selling underground cassettes and accessories to enormous mall stores to stalls that sell pirated cassettes in *pasar tradisional* (traditional outdoor markets). I also discuss how the sale of music recordings conforms to the bifurcated cultural logic of Indonesian urban life detailed in chapter 2 and raise questions regarding imported and domestic music genres as markers of social distinction and status in contemporary Indonesia.

Chapter 4, "In the Studio: An Ethnography of Sound Production," further explores the relationships among music, genre, and cultural hierarchy by examining the interactional context of the recording studio, Indonesian popular music's primary site of artifactual production.

The chapter analyzes the creative and commercially motivated decisions made by participants in three different studio environments and examines how Indonesian music producers use sophisticated recording technologies to manipulate and juxtapose regional, national, and global sonic elements in the course of producing new musical commodities for the Indonesian market.

Music videos are essential promotional tools in the Indonesian music industry, and the imagery and settings used in them reveal much about the social meanings and (imagined) audiences of the musics they advertise. Chapter 5, "On Location: Shooting Music Video Clips," describes the making of two music videos, one for a dangdut song and the other for a rock song. Operating on different budgets and levels of technical sophistication, these two videos exhibit the play of local, national, and global signs in Indonesian popular musics and also betray certain cultural preoccupations with modernity and its moral consequences.

Chapter 6, "Offstage: Music in Informal Contexts," moves from the relatively sequestered environments of the recording studio and video location shoot to the streets of Jakarta, where music originally produced in studios is discussed, performed, and used by social agents to pursue personal and collective aims. In particular, I describe the milieu of "the side of the road" (*di pinggir jalan*) as a place where mostly male, mostly working-class Indonesians deploy musics and discourses to make performative assertions about community, poverty, gender, politics, and what it means to be an Indonesian in the contemporary world. The chapter proceeds to examine middle-class leisure spaces where musical performance takes place, including public areas on university campuses. In these different settings, musical performance plays a central role in a largely masculine culture of "hanging out" (*nongkrong*), which cuts across class lines. I reveal how "hanging out" is part of a particular orientation toward the presence of others, evident both in side-of-the-road interactions and on university campuses, which I call the "ethic of sociality." I conclude by demonstrating how this ethic of sociality exerts a strong influence on the ways in which global and Indonesian national music genres are used and interpreted by Indonesian youth.

The three ethnographic chapters in part 2 analyze particular concert events featuring the principal music genres explored in this study: dangdut, pop, and underground. To the previously introduced analytical issues of class, global/national/regional interactions, and sociality, the chapters that comprise part 2 sharpen the focus on the performance of gender—the various masculinities and femininities that emerge in the context of musical performances simultaneously coded by class distinctions and influenced by hybridized and multivalent cultural formations. Given the recent importance of gender analysis in much contemporary popular music and Southeast Asia scholarship, it may seem odd to wait until the second part of the book to focus on the performance of gender norms and ideologies in Indonesian popular musics.[13] I have chosen to proceed in this fashion in order to first highlight the equally salient role of the *performance of social class,* which has received comparatively little attention from researchers of music in Indonesia, and indeed from popular music scholars in general.

The first element of part 2 is chapter 7, "Onstage: The Live Musical Event," which examines a range of more formalized musical performances — that is, performances that involve a definite division between performers and audience and often, but not always, entail some form of payment for the performers. Live music can be encountered in a wide variety of contexts in Indonesia, and performances range from lone troubadours who play in buses and traffic intersections for spare change to elaborate stadium rock shows. Following a discussion interpreting the urban phenomenon of roving street musicians (*pengamen*), I examine more-organized performance events by analyzing the structure and logic of planned performance occasions (*acara*), using televised music award shows and a festival featuring pop, jazz, and ethnic fusion artists as case studies.

Chapter 8, "Dangdut Concerts: The Politics of Pleasure," examines two kinds of musical events in detail: live dangdut shows in Jakarta nightclubs, and outdoor dangdut performances held in the capital's working-class neighborhoods. I investigate the gendered symbolic and material exchanges that take place at dangdut performances and discuss their importance vis-à-vis dangdut as a "national" music genre. Chapter 9, "Rock and Pop Events: The Performance of Lifestyle," covers pop and rock music performances of Indonesian and Western songs in urban cafés as well as at concert events organized by committees of middle-class students, while chapter 10, "Underground Music: Imagining Alternative Community," focuses specifically on underground music events (which are also organized by committees of Indonesian youths) and explores the manner in which such occasions construct musical community through collective subcultural expression, raising additional questions about class, identity, and the cultural dynamics of global music movements. The chapter concludes with a general appraisal of the cultural role of music *acara* in modern Indonesia.

The conclusion summarizes the major findings of the study and draws on them to enter the now-familiar debate on the nature of cultural globalization. I argue that the conspicuous presence of Western and Westernized popular music in Indonesia has not obliterated a distinctive Indonesian national cultural sensibility but rather provides new means by which to resist, affirm, or reflect on what might constitute such a sensibility. Contemporary Indonesian youth identities would be unimaginable without popular music, which acts as an essential cultural referent for a range of social categories, the most important of which is class.

I close the book with two polemics. In the first, I raise the perennial question of what uses popular music has in modern societies and discuss how anthropologists have overlooked popular music's significance due to their conventional emphasis on tradition and continuity rather than cultural innovation and creativity. One of the most appealing aspects of popular music is precisely that it is "something new," and I argue that what Greg Urban (2001) has called the "metaculture of modernity" constitutes as proper a subject for anthropological inquiry as its rhetorical opposite, which he terms the "metaculture of tradition."

The second polemic challenges the still-common assumption that popular music is just another commodity for the ceaseless consumerist identity-shopping that seems to characterize contemporary life. Such a view, I suggest, overlooks music's essential social component, present even in its most mediated forms, and its remarkable ability to generate communal feeling and strengthen social bonds. Thus, in Indonesia, popular music, despite its capitalistic methods of production and distribution, is often used to defy the individualist, atomizing logic of the global economy and to encourage music makers and their audiences to form affective attachments not only to one another but also to an inclusive, democratic national vision that embraces diversity and cosmopolitanism.

Indonesians have their own approaches to popular music—to its populism, its artistic pretensions, its status as a sometimes profitable commodity, and its potential as an instrument for social and political change. Throughout this book, I attempt to portray the world of Indonesian popular music not as a unidirectional cultural flow from producer to consumer but as a set of continuously evolving discourses, practices, and performances that simultaneously implicate musicians, technicians, producers, listeners, critics, and other concerned parties. For this reason, the order of the chapters does not conform chronologically to the life cycle of a specific musical commodity. Instead, the topics they cover move back and forth between sites of production and reception, finally culminating in live performance, where these two processes occur simultaneously in the same locale. Yet an understanding of the lived reality of Indonesian popular music cannot be limited to the concert stage; all the types of musical encounter covered in the book are important, from the most reified and routinized (record-store shopping) to the most spectacular, immediate, and emergent (live performance). Each has its transformative possibilities as well as a role in the maintenance of cultural continuity and predictability in the Indonesian popular music universe.

PART ONE

Sites

1

Indonesian Popular Music Genres in the Global Sensorium

Saya suka semua jenis musik, dari jazz sampai . . . musik daerah!

[I like all kinds of music, from jazz to . . . regional music!]
taxicab driver, Jakarta

So what if we're a shitty metal band.
printed on a sticker for Puppen,
a veteran underground rock group
from Bandung, West Java

One result of Indonesian music's complex history, upon which the description in the introduction barely scratches the surface, is a wide array of music genres that coexist in the Indonesian music market and significantly shape the consciousness of Indonesian listeners. The following abbreviated list of genres is meant as an introduction. Certain national genres, especially dangdut, *pop Indonesia,* and *musik underground,* will reappear frequently in the following chapters, but all the genres discussed here are important, and examining the ways they interrelate is crucial for understanding Indonesian popular music as a whole. The list is based on categories Indonesians themselves use to discuss music, primarily in verbal interaction but also in the mass media, although their presentation here incorporates an etic viewpoint that synthesizes various data sources to create a branching taxonomy of genres. Descriptions of additional popular music genres of secondary importance to the present study appear in appendix B. The following discussion begins with Western imported music, moves to Western-sounding Indonesian pop music, and then considers two genres with prominent non-Western elements: dangdut and regional music. The final genre to be considered is underground rock music, which, while sharing many musical features with pop, is unique due to its grassroots mode of production and its specialized youth audience. As will be made clear, each of these categories carries with it expectations of musical form, assumptions about the composition of audiences, social prestige factors, and a distinct significance in the context of Indonesian national culture.

Pop Barat (Western Popular Music)

Published shortly before a general session of the People's Consultative Assembly, the cover of the August 9–15, 2000, issue of *Gamma* (an Indonesian news magazine akin to *Time* or *Newsweek*) depicts the principal political actors of the time (President Abdurrahman Wahid, Vice President Megawati Soekarnoputri, Golkar Party chairman Akbar Tanjung, and House Speaker Amien Rais) as members of the Beatles: their faces had been quite convincingly superimposed over a vintage photo of the Fab Four posing with their instruments. The caption underneath them reads (in English), *Don't Let Me Down*. In addition to being a clever way to send a message to Indonesia's perpetually squabbling leaders, this illustration on the cover of a respected Indonesian news magazine demonstrates both the familiarity and the cultural cachet of Western popular music in that country.

Imported popular music from Western Europe (primarily the United Kingdom), Australia, and the United States has long maintained a strong presence in Indonesia. The names of the most prominent international artists, from Elvis Presley to Britney Spears, are quite well known, despite the fact that most Indonesians understand very little of the English lyrics they sing (although I have been told that listening to Western pop songs is a common way for Indonesians to learn the English language). Despite its extensive promotion in Indonesia by marketing divisions of multinational conglomerates, music imported from the West constitutes a minority of the nonpirated cassettes sold in Indonesia. In the first ten months of 1999, domestically produced music outsold foreign music by 3 to 1 (Theodore 1999, 4). In 1996, before the economic crisis reduced the buying power of all but the most affluent

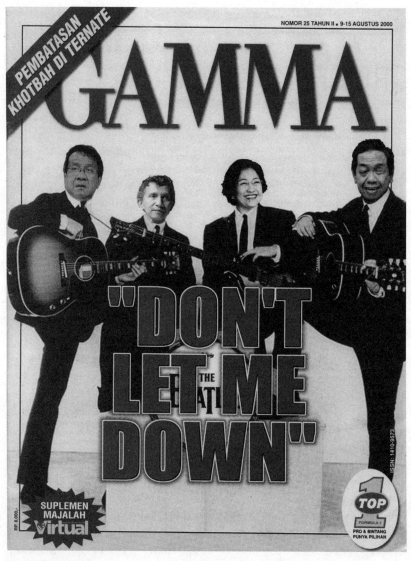

Magazine cover featuring major Indonesian politicians as the Fab Four.

(and most westernized) Indonesians, the ratio was 6.5 to 1 (ibid.). One reason for local music's dominance is undoubtedly the higher price of Western artists' cassettes relative to those by Indonesian artists (up to 40 percent higher); another is the persistent language barrier. Differing sociomusical aesthetics also play a role, however, and these will be discussed in subsequent chapters.

In general, Indonesian tastes in Western pop music tend toward two extremes: loud rock music at one end and treacly sentimental love songs at the other. Heavy metal and hard rock are among the most popular genres of Western popular music among both rural and urban youth, while the appeal of sentimental love songs is cross-generational and seems to be even greater than their appeal in the United States. Some large Indonesian record stores include an entire separately marked section for English-language love songs, many of which are produced exclusively for Asian markets and would be unfamiliar (and annoyingly, cloyingly sentimental) to Western listeners.

At the time of my fieldwork, other imported Western genres such as country, reggae, rhythm and blues, and folk maintained a more marginal status in the Indonesian market. Larger record stores occasionally devoted separate sections to them, but their audiences were limited. Western classical music (*musik klasik*) was frequently regarded as the most prestigious and refined of genres, but I found very few Indonesians who claimed they understood or enjoyed such music (a journalist told me that one had to be a "genius" just to appreciate it!). Instead, Western jazz (more precisely, the "smooth" jazz-pop fusion performed by instrumentalists such as Kenny G and Dave Koz and vocalists like Peabo Bryson) appeared to be the preferred music of the cultural and economic elite, representing a paragon of urbanity and modern sophistication.

Pop Indonesia

Pop Indonesia is the general term used to describe domestically produced, heavily Western-influenced popular music sung in Indonesian. Musically *pop Indonesia* closely resembles mainstream Anglo-American pop and rock, with the sounds of guitars, keyboards, bass guitar, and drums predominating, though the Indonesian language does lend itself to distinctive melodic contours generally not found in English-language pop songs. *Pop Indonesia* emerged as a recognized genre in the 1960s with artists such as the Beatlesque group Koes Plus and singers Eddy Silatonga and Emilia Contessa. *Pop Indonesia* rapidly supplanted the earlier national *hiburan* (entertainment) genre, which was based on Western popular music styles from before the rock and roll era, such as bossa nova and swing (cf. Lockard 1998, 83–87). Philip Yampolsky writes, "Hiburan was in all important respects a Western music, shallowly rooted in Indonesia. I suggest that Hiburan's importance to Indonesians lay more in its 'theater' than in its music: it demonstrated that

Indonesian performers and Indonesian languages could be incorporated into a clearly Western context. When Pop emerged, demonstrating the same thing with greater energy, and linking its audience to the dream-world of Western entertainment media, Hiburan dried up and blew away" (1987a, 14). Throughout its history, *pop Indonesia* artists have provided Indonesia's answer to the music of international stars such as Elvis Presley, the Beatles, Bob Dylan, and the Rolling Stones. Despite the prominent influence of Western hard rock, a style that tends to address both weightier and raunchier topics, *pop Indonesia's* primary lyrical themes are of romantic, sentimental love with some occasional light social criticism (Lockard 1998, 87–91).

Pop Indonesia is divided into several subcategories. In the period during which I conducted my research, *pop nostalgia* (also called *pop memori*) was the affectionate label given to *pop Indonesia* songs that were recorded in the 1960s, 1970s, and 1980s by such artists as Broery Maranthika, Frankie Silahatua, Leo Kristi, and Gombloh. *Pop kreatif* and *pop alternatif* were names given to newer styles that reflected contemporary global trends in rock and pop music and were usually ensemble rather than singer based. The most commercially successful bands in Indonesia in 1997–2001, including Cokelat, Dewa (formerly Dewa 19), Padi, Potret, Sheila on 7, and Wong, played this kind of pop, while top-selling solo artists like Titi DJ, Krisdayanti, Ruth Sahanaya, and Glenn Fredly sang what was sometimes called *pop kelas atas* (upper-class pop), an urbane, R & B–influenced pop style that emphasized smooth instrumental timbres, polished production, and vocal expressiveness.

Two other important *pop Indonesia* subgenres with specialized markets include *pop anak-anak* (children's pop music, usually sung by child performers—a much more significant genre in Indonesia than in the United States in terms of publicity and sales) and *pop Rohani* (pop music with Christian themes produced for Indonesia's Christian minority). Simple and catchy *pop anak-anak* tunes are the songs that initiate Indonesian listeners from different ethnic and social backgrounds into the world of national popular music. From there, the genres Indonesian young people choose to listen to depends to a large extent on their class position (see chapter 3).

Dangdut

Of all the genres of popular music in Indonesia, none has a larger nationwide audience than dangdut, a genre with a complicated and controversial history.[1] Dangdut resembles several other syncretic Asian musical styles—particularly in the Muslim world—with its nasal, ornamented vocal style, the proletarian character of its mass audience, and its association with sinful and otherwise disreputable activities (cf. Stokes 1992 on *arabesk* in Turkey and Schade-Poulsen 1999 on Algerian *raï*). Dangdut music evolved in part from popular Indian film songs re-recorded with Malay lyrics, but since its emergence in the late 1950s the style has developed along its own trajectory quite independent of the Indian film industry. In the late 1970s, as the cassette format was expanding and transforming Indonesia's music market, a singer and guitarist named Rhoma Irama "modernized" the music that had up to then been called *orkes Melayu* (Malay orchestra) by importing rock guitars (allegedly inspired by the British hard rock group Deep Purple) and sophisticated studio production techniques into the genre.[2]

The musical blueprint for dangdut created by Rhoma Irama's Soneta Group remains largely unchanged to this day when recording "original/authentic dangdut" (*dangdut asli*), which still constitutes the majority of new dangdut releases. There is only one indigenous Indonesian instrument in a Soneta-style dangdut ensemble: the *suling*, a transverse bamboo flute from West Java (where it is known as a *bangsing*).[3] The other pieces in a typical ensemble include two electric guitars (rhythm and lead), two electronic keyboards (playing piano and string sounds, respectively), electric bass guitar, electrified mandolin, tambourine, Western trap kit, and the *gendang*, a pair of goatskin-covered hand drums modeled after the Indian tabla. *Gendang* and *suling*, the two main instruments of dangdut not found in pop or rock, are regarded as emblematic of the genre (not unlike the symbolic importance of fiddle and steel guitar to the sound and iconography of American country and western music). The basic dangdut lineup is sometimes augmented by saxophones, sitar, acoustic guitar, maracas, and other instruments, particularly on commercial recordings (see chapter 4).

Whether dangdut really is "Indonesian music" continues to be debated by critics and intellectuals who point to its foreign origins (e.g., Danu 2000). On the other hand, American ethnomusicologist Henry Spiller argues that despite dangdut's musical eclecticism, the music's meanings and functions are undeniably indigenous: "The driving 'dangdut' drum pattern that gives the genre its name is, of course, a simple ostinato that hearkens back to the earliest kinds of Southeast Asian music-making—despite this particular ostinato's distinctly Indian roots. The close connection between the dangdut rhythm and dance movements in the minds and bodies of dangdut fans is a manifestation of yet another long-standing Indonesian musical process—a connection between drumming and dance, and the ability of drum sounds to animate human bodies" (Spiller 2004, 268). Whatever the reasons for its mass appeal, dangdut remains *the* music of choice for Indonesia's nonaffluent Muslim majority, and its enormous popularity cuts across region, age, gender, and ethnicity. The middle class and the elite, on the other hand, have tended to be somewhat uncomfortable with dangdut, which they associate with backward village life and sexual permissiveness (cf. Browne 2000, 11–12; Pioquinto 1998). Non-Muslim Indonesians, such as Christian Bataks and Balinese, may also feel ambivalent toward it, though dangdut is not considered Islamic music per se, and in fact many strict Muslims consider dangdut to be sinful.[4]

Although it is considered the epitome of backwardness by its detractors, dangdut music has always been open to cosmopolitan sounds and technologies. Contemporary dangdut artists and producers have continued the genre's history of eclectically absorbing outside musical influences. Recent attempts to fuse dangdut songs with electronic dance music have yielded the subcategory *dangdut trendy*, which refers to dangdut recordings in which drum machines, samplers, and synthesizers replace the *gendang* and other conventional instruments of the genre (Wallach 2004, 2005). Examples of this subcategory include *dangdut disco, dangdut reggae, house dangdut, dangdut remix,* and many other variations. Oddly enough, many middle- and upper-class Indonesians consider these new hybrids to be even more low class and backward (*kampungan*) than the "pure" or "original" dangdut (*dangdut murni, dangdut asli*) that conforms to the style and instrumentation of dangdut recordings from the 1970s and early 1980s.

Musik Daerah (Regional Music)

> Middle-class people don't like this music.
> a Solonese traditional dance instructor,
> speaking about *campur sari* music, while a band
> played *campur sari* songs to an appreciative audience
> at a middle-class East Javanese wedding

In addition to the national popular musics mentioned above, every major ethnic group in Indonesia has its own regional music idioms, which are available on cassettes produced for specific ethnolinguistic markets.[5] Much of this music, known as *musik daerah* (regional music) or *lagu daerah* (regional song), is produced in provincial capitals rather than in Jakarta, though it is frequently sold in the capital city to urban migrant populations hailing from all over the archipelago. Although I occasionally encountered people who claimed to enjoy the regional music of other ethnic groups (Javanese fans of Sundanese pop, for example), most Indonesians were not interested in the regional music of ethnicities other than (perhaps) their own.[6] "Regional music" is a catchall category that includes every style of music sung in regional languages, from the most Westernized pop to the most stable indigenous performance traditions. These two examples exist on the ends of a continuum that contains a wide array of musical hybrids of local, regional, national, and global genres.

At one end of the *musik daerah* continuum are musical styles that appear to lack any Western influence. Their instrumentation, repertoire, and musical techniques all originate in indigenous court- or village-based musical traditions that have endured since long before the current era of McDonald's and megamalls. In Indonesia, regional traditional musics are recorded in multitrack recording studios and marketed in much the same way as regional popular music, and, with a few notable exceptions, their audiences are usually just as limited to a specific ethnic group or subgroup. At the same time, the long-standing and intense interest some Westerners have shown in studying Javanese, Balinese, Batak, Torajan, and other musical traditions is a source of pride to many members of those groups, and occasionally producers of traditional recordings will target the tourist market and markets overseas as well as local consumers. Last, regional traditional musics continue to be celebrated in numerous ethnomusicological monographs written by both Indonesians and foreigners.

Pop daerah is the label given to musics in regional languages or dialects that contain nontraditional elements. The extent to which local elements other than language are present varies considerably. At one extreme, a successful *pop Indonesia* song will be translated into a regional language and rerecorded without major changes in the music or the arrangement (Yampolsky 1989). But most *pop daerah* recordings draw from a separate, indigenous repertoire of old and new songs, and they often incorporate traditional instruments, rhythms, and melodic contours into their compositions. In addition to successful genres with wide audiences such as *pop Sunda*, *pop Batak*, and *pop Minang*, a multitude of smaller, more obscure *pop daerah* varieties, such as *pop Sumsel* (South Sumatran pop) also exist in more regionally circumscribed markets (Barendregt

2002, 415). *Pop Jawa* (Javanese pop) is the most successful and variegated *pop daerah* genre, which is not surprising given the numerical, political, and cultural dominance of the Javanese ethnolinguistic group in Indonesia.

Campur sari (literally "mixture of essences") is a recent style that evolved in the late 1990s in the Central Javanese cities of Solo and Yogyakarta. It combines *keroncong* (an older style of nationalized popular music played on Western and indigenous acoustic instruments), dangdut, and Javanese traditional music, and is sung exclusively in (usually "low," informal) Javanese. The popularity of *campur sari* rivals Indonesian-language dangdut in working-class Central and East Javanese communities, while many middle- and upper-class Javanese consider it *kampungan* (yet as the epigraph introducing this section demonstrates, many enjoy it nonetheless). *Campur sari* is not considered "pop," perhaps because its embrace of genres like dangdut and *keroncong* stands in opposition to the modernity pop supposedly represents.

Jaipong is another regional genre that complicates divisions between musical categories. *Jaipong* (also called *jaipongan*) is a rhythmically exciting popular music genre, supposedly inspired by Western rock music, that was developed in the 1970s by Gugum Gumbira Tirasonjaya, a visionary Sundanese composer, choreographer, and record producer (Yampolsky 1987b; Bass 2000). What sets *jaipong* apart from most other recorded nontraditional regional genres is that it uses no Western instruments or tunings; all the rhythms, instruments, and playing techniques of *jaipong* were derived from already existing Sundanese performance genres (Manuel and Baier 1986).

In the late 1970s and early 1980s, *jaipong* became part of a nationwide dance craze that transcended ethnic boundaries (Manuel and Baier 1986; Murray 1991, 104; Yampolsky 1987b). More recently, *jaipong* has become a major ingredient for new diatonically based hybrid genres, including *dangdut jaipong*, *house jaipong*, and even *ska-pong* (a fusion of *jaipong* and ska), that use mostly Western instruments combined with Sundanese percussion (often sampled). At the same time, unadulterated *jaipong* has declined in popularity, and in Jakarta it has been relegated once again to the *musik daerah* category.

Many of my consultants were surprised (and a little disappointed) when I told them that the only "Indonesian" music that could regularly be found in American music stores was Balinese or Javanese gamelan, with Indonesian pop and dangdut nowhere to be found. (Non-Javanese and non-Balinese were particularly nonplussed.) After all, *American* popular music was ubiquitous in Indonesian record stores! Far from being emblematic of the Indonesian nation, gamelan music for most Jakartans (including many ethnic Javanese and Balinese) was just another style of *musik tradisional*—a subset of *musik daerah* appealing only to the most traditionally minded members of a particular ethnic group—and thus was rather marginal to the multiethnic national project in which Jakartan youth were routinely taught to believe.

Musik Underground

The Modern Noise Makes Modern People
slogan printed on the cover
of a 1997 issue of *Morbid Noise*,
a Jakartan underground metal zine

When I scream I would tell the truth.
Fear Inside (Bandung underground band),
"Muted Scream" (1998)

Beginning in the early 1990s, the term *underground* has been used in Indonesia to describe a cluster of rock music subgenres as well as a method of producing and distributing cultural objects. By the end of the decade, nearly every major urban area in Indonesia was home to a local underground scene, the most prominent of which were based in Jakarta, Yogyakarta, Surabaya, Malang, Bandung, Medan, Banda Aceh, and Denpasar (cf. Barendregt and Zanten 2002, 81–83; Baulch 1996, 2002a, 2002b, 2003; Pickles 2000; Putranto and Sadrach 2002; Sen and Hill 2000, 177–81).

Musik underground is composed of several *aliran* (streams); among them are *punk, hardcore, death metal, grindcore, brutal death, hyperblast, black metal, grunge, indies, industrial,* and *gothic.* As this brief list suggests, all the *aliran* are imported genres; their names and stylistic features are derived from music from overseas. But while underground musicians' orientation (*kiblat*) is toward the work of foreign bands, the way in which the music is produced and distributed is resolutely local and grassroots based. Indonesian underground bands, like underground groups elsewhere, produce their own recordings or release them through small independent labels in limited quantities. Recording studio rental rates in Indonesia are astonishingly cheap, and the number of Indonesian underground cassettes on the market increased exponentially between 1995 and 2000 despite the economic crisis. In fact, the monetary crisis may have actually encouraged the development of local underground music, since overseas underground rock recordings, which had to be purchased by catalog at Western prices and in Western currencies, became prohibitively expensive.

During its brief history, there has also been a marked linguistic shift in the Indonesian underground scene from an early predominance of songs sung in English to a larger number of songs written in Indonesian, which among other things helped expand the music's audience beyond middle-class students.[7] This shift was motivated by several aesthetic, ideological, and political factors, prominent among them an increasing awareness of and pride in the sheer scale and productivity of the Indonesian underground music movement (Wallach 2003a).

In addition to recordings, members of the underground publish "zines" (homemade magazines, short for "fanzines") that cover the local underground scene and often address sociopolitical issues. Since the late 1990s, a significant number of electronic fanzines (or "webzines"), band Web sites, and Web sites representing particular local musical scenes have appeared on the Internet. The grassroots, small-scale nature of underground cultural production is discursively linked to an (imported) ideology of "do-it-yourself" independence that rejects "selling out" to major labels (which in Indonesia also includes the large independent record companies) and celebrates artistic autonomy, idealism, community, and resistance to commercial pressures.

As in underground scenes in the United States, a certain amount of ambiguity and overlap exists between definitions of "underground" as musical style and "underground" as independent production and distribution. Recurring debates on whether bands were "selling out" because they signed contracts with large commercial record companies became more heated in the underground with the rise of ska, an energetic guitar-and-horn-based style with Jamaican, British, and American roots.[8] During my first visit to Indonesia in late 1997, ska was just another underground *aliran*. By mid-1999, however, its status as an underground style had become controversial. There were several Indonesian ska groups on major labels, and the most successful—Jun Fan Gung Foo, Tipe-X, and Purpose—were selling hundreds of thousands of cassettes across the archipelago (cf. Barendregt and Zanten 2002, 83). Also wildly popular were a number of ska band compilations with names like *Skamania* and *Ska Klinik*. Upper-class university students and street children alike knew the latest Indonesian ska tunes and the characteristic "running in place" dance steps with which to accompany them, while locally made ska T-shirts, stickers, patches, and posters featuring ska iconography's distinctive checkerboard graphics were on sale all over Jakarta in both upscale malls and outdoor markets. Ska had strayed far from its underground origins and had become, in the words of those who marketed the music, a "seasonal" (*musiman*), currently trendy (*lagi ngetrend*) music that appealed to a large cross-class youth audience.

Although other underground groups had managed to obtain major-label contracts, none had ever reached a level of commercial success commensurate with that of the new ska bands. This caused a negative reaction in the underground community, and in Jakarta the slogan *ska sucks* could be found spray-painted on walls and printed on stickers. Waiting Room, probably the first Indonesian ska band, which produced an independently released cassette in 1997, chose to abandon ska after its popularization, changing *aliran* on its second cassette (2000) to rap/funk/metal.[9] "*Ska is dead*," Lukman, the band's singer, told me, and many others in the underground scene agreed. Thus the ska boom stands as a case study of the instability of "underground" music as a category of music production versus a musical style.[10] Further consequences of the late '90s ska boom are explored in the next section.

The Formation of New Hybrids: Innovations and Juxtapositions

As will become clear in subsequent chapters, the genres listed above (and their audiences) do not exist in isolation from one another. Complex dynamics of influence, appropriation, and parody exist between them, such that dangdut rhythms sometimes appear on pop albums, dangdut bands at times play rock songs, *jaipong* groups sometimes play dangdut songs adapted to their instrumentation and tuning systems, and songs from the *jaipong* and *pop daerah* repertoires form the basis for many electronic dance music recordings. Among the more notable recent hybrids to appear on the Indonesian popular music scene are the following:

Dangdut remix (usually pronounced and sometimes spelled *dangdut remek*) is a term that denotes dance remixes of previously released dangdut songs. While dangdut remixes can be considered a subset of *dangdut trendy*, they stand out because the remix format allows producers to freely experiment with adding elements from traditional Indonesian musics, hip hop, *jaipong*, techno, and other genres to their compositions, usually through the medium of digital sampling (Wallach 2005, 142–46).

Hybrid genres *ska-dhut, ska-bon,* and *ska-pong* represented a new and unexpected phase of ska music's crossover from underground to mainstream genre. Unlike other briefly-in-vogue genres such as rap and R & B that were popular only with middle-class youth before declining and being replaced with trendier styles, ska's propulsive, danceable rhythms (which strongly resemble those used in *dangdut trendy* and *pop daerah*) have helped it to cross the social gap. The music's newfound popularity with the *orang kampung* (village/slum people) has encouraged the creation of new hybrids that combine the rhythms and sounds of ska with dangdut and *musik daerah*. The results of this innovation have met with mixed commercial success, but they certainly succeed in sheer inventiveness of a sort that can perhaps be found nowhere else in the world. One cassette released in 2000 titled *Ska Minang India* contains a song that appropriates the melody from "Kuch Kuch Hota Hai" (a popular Hindi film song), adds a programmed ska rhythm and brass arrangement, and is sung in *bahasa Minang,* a regional language spoken by the Minangkabau people of West Sumatra. The track even includes an ostinato part played with metal percussion samples resembling *talèmpong,* traditional West Sumatran tuned kettle gongs.

In the still-purist underground scene, at least two nationally known bands have experimented with combining death and black metal with Indonesian ethnic music. Kremush, a group from Purwokerto, Central Java, calls the resulting hybrid *brutal etnik,* while Eternal Madness, from Denpasar, Bali, prefers to call its music *lunatic ethnic grind death metal* (see chapter 4). These bands are extraordinary not only for their willingness to engage in cross-genre experimentation but also for the compelling nature of the results, which convincingly blend pentatonic traditional melodies and rhythmic accents with the instrumentation, vocal techniques, and musical conventions of underground metal.

"Ethnic Music" and the World Music Label

Whatever *aliran* or genre they play, Indonesian musicians tend to have some preoccupations in common. Few prominent musicians, with some notable exceptions, are immune to the desire to *go international*—an English expression, used frequently in the Indonesian mass media and in everyday conversations, which often really means making an impact in the U.S. market. An ironic twist to the desire of Indonesian pop musicians to reach an international market is that that market is more interested in Indonesian music that sounds "Indonesian" in some way than it is in thoroughly "modern" international pop music sung in an Indonesian approximation of English. The problem is that any popular music recording that draws on dangdut, *musik tradisional, jaipong,* or any other non-Western genre in order to sound distinctively "Indonesian" runs the risk of being considered *kampungan* by Indonesians themselves even as it conforms to international expectations for "world beat"-style music.

Indonesian pop and jazz musicians who have frequent contact with Westerners know that while the "world music/world beat" category may ghettoize them in the international pop music scene, this label provides their best chance for entering the prestigious and lucrative European-American market. As a result, some Indonesian musicians have experimented with adding "ethnic" elements to their compositions in an attempt to create a distinctively Indonesian brand of "world beat." The most successful of these experiments was carried out by the members of the Bandung-based jazz fusion group Krakatau (cf. Sutton 2002b, 23), who after many years of dedicated effort have received a considerable amount of international exposure for their uniquely hybridic music. This recognition was extremely hard-won, since in fact almost all of the market for Indonesian music is domestic, and the possibility of overseas promotion or distribution for the products of the Indonesian music industry is usually slim, owing to a combination of legal, economic, and ideological factors.

Dangdut Goes International

A final irony is that of all the genres of Indonesian popular music, dangdut has been by far the most successful in the international (albeit non-Western) market: Indonesian dangdut stars have found receptive audiences in several Asian countries, including Brunei Darussalam, Japan, Malaysia, the southern Philippines, Singapore, and Taiwan. In the late 1990s, a group of Japanese "world music" fans even formed their own dangdut group, O. M. Ranema, which, in the acronymic style of Indonesian dangdut group monikers, stands for *Orkes Melayu Rakyat Negara Matahari,* Indonesian for "Malay Orchestra of the People of the Sun Country." ("Sun Country" is of course a reference to Japan.) According to the group's Web site, which is available in Japanese and English but not Indonesian, the band has played several successful concerts in the Tokyo metropolitan area since the late 1990s. This kind of international recognition does not appear to have strongly influenced dangdut's domestic reception.[11]

Reacting to the chilly audience response to dangdut artist Iis Dahlia on a televised MTV Indonesia awards show we were watching, a young Javanese professional remarked, "Maybe dangdut has already *go international,* but it has yet to *go national!*" However, by 2001, a year after that conversation took place, dangdut music began to appear in slickly produced TV commercials for such global brands as McDonald's hamburgers (called "beef-burgers" in Indonesia in order not to mislead Muslims about their "guaranteed halal" status) and Sony electronics—a decision that was said to be based on solid market research (Kearney 2001; Kartomi 2002, 133). As dangdut slowly gains acceptance among urban middle-class Indonesians, it may be that dangdut's performers and producers will someday realize the wistful speculation of one Western ethnomusicologist: "Eventually perhaps *dangdut* may become as well known across the globe as Trinidad's *calypso* or Jamaica's *reggae*" (Kartomi 2002, 134). At any rate, dangdut will perhaps always enjoy the favor of one particular overseas audience: homesick middle-class Indonesian students studying abroad, many of whom never listen to the music at home.

2

In the City

CLASS, HISTORY, AND
MODERNITY'S FAILURES

Light reflects off my computer
monitor, not the glittering
rice paddy, not the sewing
machine's glittering
needle dipping like a cormorant into tomorrow's
Nike shoe and this is
the Culture at work.

Sun Yung Shin 2004

Jakarta is the least exotic locale in a country famous for being exotic. Although it has all the amenities one would expect from an ultramodern, globalized metropolis (for those who can afford them), foreigners and Indonesians alike tend to view the capital as an example of a failed, dystopian modernity—a blighted urban sprawl of traffic snarls, crime, poverty, open sewers, and pollution. Despite its political, economic, and cultural centrality, I spoke to very few residents of this massive city of approximately eleven million people who seemed to like living there very much. There is a saying in Jakarta: *Ibu tiri tak sekejam ibukota*—"A stepmother is not as cruel as the capital city [in Indonesian, literally 'mother city']." The perceived lack of communal ties between people and the difficult, competitive struggle to survive that confronts residents of the city are frequently given as examples of this "cruelty." Despite these misgivings, however, few residents would deny that Jakarta is the major center of production of Indonesian national culture, and has been so for the country's entire existence. In Clifford Geertz's memorable words, Jakarta is "where Indonesia is supposed to be summarized but perhaps is manufactured" (1995, 52).

The following overview of the cultural terrain of post-New Order Jakarta serves as a prelude to the ethnographic study of popular music that follows. Three themes emerge in a discussion of the spatial organization, speech styles, and social conditions that characterize everyday life in the capital city: first, a persistent dichotomization of rich and poor in everyday discourse, often based on an erstwhile urban/rural divide; second, the relationship between Indonesian historical memory and these class-based, discursive bifurcations; and third, the ongoing process of cultural innovation by social agents from all walks of life in response to the conditions of urban life. As the following discussion makes clear, this continual process of innovation and improvisation occurs against a backdrop of sensory unruliness created by the chaos of an overpopulated, divided, and indeed often cruel metropolis.

Jakarta as an Ethnographic Field Site

> When I tell people in Jakarta that I'm from Surabaya, they say, "Oh, you're from Java!" As if Jakarta wasn't also on Java!
>
> Samir, lead guitarist for Slowdeath

Jakarta is the main field site of this study, and in many ways, it is unique. Its size, level of commercial development, multiethnic population, and political centrality set it apart from Indonesia's other major cities, all of which are nonetheless influenced tremendously by developments in the capital. In this sense, Jakarta is an "exemplary center" for the rest of the nation, a site in which cultural power is consolidated and flows outward to the periphery (see Anderson 1990, 35–38; Guinness 2000), where it is both accommodated and resisted by local agents (Steedly 1999, 444). Indonesians often consider Indonesia's capital city a separate entity unto itself. Jakarta is located in the western portion of the island of Java, but the city is a Special Capital District (*Daerah Khusus Ibukota*) not included in the province of West Java. It is certainly not considered part of

"Java" (see Pemberton 1994b and the epigraph preceding this section), which as an unmarked term in Indonesia generally refers to the provinces of Central and/or East Java, where the majority of the population is ethnic Javanese (West Java, in contrast, is dominated by Sundanese).

To many Indonesians, Jakarta represents certain trends in contemporary Indonesian society taken to an extreme, including deepening class divisions, consumerism, westernization, and the replacement of reciprocity-based economic systems by economies based on discrete single-transaction exchanges. Each of these trends is present in most parts of Indonesia, including small towns and villages, but Jakarta is viewed as the exemplar for all of them, and many Indonesians in the provinces are wary of following its lead. Most people who live in Jakarta are migrants who often speak longingly of their home villages or cities elsewhere in the archipelago, but many admit that Jakarta is the only place where they can find real economic opportunity. For them, living in the capital is a necessary evil, and many in fact choose to leave their families behind in the village, where the cost of living is lower and family members can be insulated from the "corrupting" influences of the city. Even lifelong residents of Jakarta who can rely on extended networks of economic support may find those networks threatened by state-led development and the commodification of everyday life, leading to conditions of instability and unpredictable fortunes (Jellinek 1991; Murray 1991).

In short, Jakarta is the locus for a whole host of economic and social changes that have caused the "ethnographic ground" of Indonesia to shift "in ways unsettling to anthropology's culturalist sensibility" (Steedly 1999, 432). In this view, as the city and the lifestyles of its elites come to resemble those in other high-tech, newly industrialized Asian countries, the distinctiveness of Jakarta's Indonesian "culture" is eroded. The reality, however, despite the much-remarked-upon ubiquity of malls, cybercafés, McDonald's, cellular telephones, and Mercedes Benz vehicles in contemporary Jakarta, is more complex than a purely culturalist perspective might suggest, as is the city's relationship to the global modernity to which it aspires (see Guinness 2000). It is worth emphasizing that malls and American fast food have *not* taken over all of Jakarta; these new additions coexist with an extensive informal economy (Danesh 1999) that supports the majority of the city's inhabitants—a juxtaposition of economic and cultural logics that will be explored in more detail later in this chapter.

Jakarta: An Introductory Geography

Jakarta is so vast that during my fieldwork I was unable to find any maps of the city that covered its entire area. Jakarta's 255 square miles are divided into five municipalities (*kotamadya*): North, South, East, West, and Central (Forbes 2002, 410). Market-driven and state-led development over the last three decades has transformed most of what was essentially a loose, sprawling network of villages with a colonial-style town at the center into a congested metropolis of skyscrapers, malls, and teeming shantytowns (Grijns and Nas 2000). There are still places, especially on the outskirts of the city (which blend seamlessly into the surrounding areas of Bogor, Bekasi, and Tanggerang), where there are rice paddies and open fields.

The vast majority of Jakarta's inhabitants live in *kampung*, villagelike neighborhoods of single-family dwellings with varying population densities.[1] Middle- and upper-class Jakartans live in neighborhoods of large cement attached houses; many of the most fashionable of these are located in South Jakarta (Jakarta Selatan, or Jaksel), though East, West,

A garbage-choked canal under Sudirman Street, a main thoroughfare in Jakarta's central business district.

and North Jakarta have their own pockets of affluence surrounded by the *kampung* of ordinary residents. A small number of elite Jakartans have begun to move into high-rise apartment complexes located in the city center, which until very recently were inhabited mostly by members of Jakarta's large expatriate population.[2] These few escape the harrowing commutes undertaken daily by the numerous affluent city residents who work in Central Jakarta and who live in Pondok Indah, Kebayoran Baru, Bintaro, and other upscale neighborhoods of South Jakarta. The poor often commute even longer distances, by motorbike or on battered public buses and vans of various shapes and sizes.

Central Jakarta (Jakarta Pusat, or Jakpus) is the main hub for business and commerce, and its boulevards are lined with impressive steel and glass office towers and luxury hotels. The ground floors of these buildings house banks, restaurants, discos, upscale cinemas, and nightclubs and are nighttime destinations for Jakarta's elite. Beyond (and often beside) these narrow corridors of global capitalist cosmopolitanism is a vast and complex patchwork of neighborhoods, malls, mosques, monuments, universities, embassies, canals, government buildings, markets, and slums that together constitute a heterogeneous, chaotic metropolis—one that embodies everything that many Indonesians desire, dislike, and fear about the modern world.

Carnival and Dystopia: Jakarta, Modernity, and Traffic

In recent years Indonesia has shed its exotic, fairy-tale image and emerged as a modern, enterprising nation.

> publisher's foreword,
> *Tuttle's Concise Indonesian Dictionary* (Kramer and Koen 1995)

You might be Indonesian if: [. . .] *The first thing that comes to mind when hearing the word "Jakarta" is "macet"* [congested].

> excerpt from a humorous e-mail message that circulated widely
> in the late 1990s on Indonesian student list serves

As the metropolitan core of the Indonesian national project, Jakarta influences all corners of the archipelago, particularly with regard to the question of "how to be modern" (Yampolsky 1989, 9–10). To my surprise, a group of students at the Jakarta Art Institute (IKJ) hailing from various Indonesian provinces once described Jakarta to me as *"too* modern." At first this description surprised me, but in fact modernity, despite its considerable allure, also brings with it deep ambivalences, anxieties, and feelings of loss (Ivy 1995; Ferzacca 2001; Shannon 2006). Geertz has observed that in the developing world, "modernity turned out to be less a fixed destination than a vast and inconstant field of warring possibilities, possibilities neither simultaneously reachable nor systematically connected, neither well defined nor unequivocally attractive" (1995, 138). The ambivalence many Indonesians feel toward modernity and modernization is compounded by Indonesia's subaltern position in the neoliberal global order, which prevents most Indonesians from enjoying modernity's material and social benefits or, in the evolutionist parlance of the New Order, keeps most people in a "backward" (*terbelakang*) state.

The exacerbation of social inequality is one serious consequence of rapid and uneven economic development in Jakarta and in Indonesia more generally. Of even more concern to many Indonesians is the "individualism" (*individualisme*) that Jakarta represents: the possibility that the materialism and pressures of urban life combined with prolonged separation from solidary village communities will cause people to act selfishly, without regard for their families or communities.

Contemporary Jakarta can be viewed as a textbook example of what modernization theorists have called "overurbanization" (Sovani 1964). Gerald Breese writes, "This phenomenon [of overurbanization] has been noted with particular interest and concern because of the common observation, in newly developing countries, that with very few exceptions there appears to be much too large a population in urban areas to be supported by the employment, services, and facilities available" (1966, 134). Breese correctly notes that charges of overurbanization may be beside the point, since the overpopulation of cities in developing countries tends to result from the impoverishment of rural areas, which compels their inhabitants to migrate to cities in search of economic opportunity. This certainly has been the case on the overcrowded island of Java—the most densely populated island in the world—where many feel they have no choice but to seek work in Jakarta to support themselves and their families.

For many Jakartans, the abysmal situation on Jakarta's roadways, particularly its main thoroughfares, is a conspicuous example of the downside of modernity and "progress." Jakarta resembles most other capital cities in the developing world, where increasing numbers of motor vehicles, coupled with inefficient public transportation options, have created a seemingly insurmountable traffic problem. Jakarta's motor-vehicle traffic, particularly during rush hours, is legendary for its sluggishness. The word *macet* (clogged, stopped up) and the phrase *macet total* (totally clogged, i.e., gridlocked) are indispensable in everyday conversations—particularly when giving the reason for arriving at a meeting two hours late (cf. Ziv 2002, 86).

While some Jakartans blame *bajaj* (motorized trishaws) and public buses for causing Jakarta's hopeless traffic jams, in fact the congestion is a consequence of the rising affluence of some city residents. Around 86 percent of the cars on Jakarta's streets are privately owned vehicles (*Jakarta Post* 2000, 1), a much greater percentage than in the past, and several taxi drivers complained bitterly to me that some rich families in Jakarta owned cars for each member of their respective households, including one for each servant! Such overconsumption, they claimed, is why Jakarta's streets were so *macet*.

The individualist nature of private vehicle ownership, in addition to its role in creating tremendous traffic congestion, is offensive to working-class Indonesian sensibilities. Many privately owned vehicles in Jakarta have tinted windows that make their drivers invisible to those on the outside. Like the looming steel and glass skyscrapers along the main boulevards, the glinting opaque surfaces of tinted car windows speak to the arrogance (*kesombongan*) and power of those inside. This material expression of social distance exemplifies the *individualisme* (which in Indonesian has a meaning close to "selfishness") and lack of community that nearly everyone with whom I spoke, residents and nonresidents alike, associated with contemporary Jakarta. This arrogance receives its partial comeuppance through the very problem it creates. The city's traffic jams create a kind of transient cultural space that provides the opportunity for roving vendors, beggars, and street musicians to approach cars stopped in traffic or at intersections, hoping to catch the attention of stranded motorists. This leads to a "carnivalesque" atmosphere (see Bakhtin 1984; Stallybrass and White 1986), an ephemeral reversal of social status in which the city's mobile indigent come face-to-face with the elites trapped inside their air-conditioned capsules. Often beggars and street musicians are given loose change through cracked-open car windows more out of fear and annoyance than compassion, in the hope that these walking reminders of the *social gap* will leave the driver and passengers alone.

A new wrinkle in the controversies over Jakarta's *macet* problem is the return of pedal-powered trishaws (*becak*) to the streets of the city. These human-powered vehicles were banned by the New Order regime in the 1980s in a brutally repressive campaign to "modernize" Jakarta's streets (Murray 1991, 91–92). Since the demise of that regime, Jakarta's *becak* drivers have organized and held demonstrations seeking to regain their lost livelihoods. They have united behind the slogan *Biar Kami Ada* (Let Us [exclusive] Be), and a number of drivers have begun working on the backstreets of the city, in defiance of municipal ordinances. A number of people with whom I spoke opined that if the *becak*s were indeed permitted to return en masse to the capital, Jakarta's traffic would come to a complete standstill. Nevertheless, Jakarta's dystopian transportation problems have been caused not by the "backwardness" of nonpolluting, human-powered transport but by a *surplus* of "progress": the emulation of global standards of private affluence by an increasing number of prosperous residents. The impact of *macet total*, of course, does not affect only elites: ordinary Jakartans must also struggle to get from place to place, and while large, noisy crowds of people are regarded positively by Indonesians, roads choked with motorcycles, cars, *bajaj*, and buses are seen as just another example of the harshness and difficulty of city life.

The Dichotomized Cultural Logics of "Late" and Petty Capitalism

Jangan anda lupakan untuk berbelanja kepasar tradisional
Pasar tradisional murah meriah

[Don't you forget to shop at traditional markets
Traditional markets are cheap and cheerful]

> a large sign in Pasar Santa, a "traditional" market area
> in South Jakarta, located a short distance
> from the megamalls of Blok M

As the preceding discussion suggests, Jakarta is really two cities, each based on a separate spatial, economic, and cultural logic (cf. Leggett 2005, 279). The first of these coexisting logics is based on reciprocity and loan-based petty capitalism, while the second is the product of high-technology consumer capitalism in its most recent "globalizing" phase (see Waters 1995). Thus humble food stalls cluster around multistoried malls, and one can purchase refill cards for cellular telephones either in spacious, air-conditioned stores or from street-side vendors, often for a slightly lower price.[3] Food, clothing, cassettes, even prostitutes (Hull, Sulistyaningsih, and Jones 1999, 15) are available in both the informal and the formalized economic sectors; Geertz (1963), in a study of the commercial life of Javanese towns, identifies the two types as "bazaar-based" and "firm-based" economies. This distinction is remarkably apt for describing the contemporary economic landscape in Jakarta as well.

The vast majority of Jakartans inhabit both economic worlds. Almost everyone eats at roadside food stalls; working-class *kampung* dwellers with formal-sector occupations have bank accounts and hang out in local Internet cafés (which represent an interesting intersection point of the two worlds, as I discuss later). Nearly everyone buys cigarettes from street-side cigarette kiosks (*warung rokok*) and purchases bottled water, cigarettes, and snacks from roving salespeople (*pedagang asongan*) at traffic intersections. This ethnography focuses primarily on those who are neither destitute nor rich and powerful members of the political and economic elite. Such people are generally comfortable in both economic spheres in their everyday lives.

The 2000 Jakarta Fair, held at the expansive Jakarta Fairgrounds in celebration of the city's 473rd anniversary (dated from the defeat of the Portuguese and the renaming of the city by Fatahillah), exemplified the coexistence of conglomerate- and bazaar-based economies in urban Indonesia. At the fairground entrance the visitor was confronted with rows of large, brightly lit tents showcasing commodities ranging from shiny new motorcycles to American junk food to cellular phones. In the darkened, blacktopped area behind these corporate-sponsored tents was a sprawling night market (*pasar malam*), complete with two freak shows, a *kuda lumping* ensemble (performers from East Java who execute amazing and dangerous feats while under trance), and rows of vendors selling plastic toys, pirated cassettes, street food, clothes, and other items from blankets spread out on the asphalt. Behind this night bazaar was a large stage that featured live dangdut music.

The coexistence of the two halves gives rise to a series of binary oppositions constitutive of a fundamental social distinction in Jakarta society that is far less about the difference between traditional and modern or rural and urban than about the difference between rich and poor.

Warung Capitalism

Indonesia's vast informal economy revolves around the *warung* (stall), which ranges in size from small cigarette kiosks to large tents accommodating a dozen or so customers, as well as a whole range of mobile and semimobile street vendors. Jakarta *warung* owners do not try to make their businesses stand out but rather strive to make them resemble the other *warung* in their category. They tend to choose humble, even self-effacing names like Warung Lumayan (Pretty Good *Warung*), Warung

Nasi Sederhana (Simple Rice *Warung*), or even Warung Tanpa Nama (*Warung* without a Name). Standing out is to be avoided in the informal economy; in contrast, the formal sector in Indonesia and elsewhere relies on brand-name recognition and attempts to convince consumers through advertising that a particular product is unique and superior.

Warung also tend to operate on the principle that twenty flower stalls situated in one place is preferable to each competitor operating in a different location—a strategy of concentration that keeps prices competitive but attracts many customers. *Warung* that serve specialized needs—those that sell upholstery, customized rubber stamps, banners, identification card photos, and so on—are usually found in a small number of highly concentrated locations in Jakarta. Music cassette stalls tend to follow a different strategy and are usually widely dispersed. Often there is only one *warung* that sells nonpirated music cassettes (usually along with other items) in a bazaar; temporary street markets may contain a scattered handful of vendors selling pirated cassettes at much lower prices. More common than either are pirated VCD (video compact disc) vendors who display their wares (which may include Hollywood movies, dangdut karaoke disks, and/or pornographic videos) in large clusters. In 1999–2000 they far outnumbered cassette stalls.

Most *warung* have regular customers (*langganan*) who often buy items on credit. In the competitive *warung* economy, continuing relationships with regular customers are necessary to ensure survival. And since participants in this economy strive for subsistence rather than accumulation, the inability of some customers to pay at certain times is acceptable as long as debts are eventually paid and a small amount of money does change hands.

More on the Discursive Bifurcation of Urban Life: Rich and Poor, Village and City

Katanya Jakarta ini kota, tapi buat saya, Jakarta kampung besar.

[They say Jakarta is a city, but to me, Jakarta is a big village.]
Titiek Nur, veteran dangdut singer

In the subtitled, partially censored version of the film *American Beauty* (1999) that played in Jakarta movie theaters during the period of my fieldwork, the line "I don't think there's anything worse than being ordinary," spoken by one of the teenage characters, was translated as "I don't think there's anything worse than being *kampungan* [low class, villagelike]." When afterward I asked two English-speaking, middle-class companions about this translation, they responded that under the New Order, being ordinary and not standing out was considered a virtue, but *no one* wanted to be considered low class and backward. Thus it would not make sense for a character in a movie to say she didn't want to be ordinary, but it would be understandable for her to say she would rather be anything but *kampungan*. This small example of cross-cultural translation illustrates how important the notion of *kampungan* is in Indonesian habits of self-definition. Although the root of the word (from *kampung*, "village") suggests a "village/city" dichotomous logic behind the epithet, in fact the axiomatic discursive opposition between *kampungan* and *kotaan* (citified) is more about cultural and economic capital than geographic location. Indeed, the fundamental structural opposition that shapes social perception in Jakarta is not *kampung* versus *kota* but have-not versus have. This paramount binary opposition is invoked in the following commonly heard distinctions:

1. *Mal* (mall) versus *pasar* ("traditional" market)
2. *Restoran* (restaurant) versus *warung makan* (food stall)
3. American cigarettes versus *kretek* (Indonesian clove cigarettes)
4. Dark, subdued colors versus bright (*ngejreng*) colors
5. Indonesian versus regional languages
6. English versus Indonesian
7. *Pop* versus dangdut

Very few commodities are not subject to category distinctions like those listed above. Even fruit, for example, is divided into expensive, often imported items like pineapples and strawberries, on the one hand, and "village" fruits (often sour or bitter) such as *gohok* and *salak,* on the other.[4] Just mentioning the latter fruits invariably provoked laughter among my research consultants. Likewise, in large Jakarta supermarkets, potato chips and other slickly packaged, Western-style snacks are often located in an aisle labeled "modern snacks," while shrimp cakes (*kerupuk*) and other locally produced foodstuffs that are sold in *warung* can be found in a separate supermarket aisle labeled simply "snacks."

Class, Nostalgia, and Modern Indonesian History: New Order versus Old

In the simplified binary logic of hegemonic national discourse, "traditional culture" is conflated with backwardness and poverty, and the modern becomes nearly synonymous with Western and westernized cultural elements. But examining the realities of everyday life in Jakarta reveals a more complex, nuanced range of cultural alternatives available to Indonesians. Lisa Rofel (1999), in her study of mainland Chinese factory workers, highlights how successive regimes in China have promoted divergent visions of national modernity. These "other modernities" are internalized by subjects and result in significant cultural and aspirational differences between successive generations of Chinese. In Indonesia, the New Order's developmentalist ideology generated a particular type of modernity that displaced the populist/nationalist version promulgated by Indonesia's first president, Sukarno.

The Sukarno era (1949–65) was a complicated, troubled period in Indonesian history, but it was also, particularly in the years immediately following independence, a heady time of seemingly endless possibilities. Despite the many problems and crises during Sukarno's rule, many ordinary Indonesians view the so-called Old Order (Orde Lama) with deep nostalgia as a time when they felt included in the national project.[5] In Jakarta's outdoor markets one can always find Sukarno calendars, stickers, and posters for sale, constituting a "second life" for the late president and an implicit critique of his successors (Labrousse 1994). Under the New Order (1966–98), many urban Indonesians enjoyed a dramatic increase in their standard of living as the Soeharto regime expanded the formal economy through its technocratic developmentalist policies, yet the regime seemed to ignore the aspirations of the "little people," the *rakyat kecil*, and appeared to exist for the benefit of a corrupt, exclusive caste of big businessmen, high-level bureaucrats, and military officers. Ruth McVey writes, "The New Order's triumph marked the consolidation of Indonesia's postrevolutionary elite, its achievement of self-consciousness, and its ability when threatened to reject the populism, political radicalism, and militant nationalism that had been part of its ideological baggage since the struggle for independence" (1982, 86). The rejection of populism in favor of elitism and of militant nationalism in favor of an openness to foreign investment and foreign products became central features of official culture under the New Order, particularly in its later years.

While the pursuit of material wealth, development, and modernity remains a powerful narrative for nation building in Indonesia as elsewhere, under the New Order these ideologies were deployed in a coercive fashion, and ordinary people were made to feel ashamed of their poverty and traditional village ways. Furthermore, many Indonesians were suspicious of Western-style consumerism and longed for the Sukarno years' rhetoric of self-sufficiency and national achievement. Many Indonesian Muslims also had deep reservations about idolizing the Christian West. These and other factors led to a certain amount of ambivalence toward the New Order regime's Western-oriented developmentalism, despite the allure that Western popular culture and consumer goods held for many Indonesians.

The differences between Sukarno's and Soeharto's Indonesia are still visible in the urban landscape; the crowded *warung* and outdoor bazaars in the park area surrounding Monas (Monumen Nasional, the National Monument in Central Jakarta, a structure meant to represent the newly independent Indonesian nation's greatness and the collective achievement of its people) contrast sharply with the sterile and exclusive air-conditioned megamalls in Jakarta's main shopping districts. In their own fashion, megamalls are also monuments—to the consumerism and increasing wealth of New Order Indonesia's middle and upper classes.

Modernity's Automatons: Old Order versus New

After ascending the marble stairs to the second floor of the National Monument, one enters a large atrium built around the central tower shaft. On the shaft is a tall, narrow pair of what look like elevator doors ornately decorated with green and gold woodcarvings.

Suddenly the doors crack open to the sound of an aged, worn recording of a Western-style choir and orchestra playing a patriotic Indonesian song. The portals slide apart to reveal an additional pair of inner wooden doors that open vertically. Behind this set of doors is a piece of paper under glass illuminated by a low-wattage bulb. The music stops, and the voice of Sukarno, Indonesia's first president, crackles through the speakers. It is a recording of the radio broadcast during which Sukarno read aloud the Proclamation of 1945, which declared Indonesia's independence from the Dutch. After Sukarno's speech concludes, the music begins again, and the two pairs of doors close creakily. The proclamation was a classic performative utterance (Austin 1975): with one verbal act, Sukarno constitutes an independent nation and a people (*rakyat*) where there was once only an archipelago that happened to be controlled by a single European colonial power (Siegel 1998, 22–27). The automated display at Monas attempts to re-create this foundational event in Indonesian history with a mechanical contrivance. But the overall effect is rather underwhelming, appearing almost to emphasize the quaint outdatedness of Sukarno's vision of an independent, prosperous nation beholden to no other.

It is instructive to compare the Proklamasi contraption inside Monas with another mechanical, moving display located inside Plaza Senayan, a multitiered, luxury megamall in Central Jakarta. Every hour, the large clock in the main gallery opens up to reveal six mechanical golden cherubs with generic European features. The cherubs play Western musical instruments to a soundtrack of rather eerie synthesized New Age music. The sound is pristine, and the expressionless automatons' gestures are fluid. Perhaps without intending it, the clock at Plaza Senayan is an ideal representation of New Order Indonesia—sleek, shiny, ostentatious, westernized, and possessing a disquieting unreality. While the National Monument is located in a large park open to everyone, the clock is the centerpiece of one of Jakarta's most exclusive and expensive shopping destinations, where most Jakartans—even some middle-class people—hesitate to enter. Thus two alternative visions of modernity, two "warring possibilities," to use Geertz's term, coexist in Jakarta's urban environment, one populist but perhaps outmoded, the other sophisticated and cosmopolitan but exclusivist.

A Shrine to Sukarno in Kebayoran Baru

An unusual architectural feature I encountered in a middle-class South Jakarta neighborhood illustrates the continuing attraction of the Sukarno period to some contemporary Indonesians. The feature in question was a privately owned and constructed monument to Sukarno located in the front yard of an unassuming private residence. The monument consisted of a larger-than-life white statue of the former leader surrounded by cement bas-reliefs of icons and slogans from the Sukarno era. These included *Bersatulah Bangsaku!* (Be As One, My Nation!), *Kita bukan Bangsa pengemis* (We are not a beggar Nation), *Digali diolah sendiri* ("Excavated and processed by ourselves," a reference to Sukarno's plan for self-sufficiency in the management of Indonesia's rich natural resources), and *Kita Taruhkan Kemerdekaan dengan Darah Patriot Bangsa* (We Stake Our Freedom with the Blood of the Nation's Patriots). An inscription on the base of Sukarno's statue read *Bung Karno lebih mentjintai rakjatnja dari pada dirinja* (Brother/Comrade Sukarno loved the people more than himself). It is highly unlikely that anyone would say the same about any current political leader in Indonesia.

Sukarno memorial shrine in the front yard of a private residence, Kebayoran Baru, South Jakarta.

The slogans were written in an old orthography of Indonesian that was superseded in 1972, during the New Order. Thus in the very spelling of the words, the inscriptions on the monument convey nostalgia for Sukarno's presidency and express opposition to the current state of affairs. While apparently the handiwork of a middle-class Jakartan, the nostalgia expressed by this vernacular monument for a lost historical moment is most keenly felt among the working and lower classes, for it was during the Sukarno period that they, as "the people" (*rakyat*), assumed the role of national heroes, became revolutionary patriots, and had a charismatic leader who claimed he spoke for them.

Social Bifurcation and the Jakarta Riots

Under the New Order, the Indonesian masses (*massa*) became associated not with national revolution but with antisocial chaos and criminality (Siegel 1998). The May 1998 riots that precipitated Soeharto's departure from the presidency were a prime example of this criminality—the disruptive potential of the *rakyat kecil* (little people) realized in a paroxysm of underclass rage against the gap between rich and poor. The so-called middle to upper classes (*kelas menengah ke atas*) fear the *rakyat kecil*, especially when they take the form of the *massa*, the "mass" capable of large-scale destruction of property and people. The lack of an effective police force and the ever-present threat of provocation make the *massa* especially dangerous. The mass shields its members from individual accountability, and it easily overwhelms all but the most deadly forces of law and order. Thus the mass represents the grotesque opposite of Jakarta's "individualism"—a de-individuated mob that acts single-mindedly.[6]

The gulf between the haves and the have-nots was thrown into stark relief by the violent events of May 1998. The following passage is from a published firsthand account of the riots written by Ita Sembiring, a young Batak woman active in Jakarta's entertainment industry.

Puji Tuhan sampai selepas mahgrib tidak ada kejadian berbahaya. Massa masih tetap bertahan di seputar Plaza yang belum "takluk" juga. Aku merasakan betapa tenangnya pada saat-saat begini jadi warga kampung saja. Lihat saja mereka, sangat berbahagia dan bebas menikmati udara segar. Sementara penghuni rumah kompleks mondar-mandir tidak karuan dengan penuh kecemasan dan ketakutan. Orang-orang yang selama ini tidak pernah aku lihat sekonyong-konyong bermunculan dan berjalan-jalan dengan tenang di seputar kompleks, Plaza, dan jalan raya. Laki-laki, perempuan,

*anak-anak, orang dewasa, orang tua semua sangat santai dan tenang sea-
kan tidak terjadi apa-apa. Dan memang benar tidak terjadi apa-apa dengan kelompok mereka. Betapa mereka menyadari saat seperti ini ternyata
lebih enak punya kehidupan seperti yang mereka miliki. Tidak ada kekha-
watiran akan kehilangan harta apalagi nyawa. Terlebih lagi mereka juga
seakan sangat menikmati ketakutannya para orang "berada" itu sebagai ba-
gian dari hiburan yang jarang-jarang bisa mereka nikmati. Sangat* natural.

[Praise God, until well after sunset there were no dangerous incidents.
The mass was still staying put around the plaza, which still had not
"surrendered" (to the police). I thought, how relaxing, at moments like
this, to just be a *kampung* resident. Just look at them, very happy and
free to enjoy the fresh air while occupants of the housing complex
paced back and forth aimlessly, full of anxiety and fear. People who
until now I had never seen before suddenly emerged and strolled plac-
idly around the complex, the plaza, and the main roads. Boys, girls,
young children, adults, and old people were all very relaxed and calm as
though nothing at all had occurred. And it was indeed true that nothing had happened to their group. How aware they were that at a moment like this, it turned out to be better to have the life they themselves
had. (For them,) there was no worry about losing their possessions, or
what's more, their lives. Moreover, they also seemed to enjoy greatly
(watching) the fear of the people "of means" (*berada*) as a sort of entertainment they could rarely enjoy. Very *natural.*] (Sembiring 1998, 51–52)

This striking passage portrays the social chaos and the breakdown of
civility during the 1998 Jakarta riots as a rite of reversal. The formerly
anonymous slum dwellers—the ubiquitous, mundane human backdrop
to the Indonesian affluent urban lifestyle—"suddenly" emerged to taunt
the members of the moneyed classes, whose conspicuous material
wealth equally suddenly made them vulnerable and gave them good
reason to be terrified by the encroaching angry mob.[7] For a short time
until "order" was restored, the tables were turned, and two years later
the Jakarta cityscape still bore the scars of the mob's actions. The
broken windows, burnt-out malls (many rumored to contain hundreds
of charred corpses), and gutted, blackened supermarkets that remained
visible in commercial districts around the city in 1999–2000 indexed the
collapse of the New Order's regime of social control over the masses, as
well as the battered and economically crippled state of post–New Order
Indonesia. Many Jakartans expected more massive riots to take place,
though so far they have not. Instead, social violence in the city has taken

the form of violent street crime, brutal vigilantism, and frequent gang wars (*tawuran*) between young men belonging to different schools and neighborhoods.

Soundscapes and Mediascapes: Crowded, Noisy, Fun

Locally grounded cultural meanings are influenced by a global sensorium of images, sounds, and movements, but this influence cannot be examined properly unless the *local* sensorium is also taken into account. The following section focuses primarily on Jakarta's sonic environment, which provides an aural backdrop for all the musical activities that take place there.

Jakarta is not a quiet city. The omnipresent roar of traffic, the cries of traveling street hawkers, the Islamic call to prayer emanating at regular intervals from loudspeakers over mosques, the high-pitched bleating of cellular phones, and the sounds of recorded popular music blaring from *warung* all create an atmosphere of noisy, boisterous humanity on Jakarta's streets and in its neighborhoods. In an article on the electronic soundscape of contemporary Java, R. Anderson Sutton (1996) describes how the availability of electronic amplification has helped to create a noisy aesthetic of overlapping sound sources that conforms to the positively evaluated Javanese (and Indonesian) concept of *rame* (crowded, noisy, fun), but that also perhaps embodies the chaos of the contemporary "crazy" existential condition of Javanese confronted with social transformation, new consumer technologies, and other trappings of modernity.[8] Thus, according to Sutton, the ubiquitous presence in Java of loud, often distorted, recorded sounds blaring out of loudspeakers in a variety of public spaces both extends indigenously derived sonic aesthetics and expresses the cultural and psychological dislocations resulting from the influx of new technologies, cultural influences, and life pressures.

An outdoor carnival (*pesta rakyat*, literally "the people's party") I attended in Lebak Bulus, South Jakarta, in early 2000 featured a variety of overlapping sound sources, including a loudspeaker system blasting pop, rock, and *dangdut disco* music and an overdriven megaphone set up in front of a rather lackluster *rumah hantu* (haunted house) emitting ghoulish screams, diabolical laughter, and other contextually appropriate canned sounds. By far the loudest sound source at the fair was the Roda-Roda Gila (Crazy Wheels)—also known as Tong Sten (short for Tong Setan, "Satan's Barrel")—an attraction for which one paid 1,000 rupiahs (at the time, US$0.16) to ascend a set of spiraling metal steps to a balcony around the top rim of a large wooden barrel, about fifteen feet high and ten feet in diameter. At the bottom of the barrel were two motorcycles. Once all the ticket holders were standing on the balcony, two young men entered, mounted the bikes, and gunned their engines. As they each ascended the inner walls of the barrel, riding nearly at right angles to the ground as they spiraled upward, the noise became deafening, and the air, trapped under a plastic tarpaulin covering the top of the barrel, filled with exhaust smoke. Soon the audience members began holding out 500 and 1,000 rupiah notes for the daredevil cyclists to grab as they passed. They would snatch the bills out of the onlookers' hands and let the money flutter to the ground, until by the end of their ride, as the two motorcycles spiraled downward, there were approximately 15,000 rupiahs lying on the ground below. This dramatic and raucous spectacle epitomized Jakartan working-class entertainment: crowded, noisy, fun, and dangerous, qualities summed up in local slang by the adjective *seru*—the literal meaning of which is "to shout"—which is sort of an extreme version of *rame* that is often also used to describe loud rock concerts.

The popularity of noisiness is not limited to working-class entertainments, however, as anyone who has ever watched an action or horror film in an upscale Jakarta movie theater (and heard the theater's deafening sound system) can attest. The high Indonesian threshold for loud sounds was apparent at an upscale audio-video product exposition held at the Jakarta Convention Center on February 12, 2000. The entire main hall of the convention center was filled with a raucous cacophony of action-film soundtracks, Western rock music, electronic dance tunes, and *pop Indonesia* karaoke videos. This was a high-end exhibition targeting Jakarta's adult middle class (thus dangdut was *not* among the genres represented); the electronics companies that took part originated from Japan, Korea, and the United States, including American audiophile companies Kenwood and Marantz. When I asked one of my companions why no Indonesian electronic firms were present, he replied that made-in-Indonesia electronic products were "no good" (*tidak bagus*). The high-prestige and high-priced wares on display in each booth competed for sonic space, such that even within the same company's booth different playback devices blasted different programs at the same time, creating a noisescape of overlapping envelopes of overdriven, full-spectrum sound. Such a soundscape contrasts sharply with the orderly use of recorded music in Western built environments, in which music is architecturally contained in clearly defined functional spaces (hallways, store interiors, restrooms, etc.) and in which sonic overlap, perceived as disorienting, is assiduously avoided (see Sterne 1997).

When I asked the same companion why the volume on everything was turned up so high, his reply was, "Because people want to hear what the stuff sounds like!" The middle-aged, well-dressed crowd making its way between the booths, which in addition to audio and video equipment offered everything from cellular phone plans to food processors, seemed unfazed by the high volume of sound enveloping them, even though the decibels generated by the hundreds of VCD players, stereo systems, and television sets playing at full blast approached rock-concert levels. While the exhibition visually resembled an orderly, clean, well-organized display of luxury commodities arranged to stimulate consumer desire, the aural dimension of the event was more akin to a *pasar malam* (outdoor night market), only louder.

Internet Cafés

One relatively new feature of the Jakarta landscape is the cybercafé, known locally as *warnet,* short for *warung internet.* Since the mid-1990s *warnets* have "mushroomed" (*menjamur*) all over Jakarta and other cities in Indonesia, especially those with high student or tourist populations (see Hill and Sen 1997; Sen and Hill 2000, 195–99).[9] In a magazine article about the *boom bisnis warnet,* Onno W. Purba, a local Internet expert, metaphorically connects the *warnet* concept to Jakarta's public transportation:

> *Kalau koneksi di rumah seperti naik mobil pribadi, sedangkan warnet itu seperti angkot (angkutan kota), kendaraan umum yang dipakai bareng-bareng. Ecerannya murah, jadi enteng buat masyarakat.*
>
> [If an (Internet) connection at home is like taking a private car, then the *warnet* is like the *angkot* (city transit), public transportation that people all use together. Each (rider's) share is cheap, so it's a light burden for society.] (quoted in Sujatmoko and Winarto 2000, 6–7)

Interestingly, the only time I have heard someone use the word *macet* to refer to something other than road traffic congestion was when the speaker was experiencing a slow Internet connection.

It is difficult to estimate the total number of Internet users in Indonesia. According to a 2000 news magazine article, in that year approximately one-half of 1 percent of the Indonesian population, or about one million people, were Internet users (Khudori and Winarto 2000, 16), compared with 50,000 to 100,000 users at the end of 1997 (Sen and Hill 2000, 194). The number of users continues to rise with the increasing availability of *warnet*s, which offer access at extremely low prices. The affordability of Internet cafés, which in 2000 could cost as little as Rp. 3,000 (at the time, less than US$0.25) per hour, made them wildly popular with university students and other young people.[10] An American expatriate working for one of the major Indonesian-language Web sites, astaga.com, told me that while his company had originally targeted affluent urban professionals, they soon discovered that the majority of their users were young people, approximately 45 percent of whom accessed the site through *warnet*s rather than from home or office. Since then the site's content has been modified to appeal more to the youth demographic, with features on music, fashion, and movies.

According to my observations of *warnet* behavior in Jakarta and other major cities, the two most popular activities in *warung internet* were searching for pornographic images (which are illegal in Indonesia but nevertheless easily accessible on the World Wide Web), a largely male activity, and online chatting, which involved both genders. An especially popular activity was flirtatious virtual chatting (*kencan*) with members of the opposite sex. The popularity of chatting and e-mail among Indonesian youth has given rise to a continually evolving written youth slang, with its own nonstandard spelling conventions. For example, in the early 2000s *lu* ("you" in Jakartanese) was rendered as *loe, elo, luh, lo,* or *elu; dia* (he/she) was sometimes spelled *doi;* and words containing the *au* diphthong were written with *o,* reflecting their pronunciation in colloquial speech. Adding unpronounced letters was also common, rendering, for example, the common emphasis particles *ya, sih,* and *nih* as *yach, sich,* and *nich.* Words were also elongated to show emphasis, for example, *asiiiiiiiiiiiiiiiiiiiiiikkkkkk* (cooooool!). These colloquial spellings predate e-mail (cf. Siegel 1986, 204n), but this relatively new technology appears to have accelerated the rate of orthographic change, as different spellings move in and out of fashion. More recently, many young Indonesians have begun to omit vowels from common Indonesian and Jakartanese words to save space and time when sending wireless text messages. In a sense, Jakarta's *warnet* cyberculture, in which music, fashion, humor, and social interaction (via e-mail and chat programs) are paramount, constitutes a virtualized extension of the vibrant oral culture of urban youth.

Jakartan Multilingualism and Heteroglossia

Jakarta is a city of many languages, both foreign and indigenous. It is also a city dominated by one language, Indonesian, which functions as both the language of the street and that of the official mass media. Yet the Indonesian spoken between intimates at the local *warung*, the Indonesian heard in the latest hit song, and the Indonesian used by the announcer on a national newscast are not precisely the "same" language. In his 1934–35 essay "Discourse in the Novel," Russian literary scholar M. M. Bakhtin argues that

> [l]anguage—like the living concrete environment in which the consciousness of the verbal artist lives—is never unitary. It is unitary only as an abstract grammatical system of normative forms, taken in isolation from the concrete, ideological conceptualizations that fill it, and in isolation from the uninterrupted process of historical becoming that is a characteristic of all living language. Actual social life and historical becoming create within an abstractly unitary national language a multitude of concrete worlds, a multitude of bounded verbal-ideological and social belief systems; within these various systems (identical in the abstract) are elements of language filled with various semantic and axiological content and each with its own different sound. (1981, 288)

This argument gives rise to Bakhtin's influential concept of "heteroglossia"—the profusion of diverse forms of speech in contemporary complex societies. Adding to this notion, anthropologist Deborah Durham writes, "Heteroglossia is not . . . simply a condition of society at large. It is also a condition of individual consciousness; even 'inner thought' enters into discourse with different potential meanings" (1999, 391). Thus the multiple vocabularies and ways of speaking found in Jakarta index multiple identities and subject positions that reflect the city's complex social reality and resist attempts by the Indonesian state to create a "unitary," standardized language of the nation (Keane 2003). Jakarta's nonstandard speech variants of Indonesian include those known as *bahasa Prokem*, *bahasa Jakarta*, and *bahasa gaul* (see appendix C). This heteroglossia extends into the popular music sphere as well, in the collision of different sounds, genres, and sung languages encountered in the music performed, recorded, and listened to in the city.

The linguistic creativity of Jakartan residents in creating new ways of speaking, in juggling pronominal options, and in humorous wordplay is a response to the conditions of life in the metropolis.[11] Jakarta's reflexive heteroglossia originates from the need to create solidary speech communities across ethnic and linguistic boundaries, but also from the need to consolidate social cohesion within class-based groupings. For example, as soon as a trendy youth slang style originating among students (such as *bahasa Prokem*) spreads to the working classes, it is replaced by new slang styles. Thus speakers of university-based speech variants enact their difference from the masses in their linguistic choices. Using trendy vocabulary also marks one as *gaul* (cool and "with it") and distances oneself from the accusation of being behind the times and of being *kampungan*.

Divided Masculinities

A humorous e-mail circulated on February 10, 2001, over Philadelphia's Permias (short for Persatuan Mahasiswa Indonesia di Amerika Serikat, the Union of Indonesian Students in the United States) mailing list describes an interesting linguistically marked intragender bifurcation between "men," designated by the standard Indonesian word *pria*, and "guys," designated by the Jakartanese term *cowok*. The e-mail consists of an itemized list titled *Bedanya Pria dengan Cowok?* (The Difference between a Man and a "Guy"?). Three examples from the fifteen-item total are

> P [ria]: *Pakai dasi, kemeja, sepatu bertali*
> C [owok]: (*Masih*) *pakai kaos sekolahan yang sudah buluk*
>
> P: *Seimbang antara penghasilan dan pemasukan*
> C: *Seimbang antara hutang dan pembayaran minimum*
>
> P: *Punya akuntan, penjahit dan dokter langganan*
> C: *Punya salon, kafe dan bengkel langganan*
>
> [Man: Wears a tie, shirt, and shoes with laces
> Guy: (Still) wears school T-shirt that has gotten moldy
>
> Man: Balanced between income and expenses
> Guy: Balanced between debt and minimum payment
>
> Man: Has a regular [*langganan*] accountant, tailor, and doctor
> Guy: Has a regular salon, café, and mechanic]

As a circulating electronic text, this humorous piece is intended primarily for an audience of middle- and upper-class students—including, in this case, those studying abroad. As such, the *pria/cowok* dichotomy posited by the e-mail constitutes not a class division but rather a difference in cultural orientation, toward either the hedonistic, carefree life of an adolescent student or the responsibility-laden existence of a young professional. University students are confronted with both Western-style competitive individualism and a more relaxed, sociocentric philosophy of life consonant with the informal economy's practices of buying on credit and attempting not to stand out. The *cowok*'s insistence on wearing his old, moldy school uniform is perhaps a nostalgic gesture to a time when he could be a comfortable part of a larger whole. Thus he refuses to "advance," and like his working-class counterparts, whose lack of education denies them the opportunity to choose a professional career, the *cowok* leads a precarious economic existence in the pursuit of adventure and amusement. This humorous e-mail contains a resolution to the dilemma of choosing between being a "man" or a "guy": it validates both without privileging one over the other, while questioning whether it is really a choice at all. According to the introductory text accompanying the list,

> *Tidak semua pria dewasa menjadi "pria" ada juga yang masih begitu kekanakan setelah umurnya mencapai 40. Tenaaaang, jangan keburu marah dulu dengan kenyataan ini, mungkin memang sebagian orang dilahirkan untuk jadi "pria," tapi memang ada juga yang cukup menjadi "cowok" saja.*

> *Sekali lagi, jangan kawatir, terima saja diri Anda sebagai pria (P) atau sebagai cowok (C), toh semua punya nilai lebih dan kurang tersendiri. Dan yang tak kalah penting, percayalah kadang wanita tidak peduli.*

> [Not all grown men become "men"; there are also those who stay child-like after their age has reached forty. Relaaaax, don't immediately get angry with this state of affairs—maybe indeed a segment of people are born to become "men," but indeed there are also those for whom it is enough to just be a "guy."

> Once again, don't worry, just accept yourself as a man or as a guy; after all, both of them have their own plusses and minuses. And what's most important, believe me that sometimes women don't care (either way).]

The easygoing relativism expressed in this passage is common in Indonesian popular culture more generally, and it is apparent in many popular cultural forms that combine "modern" and "traditional" elements without appearing to choose one over the other. But the stance of easygoing tolerance can also serve to mask contradictions, instabilities, persistent inequalities, and the incompatibilities that exist between distinct ways of being in the world.

Likewise, the class contradictions of the city are both smoothed over and overemphasized in the service of particular ideological goals, while the reality of coexistence without integration persists and will likely do so for the foreseeable future. Perhaps one day resource-rich Indonesia will join the ranks of prosperous, industrialized Pacific Rim countries. But until that happens the discourses of modernity and modernization will be used as instruments of class struggle, as the dominant classes seek to delegitimate the lifeways of subaltern groups. Furthermore, the division between *pasar* (market) and mall indexes not only class divisions between people but, as demonstrated above, also divided subjectivities among Jakarta's diverse inhabitants.

Indonesian popular music plays a role in the class and cultural struggles described in this chapter. Music genres and the divisions and bridges between them are implicated in the tension between the longing for a solidary, egalitarian community, on the one hand, and for modernity, affluence, individuality, and a consumerist lifestyle, on the other. The energy exerted in the denunciation of dangdut music is a salient example of how some Jakartans aspire to modernity by denigrating a cultural form that is perceived as antithetical to this aspiration. Dangdut, the music of *warung*, villages, the "backward masses," is always on the losing end of the conceptual dichotomy between cosmopolitanism and provincialism, modern and traditional, rich and poor. Yet however much it is denigrated by elites, dangdut remains wildly popular. Furthermore, although the genre emerged during Soeharto's New Order, we shall see how dangdut music's inclusive, patriotic, and populist vision strongly resembles that associated with the Sukarno era.

The next chapter continues our exploration of urban spaces by examining an obvious but frequently overlooked site where music genres are displayed, contrasted, and categorized: the cassette store.

3

Cassette Retail Outlets

ORGANIZATION, ICONOGRAPHY, CONSUMER BEHAVIOR

Despite a growing interest in mass-mediated music among ethnomusicologists, ethnomusicological studies of record stores remain uncommon.[1] This is a bit odd, since record stores are crucial sites of musical encounter in the contemporary world (moreover, most ethnomusicologists I know spend a good deal of time in them!). These specialized spaces designed for the display and sale of musical commodities provide us with an ideal entry into the world of recorded popular music in Indonesia. Against the backdrop of current trends in the Indonesian music industry, this chapter investigates shelf categories, store layouts, decorations, employee and customer behavior, and ratios of imported to domestic product that characterize the various places where music is purchased in Jakarta. Several patterns emerge from this exploration. In particular, a survey of the different types of music retail outlets reveals signs of socioeconomic bifurcation of the sort outlined in the previous chapter. Also, the hierarchical presentation of musical genres found in nearly every Indonesian cassette retail outlet exemplifies how music genre is linked to class-inflected notions of prestige and value.

For my analysis I draw on Pierre Bourdieu's *Distinction: A Social Critique of the Judgment of Taste* (1984), a landmark study of class stratification and culture in France. Bourdieu argues against a direct correlation between socioeconomic status and cultural expression, instead asserting that certain embodied forms of knowledge become sources of "cultural capital," a separate entity from economic capital. Thus in Bourdieu's view cultural status and prestige do not follow directly from the relations of production but are negotiated in a cultural field of aesthetic alternatives in which some choices are more highly valued than others.

Genre as Metaculture

The interpretive construct of music genre shapes the form and meaning of recorded music artifacts for Indonesian music consumers. Anthropologist Greg Urban has emphasized the crucial role that discursive interpretations of cultural forms, which he terms "metaculture" (that is, culture about culture), play in the reception and circulation of those forms throughout a society: "Metaculture is significant in part, at least, because it imparts an accelerative force to culture. It aids culture in its motion through space and time. It gives a boost to the culture that it is about, helping to propel it on its journey. The interpretation of culture that is intrinsic to metaculture, immaterial as it is, focuses attention on the cultural thing, helps to make it an object of interest, and, hence, facilitates its circulation" (2001, 4). In other words, metaculture promotes the circulation of cultural forms (such as recorded music) by suggesting frames for interpreting their significance in the societies that produce them. Urban further argues that metacultural constructs play an important role in the creation of the objects themselves. "Construed in this way, metacultural interpretation is a force in the world of perceptible things, not just an arbitrary conscious representation of things construed as indifferent to their representation" (2001, 37). Thus, understandings of music genre are not employed solely to organize and classify existing music; they also encourage the fashioning of particular kinds of musical sound-objects that conform to these understandings.

The metacultural constructs of genre also point *outward* to the music's social contexts, indexing social spaces, specific communities, and types of music consumers. I would suggest that the complex whole of Indonesian popular music possesses sufficient coherence for it to be examined as a metacultural field of ideological and social oppositions manifested in particular genre ideologies.[2] What follows is an exploration of how these genre ideologies are expressed in items of material culture, the design of built environments, and the everyday spoken discourse of Indonesian listeners.

Genre and *Gengsi*: Indonesian versus
Foreign Popular Music

Asking an Indonesian teenager why he or she likes a particular song, artist, or genre tends to elicit a shy smile and the response, *Ya, suka aja* (I just like it, that's all). But when one digs deeper, one discovers a complex moral economy in which music genres are ranked vis-à-vis one another based on a largely implicit system of class distinction (Bourdieu 1984), which in Jakartanese is summed up by the Hokkien Chinese-derived term *gengsi* (status consciousness, prestige). These relative rankings of social prestige and power in many cases determine which genres and artists Indonesians readily admit to liking, and which they do not.

When I taught a cultural anthropology course at Universitas Atma Jaya, a private university in Central Jakarta, I was advised to introduce my students to the term *xenosentrik* (xenocentric) in addition to *etnosentrik* (ethnocentric) on the first day of class. I knew it was customary for anthropology instructors in the United States to introduce beginning students to the concept (and hazards) of ethnocentricity, the belief that one's own culture is superior to all others, in order to contrast it to the relativistic approach of mainstream cultural anthropology toward cultural differences among human groups. Teaching students the concept of xenocentrism—the belief, common in postcolonial societies, that a foreign culture (such as that belonging to the former colonizer) is superior to all others, including one's own—was a new experience for me. Yet it soon became clear to me why such a term was necessary to teach the idea of cultural relativism to Indonesian undergraduates: "xenocentric" well described the attitudes many educated middle- and upper-class Indonesians held about a range of cultural phenomena, including business, government, religion, cinema, technology, and, not least, popular music.[3] In relation to this last item, my research findings strongly suggest that the strategies by which cassette stores displayed their wares tended to replicate and reinforce, if not create, a xenocentric status hierarchy that places Western (primarily British and American) music at the top, and ethnic and working-class Indonesian genres at the bottom of the *gengsi* scale.

Belief in the artistic superiority of Western music was not purely a function of socioeconomic class position, though there appeared to be a strong correlation between such attitudes and middle- or upper-class standing. I spoke with many working-class Indonesian music fans whose opinions of Indonesian popular music, especially dangdut, were as uncomplimentary as those held by middle-class fans, if not more so. For example, walking home from Atma Jaya University's campus one day, I was accosted by a middle-aged man hanging out on the corner of Jalan Sudirman and Jalan Teluk Betung in Central Jakarta. He seemed more than a little inebriated and was talking and joking with two women whom I had seen at local dangdut bars and whom a consultant had told me worked as prostitutes. Speaking in broken but understandable English peppered with American slang expressions, he asked me what I was doing in Indonesia. When I mentioned that I was interested in studying national popular music genres like dangdut and *jaipongan*, he became surprised and indignant. The following is a partial reconstruction of his remarks from my 1997 field notes:

> Oh, God! I can't believe you're studying *that*. Dangdut and *jaipong*—I don't know why the Indonesian people like this music. It is ah . . . [hesitation, as though searching for the right expression in English] . . . from the village. It is . . . [*"Kampungan?"* I asked him] . . . Yes! That's it. As for me, I like Grand Funk Railroad; Chicago; Deep Purple; Uriah Heep; [a name I could not identify]; Emerson, Lake, and Palmer; Jimi Hendrix; blues . . . [*"Flower Generation?"* I asked] . . . Yes, man! I'm forty—I was in that generation. When I was still in high school, twenty years ago, my friends and I were *proud* to have the posters: Janis Joplin; Emerson, Lake, and Palmer; the Beatles. But people in Indonesia—there is a problem with *apresiasi*—appreciation of good music. [. . .] Speaking for me—I don't think I'm *kebarat-baratan* [westernized], more Western than Western guys, but I appreciate Western music: blues, *klasik* [classical music], rock. That is what I think. It's interesting talking to you.

This man's comments reveal not only the easy contempt some urban dwellers hold for Indonesian national popular music genres but also the important connection between Western popular music, especially rock, and masculine generational identity. Knowledge of a particular Western musical canon, in this case rock music from the 1960s and 1970s, associated in Indonesia with the *Flower Generation,* was a source of cultural capital for the speaker. In contrast, he seemed embarrassed by the popularity of dangdut and *jaipongan,* which for him served as a reminder of the backwardness of his countrymen and their inability to appreciate "good music."

Some more-thoughtful music fans expressed ambivalence about the musical prestige hierarchy in Indonesia without denying the power it wields. The following is an excerpt from an e-mail I received from a Jakartan small businessman and former student activist in response to a query concerning his favorite kind of music.

> *Hallo Jeremy,*
>
> *Langsung aja nich . . .*
>
> *Kalau ditanya soal musik, aku paling bingung ngejawabnya. Aku memang suka musik. But what kind of music do I like? This is really confused me. Aku mau jujur aja. Sebenarnya aku ini snobist! Snobist yang sok tahu, biar nggak dibilang ketinggalan jaman, gitu. Tapi akhirnya, ya suka juga. Awalnya memang snob. Kata Harry Roesly, apresiator musik di Indonesia umumnya berawal dari snob. Banyak juga musisi negeri ini yang snobist duluan. Biar nggak dikatakan kampungan, lalu coba-coba musik barat, trus kebablasan jadi pemain. Itu biasa. Namanya juga anak muda. Coba tanya Pra, atau yang lainnya tentang latar belakang mereka bermain musik barat seperti fusion, rock, atau sekarang yang lagi trend di sini, ska. Selain itu, memainkan musik Barat tentu lebih praktis. Bayangkan, kalau main musik trad. yang instrumentnya seberat gajah sekarat, macam gong, saron [. . .] dll.*
>
> *Lho, kok jadi ngelantur. Soal apa tadi? Oh . . . ya, soal musik yang aku suka. Jelas dong, yang kusuka kan jazz kuno, macam Louis Armstrong, Mile Davis, Herbie Hancock, Oscar Peterson dll. Yang jelas saya tidak membatasi diri hanya dengar aliran musik tertentu. Hanya lebih enjoy dengan yang saya sebut tadi. Itu saja. Masa' kalau lagi disco pake lagu gituan. Pokoknya lihat-lihat kesempatannya lah!* [. . .]

[Hello Jeremy,

I'll get directly to the point.

If asked about music, I get very confused how to answer. I certainly like music. *But what kind of music do I like? This is* (sic) *really confused me.* I'll just be honest. Actually, I'm a snob (*snobist*)! A snob who's a know-it-all, just so it isn't said that he is behind the times, like that. But ultimately yeah, I like what I like. In the beginning, certainly a snob. Harry Roesli (a well-known composer, recording artist, and raconteur) says appreciators of music in Indonesia generally begin as snobs. There are also many musicians from this country who were snobs at first. So as not to be considered backward or low class (*kampungan*), they mess around amateurishly with Western music, then instantly think they've become players. That's what normally happens. You know, kids are like that. Try asking Pra (Budidharma, the bassist of ethnic jazz fusion group Krakatau) or others about their background playing Western music like fusion, rock, or the music currently in vogue here, ska. Aside from that, playing Western music is certainly more practical. Imagine, if you want to play traditional music, the instruments are as heavy as an elephant in its death throes, like *gong, saron* (. . .) etc.

Hmmm . . . I'm digressing here. What was I talking about just now? Oh . . . yeah, the matter of music I like. It's clear of course, what I like is old jazz, like Louis Armstrong, Mile(s) Davis, Herbie Hancock, Oscar Peterson, etc. Clearly, though, I don't limit myself by only listening to a particular stream of music. I only *enjoy* more the music I just mentioned. That's all. It would be impossible if I'm disco dancing to use songs like that (old jazz)! The main thing is to look around at the situation *lah!*]

After expressing discomfort with the apparent elitism of his musical taste, the writer admits he likes one of the most prestigious categories of music, Western jazz. Moreover, he prefers *jazz kuno* (old-time, literally "ancient," jazz), not the watered-down jazz-rock-pop fusion that dominates the Indonesian and international jazz market. By writing that musicians play Western music so as not to be considered *kampungan,* the writer implies that non-Western music in Indonesia, including traditional music with its impractical, heavy instruments, is backward and low class. Yet to subscribe to this view is to be a *snob,* that is, to care too much about *gengsi.* So finally the writer disavows his elitism with the quite plausible claim that he listens to all kinds of music depending on the situation and that he just happens to enjoy traditional jazz best. This easygoing relativist stance is reminiscent of the conclusion to the humorous "man" versus "guy" e-mail discussed in the previous chapter.

As an intellectual familiar with post-structuralism and postcolonial theory, the writer is uncomfortable with the argument that Western music truly is superior to indigenous Indonesian music. He even cites (somewhat unconvincingly) logistical problems with moving heavy instruments as a reason why musicians choose to play Western instead of traditional music, as though practicality were of greater concern to them than artistic value. (Performing Western music, after all, also requires heavy and expensive equipment, from amplifiers to drum kits to mixing consoles.) Nevertheless, Indonesians from a variety of social and class backgrounds share the view he describes but does not quite endorse, according to which standards of musical excellence emanate from a Western "elsewhere" (Baulch 2003). This elsewhere is spatially and sometimes temporally distant, as in the case of 1950s American jazz or 1970s British hard rock. It is not difficult to associate such an attitude with the "brainwashing" effects of globalized Western popular culture. I would argue, however, that in Indonesia such a view is also part of a *local* strategy for distinguishing oneself from "low-class" and rural Indonesians through a self-conscious display of cultural capital. Evidence for this interpretation can be found in the conspicuous class-based differences in musical consumption in Indonesia.

Genre, Class, and Status: A View of the Indonesian Music Industry

All the music retail outlets discussed in this chapter operated in the social and economic context of the Indonesian music industry, which in 1997–2001 was in the midst of a historic transition from a highly class-segmented to a more unified music market. Indonesia's class differences were obvious and frankly acknowledged, and they permeated social life. Music industry workers therefore tended to view the Indonesian popular music market not as an undifferentiated mass of consumers but as a social ladder of different socioeconomic classes. According to the marketing director of the Indonesian Repertoire and Promotions Division of a major transnational record company with extensive operations in Indonesia, these class levels were labeled A to F. She stated that A- and B-class consumers in large cities (Jakarta, Bandung, Surabaya, Medan) preferred Western music, while their counterparts in smaller cities preferred upscale *pop Indonesia*. C and D consumers preferred sentimental, melodramatic pop (*pop melankolis*, also known pejoratively as *pop cengeng*, "weepy pop"; see Yampolsky 1989) and, of course, dangdut. She added that the crowded E and F socioeconomic levels are composed of people too poor to buy music and therefore do not factor into the industry's marketing strategies.

Although most consumers do not employ these music-industry labels, they tend to explicitly associate particular musical genres with either *menengah ke atas*, "middle to upper," or *menengah ke bawah*, "middle to below," consumers. Only children's pop (*pop anak-anak*), which appeals to children of all classes, and underground music, which attracts a cross-class youth subcultural audience, constitute partial exceptions to this rule. For example, "middle-to-upper"-oriented *pop Indonesia*, often termed *pop kelas atas* (upper-class pop), is readily distinguishable from more working-class-oriented pop music by its slicker, American R & B-influenced production, jazzy arrangements, and upbeat lyrics, as well as significant differences in promotional strategy and artists' image.

The class-inflected status hierarchy of musical genres is reflected in the range of retail prices for different types of cassette. Legitimate cassette prices in Indonesia are generally *pas* (fixed, exact; not subject to bargaining) and thus are remarkably consistent regardless of the location of purchase, though at smaller stalls one is more likely to receive a slight discount when buying several cassettes at once. The following is a list of cassette prices by genre in Jakarta in late June 2000:[4]

Western Imports: Rp. 20,000 (approximately US$2.50 at the time)
Pop Indonesia: Rp. 16,000 to Rp. 18,000 (US$2.00 to $2.25)
Dangdut: Rp. 12,000 to Rp. 14,000 (US$1.50 to $1.75)
Indian Film Music: Rp. 10,000 to Rp. 11,000 (US$1.25 to $1.38)
Regional Music (*Musik Daerah*): Rp. 10,000 to Rp. 13,000 (US$1.25 to $1.63)
Underground (independently produced and distributed): Rp. 10,000 to Rp. 17,000 (US$1.25 to $2.13)

Although the price of imported Western music cassettes was rather high for most Indonesians (and was twice as much as the cost of some *musik daerah* cassettes), it was nevertheless much lower than the retail price of Western music products in the West. This was made possible by manufacturing the cassettes domestically under license from multinational media corporations. Western compact discs were also locally manufactured, but their prices were much higher than those of cassettes, which were still by far the best-selling recorded music format in Indonesia in 1999–2000.[5] In June 2000, locally produced Western compact discs could cost as much as Rp. 80,000 (at the time, approximately US$10.00), while compact discs by Indonesian artists cost approximately Rp. 50,000 (US$6.25). Since these prices were far higher than those of cassettes, compact discs were considered a format designated for A and B consumers. Very few dangdut recordings were released on compact disc; a dangdut producer told me such items would not sell well and would only be used as ideal masters for the production of pirated cassettes. Among new releases, only *pop Indonesia* albums that had already been commercially successful as cassettes were released on compact disc.

For much of the 1980s and 1990s, the sheer number of consumers in the so-called C and D markets compensated for their relatively weak

Table 3.1 Recorded music sales data for Indonesia (units sold), 1996–99

Type	1996	1997	1998	1999 (October)
Indonesian cassettes	65,396,589	49,794,676	27,635,739	30,100,077
Foreign cassettes	11,374,089	14,005,340	9,637,200	11,395,590
Indonesian CDs	265,475	778,370	315,910	532,900
Foreign CDs	474,980	2,053,840	2,732,410	2,086,290
Karaoke VCDs	19,500	701,870	1,335,390	4,196,590
Karaoke LDs	21,375	21,975	2,205	1,050
Total	77,552,008	67,356,071	41,658,854	48,312,497

Source: Theodore 1999, 10

individual purchasing power, and in fact genres such as dangdut that targeted this audience, while low on the *gengsi* scale, were quite profitable for record companies. In the early and mid-1990s it was not unusual for a dangdut cassette containing a hit song to sell more than a million legitimate copies — an unheard-of amount for *pop* records at the time. This situation changed drastically in the aftermath of the 1997–98 economic catastrophe.[6] A comparison of music sales in the years before and after Indonesia's economic collapse provides insight into the relative ability of Indonesians from different social classes to weather the crisis. Table 3.1 is sorted by foreign and local music and by consumer format. Almost all music sold in Indonesia during the period covered in the table was in the form of prerecorded cassettes, but music was also available on compact disc, video compact disc (VCD), and laser disc (LD). The latter two formats, obscure in the West, contain images as well as sounds and were often used to accompany karaoke performance. They contain primarily Indonesian music.

These figures reveal a story of the relative power to withstand economic turmoil at various levels of the Indonesian class structure. The upper and middle classes, with their high rates of personal savings, suffered far less than the poor, who had little or no savings and could not cope with the steeply rising prices of consumer goods. A striking statistic from this table is that sales of the highest-priced commodity, foreign compact discs, actually *increased* 33 percent between 1997 and 1998, during the height of the economic crisis. It is tempting to posit a perverse kind of *gengsi* logic behind this increase, and behind the fact that the number of foreign compact discs sold in Indonesia decreased the following year. According to this logic, conspicuous consumption in the form of purchasing Western compact discs during the height of an economic crisis would powerfully demonstrate one's elite status and separation from the immiserated poor, many of whom were now unable to buy even the cheapest local cassettes.

In October 1999, the sale of cassettes by Indonesian artists over the previous eight months amounted to less than half the total figure for 1996. Due to competition from the rapidly growing VCD medium (which is even more dominated by piracy than cassettes), it is unlikely that Indonesian cassette sales will ever rebound completely, even after the economic outlook of the country improves. This situation led some recently arrived multinational recording companies to conclude that the "middle to lower" market segment was no longer profitable, a result of its decreased spending power and habit of buying readily available pirated albums.

In postcrisis Indonesia, many of the most successful new recordings have been by *pop alternatif* and ska groups like Sheila on 7 and Jun Fan Gung Foo (both artists on the Sony Music Indonesia record label) that have crossed over to an economically diverse audience. This success has often occurred against the expectations of record-label personnel, who did not anticipate such high sales (Sheila on 7's eponymous first album, for example, sold over one million legitimate copies). That *pop alternatif* artists associated with urban middle-class youth have become accepted in lower social strata is evident in a claim I heard from several people in the Indonesian music industry: the current youth market in Indonesia is far more uniform across class boundaries than in previous generations, a situation attributed to the influence of MTV and other recently intro-duced outlets showcasing global popular culture. Such a claim, how-ever, does not diminish the phenomenon of widening social inequality in Indonesia in the face of both economic globalization and economic crisis. Indeed, the New Order's aggressive economic development poli-cies may well have resulted in a more unified popular culture coupled with a more polarized society.

Music Consumption at the Ground Level: A Taxonomy of Jakarta's Music Retail Outlets

If we confine ourselves to the legitimate music market and ignore for the moment pirated products, we find that the prices of products for sale in different kinds of retail outlets do not differ markedly. The manner in which recordings are displayed is also quite similar, but the *experience* of shopping for cassettes can differ widely between a large mall music store and a small cassette stall. In the former, one usually finds that well over half of the music for sale is imported, whereas in cassette stalls that operate in the informal, "bazaar" economy, Western music cassettes usually account for less than 25 percent of total shelf space. The precise ratio of imported to Indonesian cassettes varies depending on the economic circumstances of the surrounding neighborhood. For instance, the cassette stalls I visited in Kampung Muara, a poor area in North Jakarta, offered very few Western cassettes for sale but featured a wide selection of dangdut cassettes, while the stall I frequented in middle-class Kebayoran Baru, South Jakarta, had many more imported and *pop Indonesia* cassettes on offer and significantly fewer dangdut titles.

Warung Kaset

Warung kaset (cassette stalls) distinguish themselves sonically from the other stalls in a traditional bazaar by the loud recorded music they emit outward to passersby. The type of music played depends on the salesclerk, though sentimental pop ballads, often in English, are a frequent choice. These establishments are decorated spartanly, relying on the sound of the music and the colorful cassette packages on display to attract customers. Most sell a range of other nonperishable items in addition to cassettes: plastic toys, batteries, headphones, and the like. Cassettes for sale in the stall are not displayed alphabetically but are usually separated into unlabeled categories. The most common of these implicit classifications, to judge from the different artists represented in each section, are Western pop, Indonesian pop, dangdut, Javanese, Sundanese, Islamic, and children's music. The classification scheme does not separate regional pop and traditional music recordings from the same region. In these *warung,* Western music cassettes are usually placed on the highest shelves behind the counter, while Indonesian music is displayed on lower shelves and inside the counter. This practice appears to elevate foreign music to a higher status, but it may simply result from the desire to protect the stall's most expensive items from damage or theft. Nevertheless, after visiting innumerable Indonesian cassette stalls, I concluded that the spatial separation between Indonesian and foreign music was carefully maintained in a manner suggesting that more than security concerns may be at stake.

In nearly all *warung kaset*, the customer has the option of trying out a recording on the stall's sound system before purchase, to test it for defects (which are rare, in my experience) and to determine if he or she likes the music. Usually the salesclerk opens the cassette's shrink-wrap with a small knife blade (if it had not yet been opened) and then uses a small motorized device to fast-forward the tape a little to get past the leader (the blank space at the start of a tape). In Indonesia, leaders are rather lengthy—up to 20 seconds or so—as a result of the local method of duplicating cassettes. The clerk then places the cassette in the stall's tape deck and plays a segment of the first song at a volume sufficient to fill the entire space of the stall. The cassette continues to play until the customer asks to hear another song or tells the salesclerk he or she has heard enough. The salesclerk will then immediately resume playing the cassette that had been playing previously, until another customer makes a request. In this way, the musical background of the stall is never interrupted by long silences.

Jakarta *warung kaset* proprietors buy their cassettes in small amounts wholesale from distributors located mostly in the Glodok area of North Jakarta. They make choices regarding which cassettes to stock based on previous sales, and in most cases they do not buy more than one or two copies of a single title. As a result, customers wishing to purchase a popular title are often cheerfully told that that cassette has sold out. The music selection at cassette stalls, where the majority of Indonesians purchase their music, is generally comprised of about 20 percent foreign and 80 percent Indonesian titles. Stall proprietors stock only titles they believe will sell to a broad public; thus albums by more avant-garde Indonesian recording artists such as Krakatau, Harry Roesli, or Djaduk Ferianto are generally found only in large music stores (see the discussion later in this chapter), if they are available at all.

Mall Stores

Jakarta's gigantic air-conditioned malls offered a cosmopolitan alternative to shopping in traditional markets with their mud and squalor. They were places for the fashionable to see and be seen and to experience a taste of global consumer culture. Like malls in the United States, until recently, no Indonesian mall was complete without at least one store selling recorded music artifacts.[7] Targeted at middle-class and elite consumers, upscale mall music stores were typically decorated with an eclectic, bewildering assortment of images from Western culture.

A cassette store in a South Jakarta mall.

The wall decorations in a music store located in Plaza Senayan (see chapter 2) included a portrait of Beethoven, a blown-up photograph of Kurt Cobain (the late singer of the American band Nirvana), a depiction of the Mona Lisa smoking a large marijuana cigarette, a poster of a Norwegian black metal band, and a reproduction of a Bob Marley album cover. Another mall store, Tower Music, located in the fashionable Menteng shopping district, had a display of small flags on one of its shelves. The countries represented were Indonesia, the United States, Ireland, Japan, Germany, and Britain. There was no flag representing Malaysia, Singapore, or any other neighboring Southeast Asian country, suggestive of a cosmopolitan musicscape based more on cultural power than on geography. Even the name of the store evoked Tower Records, a transnational music retailer that at the time had yet to reach Jakarta.

While all record stores I visited in Indonesia sold some Indonesian recordings, music boutiques in upscale malls tended to carry mostly Western music. In my explorations of the most upscale stores, those located in Plaza Indonesia, Plaza Senayan, Pondok Indah Mall, and Taman Anggrek, I also found that compact discs actually outnumbered cassettes. Dangdut albums, if present at all, accounted for less than 5 percent of shelf space; regional (*daerah*) genres were largely absent. Mall stores usually sorted recordings alphabetically in labeled shelf categories.

These categories usually included standard Western genres (jazz, R & B, country, etc.), while locally produced recordings (predominantly *pop kelas atas,* upper-class pop) were frequently relegated to shelves labeled "Indonesia" that took up as little as 10 percent of total shelf space. Although upscale mall stores always played music in the background, there were no facilities for testing recordings one wished to buy. Clerks were not permitted to open the shrink-wrap of cassettes and compact discs for customers.

Mall music stores present themselves as portals to an imaginary realm of global consumer culture. Signs of local specificity that would place the store in an Indonesian context, including use of the Indonesian language on posters and signs, are minimized or eliminated. Indonesian music is marginalized as a marked category, while Western music and culture are represented in a spectacular fashion.

Large Music Stores

A third music retail alternative to cassette stalls and mall boutiques is the handful of large music stores located in major cities. These establishments, which stock a wide variety of indigenous and foreign musics, are located in department stores such as Sarinah or the Pasaraya at Blok M or are housed in stand-alone structures like Aquarius, a record-store chain owned by one of Indonesia's largest national record companies. The rest of this section investigates in detail the ways in which the Jakarta Aquarius store displays its wares, which run the full gamut from Western art music to traditional regional genres.

The Aquarius music store located in the Bulungan area of Blok M in South Jakarta consisted of two rooms in 1999–2000. The larger room held both Indonesian and Western compact discs (mostly the latter), Indonesian children's pop, and a large selection of Western cassettes, while a smaller one contained mostly Indonesian cassettes. Interestingly, in the center of the "Indonesian" room there was an arrangement of tape players with headphones, with which customers could test cassettes. No such array existed in the large room.[8] These tape machines resembled those found in *warung kaset,* though the experience of listening was somewhat privatized. I say "somewhat" because I often observed two or more customers trying to listen to a song through the same pair of headphones at the same time. The presence of this listening equipment appeared to be a concession to shoppers accustomed to the cassette-stall buying experience.

Table 3.2 Inventory of cassette categories at Aquarius Musik, main room

Shelf label	Contents	Shelf units
Classic	Western classical and light classical music	1.0
Instrumental	Western New Age and instrumental pop	1.0
Soundtrack	Recent Hollywood film soundtracks	1.0
Compilation	Collections of pop hits, mostly love songs	2.0
Jazz	Jazz-pop fusion, some traditional jazz	2.0
Alternative/	Western rock bands sharing a nonmainstream,	
Modern Rock	punk-influenced aesthetic	2.0
Rhytm + Blues [sic]	American R & B and hip hop	2.0
Dance	Various Western electronic dance genres	
	such as house and techno	1.0
Rock + Pop	Western rock and pop artists	17.0
New Releases	Recent titles, both Indonesian and Western	1.5
Top 40	Ranked best-selling albums,	
	from both Indonesia and the West	2.0
Children	Indonesian pop anak-anak (children's pop)	1.0

The Western music available in cassette format at Aquarius was divided into several specific subcategories, not all of which corresponded completely with conventional Western classifications. The shelf categories are listed in table 3.2. The number in the far right column indicates the number of shelf units dedicated to each named category; each shelf unit held about fifty different cassettes, depending on how they were arranged.

Indonesian children's pop was the only indigenous musical category present in the large room. I suspect that the storeowners were concerned that middle- and upper-class consumers preoccupied with social prestige (gengsi) would not even want to enter the Indonesian music room. Such consumers often buy children's pop cassettes for their offspring; this practice is not a threat to gengsi because small children are not expected to have developed cultivated musical tastes or to understand English lyrics. It may also be the case that Indonesian children's pop benefits from the fact that it lacks a real equivalent in Western pop.

The rest of the Indonesian music cassettes sold by Aquarius were located in a room to the far left of the store's front entrance. Its total inventory was a fraction of that in the large room (10 versus 33.5 shelf units), and the five categories that appeared on shelf labels did not reflect the same level of genre specificity, as table 3.3 illustrates.

Table 3.3 Inventory of cassette categories at Aquarius Musik, Indonesian room

Shelf label	Contents	Shelf units
Compilation	Various artists, mostly *pop nostalgia*	0.5
Indonesia	Indonesian pop, Indonesian rock, alternative, R & B, metal, and so on	5.0
Dangdut	Dangdut, *dangdut trendy, orkes Melayu* (dangdut's historical precursor)	1.0
Etnic [*sic*]	Primarily *pop daerah* (regional pop) from different parts of the archipelago, including Java, Sunda, Maluku, Sumatra (Malay, Batak, and Minangkabau), North Sulawesi (Manado), Irian Jaya, even East Timor. Also some Javanese and Sundanese traditional music	1.0
Unlabeled	Indonesian jazz, jazz-pop fusion, and ethnic fusion jazz; patriotic songs; *keroncong*; Indonesian house music; *nostalgia* collections	1.0
Rohani	Western and Indonesian pop music with Christian religious themes	1.0
Unlabeled subsection	Indonesian Islamic pop	0.5

In the large room near the entrance to the small one, two shelf units were devoted to displaying the forty top-selling cassettes of the week, both Indonesian and Western. This was one of the few sections of the store where imported and domestic music shared shelf space and seemed to compete with each other on equal footing. Table 3.4 is a list of the top forty best-selling albums for the week of January 22, 2000, as compiled by the Aquarius store.

This list is fairly representative: the ratio of Indonesian to foreign entries is 2:3 (16 to 24; in other weeks the balance was tipped more favorably toward the former), and it is dominated by musical genres associated with the middle class: Western pop, sophisticated "upper-class" Indonesian pop, and Western hard rock music. I never saw a dangdut cassette included in the Aquarius Top Forty. While in table 3.4 Western recording artists occupy the top three slots, in other weeks Indonesian recordings held those positions. The list also indicates the preference among many Indonesian consumers for "greatest hits" compilations (eleven in total, seventeen if one counts albums containing "live" recordings or new studio arrangements of familiar songs) over albums of new, unfamiliar material, a preference that appeared to be shared by Indonesians from all walks of life.

Table 3.4 Top forty best-selling albums at Aquarius Musik, week of January 22, 2000

No.	Artist	Album title	Description
1	The Corrs	*MTV Unplugged*	Western, quasi-Celtic pop
2	Celine Dion	*All the Way: A Decade of Song*	Western sentimental pop ballads
3	Westlife	Self-titled	Irish "boy band"
4*	Rossa	*Tegar* [Resolute]	*Pop kelas atas* (upper-class pop)
5*	Chrissye	*Badai Pasti Berlalu* [The Storm Will Surely Pass]	Newly arranged songs from a classic 1970s pop album
6*	Various	*Hard Rock FM Indonesia Klasik*	Compilation of Indonesian rock bands
7*	Padi	*Lain Dunia* [Another World]	*Pop alternatif*
8*	Dewa 19	*Best of Dewa 19*	*Pop alternatif*
9	Boyzone	*By Request*	Irish "boy band"
10*	Melly	Self-titled	*Pop alternatif*
11	Bryan Adams	*The Best of Me*	Western mainstream rock
12	Various	*Everlasting Love Songs 2*	Western sentimental pop ballads
13*	Sheila on 7	Self-titled	*Pop alternatif*
14	Metallica	*S & M 2*	Western hard rock/metal backed by a symphony orchestra
15*	Bunglon	*Biru* [Blue]	Smooth jazz–influenced pop
16	Sheila Majid	*Kumohon* [I Beseech]	Malaysian jazz–influenced pop
17	Alanis Morissette	*Unplugged*	Western alternative rock
18	Richard Clayderman	*Chinese Garden*	Western pop-classical crossover
19	Korn	*Issues*	Western "hip metal" (hip hop + metal)
20	Various	*'99: The Hits*	Western Top 40 compilation
21	Rage Against the Machine	*The Battle of Los Angeles*	Western "new school" hardcore/hip metal
22*	Sherina	*Andai Aku Besar Nanti* [When I Grow Up]	Children's pop (*pop anak-anak*)
23	Various	*Forever*	Western sentimental pop ballads
24*	Dian Pramana Poetra	*Terbaik* [Best]	*Pop kelas atas*
25*	Syaharani	*Tersiksa Lagi* [Tortured Again]	Vocal jazz
26	Savage Garden	*Affirmation*	Western mainstream pop
27	George Michael	*Songs from the Last Century*	Western mainstream pop
28	Metallica	*S & M 1*	Western hard rock/metal
29	Santana	*Supernatural*	Western Latin-crossover pop rock
30*	Rita-Sita-Dewi	*Satu* [One]	*Pop kelas atas*
31*	Romeo	Self-titled	*Pop kelas atas*
32*	Ruth Sahanaya	*Kasih* [Love]	*Pop kelas atas*
33	Various	*L Is for Love*	Western sentimental love ballads
34	Foo Fighters	*There Is Nothing Left to Lose*	Western alternative rock
35	Eric Clapton	*Chronicles*	Western mainstream rock
36*	Purpose	*Tiger Clan*	Ska
37	Various	*The End Of Days*	Hollywood movie soundtrack
38	Guns 'n' Roses	*Live Era '87–93*	Western hard rock
39	Various	*American Pie*	Hollywood movie soundtrack
40*	Noin Bullet	*Bebas* [Free]	Ska

Note: * = Indonesian title

Mobile Cassette Vendors

A final type of commercial music retailer is worth mentioning. Along with a veritable army of other mobile salesmen who traveled through my neighborhood in South Jakarta selling everything from brooms to ice cream novelties, a mobile cassette vendor would make his way through the streets pushing a wooden cart in which a car stereo system was installed. The cassettes he sold—all legitimate copies, not pirated— were intended to appeal to the servants and *warung* proprietors of the neighborhood, not its more affluent residents. Thus the selection of recordings was dominated by dangdut and regional music from Sunda and Java, including cassettes of village folk genres (such as Sundanese *kliningan*) that were difficult to find in Jakarta cassette stores.

In addition to cassettes, the "circling-around dangdut" (*dangdut keliling-keliling*) vendor sold toys, brushes, and other household items from his cart. His approach was signaled by the dangdut music blaring out of the cart's speakers as he rolled it down the street. The tape deck installed in the cart was also used by potential customers to try out cassettes in the manner of a *warung kaset*. Although Western music was

Dangdut keliling: mobile vendor's cart with built-in speakers selling cassettes, toiletries, sandals, and other items.

not wholly absent from his stock, the circling-around dangdut seller managed to circumvent—that is, circle around—Jakarta's prestige hierarchy of genres by targeting rural migrants, not city people, as his primary customers.

Sources for Underground Music

In an interview with an Indonesian fanzine, Robin Malau, the guitarist of Puppen, comments:

> *Kebanyakan cara indie jualan, sampe-sampe ngga berasa bahwa mereka itu sedang melakukan transaksi dagang . . . antar teman, promosi mulut ke mulut . . . seperti untuk kalangan sendiri gitu . . . bagus lho . . . positifnya, itu juga salah satu cara approach yang lebih akrab kepada pasar, lagian mo begimana lagi?*

> [For the most part the *indie* way of selling is such that it is not felt that they are making a commercial transaction . . . between friends, word-of-mouth promotion . . . like for their own social circle, y'know? . . . it's nice . . . the positive thing is that it's also one way to *approach* the market that is friendlier—why would you want anything more?] (Interview posted on Puppen's now-defunct Web site, www.not-a-pup.com/multi .htm, ellipses in original)

In keeping with this point of view, underground cassettes are, as a rule, not found in mall stores, cassette stalls, vendors' carts, or any other conventional retail outlet. It is in fact technically illegal to sell them, as the Indonesian government does not collect any taxes on the transaction.[9] Legitimate (nonpirated) commercially released cassettes in Indonesia usually come with a small strip of paper indicating that the manufacturer has prepaid a percentage of the cassettes' value to the government. To purchase underground music cassettes, which lack these strips of paper, one must know someone in the underground scene, attend a concert event, or visit one of a small number of urban specialty shops that sell underground music and accessories.

Every underground concert event I attended during my fieldwork included itinerant vendors who set up shop on blankets either inside or on the grounds outside the concert venue. Their merchandise included T-shirts, stickers, cassettes, compact discs, photocopied fanzines, and sew-on patches. Here imported and indigenously produced recordings were generally sold side by side; the peddlers' wares were usually not separated by their country of origin but rather mixed together, arranged alphabetically or in no particular order at all. Thus only an insider to the music scene could distinguish foreign groups' cassettes from Indonesians', since most Indonesian underground band names were in English and their album graphics made use of iconography similar to that of Western albums. Of course, the sharp difference in cassette prices persisted, though stickers with Western band logos were usually pirated and did not cost more than those with Indonesian band logos, which were sometimes also unauthorized copies.

Reverse Outfits

The oldest standing retail establishment in Indonesia for the sale of underground music and accessories was located not in Jakarta but in a quiet residential neighborhood in the West Javanese city of Bandung. Since the early 1990s, Reverse Outfits had sold both imported and Indonesian underground music; in the years after the onset of the economic crisis, the store placed increasingly greater emphasis on the latter.

Reverse Outfits was located on the property of Richard Mutter, an *Indo* (part native, part European) who was in his late twenties during the time of my fieldwork. Richard is the former drummer of Pas (Precise), an alternative rock group that originated in the Bandung underground scene and released a cassette on a small independent label in 1994, but has since released six albums for the large national recording company Aquarius Musikindo and has met with significant commercial success. The store was part of a complex that included a rehearsal/recording studio for Richard's record label, 40.1.24 (named after the neighborhood's postal code), and facilities for creating posters and graphics. Originally a source primarily for imported underground music, which the store purchased via mail order, the inventory of Reverse Outfits shifted dramatically between 1997 and 2000 as a result of two factors.

First, the economic crisis and the devaluation of the rupiah made imported cassettes and compact discs prohibitively expensive, as the store not only had to pay full price for each item in U.S. dollars, but also had to pay substantial shipping and handling costs. Thus the amount of imported music on sale at Reverse Outfits declined considerably after 1998. The lost inventory was replaced by way of a second development: the exponential increase of independently produced Indonesian underground music recordings during the same period.

Like the Aquarius store, Reverse Outfits was divided into two rooms. At the time of my first visit to the store in the fall of 1997, the inner room was used to display recordings from overseas, while the outer room contained a glass display counter, similar to those found in *warung kaset*, filled with domestically produced underground music. Neither room made use of shelf categories.

While imported underground music was usually sold in the form of compact discs, Indonesian underground music was sold on cassette. As of September 2000, only one underground label had ever released a compact disc: a band compilation produced by 40.1.24 Records in 1997 that could still be purchased at Reverse Outfits three years later. The economic crisis prevented any subsequent compact disc releases, but the number of new cassettes continued to grow. By the time of my return to Indonesia in 1999, Reverse Outfits had combined its musical inventory. Its few remaining imported compact discs were placed on the top two shelves in the front room's glass display case, while a substantial number of Indonesian underground cassettes were displayed in no particular order on the bottom shelf. Thus even in this context the hierarchical separation between foreign and indigenous music was maintained.

In addition to Reverse Outfits, by 2000 a small but growing number of underground boutiques (*toko underground*) had opened in Jakarta, Bandung, Surabaya, Denpasar, and other cities. These establishments were often owned and operated by veteran underground scene members (often those who had graduated from or dropped out of universities and were in need of a means of earning their livelihoods) and sometimes included rehearsal and recording studios. Some stores, such as Ish-Kabible Sick Freak Outfits Shop in Jakarta, produced their own T-shirts and stickers.[10] Studio Inferno, located in Surabaya, even had its own Internet café. These outlets, like Reverse Outfits, sold both foreign and Indonesian shirts, stickers, hats, and recordings and were focal points and important hangout spots (*tempat nongkrong*) for members of the scene.

Underground boutiques existed in a gray area between the formal and the informal economies, and while they depended on impersonal, commercial transactions for survival, they adhered to the underground's ethic of do-it-yourself authenticity. Although Reverse Outfits did stock Pas's Aquarius cassette releases, all the other titles it sold were released by small independent labels. The other boutiques I visited did not sell "major label" Indonesian cassettes at all, even those released by groups that were formerly part of underground scenes.

Cassette Piracy and Vendors
of Illegally Copied Cassettes

No inventory of the sites of music commerce in Indonesia would be complete without some remarks on cassette piracy. Given that most legitimate Indonesian cassettes cost over Rp. 12,000 each during the period of my fieldwork, it was hardly surprising that the vendors of illegally copied versions priced at Rp. 6,000 or less attracted many buyers. The quality of these pirated versions varied, but they were often not markedly inferior to the originals. Color copiers enabled pirates to accurately reproduce the original graphics of legitimate releases, and high-quality cassette duplication machines could approximate the original's sound quality. In addition to selling illegal copies of complete albums, pirated-cassette vendors sold unauthorized compilations of current hit songs. These were usually either dangdut or pop compilations, and their graphics, usually a collage of miniaturized cassette covers representing the different songs, varied widely in sophistication. One advantage the pirated compilations had over legitimate hits collections was that they could combine songs released by different recording companies, since they were not bound by copyright restrictions. Thus, pirated hits compilations were not only cheaper but also more likely to contain every hit song popular at a particular time.

Surprisingly, not all Indonesian musicians whom I interviewed vehemently opposed piracy. After all, if one's work is pirated, it indicates that one's music has achieved a measure of mass acceptance. During an interview in 1997, Harry Roesli, one of Indonesia's foremost composers/musicians/social critics, proudly showed me a pirated hits compilation featuring his controversial song "Si Cantik" ("Ms. Beautiful," a song about a grandchild of Soeharto who was suspected of dealing the popular drug Ecstasy) as the first track. He considered the cassette to be evidence that the subversive political messages in his music were successfully reaching the masses. Many members of the underground scene claimed that the mainstream acceptance of underground music was proven by the fact that some death metal bands' cassettes (usually those released by major labels) had been pirated and were being sold in outdoor markets alongside the customary rock, pop, and dangdut offerings.

Buyers of pirated cassettes were categorically assumed to be members of the working class by my consultants. Members of the middle class were purportedly too concerned with status (*gengsi*) to consider purchasing such items, which were thought to be of inferior quality.

The poor, on the other hand, were said to have the attitude of *asal denger aja* (as long as you can hear [it]) and to have no qualms about the uneven quality of illegally copied cassettes. Pirated cassettes thus occupied the lowest prestige level among recorded musical artifacts. They were sources of popular pleasure, but unlike underground and legitimate commercial cassettes, they could not act as expressions of cultural or subcultural capital (Thornton 1996), even if they happen to be illegal copies of otherwise prestigious Western music.

Conclusions: Recorded Music, Display, and Musical Value

Cassette stores in Indonesia display hegemonic and xenocentric understandings of music genres that ghettoize indigenously produced musics, subordinate them to international music products, and maintain segregated, unequal relationships between them. The two partial exceptions to this rule, Christian (*Rohani*) music and underground music, are notable for their connection to subcultures reliant on cultural texts and forms produced outside Indonesia as well as within. The presentational logic that places musically similar Indonesian and Western recordings in separate areas of the store preserves the myth that they are incomparable despite their sonic similarities. While perhaps preserving a sense of Indonesian cultural uniqueness, this metacultural separation can also present Indonesian popular music as second-class and less worthy of serious attention. In the larger stores dominated by Western imports, such presentational logic deceptively suggests that Indonesian-produced popular music is a minority taste in Indonesia, despite sales figures that consistently demonstrate otherwise.

In addition to the lack of differentiation between Indonesian pop genres in most Indonesian music stores, "regional" (or "ethnic") music is also a catchall category in which the most traditional and the most contemporary styles are displayed side by side. The "regional" category is thus even less differentiated than Indonesian national music, which is always at the very least divided between pop and dangdut categories.

Dangdut, the most popular style in Indonesia, is usually marginalized in store displays. Conversely, Western music, a minority taste, is highlighted and carefully categorized by subgenre. An alternate display strategy of placing Western *and* Indonesian rock, for example, in one shelf category sorted alphabetically by artist with no regard to country of origin still seems unthinkable in mainstream outlets and even in many underground music stores. One reason for this is that Western and Indonesian music are perceived as existing on different ontological as well as economic planes. The incommensurable categorical differences between Indonesian and Western music are summed up by the term *gengsi,* status consciousness. Indonesian popular music, no matter how westernized, is considered to be of inherently lesser status than international Anglo-American music. Indonesian music is believed to require less cultivation (*apresiasi*) to enjoy and is therefore more accessible to nonelites. According to the widespread xenocentric view of musical value in Indonesia, the music of the village is *kampungan,* backward and low-class, and even higher-status Indonesian pop still cannot aspire to the greatness of international pop and moreover is forever subject to the withering accusation that such music simply imitates the sounds of Western originals.

Despite the apparent investment made by music retailers in keeping Indonesian and foreign music separate and unequal, it is important to emphasize that the categorical and presentational logics of Indonesian record stores discussed in this chapter contrast sharply with those of most Indonesian consumers. In general, Indonesians do not strictly segregate their record collections into Western and Indonesian categories, and they use more differentiated genre labels to describe Indonesian popular music than appear on record-store shelves: rock, underground, rap, ska, metal, R & B, and so on. Nevertheless, I found that the discursive divide between "Indonesian" and "foreign" was very much present in statements Indonesians made about the value of different types of popular music, as was the suspicion that Indonesian versions of Western genres were derivative and inferior. Thus the Indonesian music fan is suspended between doubts about the authenticity of westernized pop music and misgivings about the village backwardness of music regarded as authentically Indonesian. But as we shall see in the following chapters, this state of ambivalent suspension leads to many creative attempts at resolution, rewarding in their own right, as the quest for an authentically Indonesian, modern music continues undaunted.

4

In the Studio

AN ETHNOGRAPHY
OF SOUND PRODUCTION

The sources of Indonesian popular music are extraordinarily diverse. Middle Eastern pop, American hip hop, Ambonese church hymns, Sundanese *degung*, British heavy metal, European house music, Indian film song, Chinese folk music, and Javanese *gendhing* are but a fraction of the influences one might detect on a single cassette. Despite this complexity, however, the question of where the music on an Indonesian popular music cassette "came from" generally has one simple, straightforward answer: it was produced in a multitrack recording studio most likely located in Jakarta.

The multitrack recording studio—by which I mean a facility enabling the recording of several musical parts, successively or simultaneously, that can then be processed, edited, and combined (mixed) to create a final musical product in which the presence of each part in the overall sound is carefully calibrated to achieve maximum aesthetic impact—has unquestionably become the most important musical "instrument" in the world over the last fifty years. The particular ways in which users of multitrack studios have manipulated sounds have transformed definitions of music itself and given rise to new, competing discourses of sonic aesthetics, musical authenticity, and creativity (Théberge 1997, 191, 215–22; see also Doyle 2005; Greene 2001; Greene and Porcello 2005; Katz 2004; Meintjes 2003; Porcello 1998; Wallach 2003b; Zak 2001). Indeed, the myriad creative practices enabled by studio technology around the world have in many places fundamentally reshaped musical sounds, concepts, and behaviors, to use Alan Merriam's well-known triadic scheme for the anthropological study of music (1964).

In this chapter I present accounts of three different Indonesian recording studios. The first, 601 Studio Lab, was a large professional studio complex with high-quality equipment used for recording dangdut and *pop Indonesia;* the second, Paradi Studio, was a smaller, state-of-the-art facility used to record Indonesian pop, jazz, and R & B artists. Both of these studios were located in residential areas in East Jakarta. The third studio, Underdog State, was a more modestly equipped facility in Denpasar, Bali, that specialized in the recording of underground rock music. In the following pages I describe the participants, situations, discourses, and "sound engineering" (Greene 1999) practices that characterized everyday life in these three recording studios. Throughout the discussion, three themes are emphasized: metacultural understandings of genre as they are applied to music production, the use of sound technology as a tool for cultural innovation involving the hybridization of existing genres, and the social dynamics among the participants. These dynamics differ markedly from those generally found in Western recording studios, and they fundamentally shape how popular music recordings are produced in all three sites discussed in this chapter.

601 Studio Lab: Mainstream Dangdut and Pop Production in a Professional Studio

601 Studio Lab is a multipurpose commercial recording complex used to record a variety of popular musics. The facility is located in an upscale housing development in Cakung, a newly developed area on the far outskirts of East Jakarta. It occupies a two-story house that had been converted into a sophisticated recording complex—though until 1999 one had to enter the vocal booth through the kitchen. Edy Singh, the music producer in charge of running the studio, explained to me that it was located so far from the center of Jakarta to discourage musicians and their entourages from spending all their leisure time there. Such people have a tendency to *nongkrong,* "hang out," in recording studios at all hours, even and especially when there is no recording to be done.

The studio offers a very impressive array of music recording technologies. At the time of my initial visit in 1997, the first floor housed a twenty-four-track analog studio used for recording dangdut, rock, and pop music, while upstairs was a thirty-two-track digital studio (with over one hundred virtual tracks) used for producing electronic dance music and creating dance remixes of dangdut songs. The studio also owned samplers, synthesizers, amplifiers, and racks full of state-of-the-art electronic effects. In another upstairs room a few powerful computers were set up; these were used for mastering, sequencing tracks, and creating cassette cover designs.

The fact that most of this technology originated in the so-called developed world was not without consequence. Raymond, the head engineer of the second-floor digital studio at the time of my first visit, told me he had struggled to learn English so that he could understand the technical manuals for the studio's equipment. He proudly reported that, after spending countless hours with an English-Indonesian dictionary, he now understood about 40 percent of the vocabulary in these manuals, and our conversations (in Indonesian) contained an abundance of English technical terms: *frequency response, gain, panpot, distortion,* and so on.

The spatialized division of labor between analog and digital recording technologies suggests that the producers at 601 Studio Lab had adopted the natural/synthetic and "dirty"/"clean" sonic distinctions often employed by popular music producers and consumers in the West (cf. Théberge 1997, 207–8). I was told that dangdut, like rock and roll, had to have a warm, rough, and unpolished sound. To record it digitally would be unthinkable, "not dangdut." Furthermore, everyone I spoke with at the studio agreed that the *gendang* drum—dangdut's central percussion instrument—sounds too thin and "clicky" if recorded digitally.[1]

Producing Dangdut

601 Studio Lab, according to Edy, was "the house that dangdut built." Indeed, the well-appointed studio owed its existence to dangdut music, more specifically to the wealth generated by hit dangdut songs released by Edy's father, Pak Paku (aka Lo Siang Fa), a successful dangdut cassette producer whose company, Maheswara Musik (a subsidiary of national independent label Musica), owned and operated the studio.

Pak Cecep, the Sundanese chief engineer of the ground-floor analog studio and a former rock musician, described for me the steps involved in producing a contemporary dangdut song. These are significant because they indicate that the worldwide spread of multitrack sound-recording technologies has not completely standardized the process of recording popular music in all parts of the world. Actual sound-engineering practices serve local needs and agendas, and they are

Pak Cecep at work in 601 Studio Lab, Cakung, East Jakarta.

shaped by preexisting aesthetic concerns. According to Pak Cecep, 601 studio personnel learned their craft by *praktek langsung, tanpa pendidikan* (direct practical knowledge, without education). Echoing New Order developmentalist discourse, Pak Cecep described dangdut as "left behind" (*ketinggalan*); for instance, while Indonesian pop producers had been using MIDI sequencers for over a decade (i.e., since the late 1980s), dangdut producers had only begun using them three years earlier (in 1994).

Pak Cecep spoke of two basic methods for recording dangdut. Some operators prefer to record all the vocals first, but he prefers to start with the instrumental accompaniment. He usually begins with rough vocals and the "piano" part of the song, which are later erased and rerecorded. With the piano and vocal tracks acting as a guide, the *gendang* (which Pak Cecep called the *tak-dhut*) is recorded over an electronic metronome, with the *tak* of the smaller, higher-pitched drum and the *dhut* of the lower drum on separate tracks. Next, the *tak* sound is reinforced by the sound of another *gendang* or by a muted electric-guitar string—a *tung*. In dangdut it is vitally important that the *gendang* be recorded and mixed properly, lest it sound too soft (*terlalu lembek*) in the final product. The instrument ideally should have an intense presence in the mix, an effect created by close miking of the drums and the use of reverberation and delay effects for the *tak*. Engineers at 601 used a special microphone designed for recording Western kick (bass) drums to record the *dhut*, so that its sonic presence (particularly its low-frequency response) was comparable to the visceral kick-drum sounds on contemporary rock and pop recordings. The audible result of these particular engineering practices is a powerful-sounding instrument that takes up the same sonic "space" as the kick, snare, and tom of a Western drum kit in contemporary pop and rock recordings. The sound of this technologically mediated *gendang* is quite distinct from the usual (also mediated) sound of tabla—the *gendang*'s organological source—in globally circulating recordings of Indian classical music, wherein the paired drums tend to sound more "natural" and less in the forefront of a mix. (An appropriate analogy would be the difference between the sounds of the drum kit on a rock versus a jazz record.)

After the *gendang* is recorded, usually by one of the top three Indonesian *gendang* virtuosos, Hussain, Madi, or Dada, an electric bass guitar is added.[2] Dangdut bass is difficult to play, requiring agility and a strong rhythmic sense, as it involves wide intervallic leaps and rapid, forceful motion resembling that found in salsa bass-playing. (The precise origin of this resemblance is something of a mystery, but in fact Latin American dance music and dangdut share many musical affinities, which could stem from Indonesians' knowledge of the former, from simple convergence, or, most likely, from both of these factors.) The recording of the bass-guitar part is followed by the laying down of rhythm section tracks consisting of a piano and a "clean" (nondistorted) electric guitar playing the chords of the song. The "piano" is always electronic—acoustic pianos in playable condition are exceedingly rare in Indonesia and are not usually found in recording studios. As in the case of the heavy bronze instruments of the gamelan, it is far easier to approximate the sound of a piano with a sampler or a synthesizer than to find room for such a massive apparatus. Pak Cecep explained that the clean electric guitar (*gitar klin*) is always recorded "dry" (*kering*) in dangdut; that is, without artificial reverberation or other effects added. This is one of the trademark features of the genre; further, the guitar's thin, percussive sound allows it to slice through the thick wall of mid-range sound generated by the other instruments.

The fifth step, after recording *gendang*, bass, rhythm guitar, and piano, is the addition of a keyboard *pad* (often a "church organ" sound) that provides harmonic/chordal accompaniment to the song.[3] The *pad* (also called the *blok* or *rendaman*) fills out the overall sound and, as its name suggests, is supposed to lie beneath the other instruments, tending to be nearly inaudible in final mixes. Two separate keyboard "string" tracks are added next. To my knowledge, actual string ensembles are never used to play these parts on dangdut recordings; they are always played by synthesizers. The strings are divided into higher and lower octaves and are used to play "fill-ins," melodic phrases that fill the spaces between vocal passages. Pak Cecep remarked that the musical phrases played by the strings resemble those found in Indian film music (*mirip-mirip India*), in which string ensembles, both actual and electronic, have historically played a prominent melodic role.

The next step in Pak Cecep's method is to add percussion instruments, which are generally sampled and sequenced unless the producer is older and inexperienced with the new technology. Every dangdut song must include a tambourine track, the function of which is analogous to that of the high-hat and ride cymbal in pop and rock. Maracas are also frequently used in addition to the tambourine. Other percussion instruments are used primarily for fill-ins and are often incorporated into introductory or transitional instrumental passages. These instruments may include sampled congas, tympanis, gongs, and trap drums.

While actual drum kits are almost always part of a live dangdut ensemble (where they fill an auxiliary role in a percussion section dominated by *gendang* and tambourine), they are very rarely used in the studio. Like those of pianos, string ensembles, and other unwieldy, difficult-to-record sound sources, the sounds of the drum kit on most dangdut recordings are created through digital means. This practice is not only more cost-effective but also significantly influences the listener's expectations, such that if a dangdut song were ever recorded with actual drums, pianos, and strings, the result would likely sound strange and nonidiomatic to dangdut fans.

After the percussion is layered atop the original *tak-dhut* rhythm, Pak Cecep records the remaining instruments, all of which are used for melodic fill-ins. Since vocals are usually present in just over half of a dangdut song's total length, there is ample room for contributions from several different fill-in instruments. Required instruments include distorted lead guitar and two *suling* (bamboo flutes), one large and one small, tuned to the same scale an octave apart. Electrified mandolins (another import from Indian film music) were once standard in dangdut ensembles, but they have become somewhat less common in both recordings and live performance. Other instruments that play fill-ins in dangdut recordings include nylon-stringed "Spanish guitars" (for flamenco-like flourishes), saxophone, sitar, trumpet, oboe, keyboards (playing accordion, organ, piano, or analog synthesizer sounds), and the occasional traditional metallophone (usually *bonang* or *saron*). Fill-in instruments play alone or sometimes in unison with other instruments; for instance, in dangdut arrangements the mandolin often doubles the *suling* melody. In late 1999 and 2000, a popular fill-in instrument on dangdut recordings was the violin (*biola*), thanks to the contributions of a versatile young Indonesian violinist named Hendri Lamiri, who also played on numerous *pop Indonesia* albums released at that time. Lamiri was often asked to contribute violin parts to the most heavily promoted first and second songs on a dangdut cassette.

Interestingly, many of the "ethnic" instrumental sounds occasionally used for fill-ins on dangdut recordings are actually digital samples imported from the West. Dangdut producers make frequent use of the controversial Proteus "World" digital sample module and other "world music" sound libraries to add convincing sitars, gamelan instruments, and other "ethnic accents" (*logat etnis*) to their recordings. Critics in the West have decried these sound libraries as cultural imperialism in a box, serving up decontextualized sounds from the world's musical traditions as exotic raw material for Western music producers (e.g., Théberge 1997, 201–3). In this view, the predatory sonic appropriation made possible by this technology is a predictable extension of the musically and economically exploitative practices of First World "world music" or "world beat" artists (Feld 1988, 1996, 2000; T. Taylor 1997). This critique, while certainly powerful, does not address the possibility of *non-*Western producers, such as those at work at 601 Studio Lab, using these sonic tools for their own sound-engineering projects (see Davis 2005).

Below is a schematic summary of Pak Cecep's preferred method for recording the instruments of a dangdut song:

1. Guide tracks (metronome, sync tone [for MIDI sequences], rough piano, and vocals)
2. *Gendang* (*tak* and *dhut*)
3. Electric bass guitar
4. Electric rhythm guitar and electronic piano
5. "Pad" keyboard
6. Keyboard string sounds (high and low)
7. Percussion (tambourine, maracas, etc.)

8. All instrumental "fill-ins"
9. Vocals and backing vocals (see the discussion later in this chapter).

Clearly there are a large number of instruments to manage in a typical dangdut recording. Of course, one plausible (though rather deterministic) explanation for why dangdut songs have such crowded arrangements is that multitrack studio technology makes them possible. There is, however, another, more important reason for the sonic density of dangdut song arrangements that relates to dangdut's genre ideology of sonic inclusiveness: rather than producing music that stands in dialectical opposition to rock, pop, disco, traditional music, or any other musical style, dangdut producers, one could argue, attempt to absorb aspects of them all. But while dangdut recordings tend to use far more instruments than are usually part of a live dangdut ensemble, nonidiomatic instruments tend to be employed sparingly, usually as "fill-ins."

Whereas some *pop Indonesia* arrangers use Western musical notation to write out parts for each instrument in an arrangement, this practice is rare in dangdut. Most dangdut musicians do not read Western musical notes (known as *toge*, "bean sprouts," among Indonesian arrangers). The only notation they utilize occasionally is a handwritten chord chart similar to those used in jazz. For melodic instruments, most musicians play by "feeling" (*filing*)—using their own intuition and knowledge of dangdut style to generate their contributions. Again, a small number of virtuosos generally play on cassettes (Pak Cecep named just five *suling* players who at the time played on almost every dangdut song recorded in Jakarta); these experienced performers have little trouble choosing appropriate fill-in parts for songs.

After Pak Cecep records all the instruments in an arrangement, he records vocals on the remaining tracks. The time spent on recording vocals varies depending on the ability of the singer and the importance of the song being recorded. Vocals on a "champion" (*jago;* Betawi, *gaco*) song—usually the first song on a cassette and the one that is promoted through video clips and radio—may take three times as long to record as the other songs on a cassette. While instrumentalists are free to improvise their fill-ins, vocalists must precisely follow the melodic line—every melismatic twist and turn—of the composition, as previously recorded on a demo tape. Vocals are usually recorded sequentially, line by line, with the performer and the studio crew stopping and redoing all mistakes and proceeding in this fashion until the entire song has been completed. This can be a long and arduous process, sometimes taking over fifteen hours of studio time to complete one six-minute-long *jago* song's vocals.

Hierarchies of Musical Value in Dangdut Production

The scheme outlined above suggests that in dangdut music, the vocals play a more central, structuring role than in rock and pop music. I found further corroboration for this hypothesis when an amateur *gendang* player advised me to study the instrument by purchasing dangdut karaoke cassettes (which separate the vocals and the instruments into separate audio channels, allowing one to add one's own amplified voice over the accompaniment) and suggested that I play along with the track containing the *vocals* and nothing else. An experienced *gendang* player is thus able to reconstruct the entire rhythm of a song with only the vocals for a guide; often when other people heard me practicing rhythms on the *gendang*, they asked me what song I was playing, when in my mind I had only been playing abstracted rhythmic patterns and accents. Another clue is that although dangdut songs usually contain extended instrumental passages between sung verses and refrains, I have never encountered an entirely instrumental dangdut recording. Such a recording would violate genre conventions, because all the melodic, rhythmic, and sonic features of a dangdut song ideally derive from a vocal melody that constitutes its most essential component.[4]

Ranking second in dangdut's hierarchy of musical value is the beat. The *gendang* is the only instrument in the mix that rivals the vocals in volume, and the search for the perfectly recorded *gendang* preoccupies many Indonesian sound engineers. Until recently a dangdut recording without a "live" *gendang* was unimaginable, but with the advent in the 1990s of *dangdut disco* and other new hybrids, along with the development of digital sampling and looping technology, this is no longer the case. Nonetheless, the most controversial aspect of *dangdut trendy* recordings, according to many fans, was that they do not contain a real *gendang*. In early 2000, a successful *pop dangdut* hit recorded by Evie Tamala, "Aku Rindu Padamu" (I Long for You), lacked the *gendang* entirely, which may have made it more accessible to a middle-class audience. According to the album's liner notes, the song was an example of something called *unpluged* [*sic*] *dangdut*; instead of being played on the standard electrified dangdut instruments, its arrangement was dominated by violin (played by Hendri Lamiri) and acoustic guitars. This particular hybrid was engineered to attract an audience that was usually turned off by the dangdut beat, while retaining the interest of the core dangdut audience by virtue of its characteristically melancholy vocal melody and simple, plaintive lyrics.[5]

Another noteworthy feature of dangdut recordings is the prevalence of unequal, alternating pairs of instruments, a characteristic also found in gamelan and other indigenous Indonesian ensembles. The *gendang* consists of a large and a small drum; songs are recorded with both a smaller, higher-pitched *suling* and a larger, lower-pitched one; and even the string synthesizer parts are divided into lower and higher voices. A similar pairing could even be said to exist between the mandolin and the lead-guitar parts in a dangdut song. All these paired instruments are not played simultaneously but rather alternate in the course of the song. Is there an underlying musical/cultural logic at work behind these pairings? Ethnomusicologist Marina Roseman (1987, 1991) describes how the Temiar of peninsular Malaysia ascribe complementary gender meanings to the unequal pair of bamboo stampers they use in musical performances, with the smaller (and higher-pitched) tube representing woman and the larger, lower-pitched stamper signifying man. These stampers are played in alternation. Although I cannot claim the same ideological significance for the unequal instrumental pairs found in dangdut music, there does seem to be a connection between Indonesian ideas of complementarity (in which the presence of one entity implies the presence of the other) and the pairing of different-sized musical instruments in a range of ensembles. Furthermore, this notion of implicative copresence and complementarity seems to operate in the sphere of gender relations as well. Later chapters develop this idea further.

High-Tech but "Close to the People"

Dangdut's producers and fans often use the Indonesian verbs *merakyat,* "to be close to the people," and *memasyarakat,* "to be close to society," to describe dangdut music (see Weintraub 2006). Populist rhetoric aside, however, dangdut cassette production is highly centralized, high-tech, and capital-intensive, not unlike commercial country music production in Nashville. As in Nashville, a mere handful of well-paid session musicians play on almost all commercial releases, and to my surprise I discovered that the parts not played by these highly skilled professionals are often played by a computer: on dangdut recordings produced by younger arrangers, all keyboards and percussion parts other than the *gendang* (tambourines, maracas, trap drums, etc.) are programmed and played by a MIDI sequencer. While unquestionably depriving many studio session musicians of work, these technological advances have not dramatically changed the sound of the music and do not detract from the overall "liveness" of the final mix.[6] Although the sound quality on dangdut recordings has improved and the performances they contain have become technically flawless, the "pure" dangdut sound has remained fairly unchanged for the past two decades. Further, given the music's extraordinary cross-generational popularity, it seems unlikely that the genre will lose its stylistic conservatism. In dangdut, then, new technology is used to create familiar sounds in a more cost-effective manner, not to create new stylistic innovations.

Low-Tech Origins

The origins of dangdut songs contrast sharply with the capital-intensive process by which they are recorded. Hopeful composers usually submit songs to dangdut producers in the form of cassettes and handwritten lyric sheets. On such tapes (which are often old dangdut cassettes that have been recorded over), the songwriter usually sings the composition accompanied only by an acoustic guitar. In other instances, the only accompanying "instrument" on the recording is an empty pack of cigarettes striking a table. This is not viewed as a problem, however; as explained earlier, the vocal melody is the most important musical component of a dangdut song, with everything else left up to the arranger, should the song be chosen for recording. Rough song demos are often recorded by members of dangdut's primary audience—working-class and unemployed men—and this point of contact between producers and their market appears to be important. Pak Paku, the owner of 601 Studio Lab, was always willing to listen to the work of unknown songwriters who submitted cassettes, rather than relying exclusively on professional songwriters with a proven ability to produce hits. Some of his greatest successes, such as the male singer Asep Irama, first came to him as penniless hopefuls bearing cheaply recorded demo cassettes. Asep Irama (who received permission from Rhoma Irama to use "Irama" in his stage name) was reportedly so destitute that he made the entire journey to Pak Paku's North Jakarta office on foot.

Singers are also frequently recruited from the ranks of local performers from humble backgrounds. Pak Hassanudin, 601's dangdut vocal coach and producer, explained to me that there is no formal training necessary for singing dangdut; one either loves the genre and learns everything by listening to cassettes, or one cannot perform it. Even successful pop singers cannot sing dangdut well, he remarked, although dangdut singers usually have no trouble singing pop!

Dangdut vocal producer Pak Hassanudin during a recording session with artist Murni Cahnia, Cakung.

Unlike Indian film music, in which a very small number of "playback singers" have dominated recordings (Manuel 1988, 1993), dangdut vocalists are expected to have their own distinctive styles that set each of them apart from all the others. A frequent criticism of younger singers made by dangdut fans is that their vocal styles are too derivative of those of established stars. For example, some newer male singers are said to sound too much like Meggi Z or Rhoma Irama. Newer female singers, on the other hand, are more likely to be accused of having no singing ability at all and relying entirely on their looks, and almost all are compared unfavorably to the stars of the past, particularly the still-active queen of dangdut, Elvy Sukaesih.

One reason why dangdut vocals take so long to record, I was told by several producers and engineers, is that many singers are chosen for their faces (*muka*), not their voices, and their vocals therefore have to be painstakingly recorded and then processed electronically in order to be "acceptable." Three months before my first visit, 601 Studio Lab had acquired an Intonator, an electronic pitch-shifting device used to correct off-key singing, for the purpose of improving vocal quality in recordings and compensating for singers' limitations. Thus even the most low-tech of dangdut instruments, the voice, may be altered and enhanced by the mediating apparatus of the multitrack studio. Yet, as Pak Cecep pointed out, in vocal tracks "the important thing is the soul" (*yang penting jiwanya*) of the performance, not its pitch accuracy.

Sound and Language: Recording *Pop Alternatif*

601 Studio Lab was truly a multimediated place, and Edy's house, located a few blocks away in the same housing complex and where I stayed over often during the course of my research, was an extension of the studio. On a typical afternoon the house was filled with an aural collage of simultaneous, overlapping sounds: digitized gunshots and explosions emanating from a computer game, obscenity-filled American English dialogue from a DVD or satellite television channel, drum and keyboard patterns being played back on the sampler equipment in an upstairs bedroom, and occasionally the idle strumming of an acoustic guitar by one of the resident musicians. Often ideas for *pop Indonesia* songs or parts of them were generated by the informal music-making activities taking place in the house. One night Edo, one of Edy's chief producer/arrangers, demonstrated to me he could produce an entire pop song in his room in under four hours with a sampler, an electric guitar, a digital keyboard synthesizer, and an extensive library of compact discs, including both commercially released recordings and specialized audio discs containing all manner of sounds and short musical passages expressly intended as raw material for sampling and looping.

Edy began branching into *pop Indonesia* when dangdut remixes, with which he had found his first commercial success, decreased in popularity. (He claimed he was not yet ready to try producing conventional dangdut albums.) In late 1999, Edy and his producer/arranger Edo started directing their energy toward producing an album by a young Sundanese singer-songwriter, who they hoped would produce a major hit for them. Patty (whose name appeared as "Fetty" on the recording studio schedule, reflecting an Indonesian pronunciation of her name) was a university student in her early twenties and a veteran of the Bandung underground rock scene. She had played in two bands previously (bass, guitar, and vocals), had some recordings to her credit, and now wished to become a solo artist. Originally Patty was to record three songs for an album to be titled *Tiga Warna* (Three Colors) featuring songs by three different women artists representing three genres: pop, R & B, and (Patty's contribution) *pop alternatif.* But when problems arose in the search for suitable pop and R & B artists, the strength of

Patty's original material encouraged Edy to scrap the Three Colors project in favor of a full-length album by Patty, which was to contain nine songs she wrote or cowrote and one cover song. The latter was the sentimental "Perjalanan" (Journey), written and originally recorded by Franky Sahilatua, a popular Indonesian folk-rock performer and songwriter of the 1980s whose music is now usually classified as *pop nostalgia*. Edy said he chose this song in order to provide the listener with a familiar guidepost on an album of new songs. Most of Patty's album, which was produced, arranged, and partially performed by Edo, fits well under the category of *pop alternatif*: catchy, guitar-based songs played over sampled rhythm loops. One slightly unusual song became known as the *ska-dhut* track because it featured a (sampled and looped) *gendang* track and a fast, upbeat-stressed rhythm.

I observed several recording sessions during which Patty sang vocals over Edo's previously recorded instrumental accompaniment. I found these sessions remarkable for their seriousness and intensity balanced by humor and an easygoing flexibility. Many people tend to be present at an Indonesian recording session, some of them not directly involved with the recording. Typically in attendance at Patty's *take vokal* (vocal recording sessions) were Edo the producer; Wandi the tape operator; Patty's friend Ira, who had come from Bandung to attend the sessions and provide moral support; Sonny from Asli Group (one of Maheswara Musik's most successful pop bands), who was there to help come up with harmony vocal lines and just to hang out; and myself, the ethnographer. At various points, Edy came into the studio to listen to what had been recorded and to give advice to Patty. He often suggested to her that she try to sound more *genit*, "flirtatious," and *keanak-anakan*, "childlike," without overdoing it and losing her own distinctive voice.[7] The main problem, Edo and Edy agreed, was that the "soul was still empty" (*jiwanya masih kosong*) in Patty's vocals. They sounded too "sad" (*sedih*) and lacked *filing*.

Despite these frustrations, the mood in the control room remained cheerful and easygoing, punctuated by moments of intense seriousness, but never impatience or annoyance. I was surprised that when the tape operator accidentally erased part of the vocal track (which had contained an unusually inspired take) due to a careless error, no one expressed anger or irritation. During a smoke break in the middle of an especially intense session, Edo walked out of the studio into the hallway and began to dance comically to the dangdut music emanating from a radio by the front entrance, using the music to "relieve stress" while

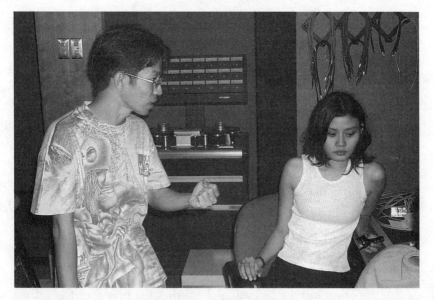

Edy Singh discusses a song with Patty in 601 Studio Lab, Cakung.

lightening the overall mood of the recording session participants (see chapter 8).

References to other musical genres and other places abounded during the session. Dangdut and Michael Jackson were brought up in discussions of sounds and techniques that Patty should avoid, although the conversation about the first of these seemed to partially contradict Edy's advice that Patty, in effect, sing more like a dangdut singer. At one point, Sonny sang a pentatonic harmony vocal line from one of Patty's songs "Javanese"-style (i.e., with a strong Javanese accent and traditional Javanese vocal timbre) for the amusement of the others. In another instance, Edo admonished Patty for swallowing syllables in her vocals and therefore sounding "Malaysian." "We're in Indonesia!" (*Kita ini di Indonesia!*), he insisted. Although at the time this seemed a rather insignificant moment in the continuous flow of conversation in the studio, I would suggest that what it means to be "in Indonesia" musically is hardly a self-evident statement. This sense of placement is constituted through cultural work such as that which was taking place in the studio at that very moment: the creation of a song in the national vernacular accompanied by a spectrum of technologically mediated sounds, providing one possible answer to the question of what it was to be a young, modern "Indonesian" in the year 2000 (cf. Yampolsky 1989, 9–10).

Recording and Loneliness

One Thursday night, considered a night of heightened supernatural activity by many Indonesians, Patty refused to finish a vocal recording shift because she was afraid. There was at least one reported *hantu* (ghost) in 601 Studio Lab—a spectral, silent young woman who was sighted in the kitchen next to the vocal booth by a few members of the staff, including Edo and Pak Cecep, the chief recording engineer. Even though Patty could see the others in the control room easily through the double glass panes, she felt isolated and vulnerable in the vocal booth. Although some may regard this incident as just an example of superstition in an otherwise modern, high-tech environment, in my view it illustrates perfectly the ethic of sociality I explore throughout this ethnography, in which the noisy presence of others is not only tolerated but valued, and its absence is considered threatening, a cause of loneliness and susceptibility to supernatural harm.

Critics of multitrack recording claim that the practice of overdubbing, of recording each part separately at separate moments in time, isolates musicians and eliminates the spontaneity of live performance. In 601 Studio Lab, the isolation of the vocal booth was sometimes construed as problematic, but not for these reasons. The separation of the performer in the sound booth from the producer, the engineer, and the hangers-on in the studio control room was considered necessary for recording vocals, and sometimes for recording instruments, but it did appear to be a cause of discomfort that studio workers attempted to overcome. A common practice for dangdut producers like Pak Hassanudin was to plug in a microphone to communicate with the person in the sound booth and leave it on, rather than using the built-in talkback system that required pressing a button to open a channel every time one wished to speak to the person on the other side of the glass. Although leaving a communication channel open could possibly interfere with the recording process, causing feedback or bleed-through, it allowed for easier and more direct communication with the singer and made it possible to put him or her more at ease, despite his or her physical isolation.

Lilis Karlina and Ethnic Techno-Hybrids

Lilis Karlina, who in 1999–2000 was one of Indonesia's most successful young dangdut singers, also records at 601 Studio Lab. Lilis's philosophy regarding musical innovation was similar to Edy's. In an interview she told me she paid close attention to international trends such as (in

1999) Latin crossover pop but also enthusiastically drew on "ethnic" elements, her trademark, when seeking new material to record. "I *am* Sundanese, after all," she explained. Many of Lilis's biggest hits have been dangdut-ethnic hybrids. Her song "Goyang Karawang" (Dance of Karawang) mixed dangdut and *jaipongan*, a combination to which the lyrics explicitly referred (cf. Spiller 2001). Her most recent hit, "Cinta Terisolasi" (which can mean both "Isolated Love" and "Love Stuck Like Cellophane Tape," the latter perhaps more characteristic of dangdut songs in its use of a prosaic simile to describe the tenacity of romantic love), contained a melancholy, "Mandarin"-style violin part (played by the ubiquitous Hendri Lamiri) reminiscent of the Chinese *er-hu* and a *jaipong*-like rhythm that Edy identified as actually originating in Banyuwangi, a region on the eastern tip of Java. Despite the difficulty of playing this nonstandard rhythm, the demand for this song encouraged many local dangdut ensembles to devise ways to perform it using the standard instrumental lineup, and in a short time it became a staple at live dangdut concerts. More recently, Lilis recorded a duet with Malaysian dangdut star Iwan that contained conspicuous Latin and disco elements, one of a handful of recordings released around the same time that experimented with combining dangdut and Latin sounds, among them Rhoma Irama's *Euphoria* 2000 album.

One of Lilis Karlina's new songs was arranged by Cahyo, a talented pop arranger on Edy's production staff (Edy told me with a smile that all his staff *had* to work on dangdut songs, whether they wanted to or not). The rough mix I heard was extraordinary, incorporating Turkish, Indian, and hip hop rhythms. It included no fewer than six drum tracks employing three different types of drums—an ordinary *gendang dangdut*, a *dholak* (South Asian two-headed folk drum), and a set of *jaipongan*-style Sundanese barrel drums—all played by percussion virtuoso Hussain. Cahyo described the track as *musik gado-gado*—literally "music that resembles a mixed peanut salad." Music makers and listeners often use this expression to describe music that incorporates numerous different styles. Unfortunately, Lilis, who loved the song, discovered that the recording's key was beneath her vocal range, so the track needed to be either transposed by an electronic pitch-shifter or rerecorded (I'm not sure what she chose to do, or if the song was ever released).

Edy then told me something that surprised me. Another song Lilis would be recording for her new cassette was written by none other than *pop alternatif* songstress Patty. Apparently, one day Patty and Edo were jamming at Edy's house with guitar and sampler, and Patty decided to write a "Malay"-style song. The resulting demo recording, which includes voice, acoustic guitar, and a sped-up sampled *gendang* loop, resembles a fast-tempo, rather aggressive dangdut song with these words in the refrain:

> *You kawin lagi!*
> *Lebih baik bunuh diri*
> *Tapi aku takut mati.*
>
> [*You* married again!
> Better to kill myself . . .
> But I'm afraid of death.]

The defiant way in which Patty sings these lines makes the song humorous and angry, both characteristics that are a little unusual in a dangdut song about heartbreak, yet it accurately expresses the predicament of many Indonesian women whose husbands take another wife (polygyny is legal in Indonesia, as Islamic religious law allows one man to marry up to four wives). The use of the English *you* instead of the usual *kau, engkau,* or *kamu* (usually the first of these when anger is being expressed) is highly unusual in dangdut or in any other genre, but it is sometimes used in coarse everyday speech. Despite these oddities, when Edy played the song for Lilis, she instantly liked it and wanted to record it. It was difficult for me to interpret how Patty felt about Lilis's request, but mostly she seemed ambivalent about the honor of being perhaps the first female *pop alternatif* artist to write a song for a dangdut star. The song itself, as performed by Patty, owes more to the "woman-scorned" angst of global pop artists like Alanis Morissette (who had played an enormously successful concert in Jakarta a few years earlier) than to the dangdut song canon (the song is neither despairing nor flirtatious), yet it seemed to fit Lilis's progressive, cosmopolitan outlook and assertive image.[8]

The Anxieties of Global English

A final ethnographic anecdote about 601 Studio Lab suggests some of the limits to the atmosphere of creative collaboration and experimentation encouraged by Edy. I was listening to another of Patty's demos, a slow, heartbreak-inspired song titled "Mungkin Terlalu Lama" (Maybe Too Long [a Time]). Toward the end of the song, after the final chorus, Patty begins singing *oh baby I love you* repeatedly over the song's chord progression. This sudden shift from Indonesian to English, which sounded like a spontaneous outburst, appeared to be the emotional climax of the song, reminding me of the many Indonesian musicians who had told me that emotional directness was easier with English lyrics (cf. Wallach 2003a, 67–68). But when I commented to Edy and Edo about that part of the song, they laughed and assured me that all the *I love you*'s would be eliminated in the final version because they were inappropriate. Although Patty and many other young Indonesian songwriters frequently sang, wrote, and even thought in English phrases when practicing their craft, these phrases were considered out of place in mainstream commercial *pop Indonesia*. One of the songs on Patty's album actually does contain some English, but only in a short introductory section. Patty sings, *Goodbye, far-e-well to you, it's time to say goodbye … but I wish you well* in an electronically processed voice that seems to float in the ether over a detuned, almost unrecognizable drum-loop sample. This would seem to be an appropriate use of English, part of a "weird" (*aneh*) introductory section framing the song and analogous to the English-language samples used in Indonesian electronic dance music (Wallach 2005, 143), but not part of the song itself, and certainly not representing its emotional high point.

Thus the conventions of *pop Indonesia*, as enforced by cultural gatekeepers like Edy, limit artistic expression. In this case, Patty's use of English *I love you*'s on the demo tape undermined the ideological mission of *pop Indonesia* by pointing to a seeming deficiency in Standard (poetic/confessional) Indonesian's capacity to express authentic emotions. By switching to English, Patty revealed Indonesian to be expressively lacking compared to a foreign language that the majority of the pop audience, especially those listeners who live outside large cities, viewed with ambivalence and incomprehension. Furthermore, Patty's apparent need to resort to singing in English calls into question the supposition that Western-style pop music can be fully Indonesianized. Such a supposition legitimates *pop Indonesia* as a patriotic, unifying force for the nation instead of an antinational example of (post)colonial mimesis.

Paradi Studio: Cosmopolitanism and Computer-Assisted Composition

Located in a quiet, affluent neighborhood in Pancoran, East Jakarta, is the showroom for Paradi, the main supplier of high-end recording and sound equipment for companies and individuals in the Indonesian music industry. During my visits in 1999–2000, Paradi's expansive, state-of-the-art equipment showroom was also a working studio, though this fact was not widely publicized. Surrounded by high-powered computers, sound modules, keyboards, effects racks, and mixing equipment, Andy "Atis" Manuhutu, an Ambonese record producer, arranger, performer, and songwriter, pursued his mission to bring a new sound to the Indonesian music market. Before arriving in Jakarta after the fall of Soeharto, Andy worked for many years in Los Angeles for Michael Sembello, a respected producer and film soundtrack composer best known for his work on two 1980s Hollywood motion pictures, *Flashdance* and *Gremlins*. Sembello also produced an album of pop ethnic fusion songs for Andy that was released in Indonesia in 1993 but has since gone out of print.

Andy's music was unusual in the Indonesian context in two main ways. First, its rhythmic sensibility, chord voicings, and arrangements were far closer to those employed in American R & B than the music of any other Indonesian producer/arranger, a result of Andy's long apprenticeship in California. Second, although the majority of Andy's compositions were in one language or the other, some combined Indonesian and English, often with one language used for the verses and the other for the chorus. Although other recording artists occasionally inserted an English phrase into an Indonesian-language song for humorous effect, I had not encountered any other who lyrically placed the languages on equal footing. The reader will recall the previous anecdote about Patty's demo tape, in which Edy deemed the English lyrics sung at the end of the song inappropriate for a commercial release in Indonesia, as well as the practice discussed in chapter 3 of keeping Western and Indonesian music spatially separate in Indonesian record stores.

Certainly Andy's decision to record songs that alternate between English and Indonesian (and, in one Latin-tinged song, Indonesian and Spanish) constituted an artistic risk of sorts.[9] But Andy was interested primarily in middle-class and elite consumers (in contrast to Edy, whose background in dangdut made him more of a populist), and in our conversations he argued that the tremendous influence of Western popular music has created a hybrid subjectivity in Indonesia, especially among youth, which embraces and identifies with global pop artists. He explained that young, affluent listeners are therefore not invested in maintaining the artificial separation between "Indonesian" and "non-Indonesian" music demanded by old-fashioned nationalist rhetoric; rather, they long for indigenous pop music that acknowledges their affective attachment to global popular culture and to English. In the course of my research among young, educated members of the multi-ethnic, urban middle-to-upper class, I found much evidence to support

Andy's argument. However, his claims seem to apply most of all to Chinese Indonesians and to Christians like himself, people who do not feel the persistent ambivalence and anxieties about Western culture felt by those Indonesians who identify themselves as members of the Islamic world.

Andy's desire to create a more globally oriented national pop music meant that he did not seek to water down his compositions to make them palatable to a mass audience. In his songs he employed the seventh and ninth chords used in American R & B rather than the standard triadic chord progressions found in *pop Indonesia* (including pop songs with hip hop rhythmic influences), and he favored a more syncopated, complex rhythmic feel on his recordings. He claimed that the sophisticated young consumer of popular music in Indonesia prefers more *"authentic-sounding"* R & B.

In addition to bringing a new approach to Indonesian pop, following his arrival in Jakarta Andy tried to introduce the American music industry's ethic of professionalism into the day-to-day workings of his production company, which he co-owned with Paradi's owner. This was not always easy. The singers with whom he worked complained that he was a harsh critic—*"His number one favorite thing to do is intimidate people!"* said one, half-jokingly—and many employees had trouble understanding why he could be stern and serious during work hours and then become relaxed and friendly after work ended. Andy also encouraged his artists to negotiate contracts carefully and to seek legal representation, both rather unusual practices in a music business where informal patron-client relationships between producers and artists were the rule.

Two singers who worked with Andy were Amanda and Anggie, sisters who came from a family of female performers. Their maternal grandmother was a *keroncong* singer; their mother sang *pop Indonesia*. The sisters chose American R & B, which they sang with skill and savvy, and they mentioned Aretha Franklin as a primary role model. Their mother used to read them the *Jakarta Post* regularly in order to teach them English, and both sisters spoke the language fluently, though during the period of my fieldwork their studio banter with Andy was dominated by colloquial Jakartanese Indonesian.

Amanda and Anggie helped write the melodies and lyrics for their songs, as Andy encouraged his artists to be involved in the writing process. Their songs were often obliquely about Christian themes, though the lyrics were always ambiguous, and the compositions could be interpreted as love songs. This was exemplified in song titles like "B My

Savior" and "Satu Bersamamu" (One with You). The sisters, who were raised in a Javanese Muslim household, had converted to Protestant Christianity (to their mother's dismay), as had many of the singers who worked with Andy.

Like many contemporary music producers around the world, Andy was able to play back an entire song from his studio computer. On the afternoon of February 14, 2000, during one of my visits, he was working on an as-yet-untitled song for which twenty tracks had already been sequenced, all of them using the electronically generated sounds stored in the memory banks of the keyboards and sound modules in the studio. The instruments that these sounds were designed to resemble, to judge from their names on the computer screen and their actual timbre, included a Rhodes electric piano, an electric bass, a grand piano, a wood block, a shaker, a tambourine, two snare drums, a kick drum, cymbals, a sitar, a string section (on two separate tracks), and an ethereal synthesizer sound called "InTheAir."

The techniques Andy used for inputting each sound varied. Often he physically played instrumental parts into the sequencer without much editing, in order to preserve a "*human feel.*" String parts, by contrast, were entered using a computer mouse to place notes on a musical staff on the screen, in order to produce the more open chord voicings characteristic of real string ensembles but difficult and counterintuitive to play on a keyboard. Bass and drums, the foundation of the song, were inputted by triggering the sounds in real time from a synthesizer keyboard. Andy then edited these parts extensively—his sequencing software allowing him to do so with great precision—until the exact rhythmic feel he intended could be realized. Using a computer keyboard, Andy could input numerical values that controlled how far ahead of or behind the electronic metronomic pulse an instrument was sounded. Andy told me he always set the kick (bass) drum at zero, exactly "*on the beat.*" The snare drum was moved slightly behind the beat, while the attack of the bass-guitar notes was usually moved considerably behind the beat, about twenty-four milliseconds, in order to produce the right "*groove*" (see Keil and Feld 1994).

Unlike the drums, whose time intervals were consistent throughout the entire song, the bass part was more flexible, and parts of the bass line that "*sounded cool*" in the original performance were kept as they were. The rest of the track could also be computer edited: discordant or extraneous notes could be deleted, specific sounds could be changed (from an acoustic to an electric piano, for example), and new sections could be created by cutting, copying, and pasting musical material in the same way that text is manipulated on a word processor.

Partway through my visit, Amanda and Anggie arrived. After a short interval of friendly small talk, Andy asked Amanda to sing her vocal line on top of the electronic playback. While she sang, Andy coached her, and Anggie occasionally inserted backing harmony vocals. The singing techniques favored in Indonesian traditional music (and in dangdut) differ from the less nasal, more diaphragmatic technique used in Western music, including R & B. During Amanda's performance, Andy shouted out reminders in English: "*Don't get lazy!*" "*Don't fade out on me!*" "*Same power!*" to encourage her to project from her diaphragm through an entire stanza, so that the final syllables of a phrase would not trail off. Since Amanda was not using a microphone, it was harder to conceal when she ran out of air while singing. She was also advised, "*Don't slide the note—hit the note!*" when she sang with excessive portamento.

Although Andy called the habits of trailing off at the end of vocal phrases and sliding up to notes "laziness," these habits are in fact quite common in dangdut and *pop Indonesia,* so much so that they are really more like techniques than habits. Indeed, descending, melismatic vocal lines that slide languidly down to the tonic are an important element in dangdut's expression of musical sensuality (R. Anderson Sutton, personal communication, August 2000). These techniques are difficult to unlearn, even for those whose primary orientation is toward Western pop, and few Indonesian singers are told to do so.

After Amanda sang the song a few times, Andy returned to adding more tracks to the instrumental accompaniment. Although very "American" in his working methods in some ways, he also had the very Indonesian capacity to perform delicate tasks in a room full of noisy distractions. Somehow while the others in the room were laughing, joking, and loudly talking on their cell phones, Andy managed to use the keyboard to play a sampled tabla part that enhanced the overall impact of the song. "*Notice I wasn't playing the tabla ethnically,*" remarked Andy proudly afterward, saying that the part instead had a "*black groove,*" "*the way an American would play it.*" In fact, Andy's choice to add a tabla to the song was influenced by "Desert Rose," the 1999 international hit song by Sting and Algerian *raï* star Cheb Mami, which contains some North African percussion. (A video for the song had appeared earlier that day on a television tuned to MTV kept above Andy's mixing desk.) The fact that tabla sounds figure prominently in dangdut recordings was most certainly not a consideration. Andy copied and pasted the tabla part so that it recurred throughout the song. He then asked Amanda to sing once more over the playback. "*Swing with the tabla now,*" he instructed.

The activities that took place in Andy Atis's studio exemplify a cosmopolitan impulse in Indonesian popular music production; they also provide a glimpse of how religious difference can be encoded into music recordings. Using sophisticated technology that allowed a single musician to create an entire multitrack soundscape, Andy brought global sounds into the Indonesian context, his mission to create world-class music entailing the avoidance of all things "ethnic," including vocal technique.

Andy's music was intended to compete directly with the imported products it resembled, yet the segregationist practices of music retail outlets prevented a relationship of equal footing between Western and Indonesian R & B; the former was considered a specific, separate genre with its own conventions that was meant to be less *easy listening* (accessible and pleasant sounding) than pop, while the latter was grouped with the other *pop Indonesia* styles, inviting inappropriate comparisons and expectations.[10] As with the other music producers discussed in this chapter, Andy Manuhutu used the recording studio as an agent of cultural change by harnessing its ability to facilitate the creation of innovative musical fusions. The final studio discussed in this chapter represents a similar strategy of techno-hybridization that is employed in the service of some strikingly dissimilar social and artistic goals.

Techno-Hybridity in the Underground: Eternal Madness and Underdog State

Our third studio offers a different perspective from those provided by 601 Studio Lab and Paradi. The Underdog State recording facility is located in a middle-class residential neighborhood in Denpasar, Bali. It is quite low-tech and low-budget compared to the recording studios discussed previously in this chapter—much of its recorded output is produced on a Tascam 424 four-track cassette recorder—yet the engineering strategies of its owner, Sabdo Mulyo ("Moel"), are equally ambitious. Moel is the bassist, vocalist, and main songwriter of Eternal Madness, a Denpasar-based metal band that holds the distinction of being one of the few Indonesian groups attempting to combine traditional (in this case, Balinese) music with the modern noise of underground metal.

Moel at Underdog State, Denpasar, Bali.

Like similar facilities in other cities, Underdog State is a favorite hangout spot. In addition to a recording studio, it contains a rehearsal space, a silk-screening workshop (for creating band T-shirts, stickers, and cassette covers), and a billiards table. The house occupied by Underdog State acts as a base camp for many members of Bali's sizable underground music scene, which is known for its strong punk, black-metal, and hardcore contingents. Eternal Madness plays death metal, a style that is more popular in the Jakarta and Surabaya underground scenes than in Bali—and plays it with a definite twist. The group, which at the time of my visit in mid-2000 consisted of Moel on bass and vocals, Putu Pradnya Pramana Astawa (Didot) on guitar, and a drum machine, has created a new subgenre for its music: *lunatic ethnic death grind metal*. In an undated Indonesian press release, the band claims its 2000 cassette *Bongkar Batas* (Break Down Boundaries) "is a work of art that responds to the blindness and deafness of Indonesian musicians toward exploiting their own identities in the concept and style of metal music." This extraordinary album, most of which was recorded at Underdog State, contains some definite "Balinese" elements: pentatonic melodies, a Balinese funerary chant, and abrupt rhythmic transitions strongly reminiscent of *gamelan gong kebyar*, the flashiest and most aggressive Balinese gamelan style (see Tenzer 2000).

Eternal Madness uses no traditional instruments, and the distorted, metallic onslaught of its music, complete with the raspy, growling vocals characteristic of the death metal subgenre, often seems to overwhelm the other elements in the music. Yet even in the most conventional passages on *Bongkar Batas* there is an audible difference that, while subtle, seems foreign to the conventions of death metal music. This sonic difference is located in the unusual rhythmic relationships between the drum machine, the guitar, and the bass, which resemble those existing between instruments in a traditional Balinese ensemble. Balinese traditional music is organized around points of rhythmic convergence at the ends of phrase units. Until those points are reached, however, the different metallophones in an ensemble are rarely struck at the same time. Instead of playing together in unison, each musician's instrument occupies a distinct place in the measure, filling up the sonic space with an interlocking, overlapping web of sound, "a dynamic intertwining of rhythms and tones" (Herbst 1997, 112). Moel revealed that this effect of "playing against" (*main kontra*) was achieved in Eternal Madness's music through the unique way in which the songs on the album were recorded.

Moel explained that when recording a song, he starts with a rhythm guitar part that plays the basic riffs (in gamelan terminology, the "nuclear melody") of the piece. Next, lead-guitar parts are added over the riffs; these parts resemble the decorative melodic phrases that ornament the nuclear melody in Balinese gamelan music. The original guitar track is then erased. Only then are the programmed drums added. Rather than the guitar following the beat of the drums, then, the drums play *around* the guitar, playing accents, filling in empty space, and marking transitions the way the *kendang* (traditional Balinese barrel drum, different from the *gendang* used in dangdut) player would in a gamelan performance.

Although Moel uses only samples of a standard Western trap-drum kit, he intentionally programs the drum machine to evoke Balinese drumming styles. He told me that he often uses the machine's sampled China-crash cymbal to play the part of the *kecrek*, loud crashing cymbals played in traditional Balinese ensembles that punctuate the core melody. Many of the drum parts Moel programs would be extremely difficult or impossible for an actual drummer to play; so far Eternal Madness has not found a human drummer capable of replacing their drum machine.

After the drums are programmed and recorded, Moel adds the bass guitar. He claimed that the bass is like the large gong in a gamelan ensemble. To my ears, the bass lines in Eternal Madness songs more often play the role of the *bonang* (tuned rows of kettle gongs). Like the *bonang*, Moel's bass plays countermelodies "underneath" the nuclear melody, while the gong marks the end of musical phrases. Moel's growled, death-metal-style vocals are recorded last.

The method for recording Eternal Madness songs (first guitar, then drums, then bass, then vocals) is quite unlike the standard technique for recording rock music employed by both Indonesian and Western producers: drum tracks first; then bass; then guitars, keyboards, and so on; then vocals. The latter method guarantees that all the instruments will follow the same rhythm (dictated by the drums) with minimal deviation. In contrast, Eternal Madness creates hybrid music through an unorthodox use of music technology that reflects Balinese aesthetics more than those of rock, allowing a greater degree of rhythmic independence for each instrument.

From the Village to the World

Studio-based sound-engineering practices tend to facilitate a certain level of reflexivity. The nature of the recording process lends itself to a particular kind of critical engagement with the work that is taking shape through it, which encourages thoughts about the music's origins, meanings, and potential audiences (Porcello 1998; Meintjes 2003). Moel has many such thoughts regarding his music. Eternal Madness's two albums, *Offerings to Rangda* (1996, now out of print) and *Bongkar Batas* (2000), both released on small, independent record labels, target an Indonesian underground audience, but again with a twist. Moel does not believe that death metal fans in Jakarta and other large cities like his music very much; they consider it too "ethnic" and therefore low-class and backward (*kampungan*), akin to the way middle-class urban Indonesians regard dangdut and *pop daerah*.[11] But Moel believes that an international audience would find his music interesting and unique. Eternal Madness received positive responses to its music during a visit to Australia, and Moel hopes his music will one day reach an international underground audience, perhaps even a world music/world beat audience, even though the latter is often comprised of "grown-ups" too old for loud youth music like metal (cf. T. Taylor 1997, 6).

Moel claims that he does not want to be an American, but rather that his goal is "to be a Balinese who plays death metal music" (*jadi orang Bali yang main musik death metal*). He doesn't want to copy an

American sound, and if that is not good enough for the America-obsessed kids in Jakarta, so be it. Instead of focusing exclusively on the urban centers of the underground music movement in Indonesia, Moel has taken his music directly to rural areas all over Java and Bali, riding ferries, buses, trains, and motorcycles to smaller villages and hamlets. Moel claims that this promotional strategy has allowed him to sell fifteen thousand copies of *Bongkar Batas,* which is more than many major-label Indonesian rock cassettes sell unless they score a big hit. He criticizes members of large urban underground scenes like Jakarta and Bandung for having what he calls a "racial" (*rasial*) view of rural listeners, that is, a prejudice bordering on racism. Moel, on the other hand, finds that this rural audience appreciates the traditional elements in the music of Eternal Madness as well as the band's occult and mythological imagery, which resembles those found in the most popular underground genre in rural areas: black metal. Thus, the music of Eternal Madness appeals to rural audiences by joining together local folklore, village music traditions, and a generation-specific musical style with both national and global dimensions. This combination seems to have had less impact on urban areas. Although city-based underground scene members with whom I spoke seemed to respect Eternal Madness's music, they were generally not interested in following the group's lead and creating their own ethnic hybrids. Indeed, EM's undertaking appeared rather tangential to the central aspirations of the Indonesian underground scene.

Moel has not lost sight of the international market; he told me he planned to rerecord four songs from *Bongkar Batas* with an actual Balinese gamelan, part of an EP intended "for export." He was collaborating on this project with Yudena, an avant-garde Balinese composer, who planned to use computer software to adjust the tuning of the gamelan ensemble to make its contribution compatible with the preexisting instruments on the recording. This project, then, is a sort of "remix," and like the addition of Sundanese and Javanese musical elements in dangdut songs, it represents a kind of "retraditionalization" of popular sounds. In this case, the objective appears to be making the "ethnic" component in Eternal Madness's music more intelligible to an international underground/world beat audience.

While the sonic juxtapositions found in dangdut could be said to be symptomatic of a characteristically Indonesian mode of coping with the heterogeneity and fragmentation of modern life, the techno-hybrid grooves of Eternal Madness, like those of Krakatau and other progressive ethnic groups, suggest fusion more than juxtaposition. Rather than evoking coexistence without synthesis, Eternal Madness uses multitrack technology to create recordings that meld together ethnic and underground sounds, such that it is often quite difficult to detect where one begins and the other leaves off. This, of course, appears to be the point. The powerful music of Eternal Madness expresses the triumph of the individual over the pitfalls of the postcolonial condition, in which modernity, on the one hand, and pride in one's traditional cultural heritage, on the other, are often viewed as mutually exclusive alternatives. Eternal Madness "breaks down boundaries" between these two poles—which might otherwise prevent postcolonial subjects from achieving a unified subjectivity—with *a wild sonic attack of twisted rhythms and howling vocals*" (Eternal Madness official Web site).

Conclusions: Technology, Hybridity, Sociality

This chapter has visited three recording-studio environments and analyzed the musical and cultural dynamics that take place in them. We have seen how processes of musical production and innovation are realized through technological means and how they are framed by particular notions of genre and subgenre. Greg Urban (2001, 55-56) suggests that anthropologists investigate "sites of replication" in contemporary complex societies, where cultural forms are primarily circulated by dissemination (rather than replication, that is, reperformance), in order to understand the specialized knowledge and skills necessary to produce new culture. An examination of recording studios in Indonesia does indeed provide important insights into how and why recorded artifacts are produced.

First, understandings of the musical genre are paramount in determining how a song is recorded and promoted; in turn, the production decisions of producers, arrangers, and other specialized personnel can transform or reconfigure these understandings. For example, the notion that dangdut should be recorded "live" with analog equipment instead of with state-of-the-art technology was once widely shared, but now the idea that dangdut music benefits from high production values, MIDI programming, and sophisticated mixing equipment has become accepted among producers and sound engineers. Developments like these reconfigure the genre expectations of performers, producers, and listeners (though sometimes they also generate a longing for older, now-obsolete sounds, a phenomenon Tim Taylor calls "technostalgia"

[2001]). On the other hand, genre expectations have a strong "inertial" component (Urban 2001), and many attempts to create novel musical forms do not succeed commercially, thus severely limiting their cultural impact. Music producers gamble on the acceptance of the new hybrid genres they invent, and if the gamble is successful, as it was in the case of Lilis Karlina's Sundanese/Chinese/Banyuwangi/dangdut hybrid "Cinta Terisolasi," the commercial rewards can be well worth the risk.

Second, it is worth repeating that despite the potential of multitrack recording and electronic music technology to isolate performers, mechanize music production, and attenuate musical interactions, studio production in Indonesia remains an exuberantly social process, and most musical decisions are made collectively. The tendency in the West to treat the recording studio as a sterile musical laboratory off-limits to nonparticipants appears not to have traveled with the technology. One reason for this, aside from the generally more sociable quality of life in Indonesia, is the lack of formally trained recording engineers who take themselves and their technical mastery seriously enough to attempt to impose a technocratic disciplinary regime on the performers who enter their domain (for counterexamples see Meintjes 2003; Moehn 2005). A second reason relates to the remarkable ability of Indonesian musicians and producers to concentrate on the performance of complex tasks in the studio while surrounded by crowds of people noisily sharing the same space. Despite all its potential distractions, participants seem to prefer the jocular unruliness of the typical Indonesian recording-studio environment to the loneliness they might feel working by themselves.

5

On Location

SHOOTING MUSIC VIDEO CLIPS

As is the case with recording studios, a discussion of Indonesian music videos must take into account the interactional dimension of cultural production: the negotiation of meaning and the concretization of metacultural abstractions that take place "on location," in this case, at taping sessions for Indonesian video clips. In the following discussion I also wish to extend my arguments regarding social class in Indonesia. While the ascendancy of mass-mediated popular culture coincided with (and arguably anticipated) the elision of class stratification and the rise of the middle class in Western countries, in Indonesia and elsewhere in the developing world the national popular cultures that have emerged in the last half century have had to respond to perseverant class distinctions—most conspicuously, the continuing presence of a poor and uneducated majority that nonetheless possesses some purchasing power. We have seen how in the Indonesian national popular music industry there arose a two-tiered hierarchy that distinguished between westernized, cosmopolitan national music and non-Western— but still national—music genres. Keeping this normative market segmentation in mind, I now turn to a discussion of Indonesian music videos and how they embody and develop assumptions about the social constitution of their audience and index class-inflected differences vis-à-vis cultural debates on modernity, cosmopolitanism, and Indonesian national identity.

Recorded Sound and Televisual Image

I view both static and moving images as contextualizing supplements to sound in popular music. My approach is therefore the opposite of the one assumed by cinema studies and generally prevalent in Western thought, which tends to elevate sight as the most "truthful" of the senses (Feld [1982] 1990). I am thus sympathetic to Andrew Goodwin's (1993) critique of studies that focus on music video's fragmented, "postmodern" character (e.g., Kaplan 1987). These analyses draw on film theory to elucidate the often disconnected, pastichelike visuals of music videos while largely ignoring their sonic dimension. Goodwin argues that it is precisely the soundtrack of music videos that provides them with coherence and affective unity, for music videos are intended to be not miniature films but rather imaginative visualizations of particular songs, and they follow a musical rather than a cinematic logic.

In general, the visual marketing of popular music tends to erect boundaries around its audience, while musical sound allows for greater ambiguity and social polysemy. This property may be intrinsic to the aural medium itself, which crosses physical boundaries with ease. Cultural critic Rey Chow writes: "While the image marks the body, in music one has to invent a different language of conceptualizing the body, that is, of perceiving its existence without marking and objectifying it as such" (1993, 392). In other words, musical sound is a felt presence that transgresses the boundaries of self and other that are traced by visual images. It is only through specific framing devices—both discursive and visual—that the embodied, affective intensity of musical encounters can be channeled efficiently into identity projects, lifestyles, and social narratives. In their attempt to promote the consumption of a specific musical artifact, music video producers make a series of explicit, if often contradictory, claims about the identities of artists and listeners by deploying a rhetoric of moving images that locates powerfully ambiguous sounds in visible bodies and in imaginary but recognizable social spaces. On a more fundamental level, exploring the tension between the polysemy of sound and the markedness of image can provide insight into a paradoxical feature of popular music everywhere: the fact that a medium that contains such powerful associations with particular social categories so easily transcends those categories in its reception.

Music Video in Indonesia

When I arrived in Jakarta in October 1999 to begin my dissertation fieldwork, the city's attention was focused on a Special Session (Sidang Istimewa) of the recently elected People's Consultative Assembly. Fears of a repeat of the massive rioting that had engulfed Jakarta in May 1998 caused the normally congested thoroughfares of the city to be eerily quiet. No one could predict what the outcome of the session would be or whether it would lead to an eruption of violence. I, too, followed the session's proceedings on television, watching the representatives of competing political parties debate and deliberate over which candidate should become Indonesia's fourth president. To my surprise, the sober-minded television coverage was periodically interrupted by Indonesian pop, rap, and rock music videos, which appeared alongside the somewhat more predictable commercials for national brands of tea, vitamins, and milk. From my perspective, this was roughly akin to an American network broadcasting a Metallica video in its entirety in the middle of coverage of the Republican National Convention. One of the newscasters on the station I was watching (SCTV) commented that the music could "calm" viewers during this time of tension and uncertainty. In fact, music videos are ubiquitous on Indonesian television, and they frequently appear as filler between regular programs in addition to appearing in programs devoted to music. Apparently, this was the case even during news coverage of a momentous occasion in Indonesian history.

Making music video clips is an essential promotional activity for the Indonesian music industry. Without an accompanying *klip* broadcast on Indonesian television (which usually involves giving some form of payola to each television network), a newly released single in a commercial genre has little hope of finding an audience. The production methods for creating clips vary according to genre and budget, and although it is beyond the scope of this ethnography to fully analyze filming techniques employed in Indonesian videos, it is possible to make a primary distinction between dangdut song clips and pop/rock clips. Dangdut clips tend to feature the leisurely paced, often narrativized visuals found in karaoke videos and are often shot on location (although one might expect them to resemble the musical sequences in Indian films, this does not appear to be the case). Pop/rock clips are usually shot in television studios and tend to feature the faster edits and stylish, striking visuals of Western music videos broadcast on MTV and other global music channels. Often *dangdut trendy* videos are of this type as well, but not always; they sometimes appear to combine both approaches. In 1999–2000, production budgets tended to be significantly higher for pop/rock videos than for dangdut clips.

Images of Tradition and Opulence: Shooting a Dangdut Clip

On November 6, 1999, I attended the shooting (*syuting*) of a dangdut video clip that took place over the course of a long seventeen-hour day in various Jakarta locales.[1] The featured artist was singer Iyeth Bustami, and the clip was for her soon-to-be-released song titled "Cinta Hanya Sekali" (Love [Happens] Only Once). Iyeth, an ethnic Malay from Riau province, had made a name for herself previously as a singer of Malay pop (*pop Melayu*), a regional (*daerah*) genre with an audience concentrated in Riau, coastal Sumatra, and Kalimantan (Indonesian Borneo). This was her first foray into a national style, and the concept behind the single was to bring together Malay pop's sentimentality with dangdut arrangements and rhythm. Maheswara Musik, the record label co-owned by Pak Paku (the father of Edy Singh, the record producer mentioned in the previous chapter), was releasing Iyeth's album, which, like most dangdut cassettes, was named after its first song—in this case, "Cinta Hanya Sekali." The shooting schedule was as follows:

9:00 a.m. to 1:00 p.m. (approximately): Shooting on location in Cijantung Mall, East Jakarta.

2:00 p.m. to 4:30 p.m.: Exterior shots of dancers and singer in the "Riau" section of "Beautiful Indonesia in Miniature" (Taman Mini Indonesia Indah), a Disneyland-like theme park located in East Jakarta that contains replicas of traditional buildings and artifacts from all of Indonesia's provinces, including now-independent East Timor.[2] Set-up for interior shots inside one of the Riau dwelling replicas.

5:00 p.m. to 9:00 p.m.: Shooting at an affluent private residence on the far eastern outskirts of Jakarta.

9:30 p.m. to 2:00 a.m.: Interior shots at Taman Mini and exterior nighttime shots on the steps of a traditional Malay wooden house (*atap limas*) replica.

This was not a high-budget production: the crew had only one camera, and their video equipment was comparable to that used for

Dancers in traditional costume perform for the camera during the making of the video clip for Iyeth Bustami's "Cinta Hanya Sekali," Taman Mini Indonesia Indah (Riau Exhibit), East Jakarta.

videotaping wedding receptions (in fact this was one of the services offered by the production company hired to make the clip). Nor was shooting on location particularly expensive: in Indonesia, outdoor filming does not take place on a "closed set"; the presence of people, cars, animals, and so on in the surrounding environment is tolerated, and there is no army of security guards to keep people out. Often shooting takes place without formal permission from the local authorities, though they are usually notified. At the theme park, Iyeth, the camera crew, and the other performers attracted an audience of park visitors who gathered around and watched them. Another music video clip was being shot simultaneously in the same exhibit area in front of a different Riau Malay structure, this one for a Muslim children's pop song. A choir of preadolescent girls wearing brightly colored Islamic headscarves gestured in unison and pretended to sing for the camera, momentarily catching the attention of passersby.

Because Iyeth was from Riau and her ethnicity was part of her musical persona, the Riau exhibit at the "Beautiful Indonesia in Miniature" theme park was chosen as a backdrop for the clip's dance sequences, which featured three male and three female dancers in traditional

Malay dress. During the editing process, these sequences would be interspersed with scenes of Iyeth wearing traditional Malay garb lip-synching the song. The interior shots in the theme park depicted Iyeth and the male actor who played her love interest dressed as bride and groom according to Malay custom (*adat*), part of a dream sequence in which Iyeth forlornly imagines her inattentive boyfriend finally marrying her in a lavish traditional ceremony.

In contrast, the scenes shot in the mall and the private residence (the house of a well-to-do public prosecutor, a friend of one of the crew members) depicted Iyeth and her onscreen boyfriend in stylish contemporary clothes. At the house, they were filmed sitting in a garden, riding in a shiny red sports car rented for the occasion, and interacting in the house's well-furnished living room. There were also scenes of Iyeth sitting alone in a bedroom, pining after her lover and lip-synching the song with tears in her eyes. (*Air mata palsu!* [Fake tears!], scoffed a crewmember.) The shooting was laborious, with frequent delays caused by equipment malfunctions, and many members of the rather large crew often had little to do other than smoke and chat. Iyeth endured the waits and the repeated takes without losing her composure, sneaking an occasional cigarette between shots. When I inquired, she vehemently denied growing weary of hearing a recording of her song played back over and over for each filmed sequence.

Unlike the nonnarrative pastiche of images found in many Western rock and pop videos, this particular clip was based on a rudimentary story. Narratives based on a song's lyrics are common in dangdut videos, and producers whom I interviewed claimed that their audience preferred stories that narrativized the lyrics of dangdut songs. In this particular clip, a young woman (Iyeth) and her handsome but neglectful boyfriend (a light-skinned young actor who appeared to be of partial European or Arab descent) are drifting apart because he is too busy to pay attention to her. In the clip, whenever the two lovers are together they are interrupted by the ringing of the boyfriend's cellular phone; he then answers the phone, begins talking, and abruptly walks off, leaving his girlfriend. Like the song itself, the clip concludes not with a happy ending or any other resolution of the narrative, but instead with the young woman continuing to tearfully lament her fate as the song's repeating refrain fades into silence.

The two main locales depicted in Iyeth's video are "traditional" "Riau" and "modern," stylish Jakarta. In a sense, the artificial traditional setting of Taman Mini's "Riau" exhibit constitutes a visual parallel to the aural representations of traditional Indonesian music in dangdut and *pop daerah*. Like the digital sampling of regional ethnic instruments, the dwelling replicas in Taman Mini are decontextualized approximations of cultural objects. The physical forms of these replicas (sonic, visual, or tactile) signify particular cultural traditions. But despite (or perhaps because of) the nontraditional methods of their creation, these cultural simulacra are powerful signs of "local culture" in the Indonesian mediascape, which, like mediated cultures elsewhere, has a tendency to reduce local cultures to a series of decontextualized, replicable artifacts that can be *re*contextualized as objects of value in a national (or international) cultural economy. Such objects derive their meaning and value not from their primary context of use but from public debates and negotiations over their significance for the nation and the market.

In the same vein, the visual juxtaposition of "traditional" settings and expressive culture with affluent, modern locales and objects (malls, middle-class homes, cellular phones, sports cars) in Iyeth's music clip resembles the layering of "ethnic Indonesian" and "modern Western" sounds in a single dangdut or *pop daerah* recording, suggesting that one can be both "Indonesian" (a national identity that for most Indonesians also includes belonging to a subnational, regional ethnicity) and "modern" at the same time. This, then, constitutes an important type of cultural work performed by videos and recordings, as they capture the fantasies and aspirations of an audience with multiple allegiances, conflicting desires, and dreams of unattainable wealth and comfort.

There is another possible interpretation of this particular video. Perhaps Iyeth's boyfriend neglects her because he has an unhealthy infatuation with modern technologies and comforts (symbolized by his cellular phone and sports car), and his abandonment of her is constitutive of his abandonment of "traditional culture," to which Iyeth, in her fantasies of a traditional village wedding, still clings. If one subscribes to this reading (which no one I spoke to on the set seemed to endorse), the video contains a critique of modern consumer culture and its erosion of traditional values. Yet the images of glamorous affluence in the mall and living room scenes nonetheless remain seductive, and Iyeth's fashionable attire in those scenes demonstrates that she is a fully modern individual despite her ties to the village. Also, the scenes in her large, private bedroom suggest that her character comes from a middle-class background. Perhaps the message the clip conveys is that one should avoid becoming *excessively* modern and leaving village customs behind completely, for this can only lead to heartbreak.

Shooting a close-up of Iyeth, Taman Mini.

Another component of the cultural work performed by music video's rhetorical manipulation of images is the visual embodiment of the music. Iyeth's facial expressions, the tears in her eyes, the traditional costumes and refined movements of the dancers, the silky blue night-gown that Iyeth wears in the bedroom scenes (which she put on over her clothes while fully dressed) all convey information to the viewer about how to move to the music and what types of desiring and desirable bodies are moved by it.[3] The clip's combination of recognizable (albeit unreal) social settings and displayed human bodies — recognizable by their costumes, movements, and emotional expressions — situates the song in an idealized social context. This purposeful "translation" of musical sound into televisual image endeavors to focus audience desires on the musical artifact as a metonym for the urban opulence, female beauty, and folkloric authenticity portrayed in the clip.

Thus successful video clips are not those that portray a plausible social world for the song to inhabit, but those that through compelling sound and spectacle suspend viewers' disbelief. Anthropologist Edward Bruner writes, "The function and the promise of national myths is to

Iyeth performing for the camera, Taman Mini.

resolve contradictions, if not in life, then in narrative and performance"
(2001, 900). National popular cultures can also perform this function
through their projection of persuasive fictions of identity that elide the
contradictions inherent in stratified societies.

Ultimately, sales of Iyeth's album proved disappointing, even though
the clip did receive some television airplay and the song was nominated
for a Dangdut Award.[4] Edy Singh attributed the cassette's lack of commercial success to Iyeth's singing technique. Because her roots were in
pop Melayu, not in dangdut, he explained, she sang with too much
Western-style vibrato, which was inappropriate for singing the vocal
ornaments (*cengkok*) of dangdut-style vocals. Thus dangdut fans reacted
negatively. Several fans with whom I spoke did say they thought "Cinta
Hanya Sekali" was too weepy (*cengeng*) to be good dangdut. Dangdut
songs can, of course, be sad (and often are), but their vocals usually do
not make use of the sung histrionics of sentimental pop: vibrato, strong
vocal projection, staccato phrasing, and wide intervallic leaps.

Iyeth's single thus represents an unsuccessful experiment in musical hybridization; to employ Greg Urban's terminology, its novel

combination of sentimental *pop Melayu* and dangdut failed to carve out new social pathways for its dissemination that could combine the audiences of different genres (2001). The album might have enjoyed greater success had it been marketed solely to a Riau audience, but problems with distribution and piracy, and the limited size of the Riau market, necessitated finding a large national, multiethnic audience for the album in order to achieve Paku's commercial goals for it. Edy blamed the album's failure to achieve those goals on a failed sound-engineering experiment that produced a musical hybrid that lacked vigor, so to speak, in the marketplace.

Shooting a Rock Clip: Netral's "Cahaya Bulan"

While Iyeth's dangdut video evoked both traditional village life in Riau and the metropolitan affluence of Jakarta, many Indonesian pop and rock videos take place in a fantastic, surreal universe that has no obvious connection to actual places in Indonesia. What follows is an account of a very different sort of video shoot: the making of a rock video for a song by Netral (Neutral), a Jakarta-based band that had four albums to its credit. Netral emerged in the early 1990s as one of the first commercially successful Indonesian alternative rock bands. Its music is heavily influenced by Nirvana, the Sex Pistols, and Metallica, and the band was once known as the "Indonesian Nirvana."[5] Netral's video for "Nurani," a song released in 1999, was one of the clips SCTV played during the broadcast coverage of the Special Session of the People's Consultative Assembly.[6]

The video shoot described next was for a video clip intended to accompany a newly recorded song titled "Cahaya Bulan" (Moonlight), one of two new songs included on Netral's upcoming "greatest hits" compilation. Because I was personally involved, in a minor fashion, in the production of this clip, at times I switch to a more autobiographical mode of narration.

The song's few lyrics are simple but poetic:

> *Cahaya bulan menemani aku* [repeat]
> *Mencumbu mesra singgasana malam*
> *Bersenda gurau hibur bintang–bintang*
>
> [Refrain:]
> *Walaupun sedih dan senang melanda hati*
> *Kau tetap cahaya bulanku.*

[The moonlight keeps me company
Fondly caresses the night's throne
Joking around, entertaining the stars

(Refrain:)
Although sadness and joy overwhelm the heart,
You are always my moonlight.][7]

In spite of the meditative tone of the text, the song is a loud, punk-influenced rock anthem with soaring electric-guitar solos and pounding drums. The words are sung with triumphant bravado by Netral's lead vocalist, Bagus Dhanar Dhana, and multitracked backing vocals, performed by versatile *pop Indonesia* and *pop Rohani* singer Dessy Fitri, echo the song's pivotal verse, "The moonlight keeps me company." After attending a portion of the recording of "Cahaya Bulan" in a West Jakarta studio complex two months earlier, I was invited to the shooting of the song's video clip, which was expected to be the primary vehicle for promoting both the song and the "greatest hits" cassette on which it was to be included. The experience of observing and participating in the production of this video clip revealed a visual logic of global-national-local hybridity distinct from that of Iyeth Bustami's video. Both clips, however, manipulate widely circulating images of social spaces, bodies, and embodied motion to create a narrative context for a particular musical encounter. Each of these manipulations, in its own way, expresses something significant about the contemporary existential condition of the videos' assumed audiences.

June 6, 2000

I arrive at Mega Sport, an expansive outdoor sports complex located in Senayan, Central Jakarta. At 9:30 p.m. on an oppressively humid Tuesday night, the complex is still filled with young people playing soccer, beach volleyball, and basketball. Walking past the crowds, I notice that the beach-volleyball sandbox farthest from the entrance is closed off from view by a tall black curtain. On the other side of the curtain a surrealistic sight greets the visitor: a long string of glowing light bulbs bunched together lies half-submerged in the sand in front of a fifteen-foot-tall cage made of chain-link fencing and wooden poles painted black, roughly 12′ x 12′ square. Inside the cage a drum kit and two guitar amplifiers are set up (the latter are unplugged, of course—there would be no actual playing of instruments during the shoot, just miming the gestures of playing). In the middle of the

Between takes on the set of the "Cahaya Bulan" video clip, Senayan, Central Jakarta.

sandlot, facing the cage and the light bulbs, an enormous, hulking camera crane stands surrounded by glowing video equipment. The whole scene is eerily lit by blue and yellow simulated moonlight, apparently inspired by the song's theme.

Around the giant sandbox are the three musicians (two band members and one additional guitarist), various technicians, makeup people, hangers-on, girlfriends, and a group of friends/extras for a planned sequence involving the cage (dubbed the *kandang ayam* [chicken coop] by those present), in which a mob of Netral fans surround and attack the structure while the band mimes playing the song. The motif of a band playing inside a steel cage while crazed audience members thrash around the cage has a long history in heavy metal music videos. Both the director and the band members, ardent fans of Western 1980s metal, were well aware that videos produced in that decade by Scorpions ("Rock You Like a Hurricane," 1983) and Megadeth ("Wake Up Dead," 1987), among others, utilized such a visual device. The use of the steel cage and the crazed fans in the "Cahaya Bulan" clip is a clear homage to those videos and an example of how televisual conventions can circulate globally.

Also present on the set are two young child actors, twin girls, made up to look like diminutive vampires. They are the "models" for the clip. In Indonesian popular music videos, the *model* is a nonmusician who plays a central character in the clip—a protagonist in a story, an enigmatic object of desire, an audience member, or just a friend hanging out with the band members. There is even a *Best Model* award category at the MTV Indonesia Video Music Awards.

One might ask what child vampires are doing in a rock video for a loud song about moonlight. James Siegel analyzes the figure of "Draculla" (who is almost always female, though usually not a child) in the popular comedic theater of 1980s Central Java, arguing that the character's "popularity depends on her foreignness" (1986, 92). In his view, Draculla represents the limits of the Javanese language to make sense of the world; she is thus "a way to accommodate the heterogeneous, given the failure of Javanese mythology to do so during the New Order" (303). Although of foreign origin, according to Jakartans with whom I spoke the Draculla (also called *vampir*) acts very much like the malevolent spirits in local mythologies (see Geertz 1960, 16-29, for an extensive inventory of Javanese village spirits). Some university students explained to me that Draculla was the "American" version of a *pocongan, gendruwo,* or other Indonesian spirit, disregarding the fact that few Americans actually believe in vampires, whereas malevolent ghosts and spirits are very much a part of everyday life for many Indonesians.

The final image of Netral's video is the three musicians sprawled unconscious in the sand with fang marks on their necks, while the vampire twins stand over them and lip-synch the song's backing vocal part. The triumph of the vampires over the band members suggests that the latter may have been too weak to resist the influence of evil spirits (Geertz 1960, 29), and it also highlights the danger of making oneself susceptible to those spirits through certain behaviors, such as letting one's mind wander or being alone at night. Thus the vampire girls are not simply characters appropriated from globally circulating horror films; they also play a particular culturally specific role in the narrative of the music video that, as I will demonstrate, relates directly to the themes of the song.

Another performer's image was later edited into the final version of the clip: a shirtless man breathing fire. Fire-eaters are a familiar sideshow attraction at Indonesian carnivals; they are usually members of traveling *kuda lumping* (Javanese trance dancer) troupes. Although fire-eaters could be considered as generic and "placeless" as Hollywood vampires, this particular decontextualized image seems to signify an unspecified Indonesian locality. Similarly, blurred shots of Netral's drummer dancing to the music, with arm movements suggesting Javanese dance, were also spliced into the final edit. Like the images of the fire-eater, these enigmatic images appear toward the beginning of the clip and seem to obliquely reference the Indonesian national context without fully invoking the discourses of traditional culture.

Having a *bule* (white person) at a video shoot in Indonesia is something of a novelty, so I am not surprised when Puput, Netral's manager, asks me to participate in the crowd scene. I agree and when the time comes, I join a group of about twenty-five enthusiastic young men standing on the cage's perimeter, waiting for the director's signal. As a tape of the song begins booming over the loudspeakers, the crowd becomes frenzied, attacking the chain-link fence with all its strength. The entire structure begins rocking violently around the band members playing inside the cage, who seem not the least bit concerned when the fence comes within inches of their heads.

During the melee I realize with dismay that the "chicken coop" had obviously not been built with safety in mind. Before long the chain links begin to break, exposing sharp metal points, and the wooden supports start to buckle under the onslaught. This causes the shooting to stop twice in order to prevent the structure from collapsing entirely; I notice that the imminent threat of the chicken coop's collapse fails to lessen the ferocity of the attacks on it. By the time the first two takes (together lasting about seven minutes) are finished, I am gasping for breath, my hands are bleeding (gashes from a broken chain link), and my shoes are filled with damp sand. The director then calls for another take, followed by several more.

Afterward, I join the crowd around a small monitor screen to watch the playback (Indonesian music video producers cannot afford film stock; they use video cameras almost exclusively). I am disappointed to find that the video footage does not quite capture the violence of the actual event, and some of our gestures even appear halfhearted and staged. I try to pick myself out in the chaotic scene, deciding that a bit of self-consciousness is justified considering the very real possibility that millions of Indonesians would soon be viewing my image on their television screens. Then the director decides to film a close-up of the drummer playing alone in the cage surrounded by the mob. I am quite relieved when the final take for this sequence fails to bring the entire structure down on our heads.

Violence and Sociality

At Iyeth Bustami's video shoot, I had certainly become familiar with the boredom caused by repeated takes and long waits between shots, but I had failed to grasp how truly exhausting performing for the camera could be, especially in the humid, stagnant Jakarta air. As a result of my experience at the Netral video shoot, I came to better appreciate the hard work Indonesian recording artists put into making videos. More importantly, I learned something about collective effort and the awareness of self and other in Jakarta. Surprisingly, aside from my hand injury and one particularly zealous participant who collapsed of heat exhaustion and dehydration (and quickly recovered), no one was hurt during the filming of the sequence. This was clearly not due solely to good fortune. Despite the violence of the proceedings, no one collided with or accidentally struck another participant, and I heard no one complain about the behavior of any other participant. I also realized that the steel cage was torn apart so quickly because, rather than thrashing about separately, all the other participants were working in concert, moving together in a manner that inflicted major damage in a very short period of time. I wondered if American youths would have been so efficient.

A bit more ominously, the behavior of the crowd also reminded me of other common forms of young men's collective action in Jakarta, including riots, gang fights, and *gebukin maling*, the beating of suspected thieves (often to death) by an angry mob, which occurred at least once a week in Greater Jakarta during the period of my fieldwork (the *Jakarta Post* called it being "mobbed to death"). In all these examples, violent, destructive acts are carried out with deadly efficiency by a group of young males, and the responsibility for those actions is diffused among them, so that as a result no one is ever prosecuted. Although all we did was perform for a rock video, I noticed certain undeniable behavioral parallels. Was it easier for the mob to continue destroying the cage because of the knowledge that no single individual would be blamed for its destruction and for any injuries that might result? This, perhaps, was the dark side of Indonesian social life, in which individual responsibility dissipates and allows groups to act with stunning violence against external targets.

Whether or not such comparisons between art and life are appropriate, paying attention to basic habits of sociality and to fundamental orientations toward physical space, the presence of others, and the burden of responsibility is part of an ethnographic perspective that is frequently missing from studies of popular music and other kinds of global media culture. Had I not joined the video mini-riot of Netral fans, I, too, might have overlooked these phenomena.

After the riot scenes, what remained of the steel cage is quickly disassembled and preparations are made for more individual close-ups of band members performing in front of a different backdrop. By this point it is well after four in the morning. I do not stay quite until the end; I have to teach an early morning class at Atma Jaya, so I gratefully accept a free ride home from a group of people leaving the set. We leave just after 5:00 a.m., when only the last of Eno the drummer's close-up scenes remain to be shot. "*Kasihan buat Si Eno* [Poor Eno!]," says Bagus as we leave Eno behind, driving away into the sultry predawn darkness.

Netral's video clip, with its visual references to Surrealism, horror movies, and Western heavy metal videos, aspires to be part of global culture. Nearly all the cultural references it contains would be intelligible to consumers of popular culture around the world. Unlike Iyeth's video, there are neither images of "traditional" Indonesian life (with the possible exception of the fire-eater and the blurry "Javanese" dancer) nor any recognizable Indonesian locales. Although the video was shot on location in an outdoor urban sports complex, the set had been transformed into a strange, fantastic landscape bearing no relationship to the settings of daily life. Yet the fact that the song in the video is sung in Indonesian and performed by visibly Indonesian musicians influences the responses of Indonesian viewers, for whom the clip's global images are recontextualized by their appropriation by an Indonesian rock band.

Moreover, an analysis of the specific images in the video reveals their connection not only to the song's lyrics but also to the general cultural themes of loneliness, fear, and the threat of the supernatural. The band plays a song about solitary contemplation of the night sky while standing inside a steel cage surrounded by crazed fans attempting to break through the metal fencing. The fans are unsuccessful, and in the end, the band falls victim to two young vampires. Are these disconnected, unrelated images, or can they be assembled into a larger narrative? Solitude is hazardous in Indonesian thought not only because it causes loneliness (*kesepian*), but also because it leaves one vulnerable to attacks by spirits. It is only fitting that a rock band that "shuts out" its fans and

Netral performing for the camera inside the "chicken coop."

compatriots (through arrogance, perhaps), preferring to be kept company by the moon alone, would be victimized by vampires—dangerous supernatural entities that, like Indonesian rock music itself, have been indigenized from a foreign source. Thus in the video clip the price the band members pay for repelling those around them is an unpleasant encounter with Draculla. But the video of "Cahaya Bulan" also tells a slightly different story: that of the fans who aggressively move to the music and form a collective body. The powerful musical sounds unite them in shared *keramaian* (crowded noisiness) and protect them from the fate suffered by the band members themselves. Although the distant moon and stars cannot protect one from Draculla, loud music and the company of others can.

Cultural Production and the Ethic of Sociality

Interactions between social agents at sites of commercial cultural production are part of larger patterns in Indonesian society that shape how people respond to music and to one another. A striking characteristic of cultural production in Indonesia is that it is nearly always an intensely social process. Solitary creation is not highly valued, though it is admitted as a possibility. But even then, creative inspiration is often derived from the surrounding social environment. The complex relationship between the hybrid, multiply positioned subjectivities of contemporary Indonesian youth and the ethic of sociality—the idea that one's well-being depends on the conspicuous presence of others—shapes everyday lives and interactions. Popular music, as meaningful cultural form and social practice, provides us with an ideal vantage point for observing how this relationship works.

6

Offstage

MUSIC IN INFORMAL CONTEXTS

What happens to the musical artifacts created in recording studios? After recordings are mixed, mastered, duplicated, packaged, distributed, promoted through video clips, and displayed in retail outlets, their fate becomes more uncertain. Some recordings become hits, others do not, depending on the number of consumers who choose to buy them. Whatever the reasons for their success, hit recordings and the songs contained on them circulate widely and become a recognized part of Indonesian public culture, available to serve diverse agendas. As a result of the limited commercial shelf life of Indonesian cassettes, a hit song often outlives its original commodity form and becomes a free-floating entity reanimated through formal and informal performances, until, if it is popular enough, it is rerecorded or the original recording of the song is rereleased on a compilation cassette.

Local, informal performances of mass-mediated music — the music created in recording studios like 601 Studio Lab — are prevalent in Indonesia, where they are part of a vibrant oral culture of informal socializing in which musical performance plays an important role. As an accessory to informal male social gatherings in particular, a guitar is nearly as indispensable as cigarettes. Indeed, one seldom sees a group of young men hanging out in Jakarta without at least one of them strumming a battered acoustic guitar. Although informal performers cannot re-create exactly the recorded artifacts that inspire them (much less the fantasy environments of music video clips), they do replicate aspects of the sounds contained in the recordings and thereby contribute to the circulation and popularity of some songs. More importantly, by exploring how songs produced in recording studios and promoted via video clips take on a life of their own in specific social settings, we can begin to address a question that preoccupies both music producers and ethnomusicologists: why do listeners choose to consume popular music?

Popular music's role in the informal leisure activities of Jakarta's youth constitutes a source of meaning and value that social actors draw on in their daily struggles with the stress and atomizing forces of urban life. Among working-class men, playing popular songs on the guitar and other instruments is considered a valued skill and an important source of entertainment for those who lack the funds for other leisure activities. It is *murah meriah* (literally "cheap and cheerful") and provides an opportunity for self-expression, collective enjoyment, and occasional reflection on the conditions of life in the capital city. For middle-class and elite youth, singing and performing popular songs can also relieve stress and create bonds of solidarity between people. In fact, the practice of creating and strengthening social bonds through informal performance does not vary much across class lines, even if the music chosen as the vehicle for such sociability often differs. In all cases, though, Indonesian popular songs provide a shared expressive resource for participants in informal socializing regardless of their class or ethnic background.

By the Side of the Road: The Art of *Nongkrong* (Hanging Out)

> *Apa artinya malam Minggu*
> *Bagi orang yang tidak mampu?*
> *Mau ke pesta tak beruang*
> *Akhirnya nongkrong di pinggir jalan.*
>
> [What is the meaning of Saturday night
> For those who can't afford anything?
> Want to go to a party, don't have money
> In the end (just) hang out by the side of the road.
> Rhoma Irama, "Begadang II"[1]

In urban Indonesia, the side of the road (*di pinggir jalan*) is a site of possibility, of adventure, and of longing for the sensual pleasures of city life that always seem just beyond reach. Jakarta has an exceedingly active street life, and musical performance is an important component of the largely masculine culture of *nongkrong* (hanging out), which pervades all aspects of street-side social activity. *Nongkrong* means literally "to squat," but in popular usage it means to socialize in groups, usually in public or quasi-public spaces. Although I have observed groups of young men on a side street squatting in a circle, talking and smoking, most *anak tongkrongan* (kids who hang out) in Jakarta do not actually squat on the ground but prefer to sit on benches in front of food stalls (*warung*), neighborhood-watch security posts, or other roadside locations. Those unable to obtain work *nongkrong* all day long, but the prime time for hanging out is from the end of *magrib* (sundown prayers), to the *subuh* prayers at daybreak. From evening on into the night, almost every cigarette kiosk located by a main thoroughfare is host to several young, working-class men sitting in a group, talking, laughing, gambling, smoking, drinking bottled tea, playing battered old guitars, and singing, their voices barely audible over the continuous roar of Jakarta traffic.

Friends and acquaintances in Jakarta frequently warned me not to associate with the young men who hung out at *warung*. I was told that they were dangerous, possibly criminals, and that they would attempt to take advantage of me as a naive foreigner. Despite these warnings, I would frequently visit with groups of guitar-playing men at food and cigarette stalls, and for the most part I found them welcoming and flattered by my attention to their performances. What follows is a description of three hangout spots, all located a short distance from my boardinghouse in Kebayoran Baru, a middle-class residential area in South Jakarta. Each site is different, but at each of them musical performance plays a vital role in social interaction.

The Warung Gaul

A small, nondescript kiosk located on Wolter Monginsidi Street, a congested main thoroughfare in Kebayoran Baru, the Warung Gaul was the designated evening hangout spot for a group of men in their late teens and early twenties when I first arrived in Jakarta. It was the type of establishment usually called a *warung rokok*, "cigarette stall," although it also sold snacks, drinks, dried instant noodles, and some minor household items.

Some of the Warung Gaul's regulars worked as security guards in nearby banks and office buildings, while others worked as waiters, assistant mechanics, or laborers. They came from a variety of ethnic and linguistic backgrounds, including Javanese, Sundanese, Betawi, and Minang. There was even a young, friendly Acehnese snack vendor who occasionally dropped by. One regular, a short, muscular man named Ucok, was born and raised in Lampung, a province on the southern tip of Sumatra. His parents both came from the West Javanese town of Tasikmalaya, and he spoke Sundanese, Javanese, and Indonesian, though he did not know *bahasa Lampung,* the Malay dialect spoken in his province of origin. All the regulars were unmarried, Muslim, and under thirty.

Gaul is an important and multifaceted word in Jakarta youth culture. In common usage it can mean sociable, cool, or trendy. *Bergaul* means to converse informally and intimately; its meaning is close to the American Yiddish expression "to schmooze." A commonly used variation is *pergaulan,* "social intercourse," while *kurang gaul,* literally "insufficiently sociable," means to be out of touch or unhip, and in Jakarta slang the word *kuper,* short for *kurang pergaulan* (insufficient schmoozing), means "uninformed" or "unaware." The Warung Gaul was located a few blocks from a hair salon that billed itself as "Jakarta's Salon *Gaul,*" and the regulars at the *warung* called the Jakartanese Indonesian they spoke with one another *bahasa gaul* (cool/social language), the language spoken between friends.[2] This language, rather than Low Javanese or any other *bahasa daerah* (regional language), was the medium of communication and sociability at the Warung Gaul.

The first Warung Gaul proprietor I met was Ridwan, a twenty-three-year-old migrant from Tegal, Central Java.[3] Ridwan, who called himself the "chairperson" (*ketua*) of the *warung* and was probably the one who gave the *warung* its nickname, was well liked by the other regulars. He lived in a nearby boardinghouse (*rumah kost*) located behind an Internet café and worked long shifts at the *warung,* from around eight in the morning to eleven-thirty at night, every day except Sunday. After dark, as cars, trucks, *bajaj,* and buses streamed by less than ten feet from the wooden benches, the group of young men gathered at the *warung* to sing, talk, tell jokes, play cards, or just lean against one another and stare into space.

At night one could often hear squealing and rustling sounds from three enormous rats who lived behind the stall. Ridwan would laugh at my discomfort when they approached us; "*mouse my friend,*" he would say in his broken English. Other characters in this nocturnal scene included traveling vendors of fried rice and *siomay* (fish dumpling), various passersby, and even the occasional customer in search of cigarettes. Early in the evening, the roar of rush-hour traffic often drowned out the music, which usually consisted of one of the *warung* regulars strumming softly on a guitar, singing in a tentative voice. As the night wore on, these solitary performances would give way to loud collective efforts when the whole group joined in the singing.

Often it seemed as though conversation at the Warung Gaul consisted of little more than reciprocal accusations of craziness. "He's crazy!" the regulars would say, pointing at a friend, or else they simply placed an index finger diagonally across their foreheads—a sign for *miring kepala*, literally "slanted head," an expression meaning a defective or lobotomized brain—and gestured toward the recipient of the joke. Humor was an important aspect of Warung Gaul interactions, and certain jokes and puns were uttered repeatedly. A favorite was to say one worked as a *pengacara* (lawyer), which turned out really to be a shortened form of *penganggur banyak acara* (unemployed [but] with lots of engagements). Another was the multilingual saying *no money, nodong; no cewek, nongkrong* (*no money*, rob [someone]; *no* woman, hang out). This was an apt statement on the culture of *nongkrong*: first, it acknowledged that resorting to crime to obtain what one could not have was always at least a rhetorical possibility for nonaffluent young men in Jakarta, when the sense of relative deprivation created by the surrounding opulence became too difficult to bear. Second, the expression indicated that while hanging out was enjoyable, it was also a consolation of sorts. The regulars at the Warung Gaul readily acknowledged that if they had money or girlfriends, they would not be spending all their time hanging out by the side of the road. It was common knowledge that most of them suffered from *kanker* (literally "cancer" but in *bahasa gaul* short for kan*tong* ker*ing*—"dry pocket," i.e., broke) most of the time. Much of the longing expressed through Warung Gaul regulars' performances of sad, sentimental songs of heartbreak and disappointment could be considered a response to this condition. Indeed, evenings in the Warung Gaul seemed to be characterized by the contrast between equal measures of the warmth of companionship and the coldness of unrequited longing.

Ridwan used to tell me that after I would leave, the rest of the *anak* (kids) would stay up all night and sometimes go hang out at Blok M, the nearby fashionable shopping district. I learned later that actually the group usually dissolved around midnight, each member returning to his boardinghouse to sleep until morning. Ridwan also boasted frequently of his many girlfriends back in Tegal and in Jakarta, about whose existence I grew increasingly skeptical. By that point I had realized the truth: that playing music and hanging out at the Warung Gaul every night was the sole source of amusement for most of the regulars.

The young men at the Warung Gaul did not spend all their time on musical performance. Gambling was another common pastime, one they were quite passionate about. (Ridwan was a notorious gambler, often losing more than a week's pay in a single evening.) But it was clear that *dangdutan* (informal dangdut performance) was central to the culture of *nongkrong*, as was the performance of slow and sentimental vintage pop compositions known as "nostalgia songs" (*lagu nostalgia*). Significantly, while a single musician accompanying himself on guitar could play *lagu nostalgia*, proper *dangdutan* usually required some sort of percussion instrument in addition to the guitar and thus was a more social activity. Vocal imitations of melodic "fill-in" instruments in dangdut songs—lead guitar, flute, mandolin, and so on—were also part of *dangdutan* performances. These were often sung with an exaggerated nasal voice imitating the instrument's timbre, sometimes after shouting out the name of the instrument on the original recording: *"suling!" "melodi!" "mandolin!"* ("bamboo flute!" "lead guitar!" "mandolin!").

Thus there seemed to be a subtle distinction made at the Warung Gaul between *lagu nostalgia* and dangdut song performance, in which the former was considered an expression of individual longing and the latter a more collective and celebratory affair. Often a solitary performer of *nostalgia* songs sang quietly to himself, ignored by the others around him, while dangdut songs usually caught the attention of the entire group.

Partway through my fieldwork, Ridwan became ill and returned to his home village (*pulang kampung*) in Tegal. His younger brother Rizal, a talented guitarist who commanded a large repertoire of Indonesian pop and dangdut songs, replaced him. Rizal's role was central in strengthening the Warung Gaul's collective identity; shortly after arriving he decorated the inside of the *warung* with drawings and photographs framed with bits of wood and plastic drinking straws. He also wrote the names and phone numbers of the regulars (including those of the ethnographer) on the wooden floor of the stall and pasted one-hundred-rupiah coins to the front panel of the *warung* guitar to simulate the volume and tone knobs of an electric guitar.

Rizal's most ambitious plan was to acquire an inexpensive *gendang* for the *warung*'s nightly *dangdutan* by pooling the regulars' financial resources. Unfortunately the regulars were unable to find a *gendang* they could afford. After three or four Sundays spent looking, the cheapest one they had found cost Rp. 60,000—too expensive, despite my own modest contribution to the fund. In fact, because 60,000 rupiahs at the time was only slightly more than eight dollars, I was tempted to simply pay for the *gendang* myself. I decided, however, that such an act would imperil the egalitarian relationship of reciprocity I enjoyed with the *warung* regulars and would lead to social discomfort. Besides, no one had asked me to contribute more than I already had.

Reciprocity and Its Hazards

It was unclear to me how the Warung Gaul made any money at all. Every time I offered to pay for my Coca-Colas and Teh Botols at the end of the night, Rizal refused. There were usually very few paying customers after dark, and some of these had to be turned away due to a lack of change. According to Rizal, most of the customers of the *warung* bought items on credit (*berhutang*). Although not an ideal business practice in some ways, the refusal of immediate payment succeeds in establishing a more lasting social relationship in which one party has an obligation toward the other. As mentioned in chapter 2, most *warung* in Jakarta have regular customers (*langganan*) who are permitted to buy on credit in return for their continued patronage.

Maintaining reciprocal relationships was paramount at the Warung Gaul. Rizal once harshly criticized one of the regulars for being a *peminta*, a "moocher," saying he was *kurang gaul* (uncool). I did not learn the exact circumstances that led to this accusation, but it was clear that excessively taking advantage of the buying-on-credit system imperiled the relationship of equality and reciprocity that formed the foundation of *pergaulan*, just as being too quick to pay could threaten it.

Though he often told me he liked Jakarta and wanted to stay there, after four months Rizal also returned to his family's home in Central Java and was replaced by Agung, who was a nonrelative and a stakeholder in the *warung's* business. Agung was less willing than Ridwan and Rizal to let the *warung* regulars buy snacks and cigarettes on credit. His resulting unpopularity among the regulars led some to choose to move their evening hangout to another *warung rokok* located across the street. Other former regulars started hanging out after hours in the *warung internet* near where Ridwan used to live, taking turns playing Sony PlayStation games while listening to dangdut on a stereo that during business hours was set to a pop radio station. By the time my fieldwork was near its end, Agung had started closing his stall early in the evening for lack of business. The Warung Gaul was defunct, a consequence of a breakdown of reciprocity between proprietor and regular customers.

American Dreams

A recurring theme in the discourse and performances of the Warung Gaul was that of longing. Although this is hardly surprising given the subordinate social position of the regulars and the high level of material affluence that surrounded them, I was surprised to find how much of that longing was focused on the country I call home. While the knowledge of English among the Warung Gaul regulars ranged from a little to virtually nonexistent, almost everyone expressed a desire to learn the language, which they associated with the excitement of America, with its wealth and "free sex." Rizal complained that his parents had not been able to afford to send him to high school, and thus he had never had the opportunity to learn English, a complaint I heard from many working-class Indonesians. Other Warung Gaul regulars who had studied English complained that even after many years of study their grasp of the language was insufficient. They frequently asked me to translate a variety of English phrases of the sort that were ubiquitous in the Jakarta landscape. Among them:

1. Lucky Strikes (American cigarette brand).
2. "Taste the Freedom" (slogan for "Kansas" cigarettes, a so-called American brand not found, to my knowledge, in the United States).
3. Hollywood movie titles, for example, *Pretty Woman, Basic Instinct, Fatal Vision, Double Impact, Trained to Kill.*
4. Money Changer (a sign that could be found all over Jakarta but that the Warung Gaul regulars did not comprehend).
5. "Winds of Change" (a ten-year-old song by the German heavy metal band Scorpions that was still wildly popular in Indonesia).
6. Hand Body Cream (many cosmetic products in Indonesia have English names).
7. Creambath (a term commonly used in salon advertisements; at the time I had to admit that I had no idea what it meant).[4]

These examples illustrate how English was associated with popular entertainment and commodities in the experience of the young men at the Warung Gaul. Aside from wanting to learn English, the young men who hung out at the Warung Gaul (and countless other young, working-class Indonesian men with whom I spoke) were frank about their adoration of *Amrik*, the Jakarta youth slang term for the United States, and their fervent desire to go there. Ridwan even told me that he someday wanted to go on a hajj to America, using the same word he would use to describe a pilgrimage to Mecca.

A major component of the regulars' fascination with America appeared to be their oft-expressed desire for *cewek bule* (white chicks), whom they saw as both more beautiful and more sexually available than Indonesian women, although their only real contact with them was mediated by filmic and televisual images. I frequently found myself explaining to them that I had no sisters nor was I acquainted with any foreign women in Jakarta (both true, as it so happened), and I often became exasperated by the regulars' persistent fixation on *bule* women.[5] Once when Ridwan was enthusiastically discussing his plans to attract a *cewek bule* I asked him how exactly he intended to flirt with a foreign woman when he could not speak English. His solution, after some thought, was that I would do the "*dubbing*" for him, substituting English for Indonesian, so that his intentions would be made clear to the object of his affection.[6] Reflecting on this response helped me to realize that to young Indonesians the United States was not a distant, foreign land but rather an intimately familiar realm of fantasy and dreams. The Indonesian practice of subtitling American television shows and films, which familiarized Indonesians with the sounds of English and rendered their meanings seemingly transparent, created the illusion of a lack of cultural and geographical distance. Similarly, the flood of American and quasi-American commodities promoted and advertised in idiomatic Indonesian could easily be mistaken as "signs of recognition" (Keane 1997) from American cultural producers, rather than the product of locally managed branches of remote, giant multinational corporations.

Even educated, middle-class Indonesians were often surprised when I told them it took me over thirty hours to travel from New York to Jakarta. It was hard for them to grasp that places like New York City, Los Angeles, and the bucolic American suburbia depicted in Hollywood movies were so physically distant when the global media made them so phenomenologically near. Nevertheless, while the young men of the Warung Gaul may have overestimated their significance in the eyes of America, they also suspected that their relationship with the phantasmagoric *Amrik* of their dreams was ultimately one-way, a dialogue only in their imagination. Indeed, a recurrent theme throughout Indonesian popular culture was a kind of yearning for a reciprocal, affirming gesture from the country that set the standard for popular culture, despite the lingering ambivalence many Indonesians felt toward the world's sole superpower. Such reciprocity remained elusive, but the yearning continued.

One night at the *warung* one of the regulars, a Betawi security guard named Mahmud, gave me a list of Indonesian expressions he wanted me to translate into English. The first few were standard conversational phrases, but to my surprise they were followed by a list of phrases I recognized as dangdut song titles. I was uncertain as to the purpose of translating Indonesian song titles, but Mahmud seemed particularly insistent, and he showed great satisfaction when I translated them for him. Perhaps he enjoyed imagining his favorite dangdut songs as global, English-language pop enjoyed by people all over the world and respected by the elites in his own country. Perhaps he also saw the small symbolic act of translating a quintessentially Indonesian musical idiom into English as a form of talking back to the globally dominant American cultural industry. My ability to translate dangdut song titles was "proof" that the unequal producer-consumer relationship between American/global culture and Indonesian culture was potentially a two-way street. It was as though if only the former would be more receptive and less arrogant, a relationship of egalitarian reciprocity could replace the current hegemonic/subaltern relationship between the two countries.

The awareness of a lack of parity between America and Indonesia, and by extension between myself and the other regulars, led to some friction at the Warung Gaul. Some of the regulars occasionally spoke to me in a nonstandard, rough (*kasar*) variant of Javanese or Sundanese instead of Indonesian, even though they were well aware that I would have difficulty understanding them. This always generated laughter among the group. I interpreted this as their "revenge" on me for my ability to speak a language *they* did not understand, as much as they wanted to learn it, and for somehow learning their language, too.

I suspect that the language barrier was a primary reason why Western pop songs were not part of the Warung Gaul's repertoire, though this was not the only cause. The only English-language song I heard occasionally at the *warung* was "Why Do You Love Me," a song recorded decades ago by the Beatlesesque Indonesian pop group Koes Plus. Most singers did not know much of this song beyond the first line, but because the song had been recorded by an Indonesian band, they seemed to feel more comfortable with it than with English-language songs recorded by Western groups.

The Warung under the Tree

A few blocks away from the Warung Gaul, on the corner of two secondary roads and surrounded by affluent Kebayoran Baru residences, was the Warung di Bawah Pohon, "The Warung under the Tree." At least this was what the regulars called it in my conversations with them; it is possible that prior to my arrival this particular hangout spot did not have a name at all, and it was my occasional presence that led to a reflexive search for a name. (In contrast, the Warung Gaul appeared to already have had a corporate identity of sorts before my arrival.) At night a dozen or so young men, many of them servants or night watchmen for the surrounding households, regularly congregated and played music on a more elaborate level than the performances at the Warung Gaul.

On a good night, depending on who was around, the Warung under the Tree had a full ensemble of musicians who frequently switched instruments during the course of the evening. The ensemble included two well-worn acoustic guitars, one used for playing chords and the other for playing bass lines transposed to a higher octave, as well as a plastic *gendang* that was actually an office water-cooler bottle. In skillful hands the hard, unforgiving plastic skin of this instrument could approximate the different sounds made by a real *gendang* or a Western trap kit, depending on the song. One of the *warung* regulars was particularly adept at playing this *galon* (from the word for "gallon"); the others told me he was a *jago*—a "champion" or virtuoso—on the makeshift instrument. The final core component in the ensemble was a *gicik,* an idiophone made from three rows of punctured and flattened bottle caps nailed into a stick of wood about nine inches long—a kind of homemade tambourine. The *gicik* is a quintessential Jakartan street instrument, often played by child beggars to accompany their singing as they try to catch the attention of motorists sitting in traffic. Its role in the *warung*'s ensemble was to play tambourine parts in dangdut songs and cymbal parts in pop songs. The sound of the group was occasionally augmented by handclaps and empty bottles struck with metal spoons or banged together like large glass claves. Played together, these humble instruments created a surprisingly full sound.

As I watched the regulars at the Warung under the Tree perform, I was struck by the amount of laughing and smiling I saw and by the seeming lack of macho posturing, teasing, and aggression that Americans tend to expect from gatherings of young males. No one quarreled over who could play what instrument next or ridiculed someone else's playing mistakes. Anyone who was interested could join in the performance by singing or playing improvised percussion. On one occasion a quiet, awkward young man, occasionally described as "crazy" by the others, carefully placed some bottle caps in an empty cassette case and tried to shake it in time with the music. After a few attempts to follow the rhythm, he gave up. Although no one made fun of him, he seemed to become shy and embarrassed (*malu*), which kept him from continuing.

One night while the band was playing a dangdut song, a luxury car pulled up to the side of the road and two men wearing well-pressed slacks and neckties emerged. They each bought a bottle of tea, which they drank impassively while standing next to the seated *warung* regulars, who at the time were deeply engrossed in their performance. The two customers completely ignored the spirited playing surrounding them, avoiding eye contact with the musicians. Finally the thinner of the two men returned the now-empty bottles to the *warung*'s proprietor and blithely handed him a twenty-thousand-rupiah bill—a rather large denomination with which to pay for two beverages priced at Rp. 1,000 each. The *warung* proprietor managed to find enough change to give back to his customer, and then the two men returned to their car and unceremoniously drove off, safe once again behind the tinted window glass. The musicians, for their part, did not pay much attention to the customers either. They were most likely accustomed to similar demonstrations of Jakarta's social gap, the yawning gulf between the young men hanging out on the side of the road and the people they often referred to as the *kaum berdasi* (necktie-wearing caste). This incident illustrates the limits of the affective community created by *dangdutan*. One of *dangdutan*'s most important functions for men hanging out by the side of the road is to create a sense of group belonging, but the music cannot compel those who refuse to join in.

Pondok Cinta: The Watchman's Post

Begadang jangan begadung
Kalau tiada artinya
Begadang boleh saja
Kalau ada perlunya.

[Stay up all night, don't stay up all night
If there is no reason (for it)
Stay up all night, just go ahead
If there is a need.]

Rhoma Irama, "Begadang"

Pondok Cinta, literally "love shack," was the nickname the regulars gave to an elevated security post on the corner of two other secondary roads in Kebayoran Baru. It did not seem to be a very effective post, since the bamboo blinds on its three walls blocked most views of the street. The job of the night watchmen was to *begadang*, "stay up all night," and thereby (supposedly) to contribute to the safety of the neighborhood. For their efforts the official night watchmen were paid Rp. 200,000 a month (at the time around US$35), hardly a princely sum even by Indonesian standards.

The regulars at the Pondok Cinta were older than those at the two *warung*, ranging in age from late twenties to midforties; some were married, others were aging bachelors. Most were unemployed or semi-employed in the informal sector, but they were not impoverished; in fact, at least three of the men owned cellular phones. The regulars came

A performance at the *Pondok Cinta*, Kebayoran Baru, South Jakarta.

from different ethnic backgrounds: there were Sundanese, Javanese, Betawi, and one Batak, who was the recipient of a certain amount of ethnically motivated ribbing from the others. Those who dropped by occasionally ranged from an illiterate vegetable peddler from Bogor to a portly middle-aged physician who lived in a house nearby. In the course of a long night of hanging out, the regulars smoked, played cards, drank hot tea, and occasionally ordered Indomie (Indonesian instant ramen noodles) from the open-all-night *warung* across the street. In addition to performing music, the men also enjoyed sharing their knowledge of Indonesian vernacular wordplay, particularly by creating humorous abbreviations and acronyms (*singkatan*) as well as puns (*plesetan*). One typical (though rather offensive) example of the made-up acronyms I heard at the Pondok Cinta is this list of names of Indonesian ethnicities:

Betawi = beta*h di* wi*layah* (enjoys being in the area [of Jakarta])
Sunda = su*ka da*nda*n* (likes makeup, personal adornment; a reference to
    the reputation of Sundanese men and women for glamour and vanity)
Batak = ba*nyak* tak*tik* (many tactics; a reference to supposed Batak
    treachery and deceitfulness)

Such wordplay was a form of idle amusement to fill a long night, but it also functioned to create solidarity in the group. Like musical performance, verbal games created shared references among group members, and the (often obscene) humor they contained could lead to reflections on ethnicity, sexuality, language, and other facets of the group's everyday experience.

Of the three street-side locations discussed in this chapter, the regulars at the Pondok Cinta took music the most seriously. They used a real *gendang,* occasionally a real tambourine, and a guitar that could stay in tune. Sometimes one of the regulars even brought a portable electronic keyboard, on which he played "piano" accompaniments and "string" melodies for dangdut songs. A book filled with handwritten song lyrics was kept at the post. A few of the regulars, including the *gendang* player, occasionally played semiprofessionally at weddings and other performance occasions.

The Pondok Cinta repertoire consisted primarily of dangdut compositions. The regulars performed many of the same songs as local dangdut bands, but their repertoire was weighted toward those originally recorded by male singers. When one of the men did sing a song originally sung by a woman singer (sometimes singing an octave lower, sometimes in falsetto), he would not alter the lyrics to reflect a male perspective. At the Pondok Cinta, I was asked to translate dangdut lyrics into English and sing them, something the regulars seemed to enjoy hearing. I suspect the reason for this was the same as that for the positive response I received when I provided translations of dangdut song titles at the Warung Gaul.

The regulars at Pondok Cinta would often play without interruption from around eleven at night until the next morning. As soon as they heard the call of the muezzin from a nearby mosque loudspeaker, all music immediately ceased "out of respect." Shortly thereafter, the group dispersed, riding away on motorcycles or leaving on foot.

The Ethic of Sociality and the Culture of Hanging Out

Musical performance in these varied street-side settings conformed to a larger ethic of sociality prevalent in Indonesia. Music making in such settings was intended primarily not for impressing others but for creating an atmosphere of camaraderie and relaxation. In fact, performances by the side of the road were essential expressions of this ethic, manifested in the relationships between different participants and often in the sung texts themselves.

Many dangdut songs, like "Begadang II," the Rhoma Irama composition quoted earlier, make explicit references to street-corner life. At the Warung Gaul, the line *akhirnya nongkrong di pinggir jalan* (in the end hang out by the side of the road) was sometimes replaced by the enthusiastically sung, "*akhirnya nongkrong di Warung Gaul*" (in the end hang out at the Warung Gaul). On one occasion, Ucok, one of the regulars, began singing a long, improvised variation on a pivotal line in the song: "*mau ke pesta tak beruang*" (want to go to a party, don't have money). While strumming a repeating open chord progression on the *warung*'s guitar, he chanted:

> *Mau jalan tidak punya . . . uang*
> *Mau makan tidak punya . . . uang*
> *Mau pesta tidak punya . . . uang.*
> (etc.)

> [Want to go places, don't have . . . money
> Want to eat, don't have . . . money
> Want to party, don't have . . . money.
> (etc.)]

As he sang, he encouraged the others to join in on the last word, "money," creating a kind of call-and-response pattern. The undercurrent of menace beneath the humorous veneer of his performance was apparent. His musical complaint, with its insistent repetition, expressed the unceasing frustration of life by the side of the road and dissatisfaction with never possessing the means to participate in the phantasmagoric realm of leisure and consumption depicted in advertisements and television programs and represented by the mansions, bars, malls, and restaurants of affluent South Jakarta.

In addition to being a lament of sorts, and perhaps a commentary on my presence at the hangout session, Ucok's song, I suspect, was also a protest directed at the government, the wealthy, and anyone perceived as having the power to change the situation of ordinary Indonesians and yet choosing not to do so. Later that night, during a long, animated conversation about Indonesian politics, Ucok stated that Indonesia was rich in natural resources, but that the nation's wealth was not utilized (*mengolah*) wisely and in a way that benefited the many. The others agreed; the perception that Indonesia would be a prosperous country if the *koruptor*s at the top would just share their wealth fairly was widespread among working-class people in Jakarta. Indeed, much working-class support for the movement to bring Soeharto to justice was predicated on the rather unlikely possibility that the Indonesian government would be able to confiscate the billions of dollars the former dictator had siphoned off from the people and use the money to pay off debts and alleviate poverty in the country. To nonaffluent young men in Jakarta surrounded by glaring evidence of tremendous wealth illegitimately gained and conspicuously flaunted, facing a life of limited means was thus a reason for vociferous protest, rather than for fatalism and acquiescence.

In a sense, Ucok's performance can be contrasted with the usual dangdut and *nostalgia* repertoires at the Warung Gaul; although the songs in those repertoires often express resignation, give aesthetic form to a shared sentiment of longing, and invite listeners to commiserate, in most cases the cause for the misery is ostensibly heartbreak, not class oppression. It is quite possible that my presence as an outsider encouraged Ucok's musical outburst, though I will never know for sure, but regardless his vehemence definitely seemed to make the other regulars uncomfortable.

In addition to "Begadang" and its musical sequel "Begadang II," both quoted earlier, numerous other Rhoma Irama compositions were performed at the Warung Gaul. The *warung* performers enjoyed singing Rhoma's songs not necessarily because the men endorsed the didactic messages those songs contained, but because the lyrics addressed the circumstances of their lives. Rhoma Irama has recorded songs about gambling ("Judi"), bachelorhood ("Bujangan"), staying up all night ("Begadang"), drug use ("Narkoba"), stress ("Stres"), and other commonplaces in the lives of young, nonaffluent Indonesian men. The song "Bujangan" (Bachelorhood) is exemplary in this respect:

> *Katanya enak menjadi bujangan*
> *Ke mana-mana tak ada yang larang*
> *Hidup terasa ringan tanpa beban*
> *Uang belanja tak jadi pikiran.*

> [They say it's nice to be a bachelor
> Going here and there, there's nothing off-limits
> Life feels light, free of burdens
> Spending money is not given a thought.]

A later verse is

> *Tapi susahnya menjadi bujangan*
> *Kalau malam tidur sendirian*
> *Hanya bantal guling sebagai teman*
> *Mata melotot pikiran melayang.*
> *O bujangan.*

> [But the hard thing about being a bachelor
> Is every night sleeping alone
> Only a long pillow to keep you company,
> Your eyes wide open, your thoughts drifting.
> Oh, bachelorhood.]

In the informal performances I observed, the eventual moral of the song, that it is better to marry and settle down than to risk having too much fun as a bachelor, was beside the point, and most performers and listeners preferred to hear the tune as a humorously ironic celebration of the life of a working-class bachelor. Often the didactic messages of Rhoma Irama songs became targets of *warung* humor. For instance, the *anak Warung Gaul* often sang "Begadang," the song admonishing listeners for staying up all night for no reason, right after someone declared his intention to do so.

The Threat of Arrogance

Despite the strong element of inclusiveness in *nongkrong* sociability, in-clusiveness and acceptance did have their limits. An important term in *nongkrong* discourse, and in Jakartan speech in general, was the Jakarta-nese word *belagu* (proud, arrogant), roughly equivalent to the Standard Indonesian *sombong*. Someone who was considered *belagu* was often, quite simply, one who refused to *bergaul*, to socialize with others. *Belagu* behavior violated the ethic of sociality that structured interactions between equals, and it placed this equality in question. If one did not hang out with others, it was taken as a sign that one felt superior to them. Often acquaintances who walked by the Warung Gaul without stopping to sit and chat (often because they were on the job) were called *belagu* in a semi-joking way by the men hanging out. Moreover, in the discourse of the street corner, this term's meaning was extended beyond the interpersonal realm of *nongkrong*. The proindependence Acehnese and the newly independent East Timorese were deemed *belagu*, as were Chinese Indonesians, who were criticized for not "mixing" with *pribumi* (native, non-Chinese) Indonesians (cf. Siegel 2000). Media celebrities who cut themselves off from ordinary people were also labeled *belagu* (I was to find out later that celebrities in Indonesia try hard to avoid creat-ing this impression among their fans), as were women who were not open to amorous male advances. *Belagu* celebrities were said to "forget themselves" (*lupa diri*) as a result of their fame. This was also said of people who had moved up in social status and displayed arrogance when interacting with their old friends.

As a foreigner, an American whom everyone assumed was wealthy, I was constantly at risk of being considered arrogant, of being *belagu*. If I had not stopped by for a while or if I didn't stop and chat every time I passed, I was especially vulnerable to that accusation. Such accusations can be dangerous. Too much arrogance invites a violent reaction—as mentioned above, many Jakartans told me that they perceived Chinese, East Timorese, and Acehnese to be *belagu* or *sombong* and implied that the arrogance of these groups justified their victimization at the hands of the Indonesian majority. Those who warned me against associating with the *anak tongkrongan*—"guys hanging out"—also framed their warning in terms of arrogance: having a white foreigner associate with them would go to the men's heads, and they would be more brazen in their behavior toward others, particularly women passersby, and feel superior to other roadside groups. (I did not observe this among the *anak tongkrongan* I knew.)

One Night in Kebayoran Baru

To give the reader a sense of the goings-on of a typical night, following is a description based on field notes from the night of February 16, 2000, a Wednesday. On this night, after having to cancel a trip to Bandung due to a lingering stomach illness, I decided to visit some of the local neighborhood hangouts. This night also marked the first time I stopped at the Pondok Cinta security post.

1. The Warung Gaul, approximately 8:20–10:50 p.m. When I arrive only Rizal, the proprietor, and his friend Andie are there, sitting on a bench and strumming a guitar. Agus, Mahmud, and another young man are inside the office building of Agus's employers, watching dangdut video clips on television. On the screen I catch a glimpse of Iyeth Bustami's video for "Cinta Hanya Sekali," the shooting of which I attended [see previous chapter]. I decide not to mention this fact to those present. When I ask why they are not hanging out outside at the *warung*, they reply that outside it is too *sepi* (lonely, deserted), even though they in effect are causing the "loneliness" by choosing to remain inside. Within an hour or so other young men begin to arrive, and the three watching television go outside to join them. I remark to the group that I have not been feeling well (*kurang enak badan*, literally

Dangdutan at the Warung Gaul, using the body of the guitar as a percussion instrument, Kebayoran Baru.

"body is less than pleasant"), which results in my becoming the recipient of two unsolicited and rather rough shoulder massages.

Over the next two hours, an uninterrupted soundtrack of dangdut and *nostalgia* songs accompanies the talking and joking of the *warung* regulars. The songs are played with voice, guitar, and various improvised idiophones, including bottles, a key chain, and a wooden bench, as well as the body of the acoustic guitar itself, which one performer beats rhythmically, *gendang* style, while another strums.[7] The participants pay varying levels of attention to the music, depending on who is playing what. At times the whole group sings together when they know the words to a particular line of a song. Toward the end of my stay, Ucok monopolizes the guitar once again, playing the same open chord progression (C–G–F) over and over and singing semi-improvised lyrics. Those surrounding him, for the most part, seem to ignore his performance. I finally excuse myself shortly before eleven, one of the first to leave.

2. The Warung under the Tree, 11:00 p.m.–12:20 a.m. After a short conversation with the workers at the open-all-night *warung seafood* down the road from the Warung Gaul, I head in the direction of the Warung di Bawah Pohon. On this night, there is only one guitar; it is accompanied by the *gicik* (homemade tambourine-like instrument) and the *galon* (plastic water-cooler bottle). I am asked to play a song on the guitar, and I try to oblige by playing "Ball and Chain," a 1990 song by the California punk band Social Distortion. Although the seven participants are unfamiliar with the song, they follow along enthusiastically, trying to approximate the sounds of the English lyrics. They are more successful in following the song's melodic contours, which by the second chorus they have mastered. They then demand I sing the song translated into Indonesian, which I do, rather awkwardly. While I play, Yusuf adds a dangdut rhythm to the song on the *galon*, which further amuses the group.

It is getting late and we are running out of songs, so I suggest an Indonesian children's song conventionally sung at the end of gatherings and performances. The song's refrain, which can be subject to an unlimited number of repetitions, is

> *Pulang, marilah pulang*
> *Marilah pulang*
> *Bersama-sama.*

[Go home, let's go home
Let's go home
All together.]

Our version of the farewell song lasts over six minutes and undergoes several rhythm changes. After it ends, we all say good night and go our separate ways, walking out of the gaslit area around the *warung* into the surrounding warm, quiet darkness.

3. The Pondok Cinta, 12:22 a.m.–3:10 a.m. Weary from illness and a night of performing and socializing, I walk back to my rooming house. I am less than a minute away when I hear some acoustic dangdut music emanating from an elevated bamboo platform on a street corner, with its back facing the street. Moving closer to investigate, I see three men seated on the platform, one singing and playing a guitar, another playing a small *gendang*, and the third sitting behind him listening. I approach and they acknowledge me silently and continue playing. The guitarist is about twenty-five, younger than the other two men, and his instrument is in better condition and in better tune than those played by most roadside musicians. After a few classic dangdut songs, the two musicians switch to playing a socially conscious Indonesian rap song titled "Putauw" (Heroin), by Neo, a popular hip hop group, and then return to the dangdut repertoire. I am impressed by the *gendang* player's ability to mimic hip hop beats on his drums.

The three men are soon joined by a heavyset man who accompanies the music with an ingeniously constructed idiophone consisting of a pair of metal spoons and a metal knife. He uses this improvised instrument to create high-pitched, metallic sounds resembling those of a tambourine. I am impressed by the skill of all the musicians, especially the *gendang* player, who manages to produce pleasing sounds using an undersized drum with a torn skin *tak* head and a cheap plastic *dhut* head. The guitarist is no less skilled—in addition to dangdut and *pop Indonesia*, he flawlessly plays the guitar parts to Eric Clapton, Eagles, and Metallica songs, though he does not sing them.

More people, all men in their late twenties to early forties, begin arriving, despite the late hour. Some of them take turns singing with the musicians. Among the later arrivals is a local physician as well as an intense, fortysomething man named Ismail who was once an aspiring dangdut singer. Pak Ismail tells me that aside from Latin music, he dislikes all *lagu Barat* (Western songs) and only listens to dangdut, which he studied intently from audiocassettes for over three years when he was trying to build a singing career. After someone tells him that I am visiting Indonesia to learn more about dangdut music, he spends over two hours talking to me between songs about dangdut's early history (mentioning Mashabi and several other *orkes Melayu* stars), the complicated melodic ornamentations (*cengkok*) that a good singer must master, and how Meggi Z's vocal style is superior to Rhoma Irama's because it is "purer" and less rock influenced. Ismail expresses skepticism about current trends in youth music, saying that the musical preferences of the "young kids" (*anak muda*) are "not yet settled" (*belum stabil*, a phrase often used at the time to describe the Indonesian polity). I finally excuse myself around 3:10 in the morning, saying politely that I need to go home because I do not want to forget anything Ismail has told me. In truth, I am also exhausted; I have stayed out far later than I had planned.

According to Ismail, eventually all the Indonesian kids rushing to follow the latest pop music trend will settle down and embrace their true music: dangdut. This notion that dangdut, in contrast to pop, is somehow immune from changing fashions and represents musical maturity was shared by many working-class men who spoke to me about Indonesian music. It is worth noting that while the younger regulars at the Warung Gaul and the Warung under the Tree expressed enthusiasm for contemporary rock and pop songs, their actual performing repertoire consisted of older pop songs that had withstood the test of time and dangdut compositions. Thus it is conceivable that by following musical trends these young people were simply enlarging their musical vocabularies without abandoning their parents' music for their own. In addition, dangdut and *pop nostalgia* were recognized as contextually appropriate for hanging-out activities. They were, in effect, the requisite soundtrack to life by the side of the road, whether they were one's favorite style of music or not.

Gendered Spaces

In the course of her research with street children in the Javanese city of Yogyakarta, Harriot Beazley reports encountering among her consultants explicit statements regarding behavioral norms for women, especially concerning nighttime behavior.

For example, when I talked to boys and girls on the street, they often mentioned how girls were "supposed" to behave. I was intrigued by this rhetoric and asked them to tell me exactly what was expected of young women by Indonesian society. The children (both boys and girls) answered that women in Indonesia cannot go out after 9:30 in the evening, they cannot go where they please, they cannot drink alcohol, they cannot smoke, they cannot have sex before marriage, they cannot wear "sexy" clothes, and they cannot leave the house without permission. They must be good, nice, kind and helpful, and stay at home to do domestic chores and to look after their children or younger siblings. These answers from the children are a clear example of how gender roles are internalized at an early age. (Beazley 2002, 1669)

While Jakarta is often considered more cosmopolitan and permissive than smaller, more "traditional" cities like Yogyakarta, the statements Beazley relates sum up rather well the attitudes I encountered among Jakarta's working-class youth. Nighttime hangouts were clearly male-oriented, largely homosocial spaces. One night a friend of Rizal's visited the Warung Gaul. He arrived on a motorcycle, his girlfriend riding behind him. While her boyfriend joked around for about fifteen minutes with the young men at the *warung,* she sat silently on the motorcycle, looking more than a bit uncomfortable. She waited there with averted eyes until her boyfriend returned to the motorcycle and they drove away. Similarly, when I asked Jono Z, one of the Pondok Cinta regulars, why his wife did not hang out with him at the security post, he said it was because he wanted to keep her away from the "naughty mosquitoes" (*nyamuk nakal*), by which he meant disreputable men hanging out at night, much as he was. Despite these sentiments (which I heard voiced many times by working-class Indonesian men), two other regulars' wives frequently showed up at the Pondok Cinta with their husbands, and they often joined in the singing.

I concluded that women had to be a little brave to hang out at night, but that women who opted to do so were not excluded. Women who chose to hang out at night were usually older and married; I was told that young girls were either at home protecting their virtue or, alternately, out in search of males with a bit more money than those who hung out all night by the side of the road. The situation was quite different among Jakartan university students, where women, while usually a minority, would hang out and socialize with young men without risking censure. This difference in gender norms is inseparable from class distinctions and the ways in which such distinctions index differing attitudes toward Western secular values regarding social interactions between unmarried men and women. The next section explores the culture of *nongkrong* in Indonesian university life, where popular music fills a role similar to the one it plays at *warung*, that of facilitator of social intercourse and group solidarity.

On Campus: Middle-Class Hangouts

Even during the New Order, many Indonesian students saw their campuses as safe havens. In late 1997, when Soeharto's grip on power still seemed unbreakable, students at the Institut Kesenian Jakarta (IKJ) told me that they were free to do what they wished on their campus, including smoke marijuana and sing about politics, without the military and the police harassing them. In post–New Order Jakarta, I found that college campuses had not changed much, aside from the prevalence of posters and banners sporting brazen political slogans. Groups of students still hung out together on campus, often with guitars, and unlike their counterparts by the side of the road, often in mixed gender groups. University campuses were considered *rame* (crowded, noisy, sociable, fun) places. At the private university where I taught classes one semester, Western and Indonesian pop music blared out of the office of the student music activity group at all hours of the day, loud enough to be heard in many classrooms. Often one also heard someone trying to play along with the music on a worn old drum kit kept in the office; this show of musical prowess could be quite distracting to class instructors.

The everyday existence of most of the Jakarta university students I knew differed little from that of the Warung Gaul regulars: they did not have much money, they lived in cheap boardinghouses (*rumah kost*) or with their families, ate at inexpensive *warung*, and spent much of their time hanging out with their friends. They had also begun hanging out at *warnet*s (Internet cafés) chatting and surfing the World Wide Web, as had an increasing number of nonstudent youth in Jakarta. The main difference between the students and the Warung Gaul regulars was the students' potential for social mobility, of someday having enough money to participate in a middle-class world of consumerism and individualism (see the discussion at the end of chapter 2). Thus the similarities between students and nonstudents were temporary and are counterbalanced by significant differences in both everyday behavior and prospects for the future.

I attended a particularly memorable campus *nongkrong* session that took place at Universitas Prof. Dr. Moestopo, a private university in Senayan, Central Jakarta. I had gone to Moestopo's campus to interview Wendi Putranto, the editor in chief of *Brainwashed*, one of Jakarta's oldest and longest-running underground zines.[8] A senior in Moestopo's Faculty of Communications, he had also recently begun working for an Indonesian-language, student-oriented Web site, bisik.com (*bisik* = whisper), writing music reviews and editing the portion of the site dedicated to underground music.

I met Wendi at the entrance to campus, and we walked a short distance to the Faculty of Communications student senate office, a small, partially air-conditioned room decorated with political posters and flyers. One wall of the office was adorned with two battered and vandalized plastic riot police shields and a gas mask, "spoils of war" from the clashes between Indonesian soldiers and student demonstrators in 1998–99. On one of the shields, the slogan *aparat keparat*, which paired the Indonesian word for "troops," *aparat*, with *keparat*, an obscenity meaning "bastard" (yielding "barracks bastards"?), was etched in large block letters on the clear plastic. A large poster on another wall depicted former president B. J. Habibie standing over a map of Indonesia and sporting a Gorbachev-like birthmark on his bald head. Over his head was written *Bapak Disintegrasi*, "Father of Disintegration," alluding to a similarity between the violent movements for independence that troubled Habibie's brief presidency and the breakup of the Soviet Union under Gorbachev. The office also included a library/bookstore consisting of old and new books on Indonesian politics and culture, among them a battered hardcover copy of Sukarno's *Di Bawah Bendera Revolusi* (Beneath the Banner of Revolution), a weighty tome that was banned during the New Order and had yet to be reprinted. Wendi explained to me proudly that existing copies of the book were quite valuable.

In addition to acting as the home base for the *Brainwashed* zine (which had acquired a fairly large staff in its five years of operation) and a preferred hangout for South Jakarta's punks, the Faculty of Communications was also home to a cottage industry that manufactured T-shirts with politically subversive slogans. Wendi was wearing an example, a black shirt featuring the text *"Fuck Capitalism!"* Many local punk and hardcore bands also produced their merchandise at this facility.

I asked Wendi if he often stayed up all night hanging out in the senate office. Not as much as before, he replied. During the months of student demonstrations preceding Gus Dur's election, the office became a kind of headquarters, and he frequently spent the night there with other campus activists. At the time, the office had a computer with Internet access, which the students used to communicate and record their experiences. Unfortunately the computer was stolen; Wendi suspects "provocateurs" were behind the theft.

Wendi introduced me to the Mohawk-wearing guitarist of a punk band named Error Crew, whom he joked was a *punk intelek,* meaning both an intellectual punk and a punk "in *telek* [Javanese for 'shit']." Several other members of punk and hardcore bands also came by, as well as some politicos. Soon a hanging-out session, complete with guitar sing-alongs, was in full swing, and would last until early in the morning.

In addition to performing their favorite rock and underground songs, the students had much to say on the topic of Indonesian popular music, no doubt due in part to the presence of a curious American music researcher. They debated whether dangdut was "hegemonic," but at the same time they decried the hypocrisy of MTV Indonesia for introducing a dangdut video show but refusing to include dangdut artists in its annual video music award contest. (As it happened, a few months later, MTV introduced a *Best Dangdut* category at its 2000 awards show.) Although for the most part they viewed dangdut as "mass culture" music in the purest Adornonian sense, some of the students spoke admiringly of a punk band from Yogyakarta named Soekarmadjoe (the name means "difficult to advance/progress"), which had switched to playing dangdut music after deciding that dangdut, not punk, was the true "*working class*" music of Indonesia. (According to the members of Soekarmadjoe, whom I later met, this story is not entirely accurate. See chapter 10 for more on this group.)

The subject of *pop Indonesia* brought out other controversies. A campus activist criticized *pop alternatif* bands like Potret and Dewa 19 as being purely derivative of Western groups. He also expressed skepticism regarding underground music as an effective force for political and social change. Other students defended the underground, as long as it maintained its ideological purity. Wendi told me to ask some of the punks what they would say if their bands were offered a major-label contract. Their emphatic response: No! One added that he would actually accept but then just steal the money and run.

The students were divided on the issue of language choice in song lyrics. While Error Crew's guitarist said that in the future there could be Indonesian punk bands that sang convincingly in Indonesian, other punks opined that English was more "international" and more appropriate for underground music. "Indonesian is good for dangdut," said one disparagingly. Punks are the most ideologically driven subsection of the underground, the only group for whom "lifestyle" tends to matter more than the music. Thus it is not surprising that they have clung most stubbornly to singing in English, no matter how ungrammatical and incoherent. I had assumed that this choice meant that punk music really was sellout-proof in the Indonesian-language-dominated mainstream music market. As it turned out, I was mistaken; later that month in a mall record store I encountered a cassette of punk songs sung in fractured English by a group called Rage Generation Brothers (*Our Lifestyle,* 2000) released on a large, commercial record label.

We debated, well into the night, the works of the Frankfurt School, postmodernism (*posmo*), methods of qualitative communications research, Anthony Giddens's concept of the Third Way (one of the most influential ideas among Indonesian intellectuals at the time), Noam Chomsky's *Manufacturing Consent,* and the writings of Karl Marx and Antonio Gramsci. At various points, nearly two dozen people crammed into the office to participate in the discussion or just to listen. While the students were sympathetic to leftist and social democratic thinkers from the West, they also were critical of Western ethnocentrism and hypocrisy. For example, they were especially opposed to international intellectual property law, which they perceived as limiting free trade (and thus contradicting the neoliberalism that is otherwise hegemonic in the West), and which they critiqued for putting developing countries at a disadvantage, since patents and copyrights tend to be owned by entities based in the developed world.[9]

I was consistently impressed with the level of knowledge I encountered; the experience was certainly at odds with the accounts I had read by both Indonesian and foreign scholars of the alleged laziness and mediocrity of Indonesian students and intellectuals (cf. Mulder 2000, 232–33). These students were knowledgeable and socially aware, and through hanging out, listening to and creating music, and debating ideas, they forged a collective but nonexclusive identity for themselves. Unlike the regulars at the Warung Gaul and their more apathetic classmates, these students approached American and Indonesian popular culture not with longing but with a critically engaged stance, aware of both the injustices and the emancipatory possibilities of the contemporary world.[10] What was striking was the importance of underground music in developing this critically engaged stance: if Chomsky's words provided a guideline for oppositional thought, then the music of the American group Rage Against the Machine, or of the numerous Indonesian rock groups that band influenced, gave a sense of what being oppositional *felt* like. Moreover, interest in that band often preceded interest in the progressive author. Wendi himself credited Rage Against the Machine for first teaching him about "ideology and oppressed people" (*ideologi dan orang tertindas*), its music providing an impetus for his political activism.

Sociality, Solidarity, and Musical Meaning

Other contexts of informal musical performances and conversations about music in Jakarta include karaoke sessions in all manner of public and private spaces as well as performance and listening activities in living rooms, dorm rooms, bedrooms, and servants' quarters. In each of these contexts, popular music is a shared reference point for people from diverse ethnic backgrounds. Like the Indonesian language itself, especially its colloquial variants and verbal art genres, music promotes social harmony (*rukun*) across ethnic, regional, and other social boundaries by creating a participatory space for collective enjoyment, and occasionally by providing an impetus for reflexive interpretation of one's social position.

It is perhaps unfashionable to claim that shared values and meanings exist across socioeconomic boundaries, as though different groups in a society share a "deeper" underlying culture that somehow transcends radical differences in life experience and opportunities for social advancement. Nevertheless, I found that certain similarities exist, to the point that working-class urban Indonesians resemble university-educated middle-class Indonesians in their social interactions far more than might be expected in such a polarized society. This resemblance does not, of course, erase the wide gulf that exists between haves and have-nots in Indonesian cities, but it points to a cross-class affinity that might some day have sociopolitical ramifications.

Indonesian nationalism arguably succeeds not only due to the ethnic neutrality of the Indonesian language and Indonesian popular culture, but also Indonesians' longstanding ethic of tolerance for various forms of social difference. The culture of *nongkrong* exemplifies this ethic of tolerance and informality, as well as the value of achieving social harmony without erasing the differences that exist among individuals. Even as a non-Muslim American, I became accepted at the Warung Gaul as long as I participated and showed up consistently over weeks and weeks—though it remains true that such acceptance would probably be more difficult for a Chinese Indonesian to gain.[11] *Nongkrong* sociality is predicated on an ethic of reciprocity in which the obligations are equal for both parties, and the nonhierarchical, open, and accepting nature of hanging-out culture makes the refusal to *bergaul* seem offensive and indicative of *kesombongan*, of an attitude of arrogant superiority, on the part of the refuser.

Finally, *nongkrong* sociality illustrates one of the central points of this ethnography: that in Indonesia music making is irreducibly social. Moreover, I want to suggest that it is possible to view almost all music-related activities in Indonesia, from recording to performing to listening, as shaped and informed by an interactive sensibility derived from *nongkrong* sociality. From this perspective, the cultural work of hanging out is anything but trivial.

PART TWO

Genres in Performance

7

Onstage

THE LIVE MUSICAL EVENT

We now move from the informal performances of everyday urban set-tings to more-structured performance events where, unlike at local hangout spots, a perceptible division exists between performers and audience. These sites include public places where humble street musicians perform with hopes of monetary gain and social recognition as much as the elaborate stages of stadiums and television studios. At all levels of formal performance, issues of sponsorship, sociality, and the collective negotiation of multifaceted identities shape the form and meaning of the music being performed.

Lebak Bulus Stadium, Jakarta, March 9, 2000
   The rock band onstage launches into its signature tune, garnering an immediate, enthusiastic response from the audience. Soon it seems as though the entire stadium of normally restrained and laconic young students are dancing, smiling, and singing the words of the song together. A few dozen dancers form a growing "conga line" of connected bodies that jubilantly snakes it way through the crowd. The song is "Radja" (King), in which the song's protagonist dreams of being king. The refrain is

> *Tapi aku bukan Radja,*
> *Ku hanya orang biasa*
> *Yang selalu dijadikan alas kaki pada Sang Radja.*

Aku hanya bisa menahan dan melihat
membayangkan dan memimpikan tuk menjadi seorang radja.

[But I'm not a king
I'm just an ordinary person
Who is always made to be the sole of the king's foot
I can only endure and watch
Imagining and dreaming about being a king.]

After the guitar solo and third repetition of the refrain comes the high point of the song, in which the lyrics of the whole song are summarized and accompanied by easy-to-follow melodic vocables.

Na na na na hei ya
Na na na na hei ya
Na na na na hei ya
Na na na na
Ku bukan seorang radja!

Hei ya na na na na na hei ya
Na na na na hei ya
Na na na na
Ku hanya orang biasa!

[Hei ya . . .
I'm not a king!

Hei ya . . .
I'm just an ordinary person!]

For the brief duration of the song, nervous questions of national identity, Western culture, socioeconomic class, and cultural difference dissolve into an ecstatic communitas of shared musical experience, and the audience exults vicariously in the predicament of the ordinary (Indonesian?) person portrayed in the song. Caught up in the spirit of the moment, I decide that the performance exemplifies one of the great things about popular music—the celebration of ordinariness over the drive for wealth and status (which otherwise preoccupies the middle-class Jakartan youth in the audience), accompanied by a thinly disguised critique of power.[1]

The by-now-familiar themes of genre, social class, gender, sociality, and hybridity are important in an examination of the many forms of onstage live musical performance in Indonesia. For the present purposes, I define "onstage performance" as any performance situation in which there is a socially recognized division between performer(s) and audience and some form of payment is offered to or expected by the performer(s) from the audience and/or from a third-party sponsor. To gather material for this chapter and the three chapters that follow it, I attended a total of eighty-three concert events in venues on the island of Java in 1997 and 1999–2000. I also observed and recorded numerous other less-structured performance occasions in malls, buses, train cars, clubs, and other public spaces. From these varied experiences I have developed a tentative, general account of the live musical event in Java.

Performances, Audiences, and Inclusiveness

The "performance event," a phrase that has become increasingly important in ethnomusicological and anthropological research, is regarded as a privileged locus for the examination of locally situated musical and cultural meanings, where sound and behavior can be analyzed together as constitutive of a larger whole (Stone 1982). Developments in the other human sciences have encouraged this focus. The foundational texts of what has become known as the "performance approach" were written by folklorists and linguistic anthropologists interested primarily in performed speech genres. In one such work, Bauman ([1977] 1984) describes performance as involving (1) some type of *framing device* (see Goffman 1974) that sets it off from the normal flow of events; (2) an acceptance of responsibility on the part of the performer; and (3) an "emergent" quality, which holds the potential for unexpected outcomes. Bauman and Briggs (1990) suggest further that performance events can be viewed as occasions for critical reflection on social life. Ethnomusicologist Regula Qureshi writes, "A performance becomes a locus in which old meanings are tested and new ones are negotiated; where rules are enforced, broken, and rewritten; and where musical meanings are interpreted and felt anew, as memories are fashioned into icons relating to the present moment" (2000, 827). Musical performances in Indonesia, through demystifying aspects of social existence (such as class and gender categories), evoking memories, and offering affectively compelling experiences, generate reflection and even transformations in consciousness. We will see how the emergent meanings of the onstage performance event are subject to the varied and often conflicting agendas of participants, and how meanings are negotiated in response to multi-sensory experiences of musical sound and spectacle.

Popular music performance events in Indonesia, like performances everywhere, ultimately resist any single agenda, and both complicity and resistance to hegemonic forces, from consumer capitalism to Indonesian official nationalism, may be present at the same moment. In the following discussion, however, I am less interested in the cultural politics of live musical events than in the importance of musical performance in the formation of subjectivities on both the individual and the collective levels. We have seen how characteristic processes of creative innovation and hybridization in Indonesian popular music production have uncertain and multiple social effects. The immediacy and emergent quality of live musical performance intensifies this unpredictability, as audiences actively coparticipate in establishing the meanings of an event. The process of ongoing interpretation involves all the participants in a performance situation and primarily operates via the realm of affective experience, simultaneously personal and shared. On the social and individual dimensions of musical performance Qureshi writes: "The physical sensation of sound not only activates feeling, it also activates links with others who feel. In an instant, the sound of music can create bonds of shared responses that are as deep and intimate as they are broad and universal. The ephemeral bond of a sonic event does not commit to physical contact — though it may elicit it. Experiencing music together leaves the personal, individual, and interior domain unviolated. At the same time, the experience becomes public, shared, and exterior" (Qureshi 2000, 810).

The ability of particular musical events to create social bonds without necessarily dissolving self/other boundaries has been commented on by psychoanalysts (e.g., Nass 1971), and the creation of collective sentiment and social solidarity through musical performance has been discussed by music researchers in a wide variety of cultural settings, from rain forests to raves (e.g., Feld [1982] 1990; Seeger 1987; Thornton 1996). Researchers in European-American popular music in particular have asserted the existence of a close link between self-conscious, individual identity formation and the generation of collective sentiment in the flow of performance (e.g., Berger 1999; Fikentscher 2000; Nelson 1999; Shank 1994). Indeed, if one accepts the notion that identity and subjectivity are constructed through dialogue with others (C. Taylor 1991), musical performance events constitute an important, emotionally heightened arena where such interactions take place.

Popular music performances in Indonesia, as in the United States and elsewhere, have significant implications for questions of identity and affect, but they also follow particular cultural logics of hybridity and sociality peculiar to Indonesian representational practice. In particular, musical performance events in Indonesia enact an ethic of *inclusiveness*, within which musical differences indexing social differences between people and their divergent allegiances are rhetorically transcended. Through the juxtaposing, parodying, and blending of musical genres, performers and audience collaborate in the creation of a hybridic, self-aware, ephemeral community in which unassimilated differences coexist as a dizzying array of alternatives—Indonesian, modern, traditional, trendy, American, global, populist, elitist, Muslim, ethnic, and so on—that not only do not line up easily into simple binary oppositions but also cannot be placed easily into a single coherent framework. This performed multiplicity nevertheless conforms to an ethic of radical inclusiveness and the promotion of social solidarity, both of which are key components of a vernacular Indonesian nationalism that is perhaps expressed more eloquently in popular music than in any other Indonesian mass medium.

Benedict Anderson elucidates the grassroots appeal of Indonesian nationalism among Javanese in the following passage: "The urge to oneness, so central to Javanese political attitudes, helps to explain the deep psychological power of the idea of nationalism in Java. Far more than a political credo, nationalism expresses a fundamental drive to solidarity and unity in the face of the disintegration of traditional society under colonial capitalism, and other powerful external forces, from the late nineteenth century on. Nationalism of this type is something far stronger than patriotism; it is an attempt to reconquer a primordial oneness" (Anderson 1990, 37). While Anderson is speaking specifically of Javanese, I found that the achievement, through performance, of a national "primordial oneness" underlying surface social and musical diversity was a recurrent theme in live musical performances in multiethnic urban contexts. But this sense of underlying unity differs from that of the integrated, well-ordered hierarchical universe that Anderson describes as the idealized Javanese "traditional society." James Siegel (1986) has argued that the boundaries of the latter ideal society are coterminous with the High Javanese speech community, and that linguistic heterogeneity, translation, and the failure of linguistic communication itself threaten its coherence. I would argue that the "oneness" of modern Indonesian nationalism, by contrast, is polyvocal, multilingual, heteroglossic, cosmopolitan, and inclusive, and its boundaries are inherently porous.

This discussion thus builds on the insights contained in chapter 6 regarding Indonesian "sociality" and the polyphonic unity and solidarity achieved through "hanging out" and other collaborative, participatory endeavors. At Indonesian popular music events, genres become virtual participants in an interactive, intersubjective space in which identities are forged, questioned, reinforced, pried open, and reconfigured in a spirit of play and experimentation. Despite these events' seeming frivolity and shallow eclecticism, and the undeniable pleasures they provide, this is a serious game that has high stakes as it confronts and interrogates *non*virtual social categories based on class, gender, religion, and ethnicity that impact people's lives in concrete ways.

Taking all these issues into account, we turn first to the variety of onstage performance events that one encounters in Jakarta.

"Live Music" in the Capital: From Streets to Stadiums

Terms for live performance vary in Indonesian: the English phrase *live music* is frequently used, as is *musik langsung* (literally "direct music") and *musik hidup* (live music). Performing musicians are everywhere in urban Java: at train stations, aboard trains, in mall food courts, at *warung*, in city buses, and of course at nightclubs, cafés, outdoor stages, and other specialized performance venues. In Jakarta, almost all the music performed in these various settings is popular music, mostly national Indonesian or Western genres. The few exceptions include occasional Western classical music concerts sponsored by European cultural institutes and the live gamelan music found in five-star-hotel lobbies and at lavish ethnic Javanese weddings.

Live performance is not heavily mythologized in the Indonesian popular music scene. There is little sense that concerts are somehow prior to or more authentic than recordings; this is not surprising given that recordings generally determine the sound of live performances and that popular music fans generally emphasize recorded songs over artists. Live performance is simply one of many modalities through which music is experienced, though it is certainly one of the more intense and pleasurable. In urban Java there is a robust demand for live music. Successful Indonesian recording artists, particularly dangdut singers, can earn sizable incomes from live appearances. Often this income far exceeds what they earn in royalties from album sales (mostly due to disadvantageous arrangements with recording companies and the ever-present problem of cassette piracy). In Jakarta, established artists regularly perform in stadiums, at five-star hotels, at prestigious nightclubs, and in television studios for live or prerecorded music broadcasts.

Yet media stars participate in only a small percentage of the live performance events taking place on any given night in the capital city. Jakarta stages are mostly inhabited by amateur, semiprofessional, and undiscovered artists, and these performers are the focus of most of the discussion that follows. My account of live music in Jakarta commences at the far opposite end of the performer spectrum from the high-paid stars, with performers whose "stage" is the city streets or the interiors of buses, trains, and food stalls: humble street musicians slinging battered, colorfully decorated guitars, who roam through the city in search of spare change. The work of these performers, known as *pengamen*, constitutes the most abundant (if banal) source of live music in Jakarta, and for this reason they deserve more than passing mention.

Pengamen (Street Musicians): Contested Performance

Jangan kau nyanyikan lagu sumbang itu
Sebab,
Aku dengar petik gitar semalam
Yang kau bawa di keramaian kota.

Kau yang tegar dalam sebuah
perjalanan
Kapan kita nyanyikan, akhir sebuah
lagu malam.
Tanpa suasana kita terus bernyanyi
Berdendang teriknya penghidupan.

["Do not sing that indecent song
Because,
I hear the strumming of your guitar all night long
That you carry around in the hustle and bustle of the city."

You who stubbornly continue on your
journey
When will we sing to the end a
song of night?

Without warmth or openness, we sing on and on,
Singing of the stifling deadness of our lives.]
"Tembang Bagi Pengamen"
(A Song for Traveling Street Musicians),
in Badjuridoellahjoestro 1994[2]

Not everyone I met while in Indonesia shared this poet's sympathy toward street musicians. *Pengamen,* traveling performers/mendicants in Indonesian cities, were often criticized as little more than beggars who were unwilling to work (*malas kerja; ngga' mau usaha*). Taxicab drivers were particularly vociferous in their criticism, weary of being approached at intersections by armies of young men carrying out-of-tune guitars and singing off-key *pop nostalgia* songs.

While the majority of *pengamen* play battered acoustic guitars, some also play ukuleles, violins, hand drums, empty plastic water bottles, and tambourines. More accomplished street musicians often play in mobile ensembles of these instruments. Other *pengamen,* usually older, play traditional instruments such as the Javanese *celempung* (zither) or *kendang* (barrel drum); in Jakarta those musicians are less common than in other Javanese cities. Another category of *pengamen* consists of sight-impaired men who carry portable sound systems from bus to bus and sing along to dangdut karaoke cassettes through inexpensive, distorted microphones. *Waria* (ladyboys; transgendered cross-dressers) also sometimes work as *pengamen,* with karaoke equipment or without.

Many of the more skilled amateur musicians I met who played informally by the side of the road (see chapter 6) worked as *pengamen* (verb form: *ngamen*) from time to time to make some extra money, sometimes even traveling to other cities to do so. But since the most common donation given to most *pengamen* (and beggars) in Jakarta was a one-hundred-rupiah coin, and the cheapest meal with rice at the time was around Rp. 3,000, the possibility of having significant earnings left at the end of the day was slight for most street performers. A trio of *pengamen* who played on buses told that me on a good day they could make Rp. 10,000, still barely enough to pay for meals. Nevertheless, they told me that they enjoyed performing, and that playing music was better than a life of crime and better than working a regular job.

Some famous Indonesian singers began their careers as *pengamen,* most notably rock legend Iwan Fals (considered by many to be Indonesia's answer to Bob Dylan and Bruce Springsteen), who was a sort of patron saint revered by legions of street musicians. Inspired by "Bang" (Older Brother) Iwan, some *pengamen* wrote their own songs with topical, politically satirical lyrics; traveling street poets also recited verses on political issues, including resistance to anti-Chinese racism and military violence. The *pengamen* I met could play several Iwan Fals songs, though they usually played more crowd-pleasing tunes—current pop hits and *pop nostalgia*—when seeking donations. I found that the skill and enthusiasm with which these *pengamen* played Iwan Fals compositions when requested to do so often contrasted sharply with the lower quality of their renditions of songs by other artists.

Anak Jalanan

In Jakarta I encountered groups of children, often siblings or cousins, who roamed the streets of busy areas like Blok M until late at night, approaching pedestrians and motorists in a quest for rupiahs. They sang schoolchildren's patriotic songs or performed their own compositions about life singing on the streets, accompanying themselves on ukuleles and *gicik*. Some of these children help support their families instead of attending school, the fees for which many families cannot afford. In Indonesian popular culture the "street kid" (*anak jalanan*) is a tragic but hopeful figure, representing the failure of the Indonesian government to provide for all its citizens but also the creativity and enterprise of Indonesian youth. The *anak jalanan* who sings for his or her sustenance is an especially enduring social stereotype in Indonesia, but the reality street children face is one of marginalization and harassment (Beazley 2000, 2002). Experienced child singers command a sizable memorized repertoire that includes pop and dangdut songs.

Adult *pengamen* are almost always male and appear to represent a particular Indonesian male ideal—that of the free traveler who gets by through his wits rather than through employment. Yiska, a seventeen-year-old *pengamen* in the city of Bandung, told me that she made more money than most because it was so unusual for people to see a female street performer, and that since she had already been singing in the street for four years she was accustomed to the heat and exhaust fumes from the local buses. She added that during those years she did not attend school. Privately, a male friend of Yiska's told me that her career of singing and playing guitar on buses was far better than "selling herself" (*jual diri*), in other words, better than following many other teenage girls from poor families into prostitution.

The guitar-slinging young men who loiter at traffic intersections and play in front of windows of halted cars (briefly mentioned in chapter 2)

Anak jalanan (street children) singing for money, Lebak Bulus, South Jakarta. The child
on the right is holding a *gicik*.

often neither sing nor play very well. They typically endeavor to make
enough noise to cause motorists to crack open their window and hand
them some rupiah coins just to be rid of the nuisance. These *pengamen*
immediately cease performing once they are paid and move on to the
next stopped vehicle (cf. Siegel 1986, 119, and the poem quoted above).
Street musicians on buses and trains tend to be more skilled and less coercive. Performances on buses often begin with a short speech by a solo
musician or one member of an ensemble, addressing the "audience" and
expressing hope that the passengers will enjoy their humble musical offerings. After one or two songs, a member of the group or a companion
passes around a used plastic candy bag, the top edge neatly folded over,
to collect monetary contributions. Usually no more than a handful of
commuters throw coins in the bag, an action for which they are politely
thanked. The *pengamen* then jump off the next time the bus stops and
move on in search of other audiences.

Street musicians occupy the lowest level of public musical performance, and the "breakthrough" into performance (Hymes 1975) they attempt is contested by the others present. By withholding contributions

and by ignoring the musicians, members of the captive "audiences" of *pengamen* attempt to deny the existence of a performance frame. If what is taking place is in fact not a performance but something more mundane, such as a request for alms, onlookers are not obligated to reciprocate or even pay attention. Indeed, the word *pengamen* is often translated simply as "beggar" (though in Jakarta mendicants who do not sing or play instruments are usually called *pengemis,* not *pengamen*).

Pengamen and Musical Replication

Whether their audience regards them as public nuisances or as welcome entertainment during a long, exhausting commute, *pengamen* are important agents of musical replication who operate outside the official mass media. They respond, of course, to market forces and musical trends but, like the amateur musicians by the side of the road, also reclaim commercially recorded songs as grassroots music of "the Indonesian people," reanimating high-tech recorded performances through low-tech live renditions. In mid-2000, it was common to hear the hit song "Jika" (If), a duet by *pop alternatif* stars Melly Goeslaw and Ari Lasso, played by street musicians throughout Jakarta. The song was sometimes hard to recognize when performed solo with an acoustic guitar, without the complex, multilayered electronic accompaniment on the recording, but listeners seemed to enjoy hearing these renditions, which were the closest most of them would ever come to hearing the "real" song (that is, the version on the recording) performed live.

If one refrains from treating national identity as a given, the role of *pengamen* in domesticating the products of the Jakarta-based national culture industry deserves consideration. If *pengamen* are living icons of "the folk" (*rakyat*), as so many of them claim, then the music played by *pengamen* is ipso facto folk music, representing ordinary Indonesians and constituting a musical heritage shared by all citizens, from the humblest to the most affluent. The street musician's command of the Indonesian popular music repertoire can be said to prove that Indonesian songs are for everyone, that even the most destitute are included in the national community the songs presuppose but, to paraphrase Clifford Geertz, in fact help to manufacture. *Pengamen* act as living radios, playing the songs the people want to hear in a performance economy that includes Indonesians from all levels of society, including those who are too poor to afford radios or cassettes of their own and do not figure into the marketing calculations of record companies. However, the fact that *pengamen* lack the patronage of a record company or other source of power and wealth makes them fraudulent performers in the eyes of many Indonesians. The modest contributions *pengamen* gain in the course of a day can be regarded as alms, not sponsorship, and their lack of institutional support, while constituting the source of their grassroots credibility, also becomes a reason to dismiss them.

The Social Organization, Structure, and Functions of *Acara*

A more formalized, less contested type of musical performance is known as the *acara* (event), a term that generally refers to any organized occasion featuring an audience and a performance of some type. While the presentations of *pengamen* take place on contested terrain and are not always accepted by the audience as actual performances, *acara* are considered legitimate contexts for live music, not least because, unlike street performances, they enjoy the material support of sponsors.

The *acara* is an important category in urban Indonesia, and the term denotes a more culturally salient phenomenon than "concert" (*konser*). *Acara* are not necessarily music related; they can be symposia, for example, or presentations, but they usually involve live music of some sort. They can be held to raise money for a charitable cause (*malam peduli*), to honor a university or high school graduating class, to celebrate a national holiday, to advertise a new consumer product, to launch a new Web site, or for a variety of other reasons. All *acara* have a sponsor or sponsors and are usually organized by a committee (*panitia*). *Event organizers* are respected professionals in Jakarta; they are frequently hired by committees to help find sponsors, hire security and soundmen, and assist with various other arrangements.

The most indispensable player in the *acara*, regardless of the type of entertainment featured, is the master of ceremonies. Emcees are usually paid much more than musicians, and their role in keeping the crowd happy is crucial to the event's success. According to a semiretired dangdut emcee living in a village in Central Java, a good emcee must be able to "look at the situation" (*lihat situasi*) and comprehend what the crowd wants without letting things get out of control. He told me that faster songs (*dangdut hot*) should be played at the beginning of the evening, whereas balladlike dangdut songs (*dangdut slow*) should be played toward the end, to calm the crowd. A sensitive emcee knows the precise moment at which to instruct a band to switch from one style to the other in order to avoid unrest and dissatisfaction.

Strong parallels exist between different kinds of *acara*. Dangdut shows always have an emcee, as do most underground concert events. Often the emcee at larger events is an entertainment personality—an actor, a model, or a comedian—while at smaller-scale events the role may be filled by a particularly charismatic member of the organizing committee. The emcee at dangdut shows is always male, and he usually sings a few songs in the course of the evening in addition to performing the important tasks of welcoming guests, introducing performers, and acknowledging sponsors. At *acara* featuring other types of music (e.g., pop, rock, and underground), women emcees are as common as men, and emcees of both sexes commonly work in pairs or groups. These emcees also address the crowd and introduce musicians, but rarely sing with them. A central task for emcees at pop and rock events is to promote the corporate sponsors' products through door prizes, audience contests, and frequent "plugs" inserted into their customary banter.

The Cultural Work of Performance

Acara serve many purposes, but among the most significant is providing an opportunity for reflection on the conditions of contemporary Indonesian cultural life. The use of performance occasions to confront cultural contradictions and social changes has been well documented in Indonesia; an early example is James Peacock's study of *ludrug* in Surabaya (1968), which describes performances of this proletarian theatrical genre as "rites of modernization," in which distinctions between what is modern versus what is old (*kuno*) in then newly independent Java/Indonesia were central to the narrative, displacing conventional Javanese cultural themes of refined (Javanese, *alus*) versus coarse (*kasar*). Similarly, the popular music performances I attended in Indonesia in 1997–2000 also addressed the existential conditions of their audiences.

One of the most striking aspects of *acara* is their innovative juxtapositions of local, national, and global cultural forms. These hybrid constructions can be provocative, reassuring, humorous, or some combination thereof to audiences preoccupied with questions of identity and allegiance in a rapidly changing society.

Geertz (1995, 145–51) describes a curious performance event in an East Javanese village staged by the graduating members of an English class at a *madrasah*, a Javanese Islamic school. He first notes the eclectic sounds and images on display at the event, including blaring recorded popular music and the decorations onstage. "Even before it started, the event—[decorative] coconut fronds, folding chairs, Muslim dress, 'The

Protocol' [a strange English-language reference to the two female emcees], rock-and-roll, the religious high holiday, and an imperfect, urban-type banner—had a definitely contestatory, multicultural feel about it. Homemade post-modernism, designed to unsettle" (1995, 146).

In Geertz's account, a climactic segment of what was an increasingly bizarre series of skits and performances involved a group of clowns singing a strange song with English lyrics, after pantomiming a street brawl. "They sang this ditty over and over again in a series of over-the-top parodies of popular song styles: the Indonesian ones called *dangdut* and *kroncong*, Bob Dylan, hard rock, country, what may have been Elvis, and a number of others I didn't certainly recognize" (1995, 148). This serial montage of musical genres resonates with much that took place at the urban musical *acara* that I attended. Due to its rural, religious Muslim setting, this particular performance elicited, according to Geertz, a feeling of extreme unease in the audience, which was composed of parents and elders. Such a spectacle would likely earn a more positive reaction from an urban youth audience. Geertz attended this unusual *acara* in 1986. Had it occurred in the year 2000, ska, punk, and black metal may well have been included among the genres parodied by the students, as the town of Pare where the *acara* took place (and the site of Geertz's original fieldwork in the 1950s) was by then home to an active local underground scene and a regional fanzine called *Dysphonic Newsletter*.

Geertz concludes: "The evening was a stream of moralities, mockeries, ambivalences, ironies, outrages, and contradictions, almost all of them centering in one way or another around language and the speaking (half-speaking, non-speaking) of language. Uncrossable lines were crossed in play, irrationalities were displayed in heavy quotation marks, codes were mixed, rhetorics were opposed, and the whole project to which the school was dedicated, extending the impact of Islam, perhaps the most linguistically self-conscious of the great religions, on the world through the learning of a world language [English], was put into question" (1995, 151). Geertz then adds that this was the only *acara* he attended in four decades of contact with this particular village that was conducted entirely in Indonesian and English, with no Javanese at all spoken onstage. In fact, the *acara* he describes seems to resemble, in both language and content, less the usual events in a Javanese village than those *acara* I observed in Jakarta, Bandung, and Yogyakarta. Much like the urban *acara* I attended, it drew from national and international sources more than from the local performance traditions one might expect to see in a village.

Although Geertz highlights the use of language and code switching in the event he describes, he also mentions other dimensions—sartorial, aural, iconographic, musical—as contributing to the overall "contestatory" feeling of the proceedings. The following discussion of musical *acara* in Bandung and Jakarta, which are more secular and less conflicted about Western popular culture than rural East Java, deals as well with the themes of parody, mimesis, and juxtaposition of local, national, and global cultural forms. These themes are detectable at many levels of the event, musical and nonmusical, including the spatial layout of the stage itself. Below is a description of the stage at a particularly elaborate music *acara* held in Bandung in 1999 and sponsored by the cigarette brand Bentoel Mild. The event was titled "Mildcoustic" and was based loosely on the "unplugged" concept invented by MTV, in which televised musicians play miked acoustic rather than electronic instruments onstage in order to generate a sense of liveness and immediacy (cf. Auslander 1999, 94–111). The event showcased an unusual combination of Indonesian rock, Indonesian jazz, and ethnic fusion ensembles. The music of the headlining group, the Bandung-based Krakatau, in fact combined these three genres, and several others, into a unique musical blend.[3]

December 7, 1999

The stage is enormous, and its decor appears to have been influenced by the studio sets used in "MTV Unplugged" concert videos. On either side of the stage are traditional Sundanese instruments: gongs, kettle gongs, barrel drums, and the like. In the center section traditional metallophones share space with four Western trap drum kits, instrument amplifiers, and, most impressive of all, a Yamaha acoustic grand piano on its own riser to the right of center stage. Krakatau bassist Pra Budidharma's electric fretless bass guitar stands proudly near the rear of the stage in its upright stand during the entire show, as though surveying the scene.

Audience members arriving early can watch continuously playing television ads for Bentoel Mild clove cigarettes, with their accompanying slogan *jangan anggap enteng* ("don't consider [them to be] lightweight," a play on the Indonesian word *enteng*, which also means "mild"), projected on three large video screens, one on each side of the stage and one looming behind it. During the actual performances, the three screens show closed-circuit video images of the bands performing; these images are alternated with canned footage of Balinese dancers, photographs of ancient Hindu-Javanese statues, an image of a human eye opening and closing, and colorful computer animation sequences incorporating the bands' monikers. The Bentoel ads are also replayed (without sound) during the performances, as are some distractingly gory animation sequences culled from *The Wall*, a surrealistic 1979 film created by the British progressive rock band Pink Floyd.

Like many other aspects of this *acara*, the material projected on the video screens presented global, national, and local cultural objects juxtaposed through technological means. Images of Indonesian jazz and rock bands, traditional dancing, and fragments of a canonical rock film jostled against one another, forming an electronic backdrop to live performances that themselves creatively combined elements from each cultural source. In this case, the reduction of culture to electronic images allowed for the placing of elements from different cultures on equal footing, as part of a repetitive series. And as in other examples of techno-hybridity in Indonesian popular culture, the "traditional," "ethnic" elements were arguably the most decontextualized and distorted by this process, which tends to serve the modern capitalist interests that give life to *acara*.

More on the Logic of *Acara*: Televised Award Shows

Award shows featuring mediated and live entertainment are a common and popular event on Indonesian television, and the features of such events—emcee banter, videos projected on large screens, and the distribution of awards—have been adopted by other, nontelevised *acara*. Award shows celebrate the people and products of the Indonesian entertainment industry, and they are popular enough that the names of accomplished directors and music producer/arrangers are almost as familiar to the Indonesian public as those of actors and musicians. The music for these *acara* is usually recorded in advance and played back as musicians mime their performance. Usually the singer adds live vocals on top of the prerecorded accompaniment, but he or she may choose to lip-synch as well.

Indonesian award shows are both national and transnational in character. The events themselves are modeled after globally circulating shows like the Academy Awards (which is broadcast every year on Indonesian television) and proceed along globally familiar lines: national celebrities, usually in pairs, introduce award categories, name the nominees, open a sealed envelope, and announce the winner. The audience then responds with applause. This repeated sequence of events is interspersed with comedy skits, musical performances, and commercial breaks (during which the live audience in the studio is entertained by the improvised antics of professional comedians). Western popular music is largely absent from awards *acara*, since these events are intended to celebrate the creativity and excellence of the Indonesian culture industry—thus, they participate in the comfortable but untenable fiction that the national entertainment business is the main provider of popular culture in Indonesia. In reality on a typical broadcast day local television productions share air time with American sitcoms, Indian film musicals, Hong Kong kung fu epics, Latin American and Middle Eastern telenovelas, Hollywood movies, and other imported programs, and radio airwaves, movie theaters, and record stores are similarly multinational in their offerings.[4]

Although the form of the award *acara* is ostensibly global, nationalistic themes and representations of the lives of ordinary Indonesians abound at these events, particularly in the prerecorded video segments spliced into the broadcast and projected on large screens for the live audience. At the 2000 MTV Indonesia Video Music Awards held on June 3, 2000 (and broadcast eight nights later), each category was announced in a short film featuring an Indonesian celebrity playing the role of a working-class Indonesian: a *tukang jamu* (traditional herbal-tonic seller), a *becak* driver, a snack peddler, and so forth. At the end of each segment (usually around thirty seconds long), the celebrity would address the audience and give the name of the next award. Award categories were always in English, so the incongruity of seeing a famous comedian in the role of a *sate* vendor or a street-side monkey trainer, or seeing a beautiful singer in the guise of a harried, overworked office assistant was matched by the incongruous words they spoke—each segment ended with the character suddenly breaking the dramatic frame by abruptly facing the camera and announcing the next category (*Best Director*, etc.). These introductory segments for each award were among the most creative and entertaining portions of the event, a humorous reminder of the particular national context of this replica of a global institution.

And yet much of the award show sought to distance its subject matter and its audience from ordinary Indonesians. "*MTV is about music, entertainment, and lifestyle,*" said one smiling presenter, a well-known radio personality, before launching into an Indonesian speech about the contributions of costume designers to music video. His English-language statement was met with applause—the young, affluent audience celebrating perhaps the cosmopolitan sophistication of both the speaker and itself. The speaker's mention of "lifestyle" is highly salient. In Indonesian, this English loanword is consistently associated with middle-class popular culture, youth, and consumerism. No one would ever state that dangdut was "about lifestyle."

The many English phrases used in the MTV awards show were left untranslated. In contrast, at a dangdut awards *acara* I attended, which was televised on the privately owned TPI (Televisi Pendidikan Indonesia, "Indonesian Educational Television") network, all three times the winners in categories for *Cover Song Terbaik* (Best Cover Song) were introduced, the announcers first took pains to explain what a *cover song* was: a song made popular by an earlier artist that had been rerecorded by another.[5] Unlike other award *acara* I had viewed or attended, all of which used English words, this dangdut award show did not presuppose any knowledge of English on the part of its audience. Apart from the use of the phrase "cover song," even the award categories were in formal Indonesian (i.e., *Lagu Terbaik* instead of "Best Song"). The event also lacked the spirit of humor and play with Indonesian working-class stereotypes that characterized the MTV award video segments. Such ordinary Indonesians were instead assumed to comprise the primary audience of the dangdut award show. Nonetheless, the evening was not without references to global culture: one example, a highlight of the event, was a dangdut version of the Three Tenors. Instead of international opera superstars Luciano Pavarotti, Plácido Domingo, and José Carreras, veteran dangdut singers and songwriters Meggi Z, Mansur S, and Basoefi Soedirman came onstage in tuxedos and took turns singing a classic dangdut tune.[6]

In all the *acara* discussed here, technological virtuality sets the stage for a particular sort of cultural collision in which the "Indonesian" is performatively constituted through the appropriation of sounds, images, objects, and languages into a national project in dialogue with Western modernity. The national is the meeting ground for both the local and the global, where allegiances constantly shift and collide. It is not sufficient therefore to assert that Indonesian national culture is "a" hybrid. More precise is the statement that Indonesian national culture is performed as an interactive field of hybridic possibilities that at times engage with each other but more often just coexist, like the disparate images on the "Mildcoustic" video screens. Thus what distinguishes Indonesian popular culture is not dialogue or synthesis but polyvocality and simultaneity. As these examples have shown, this simultaneity is exploited and presented as spectacle by commercial interests. But these interests must in turn respond to consumer demand, a complex, multifaceted entity created by the amalgamated desires, aspirations, identity projects, and affective investments of the Indonesian audience, or some segment of it.

Taking the preceding discussion into account, in the three chapters that follow we turn to an examination of the main genre categories covered in this book and their multiple realizations in performance. In keeping with our focus on inclusiveness, however, we will pay special attention to the noisy, disruptive presence of other genres at performances ostensibly dedicated to a single kind of music, whether it is dangdut, pop, or underground. Also important to the interpretations offered in the following chapters is the performance of gender, class, and national identity within the metacultural performance frame of a particular genre. Each genre's performance conventions reveal distinct strategies of incorporation, exclusion, and hybridization in performance contexts vis-à-vis the various sorts of social and musical differences that present themselves in the performance frame. These strategies reveal the complex and divergent responses of popular music audiences to the ethical and cultural challenges of life in a multiethnic, modern capitalist nation stratified along lines of gender and class.

8

Dangdut Concerts

THE POLITICS OF PLEASURE

Whether the event took place in a smoky, darkened nightclub, at a wedding celebration in a cramped *kampung* backyard, or among thousands of revelers at a large outdoor festival, I found that the structure and personnel of dangdut *acara* were remarkably consistent. The key performers were a master of ceremonies, several singers of both genders, and an instrumental ensemble consisting of *gendang, suling,* two electric guitars, electric bass guitar, two electronic keyboards, tambourine, trap drum set (often played by the same musician who played the *gendang*), and, in some cases, electrified mandolin and/or a brass section. Singers generally operated independently of instrumental groups and sang with several different local ensembles.

Instrumentalists were nearly always male. Kendedes Group, named for Ken Dhedhes, the legendary queen of the thirteenth-century Javanese kingdom of Singasari, was formed in 1976 by singer/*gendang* player Titiek Nur and was the only all-female dangdut ensemble active in Jakarta in 1999–2000. Although I have witnessed Titiek sing and play *gendang* at the same time, this mode of performance was highly unusual. In every other dangdut performance I attended, male and female dangdut performers sang and danced but did not play instruments onstage, and their backing bands were composed entirely of men.

Usually the band began with an all-instrumental introductory song to get the audience's attention. This lasted for three to five minutes and was followed by a lengthy speech (often two minutes long or longer) by the master of ceremonies welcoming the crowd, commenting on the

Dangdut recording artist Titiek Nur playing the *gendang* while singing at the author's farewell party, Cinere, South Jakarta.

occasion, and finally introducing the first singer of the evening. After the speech, the band "called" the first vocalist by playing a *selingan,* a short musical interlude that lasted one or two minutes, during which the first performer would take center stage and prepare to face the audience. *Selingan* were often instrumental versions of dangdut songs but did not have to be: some groups played *pop Indonesia* or *keroncong* compositions; even instrumental renditions of Western pop songs (including "The Cup of Life," the 1998 World Cup theme song performed by Puerto Rican pop star Ricky Martin, and "The Final Countdown," a 1986 hit by the Swedish hard rock group Europe) were sometimes played.

The band would end the *selingan* as the first singer, who was always a woman, picked up the microphone to address the crowd. After the customary Islamic greeting, *Wassalamulaikum warakhmatullahi wabarakatuh* (Arabic, "Peace be with you and may God be merciful and bless you"), to which the audience would reply *Walaikum salam!* (Arabic, "Unto you, peace!"), she would deliver a short speech in formal Indonesian welcoming the audience and acknowledging the sponsors of the event, then introduce her first song.

Usually singers only sang two songs each while the backing band's personnel remained constant throughout the performance. After the first singer's second song ended, the master of ceremonies would speak again, the next singer (usually also female) would be introduced, the band would play another instrumental interlude, and the whole cycle would repeat itself. It is worth noting that while singing two songs might not seem difficult, the average dangdut song is twice as long as most pop tunes, and the band could decide to lengthen a song depending on the crowd's reaction. A well-received performer could repeat a song's refrain three or four times more compared to the recorded version. On the rare occasion when a singer did not garner a positive reaction from the audience or was obviously unprepared, the band would cut the first song short, and the next singer in line was called to take his or her place. Although songs were never repeated in the course of a single event, they were mostly taken from a rather limited repertoire of old chestnuts and new hits, so different dangdut shows would have similar set lists. Dangdut performance events usually lasted several hours, often from 9:00 p.m. until after 2:00 a.m. Daytime performances in urban neighborhoods from roughly 10:00 a.m. to 4:00 p.m. were also common. The performance would end with a final instrumental *selingan* by the band, often the children's tune "Marilah Pulang" ("Let's Go Home"—the same final song that was played by the Warung under the Tree band in chapter 6), which was performed as the exhausted audience slowly filed out and the emcee bid the audience farewell. The entire structure of dangdut *acara* was meant to be orderly and predictable and was intended to contain the unruly forces unleashed by the sensual performance of dangdut music and the presence of crowds of young working-class men.

Woman dangdut singers' outfits were markedly different from everyday Indonesian clothes. They fell into two main categories: long evening gowns and high heels or skimpy outfits usually involving miniskirts, black leather, and knee-high boots (cf. Browne 2000, 25). Male singers and male instrumentalists often wore brightly colored, matching jackets and ties, also unusual dress in Indonesia, particularly in poor and working-class communities, where the urban elite was contemptuously referred to as the *kaum berdasi*, "necktie-wearing caste." Such extravagant costumes indexed wealth, prestige, and Western-style urbanity—village clothing styles were rare in the performance of a music forever tainted by the association with backward village life. On the other hand, the cheap fabrics and bright (*ngejreng*) colors of dangdut costumes and the "scandalous" outfits worn by some female dangdut singers indicated a distinctly working-class sensibility, and dangdut fashion differed not only from the traditional costumes of "regional music" performers but also from the MTV-inspired sartorial choices of Indonesian pop and rock artists. Thus, like dangdut music itself, dangdut costumes were not considered "traditional" yet were not quite "modern" either (cf. Sutton 2003, 329–30).

Dancing Behavior at Dangdut Concerts

The dangdut concerts I attended were highly participatory events. During a successful performance the audience was not expected to listen passively but rather to dance enthusiastically to the music. The characteristic dangdut dancing activity was known as the *joget* or *joged*. *Joget dangdut* styles varied considerably from one individual to another: movements ranged from complicated arm gestures reminiscent of Javanese and Sundanese traditional choreography to barely moving at all. The dance itself was simple in its most elemental form: to *joget* one takes two steps forward, then two steps back, or the other way around. *Joget*ting was almost always done in pairs, which could be male-male, female-male, or female-female; the first combination was the most common.[1] Partners faced each other and coordinated their moves: one stepped back when the other stepped forward. While executing these steps the arms were frequently held up, with the hands in fists tucked close to the front of the chest, thumbs pointing upward. As one stepped back and forth, the fists moved up and down in a circular motion, as if they were slowly pedaling a bicycle. There was no intentional physical contact between partners, and dancers usually avoided making eye contact with each other. Dancers *joget*ted with either a neutral facial expression or a wide grin and often appeared to be oblivious to those around them. *Joget*ting was considered a pleasurable activity in itself, apart from the quality of the music, and it was believed to have the ability to "relieve stress" (*hilangi stres*). Writing about audiences at dangdut concerts, Philip Yampolsky comments, "Indeed, the aim of their dancing is apparently to be transported to a state where they are unaware of their surroundings, free of self-consciousness and inhibition" (1991, 1).

The origins of the dangdut *joget* are unclear. It does not strongly resemble the dance moves of Indian film music—the probable origin of the dangdut rhythm—nor any traditional Indonesian dances. One dangdut fan told me that the *joget* came from the cha-cha, a claim that is entirely plausible. Beyond the basic *joget* steps, dancers could execute slow turns (*pusing*) and add hip and arm movements, but these embellishments were not necessary. *Joget*ting was not supposed to require special skill, and nearly everyone, from very young children to the elderly, could *joget*, though in public spaces the dance was most often associated with young adult men. There were no consistent gender differences in *joget* style, though women were more likely to incorporate hip movements and other gestures typical of dangdut singers, whose dance was of a different sort.

In contrast to the audience, woman dangdut performers were expected to *goyang*, a word that literally means "to sway." This movement required more skill than the *joget*, and singers were expected to perform it while singing. The *goyang* involved a slow, circular, undulating motion centered on the hips that could progress up and down the body or stay in one place. This dance move was responsible for much of live dangdut's reputation for sensuality and eroticism (*erotis*). Particularly skilled female performers were said to possess a *goyang yang aduhai* (an astounding undulation), a phrase that recurred in emcees' spoken introductions. Male dangdut performers sometimes gestured and danced onstage, but they were evaluated based on their vocal rather than their dancing skills. Women performers, on the other hand, were evaluated based on their singing ability, dance movements, and physical appearance. Often strength in one category could offset criticism in another. Titiek Nur

once remarked to me that the only reason dangdut performers performed suggestive and sensual dance movements onstage was to draw
attention away from their deficiencies as singers.[2]

Dangdut and Gender Ideology

The scholarly encounter between gender studies and the anthropology
of Indonesia has been extraordinarily fruitful (Steedly 1999, 437–40).
The valuable insights contained in studies and edited volumes on the
subject (e.g., Brenner 1998; Cooper 2000; Ong and Peletz 1995; Sears
1996; Tsing 1993; Williams 2001) derive in part from the ability of their
authors to reflect productively on the contrast between the two competing gender ideologies, one broadly Western, the other broadly Southeast Asian, that inhabit such studies. To simplify a bit, the first views
men and women as two often hostile groups locked in an unending and
unequal struggle for power, a struggle in which women's bodies are ob-
jectified and made to serve a patriarchal order. The second concept of
gender difference is more prevalent in traditional Southeast Asian societies and regards men and women as making up two halves of a complementary whole. Ideally, in this view both groups struggle to preserve
harmony between the genders through their respective spheres of influence. According to anthropologist Nancy Cooper, in Java, "[a]lthough
the scales of gender balance tilt in favor of men, misogyny is rare; harmony is usually maintained, and (noninstitutionalized) violence kept in
check" (2000, 610). Contemporary urban Indonesia is influenced by
both views. Patriarchal capitalism and the commodification of female
sexuality coexist uneasily with older (equally patriarchal) discourses of
complementarity and respect for women's power (see Cooper 2000,
608–9; Brenner 1998). In Jakarta, the resulting tension is partially re-
solved through the figure of the *janda*, the widow or divorcée.

"Most women in dangdut clubs," a married, middle-aged Betawi
man once told me with obvious distaste, "are women who do not have
husbands [*yang tidak punya suami*]." *Janda*, the women who did not
have husbands but were once married, were seen as vulnerable and sexually available, and in everyday male parlance they were contrasted with
"virgins" (*perawan*) or "maidens" (*gadis*), never-married women whose
virtue must be respected and guarded. Young *janda* without children
were called "flower divorcées/widows" (*janda kembang*) and were considered desirable but of questionable morality. Thus it was regarded as
permissible to exploit those women who defied normative expectations;

the women who were neither still "virgins" nor half of a married couple were fair game for objectification and sexual commodification, while women who were married or not-yet-married were "kept safe" by a patriarchal code that supposedly "respected" (*menghormati*) women's power but in fact most valued female subservience to men.

The majority of the professional dangdut singers whom I interviewed were *janda* with children. Unlike the traditional singer-dancers described by Cooper, these dangdut singers did not have a respected Javanese or other ethnic "tradition" they could use to legitimate their vocation, and in the face of dominant cultural values they could only cite economic motivations resulting from a condition of poverty and want to explain why they sang (cf. Pioquinto 1995). "I only sing to get money [*cari duit*]," one club singer told me matter-of-factly. The husband of this particular singer had taken a second wife, leaving her essentially to her own devices to support herself and her young daughter. Often she had to leave her child at home alone when she was out at night singing at the clubs; on those occasions she gave the neighborhood watchman some "pocket money" (*uang saku*) to check on her daughter periodically during her absence.

But while the economic motivations for singing dangdut were painfully real, they could not account for the pride with which one singer told me she knew over one hundred songs, nor for the fact that the singer quoted in the preceding paragraph enjoyed singing dangdut at informal gatherings of musicians and had taught her daughter (who was in fact quite talented) to sing dangdut as well. While women rarely danced to dangdut music in public for their own enjoyment, dangdut producers told me that married women (*ibu rumah tangga*) constituted the majority of those who bought dangdut cassettes, and indeed the thematic material contained in most popular dangdut songs portrayed the typical agonies and heartbreaks of working-class Indonesian women's lives: husbands remarrying, husbands' infidelity, and abandonment by deceitful lovers. It is therefore entirely plausible that some dangdut singers sing about their own feelings and experiences and perform for their own enjoyment as well as for the purpose of entertaining a crowd. Thus, although dangdut concert stages can easily be viewed as places that objectify and exploit women, dangdut *songs* appeal to both genders, though perhaps for different reasons: while the music's danceability appeals to men, the lyrics appeal to women, and listening to and performing dangdut songs may in fact provide one way for Indonesian women to "relieve stress" in their own lives.

Audience Participation: The Wages of Sin?

The most common interaction between performers and audience was known as *saweran*, the public offering of monetary gifts. To *nyawer* meant to hand one or more rupiah bills to the singer while he or she was singing onstage. A single *saweran* ranged from the equivalent of US$0.08 to US$8.00 or more. Audience members would give an assortment of bill denominations that usually added up to small amounts at outdoor concerts and large sums at indoor nightclubs. Unlike the street musicians discussed in the previous chapter, dangdut singers never solicited monetary contributions. Offering them rupiah bills was a "sign of recognition" (Keane 1997) not only that a performance was taking place but also that it was a particularly effective performance. After graciously but wordlessly accepting the money, the singer, singing all the while, would casually toss it onto the floor near the back of the stage. The total amount of *saweran* was later split among the singers and musicians at the end of the night. At dangdut concerts audience members also sometimes climbed up to the stage and danced with the singer. Most were not brazen enough to actually try to *joget* with the singer, but rather ascended the stage in pairs and *joget*ted on either side of him or

Singer and fan holding *saweran* (monetary offerings), Cikanjur.

her. During their dance, one or both audience members would present *saweran* to the singer before finally descending from the stage.

Male dangdut singers also received money from the audience, but with female singers in particular the presentation of money by male audience members appeared to bring a release of built-up tension between the singer, the audience member, and the onlookers. In her study of "seduction scenarios" in rural Java, Cooper discusses how performances by women singer-dancers called *waranggana* (a more polite term for the more widely used *talèdhèk*) provide the opportunity for men to express their "potency" by their remaining "impassive in the face of temptation" (2000, 618). She writes, "In these seduction scenarios, men are publicly exposed to situations involving women who test their personal control and thus their ability to avoid a commotion and preserve the general harmony" (620). Although urban dangdut differs in numerous important respects from Javanese village performance traditions, the presentation of money to dangdut singers by male patrons also exhibits men's self-control and power, and for the audience it is a cathartic event, since it signifies the giver's intention to refrain from embracing or otherwise initiating improper physical contact with the singer, in spite of her charms as a "temptress."

The monetary offering thus has value not just as a display of personal wealth but as an index of personal restraint: the patron rewards the singer and the musicians for providing an opportunity to test his resolve in the face of sensual temptation. The greater the temptation, the higher the reward. *Saweran* is thus an example of gendered role playing in dangdut that illustrates the tensions in Indonesian working-class life between village-based conceptions of female and male power, on the one hand, and urban culture's tendency to commodify (and thus remove agency from) female sexuality, on the other. In a sense, then, dangdut singers and their male audiences live out the uneasy coexistence between different constructions of gender and agency by engaging in cultural practices such as *saweran* that, arguably, both respect and objectify the female performer whose performance is simultaneously a commodity and a channeler of powerful cultural forces.

Dangdut Clubs: Gender, Sexuality, and Relieving Stress

Dangdut concerts in Jakarta take place in a variety of performance settings, but they can be divided into two basic categories: those that take place in indoor nightclubs and those that take place on outdoor stages (*panggung*). The latter are sponsored events that are open to the public or charge a small admission fee, while the former are more expensive and cater to a well-heeled, mostly male clientele. Large and small live dangdut concerts of the second type are regular occurrences in poor urban neighborhoods, and they constitute one of the primary forms of popular entertainment for working-class city dwellers (cf. Murray 1991, 83; Browne 2000).[3]

Dangdut nightclubs were largely a Jakarta phenomenon. These establishments catered to working-class men with a modicum of disposable income, of whom there were many in Jakarta. ("Even a *tukang becak* [pedicab driver] can afford to come here!" claimed one nightclub patron. When I asked him to clarify how such an individual could possibly afford the nightclub's high prices, he added that it would have to be a *"tukang becak* who's just sold some land!") Dangdut clubs tended to be dark, loud, stuffy, and un-air-conditioned. (Many working-class Jakartans I met did not like air-conditioning, complaining that it made them too cold and caused susceptibility to illness.) They were considered places of ill repute by many Jakartans, and indeed, paid female companionship, outright prostitution, and the imbibing of alcoholic beverages (forbidden in Islam) were ubiquitous in, if not essential to, these establishments.

The dozen or so dangdut clubs I visited during the period of my fieldwork ranged from small, cramped rooms in outlying areas of Jakarta featuring small-time local performers to the lavish subterranean club Bintang-Bintang (Stars) located in an underground parking garage near the Blok M Bus Terminal, which attracted nationally known dangdut recording artists, including Iis Dahlia, Murni Cahnia, and Iyeth Bustami. The vast majority of dangdut singers, even at the upscale venues, were *kelas cere* (Betawi, "minnow class") performers who had little chance of becoming recording artists and who spent their careers performing songs from cassettes recorded by more successful entertainers.

The music at dangdut nightclubs was provided by an all-male house band and a rotating group of singers, usually five or six women and two or three men. The patrons were almost all men; women at dangdut clubs typically fell into three main categories: hostesses employed by the club, "freelancers," and singers. In many establishments, official hostesses (known in polite Indonesian as *pramuria*) wore uniforms or had identification cards clipped to their clothes to distinguish them from freelancers.[4] Women who engaged in *freelancing* (the English term was used) were sometimes prostitutes, sometimes simply young women looking for kicks. They were not employed by the club, but their presence was

Flyer for a March 2000 concert featuring recording artist Iis Dahlia at Bintang-Bintang, Blok M's most luxurious dangdut nightclub.

usually tolerated, since in the course of an evening they would order numerous expensive (but nonalcoholic) drinks at the bar for which their male companions were expected to pay, thus providing a source of additional revenue for the club.

Unlike most other places I visited in Jakarta, dangdut nightclubs were sites of significant alcohol consumption, despite the high prices of drinks at these venues. A middle-aged male dangdut fan and amateur singer told me that if one drinks alcohol while *joget*ting, one becomes not drunk, sick, and dizzy (*mabuk*) but just more relaxed, and the dance becomes more pleasing (*enak*). Alcohol also appeared to be a factor in determining the amount of *saweran* presented to performers by patrons. Visibly intoxicated men were often the most generous patrons, perhaps because the alcohol lessened their tendency toward frugality, but also because the temptation to lose one's self-control, which they were paying off, so to speak, with their gift of cash, was that much greater as a result of their compromised state. I occasionally observed visibly intoxicated patrons who did in fact initiate intimate physical contact with women on the dance floor, but this complete surrender to desire was unusual and certainly not valued by the other patrons. Such behavior was never directed toward a singer while she was performing.

One reason many men gave for liking dangdut is that it was "good to move to" (*enak bergoyang*) or "good to *joget* to" (*enak dijogetin*). It is worth noting that in my observation the majority of male patrons at dangdut clubs were content to dance with each other rather than with hostesses or freelancers. (This practice also meant a less expensive night out.) In fact, despite their unsavory reputation Jakarta's dangdut clubs were not considered major hubs for prostitution. Men who were mainly in search of sexual encounters tended to go elsewhere, to brothels or to the city's abundant discos, massage parlors, hotel coffee shops, and karaoke bars that specialize in sexual services (Hull, Sulistyaningsih, and Jones 1999, 57–62).

The "free," unchoreographed dancing at dangdut clubs relieves stress and is a tremendous source of pleasure for Indonesian men, especially when accompanied by a pulsating rhythm and a sensuous female voice (Spiller 2001). Dancers at dangdut clubs often wear an expression of unself-conscious bliss, eyes closed, mouth in a broad smile. This expression contrasts sharply with the neutral, deadpan face most adult male Jakartans tend to wear in public places and formal portraits. Dangdut performance, then, is more than musical entertainment. Live dangdut music at clubs creates a gendered social space where public displays

Dangdut singer Oppie Sendewi performing at Club Jali-Jali, Parung.

of euphoric emotions by men, generally uncommon in Indonesian society, are permissible.

More on Dangdut and "Stress"

"Getting rid of stress" (*hilangi stres*) was the most commonly voiced justification for male behavior in dangdut bars. Activities like dancing to dangdut music, watching attractive singers, and consuming alcohol were deemed necessary for relieving stress, which many men viewed as caused less by one's problems than by constantly worrying about them. Stress, according to one young Betawi dangdut enthusiast in his late twenties, results from "too much thinking about something" (*terlalu banyak mikirin*) and can be cured by "refreshing" (*represing*) activities such as *joget*ting, traveling to the countryside, and going to dangdut bars. But, as his father (also a longtime dangdut fan) commented, too much "refreshing" can also anger one's wife. I asked him what married women (as opposed to the unmarried women who frequent dangdut bars) do when they feel stressed. "They keep it stopped up inside [*membuntu*]!" was the lighthearted reply, and he held his breath and puffed up his cheeks to demonstrate.

Brenner (1998, 149–57) argues that in Solo, Central Java, men are expected to engage in "naughty" (*nakal*) activities and spend money irresponsibly in order to satisfy their "desires" (*nafsu;* Javanese, *nepsu*), while women, considered the anchors of the domestic sphere, are expected to repress their passions for the sake of the household. The difference in Jakarta is that the Western-influenced concept of "stress" is invoked to explain or excuse male behavior—an example of the heterogeneity of discourses surrounding Jakartan dangdut performance. Every aspect of the dangdut nightclub experience is designed to both relieve stress and extract money from patrons: the paid female companionship; the expensive, potent alcoholic beverages; the physical beauty and lavish dress of the singers; and of course the amplified sound of dangdut music performed live. Of course, spending all one's money at a dangdut club might in the end increase one's stress level, but this possibility did not seem to concern the male patrons with whom I spoke.

"Stage Dangdut": People's Music in the Urban Village

At Jakarta's dangdut clubs, the nightly dangdut performances were routinized and through repetition lost some of their "eventful" character. In

The author videotaping a neighborhood dangdut concert featuring the Betawi ensemble OMEGA Group, Lebak Bulus, South Jakarta. Photograph by Donny Suryady.

contrast, open-air concerts were relatively infrequent, special events. These outdoor performances in urban neighborhoods were the occasions where dangdut was closest to the people, the music at its most inclusive and participatory. Professional and semiprofessional dangdut bands played at festivals, at weddings, and at other sponsored affairs that were usually open to the general public free of charge or cost a nominal admission fee. They took place in open fields and backyards and could draw thousands of spectators from the surrounding *kampung* and beyond.

Many of those in the audience were young men who would *joget* in the crowded area in front of the stage, but children, older men, and married women, who usually stood around the dancing area in a large semicircle, were also present in large numbers. Young women were less common, particularly at nighttime events; those who did attend these performances, especially without boyfriends or husbands, were said to be "brash" or "brave" (*berani*).

For the most part, outdoor dangdut shows were intended for local young men, most of whom could not afford to frequent nightclubs, and at a successful show they would *joget* enthusiastically into the night, ogle the female performers, and shower them with money. According to

Susan Browne, "in a society where the poor have no economic, social, or political power, for male audiences at *dangdut kampungan* [*sic*] performances, singer-dancers represent an escape from their lack of power into a classless world of gendered power" (2000, 34). This "classless" world is dominated by glamorous spectacle, musical pleasure, and the dissolving of boundaries between participants, even as the complex dynamic of gendered exchange described above continues to operate between female performers and male audience members.

As mentioned earlier, the pleasure of *joget*ting is very much tied to the genre ideology of dangdut as a music that gets rid of stress. The following description is from an unusual *acara* at a wedding in a Betawi *kampung* on the far southern outskirts of Jakarta that began not with dangdut music but with music from a related genre that has a vastly different metacultural ideology attached to it.

Cirendeu, Saturday night, July 15, 2000
    The taxicab drops us off at the soccer field, the site of the evening's concert. It is a familiar scene: vendors' carts selling snacks and drinks line the path to the entrance and the perimeter of the concert site, the dim light from their kerosene lamps our only guide in the darkness. Mud and lack of visibility make the path treacherous as crowds of spectators make their way to the *acara*. Up ahead a brightly lit stage approximately eight feet high comes into view. Onstage are nine performing musicians in matching red uniforms playing music that sounds like dangdut. What strikes me as unfamiliar is the gaping, empty semicircular space in front of the stage, an area usually filled with swaying and shouting male audience members. A solitary figure gyrates eccentrically to the music; no one else seems to pay him any attention. He dances alone in the semicircle, seemingly in a trance, swaying back and forth without lifting his feet. He is occasionally joined by a few small boys between the ages of seven and ten who squat down in the mud and watch the show for a while before rejoining the large crowd gathered around the semicircle. Everyone else is holding back.
    I ask why almost no one is dancing. An audience member tells me that the music playing isn't dangdut but *qasidah* or *gambus* (he says he isn't sure which one, though it is almost certainly the former)— syncretic, Islam-identified genres sung in Indonesian and Arabic. The instrumentation is identical to that used in dangdut, save for the addition of a green electric violin, which is played by an older man who

also acts as the event's master of ceremonies. The sound is very similar to dangdut, but the vocals are less sensual and more florid. The young woman singers are all wearing colorful evening gowns and brightly colored Muslim headscarves; the latter appear to have the effect of restraining the large young, male audience from interacting with them. During the emcee's lengthy orations between songs, members of the audience impatiently shout, "Dang-DHUT!" Their hoarse demands are ignored, but finally the last of the *qasidah* songs is played, the singers suddenly lose their headscarves, and less than a minute into the first new song the semicircle in front of the stage is packed with dancing young men. Older men, women, and children remain in the crowd surrounding the de facto dance floor. The same singers sing as before, with the help of a middle-aged, offstage singer who doubles their vocals. Now the singers in front of the stage have to contend with the more brazen members of the crowd below them grabbing their dresses and reaching out their hands when they draw near. The singers are now also occasionally joined onstage by a series of male dancers from the audience who ascend in pairs and present small-denomination rupiah bills to the singers as they dance on either side of them. In other words, the event has been speedily transformed into a typical dangdut concert in every respect.

Although musical performance's ability to create a feeling of social solidarity among participants is taken as a given by many music scholars, how this actually occurs is a murky issue. The example described above underscores the ways such claims should be qualified. Dangdut concerts bring people together in part through sonic characteristics deemed attractive by listeners, such as danceable rhythms, attractive melodies, and the comfortable familiarity of a standard song repertoire. Beyond this, the essential ingredient is a metacultural understanding of the dangdut genre that defines the music as quintessentially Indonesian (*ciri khas Indonesia*), intensely pleasurable (*asyik*), and belonging to everyone (*musik kita-kita*, "the music of all of us"). Thus while the *qasidah* played by the band at the *acara* described above was musically not very distinct from dangdut, its metacultural definition as an "Arab" music of Muslim piety and seriousness discouraged dancing and euphoric feelings among all but the most oblivious members of the audience, children and madmen. Once music recognized as "dangdut" started, a feeling of *communitas* appeared to arise among the now actively engaged audience members as they danced together in front of the stage.

Audience at an outdoor dangdut concert in Cikanjur.

Of course, genre ideology is by itself not sufficient to create *communitas*, that state of undifferentiated oneness with the assembled collective that Victor Turner (1967) identifies as a central goal of ritual. To be efficacious the performance must be good according to established aesthetic criteria. The evaluative dimensions I heard most often from fans included the quality of the sound system, the skill of the *gendang* player, the singer's voice, and the appearance and dancing ability of female performers. Dangdut performances that excelled in these criteria were sure to create a feeling of unity in the audience, and the local reputations of the band and the singer would benefit accordingly.

Dangdut Hybridity

The drive for inclusiveness, itself an outgrowth of everyday Indonesian sociality, characterized dangdut performances. In addition to the musically eclectic *selingan,* the instrumental interludes that connected the different singers' turns at the microphone, other musical genres regularly emerged at dangdut concerts and could take surprising forms. In dangdut nightclubs, the band often took a break during which *house dangdut, jaipong, house jaipong, dangdut disco,* and Western house music cassettes were played and the dance floor filled with patrons attempting to dance to these alternative rhythms. In one nightclub I visited, the band itself played a long instrumental *jaipongan* piece, cleverly using the electric dangdut instruments in ways that convincingly mimicked the sounds of the Sundanese gamelan instruments that usually performed this genre. According to a singer at the club, music played in this fashion was called *pong-dhut* (*jaipong* and dangdut).[5]

Outdoor concerts may represent dangdut in its quintessential state—a people's music available even to those who cannot afford to buy cassettes—but even at these events dangdut often coexisted with other genres. In the spring of 2000, the popular Indian film song "Kuch Kuch Hota Hai" (Hindi, "Something, Something Generally Happens") was often performed at dangdut concerts. Two popular Indonesian ska songs, one a *ska Cirebon* composition sung in a Cirebonese dialect of Javanese, the other a more conventional ska song performed in Indonesian by Tipe-X, entered the "stage dangdut" (*dangdut panggung*) repertoire. Oppie Sendewi, a popular local dangdut singer, described these ska songs as "*ska-dut*" since they were played with dangdut instrumentation (which in fact was not that different from that of a traditional ska group). The young male audience responded enthusiastically to these

Oppie Sendewi and fans at an outdoor concert, Serpong.

songs, shifting from *joget*ting to the more aggressive "running in place" dancing style associated with ska. At one concert, young men formed ska dance circles with their arms around one another. Thus the inclusive universe of dangdut continues to expand outward, embracing (nationalized) global musical trends as source material for populist national entertainments.

The inclusion of non-dangdut genres in dangdut performance events as "breaks" is matched by dangdut's shadowy presence at pop and underground concerts. But rather than constituting only an embellishment and a gesture toward inclusiveness in the performance frame, dangdut's incursions into concerts featuring these more westernized genres are more likely to resemble a return of the repressed.

9

Rock and Pop Events

THE PERFORMANCE OF LIFESTYLE

Chapter 7 investigated the *acara* as a culturally meaningful unit, and the preceding chapter applied those insights specifically to the world of dangdut performance. We learned how musical performance could break down social boundaries and explored the central role of genre and gender ideologies in conditioning concert-related behaviors. This chapter extends the analysis to include two middle-class-oriented rock and pop events: bands performing at upscale cafés, and student-organized concert festivals. We will see how traces of dangdut and other excluded genres appear in these settings, often in unexpected ways, and also how these types of *acara* contribute to national cultural debates over class, gender, and Indonesian identity in the contemporary world.

Café Music: *Top Forty* Cover Bands

Most young, upwardly mobile Jakartans with whom I spoke (including those in the dangdut recording business) expressed fear of and disgust toward dangdut nightclubs and could never imagine setting foot in one. For them, nightlife in the city consisted of an assortment of trendy cafés and bars featuring Western-style rock/pop bands playing the latest imported and Indonesian hits plus some old chestnuts. I found that the instrumentation of these bands (generally known as *Top Forty* groups) was almost as standardized as that of live dangdut ensembles. The typical *Top Forty* lineup consisted of three singers—one male, two female, usually wearing tight black clothing—backed by an all-male band composed of an electric guitarist, a keyboardist, an electric bassist, a trap drummer, and a percussionist. The latter played congas, bongos, timbales, cymbals, and the like—all foreign imports—rather than any indigenous percussion instruments. Generally, the male vocalist also acted as the emcee at the band's performances, addressing the audience and soliciting song requests. Groups of this sort played regularly in café districts like Kemang; in fashionable Central Jakarta clubs like Bengkel Night Park, Hard Rock Café, and Planet Hollywood; in upscale mall food courts (such as the one in Plaza Indonesia); and other urban venues frequented by Indonesian elites and expatriates from North America, Asia, Europe, and Australia.

During my stay in Indonesia, the repertoire of these *Top Forty* groups was remarkably uniform at any given time and consisted of about 75 percent foreign and 25 percent domestic songs. One male vocalist told me that Western hits tended to remain popular longer than *pop Indonesia* songs did, and therefore learning to play the former was a better time investment. When I asked *Top Forty* performers if they preferred Indonesian or Western pop, they invariably answered that it depended on the particular song. A male singer added that Western pop was more difficult for men to sing because it required a higher vocal range, whereas *pop Indonesia*, with a few exceptions like Dewa 19, was usually sung in a lower, more comfortable part of the male vocal range. He added that women's vocals were just as difficult in both categories, an observation with which his female colleague agreed.

In addition to Indonesian- and English-language pop (the latter including hits by artists ranging from Elvis Presley to 'N Sync), *Top Forty* bands played regional *pop Batak* and *pop Menado* songs when they were requested, and, as I discovered, most *Top Forty* groups knew how to play at least two dangdut songs. These songs inevitably included "Terlena" (Swept Away); popularized by singer Ikke Nurjanah, and "Kopi Dangdut" (Dangdut Coffee), a highly danceable song recorded by Fahmy Shahab and based on a melody pilfered from the international Latin hit "Moliendo Café."[1] It was not entirely clear why these two songs in particular were popular among middle-class audiences; it is perhaps significant that the lyrics of both songs describe being "swept away": the refrain of the former contains the pivotal line *Ku terlena asmara* (I've been swept away by romantic passion), while the verses of the latter repeats the lines

Dan jantungku seakan ikut irama
Karena terlena
Oleh pesona
Alunan Kopi Dangdut!

[And it's as if my heart follows the beat
Because I've been carried away
By the bewitching spell
Of the Dangdut Coffee Rhythm!]

If dangdut constitutes an irresistible intervention in social space, these lyrics could be interpreted as celebrating the blissful surrender of the listener to the seductions of that music. This theme seems rather appropriate for dangdut songs appealing to middle-class Indonesians who feel the sensuous pull of dangdut music in spite of themselves, and who must appear to surrender a portion of their self-control in order to enjoy it. Whatever the reasons for their popularity, "Terlena" and "Kopi Dangdut" were part of the nightly sets of many *Top Forty* bands, and if one requested a dangdut song from the group (as I did on several occasions, to the utter astonishment of the performers), one usually heard one of those two compositions.

As in many other contexts where dangdut music was introduced, the moment at which a *Top Forty* band launched into a dangdut composition after a series of pop songs produced a transformative effect on the café setting, even though the dangdut songs were performed without the trademark *gendang* and *suling* instruments. The band members onstage frequently lost their usual serious demeanor, which conveyed concentration and professionalism, and smiled openly at one another and at the audience. Some musicians would even start to *joget* onstage as they played their instruments. Interestingly, these gestures and facial expressions were markedly different from the stone-faced, sober expressions usually worn by "real" dangdut instrumentalists performing in clubs, on outdoor stages, and on television (cf. Browne 2000, 24); instead they resembled the blissful behavior of dangdut *fans*. The performers in a sense became their own audience: they were entertained by the music they themselves were playing, and their onstage comportment enacted the "relieving stress" effects of dangdut for the vicarious enjoyment of the spectators. Significantly, in addition to fulfilling certain genre-based expectations of dangdut's euphoria-inducing properties, the performers' stance also distanced them somewhat from the composition that they were playing, as if both they and the audience were coconspirators in a game of simultaneous enjoyment and disavowal.

Often the audience was unwilling to actually dance when café bands played dangdut songs but was nonetheless quite appreciative—deciding, perhaps, that an upscale café was a safe place to enjoy the occasional dangdut song without being considered *kampungan*. In 1999–2000, in addition to songs by the likes of Santana, Whitney Houston, Backstreet Boys, *pop alternatif* group Sheila on 7, and Indonesian singer/songwriter Melly Goeslaw (particularly "Jika," her hit duet with former Dewa 19 vocalist Ari Lasso), *Top Forty* bands often played "Terlena" and "Kopi Dangdut" toward the end of their set, and these two songs often received the most enthusiastic responses of the night. Many middle-class urban Indonesians admitted to me that although they disliked most dangdut songs, they really enjoyed "Terlena" and "Kopi Dangdut"—the reason they gave for this was that these songs could be heard in the nightspots they frequented. These two songs, which were also well known and popular among members of dangdut's core audience (among my field recordings is an impassioned male falsetto version of "Terlena" performed at the Pondok Cinta; see chapter 6), provided the opportunity for café musicians and audiences to indulge in dangdut's guilty pleasures. The popularity of these compositions lends evidence to the oft-voiced argument that urban middle-class Indonesians secretly enjoy dangdut but for reasons of status and prestige (*gengsi*) pretend that they do not.

Though they inhabit very different social and musical worlds, in some respects Indonesian *Top Forty* bands resemble *pengamen*, the roving urban street musicians discussed in chapter 7. Performers in both categories attempt to please an audience and make a living by embodying through performance a particular musicscape, and both try to maintain a repertoire of currently popular songs. On the other hand, café musicians are conduits for global sounds, and their polished renditions of pop hits bring an aura of cosmopolitan leisure and sophistication to the spaces they inhabit. Street musicians do not have access to these channels of cultural and material power and instead, with the limited means at their disposal, reproduce familiar songs that gesture not to the phantasmagoric, glamorous world outside Indonesia, but to everyday life with all its hardships. *Pengamen* are considered a nuisance because their humble, impoverished presentations are devoid of escapism—they embody the grim realities of life that deflate the pop fantasies of the songs they sing. In contrast, *Top Forty* bands' performances, like malls, invite members of Indonesia's affluent minority to pretend they are in an imaginary, postnational elsewhere removed from the squalor and want of Jakarta's streets.

Student-Organized Musical Events

Unlike the entertainment at awards shows discussed in chapter 7, the repertoires of *Top Forty* groups index the transnational character of the contemporary popular musicscape in Indonesia, though they also show a marked tendency toward xenocentrism. To appreciate the full range of musical options that exist for urban Indonesian youth, we must turn to the less self-consciously urbane, more grassroots-based types of performance events organized by and for young Indonesians themselves.

A common type of popular music event in Jakarta and other large Indonesian cities at the turn of the millennium was the daylong music festival organized by university or middle-class high school students. Such events could last over twelve hours, with forty or more amateur, semiprofessional, and professional performing ensembles participating. The most elaborate of these festivals were held in soccer stadiums, attracting thousands of spectators—mostly fashionable, cell phone-toting middle-class youth. These young people were able to afford the price of admission, which in 1999–2000 ranged from 11,000 to 15,000 rupiahs (at the time, less than US$2.00), a substantial sum for working-class Indonesians. As mentioned in chapter 7, the two key components of student-organized *acara* were a committee (*panitia*) composed of peers, which coordinated the affair and a sponsor or sponsors, usually corporations that covered the costs of mounting the event in exchange for the opportunity to advertise their products at the site. These *acara* were advertised through colorful flyers that listed the sponsors, headlining bands, and the time and location of the event, and were posted on university campuses and other locations where middle-class youths congregate.

Because most *acara* in Jakarta obtained sponsorships from major corporations, they tended to be larger and more elaborate affairs than student-organized events in the United States. Standard provisions included an enormous stage with professional-quality sound and lighting, a wide assortment of instrument amplifiers, two large video-projection screens on either side of the stage, and (invariably) a fog machine. The most humble student rock group participating in the event had the

Kresikars 2000, a student-organized *acara* in Kuningan Stadium.

opportunity to play on the same stage and through the same sound equipment as the headlining artists. Also, committees could often afford to invite the most popular recording artists of the day to perform at their events. These headliners, who played short sets of five or six songs, commonly took the stage at ten or eleven at night, more than twelve hours after the official start of the event. At first I was surprised to find successful recording artists like Gigi, Melly Goeslaw, Netral, Padi, and /rif good-humoredly tolerating extremely Spartan backstage accommodations—often little more than a cramped, windowless dressing room with no indoor plumbing and a thin curtain for a door—in order to play at these events. The reward for tolerating these conditions was the opportunity to play before a large, enthusiastic audience of young music fans—though many in the audience, after having spent an entire day under the hot sun watching less-established groups perform, would be quite exhausted by the time the headlining acts took the stage.

As one might expect in such a self-conscious cultural arena, references to local, national, and global musical genres, both present and absent, abounded at student-organized *acara*. Dangdut was a frequent subject of attempts at humor; the very presence of (prerecorded) dangdut music at such events often sufficed to provoke embarrassed and riotous laughter from the audience. At one event, when the stage was momentarily lit by yellow lights, an emcee commented that it was "like a dangdut concert" (Indonesians with whom I spoke considered yellow to be an especially low-class color). At another, clowns and cross-dressers indulged in lascivious dances when a dangdut song played on the prerecorded soundtrack; this received an uproarious response from the middle-class student audience.

Most bands that performed at student-organized *acara* were relatively inexperienced and played other bands' songs. In Jakarta and Bandung, they seemed to cover English-language songs exclusively, while at concert events in Yogyakarta I witnessed bands performing songs by Indonesian rock bands Gigi, Pas, and /rif. Bands that played at *acara* were divided into three categories: *band seleksi* were amateur bands that paid a fee to audition and were selected by the organizing committee, *band dukungan* (supporting bands) were more experienced and accomplished student groups invited to perform at the event, and *bintang tamu* (guest stars) were often full-time professional musicians and included nationally recognized recording artists.

"Guest star" bands were paid for their appearance; they included bands that performed skillful covers of Western groups and those that played their own compositions. Most artists in the latter category, which included established underground groups as well as bands signed to large commercial record labels, had recorded their own albums, while those in the former group had not. Each of the *bintang tamu* cover bands specialized in one Western style or artist; for example, Tor, one of the more creative Jakarta-based performing groups, specialized in covering the songs of 1960s rock legend Jimi Hendrix. Similarly, a Jakartan group called Rastafari played Bob Marley songs and other examples of 1970s reggae, the popular cover band T-Five was known for its versions of 1990s hip hop and R & B songs, and a dozen or so groups specialized in replicating the sounds of "hip metal" artists such as Korn and Limp Bizkit. These groups often endeavored to reproduce not only the sounds of the bands they covered but also their costumes and stage moves, which they learned through studying live concert videos. In general, the guest-star cover bands' repertoires differed little from those of the younger groups that preceded them. At a single event it was not unusual to hear the same Rage Against the Machine or Korn song performed five or six times by different bands possessing vastly different skill levels.

Not all cover bands aimed to create exact replicas of preexisting songs. Tor, the band mentioned earlier, was unique among the cover

Hendrik, Tor's *gendang* player, performing at Kresikars 2000.

groups I observed in that it included in its lineup a traditional
musician—a Sundanese *kendang* (barrel drum) player—who added his
own parts to the Western pop and rock songs performed by the band.
Often the rock instruments in the ensemble (the band also had a drummer, a guitarist, a bassist, and a keyboardist) completely drowned out the
kendang, though Tor did play one song—a departure from their usual
repertoire of Jimi Hendrix covers—that featured it prominently: a humorous version of the New Kids on the Block song "Step by Step." Not
only was it unusual for a group specializing in classic rock covers to play
a song made famous by the quintessential 1980s "boy band," this particular rendition featured a lengthy and virtuosic *jaipong*-style *kendang* solo
in the middle of the song that garnered an enthusiastic response from
the audience.

But why were the students cheering? The answer is no doubt complex; certainly the audacious aural and visual juxtaposition of traditional
drumming with a song regarded as a paragon of Western pop commer-
cialism appeared to be an undeniable source of pleasure for audience
members. In Tor's performance, the "local," represented by an "ethnic"
musical tradition, could be heard and seen "colonizing" a globally hegemonic music product, and the response was laughter and applause. Significantly, Tor *chose* to incorporate traditional music—they were not

"resorting" to ethnic sounds because of an inability to perform global popular music correctly. In fact, the band's ability to master Western rock was well demonstrated elsewhere in their set by their energetic and tight renditions of the Jimi Hendrix compositions "Crosstown Traffic" and "Purple Haze."

Tor, like most other cover bands, aspired to write original material and record an album, though by their own admission they had not yet begun taking steps to achieve this goal. In fact, many successful Indonesian rock and pop groups began as cover bands on the live performance circuit, and many remain strongly associated with the Western groups whose songs they used to play. For example, the rock group The Fly was well known among Jakarta students as a U2 cover band before they began to record their own material, which, not surprisingly, resembles the Irish band's music.

Deena Weinstein's sociological analysis of heavy metal concerts in the West divides participants into three spatially and socially distinct groups: performing artists, "backstage workers" (technicians, roadies, stage managers, etc.), and audience (1991, 199–205). I found that a distinguishing feature of live rock and pop music performances at Indonesian student-organized events is the lack of a strict separation between classes of participants, in particular the visibility of backstage personnel and audience members onstage—on the performer's turf, so to speak. Although some distinctions between groups of participants persist, they are blurred in the course of the concert event. The committee (*panitia*) plays a special mediating role. Its members generally lack technical roles in the proceedings but are free to watch from the stage, sharing space with performers in full view of the audience, their matching, custom-made T-shirts setting them apart from other participants. I took photographs of performers onstage at most of the *acara* I attended, and I noticed that I always had difficulty photographing bands' drummers. Due to their customary position toward the back of the stage, drummers were often completely surrounded by *panitia* members who preferred to watch the show from that position. Often these nonperformers completely or partially blocked the drummer from the audience's view, especially if he or she was playing with an especially popular group. No one ever asked these onstage onlookers to move out of the way. One band photographer, Helvi from Bandung, solved the problem by shooting pictures while standing atop a riser at the rear of the stage in order to gain an unobstructed, bird's-eye view of the drummer.

The Economics of Student Music Festivals

An important task of the *panitia* is to obtain sponsors for the event; this is usually not difficult. A number of companies—both international and Indonesian—that target their products at affluent youth have sponsored music *acara*. Major sponsors for musical events I attended included Close-Up toothpaste, Sprite, Arby's, McDonald's, Zevit-C vitamins, Teh Kita ("Our [inclusive] Tea," a national bottled tea beverage), Chips Ahoy! cookies, Bisik.com (a student-oriented Web site [*bisik* = whisper]), *Hai* (a youth-oriented pop culture magazine), Baskin-Robbins ice cream, and the national dairy-product company Indomilk.

Although not usually involved with school-affiliated concerts, Indonesian *kretek* (clove cigarette) brands such as Djarum Super, Gudang Garam, Bentoel, and Sampoerna frequently sponsored other youth-oriented live musical events, and audience members often received a free pack of cigarettes with the price of admission. Sponsors' products were heavily promoted at *acara*. Fast food companies operated well-staffed booths selling refreshments during the event, banners and posters advertising the sponsors' wares decorated the stage and the surrounding area, and television advertisements for the products were played repeatedly on large projection video screens between acts (recall the *Mildcoustic* event discussed in chapter 7).

Televisual images were an integral part of most pop and rock *acara*, and not just those that were broadcast for a home television audience. In addition to showing sponsors' advertisements, *acara* video screens were also used to project Western rock videos and concert footage during the breaks between bands. These sequences of imported videos, which were painstakingly assembled beforehand in a video editing studio, generally received a positive response from the audience, often far more positive than that generated by most of the local bands. Also, many *acara* screened their own custom-made computer animation sequences, which incorporated the event's logo and the list of event sponsors. These multimedia presentations were not "supplements" to the live performances but were an integral part of the *acara*. In fact there is no reason to assume that the bands' presentations were any less "mediated" than the video sequences, since their performances were often themselves self-conscious replications of the sounds, movements, and images of imported concert videos.

Acara Expresi: "Noceng Nodrugs"

The following is description of an *acara* organized by the Faculty of Communications at Moestopo University, Jakarta. The title of the *acara*, "Noceng Nodrugs" (No Drugs 2000), was created by a combination of Jakartanese (*Noceng* means "two thousand," a term borrowed from Hokkien Chinese) and English words; together they described the main theme of the event.[2] Many youth-organized *acara* of the time shared the "say no to drugs in the new millennium" theme, as awareness of the problems of drug abuse grew more widespread among Indonesian youth in the late 1990s.

12:30 p.m., July 30, 2000

It is a sweltering afternoon in the Senayan Sports Complex in Central Jakarta.[3] Student rock bands have been playing since morning, but very few audience members have arrived to watch them. A tent covers the stage; the unprotected, sun-drenched concrete basketball courts in front of the stage are still devoid of people. Behind the basketball courts is a larger tent housing a series of booths: food stands, a student photography exhibit, a display of leftist books and T-shirts run by the Universitas Moestopo School of Communications, an exhibit advertising a drug rehabilitation facility, and a large stand operated by a store called Underground, which has branches in Bandung and Bintaro, South Jakarta. The stand is selling pirated Western recordings and videos and a few nonpirated Indonesian underground cassettes. Also on sale are T-shirts, wool hats, jewelry, bandanas, sunglasses, and other accessories, as well as a row of large posters, mostly of popular Western bands like Blink 182, Slipknot, Rancid, and the Beastie Boys. There is even a colorful Che Guevara print.

The student photo exhibit provides a fascinating glimpse into middle-class Indonesian student culture. The display includes several photographs of the November 13, 1998, "Semanggi Tragedy," a notorious incident during which as many as eight unarmed student protesters were killed by soldiers during a demonstration in Central Jakarta.[4] The photographs include a violent confrontation between protesters and riot police, a group of student protesters observing evening prayers (*syolat maghrib*), a profusely bleeding student being carried off by his comrades, and a large picture of cars set ablaze in front of Atma Jaya University, which is located in the Semanggi area.

Another category of photographs portrays typical scenes from Indonesian life: schoolchildren in uniform, a young *kampung* mother and child, a garbage-strewn Jakarta cityscape. Finally, there is a still life, an abstract figure study, and two pictures of Indonesian rock singers performing (Armand Maulana from Gigi and Andy from /rif). I conclude that the exhibit combines some recurring themes in student life: a somewhat detached and aestheticized view of the life of ordinary Indonesians, the desire for artistic self-expression, and at least a sentimental attachment to politics. The day's performances provide further examples of these central themes.

The headlining "guest stars" at this particular *acara* included alternative rock band Netral, veteran Jakarta hardcore group Step Forward, alternative pop band Padi (which would later release one of the most commercially successful recordings in Indonesian history), Balcony, a Bandung-based "emo-core" (emotional hardcore punk) band, and a cover band specializing in the music of the 1960s American rock group The Doors. But these bands would not take the stage until long after sundown. Until evening arrived, a more eclectic than usual assortment of ensembles performed in the hot sun for a small but growing crowd.

3:30 p.m.–10:00 p.m.

The musical offerings at the start of the day are rather predictable. The stage is occupied by a succession of high school–and university student–aged bands covering songs by contemporary Western rock groups. Their audience consists of a mere ten people huddled under the shade of an umbrella below the stage. To the right of the performers the event planning committee (*panitia*), all dressed in matching white T-shirts emblazoned with the *acara*'s name, gather under the shade of a small grove of trees. They drink from their own water cooler, off-limits to regular audience members.

As the day progresses, there is greater variety in the performances. A group of young women in traditional, folkloric dress sing and perform an Acehnese dance. I later learn that the members of the troupe are students from SMA 70, a Jakarta high school, and that none are actually from Aceh, a province in northern Sumatra that has long been the site of a separatist rebellion against the Indonesian government. There is also a clown (*pelawak*) act, a demonstration by a *silat* (Indonesian martial arts) troupe, a cheerleading routine complete with pompoms, and a male a cappella group that performs songs from a number of different genres, from a Bob Marley reggae composition to 1970s American soft rock to 1950s rock and roll. Their clever all-vocal arrangements of two dangdut songs receive an especially positive reaction, and a few audience members even begin to *joget* enthusiastically in response. The group performs a rhyming, spoken passage in the middle of their second dangdut song, the ever-popular "Kopi Dangdut," in an aggressive American rap style, to the audience's amusement.

By sundown, after the break for evening prayers (which, as usual, I see no one actually performing), the audience has grown to around 250 people. As the evening progresses, the emcees—one man and one woman—stage dancing contests, quiz the audience, and give out prizes provided by the event's sponsors in the intervals between band performances. They also spend a considerable amount of time speaking with a mentally handicapped audience member, their gentle teasing eliciting laughter from the audience while at the same time establishing his significance as a participant in the event.

This description captures some of the basic patterns of the *acara* and highlights its juxtaposition of folkloric performance, humor, Western rock music, and consumerism. At the event described above, regional music from Aceh was appropriated in the name of the nation, aspects of global youth culture were appropriated in the name of trendiness and fashion, and national cultural forms were performed, parodied, celebrated, and hybridized.

Women and Performance Revisited

At student-organized *acara*, the gender roles that predominate at dangdut concerts, in which women are dangerous objects of desire and men exhibit their mastery over their passions as a way of relieving stress, are largely absent. In their place are equally complicated constellations of gendered meanings saturated by class differences and global popular culture influences. Women musicians were a small minority at *acara* I attended, but women's contributions to the event often took forms other than musical performance. Between bands there were sometimes "fashion shows" during which young models wearing student-designed outfits strode across the stage to the sound of loud, prerecorded, usually Western, music. In Jakarta, student events often featured troupes of young women in tight-fitting, matching outfits who, much like cheerleaders at an American athletic event, performed precisely choreographed dance routines to a prerecorded soundtrack. These troupes collectively composed their own choreography, and their internal organization seemed to parallel that of the male-dominated rock bands. "Women are soft/graceful" (*wanita lembut*) was the reason one male audience member offered to explain why women formed dance troupes, but I suspect that another reason was that, like the mostly male members of cover bands, they too wanted to experience embodying the icons of Western popular culture through mimetic performance.

The women's moves and costumes were extremely suggestive and risqué by Indonesian standards, and for that reason their performances often received an enthusiastic response from male audience members. The soundtrack for their dances was usually a cassette containing a homemade montage of electronic dance or R & B songs, each segment usually lasting less than a minute before an abrupt transition to the next. The dance moves occasionally drew on traditional sources (many middle-class Indonesian girls take classes in Balinese and Javanese traditional dance in a manner similar to the way many Western girls study ballet) but were clearly mostly inspired by the dancing in Western hip hop and R & B music videos. Unlike dangdut singers or the "women without husbands" who dance at dangdut clubs, the young women's performance did not seem to signal a lack of virtue or sexual availability. Their cosmopolitan style resulted from a playful, collective impersonation of global divas. In a sense, the "truth value" of their impersonations was analogous to that of a cover band playing a Western pop song.

One composition frequently performed by both café and student cover bands was Sting's "An Englishman in New York." When the vocalist sang the line in the refrain, "I'm an Englishman in New York," the audience was well aware that the singer was neither British nor residing in New York City. Similarly, the sensual moves of the Indonesian dancers were not intended to permanently liken their (assumed to be virginal) bodies to the dancing, sexualized bodies of the virtual (but not virtuous) Western women who originally performed these movements. This mimetic relationship differs somewhat from that between the Acehnese song and dance and the non-Acehnese performers at the Noceng No Drugs concert event. In the latter case, the women in the ensemble were not members of the Acehnese ethno-linguistic group, but they shared the same nationality as the Acehnese. Appropriating the expressive culture of Aceh was therefore an example of the folkloricization that accompanies nation-building projects (Bruner 2001), though in this instance it appeared to be the product of a grassroots initiative, rather than a direct intervention by the state.

Marc Schade-Poulsen (1999) describes male Algerian *raï* fans' perceptions of women as divided into three categories: "good" Muslim women; "bad" Muslim women who only want money; and Western women, who are perceived as attractive and offering unconditional love and devotion, standing somehow outside the moral standards and expectations of reciprocity that characterize Algerian society. The third category existed largely in the imagination of Schade-Poulsen's informants, yet it nonetheless had powerful effects on their attitudes toward the opposite gender. These three categories correspond remarkably to those discussed by contemporary Indonesian youth. The women in the dance troupes temporarily inhabited the roles of Western women—like those on MTV—whose sexuality was not subject to the moral reprobation of Islam or of "traditional" Indonesian values. As a result of this cultural mimesis, they had a freedom of expression that women in other parts of Indonesia, even in other cities, lacked.

The relative flexibility of gender roles at student-organized events indicates the presence of more westernized and flexible notions of masculinity and femininity, whereas dangdut concerts exhibit traditional gender understandings as mass, commodified entertainment. However, the differences between dangdut performance and the performance of women dance troupes are less the product of cultural differences between the more conservative lower classes and the more cosmopolitan middle-to-upper classes than they are the result of *class difference itself.* The young women onstage were not *janda* (divorcées/widows), and they were not performing for economic survival. When asked, their members explain that their troupes were formed "just for fun" (*iseng-iseng aja*), and that they, like amateur rock musicians, were merely pursuing a "hobby" (*hobi*), with all the wholesomeness that term implies in both English and Indonesian usage.

The privileged status of these middle-class, educated teenagers gives them an "obtuse purity," even when they choose to become "experimental girls" (*perempuan eksperimen* or *perek*) from the middle or upper class who engage in premarital sex for money or kicks (Hull, Sulistyaningsih, and Jones 1999, 18; see also Murray 1991, 119–20). According to a published study of prostitution in Indonesia, "[t]he behavior of these [experimental] girls, many of whom are middle class and still at school, represents a considerable challenge to official norms. It is strongly influenced by materialism and rising expectations fuelled by the media and advertising; it stresses individualism, [and] having sexual relations with whomever they like, whether paid or unpaid" (Hull, Sulistyaningsih, and Jones 1999, 18).

While female dangdut singers display themselves on stage for economic reasons, and because of their impoverished condition may be available for paid sexual encounters, becoming an experimental girl is a *lifestyle choice*, albeit an extreme (and probably rarer than commonly reported) one. Dangdut singers and professional prostitutes are driven by economic necessity, but middle-class adolescents and postadolescents possess the economic security and cultural capital to play with the sexual and social identities made available through "the media and advertising." Although most do not become sexual adventurers, some young middle-class women may choose to perform borrowed cosmopolitan identities in the safety of a student-oriented event that celebrates the ability of upwardly mobile young Jakartans to make their own temporary identity choices in a boisterous cultural marketplace of heterogeneous commodities, images, styles, and sounds.

10

Underground Music

IMAGINING

ALTERNATIVE COMMUNITY

Underground music is the third genre category in our discussion of live musical performance. While the rock and pop festivals discussed in chapter 9 frequently included underground groups, this chapter investigates the social meanings of *acara* that were exclusively devoted to underground music and the communities those *acara* purported to represent. These events resemble the more heterogeneous rock and pop events in many ways, but interestingly, though they seem to offer youth greater autonomy from the dominant adult-controlled mainstream, the range of gendered subject positions underground concerts allow are, if anything, more restrictive. Young men wear similar uniforms depending on the genre of choice and a portion of them partake in specific, predictable dance behaviors. Women audience members, who usually make up a small minority at underground shows, seem freer to defy the unofficial dress code, but on the other hand are likely to refrain from dancing or other forms of active participation in the proceedings. Female performers are likewise rare, and generally are relegated to supporting roles.

My analysis of underground music events further extends my general argument that popular music performances in Indonesia are important loci of playful contestation over alternative modernities based on different articulations of local, national, and global forms. Nonetheless, despite this contestation, the desired outcome of live performance, regardless of the particular genre(s) being played, is a positive feeling among the participants, one of experiential "sharedness" that suspends, at least temporarily, the preexisting social differences that impede the production of solidarity. Underground concert events, despite their often overtly oppositional stance toward the national mainstream, are not exceptions to this general aim. What makes underground concerts distinctive is the *imagined alternative community* such solidarity evokes, a community based on belonging to a global subculture of musical production and consumption.

Daniel Miller, an innovator in the anthropology of consumption and consumers, argues that contemporary consumption practices can and do generate novel forms of identity and community around the world. He suggests the phrase "a posteriori diversity" to describe the condition resulting from this process and argues that it is qualitatively different from "a priori diversity," which is created by separate local histories that predate the consumption practices of modernity. Miller describes a posteriori diversity as "the sense of quite unprecedented diversity created by the differential consumption of what had once been thought to be global and homogenizing institutions" (1995, 3). He adds, "The idea of a posteriori diversity allows for the possibility of more radical rupture under conditions of modernity, but does not assume that homogenization follows. Rather it seeks out new forms of difference, some regional, but increasingly based on social distinctions not easily identified with space. It treats these, not as continuity, or even syncretism with prior traditions, but as quite novel forms, which arise through the contemporary exploration of new possibilities given by the experience of these new institutions" (ibid.).

In Indonesia, underground rock music has become a remarkable source of a posteriori diversity among young people, especially as increased globalization of the music industry has precipitated a proliferation of musical alternatives to established national genres (see Baulch 2002a, 2002b). Indeed, the unprecedented rise of an Indonesian music underground dedicated to performing a diverse array of specialized imported genres is a most dramatic example of new identities and solidary communities forged in response to the new consumption possibilities opened up by global institutions such as MTV and the Internet. These "communities" may be short lived and temporally confined to a single generation, but they are nonetheless powerfully present in the lives of their participants. To understand a bit more about these communities, we take a short detour to an analysis of the printed acknowledgments found in the liner notes of underground album releases.

Representing Community:
Thank-You Lists in Underground Cassettes

Although writing thank-you lists in album liner notes is a textual practice that originated in the West, in the hands of Indonesian musicians these lists have become more elaborate and inclusive. Globalizing forces themselves are manifested in many thank-you lists, which include expressions of gratitude toward international recording artists cited as influences and sources of musical inspiration. These groups are not members of the Indonesian music community but are nonetheless included and praised, their appearance in the text indexing the globalization-influenced "unbounded seriality" of underground identities (Anderson 1998, 29–45). Thank-you lists can be written in a variety of styles, but usually underground bands divide them into acknowledgments written by the entire band followed by separate lists from each individual band member. Often there is an additional section expressing gratitude to fellow bands, and another acknowledging the support of underground fanzines, production companies, distributors, and other scenic institutions involved with the promotion of underground music.

In almost every case, regardless of the particular underground subgenre (including those preoccupied with satanic and occult themes), the first thanks is to God. References to God vary depending on the religion of the musicians: sometimes Allah S.W.T. (Arabic, Allah Subhanahu Wa Taala, "Allah the Almighty and Most Worthy of Praise"), sometimes Tuhan Y.M.E. (Tuhan Yang Maha Esa, "God the All-Powerful"), and sometimes Tuhan Yesus Kristus (Lord Jesus Christ). In Java, Muslims and Christians often play together in the same band; thus in their individual thank-you lists they thank their own version of the deity while the bands' collective thanks is to Tuhan Y.M.E., a generic title compatible with both religions. Individual thank-you lists generally acknowledge family members after God, then proceed to thank friends and colleagues, and end with a final apology to "anyone whose name was not mentioned." Here is a typical, though relatively short, example from the album *Abandon [sic], Forgotten, & Rotting Alone* (1999) by the extreme metal band Grausig:

> *Ricky* [the band's lead guitarist] *thanks to:*
> Allat [sic] SWT, my parents, Wike Sulasmi, Sony, My Wife Asri &
> Shena "Altaf," Bogor family, "Pai," Iksan, Adi, Ade, Niko "Bandung,"

Dwi "uwi" Farabi, Ki Sulaiman, Ustad Allul, Oele Patisilato, Kadek, Hendry, Chery, KH Kiansantang, Peggy, Ute, Windi, My brother band Benkel Seni, Sidick Rizal para bandit Tanjung Priok, Drs. Kasmianto and family, all Farabi gank, Deden Tobing, prumpung and the gank, Heru, Tanduk, Astreed gank, Didi, "usuf," Alex Lifeson of Rush.

This list includes the names of friends (referred to by nickname), adults (referred to by formal titles), places (Bandung, Tanjung Priok, the Farabi music school), and collectivities (Farabi *gank* [gang], Astreed *gank*), as well as the name of the guitarist from the Canadian progressive rock band Rush. Most thank-you lists follow this pattern, though many are far more elaborate.

Much like the acknowledgments section of a book, thank-you lists assert the existence of a community of friends and colleagues; hence, it is not surprising that underground music cassettes contain quite elaborate lists—more extensive than those found in the liner notes of cassettes of other genres—since underground music relies on a national network of local, self-supporting scenes for its survival outside the commercial music industry. "In order to study the underground you need to study the places where we all hang out," Wendi Putranto, the editor of *Brainwashed,* a Jakarta fanzine, told me. He emphasized that the activities of socializing and sharing ideas at specific hangouts located in Blok M and other places were essential to the development of the Jakarta scene. The thank-you lists textualize this web of voluntary association and support, and by addressing the reader directly, explicitly include him or her in this expanding musical community. The purchaser of an underground cassette thus strengthens and supports the local scene and furthers its goal of existence outside the official channels of commerce. Many thank-you lists conclude with a message directed at the reader; in underground liner notes, this message is frequently an exhortation to support Indonesian underground bands and "your local scene" or a general expression of thanks to all the band's enthusiasts, such as this example from an underground industrial cassette:

> *Dan untuk seluruh fans Koil yang super setia: Top of the morning to you, kids.*
>
> *Cheers.*

> [And for all the *super*-faithful Koil *fans: Top of the morning to you, kids. Cheers.*][1]

As mentioned, a separate section in the acknowledgments is frequently reserved for fellow bands. Band names often appear followed by their city of origin in parentheses or preceded by the name of one of their members. Such lists assert the existence of a national musical community by indexing an extended network of interdependent relationships founded on shared enthusiasm and cooperation. This network is not only the conduit through which underground music flows but is also the underground's crowning achievement: the subculture's ideological commitment to musical independence finds fruition in a nationwide web of like-minded individuals dedicated to cultural production outside the sphere of the mainstream commercial entertainment industry. The significance of thank-you lists is evidenced by the many underground bands whose cassette inserts include extensive thank-you lists on behalf of the band as a whole and from each individual band member and yet omit printed lyrics.

An interesting variant of the thank-you list is the "no-thank-you" list, which sometimes appears at the end in a separate section or is incorporated into thank-you lists. In these lists, various parties are singled out as particularly undeserving of thanks of any sort and are instead targets of the musicians' ire. Frequently included in no-thank-you lists are ex-president Soeharto, the Indonesian military, "poseurs," and the police. The following is from the liner notes of metal band Purgatory's 2000 (major label!) album *Ambang Kepunahan* (Threshold of Extinction):

> *No Thank To: Political Clowns Who Gots The Double Face and also To Indonesian Army Who Repressing The Students and Indonesian People since 30 years ago until NOW!!!*

More comprehensive still is the following vivid excerpt from the album notes for *Systematic Terror Decimation* (1999), by the Jakarta-based underground band Vile, which establishes the musical underground as a source of oppositional consciousness:

> *WE ALSO WOULD LIKE TO VENT OUR ANGER AND REVENGEFUL HATRED TO THESE FEW FUCKING ASSHOLES:*
> *Fuckin' Suharto & his crony bastards, Fuckin' [General] Wiranto & TNI [Indonesian Armed Forces] (brainless psychopathic mass murderers), Habibie, Golkar, facist & Racist, Fuckin' Provocators, False Religious Fucks (don't use a holy religion to mask any fucking decayed purposes!), Money Suckers, Fuckin' Big Mouth, Traitors, Backstabbers, Meaningless*

bastards whom doesn't know how to appreciate of what we've done,
Fuckin' Rip Offs, . . . etc . . . your life is worthless than your fucking shits!!! . . .
huahahaha . . . !!!

Benedict Anderson's seminal discussion of "print capitalism" ([1983] 1991) provides a way of tracing how textual production and mass reception encourages the imagining of translocal social entities. Cassette liner notes help listeners imagine concentrically organized musical interpretive communities—local, national, and global. The imagined social entities indexed by thank-you lists help to contextualize the music for the listener.

The origin of underground music in a particular interpretive community is supposed to be an essential feature of the listener's encounter with that music. In the underground's "jargon of authenticity" (Adorno 1973), a poseur is someone who consumes underground music but does not participate in the life of the underground community and does not interpret the music primarily as an extension of a particular scene. The occasional discursive presence of "poseurs" in cassette liner-note texts helps define the boundaries of the underground community. The community boundaries nevertheless always implicitly include the reader of the texts.

One consistent feature of thank-you lists is multilingualism. The majority of underground cassette thank-you lists are written in English with some Indonesian. Regional languages are also used—usually for personal messages included in parentheses after someone's name. Thank-you lists thus express the multilayered identities of their authors—local, national, and global—to a national audience. They demonstrate how underground scenes, examples of consumption-generated a posteriori cultural diversity, do not embrace radical individualism (exemplified by the "cruel" capital city of Jakarta) but rather reject it in their utopian quest for an authentic music-based youth community that is both profoundly rooted in local realities and potentially global in scope.

Underground Concert Events

Underground *acara* provide the context in which the imagined alternative community of the musical underground—constructed textually through sound recordings and print culture—coalesces into a palpable reality. All-day concert events featuring underground music bands representing a single subgenre or related subgenres were an important type of student-organized *acara*. Such events tended to have colorful titles that sometimes revealed their featured subgenre (*aliran*), sometimes not. In Jakarta and Bandung, these included "Nocturnis Orgasm" (underground metal), "Bumi Satoe" ("One Earth," punk and hardcore), "Independent Youth" (various, more melodic underground styles classified as *indies*), "Jakarta Meraung" ("Jakarta Roars," metal), and Jakarta Bawah Tanah ("Underground Jakarta," metal). The following is an excerpt from my field notes written while attending this last event:

Poster Café, South Jakarta, October 4, 1997
    The air is thick with perspiration, despite the air-conditioning. The entire crowd is wearing black concert T-shirts, many long-sleeved and double-layered despite the heat outside. (Nino, the lead singer of Trauma, explained that the long-sleeved, layered look was *keren*, "cool.") Most of the overwhelmingly male audience members have long, flowing hair that they flail around wildly to the rapid beat of the music. Hundreds of long-haired, black-clad Jakarta metalheads stream in and out of the concert hall, splitting their time between watching the bands onstage and hanging out outside on the wooden benches set up by the front entrance. Many of the bands performing have two alternating vocalists: one is responsible for low growls, the other for the songs' high shrieks. Was this yet another example of unequally sized paired instruments in Indonesian music? When I ask an audience member why so many groups have two vocalists, the response is that it is *lebih rame* (more crowded, noisy, fun) that way. Two of the day's headliners are grindcore group Tengkorak (Skull) from Jakarta and death metal band Slowdeath from Surabaya, East Java. The members of Slowdeath tell me they have traveled twenty hours by train to play at this concert event. (The slower trains were cheaper.) The concert starts around ten in the morning; headliners take the stage around five, and lesser-known bands play to a dwindling crowd afterward until the event's conclusion around seven in the evening. Later that night, the Poster Cafe (named for the posters of Anglo-American rock icons, from Jimi Hendrix to Kurt Cobain, that decorate its walls) will revert to a mainstream rock club catering to a slightly older, more upscale clientele.

Underground *acara* tended to be organized by smaller committees than those featuring mainstream pop and rock groups. They were also less likely to be officially affiliated with schools or universities and hence were often sponsored by cigarette companies. Although profit was certainly a motive for some *panitia* (committee) members and not all organizers were fans of underground music, for many committee members money was not of paramount concern. Although there were potential economic windfalls, these *acara* could also lose money or barely break even.

A 2001 concert report from the city of Pontianak in West Kalimantan (Indonesian Borneo) posted on a now-defunct underground music Web site (bisik.com) tells the story of a *panitia* that unexpectedly lost a cigarette company's sponsorship for an on-campus concert because of the regulation against promoting cigarettes on university grounds. As a result, the *panitia* members faced a substantial financial loss, yet they decided to persevere, and they mounted a major concert event featuring a wide variety of musical genres titled "Pontianak Bersatu" (Pontianak United). According to the author, afterward the organizers felt the concert was well worth the effort and the financial loss they sustained. The conclusion of the article reads:

> *Pontianak Bersatu! Akhirnya digelar juga, hal yang menarik memang melihatnya. Dimana perbedaan Genre musik tidak lagi menjadi persoalan. Semuanya terlihat satu, dan memang ini kami namakan musik Pontianak.*
>
> *Indah saat Punk melaju, kemudian musik etnik mengalun, grunge, pop, sampai khasidahan berdendang dan disambut teriakan death, grind, hardcore yang mengalun kencang. Saatnya bersatu, idealis bermusik-mu untukmu, Idealisme-ku untuk-ku!*
>
> *Semuanya satu diatas panggung, tidak ada lagi perbedaan. Hal ini kami mulai sebagai yang pertama di Pontianak. Dengan total kerugian 6 juta lebih, panitia masih bisa tersenyum. Kita kaya! Kita damai! Kita bersatu! Karena kita adalah satu, Pontianak Bersatu! Support Your Local Musicians!!! Apapun itu.*

[Pontianak United! In the end, it was really staged, something indeed interesting to behold. There the differences of musical genre were no longer a problem. They all appeared as one, and indeed this we (exclusive) could truly call "Pontianak's music."

Beautiful the moment when *punk* music played rapidly, then ethnic music moved steadily; *grunge, pop,* to *qasidah* sang happily and were answered by the screams of *death* (metal), *grind,* and *hardcore* at a rapid tempo. The moment of unity, your musical idealism for you, my idealism for me!

All was as one onstage; there were no more differences. This phenomenon we (exclusive) began as the first in Pontianak. With a total financial loss of over six million (rupiahs), the committee could still smile. We (inclusive) are rich! We are at peace! We are united! Because we are one, Pontianak is united! *Support Your Local Musicians!!!* No matter what.] (Mallau 2001)

This remarkable text exemplifies the underground rhetoric of scene unity, which here appears to extend to all the musical genres present at the *acara* and to the entire imagined musical community of the city of Pontianak. In the text, the author shifts back and forth between exclusive and inclusive first-person plural pronouns. The former appears to refer to the *panitia* members, while the latter's reference extends outward to all the participants present at the concert, who at the concert's end celebrate their newfound unity. Also significant is the slippage between different forms of unity: musical, social, geographical. While some underground musicians view their music as antithetical to dangdut, the anticipated effects of underground *acara* are perhaps not very different from those of dangdut concerts, except that the erasure of social divisions operates along different lines.

Moshing and Other Underground Dance Practices

Like dangdut performances, underground concerts involved dancing and embodied exchanges between performers and audience members. But instead of *joget, goyang,* and *nyawer* behavior, underground audiences engaged in less-"indigenous" practices such as moshing and stage diving.[2] Dance behavior at underground concerts was strongly influenced by the conduct of underground audiences in the West. Music videos and videotaped live performances by Western groups were readily available in Indonesia, and they provided models for concert behaviors that have become widely diffused. However, significant differences in dancing behavior nonetheless existed.

In general, I found that Indonesian concert audiences were somewhat more restrained than those in the United States. Their applause and dancing tended to be more subdued, though on occasion they would enthusiastically sing along with the performers (usually on-key) when popular songs were played. Even at underground events, the majority of the crowd would stand or sit nonchalantly while the music played, and a relatively unknown band with limited performing skills often faced an audience of disengaged, passive, seated listeners. When a better-known underground band, especially one of the "guest stars," took the stage, the crowd's actions would change dramatically. A "pit" would form in the space in front of the stage as members of the audience (no more than a third of the total, often much less than that) surged forward and began engaging in the three characteristic pit activities, which were known in Indonesian by their English names: *moshing, stage diving,* and *crowd surfing.*

Moshing, also called slamming, is an aggressive dance familiar in underground scenes the world over. While occasionally taking the form of a slow-moving circle dance (cf. Weinstein 1991, 228), moshing generally involves a group of individuals crowded together in an enclosed space (the pit) intentionally colliding with and shoving one another. Stage diving refers to the practice in which an audience member climbs up to the stage, sometimes interacting with the performers, sometimes not, and then after a short interval dives face first into the crowd (this practice resembles the ascending-the-stage behavior of some audience members at dangdut concerts, though underground music fans do not generally acknowledge this resemblance). If he (women stage divers are extremely rare in Indonesia) is fortunate, he is caught by the people standing below him and is then held aloft and passed from hand to hand, a practice known as crowd surfing. Stage diving, even more than moshing, can result in injuries, both to the audience members beneath the diver and to the diver himself, particularly when the crowd is too thin to support the diver's weight and he falls to the floor (I occasionally witnessed this occurrence). Nonetheless, serious injuries were uncommon in Indonesia as elsewhere.

While it is certainly a hazardous activity, stage diving is celebrated in underground scenes not only as a show of daredevil skill but also as a corporeal way of breaking down the separation between performer and audience (Goshert 2000, 99). Overcoming the separation between musicians and audiences is an important goal of underground concerts the world over, with their explicit rejection of an alienating media star system that places a wedge between performers and fans. In addition to audience members' stage diving, some singers onstage occasionally cross over from the other direction, diving into the crowd from the stage, with microphone in hand and microphone cable trailing behind. Hariadi "Ombat" Nasution, the lead singer of Tengkorak, was notorious for doing this during his band's performances.

At first moshing, stage diving, and crowd surfing might appear to be antithetical to the stereotypical Indonesian traditional values of order, social harmony, consideration for others, and self-restraint. Such practices instead seem to epitomize violent individualism, as audience members engaged in them appear to be heedless of the possibility of hurting those around them. The mosh pit also exemplifies a darker aspect of Indonesian cultural life: the dissolution of individual responsibility in collective actions (see the discussion in chapter 5 about the breakdown of the steel cage in Netral's video). Dancers are seemingly unconcerned with the consequences of their violent actions because they are acting not as individuals but as members of a collective body, yet I believe that it is this feeling of collective belonging that mitigates the individualism of the pit participants. While appearing to valorize violent egoism, the dancing in fact celebrates membership in a larger whole: the ephemeral collective consisting of those onstage, those in the audience, those straddling the line between stage and crowd, and, by extension, the whole underground scene itself. Indeed, although they sometimes result in the infliction of unintentional harm, stage-diving and crowd-surfing activities embody a collectivist ethos: the diver places his physical well-being in the hands of his compatriots, whom he trusts to catch him and keep him aloft.

As mentioned previously, while the characteristic underground dance practices originated in the West, in Indonesia they have been indigenized to a degree and differ in some ways from Western practices. For instance, dancers at concerts commonly coordinated their movements with others around them. A row of metal enthusiasts, arms around each other's shoulders, performing the up-and-down "headbanging" movement in unison (looking like a heavy metal version of the Rockettes) was a common sight at Indonesian metal concerts but virtually unknown in the United States. (As mentioned in chapter 8, characteristic ska dance moves were also executed in this fashion; the result resembled a chorus line.) Indonesian mosh pits often took on a collective character and ebbed and flowed as a unit. Thus dance moves thought to signify violent individualism and alienation in the West are communalized in the Indonesian context and appear to index intense collective sentiment more than individual angst.

Dangdut Underground?
The Emergence of Student Dangdut Bands

This book has focused on the ideological contrasts that exist between different popular music genres in Indonesia. Of all these contrasts,

Pemuda Harapan Bangsa (Youth, Hope of the Nation) performing in Bandung, West Java.

arguably that between dangdut and underground is the most stark—the former indigenous, mass-market oriented, proletarian, and musically accessible; the latter imported, selective in its appeal, associated with university students and middle-class youth, and musically challenging. Yet an equally salient theme in the current study has been the self-conscious creation of musical hybrids, a process that often playfully transgresses historically and discursively constructed boundaries between genres and by metonymic extension, social categories as well. Perhaps it was inevitable, then, that some student musicians would begin to experiment with playing dangdut songs with the attitude and musical trappings of underground music.

Like the café bands discussed in the previous chapter, these ensembles played dangdut songs with rock instrumentation. None had the full complement of musicians found in dangdut groups, nor did any of the groups at the time I met them have a *suling* player. I found representatives of this unusual genre in a few Indonesian cities; they included Sekarwati (from Jakarta), Soekarmadjoe (Yogyakarta), Kuch Kuch Hota Hai (Surabaya), and Pemuda Harapan Bangsa (Bandung). While student dangdut was clearly a transregional phenomenon, the small number of student dangdut bands hardly constituted a movement—and for the most part the bands were not even aware of one another's existence. Nevertheless, the bands had certain characteristics in common:

1. The groups' members were often art students at prestigious institutions such as the Institut Kesenian Jakarta (Jakarta Art Institute), Yogyakarta's Institut Seni Indonesia (Institute of Indonesian Arts), or Bandung's Sekolah Tinggi Senirupa dan Desain (High School of Art and Design).
2. All the groups were extremely popular and received many invitations to play at *acara*. During their performances, members of the audience, both men and women, would *joget*, cheer, and applaud, and sometimes even offer money to the performers in a parody of the practice of *saweran*.
3. Band members who had previous performing experience had played rock and/or underground music; I spoke to no one who had prior experience or training playing dangdut music. Indeed, for the most part these bands exhibited very little musical mastery of the genre.
4. Band members claimed to dislike contemporary dangdut, which they saw as corrupted by disco and house music, and preferred older, "pure" dangdut songs from the 1970s and 1980s by established artists like Elvy Sukaesih, Rita Sugiarto, Rhoma Irama, and Meggi Z.
5. Onstage costumes resembled those of underground ensembles rather than the usual uniforms of dangdut musicians (see chapter 8).

In addition to dangdut, two of the groups played songs from other working-class-identified genres: the Surabaya group Kuch Kuch Hota Hai played the Hindi film song from which it took its name and a few songs from another *kampungan* imported genre, Malaysian *slowrock* (see appendix B). When Soekarmadjoe added a popular *campur sari* song to their repertoire, they received an enormously positive crowd response.

Student dangdut groups may turn out to be part of a short-lived trend in a larger and longer history of humorous student performances, but I contend that the synthesis they represent is motivated by specific and important cultural agendas. In essence, student musicians appropriating dangdut music are suggesting an alternative to the elitism and foreignness of underground music, while at the same time making a provocative claim about conspicuous formal musical similarities between ideologically opposed genres. After all, dangdut and underground music use similar electrified and electronic Western instruments and technologies, share common minor-key chord progressions, and are strongly influenced by hard rock, heavy metal, and reggae.

Soekarmadjoe (Difficult to Advance) performing in Yogyakarta. Note the members' facial expressions.

But why dangdut? A conversation with Nedi Sopian, the lead singer of the sarcastically named group Pemuda Harapan Bangsa (Youth, Hope of the Nation) suggests a concern for national authenticity in response to global musical influences. This excerpt is from an interview held backstage after a performance conducted in the rowdy presence of more than a dozen of the band's fans.

Nedi Sopian: *Saya influence artisnye . . .*
JW: *Ya?*
Nedi: *Smashing Pumpkins . . .*
JW: *Smashing Pumpkins, ya . . .*
Nedi: *Eh . . . Rotor . . .*
JW: *Rotor? Grup Indonesia ya?*
Nedi: *Grup Indonesia, ya, Indonesia. Terus, Biohazard. . . . Saya nggak suka dangdut sebenernye . . .*
JW: *Tidak suka?*
Nedi: *Tidak suka dangdut saya.* Tapi karena jiwa saya Melayu . . .
      [uproarious laughter and applause from onlookers]
Nedi: *Semua di sini juga Melayu, cuman sok bule gitu . . .*
          [more laughter]
Nedi: *Bener gak? Bener gak? Bener, khan?*

[Nedi Sopian: My (recording) artist *influences* are . . .
JW: Yeah?
Nedi: Smashing Pumpkins (American alternative rock group) . . .
JW: Smashing Pumpkins, okay . . .
Nedi: Um . . . Rotor (Indonesian thrash metal/industrial group) . . .
JW: Rotor? That's an Indonesian band, right?
Nedi: Yeah, an Indonesian group, Indonesian. Also, Biohazard
    (American hardcore/metal/rap group). . . . I don't like dangdut
    actually . . .
JW: (You) don't like (it)?
Nedi: I don't like dangdut. *But because my soul is Malay* . . .
        (uproarious laughter, applause from onlookers)
Nedi: Everyone here is also Malay; they're only wannabe whites!
        (more laughter)
Nedi: Right? Right? Am I right or what?]

In this brief but telling exchange, Nedi disavows his attachment to dangdut music only to reassert it for racialistic reasons. Rather than pretend to be "white" (*bule*), like certain others among his peers, his music expresses his "soul's" true identity as a "Malay"—a biological category that every Indonesian schoolchild learns encompasses the indigenous populations of Indonesia, Malaysia, Singapore, Brunei, and the Philippines. This is the case despite his inclusion of "white" American rock bands (and one Indonesian industrial metal group) in his list of influences. Such ambivalence toward the compelling aesthetic pull of global rock music and the contrasting musical and ideological attractions of dangdut are perhaps what made Pemuda Harapan Bangsa's hybrid music so appealing to its middle-class student audience. Both band members and fans interviewed at the concert expressed the opinion (not particularly facetiously) that dangdut was *nasionalis,* an Indonesian word that is generally synonymous with "patriotic." In any case, the popular response to student dangdut bands also illustrates how the most socially transgressive musical hybrids are often the most successful.

Dangdut and Student Culture

The appropriation of classic dangdut music by Indonesian postsecondary students parallels certain revivalist phenomena in other times and regions, such as the 1950s and 1960s popularization of American "folk" music by college students in the United States, and the *nueva canción* student movement in Latin America, in which appropriated Andean folk music became a vehicle for social protest (Manuel 1988, 68–72). But in several important respects the rise of student dangdut bands differs from these earlier movements. Although the student dangdut musicians' preoccupation with "pure" dangdut songs from earlier decades may resemble the folk revivalists' concern with authenticity, no rhetoric of a pure, precapitalist past or of preservation accompanies their performances. Such a discourse would be fairly absurd in that context, given dangdut's tremendous popularity and commercial origins, and such thinking was clearly not reflected in the impure, hybridizing habits of student dangdut bands.

More importantly, while popularized folk music was often promoted as an austere, not very danceable alternative to mindless mass-market pop music, dangdut played by student bands appeared to be an antidote to the austerity and nondanceability of imported underground rock music, with its "serious" themes and jagged, lunging rhythms. Dangdut music appeared to free the audience from its inhibitions, and the atmosphere at student dangdut concerts combined the exuberance of the mosh pit with the intense pleasures of a neighborhood dangdut show. Thus the appropriation of dangdut bears a certain similarity to the appropriation of different types of working-class music by middle-class youths in the United States in the second half of the twentieth century, which was accompanied by the appealing notion that the sensual enjoyment of organic grooves from below would dismantle structures of repression in middle-class American life.

Performing Relationships to Global and National Musical Commodities

The rise of student dangdut groups can been further illuminated by comparing it to analogous developments in Western rock music history. In an essay titled "Concerning the Progress of Rock & Roll," Michael Jarrett addresses what he views as a central problem with accounts of the development of Anglo-American rock music, namely, how the genre has been able to periodically revitalize itself despite the ongoing commercialization and dilution of rock music, which he likens to "an aesthetic version of entropy as heat-death" (1992, 169). Jarrett locates innovation in rock music in a particular cultural dynamic of growth out of entropic decay, which he compares to mushrooms growing on a compost heap. He writes that the popularization and subsequent banalization of rock music "fosters artistic renewal by generating conditions that allow for aberrant readings" (174). Thus he reads a series of canonically innovative moments in rock and roll history—the emergence of Elvis Presley, the rise of the 1960s counterculture, and the late 1970s punk rebellion—as the result of musicians perversely "misreading" the musical compost heap created by all the pop music that had come before. In Jarrett's view, American rock legends such as Little Richard, Bob Dylan, and the Ramones were great because they played inept and refracted versions of rhythm and blues, country, American folk music, and the 1960s girl-group sound. (And perhaps I should note parenthetically that, like many student dangdut group members, numerous Anglo/American rock innovators, from John Lennon to Eric Clapton to the Talking Heads, happened to be students of the visual arts.)

Though Jarrett does not acknowledge this explicitly, the cultural dynamic he describes relies on the materiality and circulating capabilities of music recordings. Recordings from remote times, places, and cultures make up the cultural "compost heap" on which, according to Jarrett, innovative rock music developments thrive funguslike on an eclectic diet of decontextualized sonic objects. Thus one does not have to be from a particular place or have a specific cultural background in order to innovate within the rock "tradition" as long as one has access to recordings. Indonesian student dangdut groups in performance replicate the sounds of twenty-year-old dangdut cassettes and three-year-old imported Western rock music compact discs. Their relationship with these sounds is mediated by the recorded musical artifact, which through its very materiality flattens the temporal, geographical, and social distance that separates its producers from its consumers. The members of Soekarma-djoe, Pemuda Harapan Bangsa, and their compatriots thus perform an inspired hybrid from the jumble of heterogeneous national and global artifacts that comprise their musical biographies. I would venture to say that in doing so they demonstrate that Indonesian musicians have mastered the art of creating original and innovative rock music.

But which genre is being revitalized here? When Pemuda Harapan Bangsa was signed to a major label in 2001, it was promoted not as a rock band but as a dangdut group, appearing on dangdut-oriented television music variety shows and producing an album in which their stripped-down song arrangements were filled in with the standard multitracked instrumentation of dangdut recordings. In an April 2001 e-mail, Temtem, Pemuda Harapan Bangsa's rhythm guitarist, expressed some ambivalence about his record company's class-based promotion strategy.

Kita juga lagi berjuang buat diterima di masyarakat. Kita udah bikin videoclip, tapi stasiun TV cuman mau nayangin di program2 dangdut, terus terang, kita gak suka dikotak2in begitu. Mungkin mereka nganggap kami musik dangdut, it's o.k . . . tapi selanjutnya kita malah susah untuk bergerak, karena sebagian masy. Ind masih beranggapan bahwa dangdut itu milik masy kelas B, C (low class). Kita pengen musik kita diterima seluruh masy—tanpa terkecuali. Selain itu kami juga meramu musik—bukan hanya dangdut, tapi ada keroncong, pop, arabian, rock dan macem-macem deh.

[We are also struggling to be accepted in society. We made a *video clip*, but the TV stations only want to screen it on dangdut programs; frankly, we don't like being boxed in like that. Maybe they consider us dangdut; *it's ok* . . . but then it follows that it's quite difficult for us to maneuver, because a segment of Indonesian society still considers dangdut the property of the society of classes B and C (*low class*). We want our music to be accepted by the entire society, without exception. Besides that, we also mix music together—not only dangdut, but *keroncong*, pop, Arab music, rock, and really all sorts of things.]

As mentioned in chapter 3, the Indonesian music industry classifies the record-buying public into socioeconomic classes labeled A to D, in which class A includes young professionals and the coveted affluent teenager demographic. (In Edy Singh's words, "Teenagers don't think about how money is hard to come by!" [*Remaja sich kagak pikirin duit susah di cari!*].) Using record-company terminology, Temtem protests that PHB's music is for everyone, not just people from classes B and C (categories roughly corresponding to lower-middle class and working class). While his protest may reflect a desire to reach the most lucrative market segment (class A consumers), it may also hint at an underlying nationalist idealism that motivates musicians like the members of Pemuda Harapan Bangsa to attempt to forge a hybridic music accessible to all Indonesians regardless of class position. One could argue that by enthusiastically embracing dangdut, Indonesian students, both onstage and in the audience, are embracing the old nationalist dream of a modern, unified Indonesia and (symbolically) rejecting the tyranny of class hierarchy. But although it is true that with the demise of Soeharto's regime came a new round of negotiations between modernity's "warring possibilities," the glaring social inequality that characterized New Order society persists, as does the Indonesian elite's need to blame modernity's troubling failures in their country on the "backward" village culture of ordinary citizens (which dangdut music supposedly exemplifies) rather than on economic and political injustice.

Conclusions:
Lifestyle versus Inclusionary Community

Acara perform a variety of functions, from the most humble student-sponsored event to the most polished televised award show, from the local dangdut ensemble playing a neighborhood gig to the *pop Indonesia* star performing at a concert in a five-star Jakarta hotel. All *acara*, however, provide a space for the negotiation of meanings from local, national, and global sources. Participants—emcees, performers, audience, organizing committee members, and so on—take part in this process through musical, linguistic, sartorial, iconographic, televisual, and kinesthetic channels. These different media present performed hybridities of foreign, local, and national elements—juxtapositions often accompanied by self-conscious humor. In the context of this study, musical *acara* remind us that *hybridity does not necessarily equal synthesis*. Totalizing syntheses of genres do not occur in Indonesia or anywhere else. The reality is that in *acara*, "foreign," "Indonesian," and "regional" genres coexist with various hybrids of those genres—hybrids that rarely, if ever, entirely subsume their constituent elements.

One key concept that can help us distinguish between pop/rock and underground concerts, on the one hand, and dangdut concerts, on the other, is "lifestyle."[3] Indonesians occasionally translate this term into Indonesian (*gaya hidup*), but in Jakarta the English term is used most often. In Jakarta, *lifestyle* connotes exclusiveness, a voluntarily chosen set of behavioral and consumption practices that presumably cohere and identify the individual as differentiated from the mass public. Youth are particularly interested in *lifestyle*, and industries such as the cassette business cater to this interest by creating products that construct and reinforce youth identities based on trends. In Indonesia, lifestyle choices are thought not necessarily to express an individual's uniqueness, but rather to underscore his or her allegiance(s) to a particular desirable societal subgroup. "Coolness" therefore is defined less by character traits and personality than by one's ability to socialize (*bergaul*) with the right people and therefore keep abreast of what is "currently trendy" (*lagi nge-trend*).

In early twenty-first-century Indonesia, dangdut represents a refusal of the logic of *lifestyle* and by extension a rejection of the individualizing logic of global consumer culture. In contrast to *lifestyles* promoted in

Lifestyles vs. a life of struggle: "Which Kid Are You?" Cartoon by Mice. See page 297, note 3, for a translation.

youth-oriented popular culture (including pop/rock and underground *acara*), dangdut bridges generations, from the smallest child to the oldest grandparent, and the imaginary ideal audience for dangdut is a community without distinctions of class or status. This is perhaps one reason why performed music recognizable as "dangdut" has such powerful and immediate social effects, whether it takes place in an upscale café, a student-organized underground event, or at more-conventional dangdut concert venues.

The contrasts that separate pop/rock, underground, and dangdut *acara* illustrate the tensions that exist among conflicting modernities, all of which revolve in different ways around desire, social prestige, and the project of identity in a globalizing world. In examining the different trajectories of popular music genres in Indonesia, it does not suffice to simply reiterate the argument that local agents appropriate global cultural products for their own purposes. This phenomenon certainly occurs, but it is also true that *the purposes themselves are changed in the encounter.* Nor is it sufficient to claim that meanings at *acara*, and in Indonesian popular culture more generally, are "contested," thereby implying that the ultimate condition of these cultural performance events is incoherence and fragmentation. Anthropologist Edward Bruner writes, "I maintain that culture can be conceptualized as both contested and shared, in part because *in the contestation there is sharing*" (1999, 474, emphasis mine). In all popular cultures, an important component of what is shared is an awareness of the interpretive arena in which struggles over meaning and power take place. This overarching framework resembles Urban's (1993) notion of "omega culture," a system of meanings that governs the relationships between "alpha cultures"— the various subcultures that together constitute contemporary multicultural societies. I would argue that the *acara* acts as a physical manifestation of national "omega culture," an arena in which the competing sociomoral visions of music genres, cultures, nationalities, classes, genders, and taste publics are displayed, parodied, and juxtaposed. It is the role of the performers, the audiences, and the mediators to collaboratively make sense of this exuberant cacophony of "alpha cultures" and in the process to forge an ephemeral but deeply gratifying solidary community of participants. In this process, social differences and power differentials are not dissolved but instead are made into objects of play through the reflexive performance of musical hybridities that bring together local, global, and national cultural forms in new and unforeseen constellations.

Conclusion

INDONESIAN YOUTH, MUSIC, AND
GLOBALIZATION

Obviously critical study should retain self-doubt, especially about the
status of knowledge. But for anthropologists to wait around until
someone gets epistemology right would be like Sisyphus waiting for
Godot.

D. Miller 1995

Fieldwork is practical, messy, empirical, difficult, partial, step-by-step,
but it grounds our explanations in the dialogue between self and other.
It counteracts the intellectual tendency to theorize the world without
living in it.

Titon 1997

Our journey is nearly at its end. In this book I have attempted to capture
the musical life of young urban Indonesians at a unique historical moment. Through ethnographic accounts of various musical practices—
recording, performing, listening, purchasing—I have also tried to reveal
some fundamental dynamics in contemporary Indonesian national culture and to explore their implications for the identity projects of contemporary Indonesian youth.

In this final chapter, I return to four main themes of this study—
globalization and the nation, sociality, social class, and hybridity—and

discuss my major findings in each category. I close with some tentative predictions about the future evolution of Indonesian popular music genres and suggest how the disciplines of anthropology and ethnomusicology can benefit from ethnographic studies that take popular musics seriously as meaningful loci of cultural contestation and consensus in modern complex societies.

The Global Sensorium

The Indonesian archipelago has a centuries-long history of absorbing and indigenizing foreign cultural influences, from Hinduism, Buddhism, and Islam to the ideology of modern nationalism. It is therefore hardly surprising that the current wave of worldwide cultural globalization has had a dramatic impact on Indonesian society and culture. The United States of America has emerged as a geographically distant center of power with a palpable impact on the fantasy life of Indonesian youth, and global institutions, from fast-food chains to MasterCard, have become familiar presences in urban daily life. Global (predominantly Anglo-American) popular culture enjoys great prestige and exerts a formative influence on developments in Indonesia's "national culture-under-construction" (Suryadi 2005, 131). Thus globalization in Indonesia has transformed not only the physical and visual landscapes of settings such as Central Jakarta but also the cognitive and emotional landscapes of acting subjects (cf. Greene and Henderson 2000; Liechty 2003; Mazzarella 2003). A key indicator of this change can be found in recent innovations in the milieu of Indonesian popular music, the most grassroots-derived and populist branch of the mass media, and in the ways those innovations (re)configure relationships between local, national, and global cultural forms.

Following Urban (2001), I view the local and the global as metacultural constructs. In Indonesia, "global culture" is culture that is present in the form of particular signs and objects perceived to have come from a distant "elsewhere" (cf. Baulch 2003), while "local culture" originates in particular, proximate, physically accessible places, or at least appears to do so. Recognizing "the global" in everyday life always requires a leap of faith aided by "the work of the imagination" (Appadurai 1996, 5). An example in Indonesia is the Kansas brand of cigarettes, the motto of which is (in English) *Taste the Freedom*. Kansas is actually not a common brand in the United States (if it exists there at all), but its advertisements in Jakarta would lead one to think so, and the Kansas advertisement

poster affixed to an outer wall of the Warung Gaul (see chapter 6) generated much curiosity about "American" cigarettes among the *warung*
regulars. Yet identifying "the local" *also* requires a leap of faith—though
it is not always recognized as such—since products that seem to come
from nearby places may actually originate in a distant elsewhere or contain conspicuous elements that come from other locales.

Consumption of global cultural forms may discipline and channel
desire (toward Western women, for instance) and reinforce hegemony
(for example, the seemingly undisputed ontological superiority of Western popular music), but it may also open up new ways of making sense of
the world. The explosion of new youth-oriented musics in Indonesia
appears to have had little impact on either family relationships or religious belief or practice. Indeed, as conspicuous as cultural globalization
seems in Jakarta and in other major Indonesian cities, many of its effects
could be viewed as limited primarily to the ephemeral patterns of youth
culture. These patterns are not inconsequential, however. In the words
of "Monster," an underground metal musician in Surabaya, explaining
the typical age range of underground music fans, "The years between
fifteen and twenty-five are the time to search for one's identity [*mencari
jatidiri*]!" The identities forged in social encounters with the products of
global culture can carry implications for the way one chooses to live one's
life, not only during adolescence but also throughout one's adulthood.

Local, National, Global

> The Indonesian nation-state is not only postcolonial but also multi-ethnic—
> an ambitiously synthetic and syncretic, irrevocably modern and modernist
> project.
>
> Ang 2001

In this book I have explained how the national level of cultural production mediates between the local and the global (see also Armbrust 1996;
Sutton 2003; Turino 1999, 2000). In Indonesia, where the appropriate
content of its modern national culture has long been a subject of intense debate (Frederick 1997) and national consciousness is generally
well developed even in remote areas, the national level of cultural production nearly always plays a role in the ongoing dialectic between local
and global entities. (Indeed, it may make more sense to speak of a "tria-
lectical" dynamic when discussing macrosocial cultural processes in
Indonesia.)

Local, national, and global are intertwined and interact in complex ways. Global cultural forms can be mobilized to resist the nation-state, as in the rise of politicized underground music during the Soeharto period. Similarly, local forms can be mobilized against national culture (for example, the rise of *campur sari,* a hybrid Javanese-language style that has competed successfully against Indonesian-language dangdut among Javanese listeners), and national or global forms can overwhelm local genres (as evidenced by the displacement of Betawi folk music by dangdut, or by the wild popularity of rock music in Surabaya). National and local forms can likewise become agents of resistance to the global, as was the case with the popularization in the 1980s of *jaipongan* (a nationalized West Javanese regional genre) as an indigenous alternative to Western dance music.

The Indonesian musicscape abounds with nationalized local forms (such as *keroncong* and *jaipongan*), nationalized global forms (*pop Indonesia*), globalized local forms (world beat, ethnic jazz), localized national forms (*dangdut Jawa* and *campur sari*), globalized national forms (dangdut's popularity in East Asia, the successful marketing of *keroncong* in Europe as "world music"), and even localized global forms (Minangkabau ska, Sundanese punk rock). Each of these combinations promotes a particular orientation toward each of the three levels. This study has demonstrated the importance of popular music in negotiating between local, global, and national appeals to affective allegiance in the lives of Indonesians. In the process, popular music genres contribute to the phenomenological realness of these levels, which are at base *imagined entities* constituted through metacultural discourses and specific social practices.

Sociality and Experiential Context

We have explored how Indonesian popular music circulates through Jakarta and the rest of the nation in the form of recordings, video clips, and live performances, through broadcast media and through social pathways that the circulating music itself creates and reinforces (Urban 2001). Traveling with the sonic artifacts and performances are a variety of metacultural constructs—some imported, some indigenous, some indigenized—that render the music comprehensible and relevant to its audiences.

Yet I contend that to simply analyze the cultural forms themselves and the explicitly articulated metacultural constructs that accompany them is insufficient and falls short of the epistemological goal of music ethnography: to understand the complex, multilayered meanings of music in the lives of actual people. This study has therefore also focused on the experiential context of Indonesian popular music. That is, in addition to analyzing the artifacts themselves and common verbal discourses about them, I have attempted to illuminate the cultural spaces, the social relationships, and the shared experiences of participants that frame the production and reception of popular music in Jakarta and other large cities in Java and Bali. Thus we have learned how musical objects and performances acquire particular meanings through specific activities and interactions, from shopping in a record store to hanging out with friends to performing onstage. These and other experiences of musical encounter are often overlooked by textualist approaches to popular culture. As theorists of popular music have pointed out (e.g., Frith 1981; Wicke 1990), the significance of mass-mediated music derives from everyday life and its variable rhythms of work, leisure, socializing, resting, and dreaming. What is important to keep in mind is that these mundane aspects of existence are not the same everywhere. For example, in general Indonesians prefer to spend more time in groups and less time alone than do Americans. There is evidence to suggest that this aspect of daily life is manifested in Indonesian popular musics by a lyrical preoccupation with combating loneliness, by the common practice of singing popular songs at social gatherings, by the importance of collective participation and dancing at concerts, and by a willingness to combine different music genres.

The topical concerns of song texts, the "busy" musical textures, and the strikingly hybridic elements found in Indonesian popular musics are inseparable from the ethic of sociality, which creates an experiential context for daily life that includes sociability, tolerance of difference and contradiction, and the attempt to elide or suspend hierarchy and status for the sake of unity and social harmony. I have concluded from my research that it is more appropriate to view Indonesian popular musics, from dangdut to underground, as soundtracks for "hanging out" with others than as facilitators of private, contemplative listening. In other words, in Indonesia, musical encounters are usually social affairs, and they derive their meanings and emotional resonance from intersubjective experiences.

Popular Music Genres and Social Class: Bridging the Gap?

The ethic of sociality—the necessary and desirable copresence of others and the valuing of social intercourse above solitary activities—appears to be nearly constant across the social boundaries that otherwise divide Indonesian youth. Nevertheless, these boundaries play a central role in the cultural politics of popular music genres. Although Indonesia's multiethnic character has attracted considerable interest among scholars concerned with the ways in which different ethnic, regional, and religious identities are reconciled in the name of national unity and integration, it is really class hierarchy that most threatens the Indonesian national project in the post-Soeharto age—and that factor, not coincidentally, most consistently divides the music audience.

For most of Indonesian history, especially since the beginning of the New Order, the working- and lower-class national majority—the *rakyat kecil* (little people)—have had little voice in national public discourse (Weintraub 2004, 127). As a consequence, the most prominent expression of their identities, aspirations, and sufferings in the public sphere has been through popular music, especially in the form of the celebrated but highly controversial dangdut. The sociological fact of dangdut's vast nationwide audience (though its appeal is far from universal) makes it the de facto popular music of Indonesia, even if the majority of its disparate sonic ingredients are easily traceable to exogenous sources in India, the wider Muslim world, Latin America, and the West.

The problem of dangdut's acceptance by the middle class has existed from the origins of the music in urban folk styles such as *orkes melayu*, and it has been further complicated by the music's obvious borrowing from prestigious Western popular musics such as rock (Siegel 1986, 215–17). I assert that the continuing conflict between dangdut and the more middle-class-oriented and westernized *pop Indonesia*, not to mention Western imported music itself, can be viewed as nothing less than a battle between competing visions of Indonesian national modernity: the collectivist, egalitarian national vision of the Sukarno era versus the individualist, status-obsessed developmentalism of Soeharto's New Order. Arjun Appadurai writes, "The megarhetoric of developmental modernization (economic growth, high technology, agribusiness, schooling, militarization) in many countries is still with us. But it is often punctuated, interrogated, and domesticated by the micronarratives of film, television, music, and other expressive forms, which allow modernity to be rewritten more as *vernacular globalization* and less as a concession to large-scale national and international policies" (1996, 10, emphasis mine). In precisely this way, New Order discourses of development were "interrogated" by dangdut and other hybridic Indonesian popular music genres appealing to the nonaffluent; *pop Indonesia* "domesticated" such discourses for its assumed-to-be-middle-class audience, Indonesianizing the globally circulating "megarhetoric" of developmental modernization; while the "vernacular globalization" represented by the Indonesian musical underground suggests possible alternatives to that megarhetoric.

The demise of the Soeharto regime and Indonesia's subsequent democratic transition brought about a period of cultural dynamism and experimentation that challenged received New Order wisdom about class, modernization, development, and nationalism. These New Order–era values, which had become orthodoxy for the middle class and the elites, had never been fully absorbed by the *rakyat kecil*, who largely held on to Sukarnoist notions of self-sufficiency and community. The current popularity of dangdut music among members of the middle class, albeit hardly a new phenomenon, stems in part from a reevaluation of New Order ideology vis-à-vis the future of the nation. That some student rock bands accustomed to playing hardcore, metal, and other imported genres have begun to play dangdut songs might hint at a growing resistance to the idea that stark social inequality is a necessary fact of life in a developing nation-state.

Those who continue to play Western-derived underground music increasingly view their activities in terms of a national, cross-class community of enthusiasts, and in doing so many have turned to singing in Indonesian instead of in English (see Wallach 2003a). The most striking aspect of this process of musical indigenization is the ease with which middle-class underground participants have assimilated the imported underground ideologies of "Do It Yourself" (*D.I.Y.*), cultural autonomy, grassroots populism, and scene unity to the parallel rhetoric of the early days of Indonesian independence—rhetoric that praised national self-sufficiency, national unity, and egalitarianism. Rather than diminishing a sense of national identity in favor of the imaginary global identity marketplace, the rise of the underground may thus represent nothing less than a modest revival of Sukarnoist nationalism among educated, middle-class Indonesian youth in the guise of a global musical movement.

Dangdut music—as manifested in the hybridizing practices of cassette producers, the multigenerational collective effervescence at concerts, and its presence in informal roadside performances—erases social boundaries and attempts to create a utopian community in which identity is reduced to the inclusive ideological category of "Indonesian-ness," with gender as the sole remaining divide. Just as Sukarno tried to encompass the contradictory streams of communism, nationalism, and political Islam within a larger, integrated whole (Anderson 1990, 73–75), dangdut music attempts to encompass the entire gamut of popular sounds: the polished production techniques and sweet timbres of pop; the sensual, ornamented singing of the Islamic world; the tantalizing dance rhythms of Indian film music; the energy and power of Western hard rock; and the "ethnic nuances" of Indonesia's regional musical traditions. Indeed, there is very little in the contemporary Indonesian popular music scene that has *not* been introduced and incorporated into the dangdut sound. Even hip hop and electronic dance music have found their way into *dangdut trendy,* as has an unprecedented array of traditional instruments and sonic textures recreated through digital sampling.

Like Sukarnoism, however, dangdut ultimately fails in its totalizing mission, unable to fully engulf the individualistic, xenocentric orientation and cosmopolitan longings of the elite and middle classes within its stylistic boundaries. The developmentalist ideologies held by members of the Indonesian middle class justify the persistence of the social gap as the inevitable consequence of the perceived cultural backwardness of the poor. This mentality ensures that dangdut music, a cultural form that exemplifies this backwardness, will never lose its associations with the "village," that perpetual site of ignorance, stasis, and stubborn resistance to the project of modernity. The fact that even the urban poor are considered "villagers" (*orang kampung*) reinforces the stereotype and conflates the traditional/modern dichotomy of old-fashioned modernization theory with the persistent economic inequalities produced by uneven and corrupt patterns of national development. Dangdut's obvious deviations from the sound and style of global pop music genres make it an "abject" form, neither traditional nor modern, that to its critics expresses nothing more than the nonaffluent majority's cultural inauthenticity and lack of cultivation. The modern must be defined by what it is not—this holds as true for followers of modernist Islam as for developmentalist technocrats—but dangdut music does not exclude any possibilities. Instead, it incorporates them all into an unruly and impure hybrid formation that elicits disgust and disavowal from modernists even as it invites them to join the dance.

Pop Indonesia's ideological role in the Indonesian class structure is distinct from that of dangdut or that of the underground, and this role seems to be the most conflicted of the three. The attempt by members of the underground music scene to construct an independent, autonomous cultural and economic system outside the corporate entertainment industry echoes Sukarno's defiant stance toward international aid organizations and the agents of world capitalism. *Pop,* by contrast, can be seen as representing acquiescence to global corporate hegemony. As a national genre, *pop Indonesia* must confront the "spectre of comparisons" (Anderson 1998) that haunts all such institutions. The point of *pop Indonesia* music is neither to be distinctively "Indonesian" nor to be an exact copy of Western popular music, but rather to be a style comparable to the westernized popular music of other nations sung in national vernaculars. Thus, despite conspicuous musical differences between "pop" and "rock" and the recent proliferation of Indonesianized Western genres from R & B to ska, *pop Indonesia* remains an undifferentiated category on record-store shelves. Its particular musical content is less important than its place of origin and the fact that it is sung in the national language, unlike international or regional pop.

Moreover, unlike regional pop, which frequently incorporates elements of local musical traditions, *pop Indonesia* is supposed to sound like a national version of international music, which is nearly always assumed to be Western music. As such, *pop Indonesia* must be musically interchangeable with Western pop, or it risks falling short of a transnational ideal. Like the national bank or the national anthem, *pop Indonesia* must unproblematically fit into the international grammar of national institutions. Any deviation risks compromising the nation's modernity. It is no wonder, then, that attempts by Krakatau and other Indonesian jazz and pop musicians to create Indonesian "world beat" music, no matter how high-minded and tasteful, have met with limited popular success in Indonesia, whereas completely Western-sounding pop (such as the slick jazz-pop music Krakatau played in the 1980s) enjoys a large audience. As a result of these stylistic restrictions, the Indonesian pop audience is composed primarily of middle-class and elite listeners.

Pop Indonesia also poses a problem for working-class music fans precisely because it participates in the generic fiction of the modern nation-state, which entails an assumption of a relatively affluent audience of consumers comprised of atomized individuals separately navigating the cultural marketplace. This is why *pop Indonesia* is the music of malls and businesses—it is the music of capitalist consumption, of *homo economicus.* But neither the assumption of prosperity nor the ideal of the isolated, consuming subject resonates with the experiences of Indonesia's nonaffluent majority. Thus *pop Indonesia* is viewed by many members of this majority as egoistic (*egois*), and as fundamentally belonging not to "the people" but to an exclusive elite excessively concerned with its country's image abroad. Hence *pop Indonesia*, unlike dangdut, can never be *musik kita-kita* (all of our music) because it is a product of the artful domestication of global musical sounds by talented individuals, rather than a collectively owned and celebrated musical heritage.

In the course of my research, I encountered a great deal of anxiety among fans, record producers, and musicians about whether Indonesian pop was of comparable quality to pop music from the West. No one ever entertained the notion that it might be superior. This is because it is in the very nature of *pop Indonesia* to be derivative, so by definition its artistic value can never surpass Western pop, no matter how well-produced or well-played the music, and no matter how talented the singer or the songwriter. This does not mean that Indonesians prefer Western to Indonesian pop music. Quite the opposite is the case. Yet many Indonesians interpret the preference for *pop Indonesia* songs as resulting from the Indonesian public's lack of sophistication, their need for mediation between the global musicscape and their local sensorium. As this perceived need diminishes for a new generation raised on MTV and the Internet, *pop Indonesia* will need to reinvent itself to survive.

If to place *pop Indonesia* on equal footing with *pop Barat* (Western pop) is to deconstruct the entire concept of nationalized pop, the crisis *pop Indonesia* faces is caused by its growing parity with Western pop, made possible by increasing flows of knowledge, capital, and technology to the developing world. *Pop Indonesia*'s internal differentiation threatens to rival the West with regard to stylistic diversity, and the equalizing effects of computer-driven record production make it harder than ever to distinguish domestic from imported musical products on a purely sonic level.

Pop Indonesia must adapt to the changing conditions of the global musicscape. Global youth music genres such as rap, metal, and alternative rock are stylistically (and sonically) opposed to the saccharine and innocuous music that was once the mainstay of Indonesia's popular music industry, and it is unlikely that these new forms of music will comfortably fit under the *pop Indonesia* rubric for long. Nor do they conform to the ideal national popular culture of banal love songs meant to accompany affluence and consumption, the longing of romance metamorphosing into the longing for commodities. One significant threat posed by the new pop genres is linguistic in nature, because they disrupt the previous hegemony of poetic Standard Indonesian in song lyrics. Rock and rap styles have introduced heteroglossia (Bakhtin 1981) into *pop Indonesia*, adding Indonesian colloquialisms, Jakartanese, youth slang, regional languages, and even English to the range of linguistic possibilities employed by pop songwriters (cf. Bodden 2005). No longer the monologic voice of an imaginary affluent society, *pop Indonesia* has become increasingly responsive to the aspirations and multiply articulated identities of the nation's youth, and in the process it may cease to resemble "pop" altogether.

Pop producers and artists long for the prestige, wealth, and global stature of their Western counterparts, while dangdut producers and artists long for the prestige enjoyed by *pop Indonesia*. They dream of a day when dangdut music assumes its rightful place as the proud musical representative of a fully modern, self-possessed nation. Young working-class dangdut fans long for the cosmopolitan glamour of global popular culture that they experience through dangdut music, while some progressive middle-class students view dangdut as the authentic voice of the Indonesian people. Indonesian underground artists, for their part, yearn for a transnational community that provides an alternative to a national one stratified by class and ethnicity. They are all, in their own way, united by a longing for a truly modern, culturally authentic community—national or otherwise—that grants recognition to all its members.

Hybridities: Techno, Performative, and Postcolonial

> Hybridity is not like a cocktail that you can recompose back to its parts. . . .
> It's something that comes about when you're not even sure where your origins
> are coming from.
>
> Srinivas Aravamudan, discussing the work of Homi K. Bhabha
> (quoted in Eakin 2001)

Indonesia's diverse, vibrant, and innovative popular musicscape is characterized by a willingness on the part of producers to combine and hybridize musical forms in order to create music that is simultaneously local, national, and global. Such musical practices claim a kind of modernity that is recognizably Indonesian and contest the notion that cultural modernization must be synonymous with an uncompromising westernization. For example, it is significant that the polyvocal sonic texture and rhythmic organization of Indonesian dance musics such as *house jaipong* and *dangdut house*, with lower-pitched instruments moving at a proportionally slower rate than higher ones, strongly resembles gamelan and other indigenous Indonesian musics. This resemblance is intensified by the frequent use of *bonang* (kettle gong) and *suling* (bamboo flute) samples and complex interlocking synthesizer lines that evoke the characteristic patterns of high-pitched Indonesian metallophones in traditional ensembles.

Hybridity has become one of the principal concepts of postcolonial theory (e.g., Ang 2001; Bhabha 1994). Yet despite the aggressive theorizing that has surrounded the concept, there has been very little research, ethnographic or otherwise, into the range of possible forms that hybridity can take and the significance of that variation. The integrationist ethic of hybridization found in dangdut and regional pop—in which instruments, sounds, genre labels, and production techniques are juxtaposed to create multitextured hybrid musical artifacts—has its roots in Sukarnoism and perhaps in traditional Indonesian notions of power and incorporation (see Anderson 1990). Such an approach differs markedly from the seamless, disciplined techno-hybrid fusions of Eternal Madness and Krakatau. Yet another type of hybrid cultural production—one with its own separate set of motivations—is the use of Indonesian-language song lyrics by Indonesian underground rock musicians playing otherwise Western-sounding music.

What I have attempted to demonstrate in this study is that musical hybridities are *strategic,* subject to the artistic, commercial, and social purposes of their producers (see Berger 1999). "Sound engineering" (Greene 1999) practices in recording studios and performative gestures onstage at *acara* combine elements of the local, the national, and the global in order to attract new audiences (dangdut remixes), comment on the nature of Indonesian musical hierarchy (student dangdut groups), make bold political statements (Indonesian-language hardcore punk), and generate alternative ways to be global cosmopolitan subjects (Krakatau, Eternal Madness).

Ironies abound with musical hybridity: Moel from Eternal Madness; Dwiki, Pra, and Trie from Krakatau; and Edy Singh and his production staff are all far more familiar with Western music than with the traditional music that they incorporate into their work. Likewise, the student rock bands that cover dangdut songs often have little grasp of dangdut vocal and instrumental techniques (though this does not seem to diminish these bands' popularity and perhaps even enhances it), and underground bands that sing in Indonesian bring their music closer to the cultural location of underground music in English-speaking societies—as carriers of powerful messages in clear, direct language that listeners do not need a dictionary to decipher.

The heterogeneity of styles and sounds found in Indonesian popular music is usually the result of conscious calculation; very rarely does it result from a failure to master a particular global genre (a possible exception being some Indonesian songwriters' difficulty with writing lyrics in grammatically correct, idiomatic English). Rather, the creation of musical hybrids results from the desire to move beyond the conventions of established forms, to add an "ethnic accent" (*logat etnis*) that emerges not from the inability to speak without one (an unintended and undesirable consequence of what Greg Urban [2001, 15–33] calls "inertial culture") but from a conscious effort to introduce "local" elements into a global form—*to add something new* and thus to participate in the replication of culture characteristic of the metaculture of modernity. Often this effort is facilitated by the additive sonic logic of the multitrack recording studio. For this reason I have identified "techno-hybridity" as an important subcategory of self-conscious musical mixing. It is also fortuitous that multitrack recording techniques are remarkably compatible with the Indonesian aesthetic of *rame* (crowded, noisy, fun), characterized in the sonic realm by overlapping, layered sounds originating from multiple sources, and with the interlocking colotomic structures of gamelan and other indigenous musical traditions.

The Future of "Indonesian" Music

In the current uncertain political and social climate of Indonesia, it is difficult to set forth predictions about the fate of the three main musical genres discussed here. Nonetheless, a few tentative projections are possible.

Pop

Earlier in this chapter, I discussed the possible future of *pop Indonesia*, along with the threat of obsolescence it faces. I now add my assessment that Indonesian youth will increasingly demand Indonesian pop music that not only is musically competitive with global styles but also addresses their everyday experiences and aspirations. Members of the most recent generation of pop and rock artists record songs about their lives and, by extension, those of their fans, combining social observations, depictions of everyday life, topical humor, and of course romantic relationships. The fact that the music of *pop Indonesia* artists can address the specific experiences of Indonesian youth better than imported popular music and does so in comprehensible language will continue to constitute a competitive advantage. On the other hand, music falling under the category of *pop Indonesia* is increasingly likely to be produced by global rather than national recording companies, and this particular form of musical globalization will no doubt produce unintended effects for the recording industry. It is possible that in reaction to the slick, up-to-date global sounds of current *pop Indonesia,* older pop styles, such as *pop nostalgia,* may even enjoy a revival. (Such an occurrence would greatly benefit the national companies that hold the copyrights to *pop nostalgia* songs.)

Regardless of the eventual fate of *pop Indonesia* as a genre, I am certain that the creativity and skill of Indonesian musicians and producers will ensure that commercial music produced in Indonesia, no matter how it is labeled, will remain a vital form of expression and will likely continue to outsell Western imports in the national market.

Underground

The Indonesian underground scene began with groups of urban middle school and high school students covering songs by their favorite Western bands. This was followed by the formation of bands that wrote their own songs and recorded them, usually singing in English. Gradually more and more of these groups began to record songs in Indonesian, and occasionally in regional languages, instead of in English.

Although the lyrics and social context of underground music have been indigenized to some extent, musically underground bands have generally remained within the stylistic parameters set by Western artists. The writing of lyrics in Indonesian, therefore, has been more an attempt to approximate the Western underground ideal of music capable of unmediated communication than a desire to "Indonesianize" underground rock (Wallach 2003a). Nevertheless, many members of rock and underground bands with whom I spoke did express a willingness to combine Indonesian traditional genres with their music. For example, Bagus from Netral told me he hoped one day to form a collaboration with Javanese gamelan/ethnic fusion composer Djaduk Ferianto, and Jerry, the lead singer of the hardcore band Bantal (Pillow), once mentioned he had the idea to add *angklung* (pitched bamboo shakers) and other traditional instruments to his band's songs and call the result *art-core.* Nevertheless, Indonesian underground rockers remained generally hesitant about actually attempting to "ethnicize" their music, claiming (inaccurately) that "it had not yet been tried" (*belum dicoba*).

In short, the Indonesian underground seems quite a long way from achieving any kind of grand synthesis between "Indonesian" and "Western," as genres continue to fragment (newly introduced subgenres during my fieldwork included *crustcore, brutal death,* and *hyperblast*) and as musical approaches ranging from ethnic techno-hybridization (Eternal Madness) to austere purism (punk rock) continue to coexist and compete. It is likely, however, that the popularity of underground music will continue to increase, especially among rural and working-class young men, and that the number of bands that "cross over" and record on major labels also will continue to rise. This trend will no doubt create controversy in the underground community, but as long as the scene is composed of university students and other young people who for a time do not have to worry about earning a living, musical "idealism" will live on, and the grassroots, anti-commercial networks that sustain independently produced rock music in Indonesia will not wither.

Dangdut

The metacultural controversies surrounding dangdut—its contested status as a truly "Indonesian" music, its disreputable class associations, its connection with sexual immorality, and so on—cannot be separated from the fact that so many Indonesians find the music a compelling source of undeniable pleasure, whether they admit it or not.

Andy Atis, the Christian Ambonese R & B producer whose studio I describe in chapter 4, once told me that *"dangdut is dead."* His two reasons for this claim—that the rising costs of cassettes put legitimate (nonpirated) dangdut recordings out of reach of the music's nonaffluent core audience, and that the cross-class youth market was becoming more oriented toward MTV and global pop—seemed sound, yet in the course of my research I uncovered no evidence that the dangdut genre was in serious decline. Although the economic crisis did devastate sales of dangdut cassettes, the enthusiasm of ordinary Indonesians—male and female, young and old—for this music has persisted. Furthermore, a growing number of middle-class listeners have embraced dangdut (albeit with a frequent dose of irony), perhaps, as I have proposed, as part of a general process of rethinking the pro-Western developmentalism of the New Order. Although this tentative embrace may yet lead to new, inspired hybrids (such as *dangdut underground* and various cross-fertilizations with *pop Indonesia*), the continued mass appeal of dangdut music will most likely perpetuate the relative stylistic conservatism that has typified the genre since the early days of Rhoma Irama's career.

MTV Indonesia itself featured a dangdut program, *Salam Dangdut,* which became one of its most popular offerings. The following listing appeared on MTV Asia's English-language Web site:

Get one hour of the best and most popular Dangdut music videos. Catch VJ Arie Kuncoro on MTV Salam Dangdut every Sunday at 10:00 a.m. and a repeat viewing on Wednesday at 2:00 p.m.

To capture the essence of Dangdut, the show is hosted from a mock disco Dangdut set, complete with flashing disco lights. On each episode VJ Arie gets in touch with the fans of Dangdut by reading their letters and gives us information on the lives and music of the biggest Dangdut stars around. If you are a Dangdut fan or someone who never really gave Dangdut a listen—MTV Salam Dangdut will get you saying "asik" [intense, cool, pleasurable]. (MTV Asia)

Although clearly begun as a way to exploit dangdut's preexisting popularity, *Salam Dangdut,* as this text implies, may well have won over skeptical middle-class youth to dangdut fandom as a result of MTV's unparalleled cultural authority in the sphere of youth fashion (Sutton 2003, 326).

A 2001 article in the Singaporean *Straits Times* describes dangdut's growing popularity among middle-class Indonesians. According to the article, global major label Sony Music Indonesia (which I had been told two years earlier was unwilling to produce its own dangdut music) recently started an ambitious dangdut division (Kearney 2001). One of the division's first acts was to sign artist Ikke Nurjanah, who sang one of the first dangdut songs to catch on with middle-class audiences, "Terlena." This state of affairs may indicate a sea change in Indonesian middle-class perceptions of dangdut music, but it is more likely merely the latest in a series of well-hyped attempts to expand the music's audience that nonetheless fail to completely disassociate dangdut from its *kampungan* reputation.

Anthropology, Music, Modernity, and the Creative Side of Culture: A Polemic

Even in an anthropology that is now "embodied," too rarely do we find bodies at play or sounds that set grooves in our ethnographies.

Shannon 2004

Anthropologists tend to be ambivalent about the study of music. On the one hand, they consider it as worthy an object of study as any other meaningful human endeavor. On the other, the study of music is generally believed to entail mastering an esoteric technical vocabulary, and many nonmusician anthropologists conclude that the kinds of cultural insights that potentially can be gained from a cultural study of music and musicians can be obtained just as easily (if not more so) from investigating other areas of "expressive culture" that do not require such technical training. Such an attitude overlooks the tremendous body of academic literature on popular music that does not make use of the analytical techniques of musicology; indeed, some of the best-known writers on the subject, such as Simon Frith, do not engage in technical musical analysis at all. This view also overlooks the fact that investigating musical phenomena opens up vital fields of inquiry inaccessible by other means (Monson 1999). These areas of investigation often extend far beyond the preoccupations of the anthropology of aesthetics to matters of central anthropological concern, such as the development of political consciousness, the cultural correlates of social change, and the ethical basis of social relationships.

Musical expression, a panhuman universal, has taken on a special importance in modern societies. Its ability to channel affect, open possibilities for self-expression, and foster communal solidarity (in both imagined and realized-in-the-moment communities) stimulates various attempts to control music and/or harness its power to promote ideology. In Indonesia, powerful but abstract concepts such as nationalism, modernity, unity, and "Indonesian-ness" itself are made palpable and affectively compelling through music, but they rarely take on the monovocality and semantic specificity of ideology in the process. Anthropologists of modern complex societies thus ignore music at their peril if they wish to access the heteroglossic and ambivalent social reality behind the dominant representations produced by the state and by the commercial print and visual media, or hope to enter the realm of private subjectivities and their affect-laden responses to actual social conditions.

Greg Urban's concept of "the metaculture of modernity" directs anthropological attention to the fact that innovations in cultural forms are just as "cultural" as their perpetuation and conservation through time (the orientation Urban calls "the metaculture of tradition," which is more characteristic of small-scale societies). The creative side of culture becomes all the more important in changing societies that metaculturally identify themselves as modern or modernizing or even as "backward" yet hopeful. Urban describes the production of "new" cultural forms in the metaculture of modernity as a process of combining preexisting forms and genres. This ethnography has depicted many examples of this process at work in recording studios, at video shoots, onstage, and at other sites of cultural production. It is important, however, to note that Urban's insights do not rob artistic creation of its "originality," even if they do demystify the process somewhat. Rather, in this book I have argued that in order to be intelligible to an audience, cultural forms must contain aspects of the familiar; furthermore, the creation of cultural objects occurs through the expressive agency of social actors, not as a result of an automatic, subconscious process of combination and recombination. In fact, the high level of technological mediation in contemporary cultural production encourages a certain reflexivity among both producers and listeners regarding the nature of popular forms and the intentional manipulation and juxtaposition of preexisting templates.

Popular music is a vital means through which Indonesian youth creatively explore identity and their position in the modern world and the nation. The inclusive Sukarnoist collectivism of dangdut, the oppositional consciousness of underground music, and the cosmopolitanism of Indonesian pop all in their own way address the urgent concerns of contemporary young people and the relative appeal of each of these forms to different groups of young Indonesians tends to be mediated in important ways by class, gender, and other social categories. Thus popular music, more than any other branch of the Indonesian mass media, registers the ambivalences, allegiances, and emotional attachments different segments of society feel toward the Indonesian nation and the wider world.

The world of Indonesian popular musics is one part of a larger project of national cultural production in which the "product" is a fully modern, culturally distinctive nation. The precise composition of this hybrid cultural form-in-process has yet to be determined, but I would argue that popular music is an excellent starting point for investigating the future contours of such an imagined entity. Although the Indonesian national utopia does not (yet) exist, it can still be powerfully evoked in performance.

To conclude, I hope that the research and analysis contained herein have not only added to our understanding of how struggles over national modernity are played out in Indonesian music and culture but also contributed to an emerging type of anthropological inquiry that combines the insights of popular culture studies with an examination of lived experience in specific social settings. For only through sensitive ethnographic investigation can we understand what is truly at stake in the contestatory field of public culture.

APPENDIX A

Notes on Language in This Book

Throughout this study, direct quotations in the body of the text that are translated from the Indonesian appear in Roman characters, while quotations from Indonesian sources originally in English appear in italics, as do individual English words used in Indonesian passages. Grammatical and other errors in the original are preserved in the text. Thus, the sentence *Katanya musik dangdut udah go international* would be translated as "They say dangdut music has already *go international*," and the sentence *I no good English* (I'm not good at speaking English) would appear as "*I no good English.*" All translations of lyrics and quotations are by the author.

The primary language used by the participants in this study is the Jakartanese nonstandard variant of Indonesian (see appendix C). Much of this language is based on the Javanese-, Sundanese-, and Hokkien-influenced Malay dialect spoken in colonial Batavia, and its grammar, pronunciation, spelling, and lexicon may appear strange to those familiar only with Standard Indonesian. For instance, many common words in Indonesian are pronounced with an *e* sound instead of an *a* sound. Jakartanese grammar, though far from standardized, generally has the following characteristics:

- The standard Indonesian active verb forms *meng*-[root]-*kan* and *meng*-[root]-*i* are both replaced with [root]-*in* or *nge*-[root]-*in*. This form is used for transitive and benefactive verbs and for verbs that use nouns and adjectives as roots.
- Similarly, passive -*kan* and -*i* verbs use the -*in* suffix.
- Active verbs with roots that begin with *c*- are pronounced with *ny*- as the beginning consonant, similar to verbs in Standard Indonesian that begin with *s*.

Examples:
> *membelikan* (to buy something for someone) becomes *beliin*
> *merepotkan* (to inconvenience; to impose) becomes *ngerepotin*
> *mencari* (to search for) becomes *nyariin*
> *mencoba* (to try) becomes *nyoba*

- *Nge-* can also be used to create intransitive verbs from nouns, particularly from English loanwords.

  Examples:

  > *nge-band* (to play in rock groups).
  > *nge-chat* (to engage in online chatting)
  > *nge-drink* (to imbibe alcoholic beverages)
  > *nge-drugs* (to take illegal pharmaceuticals)

Unmarked foreign terms in the text are Jakartanese, colloquial, and/or formal Indonesian. Words in other languages or dialects, such as Javanese, Sundanese, Betawi, and Arabic, are followed by parentheses in which their origin is stated before the gloss, unless they have entered general Indonesian or Jakartanese usage.

Examples:

> *nepsu* (Javanese, "desire")
> *awewe* (Sundanese, "young woman")
> *nemuin* (Betawi, "to tell")
> *magrib* (evening prayers)
> *gendruwo* (demonic village spirit)
> *angklung* (pitched bamboo shaker)

One final note: this book's spelling of the names of former presidents Sukarno, Soeharto, and Megawati Soekarnoputri follow the post–New Order conventions of the *Jakarta Post*, Indonesia's leading English-language newspaper.

APPENDIX B

Other Indonesian Popular Music Genres

Although this book focuses primarily on dangdut, *pop Indonesia,* and underground music, these are not the only major popular music genres in Indonesia. The reader may find the following descriptions helpful, as the genres listed below appear occasionally in the text.

Rock

Indonesian *rock* music is often conceptually separated from Indonesian pop even though it usually appears as a subset of *pop Indonesia* in record-store shelf displays. The label refers to loud, electric guitar–based music, what in America would usually be called "hard rock" and in Indonesian is sometimes referred to simply as *musik keras,* "hard/loud music." Mainstream Indonesian rock bands sing in both English and Indonesian, mostly the latter, and their music is influenced by a variety of Anglo-American groups, from the Rolling Stones to Limp Bizkit to Wilco. This music has a large, primarily male audience usually described with the phrase *menengah ke bawah* (middle to lower [class]). This is also the term used to describe dangdut's audience, but unlike dangdut, *musik rock* does not usually carry the stigma of being *kampungan.*

The popularity of "power ballads," songs sung by hard rock and heavy metal bands that combine distorted guitars and virtuosic solos with slower tempos and heartfelt sentiment, encouraged the development of *slowrock,* a rock subgenre that originated in Malaysia and has successfully crossed over into the Indonesian market (Indonesian and Malay are mutually intelligible). *Slowrock,* with its emotional excess, is considered *kampungan.* There is no separate category of "soft rock" in Indonesia, as such music is classified under pop.

Jazz, Jazz-Pop, and *Jazz Etnik*

Jazz is considered the most prestigious popular music in Indonesia, and Indonesia is home to a number of world-class jazz musicians, including Bubi Chen, Candra Darusman, Dwiki Dharmawan, Indra Lesmana, Pra Budidharma, Syaharani, Gilang Ramadhan, Tohpati, and Donny Suhendra. Indonesian jazz is dominated by keyboardists, guitarists, drummers, bassists, and vocalists;

accomplished horn players are relatively uncommon, perhaps due to the scarcity of high-quality brass and reed instruments in the country. Because the audience for instrumental jazz is extremely limited, many Indonesian jazz players perform on pop albums or form bands of their own that play jazz-inflected, sophisticated *pop Indonesia*.

Indonesian jazz musicians have also experimented with combining jazz with traditional Indonesian music; arguably this has as much to do with reaching an international audience (and thus overcoming the limits of the domestic market) as it does with national or ethnic pride. Nevertheless, such cross-cultural fusions are often quite compelling, and a small overseas audience has taken notice. The best-known of these "progressive ethnic" groups is Krakatau, a multiethnic band from Bandung, West Java, that makes occasional appearances in this study.

Keroncong

Celebrated as the music of the generation of Indonesians who won Indonesia's independence, *keroncong*'s complex origins are even more disreputable than dangdut's. Brought to colonial Batavia (now Jakarta) and other port cities by freed slaves from the Portuguese colonies, *keroncong* was an Iberian-sounding urban folk music enjoyed by members of the Netherlands East Indies' native working and lower classes (Becker 1975). The word *keroncong* is the name of a ukulele-like instrument that is part of this music's customary ensemble, which also includes cello (played pizzicato style), guitar, and *suling*. During the Indonesian war for independence (1945–49), *keroncong* songs sung in Indonesian with nationalist themes became popular, and the style gained a measure of respectability. Unlike dangdut — Indonesia's other major hybrid popular music genre — modern *keroncong* is slow, stately, and refined music more suited to contemplative listening than to dancing.

Keroncong's centuries-long presence in parts of Indonesia has led local musicians to combine this style with local idioms. This led to the emergence of highly syncretized *keroncong* subgenres such as *cilokaq* music in Lombok. The best known of these is *langgam Jawa*, an extraordinary hybrid in which the stringed instruments of the *keroncong* ensemble are tuned to a Javanese scale and play colotomic rhythmic patterns resembling those found in indigenous music of the region (Yampolsky 1991). The refined Portuguese bel canto singing style of original *keroncong* is also merged with traditional Javanese vocal techniques, creating a distinctive hybrid timbre. *Langgam Jawa* was foundational to the development of *campur sari* music, the highly successful genre combining traditional Javanese folk and classical styles, *keroncong*, and dangdut that emerged in the late 1990s.

As for original *keroncong* (*keroncong asli*), it remains a marginal but significant recorded genre. As an exotic yet familiar-sounding acoustic music, *keroncong* has even enjoyed modest success abroad as "world music." *Keroncong* songs are still an active part of the live performance repertoire of Indonesian street musicians and other local, small-time ensembles (Ferzacca 1997). Young Jakartans consider *keroncong* music less than modern but not especially low-class and associate the genre mainly with their grandparents' generation.

Religious Music

Indonesia is the world's largest predominantly Muslim nation, and popular music with Islamic themes plays a significant, if limited, role in the national music scene. *Gambus* and *qasidah* are Middle Eastern–influenced syncretic genres often sung in Arabic. *Pop Muslim*, also known as *nasyid*, includes conventional pop with Islamic themes and Muslim male vocal groups that sing R & B–influenced songs with or without instrumental accompaniment in Indonesian, Arabic, and English (Barengdregt and Zanten 2002, 76–80). Rhoma Irama's songs often contain a moralistic, Islamic message, though his music is still classified as dangdut—a genre many strict Muslims condemn as immoral.

Christian pop music is also recorded and sold in Indonesia, though musically most *pop Rohani* (music of the spirit) does not differ significantly from secular pop genres. There are even a few *dangdut Rohani* recordings in existence; these are usually performed by Muslims who have *masuk Kristen*, converted to Protestant Christianity. In many music retail outlets, the *pop Rohani* section is the only part of the store where domestic and foreign music are mixed together—Indonesian *pop Rohani* recordings share shelf space with international Contemporary Christian albums. Most of this imported music is from the United States.

Musical Imports from Malaysia, China, Japan, and India

Popular music recordings from other Asian countries occupy different positions in the Indonesian musical status hierarchy, in part determined by their specific country of origin. Indonesian and Malaysian Malay are similar languages, and Malay-language popular music has successfully penetrated the large Indonesian market. Malaysian varieties of pop, dangdut, rock, Muslim pop, and heavy metal are widely available and more or less correspond to their Indonesian counterparts with regard to prestige and audience.

Japanese, Mandarin, and Cantonese pop can be found in some medium- to large-sized record stores. This music has a small but significant middle-class following in Indonesia, among both *pribumi* (native) and Chinese Indonesians. The pop music from these countries often resembles *pop Indonesia;* indeed, there appears to be a pan-Asian sentimental pop song style that varies solely by language. This is perhaps one reason why Indonesians find this music an accessible and appealing, if somewhat less prestigious, alternative to Western pop.

Lowest on the scale of prestige is music from India, primarily film song, which is on the opposite end of the spectrum from Anglo-American music in terms of both class associations and price (Indian cassettes cost about half as much as Western imports and about 40 percent less than *pop Indonesia* cassettes). Indian pop music shares many characteristics in common with dangdut, and it is not unusual for a local dangdut ensemble to include a Hindi film song or two in its repertoire. In early 2000, the theme song from the Indian film *Kuch Kuch Hota Hai* (Hindi, "Something, Something Generally Happens") was enormously popular among working-class Jakarta residents. One young Betawi man told me that there were families in his *kampung* (poor urban neighborhood) who owned a copy of the song even though they could not even afford rice to feed themselves!

APPENDIX C

More on Nonstandard Speech Variants

The following ethnographic investigation of Jakarta's speech variants, an update of sorts to Errington's landmark study (1986), reveals the fluidity, multiple subject positions, and intense sociability of life in the city, and provides an important backdrop for understanding Jakartans' speech about popular music and its interpretation.

Bahasa Betawi

I once asked a taxi driver where he was from, and he smiled and replied, "*Batavia.*" He was identifying himself as an *orang Betawi*, a descendant of the original "native" working class of Jakarta during the Dutch colonial period (1619–1942), when the city was known as Batavia (*Betawi* is the Malay pronunciation), the capital of the Dutch East Indies. The Betawi people came to be as the result of a Dutch strategy of importing labor from distant parts of the East Indies in order to prevent the formation of an anti-Dutch alliance between the "native" residents of Batavia and the local Sundanese people of the surrounding countryside (Abeyasekere 1987, 65). The Betawi language that evolved as a medium of communication between the migrants was a dialect of Malay, the language used as a lingua franca by Asians and Europeans alike during the colonial period. Separate dialects of Betawi are still spoken in different Jakarta neighborhoods, and *kampung* dwellers on the outskirts of the city speak dialects strongly influenced by Sundanese.

Betawi is very likely the only language in the world that uses Arabic for its formal first- and second-person singular pronouns (*ane* and *ente*) and Hokkien Chinese for the informal (*gua* and *lu*). Non-Betawi Jakartans (and Betawi speaking to non-Betawi) tend to use the Standard Indonesian *saya* for the formal first-person singular pronoun, while for the informal "I," "me," and "my" they use *gua*, from the Hokkien. *Gua* can also be pronounced *gue,* and when it appears as the subject of a sentence, the pronunciation is sometimes shortened to *go.* This informal Betawi pronoun, and its second-person singular counterpart *lu,* are the quintessential markers of Jakartan speech and by extension, of trendy, cosmopolitan youth culture. In 2000, Pepsi Cola's main slogan for all of Indonesia, *Kalo gue, pilih Pepsi* (As for me, I choose Pepsi), relied on this association to attract a status-conscious youth market for its product. (Actually the slogan would probably read *kalo gue* milih *Pepsi* in truly idiomatic Jakartanese.)

In practice, fully distinguishing between Betawi (a fully recognized regional language, with the same status as Javanese and Sundanese) and Jakartanese is nearly impossible, akin to attempting to separate Black English Vernacular from hip American slang. The linguistic basis of Jakartanese has been identified as Modern Betawi, a loose entity that differs systematically from Old Betawi and is closer to Standard Indonesian (Muhadjir 1999, 69–70). Contemporary Jakartanese words come from a variety of languages—Javanese, Old Betawi, Sundanese, Hokkien, Dutch, Japanese, and English—and their etymologies are sometimes unclear and often unknown to speakers. Jakartanese terms, even those that have entered common usage throughout the archipelago, are always italicized in the official mass media, where they frequently appear in quotations of spoken language and are occasionally used to add flavor or emphasis to a writer's prose. (Non-Indonesian words, such as English business-management jargon or humorous Javanese expressions, also appear frequently in the Indonesian mass media and are similarly italicized.)

The discourse on language use in Jakarta does not address the urban rich/poor dichotomy explicitly, though it is clear that English is considered the most modern and most powerful language choice, while regional languages are deemed the most traditional and solidarity oriented, with both formal and colloquial Indonesian somewhere in the middle. Jakartanese (*bahasa Jakarta*) is seen *not* as an ethnic/regional language (despite its Betawi origins) but as a way of speaking that connotes trendiness, almost like English in particular contexts.

Unlike other forms of language that are considered *kasar* (coarse, low), Jakartanese does circulate publicly on a national level in the mass media. Jakartanese is especially common in youth-oriented popular culture such as student Web sites; the lyrics on some rock, rap, and *dangdut disco* cassettes; and popular magazines. Colorful uses of Jakartanese can also be found in the work of many Indonesian cartoonists, notably Muhammad "Mice" Misrad, whose "Rony" cartoons chronicle, with incisive social satire, the adventures of a working-class Betawi man. The title of a book of collected Rony cartoons (1999), *Bagimu Mal-mu, Bagiku Pasar-ku* (For You, Your Mall; For Me, My Market), is an apt illustration of one of the central themes of this ethnography. The cartoon on the book's cover features the scruffy protagonist talking (in fractured English, no less!) into a banana as though it were a cellular telephone, startling a nearby well-groomed, necktie-wearing man conversing on a real cell phone.

In addition to Jakartanese, Jakarta is home to a number of other, more specialized speech variants developed in response to the conditions of a multiethnic, cosmopolitan milieu.

Bahasa Prokem

Bahasa Prokem, also called *bahasa Okem,* is based primarily on a simple formula involving the infix *-ok-*. The infix is usually added behind the first consonant in a word, and the last syllable is dropped. For example, *duit* (money) becomes *doku, gila* (crazy) becomes *gokil, sepatu* (shoe) becomes *spokat,* and so on. The word *prokem* is actually Prokem for *preman* (criminal, thug); young criminals are supposedly the originators of this speech style, though it has more often been associated with Indonesian high school and university students (Wijayanti 2000, 129; Chambert-Loir 1990). Now considered passé by the student culture that first popularized it, Prokem is still used by some working-class youth in Jakarta, and a few words, such as *bokap* (father), *nyokap* (mother), *pembokat* ("servant"—considered extremely derogatory), *bokin* (wife), and *toket* (breast) have entered general usage in Jakarta. Like Jakartanese itself, Prokem appears to have originated to fill a need for an informal alternative to Standard Indonesian (*bahasa Indonesia baku*) that could be used to promote solidarity and intimacy within groups of people who do not share the same regional (ethnic) language. In 1990, a Prokem-Indonesian dictionary was published in Jakarta (Rahardja and Chambert-Loir 1990).

Singkatan

A feature of *bahasa Prokem* that survives into the present is the habit of creating humorous acronyms and abbreviations (*singkatan*). The Prokem word for *orang tua* (parents), for example, is *ortu.* Hundreds of these *singkatan,* which appear to parody the New Order bureaucracy's penchant for Orwellian neologisms, circulate throughout Jakarta. Popular abbreviations frequently acquire multiple, often contradictory glosses. For example, *ABG* (pronounced *abege*) stood originally for *anak baru gede* ("child just grown," literally "child newly big"), a phrase referring to young adolescents, usually women. It can now also mean *awas babe galak* ("beware, angry father"—a warning to those men who associate with *ABG* girls), *anak Betawi gedongan* (Betawi who live in mansions, i.e., Betawi nouveau riche), or, the opposite of the original gloss, *angkatan babe gue* ([from] my father's generation, i.e., old). Another common slang expression, *BT* (*bete*), used by young people to describe a subjective state of either boredom or irritation, is glossed in numerous ways by different speakers: *bad trip, boring time,* and by its opposite meaning, *binahi tinggi* (high arousal). These examples result from the grassroots creativity of young people from different social classes, and coming up with *singkatan* is a common pastime, particularly for young men (see chapter 6).

Indonesian Gayspeak and *Bahasa Gaul*

Sometimes associated erroneously with the language of male transgendered cross-dressers (known as *waria* or the less polite *banci* or *bencong*), gayspeak is primarily spoken in *gay* and *lesbi* communities in Jakarta and other Indonesian cities. (For a valuable study of the emergence of *gay* and *lesbi* identities in Indonesia, see Boellstorff 2005; see Murray 2001, 43–61, for a discussion of the heavily marginalized lesbian subculture of Jakarta and the ways in which its members are deeply divided by class differences of the sort discussed in this book.) Various terms and expressions from gay speech have been adopted by members of Jakarta's entertainment industry and by young, hip Jakarta professionals. José Capino notes a similar phenomenon in the Philippines, where urban Tagalog gayspeak, known as "sward speak," has become the in-group language of celebrities and entertainment talk-show personalities (2003, 271–72).

In the 1980s the argot spoken by gay Indonesians was known for its multiple use of the infix *-in-,* so that *cewek* (young woman) became *cinewine,* and *bule* (white person) became *binuline* (Chambert-Loir 1990). In the 1990s a new speech style emerged in the gay community that, rather than adding infixes to common words, was based on the principle of *plesetan* (puns), replacing common Indonesian words with less common ones or with the names of countries, ethnic groups, celebrities, brand names, and so on that formally resemble the original word. For example, *sudah* (already) becomes *sutra* ("silk"; also a major brand of condom in Indonesia); *malas* (lazy, to not feel like doing something) becomes *Malaysia*; *minum* (drink) becomes *Minahasa* (the name of an ethnic group from Sulawesi); *ke kiri* (to the left) becomes *ke Chrissye* (to a famous Chinese Indonesian pop singer); and *belum* (not yet) becomes *Blue Band* (a brand of imported margarine). Other words are created by adding infixes in a variety of ways (for a detailed, formalistic inventory of the different techniques of word coinage in Indonesian gayspeak, see Wijayanti 2000). For example, *apa* (what) becomes *apose* or *apipa,* and *aku* ("I"/"me" in informal Standard Indonesian) becomes *akika.* The following hypothetical sentence illustrates the word-substitution principle at work:

> Colloquial Indonesian: *Aku lapar banget. Kamu mo makan di warung ini aja?*
> English: I'm really hungry. Do you wanna just eat at this food stall?
> Gayspeak: *Akika lapangan bola. Kawanua mawar Macarena di Warsawa indang anjas?*
> Literal meaning in Indonesian: [*Akika*] soccer field. Fellow countryman rose Macarena in Warsaw winnow [*anjas*]?

Thanks in part to a best-selling dictionary compiled by a Jakarta entertainment figure (Sahertian 2000), gayspeak has rapidly spread outward from its originary speech communities, becoming a source of trendy youth slang. The dictionary, rather confusingly titled *Kamus Bahasa Gaul* (Dictionary of

Cool/Social Language), makes very little reference to the language's origins in the gay community except in a brief foreword written by an Indonesian folklorist; rather it represents the argot as part of the affluent lifestyle of young, fashionable Jakartans hanging out at *warung*, eating, gossiping, and, of course, getting caught in traffic jams. (The *bahasa gaul* expression *macan tutul* [literally "leopard"] means traffic gridlock [*macet total*].) From an etic point of view, gayspeak is linguistically distinct from *bahasa gaul*, which for most Jakartans simply denotes the slang-filled language of everyday socializing, which is not based on such an involved system of phonetic transformation. Therefore, the title of Sahertian's dictionary is somewhat misleading.

Regional Languages and Regional Slang

Jakarta is a city of many languages in addition to those based on the national vernacular. Immigrants bring to the capital city their regional languages, which have their own versions of *bahasa gaul*. The following is a brief survey of youth slang forms among speakers of Java's other two main regional languages: Javanese (Central and East Java) and Sundanese (West Java).

The majority of Jakarta's immigrants and residents are native Javanese speakers. Unlike Indonesian, Javanese has a complicated system of politeness registers. Each language level resembles a language unto itself, with different lexical items for most common words and phrases. Although all spoken Javanese is hierarchical in this way, parts of Java have a reputation for either more or less refined speech, ranging from the highly refined formal linguistic register spoken in the Central Javanese courts of Yogyakarta and Surakarta to the extremely coarse (*kasar*) informal dialects spoken in less celebrated locales like Tegal and Madiun.

The language Javanese young people employ for informal socializing among friends is *ngoko* or *jawir*, Low Javanese. Although the ability to speak refined forms of Javanese varies considerably depending on region, class, and personal inclination, the youth of Central and East Java all speak *ngoko* and Indonesian, a language they study in school beginning at a very young age. Not surprisingly, the slang spoken in Javanese cities is a combination of Indonesian and very coarse Low Javanese. In many cases, words with fairly mundane meanings such as *nguntal* (Javanese, "eat rice") and *kencot* (Javanese, "hungry") are considered so vulgar they cannot be uttered in mixed company. Such language is unlikely to ever be used in popular music or any other publicly circulating texts.

The university town of Yogyakarta has its own variant of *Prokem* in which Indonesian and Low Javanese words are transformed according to a system of consonant substitution that, I was told by some Yogyanese students, was used by Prince Diponogoro's spies in the nineteenth century. With this code, *cewek* (young women) becomes *jethen*, *motor* (motorbike) becomes *dogos*, *mangan*

(Javanese, "eat") becomes *dalak,* and *ibu* (mother) becomes *pisu.* Dagadu, the T-shirt and accessory manufacturer based in Yogya, got its name from the *Prokem* for *matamu* (literally "your eyes," a mild expletive in Indonesian). Students at Yogyakarta's several universities speak to one another in Low Javanese regardless of their island of origin or ethnic background; Indonesian is reserved for the classroom. A friend told me a story about a university colleague from Sumatra who visited his *kampung* in East Java and made the mistake of addressing the friend's parents in the *kasar* Javanese he had learned from hanging out on campus. This was a grave breach of etiquette, since elders in Java should always be addressed in more elevated forms of Javanese. Though my friend came from a progressive family and usually addressed his parents in *madya* (the middle level of politeness) rather than *krama* (High Javanese), it was still unacceptable to address them in *ngoko.* His Sumatran companion would have been far better off just using Indonesian.

Bandung, another important university town in Indonesia, is the capital of the Sundanese-speaking province of West Java. The city is close enough to Jakarta to be strongly influenced by Jakartan speech, and the language of everyday socializing among Bandung youth is a combination of Jakarta-inflected Indonesian and a very *kasar* form of Sundanese, identified by the first-person singular pronoun *aing.* Sundanese has fewer politeness levels and is less rigidly hierarchical than Javanese, but *kasar* words such as *lebok* (Sundanese, "eat") are also considered inappropriate for public speech.

Pronominal Strategies

Even if one only speaks Indonesian and/or Jakartanese, the choices among possible pronouns to refer to oneself and others are daunting, and they depend on several sociolinguistic factors. Often personal pronouns are omitted in colloquial speech; when this is not possible, the speaker must choose among the following options, which can be used in different combinations:

> First-Person Singular
> *Saya* (Formal Indonesian)
> *Aku* (Informal Indonesian)
> *Gue/Gua* (Jakartanese)
>
> Second-Person Singular
> *Anda* (Formal Indonesian)
> *Kamu, Kau* (Informal Indonesian)
> *Lu* (Jakartanese)

A more neutral alternative to all these pronominal options is to refer to oneself by one's proper name and refer to others by their names. Students in

Jakarta occasionally use this construction when speaking to peers with whom they are not well acquainted.

Which Indonesian pronouns a young Jakartan uses in a given situation with a given interlocutor depends not only on immediate contextual factors but also on ethnicity. Javanese, for example, are more likely to use *aku* in informal conversations. One reason for this is that *aku* is also the first-person pronoun in Low Javanese. Some Sumatran groups find *kamu* offensive and prefer to use *kau,* which most other Jakartans consider somewhat coarser than *kamu.* Sundanese young people are more likely to use *saya* for both informal and formal speech, sometimes using *saya mah* for the former, the Sundanese/Jakartanese particle adding a colloquial familiarity. Betawi people, and many non-Betawi Jakartans, use *gue/gua* and *lu* with friends.

Pronoun choices are also conditioned by more personal, autobiographical factors. Some residents of Jakarta, particularly Javanese who originated from other parts of the country, find *gue/lu* coarse and offensive (*kasar*) and try to use only *aku/kamu* or *saya/kamu.* The informal Jakartanese pronoun *lu* (sometimes spelled *elo* or *elu* or *loe* but pronounced the same) in particular is considered the height of *kasar,* far coarser than the informal Indonesian pronouns *kamu* and *kau.* Other newcomers to the city immediately adopt the Jakartanese pronouns. In the relatively individualistic environment of Jakarta, many variations in pronoun use exist. I met a Jakarta-born middle-class Sundanese graphic designer who used only *saya,* even with his wife, and a Jakarta-born Chinese Indonesian record producer who used *gua* in staff meetings with his employees. I have also observed several figures in the entertainment industry switch first-person pronouns in midstream, sometimes in the course of a single sentence, when being interviewed by journalists. In general, they used *saya* when discussing career-related matters or opinions on serious subjects, *aku* when commenting on their personal aspirations or feelings, and *gue/gua* for humorous asides and when joking around with the reporters. In fact, it is quite common for speakers from all walks of life to switch between pronominal options when speaking to the same person, depending on what is being said.

GLOSSARY OF INDONESIAN AND JAKARTANESE TERMS

Many of the following terms possess several meanings; the definitions below are limited to those relevant to their specific uses in the text.

acara	organized event, often featuring musical performances
aliran	literally "stream," music genre or subgenre
anak gaul	fashionable rich kid
anak jalanan	"street child," child beggar
bajaj	three-wheeled motorized buggy found in Jakarta, a cheaper alternative to taxis
banci	male transgendered cross-dresser (derogatory)
becak	pedal-powered trishaw, pedicab
begadang	to stay up all night, usually for social reasons
belagu	arrogant, proud, self-important
bencong	see *banci*
Betawi	ethnolinguistic group descended from the native laborer class of colonial Batavia, now Jakarta
Blok M	fashionable shopping and entertainment district in South Jakarta
bonang	set of tuned kettle gongs, part of a gamelan ensemble
bule	literally "albino," colloquial term for white person
cengeng	weepy, sentimental, mawkish
cengkok	melismatic ornaments characteristic of dangdut vocals
cinta	love, especially the romantic variety
daerah	region, countryside
D.I.Y.	"Do It Yourself," punk-derived ethos of autonomous artistic production
gaul	cool, social
gendang	(1) tablalike pair of drums used in dangdut music; (2) double-headed barrel drum used in traditional and ethnic music
genit	flirtatious
gicik	crude, tambourine-like percussion instrument used by street-side ensembles and child beggars

goyang	to sway, undulate; the main dance movement of female dangdut performers
jago	champion, virtuoso
jaipong	Sundanese popular dance music played on traditional instruments
janda	a woman without a husband as a result of death, divorce, or abandonment
joget	dance step performed by audiences at dangdut nightclubs and concerts
kampung	village or poor urban neighborhood
kampungan	low-class, repellently characteristic of backward village life
kendang	see *gendang* (2)
keroncong	Indonesian national popular music genre derived from Portuguese-influenced urban folk songs and performed on Western stringed instruments
kesepian	loneliness, isolation
macet	clogged, congested
menengah ke atas	middle to upper [class]
menengah ke bawah	middle to lower [class]
nongkrong	to squat; to socialize, hang out
ngobrol	to talk, chat
nyawer	to publicly bestow money on a performer during a performance
pasar	market, bazaar
pengamen	itinerant street musician
pinggir jalan	the side of the road
plesetan	a play on words, a pun
rakyat	the people, the folk
rakyat kecil	"the little people," the nonaffluent masses
ramai or rame	crowded, noisy, active, fun
saweran	money presented to an onstage performer
selingan	contrastive musical interlude, interpolation
sepi	lonely, deserted, quiet
singkatan	abbreviation, acronym
sombong	arrogant, self-important; Standard Indonesian synonym of *belagu*
suling	Indonesian bamboo flute, end-blown or transverse
waria	"ladyboy," a polite term for male transgendered cross-dresser that combines *wanita* (woman) and *pria* (man)
warnet	cyber café; from *warung internet*
warung	roadside or market stall
wong cilik	Javanese equivalent of *rakyat kecil* (see above)

NOTES

Introduction

1. For a more detailed explanation of the sonic materialist approach, see Wallach 2003b. I use this notion to establish the materiality of popular music products, as objects that intervene in and shape social life. Moreover, perceiving musical sounds as audiotactile material culture invites researchers to trace their distribution through a cultural field and examine their various uses by different social agents.

2. Multigenre ethnographic studies of popular music in the West include Finnegan 1989 and Berger 1999. These two studies have provided valuable models for the present work.

3. My notion of "musicscape" is derived from Arjun Appadurai's famous essay on the various overlapping "scapes" of the global cultural economy (1990) as well as R. Murray Schafer's influential concept of the environmental "soundscape" (1977, 1994). The musicscape is thus both a fluid, translocal and a localized, immediate phenomenon.

4. Gus Dur was appointed by the elected representatives of the People's Consultative Assembly. Susilo Bambang Yudhoyono, who became the country's sixth president in 2004, was the first Indonesian president chosen directly by the Indonesian people in a nationwide general election widely praised by international organizations for its transparency and high voter turnout.

5. In order to address translocal cultural phenomena, Ulf Hannerz divides the contemporary "social organization of meaning" into four "frameworks of flow": state, market, movement, and "form of life" (1992, 46–52). The first two frameworks are characterized by relative asymmetry of resources between producers and consumers of meaning, while the second two are characterized by more-egalitarian forms of organization (60). (I would add that popular musics are shaped by all four frameworks, often simultaneously: they are subject to state control, market forces, appropriation by grassroots social movements, and incorporation into communal lifeways.) Though the four frameworks can be separated analytically, Hannerz notes that they "do not work in isolation from one another, but it is rather in their interplay, with varying respective strengths, that they shape both what we rather arbitrarily demarcate as particular cultures, and that complicated overall entity which we may think of as the global

ecumene" (47). In 1988, the journal *Public Culture* was launched to analyze macro-level cultural "flows" (Appadurai 1990) at the local, global, and national levels.

6. The accompanying illustration on the T-shirt depicts a student protesting for Reformasi confronting a corpulent, smiling man in a suit holding a bag of money labeled *uang negara rakyat* (the people's state money). The man is holding a sign on which is written (in English) *The Best Corruptioner*; a caption pointing to his head reads *cueq aja* (just blowing it off). T-shirts like this one were sold all over Jakarta in traditional markets for 11,000 rupiahs (less than US$2 at the time). See figure on page 10.

7. Daniel Ziv, a longtime expatriate resident of Jakarta, notes sardonically, "Each year in Jakarta we optimistically repeat the same stupid joke: that this coming December *krismon* will finally be over because it becomes 'krismas'. . . . Christmas still hasn't arrived" (2002, 80).

8. See Widjojo et al. 1999 for a collection of detailed firsthand accounts of the student movement that helped topple the New Order. For an examination of the role of song in the Indonesian movement for Reformasi (and in Southeast Asian politics more generally), see Dijk 2003.

9. The Indonesian rupiah slid from 2,450 to the U.S. dollar in July 1997 to 15,000 to the U.S. dollar in January 1998; in May 1998, the month Soeharto stepped down, the exchange rate was 14,000 rupiahs to the dollar (Dijk 2001, 71, 130, 193).

10. For a fascinating, if hardly impartial, insider's account of the political machinations behind Gus Dur's ouster, see Witoelar 2002. An Indonesian TV personality and Wahid's former presidential spokesman, Wimar Witoelar sums up the ordeal as follows: "From the beginning, President Wahid was doomed because he was made president by an unholy alliance whose only purpose in electing him was to block Megawati from becoming president. And that alliance had hoped that Gus Dur would play according to their tune. But when he asserted his independence and basic values of humanism and democracy, he lost the political support" (193–94).

11. Throughout this study, English loanwords, such as *social gap*, used by Indonesians are italicized. See appendix A for more information regarding how foreign terms and translations appear in the text.

12. In later statements, this phrase *ngak-ngik-ngek* became *ngak-ngik-ngok* (Sen and Hill 2000, 186n8).

13. Inspired by the work of feminist theorist Judith Butler (1990), which highlights the constitution and/or subversion of gender identity in performance, a wide range of studies that critically examine the performance of gender in popular music have appeared since the early 1990s. Notable examples of this type of inquiry include Auslander 2006; Schippers 2002; and Walser 1993.

Chapter 1. Indonesian Popular Music Genres
in the Global Sensorium

1. See Pioquinto 1998 for a more detailed consideration of dangdut's history. One example of the pervasiveness of dangdut music throughout the Indonesian archipelago can be found in Anna Tsing's ethnography of a remote region of Kalimantan (Indonesian Borneo), where she encounters a mountain-dwelling spirit medium who claims to be possessed by the spirit of dangdut star Rhoma Irama (Tsing 1993, 245–46).

2. Addressing the earlier style, Margaret Kartomi writes, "In *orkes Melayu*, a soloist sings Malay poetry to Malay melodies, usually accompanied with thin Western harmonies on both Malay and Western instruments, including a flute, acoustic guitar, bass, harmonium, and Malay percussion—drums and optional gongs" (2002, 148 n40).

The repertoire of *orkes Melayu* ensembles often came from Malay *bangsawan* folk theater productions (popular since the late nineteenth century), and early recordings by *orkes Melayu* groups were marketed to ethnic Malays in both Sumatra and peninsular Malaysia (Barendregt 2002, 421).

3. This *suling* is distinct from the end-blown bamboo flute found in Javanese gamelan, which is also called a *suling*. Charles Capwell has pointed out that while the physical instrument itself may be indigenous to Indonesia, the *suling*'s characteristic timbre and playing style in dangdut music more closely approximate those of the South Asian *bansuri* flute heard on thousands of Indian film soundtracks than they resemble anything found in traditional Indonesian music (personal communication, December 2003).

4. Tom Goodman, an American historian who spent time in the strife-torn Maluku province in the late 1990s, reports that musical taste in the most religiously polarized region in Indonesia was indeed split along religious lines. Christians for the most part denied liking dangdut music, while Muslim Moluccans embraced it. On the other hand, Muslims were more willing to admit they liked *dansa*, a local popular music genre with roots in Christian hymnody (personal communication, June 2000).

5. The rise and influence of *pop daerah* variants have attracted the notice of ethnomusicologists and other scholars who work in various parts of Indonesia. See, for example, Williams 1989/1990 for a discussion of New Order Sundanese popular music and Laskewicz 2004 and Harnish 2005b for investigations of the influence of popular music technology and aesthetics on the traditional performing arts in Bali. Useful analyses of Javanese *campur sari* can be found in Perlman 1999; Sutton 2002b, 23–24; and Supanggah 2003. For historical accounts of *pop Minang* and reflections on its cultural significance in contemporary Indonesia, see Barendregt 2002 and Suryadi 2003; see Jones 2005 for an exploration of the popularity of national and regional popular music genres on

public transportation vehicles in the West Sumatran capital of Padang. Sutton 2002a (196–228) provides information on *pop Makassar* and a historical overview of the commercial music industry in South Sulawesi, and Suryadi 2005 gives an illuminating account of local radio and regional pop music in Riau. The growth of increasingly robust regional pop scenes throughout Indonesia has coincided with movements for more regional and cultural autonomy in the post–New Order period.

6. In fact, regional music from Sunda (West Java) has historically demonstrated the most "crossover appeal" in the national market. R. Anderson Sutton notes, "[I]n the past 20 years the music of this one region has, unlike those of any other Indonesian region, found a receptive audience in various parts of the country, due primarily to its infectious drum rhythms and also to the haunting and enticing sound of Sundanese female singers" (2002b, 23). I would add that Sundanese music's access to national media exposure as a result of the West Java province's proximity to Jakarta, and the fact that it constitutes an "ethnic" alternative to the regional music of the culturally dominant (and resented) Javanese, are likely also important factors influencing Sundanese popular music's reception among non-Sundanese listeners.

7. Although numerically few and occasionally the object of envy by the impoverished majority, university students in Indonesia have long been a vanguard of social and political change (see Geertz 1960, 307–8; Anderson 1999, 3). At the beginning of the twenty-first century, there were approximately 2.4 million postsecondary students in Indonesia, out of a total population of roughly 225 million (Arnold 2002, 89). Interestingly, Indonesia ranked eighth, right after Canada, among countries of origin for foreign nationals enrolled in U.S. universities during the 2000–2001 academic year, with a total number of 11,625 students (Secor 2002, 37). After the terrorist attacks on September 11, 2001, it became more difficult to obtain a visa to study in the United States, particularly for Muslim men, and this number went down considerably.

8. The music that became known as ska evolved out of imported American rhythm and blues and indigenous Jamaican influences in the working-class neighborhoods of Kingston in the years after Jamaican independence in 1962 (Bilby 1995). By the late 1960s, ska had been largely superseded in Jamaica by newer genres like rock steady and reggae, but ska, with its infectious, upbeat-stressed rhythms, subsequently caught on in Great Britain, where it was performed by "two-tone" bands composed of black and white musicians for multiracial youth audiences. The so-called third wave of ska bands emerged in England and the United States in the 1980s, many of which, such as Berkeley, California's Operation Ivy, combined ska's characteristic rhythms with the noisy aggression and socially conscious lyrics of punk and hardcore, forging a hybrid style known as "ska-core," which would later become the dominant ska variant in Indonesia. The next phase in ska's development brought the genre to the attention of large numbers of Indonesian music fans for the first time: for a

brief period in 1996–97, segments of the transnational music industry attempted to turn ska into "the next grunge" by introducing a rash of major-label, heavily promoted, and mostly white ska and ska-influenced groups like Sublime, No Doubt, and Reel Big Fish. Ultimately, ska lacked the staying power of what came to be known as "alternative rock," and after producing a handful of modest hits, the style sank out of sight, at least in the American mainstream. However, this relatively brief but far-reaching exposure brought the ska sound to Indonesia, and a number of rock bands in underground music scenes there subsequently began to play in that style.

9. Waiting Room took its name from a song by Fugazi, a seminal band from Washington, DC that has long championed progressive political causes and an ethos of "do-it-yourself" independence. Fugazi has never recorded with a major record label, and I was surprised and impressed that Fugazi was so well known among members of the Indonesian underground movement.

10. The purist attitude toward independent production in the Indonesian underground is summed up in the following text from the liner notes for *Human's Disgust* (1998), an independently released cassette EP by Bandung metal band Fear Inside: "*WHO SAID MAJOR LABELS IS THE SOLUTION / MAJOR LABELS MAKE ME SICKS! / DO IT BY YOURSELF OR DIE.*"

11. O. M. Ranema's Web site is home.att.ne.jp/orange/Raj_Hikomar/ dangdut/omrE.html. By contrast, the limited but positive attention dangdut has received from Western researchers does appear to affect middle-class Indonesian perceptions of the music. For example, Alison Murray claims that the publication of William Frederick's groundbreaking article "Rhoma Irama and the dangdut style" (1982) actually led to increased middle-class acceptance and "mainstream appropriation" of dangdut music in Indonesia (1991, 120–21n2; see also Pioquinto 1998, 74). If this is indeed the case, it illustrates the important lesson that the work of the researcher can create unforeseen consequences for the subjects of his or her research, and that works of scholarship, no less than popular music recordings, are cultural interventions with multiple social effects in various arenas.

Chapter 2. In the City

1. Poorer *kampung* tend to be especially crowded places. The population density of Jakarta as a whole reported in the 1995 census was an astonishing 13,786 people per square kilometer (Forbes 2002, 410).

2. According to Daniel Ziv, "[a]n estimated 20,000 *bule* [colloquial Indonesian for white foreigners] call Jakarta home. . . . They are diplomats, journalists, consultants, bankers, artists, teachers, and NGO activists" (2002, 27). Although glamorous, mass-mediated images of the Western world play a central role in the fantasy lives of many young urban Indonesians (see chapter 6), real-life Westerners working and residing in Jakarta tend to have a rather negative

reputation for drunkenness, profligate spending, and lasciviousness. In my limited interactions with expatriate businessmen living in Jakarta, I often found this stereotype to be sadly right on the mark. See Leggett 2005 for an ethnographic account of expatriate businessmen at one transnational corporation in Jakarta and their arrogant, colonialist perceptions of their Indonesian coworkers.

3. Often the two economic sectors literally overlap in space. An example is the widespread phenomenon of the *pasar kaget* (surprise market), a name given by locals to a cluster of food stalls that mysteriously springs up in empty store and office parking lots at night and is gone by morning.

4. In everyday youth parlance, a common discursive construction for indexing the social gap involves food, namely, the opposition between the *anak singkong* (cassava kids) and the *anak keju* (cheese kids). In many parts of Indonesia, cassava is used as a dietary starch for those too destitute to afford rice, while cheese remains an exotic imported foodstuff associated with expensive Western-style cuisine (such as cheeseburgers and pizza). A well-known Indonesian *pop nostalgia* song written by composer Arie Wibowo, "Cassava and Cheese," places this opposition in the context of a failed cross-class romance:

> "Singkong dan Keju" (refrain)
> *Aku suka jaipong*
> *Kau suka disco oh . . . oh . . .*
> *Aku suka singkong*
> *Kau suka keju oh . . . oh . . .*
> *Aku dambakan seorang gadis*
> *Yang sederhana*
> *Aku ini hanya anak singkong.*
>
> [I like *jaipong*
> You like disco *oh . . . oh . . .*
> I like cassava
> You like cheese *oh . . . oh . . .*
> I desire a girl
> Who is simple
> I'm just a cassava kid.]

5. Alison Murray relates the following quote from Tomo, a middle-aged Sundanese *becak* driver working in Manggarai, South Jakarta, in the 1980s: "There's no-one like Bung Karno. He was a man of the people and cared for the poor. In those days [during the Sukarno presidency] you were free to do any job; it didn't depend on your connections. Before I used to ride my trishaw all over Jakarta, even up to Pasar Ikan. Things are much harsher now; all the riders are scared of the police" (quoted in Murray 1991, 92).

6. Those responsible for the rapes and murders during the May 1998 riots were commonly thought to be hired goons, working for whoever originally orchestrated the violence and chaos—in most accounts, a faction in the

Indonesian military or Soeharto himself. Yet I heard several accounts from eyewitnesses of the riots that suggest that at least some of the violent acts were committed by ordinary people, just as there is evidence civilians participated enthusiastically in the military-backed mass slaughter of suspected Indonesian Communists and Communist sympathizers that took place in 1965–66 (see Rochijat 1985; Report from East Java 1985).

7. For an American expatriate anthropologist's firsthand account and interpretation of the riots, see Leggett 2005, 289–94.

8. Ethnomusicologist David Harnish describes *rame* as "a magnified aesthetic state of liveliness" (2006, 4). While he is defining the term in the context of a multiethnic religious festival in Lombok, I would contend that his characterization applies equally well to the performance of everyday life in Jakarta.

9. One popular *warnet* is located in a corner of the spacious twenty-four-hour McDonald's restaurant adjoining the Sarinah department store in Central Jakarta. Here customers willing to pay three times the usual hourly *warnet* rate can experience two paradigmatic symbols of globalization—the Internet and American fast food—under the same roof.

10. At the same time, even humble roadside food stalls began to offer "*internet*" in their list of specialties. But in such establishments, the term was used as a humorous abbreviation for a popular late-night Jakarta snack: hot soup containing In*domie* (instant ramen noodles), te*lur* (egg), and *kor*net (canned corned beef). Such linguistic play constitutes a symbolic appropriation of an aspect of "modern" lifestyle by working-class Indonesians who lack the educational skills and financial resources to take advantage of the "real" Internet.

11. See appendix C for a survey of nonstandard speech variants in Jakarta.

Chapter 3. Cassette Retail Outlets

1. An exception is Marc Perlman's survey of cassette stalls in Solo, Central Java (1999), which describes a bewildering spectacle of diverse musics on display, both strange and familiar to Western readers.

2. For an investigation of how music genre is indexed by cover graphics, liner notes, and sonic features of Indonesian cassette recordings, see Wallach 2002, 114–31.

3. Xenocentric attitudes regarding religion are common in Indonesia: Muslims look to the Middle East, Christians look to the West, and Hindus increasingly look to India (see Harnish 2005a) for the proper modes of religious conduct and belief.

4. Prices for recorded music rose steadily during the period of my fieldwork, a consequence of rising production costs and Indonesia's weakened currency.

5. Jazz musician and music industry figure Candra Darusman estimates that the cassette format accounted for 95 percent of Indonesian music sales in 1999 (n.d., 1).

6. Darusman, in a discussion of "creativity" in Indonesian popular music, writes, *"Reservations should be mentioned in the field of Dangdut Music which is experiencing a stagnant output in terms of creativity. Maybe the cause of this is the fact that the major decrease in cassette sales is vastly effecting* [sic] *this type of music"* (n.d., 2–3). While dangdut cassette sales did plummet as a result of the *krismon*, I do not agree with Darusman's statement that this caused the creative stagnation of the genre. Instead his words could be viewed as yet another elitist dismissal of dangdut music by a musician specializing in a more prestigious genre. For an earlier example of this tendency, see Piper and Jabo 1987.

7. Jakarta megamalls are expensive places in which to open a music store. According to Daniel Ziv (2002, 88), in 2002 monthly rent for a medium-sized shop in ultra-trendy Plaza Senayan was approximately US$10,000, and there was a six-month-long waiting list to obtain a spot.

8. In mid-2000, another playback device was installed near the entrance to the smaller room. This was a listening booth that played a limited assortment of new releases on compact disc, both Indonesian and Western, through an accompanying set of headphones. The listener was able to operate the controls in order to hear particular albums and tracks stored in the machine. Similar digital listening booths have become popular fixtures in large Western record stores; thus, rather than constituting an extension of the Indonesian practice of trying out cassettes before purchasing, the presence of this particular playback device in the Aquarius store is better viewed as an example of transnational influences in record-store commerce.

9. Puppen's 2000 self-titled cassette was a notable exception: Guitarist/manager Robin Malau decided to pay the value-added tax required by law in order to sell the album in mainstream retail outlets like Aquarius. Puppen was one of the few underground bands to take this bold and costly step, which in the end proved to be a wise investment: during one week in May 2000, Puppen's cassette was ranked at number 38 in the Aquarius store's Top Forty list, outselling the then-new album by Sting.

10. According to Robin Hutagaol, the store's proprietor, the name is an irreverent pun on *ishkabibble*, an obscure Yiddish-American colloquialism he encountered once in a dictionary of American slang. In addition to running Ish-Kabible, Robin played drums and sang with the underground band Brain the Machine, which described its sound as *industrial hardcore progressive*.

Chapter 4. In the Studio

1. Remixes of dangdut songs, which rerecord the analog tracks of the original and import them into a totally digital domain, are a different matter. See Wallach 2005 for a discussion of dangdut remix recordings.

2. Some recording companies have used other *gendang* players on their recordings besides the top three. At an ethnic fusion concert event in a Jakarta

hotel featuring the Sundanese group Krakatau, I met an Indian classical tabla player affiliated with Jakarta's Indian Cultural Center who claimed that while living in Indonesia he frequently recorded rhythm tracks on commercially released dangdut songs. He mentioned that he found playing dangdut rhythms to be easy and that playing on dangdut cassettes was a lucrative side venture for him.

3. The function of chordal polyphony in dangdut music resembles its role in Indian film song, about which Peter Manuel asserts, "The role of harmony in a song may ultimately derive from the nature of the melody, especially since almost all film songs consist of a solo vocal melody with accompaniment. In most songs using harmony [that is, employing chordal polyphony], the conception of the melody is clearly modal, such that the chordal accompaniment functions in an ornamental rather than structural manner" (1988, 183).

4. In his study of the Papua New Guinea recording industry, Malcolm Philpott includes this quotation from Mike Wild, an Australian sound engineer who worked in a major Papuan recording studio. It is worth requoting here: "One thing any newcomer notices right away [about Papuan popular music] is the melody line. They don't just sit there and set a beat, then do a melody line over the top. They set about it in reverse. They set the melody and then work out the beat underneath. Most musicians I've ever worked with played a drum beat, then they went for a chord structure over that, and finally sang a melody line over the top of that. Up here [in Papua New Guinea] it's a bit like building a house starting with the roof first, and finishing up with the basement and the foundations. Whatever, it sounds great" (quoted in Philpott 1998, 119). I reproduce this text not in order to posit a primordial connection between Indonesian and Melanesian music but to point out that the architectonic model of musical composition that Wild assumes to be normative is in many ways culturally specific. Such a model is in fact derived from historically situated rock music compositional techniques and multitrack studio practices that are far from universal. Wild's "house" metaphor reveals an ethnocentric bias; the notion that musical composition should start with a rhythmic foundation over which a melody is layered like a "roof" does not take account of the diversity of world musics, nor does it acknowledge that different sound-engineering practices, such as those described here for dangdut, might accompany this diversity.

5. Not everyone was happy with the producer's arrangement. I attended a birthday party sing-along in a working-class neighborhood where the participants made a point of adding a *gendang* and bass-guitar rhythm track on the synthesizer (*organ tunggal*) when performing a rendition of this song.

6. For considerations of the production/simulation of "liveness" with studio technology and its importance for establishing genre-specific expectations of musical authenticity, see Auslander 1999, 61–111; and Meintjes 2003, 109–45. New cassette releases are usually easily adapted to live instrumentation by

local dangdut performing ensembles, despite the complexity and polish of their arrangements.

7. Edy's advice notwithstanding, I would argue that the rise of *pop alternatif* in Indonesia in fact transformed expectations of how women singers should sound. Although some artists in that genre, such as Potret lead singer and solo artist Melly Goeslaw, specialized in breathy, girlish vocalizing (in Goeslaw's case, inspired in part by Icelandic recording artist Björk), female-led groups like Bandung's Cokelat have achieved significant commercial success with more assertive, less sexualized vocal personae.

8. Sadly, this recording was never released.

9. In addition to combining English, Indonesian, and Spanish in his songs, Andy Atis added one more, even riskier language: Hebrew. For complicated reasons, Hebrew has become a language of church worship for many Indonesian Christians, whose pro-Jewish and Zionist leanings appear to be a reaction against the anti-Jewish and anti-Zionist sentiments attributed to the more powerful and numerous Muslim population. Andy inserted a partially masked Hebrew phrase, *heveinu shalom aleichem* (we bring peace unto you), into the introduction of one of his songs on the theme of peace and brotherhood between Indonesians of different religions—an act he regarded as rather subversive, given Indonesia's Muslim majority. The phrase is sung by an ethereal, electronically processed voice similar to that employed by Patty for the strange-sounding English-language phrase at the beginning of one of her songs. It may not be coincidental that these two uncanny vocal performances, with their use of foreign tongues and wraithlike timbres, appear to index the limits of acceptable expression in the Indonesian national music market in the same way that strange (*aneh*) Javanese spirits index the limits of the human cultural and linguistic order (Geertz 1960, 28–29; Siegel 1986).

10. Music video programs, on the other hand, often alternated freely between Indonesian and overseas artists; perhaps this strategy of presentation will gradually erode the conceptual barrier between domestic and foreign music products, and Andy's prediction of a truly globalized Indonesian music market will come to pass.

11. Such dismissive attitudes appear to have changed very little. While researching the Balinese metal scene for a forthcoming documentary, filmmaker Sam Dunn was told repeatedly by prominent figures in the Jakarta underground metal world that Bali was "backward" and that he would find little of interest there (Sam Dunn, personal communication, September 2006).

Chapter 5. On Location

1. See Williams 2001 (115–16) for a description of similar visual and narrative conventions in the making of *tembang Sunda* video clips.

2. For useful analyses of this emblematic cultural product of the Soeharto regime, see Anderson 1990, 176–83; Hendry 2000, 99–104; and Pemberton 1994a, 1994b.

3. After viewing the finished video clip of "Cinta Hanya Sekali" at a Bowling Green State University Popular Culture departmental colloquium, Marilyn Motz alerted me to the ways in which the camera's gaze invites the viewer to empathize with Iyeth's character. Instead of eroticizing and objectifying the image of the woman singer (a characteristic visual strategy in Western music videos), the camera focuses on Iyeth's face and its expressive features—lips, (tearful) eyes, and mouth—rather than on other body parts (personal communication, October 2003). This filmic technique—typical of dangdut videos featuring women singers—corresponds to the female-centered nature of the clip's narrative as well as to the woman's point of view expressed in the song itself.

4. In fact, Iyeth went on to become a major dangdut star in the early 2000s, with several hit songs to her credit and frequent mentions in the Indonesian tabloid press.

5. In 1996 Netral, Nugie, and Pas opened for American groups Sonic Youth, the Beastie Boys, and the Foo Fighters (a group founded by Nirvana's former drummer) at a concert in Jakarta. This event provided a rare moment of face-to-face contact between three well-known Western "alternative" bands and the Indonesian groups they inspired.

6. *Nurani*, from the Arabic, means "innermost, pure, and radiant." One of Netral's most poignant compositions, according to Bagus, the band's vocalist, the song "Nurani" expresses a longing for a vanished era when people in Jakarta were less "individualist" and selfish, and when there was a greater level of caring and solidarity within the communities that made up the city. One Betawi fan of the song suggested that it was also about "peacemaking" (*perdamaian*) in the aftermath of the 1998 Jakarta riots, when people involved in the violence and looting refused to heed the voice of their "inner conscience" (*hati nurani*). The timing of the song's initial 1999 release bolsters this interpretation, as does the Indonesian television network's decision to broadcast its video clip during televised coverage of an event many feared would result in a renewed outbreak of citywide rioting and chaos.

7. The theme of the moon as sympathetic companion and cure for nocturnal feelings of loneliness recurs in Indonesian pop texts. "Hujan" (Rain), a song by Bandung-based *heavypop* band Cherry Bombshell, contains these lyrics:

> *Ooooooohh . . . rembulan malam*
> *Temani aku dalam lamunan*
> *Ooooooohh . . . rembulan padam*
> *Jangan aku kau tinggalkan*

Jangan kau bersedih, jangan kau menangis
Bulan kau kembali temani dirimu

[Ooooooh, night's moon
Befriends me in my dreaming
Ooooooh, extinguished moon
Do not leave me

Don't you be sad, don't you cry
Your moon returns to be your friend and keep you company.]

(From the album *Luka Yang Dalam*
[A Deep Wound], 2000)

Cherry Bombshell and Netral both worked with the same producer, Jerry Bidara of Bulletin Records, though this was probably not a factor in the lyrical convergence of "Hujan" and "Cahaya Bulan." More likely, I would argue, is that both songs convey a preoccupation with loneliness (experienced as the absence of sociality, of companionship) typical of Indonesian middle-class youth culture in general (see Wallach 2002, 143–47).

Chapter 6. Offstage

1. This song can be found on *Music of Indonesia, Vol. 2: Indonesian Popular Music* (Yampolsky 1991). Another Warung Gaul favorite, "Sengaja" (Intentionally) performed by Elvy Sukaesih, is also on this compilation.

2. This definition of *bahasa gaul* should not be confused with the trendy, playful speech variant based on Jakarta gayspeak discussed in appendix C. The regulars at the Warung Gaul were unaware of the existence of that language, which at the time was spoken mostly by celebrities, *gay* and *lesbi* Indonesians, and hip Jakarta yuppies, and they did not themselves understand it.

3. I employ pseudonyms throughout the discussion of the three *warung*. In the section on the university I use real names, as I do everywhere else in the book.

4. Creambaths are actually an Indonesian salon specialty with an English name. Years later, I came across the following definition: "A few remarks on the famous Indonesian 'creambath.' First, it's not a bath in cream, or anything quite so sensual. It is basically a thorough hair wash followed by a head, neck and shoulder massage using an herbal conditioning cream. Eventually, with the cream fully rubbed in, a steamer is applied so that the cream seeps into the pores and revitalizes the hair and scalp" (Ziv 2002, 124).

5. Beautiful Western women, to borrow a phrase from James Siegel (2000), have a "ghostly presence" in Indonesia, where for many young men they are the elusive embodiments of male sex and power fantasies. One secret of their allure, I suspect, is that *cewek bule* (white chicks) represent the possibility of a sexual

and romantic relationship that exists magically outside the normal exchanges and obligations of everyday life and the strictures of Islamic religious morality (cf. Schade-Poulsen 1999, 182–87, and chapter 9 of the present volume). A contemporary Indonesian urban legend is the story of the ugly, dark-skinned *becak* (pedicab) driver with whom a Western woman falls in love. She then devotes her life to him, and her considerable wealth saves the man from destitution.

An East Javanese friend of mine once lamented the decline of the *hitam manis* (black sweet) ideal of feminine Indonesian beauty in favor of westernized notions that stressed light skin and Caucasoid features. Although I suspect that *hitam manis* has long been a counteraesthetic in Indonesia, he may have a point when so many contemporary Indonesian actors, models, and singers happen to be *Indos*, Indonesians of partial European descent.

6. For an enlightening interpretation of "dubbing culture" in the Indonesian context, see Boellstorff 2003.

7. Marc Schade-Poulsen notes a strikingly similar phenomenon in a description of informal performances of *raï* music in Algeria. He states that in Arab and Algerian music, vocal melody and drum rhythm "cannot be dissociated from each other": "This became clear to me when I took my guitar along to beach trips or drinking sessions outside Oran. When I played songs from the local repertoire, not many seconds would pass before I had someone in the group playing the rhythm on the wood of my guitar; we were two persons playing the same instrument" (1999, 70). Dangdut music seems to follow a similar musical logic, and this leads to analogous behaviors in Indonesian informal performance settings (see figure on page 157).

8. At the time of this writing in late 2006, Wendi is a writer for the Indonesian *Rolling Stone* and is a major figure in the Jakarta rock scene as a journalist, concert promoter, and band manager.

9. American communications scholar Kembrew McLeod (2005, 60–61) notes that the United States frequently violated European intellectual property laws during its early history as a struggling new nation.

10. These radicalized university students belong to a tradition of cultural and political avant-gardism dating back to the years before Indonesia's independence. In his 1960 monograph on Javanese society, Geertz describes the members of what he terms "the emerging 'youth culture'" in the Indonesia of that time:

> [A] group of restless, educated, urban young men and women possessed of a sharp dissatisfaction with traditional custom and a deeply ambivalent attitude toward the West, which they see both as the source of their humiliation and "backwardness" and as the possessor of the kind of life they feel they want for themselves. . . . Painfully sensitive, easily frustrated, and passionately idealistic, this group is in many ways the most vital element in contemporary Indonesian society. . . . They are the Republic's hope and its despair: its hope because their

idealism is both its driving force and its moral conscience; its despair because their exposed psychological position in the avant-garde of social change may turn them rather quickly toward the violent primitivism of other recent youth movements in Europe whose inner need for effective social reform was greater than the actual changes their elders were capable of producing for them. (1960, 307–8)

Many of the young idealists Geertz describes were to succumb to this "violent primitivism"; hundreds of thousands of young Indonesians went on to participate in the horrific events of 1965–66 as perpetrators or victims of mass murder. More than three decades later, student activism emerged once again in Indonesia as a more positive source of social change, and the activists I encountered in Jakarta fit Geertz's description — written about members of their grandparents' generation — remarkably well.

11. It is difficult, but not impossible, for Chinese Indonesians to gain acceptance into *pribumi* ("native") male hangout groups. Gus, a Chinese noodle-cart vendor in his midthirties, explained to me how through hanging out he was able to develop rapport with the local toughs in the North Jakarta neighborhood where he worked and thus to ensure his safety against harassment. Gus knew well the destructive power of anti-Chinese sentiment among the *pribumi:* the multistory building that housed the bakery he once owned was destroyed in the 1998 riots, during which Gus himself was pursued and nearly killed by a rampaging mob. For a discussion of the poignantly conflicted subject positions of Chinese Indonesians, see Ang 2001, 52–74.

Chapter 7. Onstage

1. This interpretation of the /rif song is certainly open to question. Am I being a bit too idealistic here? Probably. Although I would maintain that the musical and emotional emphasis /rif placed on the line *Ku hanya orang biasa* (I'm just an ordinary person) during its performance encouraged audience members to sing along and identify with this lyric, experiencing the "ordinariness" of the protagonist as being not that different from their own. Moreover, *orang biasa* was a phrase that I often heard Indonesians use to describe themselves in contrast to the *pejabat* (officeholders) and the *koruptor*s of society, and it seemed in those contexts to contain more dignity than related expressions such as *orang miskin* (poor person), *orang kampung* (village/slum person), or *wong cilik* (little person). Following this usage, in this book I often describe working-class and underclass people as "ordinary Indonesians."

2. Badjuridoellahjoestro is a poet based in Yogyakarta who writes verse inspired by the plight of various types of working-class Indonesians. I am greatly indebted to Benedict Anderson for his suggestions on how to translate and interpret this poem. He alerted me to the fact that the speaker in the first

stanza is intended to be an irritated motorist, unwilling to listen to the street musician's song. The second stanza is the *pengamen's* reply (which in real life he would never get a chance to voice), in which he asks the speaker from the first stanza when he will listen to his song through to the end (instead of presumably cutting him off with a token payment of spare change) and join in the singing, for without openness toward one's fellow man, both musician and listener are doomed to sing forever of the "stifling deadness" of their individual lives (B. Anderson, personal communication, October 2002). In addition to its poignant portrayal of the humble street busker, the poem also expresses a central value of Indonesian sociality: the desire to *bergaul,* to interact with others, as a way to ward off loneliness and "deadness."

3. Krakatau was the only group that used electronic keyboards during their set despite the evening's "acoustic" theme. This was necessary because Krakatau's music employs a customized gamelan-based tuning system that cannot be played on an acoustic piano tuned to the standard Western equal-temperament scale.

4. See Sen and Hill 2000, 108–36, and Sutton 2003 for a historical overview of the Indonesian television industry and the controversial place of "foreign content" in national network programming.

5. TPI specialized in dangdut-related programming, which earned it the mean-spirited nickname Televisi Pembantu Indonesia (Television for Indonesian House Servants) among members of the middle and upper classes.

6. Music producer Edy Singh told me that the King of Dangdut himself, Rhoma Irama, was originally supposed to participate in the Three Tenors sequence but had bowed out.

Chapter 8. Dangdut Concerts

1. In Indonesia, the sight of two men dancing together does not carry the same homoerotic overtones as it might in the West.

2. Dangdut performer and media superstar Inul Daratista, whose controversial rise to prominence took place after the period of time this book covers, provides an obvious example of the power of erotic onstage dance moves. In the beginning, her sole claim to fame, which caused her to be targeted by religious moral watchdogs even as it won her fans from around the archipelago, was a technique known as the "drilling dance" (*goyang ngebor*). As a result of the notoriety this dance caused, Inul was able to rise from obscurity and become a multimedia celebrity, appearing on VCDs (initially bootlegged recordings of live performances), TV specials, and even an Indonesian soap opera (Mulligan 2005). For articles about Inul in the Western media see, for example, BBC News 2003; Lipscombe 2003; Walsh 2003; and Wilde 2003. For a more academic study that perceptively situates the Inul controversy in the context of contested gender ideologies in post–New Order Indonesia, see Wichelen 2005.

3. Susan Browne's (2000) monograph distinguishes between "*dangdut kampungan*" (trashy, low-class dangdut) and dangdut that is "*sopan dan rapi*" (which she translates as "respectable and orderly," though "polite and neat" is perhaps a closer approximation). Browne associates the former with live performances in *kampung* settings and the latter with recording artists, televised concerts, and nightclubs (though she also confusingly asserts that dangdut nightclub performances may be considered *kampungan* [28]). I did not encounter either phrase during my fieldwork, and the first, with its blatantly pejorative tone, would be unlikely to be used as the name of a musical category by enthusiasts (who would find it offensive) or critics (for whom it would be redundant). Though they make use of Indonesian words, the two categories appear to be entirely etic, and Browne acknowledges that the phrase *dangdut kampungan* is not specifically employed by dangdut fans or detractors (31). Although it is true that the staging and dance moves of televised dangdut events often bear little resemblance to those of outdoor dangdut concerts, the distinction that Browne claims exists between the two types of dangdut she identifies seems for the most part not to be recognized by the music's fans and producers, who generally regard dangdut as a holistic phenomenon that belongs to the common people whatever form it takes.

4. Dangdut clubs belong to a category of male-dominated leisure spaces found in many East and Southeast Asian societies that feature hostesses, alcohol consumption, and myriad forms of paid female companionship. For an informative ethnographic investigation of the cultural and psychosexual dynamics of "hostess clubs" in Japan, see Allison 1994.

5. Similar techniques of instrumental substitution were used by dangdut bands to perform Lilis Karlina's dangdut/ethnic fusion hit "Cinta Terisolasi" at live concerts. For instance, the *suling* player usually performed the song's violin parts. See chapter 4 for a description of "Cinta Terisolasi" and its nonstandard rhythm and instrumentation.

Chapter 9. Rock and Pop Events

1. An intriguing, perhaps related, example of elite appropriation of this song: in October 1998, an Indonesian all-star jazz group (tenor saxophone: Trisno; piano: Bubi Chen; upright bass and trombone: Benny Likumahuwa; drums and percussion: Cendi Luntungan) recorded a multitracked jazz instrumental version of "Moliendo Café" ("grinding coffee" in Spanish) that is included on the album *Wonderful World* (1999). Accomplished jazz vocalist Syaharani, who sang on the album but did not perform on this particular track, insisted to me it was *not* an attempt to cover "Kopi Dangdut," though the recording's prominent use of a tambourine might suggest otherwise, since this instrument is unusual in both Latin popular music and acoustic jazz but ubiquitous in dangdut music. Moreover, the tambourine is playing a dangdut rhythm!

2. Sean Williams (personal communication, February 2005) suggests that *noceng* could also be short for "no *cengeng*" (nonweepy), which would highlight the hard rock orientation of the event.

3. This sports complex was also the location of the Netral video shoot described in chapter 5.

4. See Dijk 2001, 347–50, for a detailed account of this incident and its aftermath.

Chapter 10. Underground Music

1. The inclusion of these salutes to groups' fans in cassette liner notes may stem partially from commercial motives. Carol Muller discusses a thank-you list in a South African Nazarite hymn cassette insert and suggests that with the final message to the "fans," the worship community the cassette indexes "is commodified and redefined as a potential market" (1999, 144). While in this particular South African religious sect the tension between community and market is often cast in terms of sacred and secular, in the Indonesian underground movement the opposition is between "idealism" and "capitalism," the latter concerned with commercial viability and the former with artistic expression. Both the Nazarite religious sect discussed by Muller and the Indonesian underground movement have had to confront new commercial opportunities in a postauthoritarian, market-driven society that, while widening the movements' potential reach, also threatens their integrity as cohesive interpretive communities.

2. See Weinstein 1991, 228–30, for a helpful, unsensationalized description of moshing and stage-diving activities at live concerts.

3. A memorable cartoon by Muhammad "Mice" Misrad satirizes middle-class youth's preoccupation with lifestyle choices (see figure on page 245). The cartoon depicts the Rony character asking, *"Anak mana loe?"* (Which kid are you?). The four panels that follow depict possible choices, all middle-class youth subcultural types: *anak punk* (punk kid), *anak rap* (rap kid), *anak metal* (metal kid), and *anak gaul* (trendy rich kid), but the final panel depicts a saddened Rony and a rather different social type: an *anak jalanan* (street kid) playing a *gicik* and singing mournfully of his hardship: *Betap maling nasib ku . . . gara-gara Orde Baru,* "How unfortunate is my fate . . . all because of the New Order" (1999, 29). The cartoon's incisive social satire underscores the difference between "lifestyle" and a life of struggling to survive. Mice's cartoon portrays the underground music movement, for all its earnestness and its progressive politics, as little more than an affectation for westernized, privileged kids indifferent to the suffering of the impoverished majority of Indonesians, who do not have the luxury of making lifestyle choices.

WORKS CITED

Literature Cited

Abeyasekere, Susan. 1987. *Jakarta: A history*. Singapore: Oxford Univ. Press.

Adorno, Theodor. 1973. *The jargon of authenticity*. Evanston, IL: Northwestern Univ. Press.

Allison, Anne. 1994. *Nightwork: Sexuality, pleasure, and corporate masculinity in a Tokyo hostess club*. Chicago: Univ. of Chicago Press.

Anderson, Benedict R. O'G. [1983] 1991. *Imagined communities: Reflections on the origin and spread of nationalism*. London: Verso.

———. 1990. *Language and power: Exploring political cultures in Indonesia*. Ithaca, NY: Cornell Univ. Press.

———. 1998. *The spectre of comparisons: Nationalism, Southeast Asia and the world*. New York: Verso.

———. 1999. Indonesian nationalism today and in the future. *Indonesia* 67:1-11.

Ang, Ien. 2001. *On not speaking Chinese: Living between Asia and the West*. New York: Routledge.

Appadurai, Arjun. 1990. Disjuncture and difference in the global cultural economy. *Public Culture* 2 (2): 1-24.

———. 1996. *Modernity at large: Cultural dimensions of globalization*. Minneapolis: Univ. of Minnesota Press.

Armbrust, Walter. 1996. *Mass culture and modernism in Egypt*. Cambridge: Cambridge Univ. Press.

Arnold, Wayne. 2002. Young Indonesia. *DoubleTake* 8 (1): 88-90.

Atkins, E. Taylor. 2001. *Blue Nippon: Authenticating jazz in Japan*. Durham, NC: Duke Univ. Press.

Auslander, Philip. 1999. *Liveness: Performance in a mediatized culture*. New York: Routledge.

———. 2006. *Performing glam rock: Gender and theatricality in popular music*. Ann Arbor: Univ. of Michigan Press.

Austin, J. L. 1975. *How to do things with words*. Cambridge, MA: Harvard Univ. Press.

Badjuridoellahjoestro. 1994. *Kudengar tembang buruh, puisi pilihan lima tahun: 1987-1991*. Yogyakarta: Media Widya Mandala.

Bakhtin, Mikhail M. 1981. *The dialogic imagination: Four essays*. Ed. Michael

Holquist. Trans. Caryl Emerson and Michael Holquist. Austin: Univ. of Texas Press.

——. 1984. *Rabelais and his world.* Trans. Hélène Iswolsky. Bloomington: Indiana Univ. Press.

Barendregt, Bart. 2002. The sound of "Longing for Home": Redefining a sense of community through Minang popular music. *Bijdragen tot de Taal-, Land- en Volkenkunde* 158 (3): 411–50.

Barendregt, Bart, and Wim van Zanten. 2002. Popular music in Indonesia since 1998, in particular fusion, indie and Islamic music on video compact discs and the Internet. *Yearbook for Traditional Music* 34:67–113.

Bass, Colin. 2000. Indonesia: No risk—no fun. In *World music: The rough guide,* ed. Simon Broughton and Mark Ellingham, rev. ed., vol. 2, 131–42. London: Rough Guides.

Baulch, Emma. 1996. Punks, rastas and headbangers: Bali's Generation X. *Inside Indonesia* 48. http://www.insideindonesia.org/edit48/emma.htm (accessed June 18, 2003).

——. 2002a. Alternative music and mediation in late New Order Indonesia. *Inter-Asia Cultural Studies* 3:219–34.

——. 2002b. Creating a scene: Balinese punk's beginnings. *International Journal of Cultural Studies* 5 (2): 153–77.

——. 2003. Gesturing elsewhere: The identity politics of the Balinese death/thrash metal scene. *Popular Music* 22 (2): 195–215.

Bauman, Richard. [1977] 1984. *Verbal art as performance.* Prospect Heights, IL: Waveland Press.

Bauman, Richard, and Charles L. Briggs. 1990. Poetics and performance as critical perspectives on language and social life. *Annual Review of Anthropology* 19:59–88.

BBC News. 2003. Indonesian cleric adopts "erotic" dancer. *BBC News,* March 6, 2003. http://news.bbc.co.uk/go/pr/fr/-2/hi/asia-pacific/2825529.htm (accessed May 2, 2003).

Beazley, Harriot. 2000. Street boys in Yogyakarta: Social and spatial exclusion in the public spaces of the city. In *A companion to the city,* ed. Gary Bridge and Sophie Watson, 472–88. Malden, MA: Blackwell.

——. 2002. "Vagrants wearing make-up": Negotiating spaces on the streets of Yogyakarta, Indonesia. *Urban Studies* 39 (9): 1665–83.

Becker, Judith. 1975. Kroncong, Indonesian popular music. *Asian Music* 7 (1): 14–19.

Berger, Harris. 1999. *Metal, rock, and jazz: Perception and the phenomenology of musical experience.* Middletown, CT: Wesleyan Univ. Press; Hanover, NH: Univ. Press of New England.

Bhabha, Homi. 1994. *The location of culture.* New York: Routledge.

Bilby Kenneth. 1995. Jamaica. In *Caribbean currents: Caribbean music from rhumba to reggae,* ed. Peter Manuel, 143–82. Philadelphia: Temple Univ. Press.

Bodden, Michael. 2005. Rap in Indonesian youth music of the 1990s: "Globalization," "outlaw genres," and social protest. *Asian Music* 36 (2): 1–26.

Boellstorff, Tom. 2003. Dubbing culture: Indonesian *gay* and *lesbi* subjectivities and ethnography in an already globalized world. *American Ethnologist* 30 (2): 225–42.

——. 2005 *The gay archipelago: Sexuality and nation in Indonesia.* Princeton, NJ: Princeton Univ. Press.

Bourdieu, Pierre. 1984. *Distinction: A social critique of the judgment of taste.* Trans. Richard Nice. Cambridge, MA: Harvard Univ. Press.

Breese, Gerald. 1966. *Urbanization in newly developing countries.* Englewood Cliffs, NJ: Prentice-Hall.

Brenner, Suzanne. 1998. *The domestication of desire: Women, wealth, and modernity in Java.* Princeton, NJ: Princeton Univ. Press.

Browne, Susan. 2000. *The gender implications of dangdut kampungan: Indonesian "low-class" popular music.* Monash Univ. Institute for Asian Studies Working Paper no. 109. Melbourne: Monash Univ., Centre of Southeast Asian Studies.

Bruner, Edward. 1999. Return to Sumatra: 1957, 1997. *American Ethnologist* 26 (2): 461–77.

——. 2001. The Maasai and the Lion King: Authenticity, nationalism, and globalization in African tourism. *American Ethnologist* 28 (4): 881–908.

Butler, Judith. 1990. *Gender trouble: Feminism and the subversion of identity.* New York: Routledge.

Capino, José. 2003. Soothsayers, politicians, lesbian scribes: The Philippine movie talk show. In *Planet TV: A global television reader,* ed. Lisa Parks and Shanti Kumar, 262–74. New York: New York Univ. Press.

Chambert-Loir, Henri. 1990. Prokem, the slang of Jakarta youth: Instructions for use. *Prisma* 50:80–88.

Chow, Rey. 1993. Listening otherwise, music miniaturized: A different type of question about revolution. In *The cultural studies reader,* ed. Simon During, 382–402. New York: Routledge.

Chun, Allen, Ned Rossiter, and Brian Shoesmith, eds. 2004. *Refashioning pop music in Asia: Cosmopolitan flows, political tempos and aesthetic industries.* New York: RoutledgeCurzon.

Cooper, Nancy. 2000. Singing and silences: Transformations of power through Javanese seduction scenarios. *American Ethnologist* 27 (3): 609–44.

Crafts, Susan, Daniel Cavicchi, Charles Keil, and the Music in Daily Life Project. 1993. *My music.* Hanover, NH: Univ. Press of New England.

Danesh, Abol Hassan. 1999. *Corridor of hope: A visual view of informal economy.* Lanham, MD: Univ. Press of America.

Danu. 2000. Ditekan Sedikit, Ahh . . . *Kompas,* July 9, 2000. http://www
.kompas.com/kompas-cetak/0007/09/latar/dite14.htm (accessed July 12,
2000).

Darusman, Candra. n.d. The current and future outlook of popular music in
Indonesia. Seminar paper.

Davis, Sara L. M. 2005. *Song and silence: Ethnic revival on China's southwest
borders.* New York: Columbia Univ. Press.

Dijk, Kees van. 2001. *A country in despair: Indonesia between 1997 and 2000.*
Leiden: KITLV Press.

——. 2003. The magnetism of songs. *Bijdragen tot de Taal-, Land- en Volkenkunde* 159 (1): 31–64.

Doyle, Peter. 2005. *Echo & reverb: Fabricating space in popular music recording,
1900–1960.* Middletown, CT: Wesleyan Univ. Press.

Durham, Deborah. 1999. Predicaments of dress: Polyvalency and the ironies of
a cultural identity. *American Ethnologist* 26 (2): 389–411.

Eakin, Emily. 2001. Harvard's prize catch, a Delphic postcolonialist. *New York
Times,* November 17, 2001, A15, 17.

Errington, J. Joseph. 1986. Continuity and change in Indonesian language development. *Journal of Asian Studies* 45 (2): 329–53.

Feld, Steven. [1982] 1990. *Sound and sentiment: Birds, weeping, poetics, and song
in Kaluli expression.* Rev. ed. Philadelphia: Univ. of Pennsylvania Press.

——. 1988. Notes on world beat. *Public Culture* 1 (1): 31–37.

——. 1996. Pygmy pop: A genealogy of schizophonic mimesis. *Yearbook for Traditional Music* 28:1–35.

——. 2000. A sweet lullaby for world music. *Public Culture* 12:145–71.

Ferzacca, Steve. 1997. *Keroncong* music in a Javanese neighborhood: Rehearsals
with spirits of the popular. Paper presented at the Society for Ethnomusicology, 42nd annual meeting, October 24, 1997.

——. 2001. *Healing the modern in a Central Javanese city.* Durham, NC: Carolina Academic Press.

Fikentscher, Kai. 2000. *You better work! Underground dance music in New York
City.* Hanover, NH: Univ. Press of New England.

Finnegan, Ruth. 1989. *The hidden musicians.* Cambridge: Cambridge Univ.
Press.

Forbes, Dean. 2002. Jakarta. In *Encyclopedia of urban cultures: Cities and cultures
around the world,* ed. Melvin Ember and Carol R. Ember, vol. 1, 410–18.
Danbury, CT: Grolier.

Frederick, William. 1982. Rhoma Irama and the dangdut style: Aspects of contemporary Indonesian popular culture. *Indonesia* 32:103–30.

——. 1997. Dreams of freedom, moments of despair: Armijn Pané and the
imagining of modern Indonesian culture. In *Imagining Indonesia: Cultural
politics and political culture,* ed. Jim Schiller and Barbara Martin-Schiller,
54–89. Athens: Ohio University Center for International Studies.

Frith, Simon. 1981. *Sound effects: Youth, leisure, and the politics of rock'n'roll.* New York: Pantheon Books.

——. 1996. *Performing rites: On the value of popular music.* Cambridge, MA: Harvard Univ. Press.

Frith, Simon, Will Straw, and John Street, eds. 2001. *The Cambridge companion to pop and rock.* New York: Cambridge Univ. Press.

Geertz, Clifford. 1960. *The religion of Java.* Chicago: Univ. of Chicago Press.

——. 1963. *Peddlers and princes: Social development and economic change in two Indonesian towns.* Chicago: Univ. of Chicago Press.

——. 1995. *After the fact: Two countries, four decades, one anthropologist.* Cambridge, MA: Harvard Univ. Press.

Goffman, Erving. 1974. *Frame analysis: An essay on the organization of experience.* Cambridge, MA: Harvard Univ. Press.

Goshert, John Charles. 2000. "Punk" after the Pistols: American music, economics, and politics in the 1980s and 1990s. *Popular Music and Society* 24 (1): 85–106.

Goodwin, Andrew. 1993. Fatal distractions: MTV meets postmodern theory. In *Sound and vision: The music video reader,* ed. Andrew Goodwin and Simon Frith, 45–66. New York: Routledge.

Greene, Paul. 1999. Sound engineering in a Tamil village: Playing audiocassettes as devotional performance. *Ethnomusicology* 43 (3): 459–89.

——. 2001. Mixed messages: Unsettled cosmopolitanisms in Nepali pop. *Popular Music* 20 (2): 169–88.

Greene, Paul, and David Henderson. 2000. At the crossroads of languages, musics, and emotions in Kathmandu. *Popular Music and Society* 24 (3): 95–116.

Greene, Paul, and Thomas Porcello, eds. 2005. *Wired for sound: Engineering and technologies in sonic cultures.* Middletown, CT: Wesleyan Univ. Press.

Grijns, Kees, and Peter J. M. Nas, eds. 2000. *Jakarta-Batavia: Socio-cultural essays.* Leiden: KITLV Press.

Guinness, Patrick. 2000. Contested imaginings of the city: City as locus of status, capitalist accumulation, and community; Competing cultures of Southeast Asian societies. In *A companion to the city,* ed. Gary Bridge and Sophie Watson, 87–98. Malden, MA: Blackwell.

Hannerz, Ulf. 1992. *Cultural complexity: Studies in the social organization of meaning.* New York: Columbia Univ. Press.

Harnish, David. 2005a. Defining ethnicity, (re)constructing culture: Processes of musical adaptation and innovation among the Balinese of Lombok. *Journal of Musicological Research* 24 (3–4): 265–86.

——. 2005b. Teletubbies in paradise: Tourism, Indonesianisation, and modernisation in Balinese music. *Yearbook for Traditional Music* 37:103–23.

——. 2006. *Bridges to the ancestors: Music, myth, and cultural politics at an Indonesian festival.* Honolulu: Univ. of Hawai'i Press.

Hatch, Martin. 1989. Popular music in Indonesia. In *World music, politics, and social change,* ed. Simon Frith, 47–68. Manchester, UK: Manchester Univ. Press.

Hendry, Joy. 2000. *The Orient strikes back: A global view of cultural display.* New York: Berg.

Herbst, Edward. 1997. *Voices in Bali: Energies and perceptions in vocal music and dance theater.* Hanover, NH: Univ. Press of New England.

Hill, David, and Krishna Sen. 1997. Wiring the *warung* to global gateways: The Internet in Indonesia. *Indonesia* 64:67–89.

Hull, Terence, Endang Sulistyaningsih, and Gavin Jones. 1999. *Prostitution in Indonesia: Its history and evolution.* Jakarta: Pustaka Sinar Harapan.

Hymes, Dell. 1975. Breakthrough into performance. In *Folklore: Performance and communication,* ed. Daniel Ben-Amos and Kenneth Goldstein, 11–74. The Hague: Mouton.

Ivy, Marilyn. 1995. *Discourses of the vanishing: Modernity, phantasm, Japan.* Chicago: Univ. of Chicago Press.

Jakarta Post. 2000. Leave cars at home on Earth Day: Official, Friday, April 14. http://www.thejakartapost.com/Archives/ArchivesDet2.asp?FileID= 20000414.A07 (accessed March 28, 2002).

Jarrett, Michael. 1992. Concerning the progress of rock & roll. In *Present tense: Rock & roll and culture,* ed. Anthony DeCurtis, 167–82. Durham, NC: Duke Univ. Press.

Jellinek, Lea. 1991. *Wheel of fortune: The history of a poor community in Jakarta.* Honolulu: Univ. of Hawai'i Press.

Jones, Tod. 2005. *Angkutan* and *bis kota* in Padang, West Sumatra: Public transport as intersections of a local popular culture. Paper presented at the Arts, Culture and Political and Social Change since Suharto Workshop, Launceston, Australia, available from http://www.utas.edu.au/indonesia _workshop/abstracts.htm (accessed August 13, 2006).

Kaplan, E. Ann. 1987. *Rocking around the clock: Music television, postmodernism, and consumer culture.* New York: Methuen.

Kartomi, Margaret. 2002. Debates and impressions of change and continuity in Indonesia's musical arts since the fall of Suharto, 1998–2002. *Wacana Seni* 1:109–49.

Kartoyo, D. S., and Uki Bayu Sedjati. 1997. *Biografi satria bergitar: Rhoma Irama.* Jakarta: Limo Pendowo Karyaindo.

Katz, Mark. 2004. *Capturing sound: How technology has changed music.* Berkeley: Univ. of California Press.

Keane, Webb. 1997. *Signs of recognition: Powers and hazards of representation in an Indonesian society.* Berkeley: Univ. of California Press.

——. 2003. Public speaking: On Indonesian as the language of the nation. *Public Culture* 15 (3): 503–30.

Kearney, Marianne. 2001. Dangdut hits it big in Indonesian music industry. *The Straits Times,* November 5, 2001, 46.

Keil, Charles, and Steven Feld. 1994. *Music grooves: Essays and dialogues.* Chicago: Univ. of Chicago Press.

Kesumah, Dloyana. 1995. *Pesan-pesan budaya lagu-lagu pop dangdut dan pengaruhnya terhadap perilaku sosial remaja kota.* Jakarta: Departemen Pendidikan dan Kebudayaan Republik Indonesia.

Khudori, and Paulus Winarto. 2000. Virtual office plus. *Virtual* suppl. no. 8, *Gamma* 2 (25): 16.

Kramer, A. L. N., and Willie Koen, eds. 1995. *Tuttle's concise Indonesian dictionary.* Rev. ed. Rutland, VT: Charles E. Tuttle.

Labrousse, Pierre. 1994. The second life of Bung Karno: Analysis of the myth (1978–1981). *Indonesia* 57:175–96.

Laskewicz, Zachar. 2004. Pop music and interculturality: The dynamic presence of pop music in contemporary Balinese performance. In *Refashioning pop music in Asia: Cosmopolitan flows, political tempos and aesthetic industries,* ed. Allen Chun, Ned Rossiter, and Brian Shoesmith, 183–97. New York: RoutledgeCurzon.

Leggett, William H. 2005. Terror and the colonial imagination at work in the transnational corporate spaces of Jakarta, Indonesia. *Identities: Global Studies in Culture and Power* 12 (2): 271–301.

Liechty, Mark. 2003. *Suitably modern: Making middle-class culture in a new consumer society.* Princeton, NJ: Princeton Univ. Press.

Lipscombe, Becky. 2003. Indonesia's controversial star. *BBC News,* May 1, 2003. http://news.bbc.co.uk/go/pr/fr/-2/hi/asia-pacific/2992615.stm (accessed May 2, 2003).

Lockard, Craig. 1998. *Dance of life: Popular music and politics in Southeast Asia.* Honolulu: Univ. of Hawai'i Press.

Mallau, Dion. 2001. Pontianak Bersatu. http://www.bisik.com/underground/Beritadetail.asp?idw=139&page=1&choi=1&pr=1 (accessed January 16, 2001; page no longer active).

Manuel, Peter. 1988. *Popular musics of the non-Western world: An introductory survey.* New York: Oxford Univ. Press.

——. 1993. *Cassette culture: Popular music and technology in North India.* Chicago: Univ. of Chicago Press.

Manuel, Peter, and Randal Baier. 1986. Jaipongan: Indigenous popular music of West Java. *Asian Music* 18 (1): 91–110.

Mahon, Maureen. 2004. *Right to rock: The Black Rock Coalition and the cultural politics of race.* Durham, NC: Duke Univ. Press.

Mazzarella, William. 2003. *Shoveling smoke: Advertising and globalization in contemporary India.* Durham, NC: Duke Univ. Press.

McLeod, Kembrew. 2005. *Freedom of expression™: Overzealous copyright bozos and other enemies of creativity.* New York: Doubleday.

McVey, Ruth. 1982. The Beamtenstaat in Indonesia. In *Interpreting Indonesian politics: Thirteen contributions to the debate,* ed. Benedict Anderson and Audrey Kahin, 84–91. Ithaca, NY: Cornell Univ. Press.

Meintjes, Louise. 2003. *Sound of Africa! Making music Zulu in a South African studio.* Durham, NC: Duke Univ. Press.

Merriam, Alan. 1964. *The anthropology of music.* Evanston, IL: Northwestern Univ. Press.

Middleton, Richard. 1990. *Studying popular music.* Philadelphia: Open Univ. Press.

———. 1999. Form. In *Key terms in popular music and culture,* ed. Bruce Horner and Thomas Swiss, 141–55. Malden, MA: Blackwell.

Miller, Daniel. 1995. Introduction: Anthropology, modernity, and consumption. In *Worlds apart: Modernity through the prism of the local,* ed. Daniel Miller, 1–22. New York: Routledge.

Miller, Flagg. 2005. Of songs and signs: Audiocassette poetry, moral character, and the culture of circulation in Yemen. *American Ethnologist* 32 (1): 82–99.

Misrad, Muhammad "Mice." 1999. *Rony: Bagimu Mal-mu Bagiku Pasar-ku.* Jakarta: Kepustakaan Populer Gramedia.

Moehn, Frederick. 2005. "The disc is not the Avenue": Schizmogenetic mimesis in samba recording. In *Wired for sound: Engineering and technologies in sonic cultures,* ed. Paul Greene and Thomas Porcello, 47–83. Middletown, CT: Wesleyan Univ. Press.

Monson, Ingrid. 1999. Riffs, repetition, and theories of globalization. *Ethnomusicology* 43 (1): 32–65.

Muhadjir. 2000. *Bahasa Betawi: Sejarah dan perkembangannya.* Jakarta: Yayasan Obor Indonesia.

Mulder, Niels. 2000. *Indonesian images: The culture of the public world.* Yogyakarta: Kanisius.

Muller, Carol. 1999. *Rituals of fertility and the sacrifice of desire: Nazarite women's performance in South Africa.* Chicago: Univ. of Chicago Press.

Mulligan, Diane. 2005. The discourse of Dangdut: Gender and civil society in Indonesia. In *Gender and civil society: Transcending boundaries,* ed. Jude Howell and Diane Mulligan, 117–38. New York: Routledge,

Murray, Alison. 1991. *No money, no honey: A study of street traders and prostitutes in Jakarta.* Singapore: Oxford Univ. Press.

———. 2001. *Pink fits: Sex, subcultures and discourses in the Asia-Pacific.* Clayton, Victoria, Australia: Monash Univ. Press.

Nass, Martin. 1971. Some considerations of a psychoanalytic interpretation of music. *Psychoanalytic Quarterly* 40 (2): 303–16.

Nelson, Angela. 1999. Rhythm and rhyme in rap. In *This is how we flow: Rhythm in black cultures,* ed. Angela Nelson, 46–53. Columbia: Univ. of South Carolina Press.

Ong, Aihwa, and Michael Peletz, eds. 1995. *Bewitching women, pious men: Gender and body politics in Southeast Asia.* Berkeley: Univ. of California Press.

Ortner, Sherry. 1995. Resistance and the problem of ethnographic refusal. *Comparative Studies in Society and History* 37 (1): 173–93.

Peacock, James. 1968. *Rites of modernization: Symbols and social aspects of Indonesian proletarian drama.* Chicago: Univ. of Chicago Press.

Pemberton, John. 1994a. Recollections from "Beautiful Indonesia": Somewhere beyond the postmodern. *Public Culture* 6 (2): 241–62.

——. 1994b. *On the subject of "Java."* Ithaca, NY: Cornell Univ. Press.

Perlman, Marc. 1999. The traditional Javanese performing arts in the twilight of the New Order: Two letters from Solo. *Indonesia* 68:1–37.

Philpott, Malcolm. 1998. Developments in Papua New Guinea's popular music industry. In *Sound alliances: Indigenous peoples, cultural politics, and popular music in the Pacific,* ed. Philip Hayward, 107–22. New York: Cassell.

Pickles, Jo. 2000. Punks for peace: Underground music gives young people back their voice. *Inside Indonesia* 64. http://www.insideindonesia.org/edit64/punk1.htm (accessed June 18, 2003).

Pioquinto, Ceres. 1995. Dangdut at Sekaten: Female representations in live performance. *Review of Indonesian and Malaysian Affairs* 29 (1–2): 59–89.

——. 1998. A musical hierarchy reordered: Dangdut and the rise of a popular music. *Asian Cultural Studies* 24:73–125.

Piper, Susan, and Sawung Jabo. 1987. Indonesian music from the 50's to the 80's. *Prisma* 43:25–37.

Porcello, Thomas. 1998. Tails out: Social phenomenology and the ethnographic representation of technology in music-making. *Ethnomusicology* 42 (3): 485–510.

Putranto, Wendi, with Krisna Sadrach. 2002. Mengupas sejarah metal Jakarta dengan Sucker Head! http://musickita.com/news/detail.php?id=1010480068 (accessed January 9, 2002; link no longer functioning).

Qureshi, Regula. 2000. How does music mean? Embodied memories and the politics of affect in the Indian *sarangi. American Ethnologist* 27 (4): 805–38.

Rahardja, Prathama, and Henri Chambert-Loir. 1990. *Kamus Bahasa Prokem.* Jakarta: Pustaka Utama Grafiti.

Report from East Java. 1985. *Indonesia* 41:135–49.

Rochijat, Pipit. 1985. Am I PKI or non-PKI? Trans. with an afterword by Benedict Anderson. *Indonesia* 40:37–56.

Rofel, Lisa. 1999. *Other modernities: Gendered yearnings in China after socialism.* Berkeley: Univ. of California Press.

Roseman, Marina. 1987. Inversion and conjuncture: Male and female performance among the Temiar of Peninsular Malaysia. In *Women and music in cross-cultural perspective,* ed. Ellen Koskoff, 131–49. Westport, CT: Greenwood Press.

——. 1991. *Healing sounds from the Malaysian rainforest: Temiar music and medicine.* Berkeley: Univ. of California Press.

Ross, Andrew, and Tricia Rose, eds. 1994. *Microphone fiends: Youth music and youth culture.* New York: Routledge.

Sahertian, Debby. 2000. *Kamus bahasa gaul.* Rev. ed. Jakarta: Pustaka Sinar Harapan.

Schade-Poulsen, Marc. 1999. *Men and popular music in Algeria: The social significance of raï.* Austin: Univ. of Texas Press.

Schafer, R. Murray. 1977. *The tuning of the world.* New York: Knopf.

——. 1994. *The soundscape: Our sonic environment and the tuning of the world.* Rochester, VT: Destiny Books.

Schippers, Mimi. 2002. *Rockin' out of the box: Gender maneuvering in alternative hard rock.* New Brunswick, NJ: Rutgers Univ. Press.

Sears, Laurie, ed. 1996. *Fantasizing the feminine in Indonesia.* Durham, NC: Duke Univ. Press.

Secor, Laura. 2002. Foreign relations. *New York Times,* January 13, 2002, Education Life, 36–37.

Seeger, Anthony. 1987. *Why Suyá sing: A musical anthropology of an Amazonian people.* Cambridge: Cambridge Univ. Press.

Sembiring, Ita. 1998. *Catatan dan refleksi: Tragedi Jakarta 13 dan 14 Mei 1998.* Jakarta: PT Gramedia.

Sen, Krishna, and David Hill. 2000. *Media, culture, and politics in Indonesia.* Melbourne: Oxford Univ. Press.

Shank, Barry. 1994. *Dissonant identities: The rock 'n' roll scene in Austin, Texas.* Hanover, NH: Univ. Press of New England.

Shannon, Jonathan. H. 2004. Knocking some sense into anthropology. Review essay for Meintjes 2003. *American Anthropologist* 106(2): 395–96.

——. 2006. *Among the jasmine trees: Music and modernity in contemporary Syria.* Middletown, CT: Wesleyan Univ. Press.

Siegel, James. 1986. *Solo in the New Order: Language and hierarchy in an Indonesian city.* Princeton, NJ: Princeton Univ. Press.

——. 1998. *A new criminal type in Jakarta: Counter-revolution today.* Durham, NC: Duke Univ. Press.

——. 2000. *Kiblat* and the mediatic Jew. *Indonesia* 69:9–40.

Sovani, N. V. 1964. The analysis of "overurbanization." *Economic Development and Cultural Change* 12:113–22.

Spiller, Henry. 2001. Using music video to conflate old and new in West Java, Indonesia: "Goyang Karawang" by Lilis Karlina. Paper presented at the Society for Ethnomusicology 46th Annual Meeting, Southfield, Michigan.

——. 2004. *Gamelan: The traditional sounds of Indonesia.* Santa Barbara, CA: ABC-CLIO.

Stallybrass, Peter, and Allon White. 1986. *The poetics and politics of transgression.* London: Methuen.

Steedly, Mary. 1999. The state of culture theory in the anthropology of Southeast Asia. *Annual Review of Anthropology* 28:431–54.

Sterne, Jonathan. 1997. Sounds like the Mall of America: Programmed music and the architectonics of commercial space. *Ethnomusicology* 41 (1): 22–50.

Stocker, Terry. 2002. *It happened so fast! Changing Korea, critical years 1994–1997.* Daejon, South Korea: Heliot House.

Stokes, Martin. 1992. *The arabesk debate.* New York: Clarendon/Oxford Univ. Press.

Stone, Ruth. 1982. *Let the inside be sweet: The interpretation of music event among the Kpelle of Liberia.* Bloomington: Indiana Univ. Press.

Sujatmoko, Bambang Hamid, and Paulus Winarto. 2000. Angkot Dunia Informasi. Virtual suppl. no. 8, *Gamma* 2 (25): 4–7.

Sumarsono, Tatang. 1998. *Sajadah panjang Bimbo: 30 tahun perjalanan kelompok musik religius.* Bandung: Penerbit Mizan.

Sun Yung Shin. 2004. Economic miracles. *Mid-American Review* 24 (2): 183–87.

Supanggah, Rahayu. 2003. Campur sari: A reflection. *Asian Music* 34 (2): 1–20.

Suryadi. 2003. Minangkabau commercial cassettes and the cultural impact of the recording industry in West Sumatra. *Asian Music* 34 (2): 51–90.

——. 2005. Identity, media and the margins: Radio in Pekanbaru, Riau (Indonesia). *Journal of Southeast Asian Studies* 36 (1): 131–51.

Suseno, Dharmo Budi. 2005. *Dangdut musik rakyat: Catatan seni bagi calon diva dangdut.* Yogyakarta: Kreasi Wacana.

Sutton, R. Anderson. 1996. Interpreting electronic sound technology in the contemporary Javanese soundscape. *Ethnomusicology* 40 (2): 249–68.

——. 2002a. *Calling back the spirit: Music, dance, and cultural politics in lowland South Sulawesi.* New York: Oxford Univ. Press.

——. 2002b. Popularizing the indigenous or indigenizing the popular? Television, video, and fusion music in Indonesia. *Wacana Seni* 1:13–31.

——. 2003. Local, global, or national? Popular music on Indonesian television. In *Planet TV: A global television reader,* ed. Lisa Parks and Shanti Kumar, 320–40. New York: New York Univ. Press.

——. 2004. "Reform arts"? Performance live and mediated in post-Soeharto Indonesia. *Ethnomusicology* 48 (2): 203–28

Taylor, Charles. 1991. *The ethics of authenticity.* Cambridge, MA: Harvard Univ. Press.

Taylor, Timothy. 1997. *Global pop: World music, world markets.* New York: Routledge.

——. 2001. *Strange sounds: Music, technology, and culture.* New York: Routledge.

Tenzer, Michael. 2000. *Gamelan gong kebyar: The art of twentieth-century Balinese music.* Chicago: Univ. of Chicago Press.

Théberge, Paul. 1997. *Any sound you can imagine: Making music/consuming technology.* Hanover, NH: Univ. Press of New England.

Theodore, K. S. 1999. Industri Musik Indonesia di Ujung Abad Ke 20. *Buletin ASIRI* 5 (November): 10–11.

Thornton, Sarah. 1996. *Club cultures: Music, media, and subcultural capital.* Hanover, NH: Univ. Press of New England.

Titon, Jeff Todd. 1997. Ethnomusicology and values: A reply to Henry Kingsbury. *Ethnomusicology* 41 (2): 253–57.

Tsing, Anna L. 1993. *In the realm of the diamond queen: Marginality in an out-of-the-way place*. Princeton, NJ: Princeton Univ. Press.

Turino, Thomas. 1999. Signs of imagination, identity, and experience: A Peircean semiotic theory for music. *Ethnomusicology* 43 (2): 221–55.

——. 2000. *Nationalists, cosmopolitans, and popular music in Zimbabwe*. Chicago: Univ. of Chicago Press.

Turner, Victor. 1967. *The forest of symbols: Aspects of Ndembu ritual*. Ithaca, NY: Cornell Univ. Press.

Urban, Greg. 1993. Culture's public face. *Public Culture* 5 (2): 213–38.

——. 2001. *Metaculture: How culture moves through the world*. Minneapolis: Univ. of Minnesota Press.

Wallach, Jeremy. 2002. Modern noise and ethnic accents: Indonesian popular music in the era of *Reformasi*. PhD diss., Department of Anthropology, University of Pennsylvania.

——. 2003a. "Goodbye my Blind Majesty": Music, language, and politics in the Indonesian underground. In *Global pop, local language*, ed. Harris M. Berger and Michael T. Carroll, 53–86. Jackson: Univ. Press of Mississippi.

——. 2003b. The poetics of electrosonic presence: Recorded music and the materiality of sound. *Journal of Popular Music Studies* 15 (1): 34–64.

——. 2004. Dangdut trendy. *Inside Indonesia* 78:30.

——. 2005. Engineering techno-hybrid grooves in two Indonesian sound studios. In *Wired for sound: Engineering and technologies in sonic cultures*, ed. Paul D. Greene and Thomas Porcello, 138–55. Middletown, CT: Wesleyan Univ. Press.

Walser, Robert. 1993. *Running with the devil: Power, gender, and madness in heavy metal music*. Hanover, NH: Univ. Press of New England.

Walsh, Bryan. 2003. Inul's rules: A new idol is putting some sex and sizzle into Indonesia's pop-music scene. *Time Asia* 161 (11) (March 24), www.time.com/time/asia/magazine/article/0,13673,501030324-433338,00.html (accessed May 2, 2003).

Waterman, Christopher. 1990 *Jùjú: A social history and ethnography of an African popular music*. Chicago: Univ. of Chicago Press.

Waters, Malcolm. 1995. *Globalization*. New York: Routledge.

Waxer, Lise A. 2002. *The city of musical memory: Salsa, record grooves, and popular culture in Cali, Colombia*. Middletown, CT: Wesleyan Univ. Press.

Weintraub, Andrew. 2004. *Power plays: Wayang golek puppet theater of West Java*. Athens: Univ. of Ohio Press.

——. 2006. Dangdut Soul: Who are "the people" in Indonesian popular music? *Asian Journal of Communication* 16 (4): 411–31.

Weinstein, Deena. 1991. *Heavy metal: A cultural sociology*. New York: Lexington Books.

Wichelen, Sonja van. 2005. "My dance immoral? *Alhamdulillah* no!" *Dangdut* music and gender politics in contemporary Indonesia. In *Resounding international relations: On music, culture, and politics,* ed. M. I. Franklin, 161–77. New York: Palgrave Macmillan.

Wicke, Peter. 1990. *Rock music: Culture, aesthetics, and sociology.* New York: Cambridge Univ. Press.

Widjojo, Muridan S., et al. 1999. *Penakluk rezim Orde Baru: Gerakan Mahasiswa '98.* Jakarta: Pustaka Sinar Harapan.

Widodo, Amrih. 1995. The stages of the state: Arts of the people and rites of hegemonization. *Review of Indonesian and Malaysian Affairs* 29 (1–2): 1–35.

Wijayanti, Sri Hapsari. 2000. Bahasa gaul: Fenomena kehidupan bahasa. *Atma nan Jaya* 13 (1): 128–36.

Wilde, Craig J. de. 2003. Inul Daratista: An Indonesian concert idol. *Music Business Journal* 3 (1). http://www.musicjournal.org/03inuldaratista.htm (accessed May 12, 2003).

Williams, Sean. 1989/1990. Current developments in Sundanese popular music. *Asian Music* 21 (1): 105–36.

——. 2001. *The sound of the ancestral ship: Highland music of West Java.* Oxford: Oxford Univ. Press.

Witoelar, Wimar. 2002. *No regrets: Reflections of a presidential spokesman.* Jakarta: Equinox.

Wong, Deborah. 1989/1990. Thai cassettes and their covers: Two case histories. *Asian Music* 21 (1): 78–104.

Wong, Deborah, and René T. A. Lysloff. 1998. Popular music and cultural politics. In *The Garland encyclopedia of world music,* vol. 4: *Southeast Asia,* ed. Terry Miller and Sean Williams, 95–112. New York: Garland.

Yampolsky, Philip. 1987a. *Lokananta: A discography of the national recording company of Indonesia, 1957–1985.* Bibliography Series no. 10. Madison: Center for Southeast Asian Studies, Univ. of Wisconsin.

——. 1987b. Liner notes to Idjah Hadidjah's album *Tonggeret.* Icon Records 79173.

——. 1989. "Hati Yang Luka," an Indonesian hit. *Indonesia* 47:1–17.

——. 1991. Liner notes to *Music of Indonesia,* vol. 2, *Indonesian popular music: Kroncong, Dangdut, and Langgam Jawa.* Smithsonian/Folkways SF40056.

——. 1995. Forces for change in the regional performing arts of Indonesia. *Bijdragen tot de Taal-, Land- en Volkenkunde* 151 (4): 700–725.

Yano, Christine. 2002. *Tears of longing: Nostalgia and the nation in Japanese popular song.* Cambridge, MA: Harvard Univ. Asia Center.

Zak, Albin. 2001. *The poetics of rock: Cutting tracks, making records.* Berkeley: Univ. of California Press.

Ziv, Daniel. 2002. *Jakarta inside out.* Jakarta: Equinox.

Zuberi, Nabeel. 2001. *Sounds English: Transnational popular music.* Chicago: Univ. of Illinois Press.

Internet Sites

Note: References to Internet Web sites (URLs) were accurate at the time of publication.

Periodicals

www.thejakartapost.com (*The Jakarta Post*)
www.jawapos.co.id (*Jawa Pos*)
www.tempointeraktif.com (*Tempo Interactive*)

Music-Related Sites

www.bisik.com
http://members.tripod.com/~IrvKa/index.html (Irvan's dangdut page)
www.iwan-fals.com (official Iwan Fals Web site)
www.k5.dion.ne.jp/~ranema/logo_e.html (O.M. Ranema [Japanese dangdut group] Web site)
www.angelfire.com/nm/eternalmadness (official Eternal Madness Web site)
www.geocities.com/SunsetStrip/3817/bio.htm (official Trauma Web site)
www.krakatau.net (official Krakatau Web site)
www.mellygoeslaw.com (official Melly Goeslaw Web site)
www.mtvasia.com (MTV Asia)
http://netral.hypermart.net (official Netral Web site, now defunct)
www.NewsMusik.net (NewsMusik magazine)
www.not-a-pup.com (Puppen's official Web site, now defunct). For more current information about the group (now disbanded), see www.robinmalau .net/category/puppen (accessed May 20, 2008).
www.rileks.com
www.tembang.com

Discography

Note: Catalog numbers and years of publication are provided when available. All albums are cassette format unless otherwise noted.

Balcony. *Terkarbonasi*. Harder Records H-004. 1999.
Bubi Chen and Friends. *Wonderful World*. Compact disc. Sangaji Music SM 005. 1999.
Burgerkill. *Dua Sisi*. Riotic Records. 2000.
Cherry Bombshell. *Luka Yang Dalam*. Bulletin BUI 0290700. 2000.
Cokelat. *Untuk Bintang*. Sony Music 497753-4. 2000.
Cucun Novia. *Ska Bon Versi 2000*. Inti Suara Production/PT Sani Sentosa Abadi. n.d.
Eternal Madness. *Bongkar Batas*. PT Resswara Rodakreasi. 2000.
Evie Tamala. *Kasmaran*. Blackboard/Polygram Indonesia IND-1148. n.d.

Fear Inside. *Human's Disgust*. Extreme Fear Terror/Extreme Souls Production. Independent 008. 1998.

Grausig. *Abandon, Forgotten, & Rotting Alone*. Independen (Aquarius Musikindo) P9916/APC IND 16-4. 1999.

Ikke Nurjanah. *Best of the Best '99*. MSC Plus/Polygram Indonesia MC.034-9. n.d.

Iyeth Bustami. *Cinta Hanya Sekali*. Maheswara Musik/Musica MS.0245. n.d.

Koil. *Kesepian Ini Abadi (Maxi Single)*. Apocalypse/Karat Rekord. 1998.

Krakatau 2000. *Magical Match*. Compact disc. Kita Music/HP Records/ Musica HPCD-0099. 2000.

Kremush. *Deadly Consience* [*sic*]. Independent 060997. 1997.

Lilis Karlina. *Cinta Terisolasi*. Maheswara Musik/Musica MS.0227. n.d.

Lirra Zanni. *Ska Minang India*. Tanama Record. n.d.

Melly Goeslaw. *Melly*. Aquarius Musikindo AQM9187-4. 1999.

Netral. *Paten*. Bulletin BUI 0220699. 1999.

Netral. *Netral Is the Best*. Bulletin BU-0280700. 2000.

Pas. *Psycho I.D.* PT Aquarius P9216. 1998.

Patty. *Dulu, Mimpi & Kini*. Maheswara Musik/Musica. 2000.

Puppen. *S/T.* Distorsi. n.d.

Puppen. *Mk II.* Self-released. n.d.

Rage Generation Brothers. *Our Lifestyle*. Independen (Aquarius Musikindo) P9919/APC IND19-4. 2000.

Rhoma Irama. *Euphoria 2000*. Blackboard/Polygram Indonesia IND.1179-5. 2000.

/rif. *Radja*. Sony Music 489091-4. 1997.

Sheila on 7. *Self-Titled*. Sony Music 494042.4. 1999.

Slowdeath. *Learn Through Pain*. Independent 007. 1998.

Slowdeath. *From Mindless Enthusiasm to Sordid Self-Destruction*. Independent 001. 1996.

Suckerhead. *10th Agresi*. Aquarius Musikindo AQM9219. 1999.

Various artists. *20 Lagu Dangdut Terseleski Terpopular*, vol. 15. Maheswara Musik/Musica MS 0226. n.d.

Various artists. *Metalik Klinik 3*. Rotorcorp/Musica MSC.8346. 2000.

Various artists. *Pesta Rap*. Compact disc. Musica MSCD 0095. n.d.

Various artists. *Tembang Pilihan 5 Jagoan Dangdut*. PT Anggada Irama Melodi/ Wilhan AIM-00141. n.d.

Vile. *Systematic Terror Decimation*. Dementia Records DR002. 1999.

Waiting Room. *Self-Titled*. Tropic. 1997.

INDEX

Since Indonesian nomenclature does not always follow the same rules as those used in the Western world, for the sake of convenience all Indonesian personal names, even those that include Western-sounding first names, are alphabetized here by the first word. A few select names have been listed in two places, under both the first and last elements (for example, B. J. Habibie appears both as "B. J. Habibie" and as "Habibie, B. J."). Names beginning with the honorific "Pak," however, are alphabetized by the second word. An italicized page number indicates a picture, while a page number followed by the letter "t" indicates a table. "CD" as a reference locator is used to identify artists and song titles that are featured on the accompanying compact disc.

NEW PERSPECTIVES IN
SOUTHEAST ASIAN STUDIES

From Rebellion to Riots: Collective Violence on Indonesian Borneo
Jamie S. Davidson

Pretext for Mass Murder: The September 30th Movement and Suharto's Coup d'État in Indonesia
John Roosa

Việt Nam: Borderless Histories
Edited by Nhung Tuyet Tran and Anthony Reid

Modern Noise, Fluid Genres: Popular Music in Indonesia, 1997–2001
Jeremy Wallach

CD Track Listing

1. Dangdut. "Hanya Cinta Yang Kupunya" (I Have Only Love) written by Sonny JS. Performed by the group Manis Manja. From the album *20 Lagu Dangdut Terseleski Terpopular,* vol. 15. Courtesy of Maheswara Musik.

2. Dangdut/Combination ethnic. "Cinta Terisolasi" (Isolated Love/Love Stuck Like Cellophane Tape) written by Hawadin and Lilis Karlina. Performed by Lilis Karlina. From the album *Cinta Terisolasi.* Courtesy of Maheswara Musik.

3. *Pop alternatif.* "Mungkin" (Maybe) written and performed by Patty. From the album *Dulu, Mimpi & Kini* (Then, Dreams, and Now). Courtesy of Maheswara Musik.

4. Dangdut/*Pop Melayu.* "Cinta Hanya Sekali" (Love [Happens] Only Once) written by Dino Sidin and Iksan Arepas. Performed by Iyeth Bustami. From the album *Cinta Hanya Sekali.* Courtesy of Maheswara Musik.

5. Underground: Balinese gamelan-influenced death metal. "Bunuh Diri" (Suicide) written and performed by Eternal Madness. From the album *Bongkar Batas* (Break Down Boundaries). Courtesy of the artists.

6. Underground: Metallic hardcore. "Hijau" (Green) written and performed by Puppen. From the album *S/T.* Courtesy of the artists.